P9-DXN-879

BRIAN JACQUES

REDWALL
ANNIVERSARY
EDITION

ACE BOOKS, NEW YORK

This Ace Book contains the complete text of the original hardcover edition. It has been completely reset in a typeface designed for easy reading, and was printed from new film.

This is a work of fiction. Names, characters, places, and incidents are either the product of the author's imagination or are used fictitiously, and any resemblance to actual persons, living or dead, business establishments, events or locales is entirely coincidental.

REDWALL

An Ace Book / published by arrangement with the author

PRINTING HISTORY
Philomel Books hardcover edition / 1986
Ace mass-market edition / June 1998

The Penguin Putnam Inc. World Wide Web site address is http://www.penguinputnam.com

Check out the Ace Science Fiction/Fantasy newsletter, and much more, at Club PPI!

ISBN: 0-441-00548-9

ACE®
Ace Books are published by
The Berkley Publishing Group, a division of Penguin Putnam Inc.,
375 Hudson Street, New York, New York 10014.
ACE and the "A" design are trademarks
belonging to Penguin Putnam Inc.

PRINTED IN THE UNITED STATES OF AMERICA

15   14   13   12   11   10   9

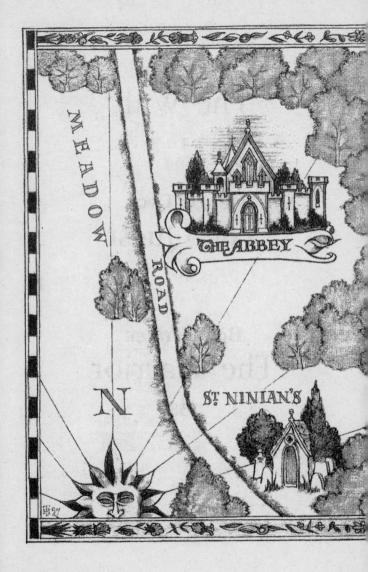

MEADOW

ROAD

THE ABBEY

N

St. NINIAN'S

QUARRY

RIVER

FARM

MOSSFLOWER WOODS

REDWALL ABBEY
AND SURROUNDING COUNTRYSIDE

Years are rarely referred to in my books; instead, seasons mark the passage of time. So, it is forty seasons, and more, since I commenced to write of Redwall, the enchanted world I discovered. What an enormous privilege it has been to share my brainchild with readers worldwide! I am certain that in the hearts and minds of all my readers, no matter how young or how old, they consider it, as I do, a flowing, timeless saga—from Mossflower's green acres, with its ancient abbey standing fast on the dusty path of the woodland fringe, to Salamandastron, mountain sentinel of the seas on the far western shores.

My chief delight and satisfaction is annually to desert the world of modern technology. When winter fades and spring blossoms into summer, I feel an overwhelming urge to travel back once more. Mouse Warriors and Badger Lords come striding through the realms of my imagination, accompanied by their companions: comical hares, rustic moles, faithful otters, and all manner of diverse creatures. Questing, feasting, singing, and battling to defend good against evil.

Forty seasons now, and forty seasons hence, if fate and fortune permit, I will still be inviting you all to continue the saga of Redwall. Come with me, my Warriors, off on the trail of high old adventure!

Brian Jacques

Recorder of Redwall Abbey,
Mossflower Country

REDWALL

ANNIVERSARY EDITION

Who says that I am dead
Knows nought at all.
I—am that is,
Two mice within Redwall.
The Warrior sleeps
'Twixt Hall and Cavern Hole.
I—am that is,
Take on my mighty role.
Look for the sword
In moonlight streaming forth,
At night, when day's first hour
Reflects the North.
From o'er the threshold
Seek and you will see;
I—am that is,
My sword will wield for me.

> *(Rhyme from beneath
> the Great Hall tapestry)*

It was the start of the Summer of the Late Rose. Mossflower country shimmered gently in a peaceful haze, bathing delicately at each dew-laden dawn, blossoming through high sunny noontides, languishing in each crimson-tinted twilight that heralded the soft darkness of June nights.

Redwall stood foursquare along the marches of the old south border, flanked on two sides by Mossflower Wood's shaded depths. The other half of the Abbey overlooked undulating sweeps of meadowland, its ancient gate facing the long dusty road on the western perimeter.

From above, it resembled some fabulous dusky jewel, fallen between a green mantle of light silk and dark velvet. The first mice had built the Abbey of red sandstone quarried from pits many miles away in the north-east. The Abbey building was covered across its south face by that type of ivy known as Virginia creeper. The onset of autumn would turn the leaves into a cape of fiery hue, thus adding further glory to the name and legend of Redwall Abbey.

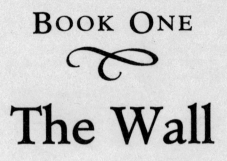

BOOK ONE

The Wall

CHAPTER

I

Matthias cut a comical little figure as he wobbled his way along the cloisters, with his large sandals flip-flopping and his tail peeping from beneath the baggy folds of an oversized novice's habit. He paused to gaze upwards at the cloudless blue sky and tripped over the enormous sandals. Hazelnuts scattered out upon the grass from the rush basket he was carrying. Unable to stop, he went tumbling cowl over tail.

Bump!

The young mouse squeaked in dismay. He rubbed tenderly at his damp snub nose while slowly taking stock of where he had landed: directly at the feet of Abbot Mortimer!

Immediately Matthias scrambled about on all fours, hastily trying to stuff nuts back into the basket as he muttered clumsy apologies, avoiding the stern gaze of his elder.

''Er, sorry, Father Abbot. I tripped, y'see. Trod on my Abbot, Father Habit. Oh dear, I mean. . . .''

The Father Abbot blinked solemnly over the top of his glasses. Matthias again. What a young buffoon of a mouse. Only the other day he had singed old Brother Methuselah's whiskers while lighting candles.

The elder's stern expression softened. He watched the little novice rolling about on the grass, grappling with large armfuls of the smooth hazelnuts which constantly seemed to escape his grasp. Shaking his old grey head, yet trying to hide a smile,

3

Abbot Mortimer bent and helped to gather up the fallen nuts.

"Oh Matthias, Matthias, my son," he said wearily. "When will you learn to take life a little slower, to walk with dignity and humility? How can you ever hope to be accepted as a mouse of Redwall, when you are always dashing about grinning from whisker to tail like a mad rabbit?"

Matthias tossed the last of the hazelnuts into the basket and stood awkwardly shuffling his large sandals in the grass. How could he say aloud what was in his heart?

The Abbot put his paw around the young mouse's shoulder, sensing his secret yearnings, for he had ruled Redwall wisely over a great number of years and gained much experience of mouselife. He smiled down at his young charge and spoke kindly to him. "Come with me, Matthias. It is time we talked together."

A curious thrush perching in a gnarled pear tree watched the two figures make their way at a sedate pace in the direction of Great Hall, one clad in the dark greeny-brown of the order, the other garbed in the lighter green of a novice. They conversed earnestly in low tones. Thinking what a clever bird he was, the thrush swooped down on the basket that had been left behind. Twisters! The basket contained only hard nuts, locked tight within their shells. Feigning lack of interest, lest any other birds had been witness to his silly mistake, he began whistling jauntily a few bars of his melodious summer song, strolling nonchalantly over to the cloister walls in search of snails.

It was cool inside Great Hall. Sunlight flooded down in slanting rainbow-hued shafts from the high, narrow stained-glass windows. A million colored dust-motes danced and swirled as the two mice trod the ancient stone floor. The Father Abbot halted in front of the wall on which hung a long tapestry. This was the pride and joy of Redwall. The oldest part had been woven by the Founders of the Abbey, but each successive generation had added to it; thus the tapestry was not only a priceless treasure, it was also a magnificent chronicle of early Redwall history.

The Abbot studied the wonderment in Matthias's eyes as he asked him a question, the answer to which the wise mouse already knew. "What are you looking at, my son?"

Matthias pointed to the figure woven into the tapestry. It was a heroic-looking mouse with a fearless smile on his handsome face. Clad in armor, he leaned casually on an impressive sword, while behind him foxes, wildcats and vermin fled in terror. The young mouse gazed in admiration.

"Oh, Father Abbot," he sighed. "If only I could be like Martin the Warrior. He was the bravest, most courageous mouse that ever lived!"

The Abbot sat down slowly on the cool stone floor, resting his back against the wall.

"Listen to what I say, Matthias. You have been like a son to me, ever since you first came to our gates as an orphaned woodland mouse, begging to be taken in. Come, sit by me and I will try to explain to you what our Order is all about.

"We are mice of peace. Oh, I know that Martin was a warrior mouse, but those were wild days when strength was needed. The strength of a champion such as Martin. He arrived here in the deep winter when the Founders were under attack from many foxes, vermin and a great wildcat. So fierce a fighter was Martin that he faced the enemy single-pawed, driving them mercilessly, far from Mossflower. During the rout Martin fought a great battle against overwhelming odds. He emerged victorious after slaying the wildcat with his ancient sword, which became famous throughout the land. But in the last bloody combat Martin was seriously wounded. He lay injured in the snow until the mice found him. They brought him back to the Abbey and cared for his hurts until he regained his strength.

"Then something seemed to come over him. He was transformed by what could only be called a mouse miracle. Martin forsook the way of the warrior and hung up his sword.

"That was when our Order found its true vocation. All the mice took a solemn vow never to harm another living creature, unless it was an enemy that sought to harm our Order by violence. They vowed to heal the sick, care for the injured, and give aid to the wretched and impoverished. So was it written, and so has it been through all the ages of mousekind since.

"Today, we are a deeply honored and highly respected Society. Anywhere we go, even far beyond Mossflower, we are treated with courtesy by all creatures. Even predators will not harm a mouse who wears the habit of our Order. They know he or she is one who will heal and give aid. It is an unwritten law that Redwall mice can go anywhere, through any territory, and pass unharmed. At all times we must live up to this. It is our way, our very life.''

As the Abbot spoke, so his voice increased in volume and solemnity. Matthias sat under his stern gaze, completely humbled. Abbot Mortimer stood and put a wrinkled old paw lightly on the small head, right between the velvety ears, now drooping with shame.

Once more the Abbot's heart softened towards the little mouse. ''Poor Matthias, alas for your ambitions. The day of the warrior is gone, my son. We live in peaceful times, thank heaven, and you need only think of obeying me, your Abbot, and doing as you are bidden. In time to come, when I am long gone to my rest, you will think back to this day and bless my memory, for then you will be a true member of Redwall. Come now, my young friend, cheer up; it is the Summer of the Late Rose. There are many, many days of warm sun ahead of us. Go back and get your basket of hazelnuts. Tonight we have a great feast to celebrate—my Golden Jubilee as Abbot. When you've taken the nuts to the kitchen, I have a special task for you. Yes indeed, I'll need some fine fish for the table. Get your rod and line. Tell Brother Alf that he is to take you fishing in the small boat. That's what young mice like doing, isn't it? Who knows, you may land a fine trout or some sticklebacks! Run along now, young one.''

Happiness filled Matthias from tail to whiskers as he bobbed a quick bow to his superior and shuffled off. Smiling benignly, the Abbot watched him go. Little rascal, he must have a word with the Almoner, to see if some sandals could be found that were the right fit for Matthias. Small wonder the poor mouse kept tripping up!

CHAPTER

2

The high, warm sun shone down on Cluny the Scourge.

Cluny was coming!

He was big, and tough; an evil rat with ragged fur and curved, jagged teeth. He wore a black eyepatch; his eye had been torn out in battle with a pike.

Cluny had lost an eye.

The pike had lost its life!

Some said that Cluny was a Portuguese rat. Others said he came from the jungles far across the wide oceans. Nobody knew for sure.

Cluny was a bilge rat; the biggest, most savage rodent that ever jumped from ship to shore. He was black, with grey and pink scars all over his huge sleek body, from the tip of his wet nose, up past his green and yellow slitted eye, across both his mean tattered ears, down the length of his heavy vermin-ridden back to the enormous whiplike tail which had earned him his title: Cluny the Scourge!

Now he rode on the back of the hay wagon with his five hundred followers, a mighty army of rats: sewer rats, tavern rats, water rats, dockside rats. Cluny's army—fearing, yet following him. Redtooth, his second-in-command, carried a long pole. This was Cluny's personal standard. The skull of a ferret was fixed at its top. Cluny had killed the ferret. He feared no living thing.

Wild-eyed, with the terror of rat smell in its nostrils, the horse plunged ahead without any driver. Where the hay cart was taking him was of little concern to Cluny. Straight on the panicked horse galloped, past the milestone lodged in the earth at the roadside, heedless of the letters graven in the stone: "Redwall Abbey, fifteen miles."

Cluny spat over the edge of the cart at two young rabbits playing in a field. Tasty little things; a pity the cart hadn't stopped yet, he thought. The high warm sun shone down on Cluny the Scourge.

Cluny was a God of War!

Cluny was coming nearer!

CHAPTER

3

Beneath the Great Hall of Redwall, candles burned bright in their sconces. This was the Cavern Hole of the mice.

What a night it was going to be!

Between them, Matthias and Brother Alf had caught and landed a fully-grown grayling. They had fought and played the big fish for nearly two hours, finally wading into the shallows and dragging it to the bank. It was nearly two pounds in weight, a tribute to Brother Alf's angling skills combined with the youthful muscles of Matthias and their joint enthusiasm.

Constance the badger had to be called. Gripping the fish in her strong jaws, she followed the two mice to the Abbey kitchen and delivered the catch for them. Then she made her farewells; they would see her at the Jubilee feast that evening, along with many other Mossflower residents who had been invited to share the festivities.

Brother Alf and Matthias stood proudly beside their catch amid the culinary hustle and bustle until they were noticed by Friar Hugo. Busy as he was, the enormously fat Hugo (who would have no other title but that of Friar) stopped what he was doing. Wiping the perspiration from his brow with a dandelion that he held with his tail, he waddled about inspecting the fish.

"Hmm, nice shiny scales, bright eyes, beautifully fresh." Friar Hugo smiled so joyfully that his face disappeared amid deep dimples. He shook Alf by the paw and clapped Matthias heartily on the back as he called out between chuckles, "Bring the white gooseberry wine! Fetch me some rosemary, thyme, beechnuts and honey, quickly. And now, friends, now," he squeaked, waving the dandelion wildly with his tail, "I, Hugo, will create a *Grayling à la Redwall* such as will melt in the mouth of mice. Fresh cream! I need lots of fresh cream! Bring some mint leaves too."

They had left Friar Hugo ranting on, delirious in his joy, as they both went off to bathe and clean up; combing whiskers, curling tails, shining noses, and the hundred and one other grooming tasks that Redwall mice always performed in preparation for an epic feast.

The rafters of Cavern Hole rang to the excited buzz and laughter of the assembled creatures: hedgehogs, moles, squirrels, woodland creatures and mice of all kinds—fieldmice, hedgemice, dormice, even a family of poor little churchmice. Kindly helpers scurried about making everybody welcome.

"Hello there, Mrs. Churchmouse! Sit the children down! I'll get them some raspberry cordial."

"Why, Mr. Bankvole! So nice to see you! How's the back? Better now? Good. Here, try a drop of this peach and elderberry brandy."

Matthias's young head was in a whirl. He could not remember being so happy in all his life. Winifred the otter nudged him.

"I say, Matthias. Where's this giant grayling that you and old Alf hooked, by the claw! I wish that I could land a beauty like that. Nearly a two-pounder, wasn't it?"

Matthias swelled with pride. Such praise, and from the champion fisher herself, an otter!

Tim and Tess, the twin Churchmouse babes, felt Matthias's strong arm muscles and giggled aloud in admiration. He helped to serve them two portions of apple and mint ice cream. Such nice little twins. Was it only three months ago that he had helped Sister Stephanie to get them over tail rickets? How they had grown!

Abbot Mortimer sat in his carved willow chair, beaming thanks as one by one the new arrivals laid their simple homemade gifts at his feet: an acorn cup from a squirrel, fishbone combs from the otters, mossy bark sandals made by the moles,

and many more fine presents too numerous to mention. The
Abbot shook his head in amazement. Even more guests were
arriving!

He beckoned Friar Hugo to his side. A whispered conference
was held. Matthias could only hear snatches of the conversation.

"Don't worry, Father Abbot, there will be enough for all."

"How are the cellar stocks, Hugo?"

"Enough to flood the Abbey pond, Father."

"And nuts? We must not run short of nuts."

"You name them, we've got them. Even candied chestnuts
and acorn crunch. We could feed the district for a year."

"Dairy produce?"

"Oh that, I've got a cheddar cheese that four badgers couldn't
roll, plus ten other varieties."

"Good, good, thank you, Hugo. Oh, we must thank Alf and
young Matthias for that magnificent fish. What fine anglers they
are! There's enough to keep the entire Abbey going for a week!
Excellent mice, well done."

Matthias blushed to his tail's end.

"The otters! The otters!"

A loud, jolly cry went up as three otters in clown costumes
came bounding in. Such acrobatics! They tumbled, balanced and
gyrated, cavorting comically across the laden tabletops without
upsetting as much as a single sultana. They ended up hanging
from the rafters by a strand of ivy, to wild applause.

Ambrose Spike the hedgehog did his party piece. He amazed
everyone with his feats of legerdemain. Eggs were taken from
a squirrel's ear; a young mouse's tail stood up and danced like
a snake; the incredible vanishing-shell trick was performed in
front of a group of little harvest mice who kept squeaking,
"He's got it hidden in his prickles."

But had he? Ambrose made a few mysterious passes and produced the shell, straight out of the mouth of an awestruck infant
mouse. Was it magic?

Of course it was.

All activity ceased as the great Joseph Bell tolled out eight
o'clock from the Abbey belfry. Silently, all the creatures filed
to their allotted places. They stood reverently behind the seats
with heads lowered. Abbot Mortimer rose and solemnly spread

his paws wide, encompassing the festive board. He said the grace.

> "Fur and whisker, tooth and claw,
> All who enter by our door.
> Nuts and herbs, leaves and fruits,
> Berries, tubers, plants and roots,
> Silver fish whose life we take
> Only for a meal to make."

This was followed by a loud and grateful "Amen."

There was a mass clattering of chairs and scraping of forms as everyone was seated. Matthias found himself next to Tim and Tess on one paw, and Cornflower Fieldmouse on the other. Cornflower was a quiet young mouse, but undoubtedly very pretty. She had the longest eyelashes Matthias had ever seen, the brightest eyes, the softest fur, the whitest teeth. . . .

Matthias fumbled with a piece of celery and self-consciously turned to see if the twins were coping adequately. You never could tell with these baby churchmice.

Brother Alf remarked that Friar Hugo had excelled himself, as course after course was brought to the table. Tender freshwater shrimp garnished with cream and rose leaves, devilled barley pearls in acorn purée, apple and carrot chews, marinated cabbage stalks steeped in creamed white turnip with nutmeg.

A chorus of ooh's and ah's greeted the arrival of six mice pushing a big trolley. It was the grayling. Wreaths of aromatic steam drifted around Cavern Hole; the fish had been baked to perfection. Friar Hugo entered, with a slight swagger added to his ungainly waddle. He swept off his chef's cap with his tail, and announced in a somewhat pompous squeak, "Milord Abbot, honored guests from Mossflower area and members of the Abbey. Ahem, I wish to present my *pièce de résistance—*"

"Oh get on with it, Hugo!"

After some icy staring about to detect the culprit, and several smothered sniggers from around the room, the little fat friar puffed himself up once more and declaimed firmly: "*Grayling à la Redwall.*"

Polite but eager applause rippled round as Hugo sliced the fish, and placed the first steaming portion on to a platter. With suitable dignity he presented it to the Abbot, who thanked him graciously.

All eyes were on the Father Abbot. He took a dainty fork loaded precariously with steaming fish. Carefully he transferred it from plate to mouth. Chewing delicately, he turned his eyes upwards then closed them, whiskers atwitch, jaws working steadily, munching away, his tail curled up holding a napkin which neatly wiped his mouth. The Abbot's eyes reopened. He beamed like the sun on midsummer morn.

"Quite wonderful, perfectly exquisite! Friar Hugo, you are truly my Champion Chef. Please serve our guests your master-work."

Any further speech was drowned by hearty cheers.

CHAPTER
4

Cluny was in a foul temper. He snarled viciously.

The horse had stopped from sheer exhaustion. He hadn't wanted that: some inner devil persuaded him that he had not yet reached his destination. Cluny's one eye slitted evilly.

From the depths of the hay cart the rodents of the Warlord's army watched their Master. They knew him well enough to stay clear of him in this present mood. He was violent, unpredictable.

"Skullface," Cluny snapped.

There was a rustle in the hay, a villainous head popped up.

"Aye, Chief, d'you want me?"

Cluny's powerful tail shot out and dragged the unfortunate forward. Skullface cringed as sharp dirty claws dug into his fur. Cluny nodded at the horse.

"Jump on that thing's back sharpish. Give it a good bite. That'll get the lazy brute moving again."

Skullface swallowed nervously and licked his dry lips.

"But Chief, it might bite me back."

Swish! Crack! Cluny wielded his mighty tail as if it were a bullwhip. His victim screamed aloud with pain as the scourge lashed his thin bony back.

"Mutiny, insubordination!" Cluny roared. "By the teeth of hell, I'll flay you into mangy dollrags."

Skullface scurried over on to the driver's seat, yelling with pain. "No more! Don't whip me, Chief. Look, I'm going to do it."

"Hold tight to the rigging back there," Cluny shouted to his horde.

Skullface performed a frantic leap. He landed on the horse's back. The terrified animal did not wait for the rat to bite. As soon as it felt the loathsome scratching weight descend on its exposed haunches, it gave a loud panicked whinny and bucked. Spurred on by the energy of fright it careered off like a runaway juggernaut.

Skullface had time for just one agonized scream before he fell. The iron-shod cartwheels rolled over him. He lay in a red mist of death, the life ebbing from his broken body. The last thing he saw before darkness claimed him was the sneering visage of Cluny the Scourge roaring from the jolting backboard, "Tell the devil Cluny sent you, Skullface!"

They were on the move again. Cluny was getting nearer.

CHAPTER

5

Down in Cavern Hole the great feast had slackened off.

So had a lot of belts!

Redwall mice and their guests sat back replete. There were still great quantities of food uneaten.

Abbot Mortimer whispered in Friar Hugo's ear, "Friar, I want you to pack up a large sack with food, hazelnuts, cheese, bread, cakes, anything you see fit. Give it to Mrs. Churchmouse, as secretly as you can without attracting attention. Poverty is an ugly specter when a mousewife has as many mouths to feed as she does. Oh, and be sure that her husband doesn't suspect what you are doing. John Churchmouse may be poor but he is also proud. I fear he might not accept charitable gifts."

Hugo nodded knowingly and waddled off to do his Abbot's bidding.

Cornflower and Matthias had become quite friendly. They were young mice of the same age. Though their temperaments were different they found something in common, an interest in Tim and Tess, the twin churchmice. They had passed a pleasant evening, joking and playing games with the little creatures. Tess had clambered on to Matthias's lap and fallen asleep, whereupon baby Tim did likewise in the velvety fur of Cornflower. She smiled at Matthias as she stroked Tim's small head. "Ah, bless their little paws! Don't they look peaceful?"

Matthias nodded contentedly in agreement.

Colin Vole tittered aloud and remarked rather foolishly, "Ooh, would you look at Matthias an' Cornflower there, a-nursin' those two babbies like they was an old wedded couple. Well, crumble my bank!"

Brother Alf reprimanded him sharply. "Here now, you keep a latch on that silly tongue of yours, Colin Vole! Don't you know that someday Matthias will be a Redwall mouse? And don't let me hear you slandering young Cornflower. She's a decent mouse from a good family. Mark my words, Master Vole, I could say a thing or two to your mum and dad. Only last evening I saw you playing 'catch the bulrush' with that young harvest mouse. What was her name now?"

Colin Vole blushed until his nose went dry. He flounced off, swishing his tail, muttering about going outside to take the air.

Matthias caught a nod and a glance from the Abbot. Excusing himself to Cornflower, he deposited the sleeping Tess gently upon his chair and went across to him.

"Ah, Matthias, my son, here you are. Did you enjoy my Jubilee Feast?"

"Yes, thank you, Father," Matthias replied.

"Good, good," chuckled the Abbot. "Now, I was going to ask Brother Alf or Edmund to go on a special errand, but they are no longer young mice and both look quite weary at this late hour. So, I thought I might ask my chief grayling-catcher to carry out this special task for me."

Matthias could not help standing a bit taller.

"Say the word and I'm your mouse, sir."

The Abbot leaned forward and spoke confidentially. "Do you see the Churchmouse family? Well, it's such a long way back home for them on foot. Good Heavens, and there are so many of them! I thought it would be a splendid idea if you were to drive them home in the Abbey cart, along with any others going that way. Constance Badger would pull the cart, of course, while you could act as guide and bodyguard. Take a good stout staff with you, Matthias."

The young mouse needed no second bidding. Drawing himself up to his full height, he saluted in a smart military fashion. "Leave it to me, Father Abbot. Old Constance is a bit slow-thinking. I'll take complete responsibility."

The Abbot shook with silent laughter as he watched Matthias

march off with a soldier-like swagger. Flip flop, flip flop; he tripped and fell flat on his tail.

"Oh dear, I'll have to get that young mouse some sandals that aren't so big," the Abbot said to himself for the second time that day.

Well, what a stroke of luck. Fancy Cornflower's family living so close to the Churchmouse brood! Matthias was only too glad to offer them a lift home.

Would Miss Cornflower like to sit next to him?

She most certainly would!

Cornflower's parents sat inside the cart, her mum helping Mrs. Churchmouse with the little ones, while her dad chatted away with John Churchmouse as they shared a pipe of old bracken twist.

Friar Hugo came out and dumped a bulky sack next to Mrs. Churchmouse. "Abbot says to thank you for the loan of bowls and tablecloths, ma'am." The fat friar gave her a huge wink.

"All comfy back there?" called Matthias. "Right, off we go, Constance."

The big badger trundled the cart away as they called their goodnights. She nodded at Methuselah, the ancient gatekeeper mouse. As the cart rolled out into the road a sliver of golden moon looked down from a star-pierced summer night. Matthias gazed upwards, feeling as if he were slowly turning with the silent earth. Peace was all about him: the baby mice inside the cart whimpered fitfully in their small secret dreams; Constance ambled slowly along, as though she were out on a nighttime stroll pulling no weight at all; the stout ash staff lay forgotten on the footboard.

Cornflower dozed against Matthias's shoulder. She could hear the gentle lull of her father's voice and that of John Churchmouse, blending with the hum of nocturnal insects from the meadow and hedges on this balmy summer night.

The Summer of the Late Rose ... Cornflower turned the words over in her mind, dreamily thinking of the old rambler that bloomed in the Abbey gardens. Normally it was in full red flower by now, but this year, for some unknown reason, it had chosen to flower late. It was covered in dormant young rosebuds, even now, well into June—a thing that happened only infrequently, and usually heralded an extra-long hot summer.

Old Methuselah could only remember three other such summers in his long lifetime. Accordingly he had advised that it be marked on the calendar and in the Abbey chronicles as "The Summer of the Late Rose." Cornflower's head sank lower, in sleep.

The old cart rolled on gently, down the long dusty road. They were now over halfway to the ruined Church of St. Ninian where John Churchmouse lived, as had his father, grandfather and great-grandfather before him. Matthias had fallen into a deep slumber. Even Constance was unable to stop her eyelids drooping. She went slower and slower. It was as if the little cart and its occupants were caught in the magic spell of an enchanted summer night.

Suddenly, and without warning, they were roused by the thunder of hooves.

Nobody could determine which direction the sound was coming from. It seemed to fill the very air about them as it gathered momentum; the ground began trembling with the rumbling noise.

Some sixth sense warned Constance to get off the road to a hiding place. The powerful badger gave a mighty heave. Her blunt claws churned the roadside soil as she propelled the cart through a gap in the hawthorn hedge, down to the slope of the ditch where she dug her paws in, holding the cart still and secure while John Churchmouse and Cornflower's father jumped out and wedged the wheels firmly with stones.

Matthias gasped with shock as a giant horse galloped past, its mane streaming out, eyes rolling in panic. It was towing a hay cart which bounced wildly from side to side. Matthias could see rats among the hay, but these were no ordinary rats. They were huge ragged rodents, bigger than any he had ever seen. Their heavy tattooed arms waved a variety of weapons—pikes, knives, spears and long rusty cutlasses. Standing boldly on the backboard of the hay cart was the biggest, fiercest, most evil-looking rat that ever slunk out of a nightmare! In one claw he grasped a long pole with a ferret's head spiked to it, while in the other was his thick, enormous tail, which he cracked like a whip. Laughing madly and yelling strange curses, he swayed to and fro skillfully as horse and wagon clattered off down the road into the night. As suddenly as they had come, they were gone!

*   *   *

Matthias walked out into the road, staff in hand. Stray wisps of hay drifted down behind him. His legs trembled uncontrollably. Constance hauled the Abbey cart back on to the road. Cornflower was helping her mother and Mrs. Churchmouse to calm the little ones' tears of fright. Together they stood in the cart tracks amid the settling dust.

"Did you see that?"

"I saw it, but I don't believe it!"

"What in heaven was it?"

"What in hell, more like."

"All those rats! Such big ones, too."

"Aye, and that one on the back! He looked like the Devil himself."

Seeing Matthias still stunned by what had happened, Constance took over the leadership. She wheeled the cart around.

"I think we'd best head back for the Abbey," she said firmly. "Father Abbot'll want to know about this straightaway."

Knowing that the badger was far more experienced than himself, Matthias assumed the role of second-in-command. "Right, Cornflower, get in the cart and take charge of the mothers and babies," he said. "Mr. Fieldmouse, Mr. Churchmouse, up front with Constance, please."

Silently the mice did as ordered. The cart moved off with Matthias positioned on the back providing a rearguard. The young mouse gripped his staff tightly, his back to his charges, facing down the road in the direction the hay cart had taken.

CHAPTER
6

The horse had gotten away safely.

It was the hay cart that suffered most damage. Bolting recklessly from side to side down the road, the blinkered animal failed to see the twin stone gateposts on its right—skidding crazily, the cart smashed into the uprights. There was a loud splintering of shafts as the horse careered onwards, trailing in its wake reins, tracers and shattered timber.

His lightning reflexes serving him well, Cluny leaped clear. He landed catlike on all fours as the hay cart upended in the roadside ditch, its buckled wheels spinning awkwardly.

Feeling braced after his mad ride and the subsequent narrow escape, Cluny strode to the ditch's edge. The distressed cries of those trapped beneath the cart reached his ears. He spat contemptuously, narrowing his one good eye.

"Come on, get up out of there, you cringing load of catsmeat," he bellowed. "Redtooth! Darkclaw! Report to me or I'll have your skulls for skittles."

Cluny's two henchrats pulled themselves from the ditch, shaking their heads dazedly.

Crack! Slash! The whiplike tail brought them swiftly to his side.

"Three-Leg and Scratch are dead, Chief."

"Dead as dirt. The cart crushed 'em, Chief."

"Stupid fools," snarled Cluny. "Serves them right! What about the rest?"

"Old Wormtail has lost a paw. Some of the others are really hurt."

Cluny sneered. "Aah, they'll get over it and suffer worse by the time I'm done with them. They're getting too fat and sluggish, by the tripes! They'd not last five minutes in a storm at sea. Come on, you dead-and-alive ragbags! Get up here and gather 'round."

Rats struggled from the ditch and the cart—frantic to obey the harsh command as quickly as possible. They crowded about the undamaged gatepost, which their leader had chosen as a perch. None dared to cry or complain about their hurts. Who could predict what mood the Warlord was in?

"Right, cock your lugs up and listen to me," Cluny snarled. "First, we've got to find out where we have docked. Let's take a bearing on this place."

Redtooth held up his claw. "The Church of St. Ninian, Chief. It says so on the notice board over yonder."

"Well, no matter," Cluny snapped. "It'll do as a berth until we find something better. Fangburn! Cheesethief!"

"Here, Chief."

"Scout the area. See if you can find a better lodging for us than this heap of rubble. Trail back to the west. I think we passed a big place on the way."

"Aye, aye, Chief."

"Frogblood! Scumnose!"

"Chief?"

"Take fifty soldiers and see if you can round up any rats that know the lie of the land. Get big strong rats, but bring along weasels, stoats and ferrets too. They'll do at a pinch. Mind now, don't stand for arguments. Smash their dens up so they won't have homes to worry about. If any refuse to join up, then kill them there and then. Understood?"

"All clear, Chief."

"Ragear! Mangefur! Take twenty rats and forage for supplies. The rest of you get inside the church. Redtooth, Darkclaw, check the armor. See if there are things about that we can use as weapons: iron spike railings—there's usually enough of them around a churchyard. Jump to it."

Cluny had arrived!

CHAPTER

7

Matthias had never stayed up all night in his life. He was just a bit tired, but strangely excited. Great events seemed to have been set in motion by his news.

Immediately upon being informed of the hay cart incident, the Abbot had insisted upon calling a special council meeting of all Redwall creatures. Once again Cavern Hole was packed to the doors, but this time it was for a purpose very different from the feast. Constance and Matthias stood in front of the Council of Elders. All about them was a hum of whispers and muttering.

Abbot Mortimer called order by ringing a small bell.

"Pay attention, everyone. Constance and Matthias, would you please tell the Council what you saw tonight on the road to St. Ninian's."

As clearly as they could, the badger and the young mouse related the incident of the rat-infested hay cart.

The Council began questioning them.

"Rats, you say, Matthias. What type of rat?" inquired Sister Clemence.

"Big ones," Matthias replied, "though I'm afraid I couldn't say what kind they were or where they had come from."

"What about you, Constance?"

"Well, I remember that my old grandad once knew a sea

23

rat,'' she answered. "Going by his description, I'd say that's what they looked like to me.''

"And how many would you say there were of these rats?'' Father Abbot asked.

"Couldn't say for sure, Father Abbot. There must have been hundreds.''

"Matthias?''

"Oh yes, Father. I'd agree with Constance. At least four hundred.''

"Did you notice anything else about them, Constance?''

"Indeed I did, Father Abbot. My badger senses told me right off that these were very bad and evil rats.''

The badger's statement caused uproar and shouts of "Nonsense. Pure speculation" and "That's right! Give a rat a bad name!''

Without even thinking, Matthias raised a paw and shouted aloud, "Constance is right. I could feel it myself. There was one huge rat with a ferret's skull on a pole. I got a good look at him—it was like seeing some horrible monster.''

In the silence that followed, the Abbot rose and confronted Matthias. Stooping slightly, he stared into the young mouse's bright eyes. "Think carefully, my son. Was there anything special you noticed about this rat?''

Matthias thought for a moment. Everyone was watching him.

"He was much bigger than the others, Father.''

"What else? Think, Matthias.''

"I remember! He only had one eye.''

"Right or left?''

"Left, I think. Yes, it was the left, Father.''

"Now, can you recall anything about his tail?''

"I certainly can,'' Matthias squeaked. "It must have been the longest tail of any rat alive. He held it in his claw as if it were a whip.''

The Abbot paced up and down before turning to the assembly.

"Twice in my lifetime I have heard travelers speak of this rat. He bears a name that a fox would be afraid to whisper in the darkness of midnight. Cluny the Scourge!''

A deathly hush fell upon the creatures in Cavern Hole.

Cluny the Scourge!

Surely not? He was only some kind of folk legend, a warning used by mothers when youngsters were fractious or disobedient.

"Go to sleep or Cluny will get you!"
"Eat up your dinner or Cluny will come!"
"Come in this instant, or I'll tell Cluny!"

Most creatures didn't even know what Cluny was. He was just some sort of bogey that lived in bad dreams and the dark corners of imagination.

The silence was broken by scornful snorts and derisive laughter. Furry elbows nudged downy ribs. Mice were beginning to smile from sheer relief. Cluny the Scourge, indeed!

Feeling slightly abashed, Matthias and Constance looked pleadingly towards the Abbot for support. Abbot Mortimer's old face was stern as he shook the bell vigorously for silence.

"Mice of Redwall, I see there are those among you who doubt the word of your Abbot."

The quiet but authoritative words caused an embarrassed shuffling from the Council Elders. Brother Joseph stood up and cleared his throat. "Ahem, er, good Father Abbot, we all respect your word and look to you for guidance, but really . . . I mean . . ."

Sister Clemence stood up smiling. She spread her paws wide. "Perhaps Cluny is coming to get us for staying up late."

A roar of laughter greeted the ironic words.

Constance's back hairs bristled. She gave an angry growl followed by a fierce bark. The mice huddled together with fright. Nobody had ever seen a snarling, angry badger at a Council meeting.

Before they could recover, Constance was up on her hind legs having her say. "I've never seen such a pack of empty-headed ninnies. You should all be ashamed of yourselves, giggling like silly little otter cubs that have caught a beetle. I never thought I'd live to see the Elders of Redwall acting in this way." Constance hunched her heavy shoulders and glared about with a ferocity that set them trembling. "Now you listen to me. Take heed of what your Father Abbot has to say. The next creature who utters one squeak will answer to me. Understand?"

The badger bowed low in a dignified manner, gesturing with her massive blunt paw. "The floor is yours, Father Abbot."

"Thank you, Constance, my good and faithful friend," the Abbot murmured. He looked about him, shaking his head gravely.

"I have little more to say on the subject, but as I see that you still need convincing, here is my proposal. We will send two mice out to relieve the gatehouse. Let me see, yes . . . Brothers Rufus and George, would you kindly go and take over from Brother Methuselah? Please send him in here to me. Tell him to bring the travelers' record volumes. Not the present issue, but the old editions which were used in past years.''

Rufus and George, both solid-looking, sensible mice, took their leave with a formal bow to the Abbot.

Through a high slitted window, Matthias could see the rosy-pink and gold fingers of dawn stealing down to Cavern Hole as the candles began to flicker and smoke into stubs. All in the space of a night events had moved from festivity to a crisis, and he, Matthias, had taken a major role in both. First the big grayling, then the sighting of the cart; large happenings for a small mouse.

Old Brother Methuselah had kept the Abbey records for as long as any creature could remember. It was his life's work and consuming passion. Besides the official chronicle of Redwall he also kept his own personal volume, full of valuable information. Traveling creatures, migratory birds, wandering foxes, rambling squirrels and garrulous hares—they all stopped and chatted with the old mouse, partaking of his hospitality, never dreaming of hurting him in any way. Methuselah had the gift of tongues. He could understand any creature, even a bird. He was an extraordinary old mouse, who lived with the company of his volumes in the solitude of the gatehouse.

Seated in the Father Abbot's own chair, Methuselah took his spectacles from a moss-bark case, carefully perching them on the bridge of his nose. All gathered around to hear as he opened a record book and spoke in a squeak barely above a whisper.

''Hmm, hmm, me Lord Abbot Cedric. It is Cedric, isn't it? Oh botheration, you'll be the new Abbot, Mortimer, the one who came after Cedric. Oh dear me, I see so many of them come and go, you know. Hmm, hmm, me Lord Abbot Mortimer and members of Redwall, I refer to a record of winter, six years back.'' Here the ancient mouse took a while to leaf through the pages. ''Hmm, ah yes, here it is. 'Late in November, Year of the Small Sweet Chestnut, from a frozen sparrowhawk come down from the far north . . .'—peculiar chap, spoke with a strange accent. I repaired his right wing pinfeather—' . . . news of a mine disaster, caused by a large savage sea rat with an extraordinary tail. It seems that this rat—Cluny they called him—wanted to settle his army in the mine. The badgers and other creatures who owned the mine drove them out. Cluny returned by night, and with his band of rats gnawed away and undermined much of the wooden shoring. This caused the mine to collapse the next day, killing the owners.' "

Brother Methuselah closed the volume and looked over his glasses at the assembly. "I have no need to read further, I can recite other misdeeds from memory. As the hordes of Cluny the Scourge have moved southwards over the past six years, I have gathered intelligence of other incidents: a farmhouse set alight, later that same year . . . piglets, an entire litter of them eaten alive by rats . . . sickness and disease spread through livestock herds by Cluny's army. There was even a report brought to me two years ago by a town dog: an army of rats stampeded a herd of cows through a village, causing chaos and much destruction."

Methuselah halted and blinked over his spectacles. "And you dare doubt the word of our Abbot that Cluny the Scourge exists? What idiotic mice you are, to be sure."

Methuselah's words caused widespread consternation. There was much agitated nibbling of paws. Nobody could doubt he spoke the truth; he was already old and wise when the most elderly among them was a blind hairless mite, puling and whimpering for a feed from its mother.

"Oh my whiskers, what a mess."

"Hadn't we better pack up and move?"

"Maybe Cluny will spare us."

"Oh dear, oh dear, what shall we do?"

Matthias sprang to the middle of the floor brandishing his staff in a way that surprised even him.

"Do?" he cried. "I'll tell you what we'll do. We'll be ready."

The Abbot could not help shaking his head in admiration. It seemed that young Matthias had hidden depths.

"Why, thank you, Matthias," he said. "I could not have put it better myself. That's exactly what we will do. We'll be ready!"

CHAPTER

8

Cluny the Scourge was having nightmares.

He had lain down in the Churchmouses' bed for a well-earned rest while his army was going about its allotted tasks. He should never have tried to sleep on an empty stomach, but weariness overcame his hunger.

In Cluny's dream everything was shrouded in a red mist. The cries of his victims rang out as barns blazed, and ships foundered on a stormy red sea. Cattle bellowed in pain as he battled with the pike that had taken his eye. The Warlord thrashed about, killing, conquering and laying waste to all in his dream.

Then the phantom figure appeared.

At first it seemed a small thing, a mouse in fact, dressed in a long hooded robe. Cluny did not relish meeting with it—he could not tell why—but the mouse kept getting closer to him. For the first time in his life, he turned and ran!

Cluny went like a bat out of hell. Glancing back, he saw all the carnage, death and misery he had caused in his career. The big rat laughed insanely and ran faster: on and on, past scenes of desolation and destruction wreaked by him, Cluny the Scourge. Floating through the red mists he could still see the strange mouse hard on his heels. Cluny felt himself filled with hatred for his pursuer. It seemed to have grown larger; its eyes were cold and grim. Deep inside, Cluny knew that even he could not frighten this oddly-garbed mouse. Now it was wielding a large bright sword, an ancient weapon of terrible beauty. The battle-scarred blade had a word written upon it that he could not make out.

Sweat dripped from Cluny's claws like stinging acid. He stumbled. The strange figure was closer; it had grown into a giant!

Cluny's lungs felt as if they were bursting. He realized that he had slowed up and the mouse was getting closer. He tried to put on an extra burst of speed, but his legs would not obey. They ran more and more slowly—more and more heavily. Cluny cursed aloud at his leaden limbs. He saw he was trapped in deep icy mud. For the first time he knew the meaning of mindless fear and panic.

He turned slowly. Too late. The enemy was upon him; he was rooted helpless to the spot. The avenging mouse swung the sword up high; a million lights flashed from its deadly blade as it struck.

Bong!

The loud toll of the distant Joseph Bell brought Cluny whirling back from the realms of nightmare to cold reality. He shivered, wiping the sweat from his fur with a shaky claw. Saved by the bell.

He was puzzled. What did the fearful dream mean? Cluny had never been one to put his faith in omens, but this dream . . . it had been so lifelike and vivid that he shuddered.

A timid paw tapping on the door snapped Cluny from his reverie with a start. It was Ragear and Mangefur, his scavengers. They slunk into the room, each trying to hide behind the other, knowing that the poor results of their search were likely to incur the Chief's wrath. Their assumption was correct.

Cluny's baleful eye watched them as his long flexible tail sorted through the paltry offerings which had dropped from their claws. A few dead beetles, two large earthworms, some unidentifiable vegetation and the pitiful carcass of a long-dead sparrow.

Cluny smiled at Ragear and Mangefur.

With a sigh of relief they grinned back at him. The Chief was in a good mood.

At lightning speed the big rat's claws shot out, and grabbed them both cruelly by the ears. The stupid henchrats yowled pit-

eously as they were lifted bodily from the floor and swung to
and fro. In a fit of rage, Cluny bashed their heads together. Half
senseless, they were hurled towards the doorway, with his angry
words ringing in their skulls. "Beetles, worms, rotten sparrows!
Get me meat. Tender, young, red meat! Next time you bring me
rubbish like this, I'll spit the pair of you and have you roasted
in your own juice. Is that clear?"

Mangefur pointed an accusing claw at his companion.
"Please, Chief, it was Ragear's fault. If we'd gone across the
fields instead of up the road—"

"Don't believe that big fat liar, Chief. It was him who suggested going up the road, not me—"

"Get out!"

The scavengers dashed off, bumping clumsily into each other
with panic as they tried to get through the door together. Cluny
slumped back on the bed and snorted impatiently.

Frogblood and Scumnose were next to report.

They bore news that cheered Cluny up somewhat. They'd
obtained over a hundred new recruits, mainly rats but with a
good scattering of ferrets and weasels, and the odd stoat. There
had been some who needed convincing. These had been press-
ganged by a savage beating from Frogblood, coupled with the
threat of horrible death. They were soon convinced that the wisest course was to enlist in Cluny's horde. Others were hungry
nomads, only too willing to join up with the infamous Cluny.
They were greedy for plunder and booty and pleased to be on
what they were sure would be the winning side. Lined up in the
churchyard, the recruits were supplied with weaponry by Redtooth and Darkclaw. Impassively they stood in ranks awaiting
the Warlord's inspection.

Cluny nodded his approval. Scurvy rats, hungry ferrets, sly
weasels, bad stoats—exactly what he needed.

"Read 'em the articles, Redtooth," he snapped.

Redtooth swaggered back and forth on the churchyard paving
as he recited the formula from memory. "Right, eyes front.
You're in the service of Cluny the Scourge now, me buckoes!
Desert and you'll be killed. Retreat and you're under sentence
of death. Disobey and you'll die. I'm Redtooth, Cluny's
number-one rat. You will obey the word of your captains. They
take orders from me. I take orders from Cluny, remember that.
Now, if any one, two, or a group, or even all of you together

want to try and beat Cluny and lead the horde, this is your chance.''

Without warning, Cluny charged headlong into the new recruits, lashing out wildly with his scourging tail. He bowled them left, right, and center with his massive strength. Baring his teeth and slitting his eye, he whipped fiercely away until they fell back and scattered in disorder, hiding behind gravestones. Cluny threw back his head and roared with laughter.

"No guts, eh? Ha, it's just as well! I don't want dead 'uns on my claws before I find a proper battle for you to fight. And make no mistake, when the right time comes I'll see you fight, aye, and die too. Now, raise your weapons and let's see if you know who your master is.''

A motley collection of evil-looking implements was framed by the cloudless sky as wild cries rang out from the newly-inducted recruits.

"Cluny, Cluny, Cluny the Scourge!''

CHAPTER

9

Abbot Mortimer and Constance the badger meandered through the grounds together. Both creatures were deep in thought. Had they spoken and voiced their thoughts, they would have mentioned the same subject, the safety of Redwall.

Down long ages the beautiful old Abbey had stood for happiness, peace and refuge to all. Diligent mice tended the neat little vegetable patches which every season gave forth an abundance of fresh produce: cabbages, sprouts, marrows, turnips, peas, carrots, tomatoes, lettuces and onions, all in their turn. Flowerbeds, heady and fragrant with countless varieties of summer blooms from rose to humble daisy, were planted by the mice and husbanded by the hard-working bee folk, who in their turn rewarded Redwall with plentiful supplies of honey and beeswax.

The two friends wandered onwards, past the pond. Early-morning sunlight glinted off the water, throwing out ripples from the fish caught by the overnight lines which were baited and left to drift each evening by Brother Alf. Ahead of them lay the berry-hedges—raspberry, blackberry, bilberry—and the strawberry patch where every August sleepy baby creatures could be seen, their stomachs full after eating the pick of the crop. Gradually they made their way around the big old chestnut trees into the orchard. This was the Abbot's favorite spot. Many a leisurely nap had he taken on sunny afternoons with the aroma of ripening fruit hovering in his whiskers: apples, pears, quince, plums, damsons, even a vine of wild grape on the warm red stone of a south-facing wall. Old Mother Nature's blessing lay upon a haven of warm friendliness.

Now with the threat of Cluny upon Redwall, the two old friends assessed the beauteous bounty of their lifelong abode. Sweet birdsong on the still air tinged Constance's heart with sorrow and regret that this peaceful existence would soon pass. Gruffly she snuffled deep in her throat, blinking off a threatening teardrop. The Abbot sensed his companion's distress. He patted the badger's rough coat with a gentle paw.

"There, there, old girl. Don't fret. Many times in our history has tragedy been forestalled by miraculous happenings."

Constance grunted in agreement, not wishing to disillusion her trusting old friend. Deep within her she knew a dark shadow was casting itself over the Abbey. Furthermore, it was happening in the present, not in bygone days of fabled deeds.

Matthias seated himself to an early breakfast in Cavern Hole: nutbread, apples and a bowl of fresh goatsmilk. Cornflower, along with other woodland creatures granted sanctuary, was sleeping in makeshift quarters provided by the good mice of Redwall. Matthias felt that he had grown up overnight. Duty was a mantle that he had taken willingly upon his shoulders. If there were a threat to Redwall from outside it must be dealt with. The mice of Redwall were peaceful creatures, but that must not be taken as a sign of weakness. Stolidly he munched away as he confronted the problem.

"Eat heartily, Matthias. No point in facing trouble on an empty stomach. Feed the body, nourish the mind."

The young mouse was surprised to see that old Brother Methuselah had been watching him, his eyes twinkling behind the curious spectacles he invariably wore. The ancient mouse sat down at the breakfast table with a small groan.

"Don't look so surprised, young one. Your face is an open book to one of my years."

Matthias drained the last of the milk from his bowl, wiping cream from his whiskers with the back of a paw. "Give me your advice, Brother Methuselah," he said. "What would you do?"

The old mouse wrinkled his nose. "Exactly the same thing

as you would—that is, if I were younger and not so old and stiff.''

Matthias felt he had found an ally. "You mean you would fight?''

Methuselah rapped the table with a bony paw. "Of course I would. It's the only sensible course to take.''

He paused and stared at Matthias in an odd manner. "Hmm, y'know there's something about you, young feller. Did you ever hear the story of how Martin the Warrior first came to Redwall?''

Matthias leaned forward eagerly. "Martin! Tell me, Brother, I love hearing about the warrior monk.''

Methuselah's voice dropped to a secretive whisper. "It is written in the great chronicle of Redwall that Martin was very young to be such a warrior. He could have been the same age as yourself, Matthias. Like you, he was impulsive and had a great quality of youthful innocence about him when he first came to our Abbey. But it is also written that in times of trouble Martin had the gift of a natural leader, a command over others far superior to him in age and experience. The chronicle says that they looked to Martin as some look to a strong father.''

Matthias was full of wonderment, but he could not help feeling puzzled. "Why do you tell all this to me, Brother Methuselah?''

The old mouse stood up. He stared hard at Matthias for a moment, then, turning, he shuffled slowly off. As he went, he called back over his shoulder, "Because, Matthias . . . because he was very like you!''

Before the young mouse could question the old one further, the Joseph Bell tolled out a warning. Sandals flapping, Matthias dashed out into the grounds, nearly colliding with the Abbot and Constance, who, like everyone else, were heading for the gatehouse.

Brothers Rufus and George had an incident to report. A large evil-looking rat, covered in tattoos and carrying a rusty cutlass, had turned up at the gate. He had tried to gain entry by pretending he was injured. Limping about, the rat explained that he had been in a hay cart that overturned into the ditch. Would they come with him and render assistance to his friends, many of whom were lying trapped beneath the cart, crying out for help?

Brother Rufus was no fool. "How many rats were traveling in the cart altogether?" he asked.

"Oh, a couple of hundred," came the glib reply.

Then why, reasoned Brother Rufus, did the rats not give aid to their own companions? Surely all two hundred were not trapped? The rat evaded the question and made a great show of rubbing his injured leg. Could they not take him in and dress his wound and perhaps give him a bite to eat at least?

Brother George agreed, on condition that the rat surrender his weapon.

The rat made as if to do so, then suddenly lunged at Brother George, only to be sent sprawling by a blow from Brother Rufus's staff. Realizing that he was up against two big, competent mice who would stand no nonsense, he became abusive and bad-mouthed.

"Ha! Just you wait, mice," he raged. "There's a whole army of us camped down in the church. When I tell Cluny how you treated me, ho ho, just wait, that's all. We'll be back, by the fang we will." With that he slunk off, cursing all mice.

The grim news was digested in silence by the assembled creatures. Mrs. Churchmouse began sobbing. "Oh dearie me. Did you hear that, m'dear? They must be living in our home at St. Ninian's Church. Oh, whatever shall we do? Our dear little home, full of dreadful rats."

Mr. John Churchmouse tried to comfort his wife as best he could. "There, there, hush now, Missus. Better to lose a house than lose our lives. A good job we got sanctuary here at Redwall."

"But what about the other creatures in the area?" cried Matthias.

"Sensible mouse," said Constance. "Is Ambrose Spike anywhere about? He'd better do the rounds and tell them to take sanctuary here at the Abbey as quickly as possible. Spike'll come to no harm. Once he curls up, there's nothing can touch him."

This idea was greeted with enthusiasm. Brother Alf went off to find the hedgehog.

The Abbot suggested they all go inside the Abbey and await

further developments. Matthias piped up again, "We'd best
mount a guard on the walls."

One of the older mice, Sister Clemence, chided Matthias as
an upstart. Her voice was stern and condescending. "Novice
Matthias, you will be silent and do as your Abbot commands."

Much to everyone's surprise, the Abbot came to Matthias's
defense. "One moment, Clemence, Matthias speaks sense. Let
us hear what he has to say. We are none of us too old to learn."

All eyes were turned on the young mouse as Matthias heard
himself boldly outline his plans for the defense of Redwall.

It was eleven o'clock on that glorious June morning. Mossflower
Wood and the meadowlands stirred to the brazen voice of the
great Joseph Bell. John Churchmouse heaved on the bellrope as
he had been told to by Constance and Matthias.

Bong! Boom! Bong! Boom! Even the small creatures in wood
and field who could understand no language save their own
knew what it meant. "Time of danger, place of sanctuary."

Carrying what simple belongings they needed, woodlanders
and their families hurried from far and near to gain the safety
of the Abbey before the storm of Cluny broke upon them—
squirrels, mice, voles, moles, otters, all save the birds of the air,
who were safe anyway. Up the long dusty road they came,
mothers protectively herding young ones while fathers provided
a rearguard.

Brother Methuselah stood at the gate with the Abbot. He
translated fully to each group of creatures the Abbot's message,
in turn construing back to the Father Abbot their grateful thanks
with pledges of help and loyalty to Redwall Abbey. For what
creature had not been freely given the aid and special knowledge
of the kindly mice? All knew that they owed their very existence
to the Abbot and his community.

Healing, aid, food, shelter and good advice were granted to
all. Now was the time to unite and repay, to give any help that
was possible. Before much longer Redwall would require the
skills and knowledge of all its woodland allies. They would be
gratefully given!

Matthias and Constance stood on top of the high perimeter
walls, watching the road. It was noon, and the sun shone directly
overhead. Despite the heat, Matthias had ordered all the mice

to put on their hoods. It served a double purpose, to shield their eyes from the sun and create a camouflage effect. Silently each one stood, armed with a stout staff. The high red sandstone walls were far too lofty to be scaled by any normal creature. Instinctively Matthias knew this was a good defense and a formidable deterrent.

Constance could feel her hackles beginning to prickle. She sniffed the air and shivered despite the heat that shimmered in waves across the meadowlands. The big badger nudged Matthias.

"Listen to that."

Matthias pricked up his ears and looked at her, questioning.

"Even the birds have stopped singing," Constance said quietly.

The young mouse gripped his staff tighter. "Yes, it's the silence we can hear. The grasshoppers have gone quiet."

Constance peered down the road as she spoke. "Strange for a summer day, little friend."

Bong!

Every creature standing on the ramparts twitched with fright as the loud voice of the Joseph Bell rang out, and John Churchmouse shouted from his position high in the belfry, "They're coming, down the road! I can see them. I can see them!"

CHAPTER

10

Cluny's army halted at the sound of the Joseph Bell. As the dust settled, Fangburn looked to his leader for approval.

"They're ringing that big bell again, Chief. Ha! ha! Maybe they think it'll frighten us off."

The Warlord's eye rested balefully on his scout. "Shut your mouth, fool. If you'd done as I ordered and come right back to report, the way Cheesethief did, we might have been inside that Abbey by now!"

Fangburn slunk back into the ranks. He hoped Cluny had forgotten, but Cluny rarely forgot anything on a campaign. The element of surprise had been lost—now he must try another ploy, the show of force. The mere sight of a fully armed horde had worked before, and he had little doubt it would prove effective now. Ordinary peaceful creatures were usually panic-stricken at the sight of Cluny the Scourge at the head of his army. The rat was a cunning general, except the times when his mad rage took control of him, but what need of berserk fits for a bunch of silly mice?

Cluny knew the value of fear as a weapon.

And Cluny was a fearsome figure.

His long ragged black cloak was made of batwings, fastened at the throat with a mole skull. The immense war helmet he wore had the plumes of a blackbird and the horns of a stag

38

beetle adorning it. From beneath the slanted visor his one eye glared viciously out at the Abbey before him.

Matthias's voice rang out sharp and clear from the high parapet, "Halt! Who goes there?"

Redtooth swaggered forward and took up the challenge in his Chief's name, as he called back up at the walls, "Look well, all creatures. This is the mighty horde of Cluny the Scourge. My name is Redtooth. I speak for Cluny our leader."

Constance's reply was harsh and unafraid, "Then speak your piece and begone, rats."

Silence hung upon the air while Redtooth and Cluny held a whispered conference. Redtooth returned to the walls.

"Cluny the Scourge says he will not deal with badgers, he will only speak with the leaders of the mice. Let us in, so that my Chief may sit and talk to your Chief."

Redtooth dodged back as his request was greeted by howls of derision and some loose pieces of masonry from the ramparts. These plump little mice were not as peaceful as they first looked.

The rats looked to Cluny, but he was eyeing the Abbot who had joined Constance and Matthias. They appeared to be consulting quietly. Cluny watched tensely. There seemed to be some disagreement between the old mouse and his two advisers. They conferred awhile; then Matthias came forward to the parapet. He pointed at Cluny and Redtooth with his staff.

"You there, and you also. My Abbot will talk with you both. The rest must remain outside."

A rumble of protest from the horde was silenced by a crack from Cluny's tail. He lifted his visor.

"We agree, mouse, let us in."

"But what about hostages for safe conduct?" hissed Redtooth.

Cluny spat contemptuously. "Don't talk fool's talk. D'you imagine a load of mice in funny robes could take me captive?"

Redtooth gnawed anxiously on a split claw. "Maybe not, Chief, but have you cast a weather eye over that badger?"

Cluny answered quietly out of the side of his mouth, "Don't worry, I've been watching her. A real big country bumpkin. No, these are mice of honor; they'd sooner die than break their word to anyone. You leave this to me."

As Cluny and Redtooth made for the gatehouse door, Constance shouted, "Put down your weapons, rats. Throw off your armor to show us that you come in peace."

Redtooth spluttered angrily. "Hell's teeth! Who does that one think she's ordering around?"

Cluny shot him a warning glance. "Quiet. Do as she says."

Both rats took off their armor and placed it in a pile on the road. Matthias cried down to Cluny, "If you really are Cluny the Scourge, then we know of your tail. It is a weapon. Therefore you will knot it tightly around your waist so that it cannot be used."

Cluny laughed mirthlessly. He squinted at Matthias and cracked his tail dramatically.

"Young mouse," he called. "You do right to ask this thing, for truly you are looking at Cluny the Scourge."

Having said this he took his tail in his claws, and pulled the poison war spike from its tip. Tossing it on the armor pile, Cluny hitched his tail in a knot around his middle.

"Now will you let us in, mice? You can see we are unarmed."

Ponderously the heavy gate inched open. The two rats passed through a bristling forest of staves. The gate slammed shut behind them.

Cluny mentally estimated the walls to be of immense thickness as he and Redtooth, ducking their heads, emerged from the tunnel-like arch into the Abbey grounds, where Constance and Matthias were waiting in the sunlight. The defenders followed the two rats closely, menacing them with staves.

Matthias rapped out a curt command, "Leave us, mice. Go back to your duties on the wall."

Unhappy at leaving the Abbot unguarded, the mice hesitated to obey the order to withdraw. Cluny addressed Matthias scornfully, "Here, mouse, watch me shift 'em."

Suddenly he whirled upon the apprehensive creatures. The single eye rolled madly in its socket as Cluny bared claws and fangs, snarling, "Ha harr! I've got a powerful hunger for mice! You'd best get aloft on those walls. Ha harr!"

Cluny leaped into the air. The mice scattered in panic.

Constance stopped the proceedings with a loud angry bark. "Here now. Enough of that, rat. You are here to talk with the Abbot. Get along with you."

*   *   *

Matthias was glad he was walking behind the rats; he blushed with shame. Cluny had sent the defenders scattering like butterflies in a whirlwind. Matthias was furious; the enemy now knew he was dealing with untrained and untested soldiers.

As the party walked towards Cavern Hole, Cluny could sense hostility emanating from the young mouse who flip-flopped behind him in overlarge sandals. Strange for one so young to be counted as a captain, he thought. Moreover, the little fellow didn't seem to fear him. Ah, but enough of that. Cluny would deal with him when the time came. Meanwhile, the big rat gazed about his surroundings in secret admiration. What an astounding place!

He allowed himself a peek at the future. One day this would be called Cluny's Castle. He liked the sound of that. Secure from attack, living off the fat of the land, in his mind's eye he saw it all: those mice and the woodland creatures enslaved, living just to serve him. He would hold sway as far as the eye could see; power; an end to his rovings; a dream come true; King Cluny!

Entering the Abbey, the party stopped to make way for a pretty little fieldmouse bearing a tray.

"Oh, Matthias," she said. "I've brought some refreshments for you and—"

"Thank you, Cornflower. Put them down on the table," said Matthias abruptly.

Redtooth nudged Cluny. "Cornflower, eh. Satan's nose, she's a pretty little one for you!"

Cluny remained silent. He stood insolently watching Cornflower set the table in Cavern Hole. A pretty one indeed!

The Abbot indicated chairs. They all sat except Cluny, who lounged against the table using the chair as a footstool. He glared at Redtooth until he stood and waited alongside his Chief. Idly Cluny picked up a bowl of honeyed milk and sampled it.

Slop! He spat it out on the floor.

The Abbot folded his paws into the wide sleeves of his habit and stared impassively at the Warlord. "What do you want at Redwall Abbey, my son?"

Cluny kicked the chair over and laughed madly. As the echoes died around the room his face went grim.

"Your son, ha. That's a good one! I'll tell you what I want, mouse. I want it all. The lot. Everything. Do you hear me?"

Matthias's chair clattered on its side as he sprang forward, breaking free from the restraining paws of the Abbot.

"Listen, rat, you don't scare me! I'll give you our answer. You get nothing! Now do you understand that?"

Shaking with fury, Matthias allowed himself to be pulled back on to the chair. The Abbot turned to Cluny.

"You must forgive Matthias. He is young and headstrong. Now, as to your proposal, I am afraid it is out of the question. Should you or your army require medical attention, food, clothing or help upon your way, you will find us only too willing to assist—"

Cluny interrupted rudely by pounding upon the table until the Abbot was silenced. He pointed a claw at Redtooth.

"Read them the articles."

Redtooth held up a tattered parchment. He cleared his throat. "These are the articles of surrender to be obeyed by all creatures who come under the claw of Cluny the Scourge or any of his commanders. *One:* surrender will be total and unconditional. *Two:* Cluny will execute the leaders of all who choose to oppose him. *Three:* all property conquered will belong solely to Cluny the Scourge. This includes homes, food, crops, land and additionally all creatures dwelling on said property: they shall be owned by Cluny—"

Thwack!

Redtooth got no further. Unable to contain himself, Matthias sent his staff ripping through the middle of the articles. As the torn document fluttered to the floor, Redtooth launched himself at Matthias with a snarl.

The rat was actually in midair when a huge blunt paw knocked him flat. He lay stunned with Constance standing over him.

"Why pick on a small mouse? Surely a big strong rat like you can deal with an old badger? Come on, try me for size."

It was only the timely intervention of Abbot Mortimer that saved Redtooth's life.

"Constance, would you please let the rat up? Much as I would like to see him get his just desserts, you must remember we cannot break the law of hospitality in our Abbey."

Redtooth staggered shakily to his feet, backing warily away from the badger. Cluny spoke as if nothing had occurred, "You,

Abbot mouse, you have until tomorrow evening to give me your answer."

Not normally given to anger, the Abbot stared Cluny in the eye, his face a mask of cold fury.

"I will not need until tomorrow, rat. You can have my answer now. How dare you come here with your robber band to read articles of death and slavery to me? I tell you that neither you nor your army will ever set paw or claw inside Redwall, not while I or any of my creatures have breath in our bodies to fight and resist you. That is my solemn word."

Cluny sneered and turned on his heel. Followed by Redtooth, he stamped out. On the stairs between Cavern Hole and Great Hall he stopped and turned, his cold voice echoing between both chambers, "Then die, all of you: every male, female, and young one. You have refused my terms. Now you will suffer the punishment of Cluny. You will beg on your knees for death to come swiftly, but I shall make your torment loud and long before you die!"

It was then that Constance did something that creatures would speak of in years to come.

Exerting the full strength of a female badger, she lifted the massive Cavern Hole dining table. It was a huge solid oaken thing that no dozen mice could even move. Dishes clattered and food spilled as Constance heaved the table above her head. Her voice was a roar. "Get out, rats! Leave this Abbey! I'm weary of your voices. Hurry before I break the laws of hospitality and ask the Abbot's pardon later. Go, while you still have skulls."

With the best grace he could muster, Cluny walked rather quickly up the stairs, followed by Redtooth, who laughed nervously. "Big country bumpkin, eh, Chief? One more word from you back there and she'd have thrown that table and crushed us."

Remembering who it was that he had spoken to in this insolent fashion, Redtooth cringed, expecting Cluny to deal him a blow for impudence. But nothing happened.

Cluny was standing transfixed.

Oblivious to all about him, even Matthias and the Abbot who had followed him out, Cluny stood staring at the tapestry.

"Who is that mouse?" he gasped.

Matthias followed the direction of the rat's gaze. He walked to the tapestry with his paw outstretched.

"Do you mean this mouse?"

Cluny nodded dumbly.

Matthias, still with his paw outstretched, declared proudly, "This is Martin the Warrior. He founded our Order, and I'll tell you something else, rat. Martin was the bravest mouse that ever lived. If he were here today he'd just take up his big sword and send you and all your bullies packing. Those of you he didn't chop up into crow meat."

Much to everyone's surprise, Cluny allowed himself to be shown out. He was like one in a daze all the way back to the gatehouse.

A hush fell over the mice on guard as Cluny and Redtooth were let out on to the road. Swiftly, the horde gathered around the Warlord and his lieutenant. They awaited orders. Deputizing for Cluny, Redtooth called out, "Form up. Back to the church, everyone."

Cluny marched automatically, shaking his head in disbelief.

Martin the Warrior. The mouse who pursued him through his nightmares. What did it mean?

As Redtooth marched away, a voice hailed him from the wall. He turned and looked upwards. The torn articles—the parchment wrapped around a fistful of rotting vegetables—splattered in his face. Livid with rage he clawed the foul mess from his eyes and saw Constance leaning over the parapet with a wicked grin of delight on her striped muzzle.

The badger shouted mockingly, "Don't forget to call again, rat. I'd be delighted to see you. We've got some unfinished business that I'm looking forward to settling. Just you and me, Redtooth!"

Before the rat could reply, she had vanished from sight.

CHAPTER

II

Later that evening Brother Alf was patrolling his stretch of wall when he noticed a movement in the ferns at the edge of Moss-flower Wood. Constance and Matthias were summoned hastily. They peered over the parapet. Brother Alf pointed to where he had seen the ferns moving.

"Over there, to the right of that aspen. Look, they're moving again."

Matthias had better nocturnal vision than either of his friends. He was the first to recognize the forlorn figure that rolled on to the grass.

"It's Ambrose Spike. He's hurt. Quick, let's get down there."

"Hold fast," Constance warned. "It may be a trap."

Matthias was loth to hang about while a creature was lying injured within his sight, but he had to heed his friend's advice. There just might be some of Cluny's rats lying in ambush for any creature that ventured into the shadowy fringes of Moss-flower. However, Matthias was growing impatient.

"We can't leave poor Ambrose lying out there, Constance. He'll die. We've got to do something."

The badger sat down with her snout between her paws. "Yes, we've got to think. Anyone got an idea?"

The two mice joined her. Hardly had Matthias sat down when he leaped up again.

"I've got it. Stay here. I'll be back in a tick!"

Brother Alf watched the little figure flip-flopping off. He gave a sigh and shook his head. "What do you suppose our Matthias is up to?"

The badger smiled affectionately. More and more she was coming to trust Matthias's natural skill as a leader and tactician. "Don't fret, Brother Alf. Whatever it is, you can bet your habit it'll be an original Matthias gem. That young mouse has got more in his head than a pile of acorns."

Brother Alf looked out at the still form in the grass. "It may be too late. Ambrose isn't even twitching. Look, he's not rolled up in a ball anymore."

Further speculation was curtailed by the appearance of Matthias. With him were half a dozen moles.

Their leader glanced out at the hedgehog. He scratched some hasty calculations on the wall with his claw, then turned to Matthias. "Oi I think we can get yon 'edgepig back, sur. You'm get us outen the gate and stan' watch."

Turning to his team, the Foremole (for that was his official title) began discussing tunnel width, coupled with reverse prickle drag, forward traction and all the other specialist details that are routine to the average qualified tunnel-mole.

Matthias whispered to Constance and Brother Alf, "Foremole and his crew are first class at rescue work. They've often rescued burrowers from cave-ins. All we have to do is stand guard by the south-east wicket gate until they're safely back."

"Right. What are we waiting for? Let's go," said the badger.

Silently they slid outside the small green-painted iron door, Matthias straining his eyes anxiously to see if there were any signs of life in the hedgehog. He still lay about a hundred and fifty mouse paces from where they stood.

The moles unraveled a rope sling. Foremole stood watching as two of his team started the dig.

Matthias looked on in wonderment. One minute they were above ground, a moment later there was a veritable shower of loam and topsoil as they vanished beneath the earth: nature's own technicians.

In a trice they were back, moist snouts poking from the excavation. They made their ground report to Foremole.

"Harr, he'm be noice an' soft, sur. Baint no rock nor root to stop us'ns, straight furrer we'm a-thinking."

Satisfied, Foremole moved towards the test hole with the rest of his team. "Oi'll dig ahead, you'm woiden workin's. Gaffer and Marge, foller up a-shorin'." He tugged his snout respectfully to Matthias and Constance. "You'm gennelbeast bide by 'ere 'til us back."

Another quick shower of soft dark earth and the moles were lost to view beneath the ground surface.

Constance sniffed the breeze as Matthias turned his ears to the nighttime woodland sounds. They watched the ground humping into a continuous hillock that progressed farther as the moles tunneled towards Ambrose Spike. The night remained calm and still, but Matthias and Constance stayed alert, both knowing if they failed to observe this rudimentary law of nature, the penalty could be fatal.

Matthias did a little shuffle of excitement. "Look, they've come up right under poor old Ambrose! My word, what splendid moles. Good heavens, he's vanished completely! They must have him inside the tunnel."

In a surprisingly short time the tunnelers were back. Emerging from the hole, they carried the hedgehog in the rope sling across their backs, refusing any help from the badger or the mouse. Foremole merely tugged his snout.

"Nay, nay, you uns on'y get yer paws durted."

As swiftly as possible Ambrose was hurried to the Abbey infirmary and sick bay. He was attended by the Abbot himself. A hasty diagnosis revealed that the hedgehog was suffering from a long jagged wound that ran from the back of his ear to the tip of his paw. Brother Alf nodded sympathetically.

"That's probably what caused old Ambrose to pass out. Pain and loss of blood. He must have traveled a fair way in that condition. D'you think he'll live, Father Abbot?"

The Abbot chuckled quietly. He cleaned the long ugly wound and applied a poultice of herbs. "No cause for alarm, Brother Alf. Ambrose Spike is made of leather and needles. Tough as a boulder, this old ruffian is. Look, he's beginning to come around already."

Sure enough, after some peculiar grunts and much curling and uncurling, the hedgehog opened his eyes and looked about. "Oh my aching ear. Father Abbot, you wouldn't see a poor son of the Spike suffering like this without a drop of last October's nutbrown ale to wet his parched gullet,'' he pleaded.

All the creatures laughed aloud with delight and relief at see-ing their old friend alive and well once again.

Matthias was astonished at the amount of nutbrown ale that Ambrose supped before he deemed himself fit enough to make a report. The hedgehog smacked his lips noisily.

''Aaaahhh, that's better. Now, let me see. I did as you asked me, gave as many creatures fair warning as I could. The Joseph Bell helped a great deal to warn everyone. Well, to cut a long story short, it must have been near noon when I stopped at Vole Bank. I told the Voles the bad news, and blow me if that little ninny Colin Vole didn't go to shrieking and screaming all over the place as to how they'd all be murdered in their beds. Believe me, there was no way of silencing the daft young thing. Any-how, his noise must have alerted a pack of those rats who were out foraging. Before you could say 'knife' they were upon us. There was such a gang of them that I couldn't do anything, I had to curl up. They carried off young Colin and his mum and dad, but try as they would there was no laying claws on Am-brose Spike, no sir. Then one of them had a go at me with a point of an iron churchyard railing. Stabbed away at me, the devil did. They reckoned I was dead. Said I was too spiky to eat, so they dragged the Vole family off and I lay still until the coast was clear. I made it as far as Mossflower and that's all I can remember. Er, is there any more left in that jug? This wound's giving me jip. I need ale for medicinal purposes, Father Abbot.''

Matthias groaned and hung his head in despair. The Vole family taken captive; death or slavery was all the wretched creatures could look forward to. Emboldened by the rescue of the hedge-hog, Matthias was about to suggest that he and Constance, to-gether with some hand-picked helpers, venture to undertake a rescue mission to St. Ninian's Church. It was as if the Abbot and Constance both read his thoughts at the same time. Abbot Mortimer sighed and shook his head at Matthias. The badger was more voluble.

''Matthias, forget it. Abandon any hopes you have of snatch-ing the Vole family from under Cluny's nose. Imagine it, a few of us going up against several hundred armed rats in their own camp. Ridiculous. A fat lot of good we'd be as defenders of

Redwall with our heads fixed to Cluny's standard. Matthias, you're a very brave young mouse, so please try to set an example to the rest by not becoming a foolish or dead one.''

On reflection, Matthias could see the wisdom of the badger's counsel. Long after they had all retired for the night he sat up thinking. A hundred mad ideas pounded through his brain, each one wilder than the last. Feeling at a loss, he wandered up into Great Hall and stood in front of the tapestry. Without consciously realizing it, he found himself talking to Martin the Warrior.

''Oh Martin, what would you have done in my place? I know that I'm only a young mouse, a novice, not even a proper Redwall member yet, but once you were young too. I know what you would have done. You'd have buckled on your armor, picked up your mighty sword, gone down to that church and battled with the rats until they released the Voles or perished beneath your blade. But alas, those days are gone. I have no magic sword to aid me, only the advice of my elders and betters, to which I must listen.''

Matthias sat down upon the cool stone floor. He gazed longingly up at Martin the Warrior, so proud, so brave. What a dashing figure he cut. Looking back down to himself in his baggy green robes and oversized sandals, Matthias felt hot tears of shame and frustration spilling from his eyes and dripping on his young whiskers. Unable to stop himself, he wept freely. The soft touch of a gentle paw on his back caused him to look around. It was Cornflower.

Matthias wished he were dead!

He quickly turned his face away, knowing she could see his tears.

''Cornflower, please go away,'' Matthias sobbed.

The little fieldmouse, however, would not go. She sat down on the floor next to Matthias. Taking the edge of her pinafore she softly wiped away his tears. For such a shy little mouse she had quite a bit to say.

''Matthias, don't be ashamed, I know why you cry and grieve. It is because you are kind and good, not a hard-hearted pitiless rat like Cluny. Please listen to me. Even the strongest and bravest must sometimes weep. It shows they have a great heart, one that can feel compassion for others. You are brave, Matthias. Already you have done great things for one so young. I am only a simple country-bred fieldmouse, but even I can see the courage and leadership in you. A burning brand shows the way, and each day your flame grows brighter. There is none like you, Matthias. You have the sign of greatness upon you. One day Redwall and all the land will be indebted to you. Matthias, you are a true Warrior.''

Matthias, with his eyes dry and his head held high, stood up; he felt himself stand taller than he ever had. He helped Cornflower to her feet and bowed to her.

''Cornflower, how can I ever thank you for what you have said? You too are a very special mouse. It is late now. Go and get some rest. I think I will stay here a while longer.''

The fieldmouse untied her headband. It was her favorite one, pale yellow bordered with the cornflowers after which she was named. She tied it to Matthias's arm, the right one, just above the elbow. A maiden's colors for her champion warrior.

Silently she crept off. Matthias could feel his heart beating against his chest. He spoke to the image of Martin.

''Thank you, Warrior. You spoke to me through Cornflower. You gave me the sign that I asked of you.''

CHAPTER

12

At the Church of St. Ninian, Cluny sat in the wreckage of what had once been a pulpit. Redtooth, Darkclaw, Cheesethief, and Fangburn lounged about at his feet on old burst hassocks. Cluny was in one of his strange moods again. He showed little interest in the captive Vole family, merely ordering that they be kept under guard until he found time to deal with them. Most of his army slept in the choir loft or the lady chapel. The rest were posted on sentry duty outside.

Cautiously, his captains watched the Warlord. Cluny's long tail swished restlessly, the single eye stared at a carved eagle holding the rotting lectern on its outspread wings. What thoughts occupied the dark devious mind of Cluny the Scourge? Finally he looked up and spoke.

"Go and get Shadow. Bring him here to me."

Darkclaw and Fangburn scurried off to obey the command. Silently the others waited, their eyes glinting in evil anticipation.

The Chief had a plan. Like all of his schemes it would be cunningly simple and wickedly brilliant. There was no better general than Cluny when it came to strategy.

Shadow had been with Cluny for many years. Nobody was sure if he was rat or weasel, or even a bit of both. He was very lithe and wiry, and his long sinewy body was covered in sleek, black fur. There was no hint of another color in his coat; it was blacker than moonless midnight. His eyes were strangely slanted, black without any brightness in them. The eyes of Shadow were like those of a dead thing.

He stood before Cluny, who had to strain his one eye against the darkness of the church to make sure he was really there.

"Shadow, is that you?"

The reply sounded like a whisper of wet silk across a smooth slate. "Cluny, I am here. Why do you want Shadow?"

The captains shivered at the sound of the voice. Cluny leaned forward. "Did you see the walls of that Abbey today?"

"I was there. Shadow sees all."

"Tell me true. Could you climb them?"

"No beast I know of could climb those walls."

"Except you?"

"Except me."

Cluny gestured with his tail. "Come closer then. I will tell you what must be done."

Shadow sat on the top pulpit step. Cluny issued his orders. "You will climb the Abbey wall. Many sentries patrol the top of the wall. Take the utmost care. If you get captured, you are of no use to me. There is no point in one alone trying to attack the gatehouse and open the door. It is too well guarded, so forget the gate."

Shadow gave no hint that Cluny had inadvertently read his mind. He remained motionless as Cluny continued, "Once you have scaled the wall, make for the main Abbey door. Should it be locked for the night you will use all your skill to open it without any noise. It is vital that you get inside. The first room you will find yourself in is the main one. The mice call it Great Hall. Walk in, turn around, and on the left wall facing you is a long tapestry covered in pictures and designs. Now listen carefully. In the bottom right-hand corner of that tapestry is a picture of a mouse dressed in armor, leaning on a big sword. I want it! Cut it, rip it, or tear it out, but get it for me. I must have it! Don't come back without it, Shadow."

Puzzlement was written on the faces of the four captains who had overheard the orders.

A picture of a mouse?

Cluny had never been known as a collector of pictures.

Fangburn whispered to Cheesethief, "What use is a picture of a mouse to the Chief?"

Cluny heard. He came to the edge of the pulpit. Grasping the sides of the lectern he surveyed his small congregation like some satanic minister.

"Ah, Brother Fangburn, let me explain. I will tell you why it is that you and all your kind will forever remain servants, while I shall always be the master. Did you not see the faces of those mice today? The mere mention of Martin the Warrior sends them into ecstasies. Don't you see, he is their symbol. His name means the same to those mice as mine does to the horde: in a different way maybe. Martin is some sort of angel; I'm the opposite. Think for a moment. If anything were to happen to me, you'd all be a leaderless rabble, a headless mob. So, if the mice were to lose their most precious omen, the picture of Martin, where would that leave them?"

Redtooth slapped his haunches. He rocked to and fro, sniggering with uncontrolled glee.

"Brilliant, Chief, diabolical! They'd just be a crowd of terrified little mice without their wonderful Martin."

Cluny's tail banged down on the rotting lectern, smashing it into several fragments.

"And that's when we'll strike!"

The powerful tail lashed backwards, wrapping itself around Shadow's body. He was dragged forward, face to face with his master. Cluny's rancid breath blasted into Shadow's face as he ground out each syllable.

"Bring that picture back here to me. Do this, and your reward will be great when I sit on the Abbot's chair in Redwall Abbey. But fail me, and your screams will be heard far beyond the woodland and meadows!"

Cluny the Scourge had spoken.

CHAPTER

13

The sun's first rays flung wide the gates of dawn. The inhabitants of Redwall were already up and about. After breakfast the Abbot issued daily orders. All those not employed defending the Abbey would husband the crops and gather in supplies for the larders in the event of a prolonged siege. Young otters collected watercress and fished; Cornflower headed a party of mice to reap the early cereal crops; more youngsters tended the salad gardens. The bright summer morning hummed to the bustle of industrious woodlanders.

Ambrose Spike, now sufficiently recovered, sat in the storeroom taking stock: lots of nuts and preserved berries from last autumn; apples and pears aplenty. Unfortunately, the hedgehog could not check the cellars; Brother Edmund and Friar Hugo had the only two keys. He licked his lips at the thought of barrels of nutbrown ale, strong cider, creamy stout and the little kegs—ah, the dear little kegs!—full of elderberry wine, mulberry brandy, blackcurrant port and wild grape sherry.

"Yurr, 'edgepig. Where'm us a-puttin' these roots an' dannylines? 'Asten up, they'm roight 'eavy."

Ambrose sighed wistfully as he attended the two moles staggering under a bundle of dandelions and tubers.

"Arr, 'old 'em liddle taters steady, Bill. Yurr, tip 'em up, leggo."

More baby moles. Ambrose pawed the bandage on his wound.
A hedgehog's work was never done.

Matthias and Constance stood in the cloisters. They had taken
charge of weapon training. The woodlanders were each showing
off their special skills. In more peaceful days, these skills had
only been used at fairs and sporting contests, but now, when the
need arose, they would be used with more deadly effect.

The otters carried bags of smooth pebbles which they hurled
from vine slings with great force and accuracy. Groups of fieldmouse archers nocked thistledown shafts to the strings of their
longbows. Many a marauding bird had been driven off by these
same tiny archers. Bands of Redwall mice practiced at thrust
and parry with staves.

Below the wall on the Abbey grass Foremole directed his
crew as they dug a trench. This was lined with sharpened stakes
by a solitary beaver. A system of ropes and pulleys carried the
baskets of stone and trench debris up to the ramparts. Defenders
piled it in heaps at the edge of the parapet.

Matthias took a group of Redwall mice to instruct in the use
of the quarter staff—he had discovered in himself a natural skill
with the long ash pole. None of the mice had ever competed in
any type of violent sport; they were awkward and timid. But as
it was a personal choice between learning cudgel and wrestling
from Constance or quarter staff from Matthias, to a mouse they
had opted for the latter.

Matthias found he had to be quite severe with them. Accordingly, he dealt out some hefty blows and hard falls to make the
more timid souls angry enough to retaliate.

"Keep that head guarded, Brother Anthony!"

Thwack!

"I warned you, Brother! Now look out, I'm coming after you
again."

Thwack!

"No, no! Don't just stand there, Brother! Defend yourself!
Hit out at me."

Thwack, crack!

This time, Matthias sat down hard, rubbing dazedly at his
sore head. Constance chuckled.

"Well, Matthias, you've only yourself to blame. You asked
Brother Anthony to hit out at you and, my word, he certainly

obliged. I'll have to recruit him for my cudgel class! He shows promise."

Matthias stood up, smiling ruefully. He rested on his staff. "Yes, he's very strong, but I do wish that we had some real weapons of war—swords and daggers and such like. We won't kill many rats with wooden staves."

"Maybe not," the badger replied. "But you must remember that we are here to defend, not to attack or kill."

Matthias threw down his staff. He took a dipper of water from an oaken pail, drinking deeply, then splashing the remains over his aching head.

"A wise observation, Constance, but you try telling that to Cluny and his horde. See how far you get."

Lunch that day was served out in the orchard. Matthias lined up with the other woodland creatures to collect his food: a bowl of fresh milk, a hunk of wheaten loaf and some goatsmilk cheese. Cornflower was serving. She gave Matthias an extra large wedge of the cheese. He rolled up the sleeve of his habit and pulled out the corner of her scarf.

"Look, Cornflower, a very close friend gave me this last night."

She laughed at him. "Get along, and eat your lunch, warrior mouse, or I'll show you my deadly aim with a piece of this cheese."

Strolling through the dappled shade of the orchard, Matthias sought out old Methuselah. Slumping down beneath a damson tree, the young mouse munched away at his lunch. Methuselah was sitting with his back against the tree, his eyes closed in an apparent doze. Without opening them he addressed Matthias. "How goes the practice war, young stavemaster?"

Matthias watched some of the tiny ants carrying off his fallen breadcrumbs as he answered, "As well as possible, Brother Methuselah. And how are your studies coming along?"

Methuselah squinted over the top of his spectacles. "Knowledge is a thing that one cannot have enough of. It is the fruit of wisdom, to be eaten carefully and digested fully, unlike that lunch you are bolting down, little friend."

Matthias set his food to one side. "Tell me, what knowledge have you digested lately, old one?"

Methuselah took a sip from Matthias's milk bowl. "Sometimes I think you have a very old head for such a young mouse. What more do you wish to know about Martin the Warrior?"

Matthias looked surprised. "How did you know I was going to ask about Martin?"

Methuselah wrinkled his nose. "How do the bee folk know there is pollen in a flower? Ask away, young one, before I doze off again."

Matthias hesitated a moment, then blurted out, "Brother Methuselah, tell me where Martin lies buried."

The old mouse chuckled drily. "Next you are going to ask me where to find the great sword of the warrior mouse."

"B-but how did you know that?" stammered Matthias.

The ancient gatehouse-keeper shrugged his thin shoulders. "The sword must lie buried with Martin. You would have little use for the dusty bones of a bygone hero. A simple deduction, even for one as old as I am."

"Then you know where the Warrior lies?"

Methuselah shook his head. "That is a thing no creature knows. For many long years now I have puzzled and pored over ancient manuscripts, translating, following hidden trails, always with the same result: nothing. I have even used my gift of tongues, speaking to the bees and others who can go into places too small for us, but always it is the same—rumors, legends and old mouse tales."

Matthias crumbled more bread for the ants. "Then the Warrior's sword is only a fable?"

Methuselah leaned forward indignantly. "Who said that? Did I?"

"No, but you—"

"Bah! Nothing of the sort, young mouse. Listen carefully to me. I have an uncanny feeling that you may be the one I have been saving this vital piece of information for."

Matthias forgot his lunch. He listened attentively.

"About four summers ago I treated a sparrowhawk who had pulled a sinew in her foot. She could not use her talons properly. Hmm, as I remember, I made her promise never to take a mouse as prey. She was a fierce, frightening bird. Have you ever been close up to a sparrowhawk? No, of course you haven't. Well, let me tell you, they can hypnotize small creatures with those savage golden eyes. Born killers, they are. But this hawk said something that made me think. She talked of the sparrows, called them winged mice, said that many years ago they had stolen something from our Abbey: a treasure that belonged to the mice. Wouldn't say what it was. Just flew off. Huh, who expects gratitude from a sparrowhawk, anyway?''

Matthias interrupted. ''Have you ever spoken to the sparrows about this 'something'?''

Methuselah shook his head. ''I'm too old. I can't climb up to the roof where they nest. Besides, the sparrows are odd birds, forever quarreling and chattering on in their strange voices. They are warlike creatures, extremely forgetful and completely savage. They'd throw you from the roof and kill you before you had a chance to get near their tribal nests. Yes, I'm far too old for that sort of thing, Matthias, and anyhow, I'm not too sure that the sparrowhawk's story was true. Some birds can be dreadful liars when they have a mind to be.''

Matthias tried questioning Brother Methuselah further, but the warm sun had worked its magic upon the old gatekeeper as he sat in the orchard savoring the peace and tranquility of a June afternoon. This time there was no deception. He was genuinely fast asleep.

CHAPTER

14

Clouds drifted across the sky, obscuring the thin sliver of moon. The Joseph Bell tolled out its midnight message to the slumbering countryside. A warm soft drizzle was falling over the parched meadows and dry woodland, bringing relief after the hot dry day, damping down the dust from the road.

In the ditch a frog opened its eyes, disturbed by some slight noise from the hedgerow. It blinked. Was that three figures creeping along, or two?

The frog remained perfectly still. There seemed to be two figures, and some sort of shadow. The moon came out from behind a cloud.

It was two huge rats . . . and a dark shadowy *something!*

They crept along under cover of the hedge towards the big dwelling of the mouse folk. Rats were hunters; thankfully they had not noticed him. The frog stayed motionless and let them pass. It was none of his business.

Cluny, Ragear and Shadow padded noiselessly towards Redwall. This was such an important mission that Cluny had decided to come along and supervise it personally. Around Shadow's waist was strapped a skin pouch. It contained a thin strong rope, a padded grappling hook, a vial of oil, some lockpicks and a dagger: Shadow's usual burgling kit.

Ragear ambled proudly along, thrilled that he had been specially picked to accompany his Chief on such a vital task. Little did he know that Cluny had only included him as an insurance. If they should get into a tight corner, Ragear would serve as an expendable fool. That way Cluny could make good his own escape.

The trio halted beneath the lofty Abbey walls. Cluny silenced them with a wave of his tail, then vanished into the night. Ragear felt distinctly nervous at being left alone with Shadow. He attempted a whispered conversation.

"Nice drops of rain, eh, Shadow? Good for the grass. Blow me, these walls are pretty high. I'm glad it's you climbing them and not me. I'd never make it. Too fat, hahaha."

Ragear's voice trailed off. He fumbled with his whiskers, wilting beneath the basilisk stare of Shadow's dead black eyes. He shuddered and fell silent.

Within ten minutes Cluny was back. He nodded up at the parapet. "I've been up and down the length of the wall for a fair distance. The sentry mice are all asleep, the fools! They've never had to do guard duty before—as soon as night falls so do their eyelids. That's what soft living does for you."

Ragear's head bobbed in agreement. "You're right, Chief. If they were in our army and old Redtooth caught them snoozing he'd—"

"Shut your trap, stupid," Cluny hissed. "Are you ready, Shadow? Now don't forget your instructions."

Shadow bared his yellowed fangs and started climbing. Slowly he made his way upwards, like a long black reptile, his claws seeking hidden niches and crevices in the sandstone. Ever upwards, sometimes stopping spreadeagled against the surface as he figured out his next movement, taking full advantage of every crack and joint in the wall. No other animal in Cluny's army could have attempted such an ascent, but Shadow was a climbing expert. He concentrated his whole being on the job in hand, sometimes clinging to the stones by no more than a single claw. Below on the ground Cluny and Ragear strained their eyes upwards. They could hardly make out his shape. He was not far from the top of the wall.

Shadow shifted position and levered with his back legs and tail. Now he wedged his claws into a fissure and stretched upwards, gaining inch by inch.

*   *   *

On top of the wall Brother Edmund was snoring gently. He was nestled in a pile of rubble, wrapped in a warm blanket with his hood up against the light rain. Edmund was oblivious to the long sharp claws that latched themselves over the parapet edge. A moment later the sleek black head appeared; two dense obsidian eyes stared at the sleeping mouse. Shadow had succeeded in climbing the Abbey wall.

Like a sinuous black lizard he slithered past slumbering creatures and around rubble heaps, never once making a sound. Friar Hugo mumbled gently in his sleep, and moved his head so that his cowl slid off. Drizzle fell upon the fat friar's face, threatening to wake him. Gently as a night breeze, Shadow replaced the hood. Pausing for an instant, Shadow looked about before descending the stone steps from the ramparts to the cloisters. Using shrubs and bushes as cover he moved furtively forwards, never taking any needless chances or making sudden movements. Sometimes he stopped and waited, letting the minutes tick away as he planned his next progression, gliding like a cloud's shadow cast upon the ground by the moon.

The door to Great Hall was not locked. Shadow judged that the latch was probably old and creaky. He took out the vial of oil and lubricated the latch and hinges. Carefully he inched the door ajar—apart from a tiny squeak it swung effortlessly open. Sliding inside, he released the door by mistake. A swift night breeze slammed it shut with a dull thud.

Shadow cursed inwardly and flung himself behind a nearby pillar. He lay inert, not daring to breathe; one, two, three minutes, good! Nobody had been disturbed by the noise. He ventured out to inspect the tapestry that hung upon the wall.

A black moth on a moonless night would not have escaped Shadow's notice. He needed no lamp to scrutinize the thing before him. So this was the picture of the warrior mouse that Cluny lusted after. Using his razor-sharp fangs he began gnawing into the ancient tapestry, working from the tasseled hem upwards.

Matthias tossed and turned in his bed, exhausted, but unable to sleep. His mind revolved around a host of problems and schemes: the sword, Martin's grave, defense of the Abbey, Cornflower. Finally, after much kicking and rumpling of sheets, sleep started to take over. He was somewhere in a long deserted room, not unlike Great Hall. A voice called to him, "Matthias."

"Oh, go away," the young mouse muttered drowsily. "Get someone else. I'm tired."

But the voice persisted, boring into his mind. "Matthias, Matthias, I need you."

He peered down the length of the darkened hall. "What is it, why do you need me?"

Matthias began to walk towards the voice. He could hear a wicked snigger followed by a cry of despair. "Matthias, help, don't let them take me."

He ran forwards. The hall seemed to grow longer.

"Who are you, where are you?"

Far ahead in the murky darkness Matthias could vaguely distinguish a figure leaning out from the wall. It was a mouse in armor.

"Please, Matthias, you must help me quickly!"

Bump.

Matthias landed on the floor of his bedroom. Sheets were tangled about his body. Slowly he sat up and rubbed his eyes. What a strange dream: the long hall, the plea for help, the armored mouse. . . .

Matthias felt the fur on the back of his neck rising.

Of course, it had to be!

Great Hall. Martin the Warrior. Something terrible was going on downstairs. He was needed urgently.

Matthias kicked the sheets from him as he leaped up and dashed headlong from the bedroom, along the dormitory corridor and helter skelter down the spiral staircase. Through Cavern Hole he clattered in the darkness, stumbling and tripping over furniture, his heart hammering loudly and legs pumping like twin pistons. Matthias fell over the top stair and went sprawling into Great Hall. He lay on the floor, gazing through the gloom to the tapestry. Martin was still there, but . . . *he was moving.*

Was it the breeze? No, it couldn't be. The likeness of the warrior mouse was jiggling about as though it were being tugged in some way. Matthias could see a shadow, but there was nothing to cast it. He jumped to his feet and ran forwards as the picture of Martin was ripped away from the tapestry.

A rat held it!

There was no doubt in Matthias's mind. It was a rat, entirely black from tip to tail, barely distinguishable from the night itself.

Shadow heard the footsteps on the floor behind him. With cold, calculated detachment he wheeled about as his opponent charged. He was certain to defeat such a small creature in combat, but his orders were to get the picture, not to fight little mice. Besides, there was always the additional hazard that the mouse might hang on to him and shout for help until it came. Like a wraith of oily smoke Shadow completed a clever double maneuver. Bowling his body into a forward roll, he knocked Matthias down like a skittle. Bounding up he slipped around the door, slammed it and fled off through the cloisters.

Matthias sprang up, roaring at the top of his voice, "Stop that rat! Stop that rat!"

Immediately the mice on sentry duty were alerted. As Shadow ran he saw Constance dash across the grounds at an angle which cut him off from the stairs up to the ramparts. Switching direction, he made for the next set of stairs, silently cursing the badger. Now he would have to use his climbing rope to descend quickly to the road.

Matthias emerged from the Abbey. He saw Shadow change direction. Thinking fast, he ran diagonally, catching up with the thief at the foot of the stairs. Throwing himself in a flying tackle, Matthias grabbed Shadow by the legs, sending him crashing on to the lower steps.

Still clinging to the tapestry, Shadow wriggled like an eel. Turning over on to his back, he kicked savagely at the young mouse's head with a free foot. Matthias tried valiantly to hang on, but his larger and heavier opponent kicked him viciously in the face, again and again. The big bony foot with its sharp claws pounding and gouging away soon took its toll. Matthias went limp and blacked out.

Constance had mounted the far steps. Gaining the ramparts, she ran along, dodging the heaps of rubble. She saw Matthias go down under the onslaught of kicks and ran even faster, impeded by mice all around who scattered in panic, thinking they were under mass invasion. The only one besides Constance who had the sense to see what was happening was Cornflower's father. Being nearer the top of the stairs than the badger, he ran straight into the intruder. Shadow was struggling to get out his climbing rope.

"Surrender, rat, I've got you," cried Mr. Fieldmouse as he grabbed hold of the thief. But, rummaging in his pouch to free the rope, Shadow's claw had closed on the handle of his dagger. He drew it out swiftly and drove it twice into the fieldmouse's unprotected body.

Constance arrived just as the victim fell wounded. Shadow turned on her with the dagger upraised. Constance swung her paw round in a mighty arc, and it caught Shadow square on the chin. The force of the blow lifted the thief clean off his feet, and, before Constance could grab hold of him, he overbalanced and hurtled over the edge of the parapet with a horrible scream. Downwards he plunged, his body thudding off the unyielding masonry. He landed in the wet roadway with a sickening crunch.

Cluny came dashing towards the stricken Shadow, with Ragear scuttling in his wake. Despite his appalling injuries, Shadow managed to lever himself up on one paw.

"Cluny, I'm hurt, help me," he gasped.

The piece of tapestry lay upon the road. Cluny snatched it up eagerly. Behind him he could hear the gatehouse bolts being withdrawn amid the shouts of angry mice. Ruthlessly he kicked at Shadow's broken body.

"Get up and run for it or stay there, fool. I don't carry cripples or bunglers."

Leaving the injured Shadow to the mice, Cluny sped off across the road. He covered the width of the ditch with a mighty leap and ran off across the meadows. In open country he could outdistance any mice that dared follow him. Waving the tapestry, Cluny laughed in exhilaration as he put on an extra burst of speed.

Ragear had panicked completely. He could not jump the ditch, so he scuttled off down the road in the opposite direction from the way they had come.

A group of mice led by Brother Alf tried fording the ditch and climbing up into the meadow. Unfortunately, the rain had made the going hard and slippery. Cluny was long gone, and the tapestry with him.

Turning back to Redwall, the pursuers came upon Matthias. He was leaning on Friar Hugo's arm in a dazed condition. Painfully he staggered up the road to where Shadow lay. Wincing, he cast about, searching the muddy roadway for the fragment of tapestry.

"It's got to be here somewhere," cried Matthias. He fell upon the injured Shadow, searching his waist pouch.

His flat black eyes clouding over, Shadow watched Matthias. Laconically he spoke. His voice was strangely calm. "Too late, mouse. Martin is with Cluny now."

It was the last thing Shadow ever said. He gave one final shudder and lay dead.

Chapter

15

Dawn arrived as if it were aware of the previous night's events. Heavy grey skies and steady rain prevailed over Redwall and the Mossflower area.

Abbot Mortimer looked old and stern as he addressed the assembly in Cavern Hole. The atmosphere was decidedly subdued.

"Sleeping at your posts, allowing the enemy into our Abbey to steal that which we hold most dear! Is this the way you defend us?" The Abbot's shoulders slumped wearily. There was an awkward hush—anger and guilt lay thick upon the air. The kindly old mouse shook his head and held up a conciliatory paw.

"Forgive me, friends, I criticize you unjustly. We are all creatures of peace, unskilled in the art of war. Yet when I saw the late rose this morning, I could not help but notice that its leaves are all shriveled; the tiny rosebuds have died. Martin the Warrior is gone from our Abbey. He has left Redwall. We are forsaken. There will be hard and sorrowful days to come without him among us." The mice and woodland creatures shuffled their feet and gazed at the floor. They knew the truth in their Father Abbot's words. But hope springs eternal. There was one voice raised, that of Matthias:

"A bit of good news," he said. "I have just come from the

infirmary. Mr. Fieldmouse is out of danger. He will live.''

The relief was audible throughout Cavern Hole. Tensions were eased; even the Abbot temporarily forgot his gloomy predictions.

"Thank you, Matthias," he cried. "What heartening news. I must say that the terrible injuries received by Mr. Fieldmouse almost had me believing the worst. But look at yourself, my son. You should be resting. Your face is still swollen after the fight with the black rat.''

Matthias gave a lopsided grin. He shrugged cheerfully. "Don't worry about me, Father Abbot. I'll be all right.''

The mice smiled with pride. A brave little warrior, Matthias; he put new heart into them. Their resolve strengthened as he continued, "Huh, black rat indeed! He didn't even scratch me. Well, only a bit. But where is he now, this sly one? Deep under the soil, if the insects are doing their job properly. Listen to me, friends. We of Redwall are a tough lot to kill off. They couldn't finish Ambrose Spike, could they? Why, even the black one armed with a dagger couldn't slay Mr. Fieldmouse, so what's a scratch or two to a mouse like me.''

Cheers for Matthias's speech rang to the rafters. Constance sprang up beside him, shouting heartily, "That's the spirit, friends! Now let's see you all back out there at your posts. We'll be wide awake this time, and heaven help any dirty rats that come marching up to Redwall this day!''

With wild yells very uncharacteristic of peaceful mice, the friends seized their staves and charged out, fired with new zeal. After a while Constance accompanied the Abbot to see Mr. Fieldmouse, while Matthias went with Methuselah to Great Hall. Together they surveyed the torn tapestry.

The young mouse stood with his paws folded, an expression of disgust upon his features. The old gatekeeper patted his shoulder. "I know how you feel, Matthias. I could see you were only putting on a brave face for the benefit of the others. That is good. It shows you are learning to be a wise leader. You hide your true feelings and encourage them not to give up hope.''

Matthias gingerly touched the swellings on his face. "Aye, that's as may be, old one. But you can see as well as I that Martin is gone. Without him I do not think we can win.''

Methuselah nodded in agreement. "You are right, my young friend, but what's to be done?''

Matthias staggered slightly. He leaned against the wall, rubbing a paw across his brow. "I don't know. In fact, the only thing I know right now is that the Abbot was right. I think I'd better go and lie down for a bit."

Refusing Methuselah's help, the young mouse left the old one gazing at the torn tapestry. He tottered off unsteadily in the direction of the dormitory.

On the spiral staircase he met Cornflower.

"Hello there," he said, as cheering as he could. "How is your father?"

Cornflower looked at Matthias solicitously. "He's doing fine, thank you, Matthias. I'm just going to get some herbs for the Abbot. Shouldn't you be lying down? Your face looks terribly puffy."

Matthias winced and leaned against the banister. "Yes. As a matter of fact, I'm just going to my room for a good long rest. But don't you worry, before long I'll make those rats pay dearly for hurting your father."

Matthias staggered weakly into his room—but the moment he closed the door he became a different mouse. With bright eager eyes he groped under his bed and brought forth the waist pouch that had belonged to Shadow. Tucking the long dagger into his belt, he wrapped the climbing rope around his shoulder and said aloud to himself, "Right, Cluny, you and I have a score to settle."

Keeping a mound of earth between himself and Brother Rufus, Matthias silently looped the rope around a projection at the edge of the parapet. Fortunately for him, Rufus was looking in the opposite direction. Matthias started to slide down the rope on the Mossflower side of the wall, where the woods came close up to the Abbey.

He had imagined the descent would be very difficult, and surprised himself by handling it with ease, his confidence growing as he slid swiftly and noiselessly to the fern-covered ground. Crouched in the undergrowth, he mentally rehearsed his plan of action. He would go through the woods to St. Ninian's Church, avoiding the road that was being watched by sentries. Once at the church he would discover where the piece of tapestry was kept; then he would create a diversion of some kind. While

Cluny's horde was occupied he would snatch the tapestry and get back to Redwall with all speed.

Matthias ducked deeper into the ferns and was soon just a silent ripple making through the lush summer green of Mossflower towards the Church of St. Ninian.

CHAPTER
16

At the camp of Cluny the Scourge, the rat army was girding itself up for war.

Weapons were being sharpened upon churchyard headstones. Under the critical eye of Redtooth a band of rodents was gnawing off a length of planking from a rickety lych-gate fence at the rear of the church. Others collected stones to provide ammunition for slings, while some coiled ropes about their bodies.

Inside the church Cluny sat up in the choir loft, the image of barbaric authority. He held the scourging tail in one claw, while gripped in the other was his war standard, topped by the ferret skull with the addition of the tattered tapestry square depicting Martin the Warrior. He gazed proudly at it as his armorer dressed him for war.

At Cluny's feet were the Vole family. They were bound. He flicked his tail at them and sneered. "Ha, look at me, you spineless little creatures! Did you ever see such a leader of fighting animals as Cluny the Scourge? Soon I will have every creature that moves down on its bended knees to me."

Mr. Abram Vole glared defiantly at his captor. "You filthy great bilge rat, why I'll—"

"Silence!" roared Cluny. "Hold your tongue, vole, or I will deal with you and your family here and now before I set out to conquer your precious Abbey. Do you see my new battle flag? That is Martin the Warrior. Yes, the same one who is supposed to protect that doddering old Abbot and his witless mob of mice. Now Martin is mine, it is more fitting that he travels at the head of real warriors. He will lead us to victory!''

Cluny ranted and raved on, the light of madness in his eye. ''Death and desolation shall be the reward of those who dare stand against Cluny. The only ones I will spare are those I might choose to serve me.''

Mrs. Vole struggled upright but was forced back down by Scumnose and Fangburn. Chattering with rage she shouted at Cluny, ''You'll never bend Redwall to your evil will. Good will prevail! You'll see, Cluny. We are tied up, but our minds are free.''

Crack!

Cluny lashed out with his long tail, sending the Vole family flat upon the floor. Mr. Abram Vole struggled to shield his wife and son with his body as the tail flailed out a second time.

''A touching little speech, vole, but you wrong me. I don't want to capture the spirit of Redwall. I mean to kill it! Take these whining creatures out of my sight. Lock them in the hut out at the back. Leave them to imagine what their fate will be when I return.''

Colin Vole shrieked in terror. His mother and father struggled bravely as they were dragged off.

Redtooth marched in and saluted Cluny.

''The horde is ready to march, Chief.''

A rat armorer set the war helmet firmly upon Cluny's head. He snapped the visor down and kicked aside the rat who had fixed the poison barb on his tail.

Striding out into the churchyard, Cluny climbed up on the wrecked gatepost. His fierce eye gazed out across the mighty army: black rats, brown rats, grey rats, piebald rats, skulking weasels, furtive stoats and sinuous ferrets, all gathered round, their weapons glistening and dripping with the rain. As Cluny exhorted them, they roared back their frenzied replies:

''Where does Cluny's army go?''

''Redwall. Redwall.''

''What is the law of Cluny?''

''Kill, kill, kill.''

''Who will lead you to victory?''

"Cluny, Cluny, Cluny the Scourge!"

Springing down among his army, the Warlord waved the banner high overhead. With a mighty shout the horde of Cluny the Scourge marched out upon the road to Redwall Abbey.

CHAPTER

17

Ragear was hopelessly lost!

Separated from Cluny, he could not think for himself. Scuttling off down the road in the wrong direction, he had kept on going in a state of funk. Frightened by the sound of a bird chirping suddenly, he rushed blindly into Mossflower Wood, and pressed on, deeper and deeper into this strange new territory. It was only with the arrival of pale dawn that he stopped, slumping down under some bushes. Exhausted, soaking wet and dispirited, he curled up into a wretched damp ball and slept.

Some time about mid-morning, Ragear was awakened by the sound of footsteps. As Matthias tramped past he lay low, silently congratulating himself. What a find, a little mouse! He would take him prisoner and bring him back alive to Cluny. That way he could gain some prestige. Cluny might even forget that he panicked and deserted at the Abbey.

Matthias risked a swift glance over his shoulder. There was a rat clumsily trying to stalk him, a fat awkward-looking rodent, but nevertheless an enemy. The young mouse strode onwards, his mind working coolly and without fear, confident that he could handle the situation.

Breaking twigs underfoot, stumbling ineptly from tree to tree, Ragear watched the mouse and fantasized.

"There was six of 'em, Chief, they tried surrounding me, but

I fought like a devil! Then I says to meself, Ragear, says I, you'd better capture this last one and fetch him back for the Chief to question.'' Then Cluny'll say to me, ''Ragear, good old Ragear, I knew I could depend on you. Why d'you suppose I took you along in the first place? Mangefur, bring food and wine for my old pal, Ragear the Brave.'' Ha, yes, then I'll pat the Chief on the back and say, ''By Satan's whiskers, you old rodent! Have you never thought of retiring and letting me lead the horde? Why, with a gallant warrior like me in comm—''

Thwack!

A long whippy larch branch sprang forward suddenly. It crashed into Ragear's head, poleaxing him.

Matthias stepped out of hiding, rubbing his hands—it had been a strain holding the branch back for so long. Uncoiling Shadow's climbing rope, he bound Ragear paw and claw to a sturdy oak. The young mouse could not afford to wait around for the rat to regain his senses. There was still a deal of traveling to be done. He pressed onwards, leaving his senseless enemy bound to the tree.

The rain stopped. Within minutes the hot June sun burst down on Mossflower, as if in apology for its absence. Clouds of steaming mist arose from the woodland floor, mingling with the golden shafts slanting down through the trees. The birds began singing. Each flower and blade of grass was decked out in jeweled pendantry with necklaces of sparkling raindrops.

The sudden warmth flooded over Matthias, cheering him onwards. Humming a tune beneath his breath, he strode out with a will, almost breaking from the cover of the trees straight out into the flat meadowland. He checked himself just in time. Directly ahead lay a vast overgrown area which was neither pasture nor meadow. It was the common land that had once belonged within the curtilage of St. Ninian's.

Matthias crouched at the edge of the woods. He could see the back of the church. There were ten or twelve rats patrolling it, some distance away. Before he dealt with that problem there was still the common land to be crossed. Clumps of thistle and slight ground hummocks would be his only cover. The young mouse spoke his thoughts aloud. ''Hmm, this could present a little problem.''

A strange voice answered him. ''Problem, a little problem?

Well at least it's not a fully-grown adult problem."

Matthias squeaked aloud with fright. Whirling about, he looked for the source of the mystery voice. There was no one about. Taking a grip of himself, he squared his shoulders and called out boldly: "Come out here this instant and show yourself!"

The voice answered. It seemed to come from directly in front of him. "Show m'self indeed! How many pairs of eyes d'you want, young feller, eh, eh? Fine state of affairs, bless m'soul! What, what!"

Matthias narrowed his eyes and looked hard . . . still nothing.

"I warn you, come out and show yourself," he shouted irritably. "I'm in no mood for playing games."

As if by magic a lanky hare popped up right beside Matthias. An odd patchworked creature, his fur was an ashen hue with blots of grey and light-brown-flecked white on the underbelly. He was very tall, with formidable hefty hind legs and a comical pouched face topped off by two immense ears which flopped about of their own accord. With a courtly old-fashioned manner the hare made a leg, bowing gracefully. His voice carried a slightly affected quaver.

"Basil Stag Hare at your service, sir! Expert scout, hindleg fighter, wilderness guide and camouflage specialist, ahem, liberator of tender young crops, carrots, lettuce and other such strange beasts. Pray tell me whom I have the pleasure of addressing, and please state the nature of your little problem."

Matthias decided the peculiar hare was either slightly mad or tipsy, but his outmoded manner was certainly friendly. The young mouse humored him accordingly, bowing low with a paw at his waist.

"Good day to you, Mr. Basil Stag Hare. My name is Matthias. I am a novice in the Order of Redwall mice. My immediate problem is to cross this land to the church over yonder without being discovered by the rats who are guarding it."

Basil Stag Hare tapped one of his huge feet gently on the ground. "Matthias," he laughed. "What an odd name, to be sure!"

The young mouse laughed back as he replied, "Not half as odd as your own name. Whoever heard of a hare being called Basil Stag?"

The hare disappeared momentarily. He reappeared next to

Matthias. "Ah well, Hare's the family name, don't y'know. My parents named me Basil, though the old mater wanted me to be called Columbine Agnes. Always longed for a young lass, she did."

"But why Stag?" Matthias inquired.

"Noble creatures, stags," the hare sighed. "Did I ever tell you I wanted to be one; a magnificent royal stag with great coathanger antlers? So, I went down to the jolly old river one night and christened m'self Stag! Had two toads and a newt as witnesses, y'know. Oh yes."

Matthias was unable to hide his merriment. He sat down and chuckled. Basil started chuckling too. He sat down beside Matthias.

"I think I'm going to like you, m'boy," he cried. "Now, what about getting you to that church? Why, there's nothing simpler. But enough time for that later, young rip. How about telling me what brings you here? I love listening to a good yarn, y'know. Oh, by the way, I hope you like fennel and oatcakes. Of course you do! You'll share lunch with me—of course you will—young 'un like yourself."

In a flash Basil had lugged a haversack from the undergrowth and was spreading a repast on the grass between them. For the next half hour Matthias related his story between mouthfuls of the hare's tasty luncheon. Basil listened intently, interrupting only when he required clarification on some point.

Matthias finished his tale and sat back awaiting comment. Basil's long ears flopped up and down like railway signals as he digested his food and his friend's information.

"Hmm, rats. I knew they'd come eventually, through intelligence on me grapevine, y'know. Could feel it in the old ears, too. As for Redwall, I know it well. Excellent type, Abbot Mortimer. Splendid chap. I heard the Joseph Bell tolling out the sanctuary message. Huh, even had some cheeky old hedgehog telling me to run for it. Couldn't go, of course. Dear me, no. That'd never do. Chap deserting his post; bit of a bad show, what, what? I prefer me own company, y'know. Present company excepted, of course."

"Oh, of course," Matthias agreed. He had taken enormously to the hare. Basil sprang up in a smart military fashion and saluted.

"Right, first things first! Must get you across to the church, young feller me mouse. I say, that green thingummyjig you're wearin'—habit, isn't it? Capital camouflage. You just try lying down anywhere in the shadows. Believe you me, you'd have trouble finding yourself. Top hole-cover, absolutely!''

Basil stopped and ruminated for a moment. His ears lay flat, stood up, then pointed in opposite directions. He continued, "Now, when you've liberated your bit of tapestry or whatever, make straight back across the common. I'll be waiting, never fear. Good! Well, come on, young bucko. We can't sit about here all day like two fat rabbits at a celery chew. Up and at 'em! Quick's the word and sharp's the action! Nip about a bit, young un.''

Again Basil vanished only to reappear some three yards out on the common. "Come on, Matthias. Tack to the left and wheel to the right. Bob and weave, duck and wriggle. Look, it's easy.''

Matthias hurried to follow, keeping in mind Basil's instructions. Surprisingly, they seemed to work perfectly and before long the two friends had covered nearly three-quarters of the common land. Matthias could even count the whiskers on some of the rats. He covered his mouth with a paw to stifle a giggle.

"It's really very simple, isn't it, Basil? How am I doing?''

The hare bobbed up beside him. "Capital! Bung ho! Like a duck to water, young feller. Flop me ears if you aren't the best pupil I've ever had. By the way, is there anything I can do to help?''

Matthias stopped and looked serious. "Yes, there is, Basil. But I feel reluctant to ask you to involve yourself in my fight.''

Basil Stag Hare snorted. "Rubbish. My fight indeed! D'you fondly imagine that I'd sit there munching at the old nosebag while some ugly great rodent and his band of yahoos run about conquering my countryside? Huh, never let it be said in the mess that Basil Stag Hare was backward in coming forward! Ask away, Matthias, you young curmudgeon.''

The hare puffed out his narrow chest and stood with paw on heart, his eyes closed and ears standing straight up. He awaited orders. The young mouse, hiding a smile at Basil's noble pose, said admiringly, "Oh, Mr. Hare, you do look heroic standing like that! Thank you!''

Basil opened one eye to look at himself. Yes, he did look rather gallant; a bit like the Monarch of the Glen, or the Stag

at Eve. Not that a young mouse'd understand anything of that
nature.

Matthias expressed his wishes to the "Stag." "Would it be
possible for you to create some kind of diversion while I'm
getting the tapestry? Could you keep the rats occupied, Basil?"

The hare twitched his ears confidently. "Say no more, laddie.
You've come to the right stag. Listen carefully. You cut across
the flank to their left. They took a piece of planking out of the
fence by the lych-gate. That's where you'll slide through. When
you've got what you came for, then make your exit the same
way. I'll be somewhere about keeping an eye on you. Right, off
you go."

Matthias went swiftly, still remembering to bob and weave
as Basil had taught him. He made it with ease to the fence,
glancing back to check on his companion.

Basil went into a speedy run. He cleared the fencetop at a
bound and tapped the nearest rat on the back.

"I say, old thing, where's this leader feller? Cluny, or Loony,
whatever you call him."

Completely staggered, the rat stood slack-jawed. Basil left
him and popped up beside another rat.

"Phew! Dear, dear, don't you chaps ever take a bath? Listen
here, you dreadful creature. D'you realize that you smell to high
heaven? Er, by the way, did your parents ever call you Pongo,
or did they smell as bad as you?"

It took the rat sentries a moment or two to recover from their
surprise. Then they let out yells of rage and tried to seize the
impudent hare.

It was like trying to catch smoke with their claws. Basil ran
rings round them, keeping up a steady stream of insults and
adding to the rats' bad temper. They shouted angrily:

"Grab that big skinny rabbit, lads."

"Big skinny rabbit yourself! Catsmeat!"

"I'll stick his damned guts on my pike."

"Temper, temper! Tut tut! Such language! If your mother
could hear you!"

"Blast, he's as slippery as a greased pig."

"Some of my best friends are greased pigs, bottle nose. Oops!
Missed me again, you old butterfingers, you."

*   *   *

Matthias chuckled quietly and shook his head in admiration. He watched twelve rats falling over each other and bumping heads as they chased his friend around the common land. Every now and then Basil would pause and strike his "Noble Stag" attitude, letting the rats get to within a whisker of him. Nimbly he would kick out with his long powerful legs and send them all sprawling in a heap. Adding insult to injury, he danced around the fallen sentries, sprinkling them with daisies until they arose, cursing him, to continue the chase.

Wary that there might be other rats about, Matthias climbed into the church through a broken stained-glass window. He dropped down into the lady chapel. The young mouse wrinkled his nose in disgust. The beautiful old church was rank with the heavy odor of rats. Furniture was overturned, statuary broken, walls stained; the pages of torn hymn books lay about everywhere.

Where was the fragment of tapestry?

And where was Cluny with the rest of his army?

Instant realization sent a leaden weight thudding into the pit of Matthias's stomach!

They had gone to attack Redwall. Cluny must have the tapestry with him. Matthias felt sick at the thought.

Hastily he climbed back out of the window. Halfway across to the fence he noticed a small shed. Somebody was pounding upon its locked door and calling his name aloud.

"Matthias, quickly, over here in the hut."

Through a small gap in the door he could see the Vole family. Their paws were tightly bound. Colin Vole huddled piteously on some dirty sacking in a corner, while Mr. Abram Vole and his wife battered away at the door with their paws tied together. Matthias called through the crack to them, "Stop banging! Stay quiet! I'll have you out of there as soon as I can break the lock."

Matthias cast about for something that would force the padlock and hasp. Doubtless some rat had the key, but there was no time for that.

By a stroke of luck he found an iron spike that had been thrown at Basil by one of the rats. Forcing the spike in the hoop of the lock, Matthias levered away.

"It's not budging," he muttered.

From the corner, Colin Vole started to weep aloud. "Oh we'll be locked in here until Cluny gets back. I don't want to face him again! Do something, Matthias! Save me!''

Despite the Voles' wretched predicament, Matthias could not help showing his contempt for Colin. ''Do stop whining, Colin! It doesn't help matters, and keep your voice down. There may still be rats about. Try to be brave like your mum and dad.''

In his frustration Matthias swung the spike at the lock. It bounced off, lodging deep between the hasp and the woodwork. He grunted in exasperation, pulling it savagely towards himself to loosen it. Taken off balance, he went head over tail. The hasp had broken; it came away bringing with it some twisted rusty screws. The door swung open.

Drawing his dagger, Matthias hastily cut the bindings from the paws of the Voles, issuing orders as he worked. ''Follow me and do as I say. Move as quickly and quietly as you can.''

Cautiously, they slid through the broken fence and began making their way across the common. There was no sight of the rat sentries. Matthias guessed that they were off somewhere, still trying to catch the elusive hare.

It was mid-afternoon. The common was peaceful and sunny; butterflies perched on thistle flowers and grasshoppers serenaded each other with their ceaseless cadences. Abram Vole insisted on shaking Matthias by the paw and congratulating him. ''Matthias, thank you with all my heart for saving my family. We thought we were doomed.''

The young rescuer looked grim.

''We're not back home yet by any means, Mr. Vole, and even if we do make it back to the Abbey, I dread to think what we may find.''

Mrs. Vole nodded vigorously. ''Aye, we saw them leave the church to march on Redwall. Cluny was leading the villains with Martin's picture tied to his banner. My oh my, you never did see so many wild rascals in all your born days.''

Matthias's brow creased in a worried frown. ''I wish I hadn't sneaked off from the Abbey this morning. I do hope Constance has all the defenders on the alert.''

It was only seconds later that Matthias wished he had also been on the alert.

The sentry rats had become tired of chasing Basil. Wearily they made their way out of the woods and back to the common land. They sat on the grass behind a low hummock, taking a break together.

Matthias and the Vole family walked straight into the middle of them.

CHAPTER
18

Cluny massed his forces in the roadside ditch opposite Redwall Abbey. He stood well back in the meadow behind the ditch, surrounded by his captains. Here, where he was out of range, he could direct the entire operation.

But at the moment he was not having things all his own way. For a start, he did not have many archers. Rats are notoriously bad at bowmaking and the fletching of arrows.

From the ramparts of Redwall the field and harvest mice sent down volley after volley of tiny arrows which, while they had no great killing power, were causing much wounding and discomfort in the ranks of Cluny's horde.

Standing beneath his banner which was rammed into the earth, Cluny cracked his tail. "Redtooth, Darkclaw, tell the sling-throwers to stand ready. When I give the signal I want to see a good heavy barrage of stones hitting the top of that parapet. That'll make them keep their heads down. Frogblood, Scumnose, you two will organize the gangs with the scaling ladders and grappling hooks. See they all get up on top of that wall, and no blunders."

The rat captains marched off to the ditch to make ready. Cluny held his tail up to give the signal.

On top of the wall the mouse archers kept up their relentless hail of arrows into the ditch. Constance strode up and down, holding a heavy cudgel in her paws as she urged them on.

"That's the stuff to give 'em, mice! Keep those bows twanging!"

Knowing the supply of arrows was not endless, the badger looked to the heaps of rubble and stone along the parapet edges. "Brother Rufus! Foremole! Be ready to shift that lot overboard at a moment's notice."

Smack, clank, bang, thud!

A hail of sharp stones and pebbles whizzed upwards, rattling against the masonry as Cluny waved his tail in the meadow below. Taken unawares, several mice were felled and a mole lay stunned.

"Get your heads down, everyone! Lie flat!" Constance shouted.

The defenders instantly obeyed as the showers of missiles increased. Running along the ramparts, bent double, the Abbot cried out, "Stretcher bearers! Over here! Help me to get the casualties down into the cloisters."

Winifred the otter lay alongside Constance and whispered to her, "Hear that scraping! Cluny's lot are putting something against the walls. It's my guess they'll be trying to climb up while we've got to lie low."

Even as Winifred spoke two grappling hooks with climbing ropes attached came clanging over the parapet and lodged in the joints.

"Stay low, my friends," whispered Constance. "Give them a bit of time to get off the ground. I want plenty of rats to be high up before we make a move. Pass the word along."

Below in the meadow, Redtooth waved his cutlass and laughed wildly. "Your plan is working out, Chief! Look, there's old Fangburn and his gang nearly at the top of the wall."

Cluny lifted his visor to get a better view. It was too late to call out against what he saw happen next.

A veritable avalanche of earth and rocks cascaded over the parapet. It smashed straight on to the main ladder. Rats screamed aloud and grasped at midair as they were swept from the ladder to the road below. The ladder fell sideways, cannoning into another one that had been set up beside it. As both ladders fell there were scenes of mass chaos. Badly wounded and shocked, the survivors on the roadway tried to crawl back to the safety of the ditch, only to be buried beneath rubble which thundered down on them. Many lay trapped beneath the heavy ladders that had fallen. The air resounded with screams and moans.

Cluny ranted and swore. Leaving his standard, he rushed across the meadow. Taking the ditch in a single leap, he darted across the road. Grasping a hanging rope he began hauling himself up, claw over claw. As the solitary beaver gnawed through the last strands, the rope parted. Cluny fell from a fair height and sprawled on the dusty road in an undignified heap.

Cluny flung himself into the ditch. Regrouping the slingthrowers and a few archers, he ordered them to await his command.

At the top of the walls the last climbing rope had been severed. A hearty cheer rent the air as the Redwall defenders broke cover to survey their handiwork.

"Fire," Cluny roared.

Stones and arrows sped upward with devastating effect. Several mice and woodlanders cried out and fell. The results heartened Cluny. All was not lost. He began devising a new plan.

In Mossflower Wood, Ragear was struggling with the rope that bound him to the oak tree. He could hear far-off sounds, which meant only one thing. His Chief was attacking the Abbey.

Straining his neck downwards at an uncomfortable angle, Ragear was able to get his teeth into the tough climbing rope. If he could manage to free himself he might be able to sneak back and join the horde. He could mingle with them and deny that he had ever been missing. Cluny might also take a lenient view of his desertion if he could distinguish himself during the battle.

The rope tasted foul. Ragear could tell by its scent that it had once belonged to Shadow. He'd never liked that surly pokerfaced rodent! Ragear congratulated himself as his teeth bit through another strand.

"Ha, take that, rope, and that! No rope can keep Ragear prisoner for long, he, he, he! Poor old Shadow, if only you could see your lovely rope now!" Ragear straightened up for a moment to ease his neck.

The laughter died on his lips. A horrified gurgle bubbled from his throat. Icy claws of terror gripped his chest.

Swaying hypnotically a foot from his face was the biggest, strongest, most evil-looking adder that had ever been born.

The rat was completely petrified. The breath seemed to freeze in his lungs. The sinister blunt head moved in a lazy rhythm, its forked tongue flickering endlessly in and out, the round bead-like jet eyes never leaving his for an instant. Its voice was like dry leaves rustling in an autumn breeze.

"Asmodeus, Asmodeussssssss," it hissed. "So kind of you to untie yourself, rat! Come with me, I will show you eternity! Asmodeus, Asmodeusssssssss."

It struck with lightning speed! All that Ragear felt was a sudden sharp sting to the side of his neck. His limbs became flaccid, his eyesight shrouded by a dark mist. The last words Ragear ever heard on this earth were uttered in the adder's sibilant hiss.

"Asmodeus, Asmodeussssssssssss!"

Cluny scratched the floor of the ditch with his claw. It was all there, the design for his next move. He would attack the Abbey secretly from the Mossflower side.

It would be a surprise maneuver. A handpicked squad led by him would carry out the mission. Dressed in Cluny's war helmet and armor, Redtooth would stay back in the meadow. His disguise would be sufficient to fool the defenders from the distance of the high walls. The rats in the ditch were ordered to continue pressing home the attack until Cluny and his party scaled the walls from behind and fought their way across the grounds to open the Abbey gates.

After issuing orders to his remaining captains, Cluny, accompanied by a score of assorted rats, weasels, stoats and ferrets, crept off along the course of the ditch. They carried with them the long plank from St. Ninian's lych-gate fence. Silently they traveled in a northerly direction, until they were out of sight of the walls. Climbing out of the ditch, they crossed the road into Mossflower Wood.

Cluny sat on a fallen tree trunk and told his squad what was required of them. "I'll wait here with the plank carriers. The rest of you split up and search the area for any big, high trees growing near the Abbey walls. Make sure that the tree you pick is higher than the wall itself and not too difficult to climb. Got that? Right, get going."

Cluny watched them strike off into the undergrowth. His previous good mood had deserted him. He was working himself into a foul temper over the day's performance by his mighty conquering horde. Shown up by the simple tactics of woodland creatures and mice! He snorted and dug his powerful claws into the rotten tree trunk, sending beetles and woodlice scurrying as he tore out a chunk of the spongy timber. Oh, he had had them frightened at first. As a commander he knew the power of fright, but once they had gained the upper hand in the initial skirmish the mice lost their fear and became bolder. That was when the battle had started to go against him. Granted, he had scored one or two small victories, but they were nothing to brag about. He couldn't use them as an example to put fresh heart in his troops.

Cluny's only hope was that the mice would become over-confident and eventually make a mistake. It was the old waiting game. Just let them make one slip; that was all he needed. Mean-while, he had a greater obstacle to overcome than mice: the walls. It was those same accursed walls that were ruining all his plans. Cluny tore viciously at the rotting log until great chunks of it flew through the air. If this scheme worked he wouldn't have to worry about walls anymore. He would be inside those walls like a fox among day-old chickens.

Cluny sniffed the air. His senses told him the searchers were returning. Cheesethief and a ferret named Killconey came crash-ing out of the underbrush. They were trembling and twitching. Both looked as if they had been badly scared.

It was some time before Cluny could get any sense out of them. Cheesethief spoke haltingly, glancing back fearfully over his shoulder. "Er, er, we, like . . . we got a bit lost, Chief."

"Lost? Where?" Cluny snarled.

Killconey pointed a shaky claw. "Over that way, yer honor, and didn't we find a great strappin' oak?"

"Was it close to the wall?"

Cheesethief shook his head. "No, Chief, it was further out into the woods. Look what I found wrapped around the trunk."

He held out the chewed and broken climbing rope. Cluny snatched it. "This looks like Shadow's climbing rope. He's dead. What are you fools trying to tell me?"

Killconey whimpered pitifully. "It's Ragear, yer honor."

Cluny seized the unlucky pair and shook them soundly. "Have you both gone raving mad? D'you mean to tell me you're frightened of that fool Ragear?"

Cheesethief fell to his knees, sobbing. "But you didn't see him, Chief. He was just lying there. His face was all swollen and his tongue was sticking out. It had gone purple. Ugh! He was all sort of bloated like . . . it was horrible!''

Killconey bobbed his head vigorously in agreement. "Aye, so 'twas. Didn't we see him with our very own eyes, sir? Pore ould Ragear, and him going backwards all the time.''

"Going backwards?" echoed Cluny.

"Indeed he was," said the ferret, "and your man here says to me, says he, 'There's something pulling Ragear along.' Sure, we couldn't see what it was for all the bushes, so we pulled them to one side between us, and what did we see?''

"Well, what did you see?" barked Cluny irritably.

Killconey stopped and shuddered. He spoke incredulously, as if he were unable to believe himself. "We saw the biggest snake you ever clapped eyes on. The father of all serpents! He had poor Ragear's body by the feet and was dragging it along backwards.''

Cluny's one eye widened. "What did this serpent do when it saw you?''

"It let go of Ragear and looked at us," squeaked Cheesethief. "The serpent stared at us. It kept on saying, 'Asmodeus, Asmodeus'.''

Cluny scratched his head with a sharp, dirty claw. "Asmodeus? What's that supposed to mean?''

"Do ye not know? 'Tis the dreaded name of the divvil himself, sir," wailed the ferret. "I know because me ould mother told me so, and she always said never to look a serpent in the eye. So I sez to me mate here, 'Cheesethief,' sez I, 'don't look. Run for your life!' And that's exactly what we did, sir. Oh, you'll never know how horrible it was. I'd rather be tied in a blazin' barn than go back there, so I would! The great scaly body of the—''

"Quiet, fool," said Cluny. "I think I hear the others coming back. Now straighten yourselves up, and not a word to anyone about this serpent thing, or you'll feel my serpent across your backs." Cluny's long tail waved menacingly under their noses. They took his point.

A weasel called Scragg came running up. He reported smartly with great efficiency. "High tree near the Abbey wall, Chief, elm I think, much higher than the wall, lots of branches jutting out, just the job for climbing.''

"How far to this tree?" Cluny asked.

"About ten minutes' march to the east," Scragg replied.

When the rest of the party arrived back, Cluny had them form up in single file. They marched eastwards at a smart pace.

The high tree did prove to be an elm, an ancient giant covered in gnarled bumps and handy branches. Cluny sized it up: exactly what he wanted, the perfect distance from the wall. He turned to his commando squad.

"Listen, we're going to climb this tree. When we get up high enough I'll find a strong branch that we can bridge to the wall with the plank. If we go carefully, the mice won't suspect a thing. Before they can gather their wits about them we'll be inside Redwall."

CHAPTER
19

It was difficult to tell who was the more surprised, Matthias and his party or the rat sentries.

There was a second's pause, then they scattered. One or two of the rats were a bit slow off the mark, but not as slow as Colin Vole and his mother, who were roughly grabbed by the faster sentries.

Matthias dodged, wriggled and ran free, tripping a rat who was about to seize Mr. Vole. The young mouse ran, pushing the vole in front of him and calling out: "Run, keep going, Mr. Vole! Try to make it to the woods and hide."

The vole faltered. "But my wife—Colin—the rats have got them."

Matthias pushed him roughly forward. "They'll get you too, if you don't hurry! Move yourself, vole. You'll be no good to your family as a prisoner again."

Taking Matthias's advice, Abram Vole ran as fast as his legs would carry him. Matthias turned and picked up a heavy branch. He faced the oncoming rats.

"Only a dozen of you," he taunted. "Let's see what you rats are made of. First come, first served."

Matthias swung the branch. It whooshed through the air, causing the rats to stop in their tracks. As he advanced on them flailing the branch, he shouted at the top of his voice, "Basil, Basil Stag Hare, where are you?"

The rats tried to circle Matthias. One got too near. A hefty blow from the improvised staff sent him crashing to the ground.

"Oh, well hit, sir! Jolly well hit!"

It was the hare.

He came bounding up, for all the world as if he were on a Sunday School picnic, grinning from ear to ear. Colin and Mrs. Vole came panting in his wake. Matthias gasped with relief.

"Basil, where in heaven's name did you get to?"

The skillful creature dodged a rat, spun round and landed a fierce double-footed kick to its stomach. The rat bowled over, completely winded, all the fight knocked out of its body. Basil chuckled. "Sorry about that, Matthias, my old lad. When these chaps gave up chasing me, I scooted back to my den. Spring cleaning, y'know. A bit late, but I'm only a bachelor in single quarters, what!"

Matthias was flabbergasted. Here he was fighting off a dozen rats, trying to rescue the Vole family, while Basil was dusting out his den! The young mouse could scarcely hold his temper.

"Oh, how nice of you, Mr. Hare. So glad you could join us," he said sarcastically, as they beat off rats and hurried the Voles along. "I don't suppose you put the kettle on for tea?"

Basil bowed to Mrs. Vole and offered her his paw.

"Allow me, ma'am. Why yes, as a matter of fact I did. Nothing like a fresh pot of mint tea after some good healthy exercise, what, what?"

Matthias struck a rat square in the face with the butt of his branch. The hare was obviously insane. Mint tea, indeed!

"Well, I don't suppose you think I'm going to sit in your den drinking tea all afternoon," he yelled.

Basil had a hammerlock on a rat. He swung him and knocked two more flat on the ground. He winked at Matthias.

"I certainly hope not, old bean. You see, it'd be perishin' awkward, as I've only got a four-piece teaset, and if I'm not mistaken the small gent who took off for the woods like a scalded duck is obviously the husband of this delightful lady vole, so I'll have to invite him too, won't I?"

Matthias tripped a rat with the branch. He was learning to take Basil in his stride.

"Why, of course you will, Mr. Hare. What a bore you must think me. I'll probably sit around on the common here and teach the rats to make daisy chains."

Basil dodged around a rat and laughed approvingly. "No need to get uppity, young feller. I thought I'd best shelter the Voles and see 'em safe to the Abbey later. Obviously you need to get back to Redwall posthaste. A family of voles would only slow you up."

Matthias grinned ruefully. "I apologize, sir. I accept your offer of help gratefully, I didn't mean to be rude."

By now they were at the edge of the common land. The rats had fallen back momentarily.

Basil shook paws with Matthias. "Good mouse. Right, cut along, young 'un. I'll see you when I deliver my charges back to the Abbey."

Alone and unencumbered, Matthias struck off into the woods. Traveling doggedly on wearied legs, he realized that his entry to Redwall would have to be from the Mossflower side, as the main gate would probably be under attack. Could the defenders hold out? Was Constance organizing the retaliation correctly without him? Had the sentries stayed alert? Was Cornflower safe?

Questions raced through Matthias's brain as he fought his way through the undergrowth. Taking a check on his bearings, he began to worry a little. The Abbey walls should be in sight over towards the north-west. Perhaps he hadn't fully realized the sprawling size of the woodlands. Yes, that was it. Maybe if he kept on trekking the walls would soon come into view.

From somewhere ahead Matthias could hear the trickle and gurgle of a stream. He remembered that it had been some time since he had eaten and drunk. Changing direction, he followed the water sounds until he came to the banks of the stream.

Lying face down on a low outcrop of red sandstone, Matthias drank his fill of the cool, sweet stream water. Further down the bank he found some young dandelions. Gathering a bunch of tender leaves and buds, he made his way back to the sun-warmed sandstone and stretched out on his back, nibbling dandelions and gazing up at the cloudless blue June sky through the treetops. What an action-packed day it had been!

Matthias was glad of the brief respite after all the excitement. But he told himself that he could not afford to stay long. He must press on to Redwall. He heaved a great sigh. The life of a warrior was very tiring.

Closing his eyes momentarily, he thought of Martin the Warrior. Did he ever feel tired? He must have, defending the Abbey with his large heavy sword, wearing all that armor. Whatever happened to the sword? It had to be somewhere. Legendary weapons didn't rust and wear away to nothing; otherwise they'd never get to be legends.

A dragonfly hovered directly above the young mouse, gently stirring his whiskers. What was this strange creature doing in his territory? He glided a little closer. It was quite safe; the oddly garbed animal posed no threat to his authority as bailiff of this stretch of water. He was fast asleep, snoring like a squirrel in midwinter, oblivious to all about him.

CHAPTER

20

It was late afternoon. There had been one or two minor setbacks, but Cluny and his squad had finally made it up into the elm tree. Some of the rats were really hopeless climbers in Cluny's estimation. There had been quite a bit of jostling and slipping, and as for that idiot Cheesethief, imagine waiting until you were six yards above ground to find out that you were afraid and had no head for heights. Cluny thought angrily that if there hadn't been such an urgent need for silence, he'd have given him what for!

The Warlord began to wish that he had brought along more ferrets and weasels. They possessed good natural climbing ability, and that weasel—what was his name? Scragg—he'd been an enormous help, boosting and encouraging the others, even organizing the lifting up of the plank. Cluny made a mental note for future reference. Officer material, that one. Despite all efforts, however, they were still below the edge of the parapet. Higher up, the elm branches became thin and whippy, not strong enough to support the plank's weight.

Cluny took stock of the situation. This was really as far as he could go while still retaining some kind of safety factor on their hazardous assignment. He decided to call a halt.

"Right, take a breather. Find somewhere that you won't fall from. In an hour or two it'll be evening; there'll be lots of shadow and less daylight. The mice will have slowed up a bit by then. We'll catch them off guard. Scragg, see this lot keep still and quiet, will you?''

Scragg saluted smartly and offered a helpful comment. "This branch I'm sitting on, Chief. I've just been testing it and it feels good and strong. Maybe we should mount the plank from here to the wall. It'll reach easily enough. I know it's a bit of an uphill climb, but it shouldn't be too difficult. I don't fancy those branches higher up—they're too thin."

Cluny climbed across and sat next to Scragg. He spoke in a whisper. "Good thinking, weasel. Yes, this branch'll do fine. Stick by me, Scragg. You're a useful soldier. With some of the blockheads I've got around me I could be on the lookout for a new captain soon. You know what that means: extra loot, a bigger share of the plunder. Cluny always rewards initiative, Scragg. Play your cards right and you'll soon get promotion."

"Thanks, Chief. Don't worry. I won't let you down," Scragg murmured.

On a lower branch, Cheesethief (who had been eavesdropping on the conversation) sneered inwardly. Yes, Chief. No, Chief. Three bags full, Chief! Who did that snotty weasel think he was?

And as for Cluny promoting a weasel to captain over rats of his own kind, well Redtooth and Darkclaw and the others might have something to say about that! Upstart weasel, he'd only joined up a day or two ago. If he got half the chance, Cheesethief would fix Scragg all right.

Abbot Mortimer looked thankfully up at the sky. Evening had come. They had lasted out well; the rats had not breached the wall in any way. Most of the main fighting had gone into a lull. Cluny's horde was only making spasmodic sallies from the ditch now. Taking advantage of the interval, the defenders hauled up more rocks and rubble to the ramparts. Cornflower and her band of helpers were on top of the walls. Keeping their heads low, they moved from post to post, serving each creature with a bowl of stew, some wild grapes, and a small loaf of honeyed nutbread.

"What a calm, efficient young mouse Cornflower is," the Abbot remarked to Constance.

The badger passed a bundle of arrows to Ambrose Spike for distribution as she replied, "Aye, that she is, Father Abbot. But she looks worried. Matthias, do you think?"

"Doubtless," said the Abbot dryly. "That young mouse is on my mind as well as hers and yours."

Constance shook her large striped head. "It's not like Matthias to go off like that. I've searched everywhere in my spare moments, but he's not in the Abbey."

"Well, wherever he is," the Abbot replied, "I'm certain that he is helping our cause, so we'll just have to await his return and trust to Matthias's judgment and good sense."

The two friends thankfully accepted food from Cornflower and her helpers. Both watched, mystified as Winifred the otter and Foremole hoisted and pulled a seesaw into view.

It was a plaything, made in the distant past for the use of infant woodlanders. It had lain near the strawberry patch for as long as anyone could remember. Baby animals played on it throughout the year. As a seesaw it was in perfect working order.

Winifred and Foremole set it down on the parapet. Bent double, two moles staggered up carrying between them an enormous rock. Foremole indicated the opposite end of the seesaw. "Arr, purrum thur, that's a noice bowlder, my beauties."

When the "bowlder" was in position, Winifred and Foremole hugged each other tightly. With a nod they jumped heavily on to the near seat.

Whoosh!

The big rock catapulted over the top of the parapet. Several seconds of silence followed, then there was a crash, accompanied by screams of pain and shock from the rats packed into the ditch below. Winifred and Foremole gravely shook paws.

"Yurr, oi reckon they pesky varmints got'n an 'eadache," chuckled Foremole, as everybody on the ramparts ran to seek cover from the retaliatory missiles hurled by Cluny's horde.

The battle had started again in earnest.

Mouse archers sprang up and loosed their shafts down towards the ditch; otter sling-throwers whipped hard pebbles off with fierce rapidity; long rat javelins flew upwards, causing death and injury in the ranks of the defenders. But now there was a new hazard. Some inventive rat had devised a fearsome weapon: chunks of iron grave-railings from the churchyard, strung to lengths of cord. The rats would swing the cord round and round, gaining momentum until, judging the right direction, they loosed the cord. The missiles sped upwards, two or three

times higher than the wall, almost out of sight; then they would
plummet downwards, whistling viciously, to burst on the ramparts. Any defender struck by a missile was either instantly
killed or horribly maimed. Even if the iron missed its target, the
stones and shattered metal fragments ricocheted about dangerously.

Realizing the danger of this new device, Constance ordered
all but a chosen few to leave the wall for the safety of the Abbey
grounds. However, the strung iron bits soon proved to be a two-
edged weapon. Many that were released wrongly came hurtling
back down into the ditch, sometimes slaying the very creatures
that had hurled them. Even Redtooth, in Cluny's armor, guarding the standard in the meadow, had to make an undignified
scurry to avoid being hit, but he could see the demoralizing
effect the missiles were having on the defenders, so he ordered
the throwers to continue.

Constance bravely stood her ground on the parapet, as did
her small band of picked fighters. Whenever one of the missiles
landed intact on the rubble pile, she would seize it, standing in
full view as she whirled the corded iron round and round, re-
leasing it in a blur of speed. Constance was a far more powerful
and accurate thrower than any rat. The attackers bared angry
fangs at her from the cover of the ditch—of all the Redwall
defenders the big badger was the one they most hated and
feared.

Seated in the branches of the elm tree at the north wall of the
Abbey, Cluny watched the shadows lengthen. To the west, the
sky was crimson with sunset. Soon he would raise the plank to
the parapet. Then let them beware! No tinpot order of mice was
going to stand against the might of Cluny the Scourge.

Methuselah the gatehouse-keeper stood facing the damaged tapestry in the Great Hall of Redwall. Being too old for active battle
service he reasoned that the best way he could serve his order
was by putting his fertile brain to work.

Somewhere there had to be at least a clue, a single lead that
might tell him where the resting place of Martin the Warrior
could be found, or where he could regain possession of the
ancient sword for his Abbey. But where?

Every now and then over the years Methuselah had searched

through Redwall for Martin and his sword. Now he stepped up his questing activities, alas with no success. Vital clues and answers still eluded him. What he needed was a younger, fresher mind to assist him. What a pity that Matthias could not be found. Now *there* was a young mouse with a head on his shoulders. Long years and much mental strain had taken their toll on the ancient mouse. Wearily he swayed on his feet and, putting out a paw to steady himself, he touched the wall—the exact patch of stone over which Martin's likeness had once hung.

Methuselah gave a sigh of satisfaction and allowed a small smile to creep across his features. His search had not been in vain. Beneath his paw there was writing carved into the dust-covered wall.

BOOK TWO

The Quest

CHAPTER

I

Matthias came awake slowly. He blinked, yawned, and stretched his body luxuriously. The sun was setting, turning the little stream into a flow of molten red and gold tinged with deep shadow. He lay calm, savoring the peace and quiet of the woodland summer evening.

Reality struck him like a thunderbolt. He sprang to his feet, instantly forgetting the beauty that surrounded him. Lying there snoring and sleeping like a lazy little idiot, and all the while Redwall Abbey and his friends were under attack!

Furious with himself, Matthias strode off angrily into the darkening trees. He could find no words strong enough to express his self-contempt. It was not until he had blundered and crashed along his way for some time, wildly upbraiding himself, that he calmed down with the realization that he was well and truly lost. No tree, path or landmark looked remotely familiar. He despaired of ever seeing Redwall again. Night closed in on the small mouse wandering alone in the depths of Mossflower Wood. Strange, imaginary shapes flitted about in the gloom; eerie cries pierced the still air; trees and bushes reached out their branches to catch and scratch like living things with claws.

Trembling, Matthias took refuge in an old beech trunk that had once been riven by lightning. Gradually he became critical of himself again: the great warrior, frightened of the dark like

a baby churchmouse. From somewhere overhead he heard a
scratching noise. Summoning up all his courage he banished his
fears. Drawing Shadow's dagger he stepped out into the open,
calling aloud in what he hoped was a gruff voice.

"Who's doing all that scratching and scraping? Come out and
show yourself if you are a friend. But if it's a rat out there, then
you'd best start running, otherwise you'll have to deal with me,
Matthias, a warrior of Redwall."

Having spoken his piece Matthias felt his confidence surge
back. He stood tense and alert. However, he received no answer,
save the mocking echo of his own voice ringing back at him
through the dark woodlands.

A slight noise at his back caused Matthias to wheel about
with the dagger upraised. He found himself confronted by a
baby red squirrel. It gazed up at him curiously, sucking noisily
on its paw. Matthias practically dropped the dagger through
laughing so much. So, this was the nameless terror that stalked
the night?

The tiny creature continued sucking its paw, shifting from
foot to foot, its bushy tail curled up over the small back, higher
than the tips of its ears.

Matthias stooped, speaking gently for fear of frightening the
infant. "Hello there. My name's Matthias. What's yours?"

The baby squirrel continued sucking on its paw.

"Do your mummy and daddy know you are out?"

It nodded its head.

"Are you lost, little one?"

It shook its head.

"Do you talk?"

It shook its head.

"Do you often wander about like this at night?"

It nodded.

Matthias smiled disarmingly. He threw his paws open wide.
"*I'm* lost!" he said.

The paw-sucking continued without comment.

"I come from Redwall Abbey."

Suck, suck, suck.

"Do you know where that is?"

The baby squirrel nodded.

Matthias was overjoyed. "Oh my little friend, please could
you show me the way?" he asked.

It nodded.

"Thank you very much."

The tiny squirrel hopped and shuffled a short way into the woods. Turning to Matthias, it took its paw from its mouth and beckoned him to follow. He needed no second urging.

Suck, suck, suck.

"Well at least," Matthias thought aloud, "if I lose sight of this fellow I'll be able to hear him."

The baby squirrel smiled . . . and nodded . . . and sucked.

CHAPTER

2

Abbot Mortimer sat in the grass of the Abbey cloisters. All around him the defenders who had been sent down from the wall lay in slumber. Not knowing when the rats were going to stop fighting, and realizing that they might not, the kindly Abbot advised those who had been relieved to try and get some sleep.

Methuselah came shuffling up. With a sigh and a groan he sat down on the grass alongside his Abbot who greeted him courteously.

"Good evening, Brother Methuselah."

The old gatehouse-keeper adjusted his spectacles and sniffed the air. "And a good evening to you, Father Abbot. How goes the battle against the rats?"

The Abbot folded his paws within his wide sleeves. "It goes well for us, old one, though how I can say that anything goes well which causes death and injury to living creatures is beyond me. We live in strange times, my friend."

Methuselah grinned and wrinkled his nose. "But still, it goes well."

"Indeed it does. But why do you smile, Methuselah? What secret are you keeping from me?"

"Ah, Father Abbot, you read me like a book. I do have a secret, but trust me, all will be made known to you in the fullness of time."

The Abbot shrugged. "No doubt it will. But please make it

soon. We are not getting any younger, you and I."

"Come now," said Methuselah, "compared with me, you are still a mouse in your prime. Yet like many others that think my senses are failing, you cannot see half the things that my old eyes observe."

"How so?" inquired the Abbot.

Methuselah touched a paw to his nose knowingly. "For instance, did you notice that there is a southerly breeze tonight? No, I don't suppose you did. Then look at the top of that old elm tree sticking up above the wall. Yes, that one over by the small door. Tell me what you see."

The Abbot's eyes followed Methuselah's paw until he saw the tree in question. He studied it for a moment, then turned to the old mouse. "I see the top of an old elm tree growing out in the woods. But what is unusual about that?"

Methuselah shook his head reprovingly. "He still cannot see. Dear me! If the breeze is blowing from the south, then the elm tree would move its leaves and branches in a northerly direction as it has always done. But that particular tree is choosing to disobey nature. It is swaying from east to west. This can mean only one thing. Somebody is using that tree for a purpose. At least, that is what I think. Do you agree?"

Without replying or showing any sign of alarm whatsoever, the Abbot arose. Walking calmly over to the gatehouse wall, he beckoned silently to Constance. The badger descended the steps. She held a whispered conference with the Abbot, nodding in the direction of the elm. Less than a minute later, Constance, accompanied by Winifred the otter, Ambrose Spike and a few others, padded carefully along the top of the wall, taking great pains not to be seen.

On the woodland side, Cluny whispered commands to his followers as they pushed the plank towards the wall from their perch in the elm tree. "Steady now, Cheesethief, you moron. Keep your end up! Keep it going upwards, not down!"

Cheesethief struggled to obey. It was all right for the Chief, sitting back there giving out his orders. He didn't have to balance with one claw while pushing a silly plank about with the other. Cheesethief slipped. With a squeak of dismay he let go of the plank. It clattered against a branch.

Fortunately, Scragg the weasel was on the alert. He caught

the end of the plank, steadying it. Cheesethief regained his balance and clung miserably to his perch as Cluny hissed in rage at him.

"Clown! Bungling buffoon! Get out of the way! Shift your fat idle carcass and let Scragg take over."

Burning with resentment, Cheesethief was shoved unceremoniously aside. Cluny aimed a kick at him as the efficient weasel took his place. "You just sit there and be still," Cluny snarled. "And try not to make enough noise to waken the entire Abbey."

Scragg moved with skill and economy, issuing quiet confident directions to the others. "Up a bit, left a touch, take it forward steady now, good, hold it."

The long plank snaked out and upwards, coming to rest gently but firmly on the parapet edge. Scragg saluted Cluny. "Plank in position and ready, Chief."

Cheesethief shot Scragg a venomous glance.

Cluny climbed on to the plank and tested it. The improvised bridge wobbled and sprang a bit, but it held.

Cluny turned to the raiding party. "I'll go first. We'd better have only one at a time on the plank. When I'm on the parapet I'll steady the other end. Scragg, you come next. The rest of you follow."

Cluny held on to branches for as long as he could. Soon he was out on the middle of the plank with nothing to steady him. Trying hard not to glance downwards at the dizzying drop, he inched his way up the plank, towards the wall.

Cluny was almost in reach of his goal when Constance appeared on the parapet. She gave the plank a mighty kick, sending it off into space!

With a shout of dismay Cluny plunged earthwards, snapping branches as he went. Winifred fired off a pebble from her sling, knocking a ferret clean out of his perch into empty space. Scragg still held one end of the plank. He leaned precariously out from the elm to see where Cluny fell.

Seizing his opportunity for revenge, Cheesethief shoved Scragg hard in the back. The weasel dropped like a stone with the plank on top of him. Cluny's followers were kicking at each other and screaming as they tried to clamber down from the high elm branches.

Leaning across the parapet, Constance and her friends watched the panic-stricken animals descending. Winifred the otter managed to speed up the retreat with a few well-aimed stones from her sling. The defenders viewed their work with grim satisfaction.

Ambrose Spike squinted short-sightedly down at the darkened woodland floor. He tried to assess the casualties.

"How many did we get?" he inquired.

"Hard to tell in this light," replied Winifred. "But I'd swear that was Cluny Constance tipped off the plank."

The badger's brow creased. She shot a quizzical glance at the otter. "So you saw him too? I'm glad you did. I thought I was seeing double for a moment back there. How could Cluny be in two places at once? I'm sure I saw him standing in the meadow not ten minutes ago."

Winifred shrugged. "Well let's just hope that it was Cluny. Personally, I'd like to think that he's lying somewhere down there now, dead as a doornail."

Constance peered downwards. "Difficult to say, really. There seem to be around half a dozen or so laid out down there. Can't tell for sure; too much shadow and darkness. Still, I don't think any creature could survive a fall from this height."

"Maybe we'd better go and see," suggested Ambrose.

The defenders looked towards Constance.

"Maybe not," said the badger thoughtfully. "No, I don't like it. It suddenly strikes me that this could be a diversionary tactic to draw us away from the gatehouse wall. If it was Cluny who fell from the plank, all well and good; but if it wasn't, then he's still around the front. It won't serve any useful purpose counting dead bodies. Let's get back to the main action."

Led by Constance, the defenders filed hurriedly off.

Cheesethief slunk cautiously out of the undergrowth. It was safe to move now; the woodlanders had gone from the parapet. Behind him, limping and complaining, came the survivors of the ill-fated raiding party. Cheesethief ignored them as he moved among the bodies that had fallen from the high branches: four rats, a ferret, and one weasel. Three of the rats and the ferret were dead. They lay where they had fallen, their limbs in grotesque positions. The survivors immediately pounced upon the bodies of their fallen comrades, plundering weapons and objects

of clothing that they had coveted. Cheesethief stood riveted by
the single eye.

Cluny was alive!

Beneath the plank Scragg stirred and groaned. Amazingly, he
too had survived.

Cheesethief sprang into action, surprised that Scragg still
lived but fatalistically accepting that nothing could kill Cluny.
"Quick, get that plank over here, you lot. We've got to get the
Chief out of here."

Using the plank as an improvised stretcher they carefully
lifted Cluny on to it. Cheesethief knew Cluny was watching him.
Tenderly he lifted the dangling tail and arranged it gently alongside his leader. "Try not to move, Chief. Lie still, we'll soon
get you back to camp."

The stretcher bearers moved off slowly through the woods.
Cheesethief avoided Cluny's eye. An idea was taking form in
his mind. He sniffed piteously, wiping an imaginary tear from
his cheek.

"Poor old Scragg! What a good weasel! I think he's still
alive. Listen, you lot: carry on and get the Chief home safely,
I'll double back and see if I can help Scragg."

Cheesethief sniggered to himself as the survivors disappeared
into the night, carrying Cluny on the plank.

Matthias followed the baby squirrel through bramble and bush.
Whenever he tried to communicate, all that he received was a
nod or a shake of the tiny creature's head. They had been traveling for quite a long time. As the pale fingers of dawn crept
across the sky Matthias was beginning to doubt that his companion knew the way.

Then suddenly the little fellow pointed to the east with his
paw. In the distance Matthias could make out the shape of the
Abbey.

"There's no place like home," he said thankfully. "What a
splendid pathfinder you are, my friend."

Still sucking his paw, the small squirrel smiled shyly. He took
hold of Matthias's tail as they went forwards together, the mouse
talking animatedly, the squirrel nodding vigorously.

"I'll take you to Friar Hugo's kitchen and see that he gives you the nicest breakfast you've ever had. Now what do you say to that?''

Suck, suck, nod, nod.

When Matthias arrived at the wall he felt like patting the old red sandstone. He turned to his companion. ''This is where I live.''

A noise nearby caused them both to freeze momentarily. It sounded like some creature groaning. Instinctively Matthias and the squirrel ducked down among the ferns. Cautiously, they crept along in the direction of the sounds.

Silently parting the ferns, they gazed in horror at the dreadful scene around the base of the elm tree. Among the dead animals that lay stretched in unnatural attitudes was a badly injured weasel. He was moaning and twitching fitfully.

Before either of the friends could decide what to do, a rat appeared on the scene. They remained motionless.

Cheesethief was in a cheery mood. He hummed happily under his breath as he prodded Scragg with his foot.

''Scragg, wake up. It's me, Cheesethief. Oh come on now, I'm sure you remember me? The stupid one, the rat whose job you were going to take?''

Scragg's eyes were barely open. He groaned in agony.

Cheesethief cocked a mockingly sympathetic ear. ''What's that, Scragg, my old mate? Tired, are you? Yes, you must be, lying there like that. Tell you what, I'll help you to go to sleep, shall I?''

The rat placed his foot on the weasel's throat and began pressing down. Scragg struggled feebly, fighting for breath, unable to stop his tormentor. Cheesethief took malicious pleasure in his revenge. Cruelly he leaned his full weight upon the weasel's rasping throat. ''Hush now. Go to sleep, Scragg. Dream of the command you never had.''

Scragg made one final gurgling whimper and lay still.

Cheesethief slunk off chuckling with satisfaction.

Hidden in the ferns, Matthias and the baby squirrel held their breath in disbelief. They had seen murder committed!

Matthias and the squirrel waited until they were sure the coast was clear. At last they emerged from the ferns, and Matthias, cupping his paws round his mouth, ventured a low halloo up at the wall. There was no reply.

The little squirrel shook his head. He pointed to the floor with his paw in a gesture that Matthias interpreted as "Stop here."

With breathtaking speed and skill, the tiny creature raced up the trunk of the old elm. Reaching the thin branches above the parapet, he ran out along one. Using it as a springboard, he bounced nimbly on to the ramparts and vanished, sucking fiercely at his paw.

Matthias had not long to wait before the small door in the wall nearby grated open on its rusty hinges, and Constance peered cautiously out. Seeing Matthias, she ran to greet him, with the little squirrel perched upon her back.

Matthias was not sure what sort of a reception was in store for him. He need not have worried. Constance hugged him, patted his back and shook him by the paw.

The badger forestalled the explanation that was upon the young mouse's lips. She beckoned Matthias inside, shutting the door behind them. "You can tell us everything later, Matthias. Right now I insist that you come to the main gate. There's something you must see."

A minute or two later all three were standing on the gatehouse wall, shoulder to shoulder with countless other defenders. Cluny's horde was retreating, back down the road to their camp at St. Ninian's Church. There was a wild cheering from the ranks of the mice and woodlanders.

Cluny was being borne upon the plank in the midst of his army. Redtooth, who was still disguised in the Warlord's battle-armor, had draped a blanket over Cluny to hide him and keep up the masquerade. But nobody was fooled! Both sides of the wall had heard the tale of misadventure in all its gory detail. They knew that the strutting rat in armor was not Cluny the Scourge.

Redtooth nevertheless strode proudly along. Cluny might not recover. Besides, he reveled in the respect that he received, dressed as he was in such barbaric finery. He knew that it was only borrowed plumage, but he could always hope that the position might become permanent.

On top of the gatehouse ramparts feelings ran high. The Abbot had issued strict orders that no missiles or weaponry be discharged at the enemy in retreat. Amid the cheering there was quite a bit of resentful grumbling.

Why not smash Cluny's army once and for all?

Now that they were on the run, this was the proper time to consolidate a resounding Redwall victory!

But the good Father Abbot would not hear of it. Like a true gentlemouse he believed in tempering triumph with mercy. The jubilatory sounds died away to an eerie silence as the rats toiled raggedly off down the road, raising a column of dust in the early dawn. Dispirited and battleworn, carrying their fallen leader, the maimed and wounded hobbled painfully along at the rear, the bitter ashes of vanquishment and defeat mingling with the dust from their stumbling vanguard.

Even the silent victors began to realize that victory came at a high price. Freshly dug graves and a crowded infirmary bore silent witness to the reality of war.

Matthias felt a gentle paw intertwining with his own. It was Cornflower. Relief showed in her eyes and her voice.

"Oh Matthias, thank goodness you are back safe! It was dreadful, not knowing where you were or what had become of you. I thought you'd never come back."

"I'm like an old bad penny, I always come back," Matthias whispered.

"Oh, by the way, how is your father?"

Cornflower brightened up. "He's made a marvelous recovery. He refused to lie in bed and has been up on the wall helping out. You can't keep a good Fieldmouse down, my dad always says."

Matthias barely had time to bid Cornflower a hasty goodbye before he was ushered off to the Abbot's room for an early-morning conference. He took his seat and looked around the table. There were Constance, Ambrose, Winifred, Foremole, the Abbot, and also his friend the baby squirrel. He stood on a stool, dipping his paw into a bowl of milk and honey, sucking it with noisy enjoyment.

"I think that you would have been in trouble without Silent Sam here, Matthias," the Abbot said.

The young mouse nodded. "I certainly would, Father Abbot. So that's his name? Silent Sam? Well, he certainly lives up to it."

"Indeed he does," replied the Abbot. "His mother and father are old friends of mine. They'll pick up his tracks and be along here later to collect him. Do you know, this little chap hasn't spoken since he was born. I've tried every remedy known to Redwall on him, but none has worked, so he was named Silent Sam. But don't let that fool you, he knows Mossflower Wood like the back of his paw, don't you, Sam?''

The tiny squirrel licked his paw and smiled. He indicated a large circle with it, pointing at himself with his unsticky paw.

Matthias reached over and shook the paw heartily. "My thanks to you, Silent Sam. You are truly a great pathfinder."

During the meeting there was much useful information exchanged. Matthias told of the rescue at St. Ninian's, and his encounter with the strange hare.

"Surely you don't mean Basil Stag Hare?" cried Constance. "Well, I never! Is that old eccentric still bobbing around? I expect we'll see him turn up with the Vole family around about lunchtime. I never knew Basil to miss the chance of a free lunch back in the old days."

The assembled creatures passed on a vote of thanks to Matthias for his resourcefulness and bravery. Matthias blushed. Then he sat listening intently while those who had taken part in the battle recounted all they could remember. In the aftermath of that memorable conflict there was much speculation as to what the future held.

Would Cluny recover from his injuries? Had his horde been so soundly defeated that they had learned their lesson? Or would they be back?

It was the Abbot's opinion that Cluny and his rabble would not bother Redwall again. Their leader's injuries would doubtless prove fatal. This statement was strongly opposed by the others, and Constance was elected to speak for them.

"Cluny is still the prime factor," said the badger. "That rat is physically tougher than we could ever imagine. It is only a matter of time until he recovers sufficiently to attack us again."

Constance pounded upon the table with a heavy paw, emphasizing each word. "And make no mistake about it, Cluny the Scourge will attack Redwall again. I'd stake my life on it! Think for a moment. If Cluny were to give up the idea of conquering this Abbey, he would lose both face and credibility with the army he commands. Furthermore, and most important of all, word would spread across the land that Cluny was not invincible, that he could be beaten by mice!

"This would mean the end of Cluny as a legend of terror; so you see, when Cluny recovers he will be virtually forced to mount a second assault upon Redwall."

There was a sober silence around the table.

The Abbot arose. He had arrived at a decision.

"So be it. I have listened to your counsel and opinions, my dear and trusted friends. Although I yearn for peace, I feel that I must base my judgment on your words, which I know to be true. Therefore my power as Abbot, and any assistance that I can give are yours for the asking. It is my wish that Constance, Matthias, Winifred, Ambrose and Foremole take complete command at Redwall in the event of a second invasion. I will concern myself with aiding the injured and feeding the hungry. And now, my friends, I must adjourn this meeting, as I have other matters to attend to. Come, Sam. We must wash those sticky little paws before your parents arrive. Oh, and before I forget, Matthias, Brother Methuselah would like to talk with you. He is in Great Hall."

CHAPTER

3

Cluny the Scourge lay upon his bed, racked with crippling pains. Rat captains gathered in the corner of the sickroom. They sat silent. The terrible injuries would have proved fatal to any other rat on earth, but not to Cluny—a broken arm, a broken leg, numerous cracked ribs, a fractured tail, smashed claws and other hurts not yet diagnosed.

Redtooth and four of the others might have set upon their leader and finished him off for good.

But the fear of his legendary powers was too strong!

Nobody knew for sure the extent of Cluny's remorseless vitality. Watching him now, the barrel-like chest heaving up and down, the still-strong tail swishing spasmodically, Redtooth marveled at Cluny's strength. He was not even sure if Cluny was shamming, pretending that his injuries were severe merely as some kind of test or trap that he had set for his captains.

The twelve sentry rats were locked in the hut they had been set to guard. It was now repaired. They had been soundly flogged for letting the Vole family escape. As a further punishment for concocting lies about a big hare and a young mouse, Redtooth ordered that the twelve be starved until further notice. He had been lenient with them. Cluny would have sentenced them to death and personally killed them with his bare claws.

Outside in the churchyard the leaderless horde did absolutely nothing to reorganize. Sitting about licking their wounds and waiting for the Chief to recover seemed to be the order of the day.

Again the mouse warrior armed with his ancient sword returned to haunt Cluny's fevered dreams.

Once more he was falling from the plank on the Abbey wall, falling, falling. Below him waited spectral figures: Ragear, with a blue face bloated to many times its normal size, a rat-skeleton dressed in Cluny's own battle armor, a huge hare with enormous feet, and a thick-bodied, venomous-looking banded snake. He tried to twist away from them as he fell, but, however much he swerved and tried to change direction, Cluny had only to look down and see the fierce-eyed warrior mouse—waiting, always waiting, the sword held point upwards for him to be impaled upon. Cluny tried to cry out, but not a sound came; it was as though his throat were being squeezed tightly.

He felt the sharp sword pierce his chest.

Bong!

Once more the sound of the Joseph Bell tolling out across the fields from Redwall wakened the Warlord. Fangburn, who was trying to extract a piece of elm branch from his Chief's chest, leaped backwards in fright as Cluny's eye snapped open inches from his own.

"Get away from me," Cluny rasped.

Fangburn retreated, mumbling excuses. Cluny eyed him suspiciously—he didn't trust any of them.

"If you really want to help, go and get hold of some of those new recruits who live locally and bring them here to me," he gasped.

Within minutes Fangburn had assembled a band of the recruits around Cluny's bed.

"Where's Scragg the weasel?" Cluny growled.

Cheesethief stepped forward, wiping imaginary tears from his face with the back of a filthy claw. "Don't you remember, Chief? He fell out of the big tree. After I'd taken care of you I went back for him, but when I got to him the poor weasel was dead. What a good, kind—"

"Ah, shut your moaning face," said Cluny irritably. "If he's dead, then that's that. Here, you recruits, come closer and listen to me."

Apprehensively the little group shuffled forwards. Cluny raised himself slightly on one elbow.

"Do any of you know where a healer can be found? I don't mean one like those mice. I need a creature that knows the old ways, a gypsy, one who can cure anything for the right price."

Killconey the ferret bowed elaborately. "Ah, 'tis your lucky day, yer honor, for don't I know the very vixen."

"Foxes?" echoed Cluny.

"Aye, foxes, sir," the ferret replied. "Didn't me ould mother always used to say, 'There's nothing like a fox to fix'? There's a whole tribe of 'em livin' across the meadow, sir. Old Sela the vixen is the girl you'll be wanting, her and her son Chicken-hound. They'll fix you up as right as rain if there's something in it for them. Does yer honor want me to fetch them?"

Slowly Cluny's tail wound itself about the ferret's neck, drawing him in close.

"Get them," Cluny said hoarsely. "Find the foxes and bring them here to me."

Killconey's throat bulged as he tried nervously to swallow. "Glug! I will indeed, if you'll just let go of this pore ould ferret's neck, sir, I'll go as fast as if the divvil himself was chasin' me. You lay back now and rest your noble self, sir."

Cluny released the ferret and lay back with an agonized sigh. Now was the time to think and plan ahead. Next time would be different.

"Redtooth," he called. "Take some soldiers and scout around. See if you can find a great hard timber, a big log or tree trunk, something that will serve as a battering ram."

The mice might have won a battle, but Cluny had not yet lost the war, by the claws of hellthunder!

Those Abbey mice were going to pay with blood for what they had done to Cluny the Scourge.

CHAPTER

4

Brother Methuselah was busy with a small brush and a pot of black ink. As he brushed the dust of ages from each letter on the wall, he filled it in with ink. This would make it easier to read the message that had been graven underneath the tapestry.

"Ah, Matthias, there you are," Methuselah squeaked.

He blinked over the top of his glasses at the young mouse. "Look, this is something I want you to see. Quite by accident I discovered this writing beneath where Martin's picture once hung."

Matthias was full of unconcealed excitement.

"What does it say, Brother Methuselah?" he cried.

The old gatehouse-keeper sneezed as he brushed more dust from the lettering on the wall. "All in good time, young mouse! Here, make yourself useful. You brush the dust off the words while I ink them in. Between us we'll soon get it done."

Matthias set to work with an energetic goodwill. He scrubbed vigorously, sending up clouds of dust. Between sneezes Methuselah hurried to keep pace with him.

One hour later they both sat on the stone floor, drinking October ale to quench the dust while they admired their handiwork.

"It's written in the old hand," said Methuselah, "but I can read it clear enough."

Matthias jostled him boisterously. "What does it say, old one? Hurry up and read it to me."

"Patience, you young scallywag," chided the ancient mouse. "Be quiet and listen. It takes the form of a poem:

'Who says that I am dead
Knows nought at all.
I—am that is,
Two mice within Redwall.
The Warrior sleeps
'Twixt Hall and Cavern Hole.
I—am that is,
Take on my mighty role.
Look for the sword
In moonlight streaming forth,
At night, when day's first hour
Reflects the North.
From o'er the threshold
Seek and you will see;
I—am that is,
My sword will wield for me.' "

Matthias blinked and scratched his head. He looked at Methuselah. "Well, what did all that mean? It's a riddle to me."

"Precisely," said the old mouse. "It is indeed a riddle, but don't worry, Matthias, we will solve it together. I have sent for food and drink. You and I will not move from here until we have the answer."

Shortly afterwards, Cornflower arrived bearing a tray of breakfast for them both: nutbread, salad, milk and some of Friar Hugo's special quince pie. She was about to strike up a conversation with Matthias when Methuselah sent her packing.

"Shoo! Away with you, little fieldmouse. I need Matthias with a clear brain to help me solve an important problem, so run along."

Cornflower winked at Matthias, shook her head at Methuselah and walked off with mock dignity, her nose high in the air. Matthias watched her go until Methuselah tweaked his ear. "Pay attention now, young mouse. We must study this bit by bit. Let's take the first two lines:

> 'Who says that I am dead
> Knows nought at all!' ''

Matthias waved a paw. His mouth filled with salad, he mumbled, "But we know that Martin is dead."

Methuselah took a sip of milk, pulled a wry face and reached for his October ale. "Ah, but, if we suppose that he is dead, then the words tell us we know nothing at all. So, let us assume that he is alive."

"What? Do you mean Martin, alive and walking about?" said Matthias. "We'd recognize him! Unless, that is, he was disguised as someone else."

The old gatehouse-keeper choked, spluttering ale over his habit. "Good grief! I never looked at it that way. Very good, young one. Maybe the answer is in the next two lines. What do they say?"

> '' 'I—am that is,
> Two mice within Redwall!' ''

Matthias repeated the words, but he could make no sense of them. '' 'I—am that is.' What is? 'Two mice within Redwall.' Hmm, two mice it tells of."

"Of two mice in one," replied Methuselah.

They sat silent awhile, both racking their brains. Matthias mentioned something that was bothering him as he looked at the graven lines. "What I cannot understand is that sort of dash. Look: 'I—am that is.' Do you see, there is a small dash between the words 'I' and 'am.' In fact the same dash occurs three times throughout the rhyme: here, here and here." Matthias pointed.

Methuselah adjusted his glasses and peered closely. "Yes. You may have something there. It could be the key to the whole thing . . . 'I—am that is.' Let's say that the dash separates the line, so that we will look at the last three words, 'am that is.' Suppose we took that part out, then it would read, 'I, two mice within Redwall.' ''

Matthias shook his head. "What do you make of that?"

"Complete nonsense," replied the old mouse. "Let's stick with, 'am that is.' ''

"Sounds all mixed up to me," Matthias grumbled.

Methuselah looked up sharply. "Say that again."

"Say what again? You mean that it sounds all mixed up to me?"

Methuselah executed a little jig of delight. He patted the wall with his paw, shouting, "That's it! That's it! Why couldn't I see that? It's all mixed up, of course!"

The old mouse took a great draught of ale. Cackling with glee, he pointed a paw at Matthias. "I know something that you don't know . . . '*am that is*' . . . Matthias."

The young mouse frowned. So, the old one had finally cracked. He was in his second infancy.

"Methuselah," he said kindly, "hadn't you better lie down awhile?"

But the old gatehouse-keeper kept pointing. He began to chant.

> "*Matthias, I that am,*
> *Matthias, you that are.*"

The young mouse stood tapping his tail in exasperation.

"I wish you'd tell me what you're so excited about," he said severely. "Why are you saying my name?"

Methuselah wiped tears of laughter from his eyes as he explained. "When you said it was all mixed up, that got me thinking. Martin was talking of two mice, himself and another. Ergo, Martin is represented by the word 'I.' The other mouse is '*am that is*' all mixed up. Now do you see?"

Matthias leaned against the wall. "I'm afraid I don't follow you."

"Oh, you young booby," Methuselah giggled. "I mixed the letters up and re-arranged them. It's your own name . . . '*am that is*' . . . Matthias."

"Are you sure?" said Matthias in astonishment.

"Of course I'm sure," replied Methuselah. "It couldn't mean anything else! Your name has eight letters in it. So has '*am that is.*' An M, two A's, two T's, an H, an I and an S. Whichever way you look at it, Matthias or '*am that is,*' it comes out the same."

"Methuselah, do you realize what this means?"

The old mouse sat down beside him, nodding gravely.

"Oh yes, indeed I do. It means that Martin somehow knew that one day he would live on through you."

Matthias was staggered. "He knew about me! Martin the Warrior knew my name! Can you imagine that?"

The enormity of it overwhelmed them both. For several minutes they sat, no word passing between them. Suddenly Matthias leapt to his feet. "Right, let's get on with it. Look at these lines:

> 'The Warrior sleeps
> 'Twixt Hall and Cavern Hole.
> I—am that is
> Take on my mighty role.' "

"Well, the last two lines are pretty clear," said Methuselah. "They mean that Martin, carrying on through you, has a great task to perform."

"What about the first two lines?" Matthias said. "They seem fairly obvious, too. Between Great Hall and Cavern Hole there is a flight of stairs. Come on, old mouse."

In spite of his advanced years, Methuselah gripped Matthias's paw and ran so fast that the younger mouse had difficulty in keeping up.

Between Great Hall and Cavern Hole there were seven stone steps. The problem was, which one held the answer?

"Thinking caps on again," said the old mouse. "Let's make a close inspection of these steps."

Together they examined the stone steps minutely, going back over each one several times. Matthias sat on the bottom step. He shrugged. "They appear to be seven ordinary broad stone steps; nothing special; quite the same as any other set of stairs in the Abbey, wouldn't you say?"

Methuselah was forced to agree. After sitting awhile and letting his eyes roam about, Matthias remarked, "I've just noticed something. The name of our Abbey is carved into the wall as you go up the steps on the left-hand side, and also as you descend on the right-hand wall. It reads 'Redwall,' either way."

Methuselah walked up and down the steps, testing what Matthias had said. "Yes, so it does. Do you see that each letter is one step's width? Hmmm. Seven letters for seven steps. Surely that must be some kind of a hint?"

Again the two friends sat to ponder the mystery. This time it was Matthias's turn to become excited and point a paw at his companion.

"I know something *you* don't know."

Methuselah pursed his lips in annoyance. "You know, Matthias, for a mouse that claims affinity with Martin the Warrior, you can be singularly foolish sometimes."

"Huh. No more foolish than you were when you were saying the same thing to me not so long ago," Matthias retorted.

Methuselah coughed and cleaned his spectacles on his habit. "Harrumph. Er, yes, well, I apologize. Now please tell me what you have discovered."

Matthias explained. "If you place the word 'Redwall' running both ways as it does here, you will notice that only one letter occurs in the same place, the letter W. Furthermore, if you were to turn a W upside down it becomes a letter M, which stands for Martin, Matthias, oh, and also for Methuselah, my old friend."

"Well, curl my whiskers! The young scoundrel has a brain, and it works too. It's got to be the fourth step, the middle one up or down."

The step in question proved to be as solid and unmoving as its counterparts. Even with their combined strength, the friends could not budge it a fraction.

Matthias wiped sweat from his brow. "Take a breather, old one. I know who can handle this. Foremole and his team."

The moles were not long in arriving. They gathered around the step, sniffing and scratching. Foremole exercised his authority, clearing them out of his way.

"Yurr moles, get outten th' loight. Let'n um dog at bone thurr."

Foremole paced the length of the step then shuffled sideways over it. He tapped it with his great digging claws. He sniffed it, licked it and rubbed it with his velvet head.

"Ummm, worra you'm gennelbeast know abouten this yurr step?" he asked.

Together they related all the information to the attentive Foremole. He blinked short-sightedly as he ruminated.

"Arr, fourth'n uppards, same down'ards. Yurr, Walt, 'ark,

Doby. B'aint that same as your grandmum do foind when she'm rooten about olden toim fortications?''

"What's he saying?'' whispered Matthias.

Methuselah translated the curious mole dialect. "Foremole said, the fourth step upwards is the same as the fourth step down, that much we already know. Then he consulted the two mole brothers, Walt and Doby. It seems the step is the same as one found by their grandmother when she was exploring an old-fashioned castle or fortification. Moles are very sensible creatures, you know, and I think they have the answer to our problem.''

"Good old Foremole,'' said Matthias.

"Hush. Let's hear what Walt and Doby have to say,'' whispered Methuselah.

The two mole brothers respectfully tugged their noses to Foremole before answering:

"Urr, that be true, zurr.''

"Our grandmum, she'm foind lots o' them.''

"Aye, that she do. Never diggen or breaken, just turn 'em after dustin'.''

Methuselah interpreted to Matthias. "Apparently their grandmother was somewhat of an authority on steps such as these. The clever old mole would neither dig nor break them. Evidently she could turn the step over, once she had brushed it.''

Matthias addressed Foremole courteously. "Excuse me, sir, but do you know how to deal with this step now? If you do, then my friend and I would be only too willing to help you.''

Foremole smiled, his whole face almost vanishing into dark velvet wrinkles. He clapped Matthias on the shoulder in a chummy way. The young mouse was amazed at the weight and strength of Foremole's paw. He was glad that it was a friendly pat.

Foremole chuckled deeply. "Nay, nay, bless your li'l 'eart, Mattwise, you'n owd Methuselam be but mouses, best leave 'er to Foremole, oi'll deal with'n.''

"He says he can cope adequately without either of us,'' said Methuselah.

Foremole produced a thick, fine-haired handbrush from his tunneling kit. Bending close, he brushed furiously at the upper and lower insteps of the fourth stone. As he swept, he snuffled and blew, following the path of his brush. It soon became apparent that the stone had been cunningly jointed. The dust came away to reveal a continuous hairline crack which ran around the edges of the step.

Next Foremole rummaged in his kit and came up with a tin of grease and a strong thin bar, one end of which was flattened like a spatula. Smearing the grease liberally on top of the third step, Foremole inserted the flat metal tip against the base of the fifth step. He dealt the blunt end of the bar a smart blow, setting it firmly into the crack. With a swift movement he levered the fourth step an inch forward, exposing a long dark gap.

With a grunt of satisfaction Foremole called out to his team, "Yurr moles, gather round an' set your diggen claws in um crack."

The mole team dug their claws into the gap, chanting together as they heaved with a will.

> "Hurr she come, if'n you please,
> Movin' bowlder, sloid on grease."

To the astonishment of the watching mice, the step slid smoothly outwards on the greased stone. It turned completely over to reveal a dark opening with a downward flight of stairs running off into the blackness below.

CHAPTER

5

Old Sela the vixen muttered her charms and spells in a singsong voice. Sometimes she did a hopping little dance around the sickbed. Cluny was not fooled!

He watched as the fox sprinkled "magic herbs" on the pillow, reciting another strange spell as she did so.

"The old fraud," Cluny thought. "All that mumbo-jumbo and magic nonsense. Why does she need it when she knows that she's a perfectly good doctor?"

Sela had placed herb poultices and healing salves on all the Warlord's wounds. After bandaging them neatly she had administered a potion that would deaden the pain and induce sleep.

Cluny was satisfied. He had been treated by healers many times before. Sela was the best; all the added muttering, dancing and trickery was done merely to enhance her reputation, to pull the wool over the eyes of stupid ignorant creatures.

"She may be a fox, but she'll never outfox me," Cluny thought to himself. Sela had assured him that with three weeks' rest, combined with her healing skills, he would be fighting fit once more.

"Three weeks!" At first the rat leader had raged and sworn. He had never been out of action that long in all his life. But secretly he knew that the fox was right. Without her, Cluny would have been dead or permanently crippled.

Like all of her kind, Sela was a slippery character. What did she expect to gain from all this?

Loot and plunder from Redwall!

Sela had never been allowed past the Abbey gates. She was certain that if Cluny's army overran Redwall, there would be enough treasure to keep even the greediest creature happy for life.

Now, as the potions took effect, Cluny felt himself drifting off to sleep, lulled by the ceaseless chantings and murmurings of Old Sela. He would have come awake like a scorched tiger had he known what the fox was actually up to!

Old Sela had lived on her wits for many years. She was a counterspy by nature. In any dispute or conflict she invariably sold secrets to both sides. It was a dangerous game, but one that she had played well thus far. Her crafty, golden eyes had not been idle for a second since entering Cluny's camp.

Sela knew exactly how many rats, weasels, stoats and ferrets were able-bodied enough for combat. Also, she had seen the working party gnawing industriously at the base of a tall poplar. If that wasn't going to be used as a battering ram then Sela was a trout, and by her own diagnosis of three weeks, she knew to the day when the date of the next attack on Redwall would be.

The vixen watched Cluny's eyes closing under the influence of her medicine. These warlords were all the same—they never gave credit for brains to anyone except themselves. There the big oaf was, snoring like a fox cub in his earth on a winter's night.

She turned to the armed rats who guarded the sickroom. She issued orders in a confidential whisper, "I want no noise, please. Your Chief must have complete rest. Don't let him exert himself when he wakes. Now you'll have to excuse me."

She made her way to the door. Fangburn and Redtooth stood barring it.

"Where do you think you are off to, fox?"

Sela licked her lips. She tried to look kindly but earnest. "Actually I was going back to my den to replenish my stock of herbs, that's if you wish me to treat your leader properly, of course."

Redtooth prodded her with a spear. "Cluny gave strict orders that you must stay here until he's better."

The sly fox blustered. "But my good rats, surely you must

realize that I can do nothing without my stock of herbs? Now please let me pass."

Fangburn shoved her roughly. "Sit down. You're not going anywhere."

Sela seated herself. Her mind was racing. "Er, then at least let me go out into the churchyard. I've got to have some fresh air. Besides, I can tell my young assistant what herbs I require, and he can fetch them for me."

Redtooth was not convinced. "But the Chief said you'd got to stay here."

Sela smiled inwardly. She had them where she wanted them now.

She put on a serious expression, shaking her head gravely. "Then you had better let me have your names. That way I can tell Cluny when he awakes full of pain with festering wounds. No doubt he'll want to know who it was stopped me trying to cure him."

This crafty statement did the trick. After a few whispered words between the two rats, Redtooth turned to Sela. "Listen, fox, you can go out into the churchyard and tell your assistant to run this errand, but Fangburn here will be right beside you with a cutlass in your ribs. One false move out of you, and you'll be a dead healer. Is that clear?"

Sela smiled ingratiatingly. "By all means. Let your friend come along. I have nothing to hide."

Out in the churchyard Chickenhound, who was the son of Sela, sat sunning himself upon a tombstone.

Fangburn did not see the secret wink that passed between the two foxes. Chickenhound was as devious as his mother in matters of espionage. His face was the picture of blank innocence as he listened to Sela's instructions.

"Now listen carefully, my son. We have a very sick rat inside that church. He is in urgent need of my special remedies. I want you to run as quickly as you can back to our den. Bring me back some snakewort, cuckoo spit, a medium eelskin, three fine strips of willow bark . . . oh, there's so much to remember, I'd better write it all down for you."

Sela turned to Fangburn. "Do you carry any writing materials with you, sir?"

Fangburn spat scornfully at the fox's feet. "Are you trying

to make fun of me, healer? What d'you think I am? Huh, writing materials! The idea of it!''

Sela smiled disarmingly. "Ah, I thought not. Sorry, no offense. I'll just make do with some bark and a burnt twig. Where could I obtain such things, please?''

Fangburn pointed sullenly with his cutlass. "Over there by the cooking fire. Be quick about it.''

A few minutes later Sela had presented Chickenhound with a scroll of bark that she had written upon.

"There, that should do it. Now hurry along, my son. Don't stop for anything on the way. Isn't that right, Captain?''

Fangburn puffed out his chest, proud that the fox knew his rank. He pointed a claw at Chickenhound.

"You listen to what your mother tells you, young feller. Get back here with the stuff on that list as soon as possible. Be off with you now.''

The young fox took off like a rocket. Fangburn leaned on his cutlass. "That's the way to deal with young uns.''

Sela looked at him admiringly. "Indeed it is, sir. He never goes that fast for me. It's obvious that you've got an air of command about you.''

Fangburn colored slightly. This vixen wasn't such a bad creature after all. He gestured modestly to the church with his cutlass. "Er, I think it's time we went back inside. Orders, you know!''

"Oh quite. Can't have you getting in trouble, can we?'' said Sela in her most flattering tone.

As soon as he was out of sight of Cluny's stronghold, Chickenhound slowed to a leisurely walk. He unfastened the bark scroll and read his mother's message.

> To the Abbot of Redwall Abbey
> I know exactly when, where, and how the hordes of Cluny will attack your Abbey. What price will you give me for this important information?
>
> Sela the Vixen

Chickenhound sniggered noisily. He knew precisely what his mother required him to do. He recalled Sela's favorite saying:

"I've sold hens their own eggs back and stolen the whiskers from farmyard dogs." The young fox ambled along the dusty road to Redwall, the hedgerows echoing with the sound of his sly chuckles.

CHAPTER

6

Cornflower was having a very busy day.

Having delivered food to Matthias and Methuselah, she went out on the ramparts accompanied by her helpers. They fed the sentries and took back all the dishes. Next she found herself making an extra two trays of food up for Silent Sam's parents. The two squirrels thanked her politely and set to with an appetite. Little Sam stood watching them, sucking his paw. Cornflower had a special soft spot for the baby squirrel; she made up a tray for him too. She had no sooner finished than Constance called to ask a favor of her. Would she mind making up another four trays? Three for the Vole family who had just returned, and an extra-large one for Basil Stag Hare. Cornflower cheerfully obliged.

Later, as they all ate, her eyes grew wide with amazement. She had never seen anyone shift such vast amounts of food, not even Constance or Ambrose Spike. They were huge eaters, but mere amateurs compared with Basil Stag Hare.

Basil wiped his mouth daintily on a napkin. He had impeccable manners to match his insatiable appetite. He gushed forth praise for the Abbey victuals. "Oh excellent! Absolutely top hole! D'you know, I'd forgotten how good the old tiffin at Redwall could be. I say, m'dear, would you mind refreshing an old bachelor hare's memory? Another tankard of that fine October ale, and perhaps one more portion of your very good summer

salad. Ah, and I think I could manage another few slices of Friar
Hugo's quince pie. Superb! Ahem, don't forget the goatsmilk
cheese with hazelnuts. I'm very partial to that. Cut along now,
you little charmer. My word, what an attractive young fieldmouse girl.''

Cornflower sent two of her helpers. They had to go the long
way around to reach the kitchens. Abbot Mortimer had declared
Great Hall and Cavern Hole out of bounds to all creatures, with
the exception of those helping Matthias and Methuselah.

Below the newly-discovered steps, a pair of lanterns cast pools
of golden light into the inky blackness. The two mice made their
way gingerly down the secret staircase. The moles stayed outside, ready to help if they were needed further.

The air was chilly but dry. Deeper and deeper the two friends
went until the steps ended at the beginning of a downward-
winding corridor. It had been neatly dug and shored up with
wooden supports. Matthias suppressed a shudder. How long had
it been since any creature trod this silent musty passage? He
brushed away cobwebs which disintegrated at the touch of a
paw. Methuselah held on to his habit. Now they turned left, now
right, then another left turn, left again, then right. Methuselah's
voice sounded hollow and eerie. ''The passage was probably
dug like this to give it extra strength. Have you noticed, Matthias? We seem to be going downwards still.''

''Yes, we must be nearly underneath the Abbey foundations,''
Matthias replied.

The friends pressed onwards. They could not estimate how
long they had been following the course of this ancient winding
corridor. Methuselah had ventured slightly ahead. Now he
halted.

''Aha, this looks like the end of the line,'' he squeaked.

It was a door.

Together they inspected it. Built of stout timber, banded with
iron, beset with florin spikes, the door did not appear to be
locked. Yet it would not budge.

Matthias held his lantern high. ''Look, there's some writing
on the lintel over the door.''

Methuselah read it aloud:

    '' 'The same as the steps 'twixt the Hall,
    Remember and look to the center.

My password again is Redwall,
Am that is, you alone are to enter.' "

The old mouse did not hide his disappointment. "Humph! After all the help and assistance that I've given, countless hours of study and valuable time. Really!"

His words fell upon deaf ears. Matthias was already counting the florin spikes that were driven into the door.

Methuselah feigned indifference, but his natural curiosity soon overcame any chagrin he felt at not being allowed to pass the doorway.

"Need any help, young mouse?"

"Forty-two, forty-three, hush! Can't you see I'm trying to count?" came the reply.

The old gatehouse-keeper put on his glasses. "Well, have you solved the riddle all by yourself?"

Matthias winked at his companion. "Yes. At least I hope I have. There are three clues in the rhyme you see, the same as the steps. Look to the center, and the password is Redwall. Now, we must remember that Redwall has seven letters. If you look at these old-fashioned nails—"

"Florin spikes," Methuselah corrected.

Matthias continued, "Yes, if you look at these florin spikes, you'll find that they are in rows of seven, the same as the number of letters in Redwall. There are seven rows of spikes going from side to side and seven rows from top to bottom, forty-nine spikes in all. Therefore, the twenty-fifth spike up, down, or across is the exact middle spike. The rhyme says, '*look to the center.*' That's this one here."

As Matthias placed his paw on the spike in question, the door swung creakingly inwards.

Both mice could feel the hairs standing on their backs as the door opened with agonizing slowness.

When it stood fully open, Matthias put his paw around Methuselah's thin shoulders.

"Come on, old friend, we go in together," he said.

"But the rhyme," Methuselah protested. "It says that only you may enter."

Matthias answered in a strange, full voice. He seemed to grow in years and stature. "*I am that is*, old one. Martin is Matthias.

As my trusted friend and faithful companion, I say that you may enter with me.''

Methuselah felt himself in the presence of one many times older than he. Lanterns held high, the two mice advanced through the doorway.

It was a small, low-ceilinged chamber. A stone block rested squarely in the center.

The tomb of Martin the Warrior!

All around the sides of the stone were detailed carvings, depicting scenes from Martin's life: deeds of valor and works of skillful healing. Lying along the top of the stone was a life-sized effigy of the Warrior. He was clothed in the familiar habit of a Redwall mouse, plain, with no trimmings.

Matthias stood reverently, gazing upon the calm features of his own legendary hero in the silence of the small chamber.

Methuselah whispered in his ear. ''He bears an uncanny resemblance to you, young one.''

As the old mouse spoke, the door behind him creaked shut!

Feeling no panic, Matthias turned to look. On the back of the door hung a shield and a sword belt.

The shield was a plain round steel thing of the type carried by the warriors of old. The years had not dulled its highly-burnished front. At its center was a letter M.

The sword belt was in pristine condition, soft and as supple as if it had newly come from the tanner's bench: shiny black leather with a hanging tab to carry sword and scabbard. Its broad silver buckle gleamed in the lantern light.

Without a word Matthias undid his novice's cord girdle. Handing it to Methuselah, he took down the sword belt and buckled it about his waist. The belt fitted as if it had been made for him. With great care he lifted the shield from the door and tried it on his arm. It had two grips, one below the elbow, the other for the paw to grasp. It felt oddly familiar to Matthias.

There was more writing where the shield had hung upon the back of the door. Methuselah read it:

> '' 'By the moonlight, on the hour,
> In my threshold space lay me.
> Watch the beam reflect my power,
> Unite once more my sword with me.

I—am that is, stand true for all.
O Warrior Mouse, protect Redwall.' "

As in a dream, Matthias gave the door a gentle tug. It opened. By the lantern lights the two mice made their way back from the lonely chamber. Back to the familiar warmth and cheer of Redwall Abbey. Back to the hot June noonday sun.

CHAPTER

7

Constance stood on the ramparts. She leaned over the parapet, watching as a young fox approached along the dusty road, bearing a stick with a white rag of truce tied to it.

The big badger was uneasy. She knew this one, a fox from Old Sela's brood. You needed eyes in the back of your head to watch that lot!

"Stop right there and state your business, fox," Constance called gruffly.

Chickenhound sniggered, but seeing the badger's stern expression, he quickly took control of himself.

"I want to see your Abbot," he called.

The reply was abrupt. "Well, you can't!"

The fox waved his flag, squinting up at Constance. "But I must see the Abbot! I come in peace. I have important information for sale."

The badger was unmoved. "I don't care if you've got the rumbling foxtrot, you aren't getting inside this Abbey. If you want to speak to anyone, then speak to me."

Constance watched the crestfallen fox, then added as an afterthought: "And if you don't like it, well, you can sling your brush back up the road."

Chickenhound was dismayed. This last insult had taken the wind completely out of his sails. He tried to think how Sela would have handled a situation like this. Eventually he unrolled the bark scroll and waved it up at Constance.

"This message is for the Abbot's eyes only. It's important."

The badger eyed him coldly. "Then chuck it up here. I'll see that he gets it."

No amount of wheedling and blandishment would cause the cynical badger to change her mind. She was adamant. In the end, Chickenhound had to throw the scroll up. He made several puny attempts, each one weaker than the last. As the scroll fell back down into the road yet again, Constance called aloud, "Put some energy into it, you little milksop. I'm not hanging about here all day."

Chickenhound heaved the scroll with all his strength. He was gratified to see Constance lean out and catch it. Hopefully he called, "I'll wait right here for an answer."

The badger grunted noncommittally. She sat down below the parapet out of sight of the fox, and scanned the message. Constance stayed where she was until a reasonable time elapsed, then stood up, panting heavily for effect.

"Tell Sela that the Abbot will see her two days from tonight at ten o'clock in Mossflower Wood. She must come to the old tree stump, and mind you tell her—no tricks!"

Chickenhound waved the flag. He went into a bout of uncontrollable sniggering. "Right, I've got the message, fat one! Be sure your Abbot brings lots of valuables with him. Goodbye, old greyback."

Constance poked an angry snout down at the insulting young fox. "You'd better get running, frogface! I'm coming down there to put my paw behind you right now!"

Again Constance dropped behind the parapet. She hammered her paws loudly against the stones. Standing up, she watched the terrified Chickenhound racing off down the road in a cloud of dust.

"Snotty-nosed little upstart!" she muttered.

There was no need for the Father Abbot to concern himself with the underhand dealings of traitor foxes. Constance would be well able to deal with the situation herself.

Matthias was famished. He sat down and took his lunch with Mr. and Mrs. Squirrel, the Vole family, Silent Sam, and Basil the garrulous hare. The young mouse ate mechanically. He did not really want conversation. This latest discovery of a new and baffling rhyme concerning moonlight, the north and an unknown threshold nagged at his brain. Methuselah had gone off to seek the solitude of his gatehouse study, where he claimed he could think more clearly.

Matthias was not the liveliest of table companions. He smiled and nodded, paying little attention to the chatter of the Voles and Squirrels. He was not even distracted by Silent Sam who sat upon his knee, stroking his whiskers with a sticky paw. Basil Stag Hare eyed the food which Matthias had hardly touched.

"Beg pardon, young mouse, old chap, but if you can't finish that blackberry muffin or that red-currant tart . . ."

Matthias absently pushed his plate across to the hare. Basil needed no second bidding.

Abbot Mortimer entered. Seeing the look on Matthias's face, he leaned across and murmured in his ear, "All work and no play makes Matthias a dull mouse. Cheer up, my son."

"What! I mean, sorry, Father Abbot, I didn't mean to be rude. I was trying to solve a problem, you see."

The Abbot patted Matthias indulgently. "I understand, my son. Methuselah has told me of some of the difficulties facing you both. My advice is, don't let it get on top of you. Relax a little. Time provides all the answers. You've done splendidly so far, Matthias. Meanwhile you must not forget your manners at table with the guests of our Abbey."

Matthias snapped out of his reverie. Silent Sam was admiring his sword belt. He laughed. "Do you like that, Sam? It's the sword belt of a famous warrior."

The little squirrel leaped upon the table. He darted up and down, thrusting out his paw as if he held a sword in it, stabbing away at thin air. He pointed at Matthias. The young mouse gave him a hug. "No, bless you, Sam. I haven't got a sword of my own yet, but I will have some day."

Silent Sam pointed to himself, cocking his head on one side. Matthias prodded his fat little stomach. "A sword for you too, Sam? Well, I don't know about that. Your mum and dad might not want you going about armed to the teeth."

Basil Stag Hare had the answer. He produced a beautifully made knife. It was very small, encased in a cunningly crafted willow bark sheath. The hare beckoned Sam. "C'm'ere, you dreadful little rogue! I've got the very thing for you. This is a

leveret dagger. All young hares carry one. Here, let's try it on
you for size, young buccaneer, what, what!''

Basil picked up a worn and discarded sandal. He undid the
foot strap. Threading the dagger and sheath along the strap, he
fastened it around Sam's waist.

''There, by the left, you look a regular little swashbuckler
now,'' chuckled the kindly hare.

Bounding up and down with delight, Silent Sam cut a comical
figure as he fenced his way along the tabletop, thrusting and
parrying at cruets and candlesticks with his new ''sword,'' and
sucking furiously on his free paw.

Matthias joined in the laughter as Mr. and Mrs. Squirrel
thanked Basil for the generous gift to their tiny offspring. Forgetting his immediate problems, Matthias passed a happy hour
in the company of the friendly woodlanders. He enjoyed it even
more when Cornflower appeared. She shared Matthias's seat,
glad to be off her feet for a while. Basil nudged Matthias.

''Excellent little filly, that girl! D'you know, she can produce
more tuck in the twinklin' of an eye than you could shake a
stick at. You mark my words, young feller-my-mouse. A body
would be lucky to settle down with her. I say, have you noticed
the way she looks at you? Hinds look at stags like that. Noble
creatures, stags. It strikes me that you could be just the stag for
her. Why, I remember when I was only a young lancejack. . . .''

Cornflower was making such faces that Matthias was about
to silence Basil, when Methuselah popped in at the door. He
beckoned urgently to Matthias. Hastily the young mouse excused himself and left. Basil leaned closer to Cornflower. He
smiled roguishly.

''You didn't know I was a lancejack, did you, m'dear? Ah
those were the days of the old Forty-Seventh Hare Border Rang-
ers! That was the first time I ever clapped eyes on a stag! I say,
I'm not boring you, am I? Nod's as good as a wink to old
bachelor Basil, y'know.''

Methuselah was in a ferment of eagerness as he led his young
friend over to the gatehouse.

''Matthias, I've found out where the threshold is!''

The ancient mouse refused to say more until they were safely
inside his gatehouse study with the door firmly shut. Even then
he said nothing that made any real sense, shoving Matthias to

one side as he delved through old parchments and manuscripts, scattering books left and right.

"Where is it? I had it not five minutes ago. Hullo, what's this? Oh, the treatise on *Bee Folk of Redwall*!" Methuselah hurled the dusty volume to one side, narrowly missing his companion. "Wait a tick. I think I may have put it down over there."

Matthias gazed in bewilderment at the overcluttered study. Books, scrolls and manuscripts littered the small room. In his excitement Methuselah opened a desk and practically disappeared under an avalanche of paperwork.

"Hey! Steady on, old mouse! What are you up to?" cried Matthias.

Methuselah emerged jubilant, clutching a yellowed book. "Eureka! This is it! Sister Germaine's literal translation of Martin the Warrior's Abbey blueprints."

He flicked swiftly through the dusty pages of the aged volume. "Let's see: 'Gardens,' 'Cloisters,' 'Belltowers' . . . ah, here it is, 'The Great Wall and its Gates'."

The old mouse winked at Matthias gleefully as he adjusted his glasses. "Listen to this: 'On the west wall will be situated a main gate so that creatures may come and go, obtaining entrance to or exit from the Abbey of Redwall. This entrance will be guarded both night and day, for it is the main gatehouse, and as such is the very threshold of our Abbey.' "

The two mice hugged each other. They danced around amid the chaos of paper, chanting with joy,

> "The gatehouse is the threshold,
> The gatehouse is the threshold."

The Abbot, who was passing by, heard the noise. He shook his head at Ambrose Spike who was coming from the opposite direction.

"Mayhaps they've been at the October ale a little too much, Father Abbot," said the hedgehog.

The Abbot chuckled at the idea. "Well, if it helps them on their mission of discovery, Ambrose, perhaps they ought to drink some more, eh?"

"Aye," Ambrose agreed. " 'Tis enough to inspire any creature, good October ale. Perhaps it might inspire you one day to make me keeper of the cellar keys, Father.''

Inside the gatehouse study the two companions were once more at work, trying to break the code of the Great Hall rhyme.

"Well, that's another piece of the puzzle in place,'' said Methuselah. "But we've jumped ahead of ourselves a bit. There are four lines before that to crack yet:

> 'Look for the sword
> In moonlight streaming forth,
> At night, when day's first hour
> Reflects the north.' ''

Matthias interrupted. "Those first two lines sound as if they could only be solved in the darkness. 'Look for the sword in moonlight streaming forth.' ''

"I agree,'' replied Methuselah, "but the next line is of vital importance. It tells exactly when to look—'at night, when day's first hour.' ''

"Hmm,'' Matthias mused, "let's look at this logically. Go through it word by word.''

Slowly they repeated the line together, '' 'At night, when day's first hour.' ''

Methuselah slumped in his armchair. "I'm afraid it doesn't mean anything to me—''

"Wait!'' cried Matthias. "Midnight is the last hour of the old day, so by the same token, one o'clock in the morning is the first hour of the new day, but we still tend to class it as nighttime. It is as the rhyme says, 'at night when day's first hour.' ''

"I believe you are right,'' said the old mouse. '' 'Day's first hour' is not when it becomes light. It's one in the morning, still dark.''

Matthias leaned wearily against a stack of books. "But if the gatehouse is the threshold, where are we supposed to stand to see anything an hour after midnight?''

"That's easy,'' grinned Methuselah. "The rhyme says, 'from o'er the threshold seek and you will see.' It's simple! What is above our heads right now?''

Matthias shrugged. "The wall, I suppose.''

Methuselah banged his paw down on the arm of the chair.

"Exactly. And where is the only place you can stand on a wall but on top of it."

Suddenly it became clear to Matthias. "Oh, I see," he cried, " *'From o'er the threshold'* means that we must stand on the wall directly above the gatehouse."

As fast as they could run, both mice hurried up the steps to the top of the wall. With Matthias in the lead they pounded along the ramparts. Matthias stopped above the gatehouse and stamped his foot upon the stones.

"I'd say about here. Would you agree?"

Methuselah looked a trifle doubtful. "It looks to be a very rough approximation."

Matthias had to concede. He looked sheepishly about. The stones where they stood were no different from any other part of the wall. The trail seemed to have gone cold again. Dejectedly Matthias sat down on a heap of rock and rubble that had been there since the invasion.

"Huh, what are we supposed to do now? Hang about up here until after midnight and wait for a miracle?"

The old gatehouse-keeper raised an admonitory paw. "Patience, young one, patience. Let us take stock and review the facts. Lend me your knife for a moment."

Matthias drew Shadow's dagger from his belt and gave it to his friend. He sat watching as the old mouse began writing in the dust from the rubble.

Item one: Martin is Matthias.

Item two: We have found Martin's tomb.

Item three: We have also found his shield and sword belt.

Item four: Our task is to find Martin's sword.

Item five: Where? From here, the top of the gatehouse wall.

Item six: When? At one in the morning when moonlight streams forth.

Item seven: In which direction? To the north.

They sat in silence, digesting the facts on the list. Then Matthias spoke: "Suppose we look to the north."

Both mice turned their heads northwards.

"Well, what do you see, young one?" queried Methuselah.

Matthias's voice was tinged with disappointment. "Only the Abbey, part of the beehives, the north side of this wall, and the treetops beyond. What do your eyes see, old one?"

"Exactly the same as yours do, though perhaps a bit dimmer.

Don't give up hope, though. Let us keep looking. Maybe we'll see something.''

The surveillance continued. Apart from retrieving his dagger, Matthias sat very still, peering northwards. Eventually he had to give up, as his eyes were beginning to water and he was getting a crick in his neck. Methuselah had fallen asleep in the afternoon sun.

Angrily Matthias slammed his dagger point deep into the edge of the rubble heap. "I told you it was a waste of time. Can't you stay awake for five minutes? Must you go to sleep on me?"

The old mouse awoke with a start. "Eh, what's that! Oh, Matthias, there you are. Dear me, I must have dropped off for a moment. Sorry, it won't happen again."

Matthias was not listening. He was digging in the rubble with his dagger. Methuselah watched him curiously.

"What in the name of goodness are you up to now?"

The rubble scattered as Matthias dug away madly. "I think I've found what we're after! There's some sort of shape in the stone down here. Trouble is, there's too much rubbish on top of it. I think we need Foremole's help again."

Foremole and his team arrived panting, with Matthias running ahead. The moles collapsed on the rubble, breathing hard.

"Yurr on'y gotten biddy short legs, us moles do, oi takes it you'm gennelmice needin' our 'elp agin."

This time Matthias understood. "Yes please, Mr. Foremole. Do you think that you and your team could possibly move this pile of rock and rubble? There's something we need to get at underneath it all."

Foremole spread his stubby paws wide. He smiled winningly. "Hurr, no soon as said'n done, young un. Wurr ud you'm loik 'er shiften to?"

Matthias shrugged. "Oh, anywhere, I suppose, as long as it's not in our way."

Foremole spat on his paws and rubbed them together. "Arr roight, mateys, best dumpen this lot whurr it comed from."

The two mice had to jump aside smartly as the mole team took over. With much "Hurr-ing" and "Arr-ing," they waded busily in, bulldozing the enormous heap of rock and rubble off the top of the ramparts. It tipped downwards in earthy showers, back into the trench in the Abbey grounds whence it had first come.

Matthias watched admiringly. "What splendid workers these moles are, Methuselah."

As the hill dwindled his friend heartily agreed. "Indeed they are, their skills and knowledge are passed on through families, you know. Earth, rock, shale or root, they can handle it all. Do you know, it was the moles that dug the foundations for this very Abbey. Foremole can claim direct descent from the mole who was in charge of the operation. In fact, it was Martin who bestowed the title Foremole upon his ancestor."

As the mice conversed, the moles hurled the last of the rubble from the ramparts, then set about brushing the stones clean.

Foremole tugged his nose in salute. "Harr, we'm dum now, zurrs, oi'll bid ye g'day."

Ten seconds later they were all gone.

"Moles aren't too fond of heights," observed Methuselah. "Right, let's see what they've uncovered."

It was a circle cut into the stone.

On one side it was cut shallow, while at the opposite side it was carved deeply. The center was domed with two slots graven into either slope. At the apex of the dome was the letter M. Beneath it were carved thirteen small circles, each with a smiling face upon it.

Constance came rambling along the wall, checking on the road beneath. "Hello there, you two! Are you staying up here all day? You'll miss afternoon tea if you don't hurry. There'll be precious little left with three squirrels, three voles, and Basil Stag Hare as guests."

Studying the carvings, Matthias waved absently at the badger. "You carry on, Constance. We'll be down shortly."

The badger's natural curiosity was aroused. She came over and stood between the two mice. After a cursory glance she threw up her paws in mock despair. "Oh no, not more puzzles and riddles?"

Methuselah gave her a severe stare over the top of his glasses. "My dear Constance, kindly do not pour scorn on things you know nothing of. Leave it to those with specialized knowledge."

Turning to Matthias, the old mouse continued, "Yes, most

interesting. These thirteen small circles with smiling faces. What do you make of them?''

Matthias could only shake his head. He could not think what the circles might mean.

Constance interrupted. ''What, do you mean those things? Huh, they're obviously the thirteen full moons of the year.''

Methuselah was distinctly piqued. ''How do you know that? Explain yourself.''

Constance scoffed. ''Ha, any badger worth its salt knows all about the moon. Do you want me to recite all its phases? I can, you know.''

Matthias was suddenly back on the track again. He counted along the moons, stopping at the sixth one.

''That one will be this month, June! When is the full moon due in June, Constance?''

''It's tomorrow night,'' came the prompt reply. ''Why, is something supposed to happen then? Some magic or a miracle?''

Methuselah ignored the badger's attempt at levity.

''If we stand up here at one o'clock in the morning on the night of the full moon, we may be able to find the sword of Martin the Warrior,'' he said, rather sternly.

Constance scratched her muzzle. ''How are you going to manage that?''

Matthias ran his foot around the edge of the circle. ''We're not quite sure yet, but we are trying to figure it out. You see, it's all linked closely with the rhyme from the wall of Great Hall, Martin's tomb, and the stuff we found in it, this sword belt, a shield, another rhyme on the back of a d—''

Constance interrupted, ''What type of shield?''

''Oh, pretty much the standard kind used by warriors,'' Matthias replied. ''A round steel affair with hand- and arm-holds.''

The badger nodded knowingly and continued where Matthias had left off. ''Yes, I've seen that sort of thing before. Not much to look at; in fact, just the type of shield that would fit precisely into this circle. Can't you see the slots for the arm-holds? But then again, if you look at that carved circle, you'll notice that it is cut so that the shield would tilt, probably to reflect the moonlight. . . .''

Both mice stared at the badger. There was awe and respect written upon their faces.

Matthias shook her paw with great ceremony. "Constance, wonderful badger, old friend. Don't worry about afternoon tea. You just sit yourself down right there, because I, personally, am going to bring you the largest, most delicious tea that has ever been served within the walls of this Abbey."

The warm, red stone ramparts rang to the echo of the three friends' delighted laughter.

CHAPTER
8

Cluny lay with his one good eye half open.

From beneath its slitted lid he watched Sela the vixen.

The sly old devil was definitely up to something, he was certain of it.

Cluny had secretly questioned Fangburn about the conversation that had gone on between Sela and her son. There was no doubt about it, the foxes were trying to dupe the Warlord.

Cluny had cursed Fangburn for twenty different kinds of an idiot. Fancy not being able to read, and allowing Sela to write out a message! Imagine letting Chickenhound go free without first getting the scroll read.

If he had been a little fitter, he would have personally slain his oafish captain. But as it was, Cluny kept silent about it all. Even if Sela was playing a double game, he needed the fox's healing powers to regain his health and strength.

Meanwhile, Cluny the Scourge made his own counter-espionage moves. He allowed Sela to minister to his wounds, but he secretly stopped taking the herbs and potions to help him sleep.

Early next morning Chickenhound returned. He carried a bag laden with medicinal ingredients. Cluny feigned sleep, but secretly he observed the foxes closely. They nodded and winked at each other quite a bit. When they were reasonably sure he was asleep, the two held a hurried whispered conversation. And though, unfortunately, he could not hear what they said, their behavior was secretive enough to make Cluny sure he was right. They were planning a double cross!

Cluny did not tell any of his officers of his suspicions. He kept everything to himself. This way there could be no possible leak of secrets. Cluny was content to watch and wait, getting a little stronger each day.

Then after a while he came up with a fiendishly simple idea. He ordered that the room be cleared: he wished to be alone so that he could rest. When he was quite sure that he would not be disturbed, Cluny took a quill and parchment from the bedside table. He drew a diagram, complete with pointing arrows, horde positions, lines of attack and defense, together with written instructions. It was a plan for the second full-scale invasion of Redwall Abbey. Cluny made it clear that the success of the attack depended solely on the battering ram breaking through the main gate.

When he had finished writing, Cluny pushed the parchment under his pillow, taking care to leave just a small corner of it jutting out. His officers would be too slow and dull to notice it—a tiny scrap of parchment showing from beneath the pillow. Even if they should, they would attach no importance to it.

But Sela the fox would!

Cluny settled down to wait.

Redtooth and Fangburn returned with their captive guest an hour later. Cluny stretched himself luxuriously and yawned aloud.

"Aaaah, I had a nice peaceful nap without you three clattering about the room and creating a noise. How's that tree-felling coming along?"

Redtooth leaned upon his spear. "Shouldn't take much longer now, Chief. I've ordered some of them to get a good blaze going so that the trunk can be fired and hardened."

Cluny flexed his injured tail slowly. "Good, make sure that all the large branches are cut off close to the trunk. It'll make it easier to carry. Now, fox, how about changing these bandages and giving me something to make me sleep tonight. That stuff you gave me yesterday wasn't much use. I was tossing and turning for hours before I got any rest."

Sela made a sweeping servile curtsey. "Now that my son has brought my new ingredients I can certainly give you medicine to make you sleep, sir. I guarantee you'll go off like a bug in a blanket, if you'll pardon the expression, sir."

"Just as long as it gets me to sleep," said Cluny, smiling inwardly.

That night, Cluny allowed Redtooth and Fangburn to guzzle their fill from a cask of barley wine that had been found in the church cellars. He gave Sela permission to drink also. Cluny watched as the fox pretended to drink as much of the barley wine as the rat captains. While she was doing this, Cluny also pretended to take his sleeping medicine. Cluny and Sela continued with their pantomime, neither letting a drop pass their lips.

It was late night. Cluny joined in the snores of his drunken officers. The room was comfortably warm. A lone candle flickered in its socket. Cluny felt the pillow move slightly.

Sela was taking the bait!

Cluny gave a big imitation snore and smacked his lips contentedly. Some day he must learn to play chess. He bet himself that he would be unbeatable.

Cluny also made a wager with himself that the plans would be back, safely tucked under the pillow, by morning, and that Sela would have an accurate copy of them hidden away somewhere. Now he could catch a few hours' sleep.

No doubt the mice would be interested to learn of his scheme to attack the main gate with a battering ram. They would strengthen the gatehouse and deploy the main body of defenders in the immediate area. Cluny could have laughed out loud.

While they were defending the gate, he would be tunneling under the south-western corner of the Abbey Wall!

CHAPTER
9

The deep, warm, brazen voice of the Joseph Bell tolled across the tranquil meadows, its echoes fading in the leafy depths of Mossflower Wood. It was eleven o'clock on the night of the full moon.

Inside Cavern Hole the candles burned bright. Most of the woodland defenders and Redwall mice had retired to their beds. Those who preferred to stay awake were gathered by invitation of Matthias and Methuselah to a party supper. All who attended wished them well on their quest. Abbot Mortimer took the floor.

"My friends, Redwall mice and honored guests, we are gathered here tonight, not only to pay tribute, but to add our heartfelt good wishes to Matthias and Brother Methuselah. May they have success and fortune in their venture this night, and may our Abbey soon be enhanced by the restoration of the sword that belonged to Martin the Warrior."

The Abbot took his seat among cries of, "Hear, hear." There was much paw-shaking and fur-patting. Matthias felt deeply honored, but very impatient. The hourglass had to empty twice more before the crucial time he awaited. He stole a sideways glance at his companion. Methuselah could hardly stop his eyelids from dropping. The hard work they had done, combined with the nervous tension, were beginning to tell upon the old gatehouse-keeper. Matthias nudged him gently.

"Wake up, old one. If you're tired I'll help you to your room.

Constance and I can take the shield up to the threshold. You get a good night's sleep. We'll tell you all about it in the morning."

Methuselah came wide awake with indignation. "You'll do nothing of the sort! You young scallywag, I could give you a ten-second start and still beat you to the top of the wall! D'you want to try me?"

Constance coughed and spluttered upon a candied chestnut. She roared with laughter. "Ha ha ha, ho ho ho, I wouldn't attempt it if I were you, Matthias. He's liable to beat you hollow in his present mood."

The old mouse, seeing the humor of the situation, began to chuckle. "And don't think I couldn't, you great stripey lump. Here, what do you say we put this young mouse up in the dormitory? It's way past his bedtime. You and I could go to the threshold together."

Constance and Methuselah collapsed against each other, laughing helplessly. It was all Matthias could do to keep a straight face. He pretended to take offense at Methuselah's statement.

"Why, you old pair of relics! It wouldn't take me two ticks to bring you some warm milk and tuck you in your own beds. Then I'd be free to get on with the job myself."

The three friends laughed until tears streamed down their cheeks. Methuselah held his sides as he spoke between gusts of merriment. "I say, Constance—ha ha ha—you old fogey—oh ha ha ha tee hee!—you'd better come along with us—ha ha ho ho oooh!—Matthias is a bit old for this sort of thing! Hahaha-hahahaha."

Matthias had fallen off his chair. He waved his paws, pleading for the joking to stop, as he rolled about on the floor, exploding from bouts of giggling to fits of laughter.

Basil Stag Hare tut-tutted severely as he remarked to Ambrose Spike, "Tch, tch. Dreadful table manners. Just look at those three, kicking up a hullaballoo like that! Eating's a serious business. They haven't touched a bite of supper, y'know."

"Aye, so I see," grunted the hedgehog. "Here, you don't suppose they'd mind, do you?"

"Not at all, not at all, dear fellow," said Basil regally, as he shared the contents of the three plates between himself and Ambrose. "Saves it all going to waste, what, what?"

*　　*　　*

It was fifteen minutes before one o'clock in the morning. Three figures crossed the Abbey gardens as the moon broke from behind a drifting cloudbank. The nearby pond was bathed in a silver sheen, parts of the sandstone wall reflecting back a wavery bluish light. Constance and Methuselah carried lanterns; Matthias bore the Warrior's shield upon his arm. They ascended the wall steps in single file, acknowledging the murmured good wishes of those on sentry duty.

Matthias had decided against trying the shield in its niche before the appointed hour. He felt somehow that they must abide by the rules of the verse, waiting until day's first hour on the night of the full moon. It just had to be so. No use tempting fickle Dame Fortune.

Solemnly the three friends gathered around the carving upon the ramparts. Matthias clutched the shield tightly, waiting for the stroke of one. High above the small world of Redwall the moon also waited, suspended in velvety space like a pale gold coin. It seemed that the minutes stretched into an eternity in which silence reigned over all.

The great Joseph Bell boomed out once. It was one o'clock—day's first hour. Slowly, reverently, Matthias lowered the shield of Martin, down on to the stone circle that had been carved many long years before to receive it. The shield made a mild clanking sound as it was laid to rest in its niche. It fitted perfectly into the stone receptacle. All three creatures stood back a pace to see what might happen. Matthias was first to cry out.

"Look! The shield is reflecting the moonlight back into the sky!"

Moonlight seemed to concentrate upon the highly-polished steel dome in its designated position, sending an intense beam of white light back off into the night sky.

Methuselah blinked. Holding his paw across his eyebrows, he stared into space, trying to follow the path of the reflected moonlight. "Truly it is a most beautiful, wondrous sight," he breathed. "Alas, my old eyes are not what they were. All I see is a light shooting off into infinity."

"Wait. Look at the Abbey roof," Constance murmured. "The beam cuts right across the top gable. I can see the weather vane as clearly as if it were day."

"Good heavens," Matthias squeaked. "You're right! The

Abbey weather vane, it's the one thing that's caught in the path of the light.''

"The North! The North!" Methuselah shouted. "It's the weather vane arm that points north! That's where the sword must be!''

Solemnly the three friends placed their paws one on top of the other. At long last the mystery was solved. They knew now where the sword of Martin the Warrior had been for countless years.

On the arm of a weather vane, pointing north!

However, it was three rather disconsolate creatures that sat down to early breakfast after a few hours' fitful sleep. They had encountered a major problem: how to get the sword down?

"What a pity we haven't got about thirty or forty extra-long ladders that we could tie together to reach the roof," muttered Constance.

"Oh, do be quiet, Constance," Matthias grumbled. "That must be the tenth time you've said that in the last hour."

"Sorry, only trying to help," she mumbled.

Methuselah pushed his porridge aside. "There are only two ways that you could help, my friend. One, by keeping silent. Two, by turning yourself into some creature that could climb all the way up to that roof. A bird, or a squirrel or something.''

They sat and stared at Methuselah in amazement. A solution of stunning simplicity had been found.

"I do hope that Mrs. Squirrel hasn't decided to sleep in," said Matthias. "She'll need an early start if she's going to make it back by lunchtime.''

Mrs. Squirrel (or Jess, as she liked to be called) was only too pleased to oblige her friends from Redwall.

Having been given full instructions by Matthias, Jess stood at the base of the immense Abbey building. The squirrel performed what looked like an intricate acrobatic dance, followed by several cartwheels at lightning speed.

"She's just limbering up," Mr. Squirrel explained to Matthias.

A large crowd of mice and woodlanders had gathered to witness the epic ascent. Not even in the oldest recorded writings was there any mention of a creature venturing to climb as high as the Abbey roof. It was a most formidable task, for the roof soared to nearly twice the height of the bell tower.

Jess elbowed her way through the throng. She kissed Mr. Squirrel, patted her son Silent Sam upon the head, then shook paws with Constance, Matthias and Methuselah. With a brisk cheery manner she scooped up a handful of soil, rubbing it into her paws to give some extra gripping power.

"Lovely day for a climb," she remarked off-handedly.

Then away she went, paw over paw, up the massive Abbey face.

The lower wall with its arched sandstone window frames held no difficulties for the tough squirrel. She climbed with speed and alacrity. Lifting herself over the gutter with a neat flick of her bushy tail, Jess clattered across to a small slate side roof. She was temporarily lost to view at the start of the second stage. As she came into sight again, the watchers below could not help but notice that the climb was more difficult, progress was slower.

Mr. Squirrel cupped his paws and called up, "Are you all right there, Jess?"

Latching her tail around a projecting gargoyle, Jess shouted back, "Well, I'm making headway, m'dear. This stone though— it's a bit rough on the old paws and claws. Not like good old wood or tree bark."

Chins went up, heads tilted back, the crowd below followed the ascent of the plucky Jess Squirrel. By this time she seemed to the watchers to be rapidly diminishing in size as she forged upwards.

Foremole (who was never too keen on heights) covered his eyes with a paw. "Gurr, moi dearie, dearie me. She'm loiken an owlyburd allaways up thurr. Nay, oi'm afeared to look."

Although Matthias had to agree with Foremole, he continued looking upwards. Jess was reduced to a mere speck now. The young mouse gritted his teeth, willing the brave squirrel onwards. "Go on, Jess, you can do it! Not far to the gable now!"

The crowd fell silent. All that could be heard was Silent Sam sucking his tiny paw as he clutched on to his father's tail.

Suddenly Winifred the otter broke the quiet: "Look, Jess has made it over the gutter! She's on the roof."

A mass cheer went up. The squirrel was on the last lap. Now she would have to call into play all of her climbing ability to keep going up the treacherously steep smooth slates.

Methuselah polished agitatedly at his spectacles. "Where is she now? Will someone please enlighten me?"

"She's on top of the roof, walking with a foot either side of the apex towards the gable," yelled Abbot Mortimer.

Methuselah sniffed. "No need to shout, Father Abbot. I'm only hard of sight, not hearing."

Mr. Squirrel clapped his paws joyfully. "Oh she's made it! My Jess has made it!"

Amid the riot of jubilation Matthias watched. The weather vane moved slightly, indicating that Jess, actually out upon the north pointer, must be trying to retrieve the sword.

What a daring climb! What a courageous creature! Jess Squirrel would surely take her place in the annals of Redwall Abbey.

Mr. Squirrel held Silent Sam up in his arms. "Look, Sam. Mum's done it! She's on the way back down now."

Silent Sam clenched his little paws over his head. He shook them like a tiny champion. Nobody in all the world was a better climber than his mother.

Matthias waited for a glimpse of the sword, but Jess was not halfway down when a shout of consternation arose from the crowd below.

"Look out, she's being attacked by sparrows!"

Sure enough, the fierce birds were whirling in close to the intrepid Jess. They tried to peck at her, seeking to dislodge her, or distract her enough to make her fall. It was a fearsome, sickening drop should she lose her grip.

Matthias took command. He acted swiftly.

"Hurry, get the six best field and harvest mouse archers! Those birds have got to be stopped immediately."

The angry sparrows persisted with their savage assault. Jess kept on descending resolutely. She couldn't seem to defend herself.

The Abbot and Constance had to leap forward to restrain Silent Sam. He had left his father and was trying to scramble up the base of the Abbey wall with the small dagger clenched in his teeth.

Constance attempted to reason with Sam. "Stay clear, little one. You'll only distract your mum. Look, she's doing splendidly! An old bunch of sparrows can't bother her. Stand back now; here come the bowmice!"

Speedily notching shafts to their strings, the archers angled their bows upwards.

"Do not aim to kill any of the birds," the Abbot cried. "Shoot to frighten them off."

"Shoot," Matthias yelled.

The first volley of arrows was launched. They fell short of the sparrows. Jess carried on scrambling downwards, beating off attackers whenever she had a free paw.

"They're getting within range now," shouted Matthias. "Aim, fire!"

The mouse archers sent off a hail of arrows that came close enough to cause a scatter among the sparrows. Taking advantage of their brief confusion, Jess clambered down on to the small side roof.

The tenacious birds regrouped and came at her again. Below, the bowmice stood ready.

"She'll make it down," Ambrose Spike yelled. "One more good volley should scare them off."

"Ready, fire!" called Matthias.

The deadly shafts hissed upwards, causing a mad flurry among the attackers. Purely by accident a stray arrow struck one young sparrow. It came tumbling down the slope of the small roof, dropping to earth like a stone, the arrow sticking in its leg just above the knee joint. Cheated of their intended victim, the sparrows flew off, chirping bad-temperedly.

Constance snatched up a woven rush washing basket. Holding the small sparrow firmly with her paw, she gripped the arrow in her teeth and yanked it clear from the bird's leg. The badger then upended the basket, imprisoning the maddened sparrow beneath it.

Shouts of joy mingled with relief greeted Jess Squirrel as she dropped wearily to the grass.

"Phew!" she gasped. "What a wild bunch of savages those sparrows are! I thought they had me once or twice back there."

Before the heroic squirrel could be united with her family, Matthias came dashing across.

"Jess! Where is the sword?" he panted.

The squirrel shrugged and shook her head. "It wasn't there, Matthias. I climbed out along the north pointer and actually saw the shape of the sword in the holder where it was supposed to rest. There were even some loose rusty wires that may have held it in position at one time or another. But there was definitely no sword. I'm sorry, Matthias, I tried my best.''

"Of course you did, Jess," said Matthias, hiding his disappointment. "Thank you very much for your valiant efforts.''

Half an hour later, the crowd had dispersed and gone about their business. Matthias sat with his back against the Abbey wall, his mind in a turmoil. All that hard work, solving the clues, burning midnight oil, endangering the lives of his friends, it had all come to nothing. He beat his paws against the stones of the Abbey, a tear of frustration gleaming in his eye.

"Why, Martin, why?" he moaned.

The captive sparrow fluttered her wings against the upturned basket. "I killee you!" she chattered angrily at Matthias. "I killee mouse, let Warbeak free, you dirty worm.''

Matthias peered through the cracks at the insulting prisoner. "Oh, shut your beak, you little monster!" he muttered. "You're in no position to kill anyone.''

The sparrow's venomous temper increased. "King Bull Sparra, he killee you. Make dead quickfast.''

Matthias laughed mirthlessly. "Will he indeed? Well, you tell King Thingummy if you should bump into him again, that you've met Matthias the Warrior, and I don't kill that easily, my bad-tempered little friend.''

This last statement sent the young sparrow off into a veritable dance of rage. "Mouse no friend of Warbeak! K-Killee, k-k-killeet!''

Matthias tapped the basket with his foot. "Listen, Warbeak, if that's your name. You'd better improve your temper, or you'll find yourself without food to eat or any medical attention. So if I were you, I'd sit quietly for a while and think about that.''

Matthias spun on his heel and marched off, the enemy sparrow's chirps still ringing in his ears: "No wanta food, no needa 'tenshun. Warbeak Sparra, all brave, killeet.''

Matthias sighed wearily.

There was just no talking to some creatures.

CHAPTER

10

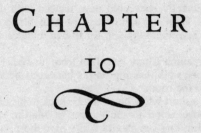

Sela the fox continued to complain. She must have a certain type of herb that was not in her kit. It could only be found in Mossflower Wood at the dark of night.

Cluny listened to the fox's pleas, knowing that they were merely an excuse to gain her freedom. He paused as if to deliberate, watching the hopeful expression on Sela's face.

"Hmm, I can see that you need this herb, so why don't you send your son Chickenhound to get it?"

Sela was never stuck for a ready answer. "No no, I'm afraid that's useless, sir. He's too young and inexperienced. Chickenhound wouldn't know where to start looking."

Cluny nodded sympathetically. "Aye, you're probably right. I suppose I'll have to stretch a point. You can go off to the woods to search for this vital herb. But be warned, fox! There will be two rats with you all the time. One false move and I'll have that bushy tail of yours to trim the collar of my war cloak. Is that understood?"

Sela's head bobbed vigorously. "Of course, sir. What reason would I have to play you false? I'm looking forward to a good share of plunder, once I've healed you and Redwall is conquered."

The huge tail snaked out and caressed the fox. "Of course you are, my friend. How silly of me."

Cluny actually smiled. Sela shuddered.

*   *   *

That evening Sela left the church, accompanied by Redtooth and Fangburn. Secretly she could have danced with delight. Only two guards! With her knowledge of Mossflower, Sela could quite easily give them the slip for fifteen minutes or so.

Back at the church Cluny had risen from his bed. He attempted an exploratory walk, leaning on his banner as he stumped gingerly around the room.

Good! In a short while he would be back to his old self again.

Cluny spoke aloud to the picture of Martin, bound to his standard: "Ha, that fox should easily give those idiots of mine the slip. Then she can deliver my false plans to your Abbot. It's all going along quite smoothly. Bit of a blow for your side, eh, mouse?"

Twilight tinged Mossflower Wood. Sela sniffed the breeze. She glanced up at the sky. It would soon be dark and she could keep her rendezvous with the mouse Abbot at the old stump.

Redtooth and Fangburn were both unhappy and uncomfortable. For the last hour Sela had led them through stinging nettles, swarms of midges and marshy ground. They blundered along, hacking at the undergrowth with cutlass and spear.

"I think we must be somewhere near the mouse Abbey," Fangburn said.

"Stow the gab! Keep your eyes on the fox," Redtooth snarled.

"I wish I'd brought some lanterns along with us," Fangburn whined.

Redtooth's already dangerously-thin patience snapped. He grabbed hold of his sniveling crony and started shaking him. "Listen, thickhead! If you don't stop your moaning I'll chop your tongue out with my cutlass! D'you hear me?"

Fangburn struggled free. Angrily he jabbed at Redtooth with his spear. "You dare try anything with that blunt old breadknife, and I'll spear your gizzard before you can blink an eye!"

"Oh you will, will you?"

"Yes, I will, smarty rat!"

"Then take that, big mouth!"

"Ouch! Punch me, would you? I'll soon show you!"

Together the rats crashed into a prickly bush, kicking, biting and pummeling each other. Claws, tails and teeth came into play. They went at it hammer and tongs for several minutes until Redtooth emerged the victor. His nose was bleeding and he had lost a tooth, but he was in better shape than his opponent.

Fangburn crawled miserably out of the wrecked bush. Both eyes were blacked, a chunk of his left ear was missing, and his whole body was covered in long raking claw marks and prickles. He bent painfully to retrieve his spear. Seizing the opportunity, Redtooth landed him a mighty kick on the bottom. His nose plowed up a furrow of soil.

Panting furiously, Redtooth berated Fangburn: "You half-witted fool! Now see what you've done! While you were busy assaulting a superior officer, you let the fox escape."

Fangburn sat up. He winced through discolored eyes. "*I* let the fox escape? Me? Oh no. You're the one in charge! *You* let her get away, not me. Wait'll I report this to Cluny. I'll tell him that you—"

"Will you shut up?" Redtooth yelled. "It's no use us standing here arguing. We'd better get searching for the fox. I'll go this way and you go that way. The first one to find her keeps shouting until the other arrives. Have you got that? Now get moving."

The two rats stumbled off through the woods in different directions.

Meanwhile, in another part of Mossflower Wood, Sela sneaked along looking from left to right. There was the three-topped oak, there was the Abbey wall. Ah, here it was, the old stump.

The moonlight illuminated the scene clearly. She was alone. Where was the mouse Abbot?

A heavy paw clamped itself around Sela's neck from behind. Her tongue shot out. Struggling uselessly, she gagged and choked.

Constance's gruff voice growled into her ear, "Be still, fox, or I'll snap your neck like a dead twig!"

Sela froze. There was nothing more dangerous than a fully-grown badger. Their strength and ferocity were renowned.

Constance's free paw snapped the herb pouch from the fox's belt. She shook the contents out on to the stump. Grabbing the copy of Cluny's invasion plans she studied it briefly, then stuffed it into her belt.

"Your Abbot was supposed to meet me with a reward," Sela whispered.

The badger's eyes blazed with contempt as she spun the vixen around. "Here's your reward, traitor!"

Whump!

Constance dealt Sela a sharp blow between the ears. The fox fell in a senseless heap. Constance ducked behind a tree and called out in a high-pitched voice, "Over here! I've got the fox! Quick, over here!"

Redtooth was first to arrive. He came dashing through the bushes and halted at the sight of the unconscious fox among the ferns.

"Hell's teeth, fox. Where's Fangburn? What the devil do you mean slinking off like that? Get up on your feet and answer me."

Constance emerged from behind the tree. "I don't think she'll wake up for a while yet. Fancy meeting you here, rat."

Redtooth got over his surprise quickly. Seeing the badger unarmed, he swished his cutlass through the air and smiled menacingly.

"Well, well. It's the friend of the mice! So, we meet again, badger!"

Constance stood tall, her huge paws folded. "Redtooth, isn't it? I see you still remember me from your defeat at the wall. I told you then we had a score to settle."

Redtooth bared his teeth and snarled. "I'm going to enjoy this, badger. I'll make sure you die slowly."

The rat leaped at Constance, swinging his cutlass expertly. For a heavy badger, his adversary moved lightly and skillfully. Neatly sidestepping a cutlass thrust, she cuffed the rat smartly on the point of the nose. Stung into retaliation, Redtooth charged Constance with the point of his blade.

A fierce kick in the ribs and a swift chop to the claw sent the rat and the cutlass in opposite directions. Redtooth lay winded upon the ground. Constance leaned over him.

"Get up and retrieve your weapon," the badger growled.

As Redtooth stood, he grabbed a handful of earth and flung it in Constance's eyes. The big badger staggered back, rubbing at the grit which clogged her vision. The rat picked up the cutlass and swung it, slashing wildly at his enemy's thick fur. He scored several hits.

Suddenly panic gripped him. The wounded badger had seized the blade regardless of its keen edge. Constance pulled Redtooth in close. She gave a sideways push, snapping the cutlass blade in two pieces. Kicking the rat over on his back, she flung the broken blade away and grabbed the rodent's tail tightly with both paws.

Redtooth screamed in terror as he felt himself leave the ground to go spinning aloft over the badger's head. With his tail pulled taut and the wind whistling through his fangs, Redtooth howled as the trees went by in a green blur. Like an athlete throwing the hammer, Constance whirled on her hind legs, faster and faster, until suddenly she threw her burden with a colossal heave.

Redtooth would have flown a record distance had there not been a stout sycamore tree several yards away. . . .

Ignoring her injuries, Constance called into the surrounding woods, "Over here, he's over here!"

Then she limped swiftly off in the direction of Redwall with the captured plans.

Only moments later Fangburn came blundering through the ferns. He tripped upon the groaning fox who was just coming round.

"Here, what's happened? Where's Redtooth?" he asked anxiously.

Sela sat up, rubbing her head, trying to recognize her surroundings. She saw the old stump littered with her herbs and potions. The pouch lay nearby. Holding her head with both paws, she tried to halt the thumping ache.

Damn that badger's hide! She'd taken the plans from Sela as if she were confiscating acorns from a baby mouse. So much for the "rich rewards."

Fangburn prodded Sela with the spear. "Hey you, pay attention! I asked you where Redtooth is."

Sela probed a loosened tooth with her tongue. "Leave me alone. How should I know?"

Fangburn persisted. "Now listen, fox. I want to know what's been going on here. I'm sure I heard Redtooth calling out. Hell's whiskers, wait until Cluny gets to hear about this!"

Sela pointed a shaky paw. "There's your rat, by that big

sycamore yonder. Huh, looks like he's had a spot of bother, too.''

Fangburn touched Redtooth with his foot. ''Aaaaargh! He's dead. Look, this sword's been broken in two.''

The fox and the rat stood looking at each other, their thoughts running on parallel lines. It was fairly obvious what must be done if they were to save their skins.

''Right,'' said Sela. ''We'd better work out a good story to tell Cluny when we get back. He's not stupid, so we'd better get it right.''

The unlucky pair stumbled off through the nighttime woodland, gesticulating and muttering together, weaving a fabric of lies that they hoped would satisfy Cluny the Scourge.

CHAPTER

II

Once again the Abbot's room was the scene of a late repast. The news that Constance had brought showed without a doubt that Cluny would soon be on the attack again.

Abbot Mortimer was the first to admit that he had been mistaken. "The intelligence brought to us by our friend Constance is conclusive. Cluny will never rest until he has Redwall under his heel; therefore I feel that I must apologize for my misjudgment of the situation. You, my commanders, were right, and now, thanks to Cluny, we know the secret details of the enemy horde's next attack."

The Abbot slapped a paw down on the plans. "It is all here, but as I have said before, I will not concern myself with the fighting of a war. It is my task to heal the injured and give sustenance to the defenders. It is the duty of you, my generals, to plan the repulse of this invasion."

Matthias held up a paw. "Father Abbot, it is our duty not only to defend but to retaliate."

There was a strong murmur of agreement from around the table.

The Abbot bowed and placed his paws within his wide habit sleeves. "So be it," he said with great solemnity. "I leave the salvation of Redwall to you, my commanders."

The Abbot bowed once more, then retired for the night, leaving Matthias, Constance, Winifred, Foremole and Ambrose Spike.

The meeting continued. They were joined by Basil Stag Hare and Jess Squirrel. Methuselah also attended to act as mediator and counselor, approving some ideas while discouraging others, calming the hothead and encouraging the timid. Much good sense was talked and the tone of the meeting was that of creatures who were determined to win at all costs. The discussion, running on sensible lines, went on until it was nearly dawn. It was a confident and satisfied group of friends who shook paws as the meeting ended.

Basil insisted on taking Constance to the infirmary to have her wounds treated. The badger tried to shrug him off.

"Pah! Such a fuss over a few minor scratches," she grumbled.

The hare chuckled admiringly. "A few minor scratches! Will you listen to the heroine? Why, my dear badger, those are honorable wounds, gained on the field of combat. I say, Jess, lend a paw here. Have you seen the dreadful gashes that friend Constance has collected? By the left, old girl, you should be hors de combat. Not even a stag could put up with slashes like that. Come on now, let's have you, there's a sensible girl."

Constance was led off muttering by Basil and Jess. All the rest retired to their beds, with the exception of Matthias and Methuselah. They strolled around the cloisters, savoring the peace of the midnight hours.

"You know, old one, I can't help thinking that a victory would be assured if only we had the Warrior's sword," Matthias said.

Methuselah nodded wistful agreement. "Indeed it would. But alas, for all our efforts, the trail is as cold as a midwinter night. I'm afraid we must resign ourselves to the fact that the sword is lost or hidden somewhere forever."

The old gatehouse-keeper leaned upon the young mouse's arm as they walked along, talking of this and that. Eventually the conversation came around to the sparrows' attack upon Jess.

Methuselah shook a warning paw. "Extremely dangerous birds, sparrows. Very warlike and quarrelsome. Luckily they keep to themselves and will only attack if their territory is intruded upon as you saw today. By the way, did you see that young one who was brought down by the archers?"

"I certainly did," Matthias replied. "Constance has got the bad-tempered little wretch imprisoned under a wash basket. What a nasty young villain. The arrow only scratched her really. It was shock more than anything else that brought her down. Says her name is Warbeak."

Methuselah was taken aback. "Do you mean to tell me you've talked with her? Remarkable! The sparrow language, or 'Sparra' as it is called, is very difficult to comprehend."

"Oh, I don't know," said Matthias casually. "I didn't find it too hard, and at least the little hooligan seems to understand what I'm saying to her."

Methuselah's curiosity was aroused. "And what has she been saying to you, this, er, Warbeak?"

"Pretty much what you'd expect," Matthias replied. "Either she, or the leader King Bull Sparra, is going to kill me. Evidently she looks on anything that can't fly as an enemy."

They strayed over by the gatehouse. The old mouse invited Matthias in for a late nightcap. Methuselah appeared very interested in sparrows. He leafed through his record books.

"Let me see. 'Summer of the Big Drought' . . . 'Winter of the Deep Drifts' . . . yes, I thought I'd find it here. Do you remember I told you of a sparrowhawk whom I treated about four years back? Well, here is my report, some small notes I made at the time. This hawk talked of the sparrows. She called them winged mice, though for the life of me I cannot see any comparison between highly civilized mice and those primitive savages. Point was, though, this sparrowhawk said she'd been told that the sparrows once stole an object of great value to our Abbey. She didn't say what it was. I thought the bird was merely trying to impress me with idle gossip: I should have questioned her further. We may have found out just what that object was."

Matthias looked pensive. "Do you think it could have been the sword?"

The old mouse sat tapping his paw upon the record book. "It could have been, Matthias, it could have been. You see, the sparrows never communicate or bother with us. They never fly into our Abbey. But up on the roof, well, that's a different matter. They consider that to be their territory. As I see it, the sword was the only object of value we had up there, although we did not know it at the time. So who else but another bird would know that the sparrows had stolen it?"

"By the whiskers, old one," Matthias said excitedly, "I think you've hit the nail on the head. Do you think that our bad-tempered captive might know something about the rumor?"

Methuselah grinned mischievously. "Lend me your dagger. I have a simple experiment that I wish to try on our prisoner. Come on."

Matthias escorted his friend to where the basket lay by the Abbey walls. There was no sound from within. Methuselah tapped the basket sharply with the blade of the dagger.

Warbeak had been caught napping. She came to life in an irate mood. "Worms, all worms, you old mouseworm! Stay 'way, Warbeak killee!"

Methuselah tried his level best to act tough. "Be silent, you little baggage, or I'll spike you on this dagger, and your king too, if he dares to come down."

In a fury Warbeak smashed her small body against the sides of the basket, causing the old mouse to take a step back.

"Ha, go on, you killee Warbeak with dagger! Wait see! You not get King Bull Sparra with little worm knife. King have a big sword! Chop all mouses up! Killee pretty quick, you betcha."

Methuselah laughed with delight. "You see! The Sparrow King owns a big sword!"

Matthias did a cartwheel. He whooped with joy. "Methuselah, you're a magician, an ancient wizard."

The old mouse shook his head modestly. "Oh, dear me, no. I like to think of myself as an aged but extremely erudite scholar."

CHAPTER

12

Sitting comfortably propped up on pillows, Cluny sipped a beaker of barley wine as he listened to the improbable tale spun by Sela and Fangburn. They both fidgeted nervously during the course of their deceitful narrative, trying desperately not to contradict one another, while at the same time avoiding the cold impassive eye of the Warlord.

"Er, it was like this, Chief," Fangburn stammered. "Me and old Redtooth were keeping our eyes on the fox here, when suddenly Redtooth hears a noise in the woods, so off he goes to investigate."

"Where was the noise coming from?" snapped Cluny.

The deceivers spoke together.

"North," said Sela.

"West," said Fangburn, simultaneously.

"Er, er, it was sort of north-west," Sela gulped, realizing how foolish she sounded. Knowing that Cluny was smarter than either of them, she wished she didn't have this big dumb rat to corroborate the story.

"So Redtooth went off to see what the noise was," Sela faltered. "We told him not to go, sir, but he insisted."

Cluny watched Sela's legs shaking.

"Go on, what happened then?" he murmured.

Fangburn took up the tale again. "Well, you see, Chief, he

was gone an awful long time. We both called out to him but there was no answer."

"So we both went to look for him," said Sela.

Cluny toyed with the beaker. His eye bored into the fox.

"We searched and searched, sir," Sela mumbled, "but all we could find was this big stretch of marshland and bog. . . ."

"Which poor old Redtooth had wandered into and been sucked down never to be seen again," Cluny supplemented.

Sela kept wishing the floor would open up and swallow her.

Fangburn sobbed brokenly. "Our poor friend Redtooth, gone forever!"

"Yes, our poor friend Redtooth," Cluny agreed sympathetically. Suddenly his voice hardened as he shot a question at Fangburn: "You! How did your face get knocked about, and where did you get those long scratches from?"

Sela jumped in hastily. "Er, er, he walked into a big thorn tree, didn't you, Fangburn?"

"What? Oh, yes. I was dashing about and I didn't see it, Chief. The fox can tell you. She saw it, and if she didn't, well, I already told her," said Fangburn, his voice trailing off miserably.

Cluny laughed mirthlessly, his fangs showing yellow and sharp. "So, you walked into a big thorn tree and got two black eyes, a torn ear and your whole hide covered in long scratches?"

Fangburn stared at the floor. He had to swallow twice before he could answer. His voice subdued, "That's what happened, Chief."

Cluny's tone was laden with sarcasm. "And then I suppose that three little pigs with wings flew down and gave you a toffee apple each?"

"Er, yes. Er, I mean, what was that, Chief? . . . Oouch!" Fangburn hopped on one leg as Sela kicked his ankle to silence him.

"You, fox!" Cluny snarled. "Where's the special herb you went to search for?"

Sela was completely nonplussed. "Special herb? I—"

Cluny hurled the beaker. It bounced off Fangburn's nose, splashing barley wine over them both.

"Get out! Out of my sight, before I have you tortured and roasted!" Cluny roared at the unlucky pair.

There was an undignified scramble. The door slammed shut

behind the conspirators. Cluny lay back and smirked. Everything was going according to plan. He had lost Redtooth, but what the devil? Redtooth had been an ambitious rat. Cluny only admired ambition in one rodent—himself.

Far off in Mossflower Wood, the night breezes stirred the treetops gently. The moon rode in a cloudless sky. Its pale light filtered through the waving foliage to create the beautiful but strange effect of a shimmering, swaying carpet on the woodland floor.

"Asmodeus, Asmodeusssssssss."

The covering of dead moonlit vegetation on the ground trembled and rustled. What better cover than a light breeze and a hunter's moon? Glittering black eyes searched the night, a forked tongue tasted the air, the small living plants appeared to shudder as the long scaly body brushed by them, trailing its way along.

"Asmodeus, Asmodeusssssssss."

Softly rustling, deceptive as the speckled shadows, the huge adder roamed his domain. Patience and stealth were acquired by long experience. Sometimes the serpent would lie totally inert, awaiting the unsuspecting paw that trod too close. Other times it would raise itself, uncoiling to look into bushes for eggs and birds on the nest. Some nights it was lean hunting. Many creatures sensed the approach of the slithering evil, or scented its dry, musty, deathlike odor. The snake had often gone hungry at times like these. But patience and stealth, patience and stealth; a lesson soon learned is a meal soon earned. At the foot of the sycamore the adder stretched itself alongside the still form of Redtooth. Well, an unexpected bonus! This was another rat that could not scurry off. No expenditure of venom or hypnosis needed. How fortunate! The huge reptile coiled itself languorously around the dead rodent.

"Asmodeus, Asmodeussssssssssss."

No need of burial parties. Nature and the woodlands took care of their own funeral arrangements. There was but one efficient undertaker. The adder's jaws opened in something resembling the nightmare of a smile. The pathway to eternity was open.

CHAPTER

13

Matthias was excused from duties at the gatehouse fortifications. The council had agreed that both he and Methuselah, plus any creature they chose to help them, were to be left to their own devices. The majority of the Redwall mice thought that Matthias was acting a little oddly, but the young mouse knew exactly what he was about. He strolled slowly through the Abbey grounds. Behind him hopped Warbeak on a lead with a collar about her neck. On the sparrow's uninjured leg Matthias had tied a brick; not a very big brick, but one large enough to stop the bird getting airborne or trying any sneak attacks upon its captor. Thoroughly disgruntled, the sparrow hopped along like a feathered convict with a ball and chain, forced to follow the young mouse wherever he chose to wander.

At first, Warbeak had raved and threatened. Death was too good for Matthias! Warbeak was going to kill him twice, then cut him up and drop him from the top of a high tree for the worms to feed upon! Matthias had merely tugged the lead sharply and quickened his pace. When the savage young sparrow showed signs of good behavior, Matthias would feed her morsels of candied chestnut.

The treatment was working.

Outside the gatehouse Matthias rested. He fed the sparrow some more of the candied nut.

"There now, you good bird, well done," he said approvingly.

Warbeak scowled fiercely, but she munched the nut readily.

Methuselah popped his head out briefly and beckoned. "Come into the study, Matthias. Oh, and bring that little horror too."

In the cluttered study the old mouse produced a yellowed volume. "Our old friend Sister Germaine's translation of the original Redwall Abbey blueprints. I think I've found what we are looking for in the main diagram. See."

Matthias studied the blueprint carefully.

"Brilliant!" he exclaimed. "You've done it again, my friend! A route to the Abbey roof from the inside."

Methuselah breathed upon his glasses, polishing them on his fur. "Really, it's thanks to Sister Germaine for keeping such fastidious records, young mouse. Now, here's where you'll start."

An hour later Matthias left the gatehouse with Warbeak bobbing behind. As they went the young mouse muttered to himself, "I'll need five or six strong climbing ropes, some spikes, oh, and a hammer. Must have a hammer. Now let's see, a good haversack to carry it all, enough food and drink, ah, and some candied chestnuts for you, my friend."

Warbeak uttered a stream of curses as she stumbled on the brick. Matthias waited as she picked herself up. "Tut tut, such language for a young sparrow."

Constance and Ambrose Spike watched the odd pair pass by. The badger tapped the side of her head with a paw.

"Bats in the belfry."

"Or sparrows," giggled the hedgehog.

Basil Stag Hare superintended the willing creatures who carried logs and filling to shore up the gatehouse entrance. The hare had brought a touch of military efficiency to bear upon the exercise. He had formed the volunteers into a living chain which constantly passed the defense materials along.

Basil brought his good-natured authority into play. "You there! Fourth from the end, chappie! Liven your ideas up, laddie buck. That's the third time you've spilled a basket of soil. Here, let me show you how."

The timid mice smiled among themselves. The blustering hare was quite a kindly creature really, all bark and no bite at all.

He shared the tasks with them, working as hard as anyone.

"No, no, Brother Whatsyourname. You pass logs along like this. Look, you go and get a bite to eat. Come on, the rest of you beautiful dreamers! Stir your stumps or I'll have your whiskers for bootlaces."

The helpers laughed and did the best they could. Now and again there would be barely stifled giggles as they watched the performance of Silent Sam. He stood behind Basil, pantomiming the hare's every movement, puffing up his tiny chest and strutting about importantly.

In the Abbey kitchens, Cornflower carefully wrapped Matthias's food in fresh dock leaves. Matthias sidled up, helping himself to a candied chestnut. Cornflower rapped his paw with a wooden ladle.

"Those nuts are for that poor little sparrow. Leave them alone, you great glutton," she scolded.

Matthias snorted indignantly. "Poor little sparrow, my eye! Listen, Miss, if I let that young hussy off her lead for five minutes, we'd all be murdered in our beds."

The young fieldmouse helped Matthias with the haversack straps. She tried not to let her concern for him show. "Matthias, I know you won't tell me where you are going, but wherever it is, please take care of yourself."

Matthias adjusted the dagger in the black sword belt. He stood framed in the doorway, smiling confidently. "Don't worry, Cornflower. I fully intend to take care of myself, for the safety of Redwall Abbey . . . and for you."

A moment later he was gone.

Halfway along the top dormitory passage, Matthias halted. A stepladder was set up underneath a wooden loft door in the ceiling. Methuselah came along, leading Warbeak. The sparrow was still wearing the collar, lead and brick shackle.

Matthias looked up to the door. "So, that's where we're going, eh."

The old gatehouse-keeper gave him a neatly-drawn map. "You'll find it all marked down there, Matthias. That door leads to a loft. Turn to your right and keep walking until you touch the wall. To your right you will find a gap in the wall. On the other side of that gap you will come out about halfway up the

wall of Great Hall. It is a ledge between the arches of the sandstone columns. From there you must climb up to a higher row
of ledges alongside the stained-glass windows. Scale the rib in
the center of the first window to the left. You will find yourself
on a wooden ridge that runs along parallel to the curve of the
roof. Further along that ridge there is another wooden loft door.
I'm sorry, but I cannot locate it exactly; you must find it yourself. When you do, go through it and you should be directly
underneath the top roof attic. From there on you are on your
own. I cannot help you, Matthias.''

The ancient mouse placed his paws on his young friend's
shoulders. His voice trembled as he bade goodbye. ''Good fortune go with you, Matthias. I wish that I were young and agile
once again so that I could accompany you.''

Methuselah embraced the young mouse as if he were his own
son, and as Matthias ascended the ladder, the old mouse called
out final instructions to him.

''If that sparrow causes you any trouble, don't hesitate to kick
her off into thin air. She'll come down as fast as the brick she's
tied to!''

Warbeak scowled but made no comment. She knew Methuselah spoke the truth. The brick was like an anchor against her
leg.

Matthias gave the loft door a strong shove upwards and slid
it to one side. He covered his eyes and coughed as the dust of
ages poured down upon his head.

Tugging the sparrow behind him, he climbed into the loft.

It was very dark and gloomy. Matthias peered over to his
right. Faintly he could make out a strip of wan, greyish light
filtering in.

''Him be gap in wall like old worm mouse say about,'' Warbeak chimed.

''Hey, keep a civil tongue in your head, sparrow! That's my
friend you're talking about,'' gritted Matthias as he strode off
to the right, tugging the lead. His concentration broken, he
stepped awkwardly upon a joist and tripped heavily into the
thick dust.

Warbeak was upon the young mouse in a flash!

The sparrow scratched hard at Matthias's neck and pecked at
the back of his head, forcing it down to the floor.

Matthias felt the suffocating dust clog his mouth as he struggled to turn his body over. Warbeak pecked and scratched frantically, her target obscured by the bulky haversack. Reaching up behind himself, the mouse felt around until he grasped the sparrow's leg. Giving it a hard pull, he rolled over, plucking out his dagger in the same movement. Matthias lay across Warbeak, pinning her to the floor, the point of his dagger pricking the sparrow's throat.

"Listen, Warbeak," Matthias panted. "One more move like that and it will be your last. Do you hear me?"

Both creatures lay still awhile, their faces close together, breathing heavily. The sparrow was still defiant. "I get chance, Warbeak killee mouse. Sparra not give up, you see!"

Matthias sprang to his feet, tugging the lead viciously. He dragged the sparrow stumbling and tripping to the crack of light. Swinging the bird forwards, Matthias pushed her through the narrow aperture, squeezing through after her with great difficulty.

They were on the first ledge, high above Great Hall.

Without warning, Matthias shoved Warbeak roughly off the ledge.

The startled sparrow shot downwards and stopped with a jerk, only thick neck feathers saving her from strangulation. Matthias held the lead tightly with both paws, straining backwards as the sparrow dangled and fluttered over Great Hall.

"Now, you promise to behave yourself, or down you go, my friend," Matthias shouted.

With her heart hammering at the surprise attack and her predicament, Warbeak realized that she was completely at the mercy of her captor. Burdened with the brick, she had no chance of flying. As she hung flapping uselessly, Matthias called down, "Make up your mind! My paws are getting tired. This lead's beginning to slip."

A forlorn little voice answered. "Warbeak not wanta die. Mouse win. Pull Sparra up. Be good. Give word."

Bracing himself against a stone arch, Matthias pulled the sparrow back to safety. Together they sat on the ledge sharing a canteen of water, both weary and dusty. Matthias was still wary of his prisoner.

"How good is the word of a sparrow?" he asked.

Warbeak puffed out her chest. "Sparra word always good.

Warbeak no say lie. Me swear by mother's egg. That big swear.''

Matthias reflected that he had used desperate measures to secure a promise, but with justification. He was being uncompromising with himself as well as his captive. No more could he afford to be the silly little novice that had bumbled about the Abbey before the start of the present troubles. He was maturing, learning the warrior's way. This mission was vital. Redwall depended upon him, just as it had once depended upon Martin the Warrior.

Warbeak cocked her head quizzically to one side. "What Matthias think about?"

The young mouse repacked the water canteen into his haversack. "Oh, nothing much, Warbeak. Come on, we'd better get on."

With an odd feeling, Matthias realized that he and Warbeak were now on first-name terms.

Cluny might be making promotions. There were now three rat officers on the list of the dead.

First it had been Skullface, killed beneath the wheels of the cart. Next to go was Ragear. There was talk of a serpent. He was never seen again. Now Redtooth, Cluny's first officer, was missing, presumed dead.

Most of Cluny's army had an eye to promotion; not only for prestige—there were the extra shares of loot to be considered.

Killconey the ferret extolled the virtues of his weasel friend, Scragg, who had met his death at the foot of the big elm tree. "Aye, let me tell you, buckos. Scragg: now there was a weasel with a head on his shoulders! Officer material he was, definitely. D'you know, I still can't figure how a smart boyo like that could let himself be killed in a fall from some old tree."

Cheesethief sneered. "Clumsiness, I'd say. I was there and saw it all. Besides, Cluny wouldn't have a weasel officer ordering rats about."

"And why not?" challenged the ferret. "I'll wager the Chief would promote any creature that showed good sense and a fightin' spirit. Will you look at me now? I'm a fine figure of a ferret. Why, if I was the Chief I'd make me a Captain just like that!" The ferret snapped his claws.

Cheesethief spat upon the ground in contempt of Killconey,

knowing there was not much chance of promotion for himself. He was only rated as a minor sort of officer. If it came to a decision, Darkclaw was the natural choice. Fangburn had fallen from favor since the incident with Sela and Redtooth. Nevertheless, the weasels, and their brethren the stoats and ferrets, argued their case hotly. Why shouldn't others be promoted? What was so superior about rats? Mangefur, Scumnose and Frogblood considered rats to be the elite of Cluny's horde. Darkclaw sided with them while trying to placate the others, attempting to keep a foot in either camp, should it come to a vote. One never knew!

Little chance there was of anything democratic being allowed by Cluny the Scourge, who lay on the bed with his eye closed, ignoring the whispered bickering and backbiting around him. He would promote only when he was good and ready. Meanwhile, just let any of his horde dare try to press the issue!

Sela and her son skulked in a corner. They felt trapped. Nobody had spoken to them since the demise of Redtooth. It was as if they were being blamed.

Suddenly, Cluny called over to Sela, "Hey, fox, take that brat of yours outside for a bit! Get some fresh air, and remember, no wandering off! Send Darkclaw in here to me, and that gabby ferret, whatsisname, Killconey."

The foxes hastened to do as they were told, glad to be out of the oppressive atmosphere of the sickroom.

Darkclaw and the ferret came marching in, not knowing whether to be confident or apprehensive. You never knew with Cluny.

They both saluted. "Chief?"

Cluny got out of bed. He paced back and forth, testing his legs. Each day they were a bit stronger. He walked past the pair and spoke without turning to face them. "Who knows anything about tunneling?"

Killconey stepped smartly forward. "Ah, the tunnels, yer honor. You're talkin' to the very creature."

Cluny rested upon his standard. "You?"

"Who else but meself, sir?" the ferret wheedled. "And don't I know some grand ould animals that could help? Ferrets like me, stoats and weasels; why, sure, we're as good as any mole when it comes to the tunnelin', so we are; shorin' and bankin', sinkin' shafts and galleries—''

Cluny banged the standard against the floor. "Enough! Where are these others that you mentioned?''

Killconey cocked a claw over her shoulder. "Sure, they're all outside, your worship. Shall I go and fetch them?''

"Go, and don't be all day about it,'' Cluny replied.

Killconey threw a fancy salute and departed. Cluny pulled Darkclaw close to him. He spoke confidentially. "Don't you know anything about tunnels, Darkclaw?''

The rat shook his head unhappily. Cluny put his claw around Darkclaw's shoulder. "Well, never mind, I've got other work for you. We can't let ferrets, stoats and weasels take all the glory, can we? You've always been a good solid rat, Darkclaw. You help me and I'll see that you get a rich reward when the time comes.''

Darkclaw nodded obediently.

Some time later, Cluny was deep in conference with Killconey and his squad. It was interrupted by a scuffle and commotion from outside. Cheesethief strode in, dragging Chickenhound and prodding Sela ahead of him with a spear.

"What's going on here?'' Cluny demanded.

Cheesethief smirked triumphantly. "It's these two foxes, Chief. I caught them with their ears against the door. They were listening in.''

He skillfully tripped Sela and Chickenhound with the spear butt. They fell in a heap at Cluny's feet, where they lay shivering and protesting their innocence.

"Not us, sir. We weren't eavesdropping.''

"We were just leaning there for a rest. We're only simple healers.''

Cluny nodded understandingly. "I see. You just wanted to help with the digging, is that it?''

Eager to please and panic-stricken, Chickenhound blurted out, "Yes, that's right, sir. Give us a chance and we'll tunnel with the best of them.''

Sela groaned despairingly as Cluny kicked her son viciously. "Who said anything about tunneling, fox? I only mentioned digging.''

Sela attempted to save the situation. "Please, sir, take no

notice of the young fool. All he meant was that when you said dig—''

A whack from the bannerstaff silenced Sela. Cluny's voice was icy with condemnation. ''Traitors! All that he meant was that you slipped up when you copied my plans for an attack with a battering ram. So now you know that I intend to tunnel into Redwall.''

Sela licked dry lips. She stared pleadingly at the Warlord. There was no mercy in the single eye.

''You know too much, vixen. You and your son played a dangerous game. Nobody outsmarts Cluny. I've won, and you have both lost.''

The foxes clasped their claws. They knelt, whimpering pitifully. Cluny stood over them, enjoying his power as judge. He signaled to Cheesethief and Darkclaw.

''Take these miserable turncoats out of my sight. You know what to do.''

Shrieking and screaming for mercy, the foxes were dragged away. Cluny turned back to the ferrets, weasels and stoats.

''Now, about this tunnel.''

CHAPTER
14

Matthias and Warbeak had made slow progress. The climb up
to the arches and stained-glass windows was long and arduous.
Matthias had relieved the sparrow of her brick hobble, pinioning
her wings, make the going easier. At intervals the young mouse
drove spikes into the joints of the stone. He was careful not to
look down: it was a terrifyingly impressive distance down to
the Abbey floor. Only once did he risk a quick glance, not certain if the dark spot on the ground might be Methuselah watching them.

There was real peril negotiating the curve at the top of the
arch. Hanging tightly to the spikes he had fixed, Matthias leaned
out dangerously. There was nothing but determination and the
strength in his paws to stop him from plunging down to a frightening death. Gritting his teeth, he made it to the apex of the
arch. He reached over the stone ledge which divided the arch
from the stained-glass windows above and, taking a firm grip,
propelled himself upwards and sideways. His legs landed further
along the ledge. With his cheek resting on the stone, he gave
one last heave and rolled on to the safety of the ledge.

Sitting up, Matthias knotted two ropes together. He lowered
them to Warbeak, who was waiting below at the base of the
arch. The sparrow looped the rope about herself. As she climbed
she aided Matthias by finding clawholds and making use of the
spikes.

*   *   *

Leaning back against the stained-glass windows they ate lunch. Warbeak gave a twittering laugh.

"Matthias all red mouse."

"Ha, you should talk, Warbeak!" Matthias replied. "Look at yourself. You're blue all over."

The bizarre effect was created by sunlight shining through the stained-glass. As they ate, Warbeak would dodge her head from side to side, changing color as she did so. "Lookeet! Now me green, blue again, now red like a Matthias mouse."

"If you don't sit still you'll be white with fright, because you'll fall," Matthias warned.

When they were sufficiently recovered to start again, Matthias tried the sandstone center rib of the window. It was carved into a profusion of curlicues and niches which made the climb considerably easier. Soon they reached the wooden ridge at the bottom of the roof curvature. It was perilously narrow. Together they edged along it, their backs bent unsafely forward with the curve of the ceiling behind.

Neither of them was aware of the inquisitive, beaked face of a sparrow who watched them from the corner of a stained-glass window. It noted the would-be intruders, then flew off.

Matthias drew his dagger. He stuck it into the wooden ceiling to steady himself as they halted to look for the next loft door.

"I can see it," said Matthias, "there, along to your left. You'll have to lead, Warbeak."

Gingerly the sparrow slid her claws along the smooth wooden ridge. Suddenly Matthias felt the dagger come free from the wood. He lost his grip and leaned outwards, teetering and waving his paws. Warbeak stopped him falling by pulling him back. The dagger went spinning down. It was a considerable time before they heard the faint clatter as it hit the Abbey floor.

"Gosh!" said Matthias in an awed voice. "I thought I'd had it then. I was certain I'd fall. Thanks for saving me, Warbeak."

Gradually they inched their way along until they arrived beneath the loft door. It was too high and difficult for either of them to reach. Matthias made several attempts before he had to admit defeat. He sat upon the ridge, kicking his legs and feeling quite angry with himself. Failure stared him in the face.

"A fool, that's what I am! A little fool, climbing all this way to be beaten by an old loft door."

The sparrow tapped him with her claw. "Why not Matthias cut Warbeak free? Then fly with Sparra wings and open little worm door."

Matthias looked blank. "Beg pardon?"

Warbeak explained again. "You no listen. Warbeak say, cut wings free, fly up and open door."

"Give me your sparrow's word that you won't fly off."

"Is good. Give Sparra word. Promise no 'scape."

"Swear by your mother's egg."

"By mother's egg, Warbeak swear."

Matthias undid the twine that pinioned the sparrow's wings, and Warbeak flapped her wings experimentally. "Long time no fly. Me good, you see."

The young sparrow launched herself off the ridge. She went into a series of zooming circles and performed a few acrobatic turns for her companion's benefit.

Matthias grinned. "Righto, I'm impressed. Now get back here, you little showoff, and open this door."

Warbeak sped back, hovering level with the loft door as she set her claws into the latch. "Watch out. . . . Door open, fall on mouse."

The young mouse backed away as the sparrow released the door. It banged down hard, flapping on its hinges.

This time Matthias was aware that there would be another shower of falling dust when the door opened downwards. Wisely he had edged sufficiently along the ridge to avoid both.

With Warbeak flying behind him as a backup in case he fell, Matthias used the open door as a ladder. He was soon up through the opening. Though the inside was dull and gloomy, he could see they were in a long trenchlike defile, one side of which was a fairly straight wall while the other side was a high curving slope, the reverse side of the arched wooden ceiling.

Matthias called Warbeak to him. He undid the collar and lead from the sparrow's neck, and packed them away in the haversack. He patted his flying friend. "Warbeak, I can no longer keep you collared. You are a free sparrow and a very good friend."

The young sparrow blinked her fierce little eyes. "Matthias, my mouse friend. I no leave. Stay with you."

Together they spent several minutes searching the high ceiling above. Warbeak, having the advantage of flight, was first to find the final trapdoor that they had guessed must exist.

It was not a hard climb for Matthias, merely an excited and rather undignified scramble up the curving wooden roofback. This time they found that the door opened inwards. It was really heavy. The two companions strained together until it creaked loudly and opened.

Matthias scrambled through, followed by Warbeak. They found themselves completely surrounded by sparrows as the door slammed shut behind them. The birds argued and chattered aloud as they sprang upon Matthias, pinning him to the lid of the door with many claws. He was unable to move a single whisker. As quickly as it had started, the noise ceased. The flock of birds parted. Matthias found himself staring straight into the bold aggressive face of a big strong-looking male sparrow. The bird glared at him with a crazy light in its bright, mad eyes.

"Mouse worm, you my prisoner! This court of Sparra! Me King Bull Sparra!"

CHAPTER

15

The bodies of Sela and Chickenhound, the two traitor foxes, lay limp in the ditch that ran alongside the road. The rats of Cluny's horde had executed them with spears and tossed them there. Sela lay still, her once bright cunning eyes glazed over in death.

But gradually Chickenhound began to twitch and groan.

He was still alive!

The fox's entire body was afire with pain. Twice they had stabbed him, once in the back leg, and again right through the loose skin and fur at the scruff of his neck. Chickenhound had screamed and fallen into the ditch, helped by the feet of the rat executioners. He had immediately blacked out. Sela's carcass landed on top of her son's body in the shallow muddy water.

The rats were satisfied that both foxes were dead, and if they were not, well, who was going to climb down through all of those stinging nettles into the slippery ooze to find out? They hurled clods of earth at the prone forms in the ditch and stood watching them for a time. When flies began to gather on the foxes, the rodents lost interest and wandered off.

Chickenhound regained his senses. He lay quite still with Sela's body draped across him. When he was satisfied that the coast was clear he struggled painfully clear of the grisly carcass that had once been his mother.

Old fool! She would never have been in this mess if she'd let a much younger and smarter fox handle things.

With a total lack of sorrow for his deceased parent, Chick-enhound began figuring out his next move. He would have to lie low in this stinking ditch until darkness fell. Even though he was severely hurt, the irony of the situation caused the young fox a silent snigger. It was he, not his mother, who had outwitted Cluny. Now he would soon be free with the revised plans of the attack upon Redwall Abbey. Surely that would be worth something?

As soon as it was dark, Chickenhound made his move. He was only too glad to do so. Flies, wasps, worms and all manner of crawlies had been thoroughly investigating him all afternoon. Slowly and carefully he rolled about in the thick mud until it formed a poultice, cooling the wounds in his leg and neck, pre-venting further blood loss. Under the cover of night he wobbled unsteadily to his feet, limping away up the bed of the ditch towards Redwall.

The going was painfully slow, but Chickenhound consoled himself on the long journey by boosting his own ego. "Maybe a silly bunch of rats could put one over on Sela. Huh, she was old and had lost a lot of her guile. Not like me! They hadn't reckoned with a smart intelligent young fox like I am. I'll show them! Revenge will be mine! They'll see what it's like to be up against an expert in espionage."

Hours later, within sight of the Abbey walls, Chickenhound discovered a slope that was not too steep and started to pull himself up out of the ditch. He gasped and cried out in agony as he climbed. Using some creepers and an overhanging bush, the young fox finally made it to the road.

Completely exhausted, he lay in the dust. How long he had been dragging his wounded body along the ditch bed he could not tell. In his present weakened condition he could not go a step farther, but fell into a state halfway between unconscious-ness and sleep.

Silent Sam was Cornflower's bodyguard on her nightly round of the ramparts. He marched solemnly by her side as she gave out mugs of hot soup to the grateful sentries that watched through the night hours. Ambrose Spike watched hungrily as she poured him a steaming mug of the delicious soup. The hedgehog thanked her profusely, hoping that there might be sec-onds after the others had been served.

"What a thoughtful little body you are, Miss Cornflower. I always say there's nothing like some good homemade vegetable soup to keep the life in my old spines. It's a fair night, but mark you, it gets a bit chill twixt dark and dawn, m'dear."

While the hedgehog and the mouse were chatting, Silent Sam was never still for a second. He trotted about on the parapet, always sucking his paw, leaping from stone to stone, fighting off imaginary foes with his tiny dagger.

At first Cornflower thought he was play-acting as usual. The baby squirrel stood on top of the gatehouse threshold. Pointing down to the road with his knife, he beckoned Cornflower and Ambrose with his well-sucked paw to come and see something.

The young fieldmouse wagged her ladle. "Put that dagger away and stop your climbing, you little scamp."

Silent Sam remained as he was, like a well-trained pointer dog.

"P'raps he's trying to tell us summat, Miss?" grunted Ambrose. He waddled over to the parapet and looked down to where Sam pointed.

"Well, bless m'soul, Miss Cornflower. I do believe that our little soldier 'ere has spotted a hobject. There's a creature a layin' down there, but I'm blowed if it's fish or fowl, there's so much mud and dust plastered on it," whispered the hedgehog. "You stay put, Missy. I'll go and fetch help."

Cornflower and Silent Sam stood looking down from the parapet. Ambrose, aided by Jess Squirrel and Foremole, ventured out into the road to investigate. At their back stood a dozen stout mice guarding the gatehouse door under the command of Basil Stag Hare.

"Steady in the ranks there," said the hare quietly. "Keep your eyes peeled for signs of ambush, and no talking now."

Chickenhound was lugged inside as rapidly as possible. Unable to contain their curiosity, the defenders questioned the limp, half-awake fox as they carried him across the Abbey grounds.

"Did your friends the rats do this?"

"I suppose it's sanctuary you want now?"

"Harr, warra you'm be about, a layin' in yon road?"

Chickenhound's head flopped from side to side as he was borne along. He would only say one thing. "The Abbot. I must see the Abbot. Keep that badger away from me, or you'll learn nothing.''

Basil dismissed the rearguard and caught up with Ambrose. ''I say, you'd best get that rascal straight to the jolly old Abbot. Let him make his statement before he pegs out, don'cha know.''

Chickenhound was hauled into the Abbey building and laid out on a bench. Abbot Mortimer shuffled up in his nightshirt, rubbing sleep from his eyes. He inspected the fox's wounds with a critical, practiced look and spoke dispassionately, ''Well, fox, what do you want from us? No doubt Cluny your master has sent you here to spy.''

Chickenhound shook his head in weak denial. ''Please, I must have some water.''

Jess Squirrel picked up the water jug but withheld it.

''Tell the Father Abbot what you want, sly one,'' she rasped sternly.

The fox reached out feebly for the water jug. Much to the Abbot's dismay, Jess still held it at a distance.

''Speak first. You'll get water when we get information,'' she insisted.

The sight of an injured animal distressed the Abbot, but he decided wisely to leave matters to Jess. The squirrel knew what she was doing.

''Cluny's horde did this to me,'' croaked the fox. ''My mother, Sela . . . they killed her. I know of Cluny's new plans. Care for me and I will tell you all.''

Chickenhound fainted clean away.

''Huh, I certainly wouldn't waste good time and medicine on this one,'' said Jess coldly.

Ambrose Spike scratched his stomach speculatively. ''True, Jess, neither would I. But mayhap he has vital information, otherwise why would he drag himself 'ere in this state?''

The Abbot inspected the fox's neck-wound beneath the muddied fur. ''What Ambrose says makes sense. Would you lift the wretched creature up and carry him to the sick bay, please?''

Cornflower and Silent Sam watched the fox being carried away. Sam stood in front of her, his dagger drawn to protect them both. She ruffled his pointed ears.

''It's all right now, Sam,'' she said, gently. ''The fox cannot hurt us. Thank you for protecting me.''

The little squirrel sheathed his knife and resumed paw-sucking.

Winifred and Abbot Mortimer sat by the bed in the sick bay. They kept up their vigil until Chickenhound regained consciousness. The fox whimpered. He gazed around at the homely little room.

"Oh my neck! What is this place? Where am I?" he groaned.

Winifred pushed the patient gently back on to the pillows and held a bowl of water to the cracked, dry lips.

"Please drink this and lie still," she ordered.

Chickenhound slurped and gulped greedily at the water as the Abbot enlightened him. "You are in the infirmary at Redwall Abbey. As yet I do not know the full extent of your injuries. When you have rested, my friends will cleanse you and dress your wounds."

Chickenhound could hardly believe his ears. "You mean I can stay! But I haven't told you of the new plans yet."

The Abbot wiped driblets of water from his patient's chin. "Listen to me, my son. We would not turn you away from our gates, unless you were an enemy that meant us harm. All creatures are cared for at Redwall Abbey and it is my task to care for the sick and injured. You are my responsibility. Whether or not you choose to give information is a matter that your own heart must deal with. Meanwhile you will receive our hospitality and sanctuary until you are fully recovered."

Chickenhound lay thinking about what the kindly old mouse had said. Suddenly he blurted out, "The battering ram is only a decoy. Cluny means to use it as a diversion so that he can tunnel underneath your Abbey walls. I don't know exactly where he plans to start digging, but I do know that he will come at you from under the ground."

The Abbot shook his head reprovingly as Winifred lowered the lamp flame and drew the curtains. "Cluny is surely the spawn of darkness. He will stop at nothing, my son. Now I realize this and I believe what you tell me is true. But why did you crawl all the way to Redwall with this information—almost at the cost of your life?"

Chickenhound did his best to look sorrowful and outraged as he lied. "Because they killed old Sela, sir. She was my mother. I will not rest until justice is done to her murderers."

The Abbot patted the young fox's paw. "Thank you for entrusting your confidence in us, young one. Close your eyes now, and try to get some rest."

When the Abbot had departed, Chickenhound snuggled his filthy body down against the clean white sheets. He felt a little better already, well enough to have a quiet snigger.

There was no fool like an old fool!

This mouse was as stupid as Sela had been. Let the mice fight the rats and the rats fight the mice; what did he care? Redwall must be a veritable treasure house to a clever young fox.

CHAPTER
16

Dunwing was the widowed mother of Warbeak. She was also sister to the mighty King Bull Sparra. When her daughter was shot down by the arrow, she had given her up as dead. Now that she was back safe and sound she stroked and scolded her at the same time with relief. When she could get a chirp in edgeways, Warbeak related the strange story to her mother in the rapid Sparra dialect.

As she was doing this, Matthias lay pinned to the floor by the claws of many fierce Sparra warriors. As far as he could tell, the place was one enormous loft. This was the court of King Bull Sparra, whose wrath seemed about to descend upon him.

The sparrows lived higgledy-piggledy here in one great untidy tribe. The roof above met in the shape of an upturned V, thus making the court a long triangular structure. Under the eaves at either edge were countless scruffy-looking nests, all of which appeared to be filled to overflowing with shrieking baby sparrows. At one end the loft was blocked off by roofing slates and old nesting materials. This was the King's own private chamber. Matthias estimated that it was probably underneath where the weather vane was situated.

King Bull Sparra was not a bird to be trifled with. He noticed the young mouse's evident interest in his surroundings and quickly diverted his attention with a savage kick at the helpless figure.

"Whatta mouseworm want in court of King?" he snapped.

Matthias, realizing that this was no time for idle chit-chat, promptly shouted out in a loud, courtly manner, "O King, I come to return one of your brave young warriors!"

The statement caused an immediate hullaballoo. Bull Sparra flapped his wings once and quiet descended. He cocked his head to one side, assessing this bold young intruder.

"You lie, mouseworm. Not help Sparra! Mouse enemy," he shrieked. "King Bull Sparra say killee enemy, k-killeet!"

Instantly Matthias found himself fighting for his life. The Sparra soldiers piled in on him, jabbering, clawing and pecking. He managed to get a paw free and struck out left and right, dealing hefty blows to several of the sparrows. Matthias realized that he would soon be overwhelmed as more sparrows pressed in on him, urged on by the mad exhortations of their King. "K-killeet, k-killeet, make mousa dead, killeet!"

As Matthias battled to free his other paw he felt himself enveloped by two pairs of wings. Warbeak and Dunwing were attempting to shelter him. The mother sparrow was crying out, "No killee! Mouse good! Save my egg Sparra."

The King was not convinced. "Mouse enemy, gotta make dead."

King Bull Sparra had no fledglings of his own. Warbeak, who was his favorite niece, called out to her uncle, appealing for mercy. "No, no, King Bull. Not killee Matthias mouse! Him save Warbeak! Give Sparra word to mouse that you no killee."

The King sprang in among his warriors, scattering them like chaff. They cowered before him as he shouted out a new edict. "Foolworms! Stop! King say no killee mouse! We have Sparra word of my sister's eggchick."

The Sparra warriors backed off. Matthias picked himself up. Luckily, he had not come to much harm. He dusted his habit off. "Whew! Thank you once again, Warbeak, my friend. I owe you my life."

The King issued orders to two Sparra warriors. "Battlehawk, Windplume! Getta bag. Find out what mouse carry."

Matthias stood firm as the haversack was pulled from his back. The two warriors could not figure out how to open it.

They tore at the material with beak and claw until it gave way. The contents scattered upon the floor. Matthias stood respectfully to one side as the King rummaged through his meager possessions.

King Bull Sparra drank some water from the canteen. He spat it out.

"No worms, only mousefood," he commented.

Warbeak sighed wistfully. She looked longingly on as her uncle found the package of candied chestnuts and ripped it open. Bull Sparra dubiously sampled one. His face lit up with pleasure. "This good food for Sparra King. Not good for mouseworm. Me keep."

He tucked the candied chestnuts under his wing, then picked up the collar and lead and beckoned to Matthias. "Mouseworm, come here. You lucky King letta live."

The young mouse approached the sparrow with trepidation, not wanting to antagonize the moody, dangerous bird. The Sparra King buckled the collar tightly about Matthias's neck. Scarcely leaving him room to breathe, he attached the lead and laughed aloud. Dutifully the other sparrows laughed with him.

Matthias felt his blood boil. He tried to contain his rising temper; the court of the Sparra King was no place to have tantrums. Mentally he promised himself that he would never again use a collar on any living creature. The indignity was unspeakable.

Bull Sparra handed the lead to Warbeak. Turning to his subjects, he chuckled insanely and pointed at Matthias. "King Bull Sparra spare mouse. How you like him for pet, my niece? Mouse, you obey my sister and her eggchick, funny, ha?"

All the sparrows laughed loud and long, vying with each other to show the most merriment. The King was a completely unpredictable tyrant. When he made a joke it was always funny.

Warbeak gave the lead a tug and whispered to her friend, "Matthias, you see Warbeak and mother not make laugh. Sorry."

The young captive winked at his warder. He was beginning to hatch a plan. "Don't worry, my friend. At least I'm alive."

Warbeak handed the lead to her mother. "This Dunwing; she mother. Good Sparra; not hurt mouse. See!"

Dunwing gave the lead a light pull. She gave Matthias a smile and a nod. He decided that he liked Warbeak's mother.

The King issued his orders to Warbeak and Dunwing. "You keep mouseworm on lead. No wander, no stray. Give plenty work. Much kick, like this."

Bull Sparra raised a kick at Matthias, who dodged nimbly and started to dance and sing with a silly expression on his face.

The King stood with his head cocked to one side, amazed at the performance of this strange mouse.

Matthias pranced comically about, improvising a song as he went:

> "Up higher than before,
> I'm near the roof indeed,
> The King gave me a collar,
> His sister holds the lead."

Round and round he skipped, repeating the verse over and over.

Bull Sparra flapped his wings and laughed hysterically. "Hahahahahahaha! Look, Battlehawk! See, Windplume! Mouseworm be hurt in headbrain. He crazy! Hahahahahahaha."

Obediently everybody laughed with the mad monarch.

After a while the sparrows drifted off, some to their nests, others to hunt worms. A chosen few went with the King to play three feathers, a popular Sparra gambling game of which Bull Sparra was very fond. Dunwing and her daughter led the dancing mouse off to their nest at the rear of the court under the farthest eaves.

Despite its outwardly untidy appearance, the nest was neat and cozy on the inside. Warbeak had gathered Matthias's gear together. Repacking it into the torn haversack, she returned it to her mouse friend, eyeing him in an apprehensive manner.

"Matthias be sick in head?" she inquired.

The young mouse lay back gratefully in Dunwing's nest and smiled reassuringly at them both. "Not at all. I'm as sane as you are. However, if I act as if I'm mad then maybe your King and his warriors will not regard me as a threat. Perhaps they will leave me alone and forget about me."

Dunwing looked up from the meal she was preparing. Her eyes were serious.

"Matthias mouse do right thing," she said. "Bull Sparra be

wicked; bad temper. Sometimes Dunwing think Bull Sparra mad. Best he thinks you no-harm mouse.''

Matthias bowed deferentially to her. "Thank you, Dunwing. You are a very brave sparrow. You put yourself and Warbeak in great peril, saving me as you did."

Dunwing served them both some food. Thankfully Matthias noted that she refrained from putting worms and dead insects on his portion. The mother sparrow watched him with soft intelligent eyes. The mouse was about the same age as her daughter.

"Matthias save my Warbeak," she said. "We have no Sparra warrior to look after us. Warbeak brave like father was. Now father, he dead. I learn to stand up for us 'til Warbeak grow into great warrior some day."

The hours slipped by as the three conversed. Matthias learned much of the Sparra customs and way of life.

Dunwing, being the King's sister, was of royal blood. Her husband had been killed the previous spring in a battle with some starlings. He had saved the life of the King, whereupon Bull Sparra had vowed to care for her and her daughter: but he had instantly forgotten his promises, leaving the pair to fend for themselves. Only in moments of urgency would Dunwing remind him of his vow, knowing that Bull Sparra was a dangerous despot. So normally Dunwing maintained a diplomatic silence in his presence.

Sometimes Bull Sparra would retire to his private chamber. He would remain in there brooding for days, suddenly emerging to fire his warriors with grandiose schemes and wild ideas. No one dared to disobey him, even though half an hour later he had forgotten his previous foolhardy notions and wandered off to hunt worms. Later he would return to find that his plans had not been carried out. In a furious squabble of accusation and recrimination he would demote officers and promote the most unlikely soldiers from the ranks. Next day he had forgotten it all again and was hatching more crazy plans. Matthias was constantly amazed at the mode of life in the Sparra court. The sparrows showed no kindness or civility to one another, often fighting savagely among themselves on the slightest pretext. Warriors, and even fledglings, joined in. The injuries they inflicted upon each other were appalling.

Sparra folk knew nothing of the firemaker's art. By day the

court was illuminated by sunlight that streamed in through the
cracked and broken slates and slanted up through the eaves. All
food was eaten uncooked, worms and small insects providing
the main diet. The Sparra did not discriminate between different
species of insects. All came under the general heading of
''worm.'' Thus a sparrow might make a meal of a butterfly or
a grasshopper and refer to it as ''wormfeed.'' ''Worm'' was
also used to denote an enemy or a coward or anything alien to
the Sparra. Fresh flowers and tender shoots of vegetation were
used to supplement the worm diet, also berries and whatever
fruit a Sparra could carry in flight. Matthias was grateful for
this. He abhorred the idea of eating live worms or dead insects.

There was no strict routine of chores ever carried out. Apart
from parents feeding fledglings, everything was left undone until
tomorrow, which meant it never was done. The evidence of this
lay all about the court; dirt, dust, filth and general chaos prevailed.

Matthias gradually found that once he could keep pace with
the speedy delivery of Sparra language it was relatively simple.
Some of the Sparra chattered with such rapidity that Matthias
was sure they could not understand themselves.

Matthias was not sure whether Warbeak knew of his mission to
bring back Martin's sword; certainly Dunwing did not. The
young mouse had had a good look round most of the court, but
the sword was not to be seen. Matthias reasoned that it must be
in the one place he had not yet explored: the private chamber
of the King. He thought long and hard about how he might
obtain access to the royal apartment. He did not want to cause
trouble for his friends, nor did he want them to suspect what he
had come for. And supposing he ever did regain the sword, the
next problem would be how to take it safely back down to the
floor of the Abbey and his own kind.

Matthias figured that he had been in his new surroundings for
a night and a day. Towards the evening of that day, he was
sitting outside the nest, repairing his torn haversack and taking
stock of his personal effects. Each time a sparrow passed by he
would grin vacantly and strike up his song. No one bothered to
take much heed of him.

Warbeak flew in from a lone wormhunt. She stood watching Matthias.

"Me hunt worms," she chirped. "Bring dandelions for Matthias. Mouse like eat flowers."

Matthias replied in Sparra language, "Warbeak good hunter. Mouse like flower. Make good wormfood. Where be Dunwing mother?"

Warbeak pointed to the King's chamber. "Dunwing get Bull Sparra wormfood ready. King have no wife to make food."

Matthias acted unconcerned. He pulled at the collar to loosen it.

"Collar hurt mouseneck," he grinned.

Warbeak shrugged sympathetically. "King say you weara. No can take off. Me sorry."

Matthias continued sorting through his belongings. He came across an unopened package. What a stroke of luck! It was candied chestnuts. Hastily he slipped them into the haversack, hiding the nuts from Warbeak. Under normal circumstances he would gladly have given them to his friend, but this was different. Matthias needed them as bait.

They continued gossiping until Dunwing returned. After a decent interval the young mouse spoke to her, "You go to King's room all lotta time."

Dunwing nodded.

"Me only Sparra King Bull let into there," she laughed. "He lazy Sparra. Not make own wormfood."

Matthias shared her laughter.

"Betcha King not know how to make own wormfood," he chuckled. "What you think, Dunwing? Matthias find a gift for King?"

The Sparra mother looked up sharply. "What mouse mean. Gift?"

Matthias drew close and whispered conspiratorially. "You 'member how King Bull like mouse candynuts? Me find more. You take me. We give nuts to King."

Dunwing looked doubtful. "What for mouse wanta give nuts to King?"

Matthias spread his paws as if stating the obvious. "So King let mouse free. Wanta go back to mousehome."

Matthias held his breath and watched Dunwing. Finally her face softened. She smiled sympathetically. "All right, Matthias.

We try. Not do much harm, but 'member, not make Bull Sparra
bad temper. He killee sure.''

With an inward sigh of relief Matthias swept up the packet
of nuts.

"Thank you, Sparra mother," he said. "Mouse not make
trouble for you. Nuts make King happy, you see.''

With Matthias trailing behind her on his lead, Dunwing tapped
on the slates which formed King Bull Sparra's wall. An irate
voice came from within.

"Fly 'way, Sparra! King wanta sleep.''

Dunwing realized they had chosen a bad moment. Nevertheless she persisted, this time tapping harder. "Let in, King
brother. It Dunwing and crazy mouseworm. Gotta gift for great
King.''

A sleepy head poked round the door opening. Bull Sparra
blinked owlishly at them and yawned in their faces.

"Better be 'portant, Majesty no like to be woked," he grumbled.

As they entered the room, Matthias skipped about and sang
his ditty. Whipping out the packet he selected a nut and popped
it straight into the open beak of the astonished ruler.

"Mouseworm find more candynuts for big King Sparra,"
Matthias giggled. "Fetch here quick. Maybe mouse give King
alla nuts. King letta mouse go home free.''

The King munched and chomped greedily on the sweet nut,
eyeing the packet covetously. "Ha, mouseworm give King alla
nuts. Majesty have great things on mind. Me thinka 'bout,
hmmm, letta mouse go freehome.''

Matthias capered about. He went down on one knee, offering
the nuts. Bull Sparra snatched the parcel. Hoggishly he stuffed
far more of the nuts into his beak than it could cope with. Closing his eyes in ecstasy, he gobbled furiously. Pieces of nut falling from his beak littered his breast feathers.

Matthias's eyes roved about the chamber, searching. It was
nothing special as Sparra habitations went: a straw palliasse,
some butterfly wings stuck to the wall by way of decoration. In
one corner there was a huge overstuffed old chair. How it got
there would forever remain a mystery. Matthias's attention was
held by something that protruded out of the back of the chair.
It was an old-fashioned-looking object made from black leather

with lots of silver trimming, identical to the belt he was wearing.

The scabbard of Martin's sword!

Surely the sword must be somewhere close by?

Matthias wished that he could see around the back of the chair to confirm his discovery, but he had to bring himself back to the issue at hand.

King Bull Sparra crammed the last candied chestnuts into his beak and chomped with evident enjoyment.

Dunwing attempted to press for justice. "King eat gift. Now mouse go free?"

The King held out a grasping claw. "More! Mouseworm got more candynut gift for Majesty?"

Matthias remained kneeling. He appealed to the gluttonish ruler.

"O King, mouse have no got more candynuts. Give all to great Majesty. Now you let mouse go freehome," he said hopefully.

Bull Sparra pecked nut morsels from his feathers, his eyes gleaming craftily.

"Ah! Now King give Sparra word. I say if mouse-worm give more candynuts then go free, but must give lot." The King spread his wings wide apart. "This many lot!"

The young mouse bowed his head. "But Majesty, me got no more nut."

Unexpectedly Bull Sparra's mood changed for the worse. He crumpled the empty dock-leaf packet and hurled it into Matthias's face.

"Mouseworm get more! More, you hear?" His eyes shone madly as the feathered hackles rose around his neck. "King not argue with crazy mouseworm. You get gone now, plenty quick or me killee. Go now. Majesty sleep."

Sensing that the King had become dangerous, Dunwing did not hesitate. Roughly she dragged the mouse by the lead from the chamber.

Matthias spluttered with uncontrolled rage. "Dunwing, how you letta stupid oaf be King of Sparra?" he choked.

The mother sparrow shushed soothingly and dragged Matthias off to the safety of her nest.

Warbeak had gone off hunting again. Dunwing sat down and tried to reason with the angry young mouse. "Matthias not let

King Bull hear say him stupid oaf. You be dead wormbait much
soon.''

Matthias opened his mouth to protest. The sparrow silenced
him with an upraised wing. ''All birds know that King Bull
mighty fighter. Him save Sparra tribe many time from enemy.
He sometime lazy, sometime bad temper, but not stupid. Bull
Sparra sly like fox, only pretend to be stupid, just like Matthias.''

Dunwing had guessed that Matthias had gone to the King's
chamber for other reasons than to gain his freedom. This was a
very wise mother bird. He decided to put all of his cards on the
table.

''Dunwing, listen. I want to tell you a story,'' he said. ''It is
all about the mice who live in the Abbey beneath us, and of
one mouse in particular called Martin the Warrior. . . .''

The sparrow listened intently as the young mouse unfolded
the story of Redwall Abbey and the part that he was playing in
its hour of need. When Matthias had finished his tale, Dunwing
saw the truth of it in his open face. She drew close and said
quietly, ''Matthias, Dunwing knew! First day you come here I
see belt you wear. It all same as thing behind chair in King's
room.''

''But why—?'' Matthias interjected. Again Dunwing silenced
him.

''Young mouse sit still,'' she said. ''Now me tell you story.
Many time ago, before my mother was egg, King named Bloodfeather. He steal sword from northpoint. Sword make Sparra
folk proud, brave fighters, strong eggchicks, much wormfood to
eat. Sword hang in court of Sparra. Bloodfeather die, who know
how? Bull Sparra become King. My husband Greytail tell me
this 'fore he die. Bull Sparra wear warrior sword. Case be too
heavy. Leave case behind in room backa chair. Carry sword in
clawfeet. King Bull he much showoff. Dig worm with sword.
My husband go longa with him. One day they hunt in Mossflower trees, giantworm come, one with poisonteeth. Alla time
say 'Asmodeussss', like that. Bull Sparra drop big sword. Even
he scared of poisonteeth. Giantworm curl round swordhandle.
Bull Sparra, he order my husband, Greytail, get sword back.
Greytail try, but worm bite with poisonteeth. He hurt bad, but
fly back to court with Bull Sparra. They leave sword in Mossflower with giantworm. My husband die. Bull Sparra say hurt

in starling fight. Not true. Greytail tell me all 'fore he die. War-beak still egg; not know how father die.''

Matthias watched sympathetically as Dunwing fought back her tears. Gently he patted the widowed sparrow. "Greytail be mighty warrior to face poisonteeth alone. You glad Warbeak be his eggchick."

Dunwing smiled through her tears. "Matthias be good mouse."

There followed an embarrassed silence. Matthias spoke half aloud. "So, it seems my quest has been in vain. But what of the scabbard?"

"Scabbard mean sword case?" Dunwing inquired. Matthias nodded.

"Me tella 'bout sword case," Dunwing said bitterly. "King Bull Sparra be frighten to tella rest of Sparra that he lose sword. Huh, he not know Greytail tell me, but I watch King, Dunwing know. Bull Sparra still pretend sword in case. That way he stay King. If I tella, he killee me and Warbeak, this I know. Someday Warbeak my eggchick be Queen. She have royal blood, then Sparra folk be better, be happy. Bull Sparra rule for now, huh, lose heart, lose sword. No good crazy bird, Bull Sparra."

That night as he settled down to sleep in Dunwing's nest, Matthias had a good deal to reflect upon. So, King Bull had lost the sword to a giant worm with poison teeth. Matthias knew the description fitted only one thing: a snake!

Poison probably meant it was an adder. He had never seen an adder, nor any other type of snake. At Redwall he had learned of snakes from the talk of others. They spoke of the adder as if it were a reptile that was half legend, half nightmare. It was said that even the Father Abbot himself would flatly refuse to treat a snake, no matter how bad its condition might be. Luckily there had never been cause to. There had never been reports of an adder in the area of Mossflower, that was why most creatures tended to treat it as a mythical reptile; but wise ones like Constance, the Abbot and old Methuselah assured everyone that the adder was cold deadly fact. They said that in all the world there was nothing more feared: the strong coils, hypnotic eyes and poison fangs.

Matthias shuddered. It sounded even more fearsome than Cluny the Scourge! How could a mere mouse take the sword from this adder that Dunwing had described? The one that said "Asmodeusssss"? Matthias tried to put it from his mind. Gradually sleep overtook him.

"You come quick, mouseworm. King wanta see you."

Rough claws seized Matthias, dragging him from the nest only half awake. It was the two Sparra warriors, Battlehawk and Windplume. They lugged Matthias off without further explanation, tugging cruelly on his lead. The last things he saw before he was pulled off into the darkness of the court were the pale worried faces of Dunwing and Warbeak.

He shouted to reassure them, "Don't worry, I'll be all right. Take care of yourselves."

Battlehawk hit Matthias in the face with a stiff bony wing. "Mouseworm, shut beak or me killee."

"Not before I see your King, you won't," the young mouse retorted.

Battlehawk aimed a kick at him, but Windplume deflected it. "Leave mouse alone. You killee him, King killee us."

Windplume grinned at Matthias. "Mouse cheeky, but brave like Sparra warrior."

King Bull Sparra had finished napping. Something was disturbing him about the captive mouse. He had been too busy guzzling candied chestnuts to let it bother him. But now that he was wide awake it hit him like a ton of bricks.

The mouseworm's belt!

What had taken Dunwing a single glance to recognize had finally dawned on the King. Matthias's belt was the same as the sword case behind his own chair!

A broken piece of mirror reflecting the moonlight was the only illumination in the King's chamber. He dismissed his two warriors to wait outside. The King of the Sparra folk sat staring at the young mouse in silence.

Matthias stood his ground bravely, not knowing what to expect. Bull Sparra stood up. He strutted about in front of Matthias, then around behind him. Matthias felt his belt gripped from behind by strong claws. The crazed King whispered close in his ear.

"Where mouseworm get belt?"

Matthias swallowed hard. He tried to act casual.

"Belt? Oh, you mean this belt? Mouse always have belt for many long time. Not know where me get."

Thump!

Matthias hit the floor as the King shoved him fiercely in the back. "Mouse lie. King Bull not wormfool! Where you get? Tell, tell."

As he shouted madly, the sparrow pulled at the belt. Matthias knew he was facing death with the insane ruler in one of his lunatic rages. He must think fast.

"No got more candynuts," the young mouse cried. "Please, Majesty, give mouseword, no more candynuts. Me give great King this belt, then he letta mouse go freehome."

Matthias's plea had the desired effect upon the mad King. He sat in the big chair, his eyes glinting cunningly.

"Sparra law say King must killee mouseworm, but me good Majesty. No killee mouse. Give belt to King."

Matthias unbuckled the belt and handed it over. King Bull fondled it, then fastened it on himself. As he admired the belt, strutting in front of the broken mirror, the sparrow spoke in a normal voice.

"Nice, good belt. Mouse know of great sword?"

Instantly Matthias was on his guard. One wrong word might spell death for Dunwing and Warbeak. He must affect ignorance to allay the King's suspicions.

"Oh, Majesty, that good belt. Make King look fine, like mighty warrior. Not look so good on mouse."

Bull Sparra appeared flattered. He preened himself, then asked the question again, this time in a coaxing tone. "Surely Matthias know of great sword?"

In spite of his dangerous predicament Matthias was inwardly amused at the King's use of his name. Slumping to the floor, he sat with his head between his paws, the picture of dejected innocence.

"Oh mighty King, mouse not have more candynuts. Not know 'bout sword thing, not even have belt now. Me die if not soon go free. Please letta poor mouseworm go home."

Matthias's show of pathos seemed to cheer the King. He tucked his wingtips into the belt that he had fooled the mouse-worm into giving him. Ha, he had eaten all the mouse's nuts too! Feeling no end of a fine bird, he gave a sharp whistle that brought his two warriors on the double.

"Looka this mouseworm," he scoffed. "He not happy that I spare him. You take mouse back to my sister Dunwing. Tell her King say, take care of mouseworm. He give me good gifts, candynut, belt. Maybe mouse find more gift for good Majesty who let live. Take 'way now. Must get more sleep. Go."

As Matthias was dragged off once more, he pretended to cry out in distress. This caused Bull Sparra much amusement. He waved a wing in farewell, calling out to the prisoner, "Getta good sleep, mouseworm. Thinka way to get more gift for Majesty, hahahahaha!"

The two warriors and a nearby fledgling who was half awake laughed obediently with their King.

Matthias thanked his lucky stars that he had once more come out alive. Had he refused to give the belt he would surely have died. Anyhow, he reflected, it was only a temporary loan. As he planned on stealing the scabbard from Bull Sparra, why not the belt to go with it?

CHAPTER 17

Basil Stag Hare and Jess Squirrel were as thick as thieves. When they were not helping with the defenses, they could be found in odd corners whispering together. Nobody knew what their conversations were about, or what exactly they were plotting. But with the fastest runner and the champion climber of Mossflower, it was sure to be something spectacular!

Cornflower and Silent Sam watched them stealing off at lunchtime to continue their conspiracy beneath the trees in the orchard where they would not be disturbed.

"What do you suppose your mum and Basil are up to, Sam?" asked the young fieldmouse, whose curiosity was aroused.

Silent Sam shrugged his tiny shoulders and buried his head in the lunchtime milkbowl. He drank in a noisy, enjoyable infant fashion. Whatever Jess was planning had Sam's complete approval, simply because his mother could do no wrong as far as he was concerned.

Basil stretched comfortably in the shade while Jess sat out in the sunlight, her tail, curled overhead, acting as a sunshade.

"Ah, this is the life, Jess, me old climber." Basil yawned cavernously as he fed crumbs to the ants. "Plenty to keep the inner creature satisfied. Scorching June weather, and a top-hole billet for snoozin', what, what?"

Jess nibbled on a wedge of cheese. "Aye, and it's up to woodlanders like us to keep it that way, Basil. What sort of a neighborhood would this be for young uns like my Sam to grow up in if Cluny and his lot were to take over?"

Basil humphed through his military-style whiskers. "Good grief, doesn't bear thinkin' about, old girl! Those rats and vermin, an absolute shower of yahoos and cads! Bad influence, y'know."

They both sat nodding in agreement, faces full of grim righteousness, uttering dire home truths and generally working themselves up into a fine old state of indignation.

"Huh, Cluny the Scourge! A bully and a braggart if ever I clapped eyes on one."

"Yes, and a robber to boot. Fancy stealing Martin's tapestry from the mice! What harm have they ever done to him?"

"Y'know, it strikes me that it'd do the Father Abbot's heart good to see that tapestry back in its rightful place again."

"Indeed it would, and the troops would take new heart."

"Ha, what a blow it would be to that feller Cluny and his filthy band of robbers."

Basil bounded up and ate the last of Jess's cheese decisively. "Well, what are we waiting for then? Come on, Jess, you old hazelnut woffler. Up and at 'em. Forward the fur!"

Jess flexed her climbing claws and bared her teeth angrily.

"Just you try and stop me," she chattered fiercely.

Without telling anyone of their intentions, the two expert campaigners slid out secretly by one of the small doors in the Abbey walls. Soon they were stealing through the green, noontide depths of Mossflower Wood.

Cluny was up and about. His first decision was to put the horde through their paces. He had decided that they had become fat and lazy from lying about in the church grounds while he was confined to bed, but now that he was on the mend they were going to do some drill. Standing on a tombstone, he leaned slightly upon his standard and viewed the army in training.

Panting and sweating, a large mob of rats dashed to and fro burdened by the battering ram. The captains, hoping to curry favor with Cluny, harangued the hapless runners: "Pick your feet up, you lily-livered scum! Come on, lift that ram properly, you idle devils.''

Practice tunnels were being dug willy-nilly owing to the lack of communication between rats and other species. Ferrets, weasels and stoats, their faces smeared with moist dark earth, popped out of the ground in the oddest of places. Unaccustomed to such strenuous labor, they would stop digging as they pleased, basking in the sun until they were trodden on by columns of marching rats. A squabble would ensue until they all became aware of the watchful eye of Cluny. Then it would be heads down, resume marching, get back to tunneling.

Either side of Cluny on the tombstone stood Darkclaw and Killconey. Scornfully watching the chaotic maneuvers, the Warlord would criticize first one then the other for the shortcomings of the creatures they represented. Both squirmed under the lash of the Chief's tongue.

''Darkclaw, look at the way those rats are marching! Idiots! They look like a flock of lambs at a village school outing! Haven't you taught them anything?

''Oh hellfire! That stupid lot with the battering ram have just marched straight into a tunnel! Killconey, tell those morons of yours not to tunnel into the parade ground. Just a minute, that weasel there, the one grinning all over his face like a drunken duck: lock him up without food or water for three days! That'll wipe the daft smile off his face. Well, what a fine pair of commanders you two turned out to be. I can't turn my back a minute and you've got all hands behaving like mad frogs in a bucket.''

Cluny ranted and fumed at the animals under his banner. They were going to march, sweat, dig, carry, drill and tunnel, until they performed to his satisfaction. Sloppy idle lot! He'd show them now that he was back; he'd keep them at it all day and all night if need be. Cluny had taken a vow while he lay injured: never again would he allow himself to be thwarted by mice and woodland creatures.

At that precise moment it was two of those same creatures who stood on the fringe of Mossflower Wood, spying across the common land to where Cluny's army was exercising.

But for the gravity of the situation, Basil and Jess would have seen the chance for many a good laugh. What a difference between the antics of this rabble and the way in which the Abbey defenders went about their business of training! Jess observed that it was the contrast between slaving under a tyrant and voluntary cooperation that arose from determination and good fellowship.

The plans of the two comrades were well laid. Basil decided that now was as good a time as any to put them into operation. He turned to Jess.

"Well, you old tree-jumper. Let's see if we can't baffle the blighters with science!"

They shook paws and ventured out on to the common land: Basil Stag Hare, camouflage expert and foot fighter, in the lead; Jess Squirrel, champion climber and pathfinder, close behind him. They were like twin cloud-shadows drifting silently across the land.

Cluny had climbed down from his perch on the tombstone. He stood by the churchyard fence, intent on trying out the whipping powers of his fearsome tail upon a few rats that he had dubbed "the awkward squad." Flexing his long scourge-like tail, he gave a few experimental swishes and cracks as he shouted commands.

"Left wheel! I said *left* wheel, you buffoons. You there, don't you know the difference between your left and your right? Hold out your left paw."

The frightened rat stuck out what he fervently hoped was his left paw.

Swish. Crack!

The unfortunate rodent screamed and danced about with the stinging pain of the thick whiplike tail. Cluny foamed with ill-temper.

"Blockhead! That was your right paw. Now hold out your left, stupid! I'm going to make an example of you this lot won't forget."

A voice interrupted him. "Tut tut, officer striking an enlisted creature! Bad form, old chap, thumping bad form!"

Cluny whirled round. Just out of reach across the fence on the common land stood Basil Stag Hare, in the "at ease" position.

Cluny goggled in thunderstruck silence at the audacious Basil, who merely scowled in mock censure.

"Not the sort of thing one expects from a horde commander,

what! Personally I'd have you blackballed from the church premises.''

Cluny's voice was a strangled yell, "Get him! Grab that spy! I want his head!''

Basil chuckled. "What's the matter? Isn't your own head good enough? No, I don't suppose it is. Ugly-looking brute, aren't you?''

A mob of rats had scrambled through the fence to catch Basil, but it was like trying to catch smoke upon the wind. He was there and gone. From her hiding place Jess tried hard to stifle her giggles.

After several exhausting minutes it became apparent that neither the rats nor the dozen or so panting ferrets, weasels and stoats who had joined the chase on Cluny's orders, were remotely close to apprehending the strange hare.

Gripping the standard in bloodless claws, Cluny climbed over the fence to the common land.

The comrades' scheme was beginning to work.

Basil bobbed up alongside Cluny. "What ho, old rat! Showing a bit of initiative? Never ask the troops to do what you can't do yourself and all that! Splendid!''

He dodged playfully out of reach. Cluny snarled and went after him. Basil ducked and weaved, drawing Cluny further out on to the common. All eyes were upon the two figures. This made it easier for Jess to change hiding places as she followed them.

Cluny pursued doggedly, making no sudden moves, waiting for the hare to get overconfident so that he could strike. His soldiers moved about twenty paces behind the action. Cluny had warned them off—he wanted a one-to-one confrontation.

Cluny jabbed out with the banner at Basil. The hare inwardly rejoiced. They were getting closer to Mossflower Wood. Soon Jess would make her move. Meanwhile, he must draw the rat further out. Avoiding the stabs of the banner pole and the swift whiplike slashes of the tail, Basil realized that this was no clumsy rat he faced. He chanced a sudden glance to check if Jess was nearby. As he did, his back left leg shot down into a pothole. It twisted and Basil fell heavily to the ground.

Cluny charged in. He lifted the banner and slammed it down

on the hare's unprotected head. Basil twisted quickly to one side.

"Now, Jess. Now!" he yelled.

As Basil shouted, several things happened at once.

Jess came blasting out of nowhere like a red whirlwind. The banner thudded into the soft earth where Basil's head had been a fraction of a second before. Basil freed his leg as Jess leaped like a salmon. In midair she ripped the tapestry clean off the standard in one go.

Cluny bellowed with rage. His followers came surging across the common to aid him. Basil leaped to his feet and hobbled gamely in front of Cluny, shielding Jess. The squirrel raced about trying to distract Cluny.

Basil winced as he called out to his friend, "Run for it, Jess. I'll hold 'em off!"

Jess ducked a blow from Cluny's tail. "Not likely! If you stay, then so do I."

Basil limped about, keeping himself between Cluny and Jess. "You stubborn beast," he yelled. "*Will* you get going?"

The horde was almost upon them. Quick as a flash, Jess grabbed the end of Cluny's tail. She swung him with all of her might, throwing him off balance and sending him crashing into the frontrunners of the horde. Jess threw Basil's paw about her shoulder.

"Come on, Basil, head for the woods. We'll make it together."

Both creatures dashed from the common into the depths of Mossflower. Behind them, Cluny's horde was in headlong pursuit, yelling and shouting. As they ran, Jess panted, "Here, take this and give me the decoy! Hurry."

Basil snatched the tapestry and reached beneath his tunic. He gave Jess the crude replica they had prepared, which was in reality an old dishcloth from Friar Hugo's kitchen.

The sounds of the pursuers grew louder. They were gaining.

"Now, you drop out of sight," Jess gasped. "I'll draw them off, then you can double back through the churchyard and up the road to Redwall. They'll never think of searching along that way."

As suddenly as she had spoken, Jess glanced to one side. Basil was no longer there. A breathless military voice whispered from the undergrowth, "Will do, old chum. See you back at the Abbey. Have a good chase now, cheerio."

Basil Stag Hare, camouflage expert, had gone to earth.

Jess could see Cluny and the horde coming through the trees. She stood and waited until they caught sight of her. She saw Cluny point and shout.

"Over there! The squirrel! She's the one who's got the tapestry. Get her! Take her alive if you can."

Coolly Jess stood her ground until they were almost upon her. Right at the last second she went like a blur up the side of a horse chestnut tree, stopping just out of reach. Some of the more agile ones tried climbing to get at her. Jess merely scampered further upwards.

"Get down, you nincompoops," Cluny hissed. "Don't try to outclimb a squirrel. See if you can keep her near the ground while I think what to do."

The rats climbed down. As they did, Jess returned to the lower trunk. She had to buy as much time as possible to allow Basil's escape.

Cluny lounged nonchalantly against the tree. "Well done, squirrel. Very clever indeed. I could use someone like you in my army. Somebody smart, with brains like yours."

Killconey also demonstrated his persuasive powers. "Ah, you take the Chief's word. He's lookin' for a good first officer. Why don't you come down now and talk it over? Sure, the loot will be grand when we conquer the Ab—Ouch!"

A small green spiky chestnut still in its husk bounced off the vociferous ferret's head. Jess moved higher to a branch with a more plentiful supply. She waved the decoy tapestry at Cluny.

"Is this what you're after, ratface?"

Cluny battled to keep his temper. Darkclaw nudged him and whispered, "What about the other one, Chief? Shall I take some troops and start searching for him?"

"No, I'll deal with the hare another time. Right now I want you all here in case there's a chance of trapping this one," Cluny murmured.

Jess's keen ears caught every word the Warlord had said. The plan had worked! She threw a hard spiky nut and called to Cluny: "Hey, ratface! Do you actually think that you've got 'this one' trapped? Ha, I'm about as trapped as a skylark in the air on a clear day! There's not one of you can get near me."

"I know that, squirrel," Cluny answered. "But just think for a moment. If I win the war against the mice—and I will, you know—I've made a vow to kill everyone inside Redwall. Now suppose that you've got someone dear to you in there; you know what I mean: a mate, a little baby, some family—"

Cluny dodged about as a shower of spiky chestnuts hurtled down.

"You filthy murdering scum!" shouted Jess. "You rotten loathsome slime! If you come near my family, I'll rip that evil eye of yours right out of your face!"

Cluny knew that he was succeeding with his scheme against the squirrel as more hard chestnuts pelted down.

"Throwing things won't do you much good. Listen, I'm a reasonable creature. All I'm asking you to do is to think of your family. You haven't got to join us if you don't want to. Stay up in that tree forever if you want, it doesn't bother me. All I need is that little scrap of tapestry. It isn't much to ask, is it? Your loved ones will be safe if you hand it over."

Jess was about to hurl more nuts and insulting remarks when the form of Cluny's plan dawned on her. The rat was trying to do exactly as she and Basil had done. It was a trap to make her become careless. Two can play at that game, Jess thought to herself. The horde soldiers watching the squirrel noticed a change come over her. She appeared agitated, gnawing upon her lip and rubbing her paws together. In anguish she clutched the tapestry, hugging it to her body.

"I don't care about the others at Redwall, but I've got a husband and a small son. You wouldn't hurt them, would you, Cluny?"

The Warlord detected a sob in the squirrel's voice.

"No, no, of course I wouldn't," he said soothingly. "All you have to do is let go of that scrap of cloth and let it drift down here to me. The moment you do, your loved ones' safety is assured. Believe me, squirrel. I give you my word of honor."

Jess wiped her eyes on the decoy cloth and sniffled piteously as she answered. "Well, all right then. If I have your promise that my family will be safe, then you can have this old thing. It means nothing to me."

Jess released the piece of material. It drifted down through the branches. Cluny could scarcely restrain himself from leaping for it. Killconey hurried forward, his eyes shining with reverence. He picked the dishrag up gently, offering it to Cluny.

"Here you are, yer honor, the lovely thing itself, safe and sound."

Avidly Cluny snatched the cloth. His eyes narrowed. Something was wrong. He gave a scream of terrible rage. Instantly his followers scrambled into the bushes as their Chief ripped the tapestry into shreds, his mighty claws rending and tearing as he roared madly: "It's a fake, a copy, worthless trash. Aaaaaarrgh!"

From her perch in the tree, Jess watched with grim satisfaction. "Aye, worthless trash, rat, just as you are. The real tapestry is back at Redwall by now. You've been fooled."

"Kill her! Kill the dirty little swindler!" Cluny's cry rang out. But before a spear or a missile could be thrown, Jess had gone. She darted from tree to tree with artistic speed. Far above Mossflower ground in the upmost terraces of foliage, the champion squirrel turned her flight in the direction of Redwall Abbey.

Sometime around early evening Jess arrived back, springing lightly from a high elm branch to the parapet of the Abbey wall. She could tell by the sound of happy chattering and general jubilation that once more the picture of Martin was safely back.

Bounding down into the grounds she was surrounded by cheering friends, not the least of whom was Mr. Squirrel, who smothered her with kisses, while their son, Silent Sam, sat upon her shoulder and dampened her head by patting it lovingly with a well-sucked paw.

The woodlanders carried Jess shoulder-high into the dining hall, where sat another celebrated hero, Basil Stag Hare. He looked up momentarily at his comrade from behind a staggering mountain of scrumptious food, and pointed to his leg, which was swathed in a hugely exaggerated bandage.

"War wound," Basil muttered as he demolished a plateful of quince and elderberry pie. "Got to keep the old strength up, y'know. Lashings of nourishment; only way to heal an honorable injury. Feed it, what, what!"

Silent Sam hopped upon the table. He showed Basil a tiny scratch on his unsucked paw. The kindly hare inspected it gravely. "Egad, looks like another serious war wound! Better sit here by me, little warrior. Feed it well, that's the ticket."

They both tucked in voraciously. Friar Hugo came waddling up, his face a picture of delight.

"Good creatures," he chuckled. "The late rose is starting to flourish anew. Eat to your heart's content."

Jess placed her paws on the fat mouse's shoulders. The squirrel's face was a mixture of sadness and concern.

"Friar Hugo, old friend, brace yourself. I am the bearer of tragic news!"

Alarm spread across Hugo's pudgy features. "Tell me, Jess. What dreadful thing has happened?"

Jess spoke haltingly in a broken voice. "I fear that Cluny tore up one of your oldest and most venerable dishrags. Alas, Redwall will never see it wipe another plate!"

Behind the Friar's back Basil and Sam almost choked with laughter in the middle of an apple cream pudding.

Shafts of evening sunlight flooded Great Hall as old Methuselah worked painstakingly away with needle and thread. He was sewing Martin the Warrior back in his former position on the corner of the magnificent Redwall tapestry.

CHAPTER
18

Matthias huddled deep into Dunwing's nest. He shuddered comfortably, wriggling to get further into the dried moss, down-feather and soft grass. During the night a wind had sprung up. He peeped over the rim of the nest. It was a grey day of the kind often found at the too-brilliant start of early summer. Clouds scudded nose to tail across the sky, though it was not raining and the wind was quite warm. Nevertheless, the eaves and the roof cracks magnified the sighing and moaning of the vagrant wind, driving the young mouse back to snuggle up once more as he had often done in his own bed in the dormitory. Matthias thought of the neat cozy little bed and a wave of home-sickness swept over him. Would he ever sleep in it again?

A busy flutter of wings announced the mother sparrow's arrival.

"Matthias mousa sleepyhead! Get up! Things to be done this day."

Matthias stretched, yawned and scratched under the collar.

"Good morning, Dunwing," he said politely. "What things are to be done today?"

The sparrow settled herself. She looked gravely at the young mouse. "Today Matthias escape Sparra court. Me make plan, King not right to keep mouse prisoner."

Matthias was suddenly wide awake. The sparrow had his undivided attention. "A plan? What sort of plan? Oh, please tell me, Dunwing!"

The mother sparrow explained. "First, no can go back through loft door. King much angry, have many great slate pile on door. Stop intruders. Door not open again, me think."

Matthias whistled. "Well, the crafty old sparrow! But how am I going to get back down? Do you think you could fly me down in some way? You are bigger than Warbeak—"

Dunwing immediately squashed the idea. "Matthias talk crazy. Even Warbeak and Dunwing together not able to do that. Sparra very light, maybe strong beak, claws, but wings small, not like great birds, fall like stone carrying mouse. Huh, sometimes even worm too heavy, carry in bits, two, three journeys."

Matthias began to apologize for his ignorance, but the mother sparrow cut him short. "Dunwing think plan; pay 'tention now. Me send Warbeak to tell old gatemouse, how you call? 'Athuselah? Good. My eggchick she tell old mouse to getta big red squirrel; bring plenty climbrope; when she see you on roof she climb up, help Matthias mouse down."

"Why, of course!" cried Matthias. "What a splendid idea! I wouldn't be a bit afraid with Jess there to help me down. But what about the King and his warriors? If they see me, I won't stand a chance."

Dunwing waved impatiently. "That next part of plan. Pretty soon Warbeak come back. She tell what time squirrel meet you, good. Then Dunwing whisper big lie fib to other Sparra. It soon spread."

Matthias was puzzled. "Spreading lies; what good will that do?"

Dunwing preened her feathers, smiling craftily. "Great fibba lie. Me whisper bit here, there, about giant Poisonteeth. Say him lying hurt down in Mossflower trees, look to die, Poisonteeth have sword witha, you see."

Matthias gazed in admiration at Warbeak's mother. "Well, I never! You are going to spread a rumor that the snake has the sword and is dying down in the woods. Amazing, I can picture it now. Bull Sparra will go chasing straight down there with his warriors. Meanwhile I will escape out on to the roof. Correct?"

Dunwing nodded. "Matthias steal belt, sword case, quickfast. Climb down off roof with red squirrel."

The young mouse could not meet the mother sparrow's eyes.

He was overcome with guilt and shame. "Dunwing, I'm sorry. How did you guess?"

The sparrow placed a claw upon his paw. "Me know alla time. Matthias mouse not come to bring my eggchick safehome. Come for sword. Not get sword. Alla same, belt case belong mice. You must take away. These things trouble for Sparra. Husband dead because of sword."

Dunwing clasped Matthias's paw warmly. "Dunwing like mouse. You good friend to my Warbeak. Me think she dead 'til you bring back. Me help you steal case, belt."

Matthias was lost for words. He laid his head against the mother sparrow's soft feathers, brushing a tear from his cheek.

Warbeak came fluttering and bustling in. "Wind much strongblow. Old mouse say he tell squirreljess, you be out on roof when Josabell ring lunchworm. Squirreljess meet there with climbrope."

Matthias scarcely tasted the food that Warbeak had brought back. His mind was focused on the plan. It was extremely hazardous. There would be great danger, not only for himself but also for his Sparra friends.

Supposing Bull Sparra took the belt and sword case with him?

What if the King left them behind but hid them in a new place?

Would Jess be able to catch sight of him?

If he did not make it out on to the roof, what then?

There were so many things that could go wrong. What would Martin the Warrior have done in a situation like this? Matthias decided that Martin would have put on a brave face and trusted to a warrior's luck. And that was precisely what he was going to do.

Dunwing left the nest an hour before the Joseph Bell tolled lunchtime: she had to start spreading the tale of the snake. Rumors were often circulated among the Sparra folk. All it took was a few chosen whispers in the right places. Pretty soon the Court of King Bull Sparra would be in uproar. Later when it all turned out to be nothing, nobody would remember who started spreading the rumor—it had always been the same with the Sparra.

* * *

Matthias passed a miserable few minutes in the nest with Warbeak. When the false news broke, the young sparrow would have to fly along with King Bull and the other Sparra warriors. The two friends might never see each other again.

However, there was little time for emotional farewells. Outside the nest pandemonium was sweeping the Sparra Court.

Dunwing had performed her task well. A loud drumming like the beating of many wings against the wooden floor filled the air.

"King call alla warrior," Warbeak murmured. "Gotta go now. Me meet Matthias mouse again one day."

Warbeak undid the collar. It fell from Matthias's neck. "Mousefriend set me free. Now me set you free. Warbeak go now, Matthias. Good wormhunt."

They shook paw to claw. The young mouse said his farewell in the Sparra language: "Matthias look for Warbeak. See someday. You go now. Be brave eggchick. Mighty Sparra warrior. Great friend."

A swift rush of wings and Warbeak was gone.

Matthias kept his head well down inside the nest. He listened as the flapping of wings and chirping of sparrows grew less and less. Finally there was silence. Dunwing popped her head over the rim of the nest.

"Matthias come quick, not lose time!"

Together they hurried through the deserted Sparra court. Dunwing knew there were mothers in every nest with small chicks. These birds remained quietly out of sight when there were no warriors about to defend them. Matthias and Dunwing pushed hastily past the scrap of sacking that served as a door to the King's chamber and began their search.

The scabbard had gone from the back of the chair.

"Oh, I just knew it!" Matthias cried. "That sly old Bull Sparra has taken them with him."

Dunwing shook her head. "No, me see King go. He not take belt or case. Search hard, we must find plenty quick."

The chamber was so sparsely furnished that it required very little searching. Dunwing fluttered about but Matthias became discouraged.

"Oh, what's the use?" he cried. "It's gone, all gone! There's only bits of half-finished food, old slates, butterfly wings, and this stupid old chair."

In his frustration, Matthias gave the sagging armchair a hefty shove. One of the legs collapsed and it fell backwards, revealing crossed lattice strips of hessian on its underside.

Dunwing hopped on the upturned chair, twittering with elation. "Look see! Look see! King hide stuff under old wormchair!"

Through the crossed latticework Matthias could see the shine of black leather and silver. Hastily they ripped and tore with beak, claw and paw. Dust and aged stuffing flew everywhere. Matthias triumphantly pulled the scabbard and sword belt free of the wreckage.

There it was, supple shining black leather, chased and trimmed with the purest silver. The scabbard fitted perfectly into the well-made holder on the belt. This was truly the equipment which had belonged personally to Martin the Warrior of Redwall Abbey!

"No time for mousedream! You hurry, quick!"

Matthias paid full heed to Dunwing's plea. Sweeping the belt and scabbard up, he slung them across his shoulder.

"I'm with you, Dunwing! What next?"

The usual way for sparrows to leave the Court was to fly out from under the eaves. Not being a sparrow, Matthias felt his stomach turn a cartwheel at the prospect of what he must do next. He would have to go on his back under the eaves and, with nothing beneath him but a heart-stopping void of space, negotiate his way out and around the curving gutter to reach the steep upward sweep of the roof.

The first mistake he made was to peep over the edge of the eaves. Far, far, below, the Abbey grounds looked like a spread-out pocket handkerchief, the great wall representing its border. With the blustery howling wind pinning flat his ears, and forcing the breath back down his throat, Matthias giddily covered his eyes with a paw. He felt physically sick at the mere thought of it all.

"It's no good, Dunwing. I'll never be able to do it," he gulped.

The mother sparrow pecked him sharply upon his paw. "Matthias mouse got to do it. You no go you mouseworm. King Bull come back. He killee you. Huh, me thought you warrior."

"So did I until I saw how high this lot is," Matthias wailed.

Dunwing patted him with a reassuring claw. "You go getta climbrope. Bring here. I show how."

The young mouse rushed headlong back to the nest, rummaged in the haversack and found a stout climbing rope.

Dunwing was waiting for him. She tied it firmly around his waist. Matthias tested the knot apprehensively as the sparrow told him what she proposed to do.

"Me fly out on to roof. Hold other end of rope plenty tight. You swing out. No worry, me pullee up."

Grasping the rope in her beak, Dunwing flew out on to the roof and braced herself.

"Matthias come now, me ready," she called.

"Don't think about it," Matthias told himself aloud. "Just do it!" Clinging for dear life to the rope, he launched himself over the edge of the eaves.

Matthias closed his eyes. His heart seemed to stop as he dropped. The rope went taut and he came to a sudden halt. The boisterous wind buffeted him about like a feather. Gritting his teeth, he began pulling himself up, paw over paw, not being able to reach the wall for help as the rope was held outwards by the projecting gutter dangling him out in space.

"Climb good. Dunwing have rope plenty tight hold," the sparrow called out from the roof, her voice muffled by the wind.

Matthias's paws quivered with the strain of hauling up his own body weight. He strove gallantly upwards, reaching the gutter. It took all the young mouse's courage to let go of the rope and grab for the thin curving edge. Nerving himself, he did it in one clean move, clamping his paws heavily into the weatherworn sandstone groove. Under the unexpected weight it crumbled and broke!

Matthias plunged downwards, his feet where his head had been a second before. A chunk of stone hurtled past him on its flight to earth. The rope went taut with a jolt that drove the breath from him. Matthias dangled on the rope's end for a moment, then he started to slip slowly down.

Above him on the roof, Dunwing had lost her footing. The sparrow's claws screeched and grated on the roofing slates as the weighted rope pulled her downwards on the steep slope. Dunwing leaned back, trying to dig her claws in somewhere to check the inexorable slide. The broken gutter edge loomed up, surprisingly bringing with it a desperate chance. With lightning speed, Dunwing tugged hard on the rope, gaining a little slack. Giving a skillful flick, she jammed the rope in the niche of the broken stone edge. It slipped for a moment, then held. Flying out, Dunwing took a few extra turns upon the rope, locking it firmly off on the projecting edge. Letting go of her end, the sparrow flew down underneath Matthias. She started pushing him upwards.

Matthias climbed as he had never done before. Aided by Dunwing, he made it. Two things happened at once. He grabbed for the gutter just as the sharp newly-broken stone sawed through the rope.

Snap! Grab!

As the rope parted, Matthias clung to the gutter. With Dunwing pushing as she flew upwards, he scrambled over the edge of the gutter and rolled inwards to safety.

Dunwing joined him. They both lay completely exhausted as the wind howled around them, stunned by the danger they had come through.

The mother sparrow was first to recover. She drove her mouse friend relentlessly to his feet. "Matthias, come hurry! We waste time."

The climb of the sloping roof was extremely treacherous. Slightly unhinged by the perilous events, Matthias giggled to his friend, "It's all in the average day's work of a warrior. No use of a warrior worrying, ha ha ha."

Taking into account loose slates, buffeting wind and the occasional slide backwards, Matthias reckoned he had done pretty well as he gained the roof ridge. He straddled it with both feet, gazing straight ahead at the north point of the weather vane.

Dunwing fluttered above him. She saw the look of achievement upon his face and ruffled his ears with her claws. "Matthias mouse, me gotta go now, no can help anymore. Take care. Good wormhunt."

Dunwing flew off to her nest back at the court of King Bull Sparra. Matthias pressed forwards along the roof ridge.

He would never forget Dunwing and her eggchick Warbeak. Friends in need are friends indeed.

* * *

Bracing himself against the weather vane, Matthias shielded his
eyes and peered down into the Abbey grounds. Starting from
there he began a systematic search upwards. Most of it was too
far below him to make out anything clearly.

The Joseph Bell boomed out the lunch hour.

At first Matthias could not be certain. He slitted his eyes and
looked hard. A small dark blob was definitely making its way
up. He waited with bated breath as it came nearer.

It was Jess Squirrel!

Clinging to the vane with one paw, Matthias jumped up and
down in a frenzy. He waved frantically, shouting at the top of
his voice. "Jess! It's me, Matthias. Hurry. Oh please hurry!"

Jess was trying her best, but from the start she had been hand-
icapped by her big curling bush of a tail. The rude winds swept
it about playfully. She could not stop her own tail from dragging
and pushing her hither and thither.

The champion squirrel climbed gamely onwards. Normally
she would not have attempted the climb under such blowy conditions. She concentrated hard on the ascent. Matthias's voice
had not reached her across the vagrant wind, but someone had
heard the young mouse's shouts: King Bull Sparra!

Having found neither sword nor snake, the King had become
peeved and bad tempered. He issued orders to the search party
that they were to stay on the floor of the woods until they found
something. Meanwhile, he must go back to the Sparra court,
where he said there were important matters to attend to. Bull
Sparra flew away from the woods secretly relieved. On reflection he did not fancy a second meeting with the giant Poisonteeth whether it was alive, dead, or just pretending, as
Poisonteeth often did. Muttering and grumbling to justify himself, the King flew upwards to his court under the roof.

"Jess, up here! Look, I've got the scabbard!"

Bull Sparra's mad bright eyes glanced upwards to the weather
vane. There was the accursed mouseworm, waving and shouting
with the sword case and belt slung about him. He saw it all
now. He had been tricked, duped!

Maddened by his own berserk rage, Bull Sparra flew straight
upwards. When he was high above the young mouse, he
dropped like a stone, right on target.

Matthias screamed aloud in agonized terror as the King's beak buried itself into his shoulder. Instinctively he lashed out with his free paw and struck Bull Sparra in the eye. The furious claws almost lifted Matthias from the weather vane as the King gripped the belt, trying to drag it off him. Letting go of the vane, Matthias battered at Bull Sparra's head with both paws. He felt his feet leave the roof as the maddened sparrow heaved away at the belt, causing the scabbard to become disarranged. It flapped down across the young mouse's face.

In a fighting fury, Matthias grabbed the scabbard. He used it like a sword, smashing it mercilessly once, twice, thrice, into the Sparra King's face. The force of the blows from the weighty sword case knocked Bull Sparra senseless. He toppled from the roof out into space. Matthias screamed in panic. The King's claws were still caught fast in the sword belt.

Below, Jess Squirrel clamped a paw across her mouth in horror. She heard the scream and saw Matthias and Bull Sparra topple from the roof, locked together by the sword belt. They fell outwards into space from the topmost point of the Abbey roof.

CHAPTER

19

Chickenhound was having one of his sniggering fits, even attempting to dance a little jig. He had been left to his own devices.

The old fool of an Abbot and his stupid devoted band of creatures were all outside, shoring up gatehouses, drilling, fetching, carrying and generally being good and useful.

What a crowd of ninnies!

With a sack upon his back the wily fox roamed from room to room. The Abbey was his oyster.

"Hmm, this is a nice green glass vase."

"Why hello, what a lovely little silver plate."

"My, my, fancy leaving a beautiful gold chain like you all on your own."

"There now, I'll just pop you all into my sack. Don't worry, Uncle Chickenhound will take care of you!"

Sniggering delightedly, the fox trotted along the corridor into the next room. More and more small valuables and family keepsakes belonging to the mice and their woodland guests vanished into the thief's sack. He sniggered uncontrollably. Imagine all the hard work and fighting that Cluny was going to do, just to get at all this, and here was he having first choice.

He was Chickenhound, master burglar. He had outlived Sela, outwitted Cluny, and pulled the wool over the eyes of an abbeyful of mice. One day they would speak his name as the

Foxprince of Thieves! Chickenhound paused to admire a handsome pair of brass nutcrackers. Oh yes, very elegant indeed! Into the sack they went. He trotted down the stairs into Cavern Hole. The tables had been laid for afternoon tea. Stuffing and gorging, he moved from place to place, choosing only the tastiest morsels. On his tour of the dining hall he collected a good quantity of cutlery and some fine antique cruets. Anything that did not suit the young fox's taste was smashed or vandalized. Milk was spilt upon the floor and bread trampled into it. Candles were broken and vegetables squashed across the walls.

Chickenhound shouldered his sack and turned his attentions to the kitchen. He booted the door open and walked straight in, slap bang into Friar Hugo. The fat old mouse was bowled completely over.

The unexpected fright sent Chickenhound dashing back through Cavern Hole with the outraged Friar's shouts ringing in his ears.

"Stop, thief! Stop the fox!"

Chickenhound bounded up the stairs into Great Hall. Behind him the Friar, having regained his feet, puffed along raising the hue and cry.

"Stop, thief! Come back here, you villain!"

With great love and care, Methuselah was putting the final touches to his repair of the tapestry. Only a very sharp-eyed observer would be able to tell that it had once been torn. The warning shouts caused him to stop what he was doing. He turned to see the fox racing down towards the door with Friar Hugo trailing far behind, shouting for all he was worth.

Methuselah had but to move a few paces and he was blocking the doorway. Bravely he held up a frail paw at the oncoming fox.

"You young blaggard! So this is how you repay our kindness. You are far worse than your wicked mother!"

Chickenhound swung the loaded sack with both paws at the old gatehouse-keeper's head.

"Out of my way, you doddering old fool," he panted.

The heavily-laden sack struck Methuselah a crushing blow. He collapsed instantly on the floor and lay still.

Chickenhound froze momentarily. The sack of loot clattered from his nerveless paws. Friar Hugo halted in his tracks. The fox stared down at the pitiful crumpled figure. He had not meant to hit him so hard.

"Murderer! Oh, you barbarous creature! You have killed Brother Methuselah!"

Friar Hugo's cry galvanized the fox into action. He grabbed the sack and fled from the Abbey.

The fat little Friar fell to his knees, tears coursing openly down his plump face. He cradled the sad, small bundle that had once been the wisest and oldest mouse of Redwall.

Chickenhound sneaked along, keeping close to the Abbey. He slunk swiftly across the grounds to one of the small doors in the massive outer wall. The murderer had to get out into the woods before Hugo regained his senses enough to raise the alarm. Wrestling wildly with the stout bars and bolts, he managed somehow to open the small iron door. Without a backward glance the fox bolted off into the Mossflower woodland. As he ran the Joseph Bell began tolling out the alarm.

Chickenhound's confidence grew as he raced through the woods. He sniggered. Daft old fool! Served him right, he should have got out of the way. Hadn't he realized that he was facing Chickenhound, the overlord of all criminals?

Pressing deeper into Mossflower, he paused and listened upon the wind for sounds of pursuit. Faintly he could distinguish certain noises. Whoever it was seemed to be traveling at a breakneck pace with little regard to obstructing bush or foliage. The sound of snapping branches and undergrowth being trampled grew nearer. The fox's finely-attuned sense of smell told him that there were two creatures on his trail. One of them was a hedgehog, but the other? Chickenhound's legs began to tremble. His heartbeats echoed in his ears. There was only one creature in all the wood with that heavy unmistakable scent . . . Constance the badger!

Instinctively, the terrified fox looked wildly about for a place to hide. Running was out of the question in his present state of panic. It was as if some dark force had heard his silent plea. Not ten yards from where he stood was the ideal refuge, a hollow in the base of a dead oak. There was a space between two thick roots, partially covered by ferns. Chickenhound slung the sack down the hole and dived in after it.

To his surprise he found it quite large and dry, with a thick carpet of dead grass and leaves. It was dismally dark, but still, it was the best place at a moment's notice. He would be quite invisible and safe from detection. Let them try and find him now!

With Ambrose Spike trailing in her wake, Constance crashed through the woods. So great was the badger's anger and grief that she was oblivious to any notion of stalking or tracking. She barged along straight through anything that stood in her way, the heavy striped face a mask of cold fury. The hedgehog stayed behind Constance. Those huge blunt paws were ready to tear some creature into dollrags. No power on earth would save the murderous fox if Constance caught him. But the badger's retribution was not to be.

Quaking with fear, Chickenhound held his breath as the woodland juggernaut thundered by within a couple of yards of the hideout. He listened hopefully as the path of destruction trailed off into the distance of Mossflower. Once more the woods grew quiet.

Chickenhound finally exhaled a long sigh of relief.

Once again the newly self-titled overlord of crime had outsmarted a couple of mere animals.

Who on earth did they think they were?

When word got around of his daring exploits other creatures would come to him, foxes perhaps. Yes, he could see it all, Chickenhound at the head of a band of robber foxes, plundering and thieving wherever the whim took him. Of course he would change his name to a title more fitted to his position: Redflash, or Nightfang, or maybe Mousedeath. Yes, he liked the sound of that, Mousedeath! His band of minions would admire him, telling each other tales of his astonishing deeds, convinced that the mysterious Mousedeath had always been an infamous thief, unaware of his humble beginnings as Chickenhound, son of Old Sela.

As he crouched in the darkness the young fox decided that the coast was now clear. He could venture out again. Reaching behind, he felt for the sack that contained his first solo haul. Before he left he wanted to fondle his treasures once more, to reassure himself that they were an auspicious start to his new

venture. In the gloomy hideout his paw reached out and felt
something.

It was not the sack of loot.

"Asmodeusssssssssss!"

That evening the Joseph Bell rang out a message of sadness and
grief to Redwall Abbey.

Mice and woodlanders sat about on the stone floor of Great
Hall, each creature with its own sorrowful thoughts.

Two Redwall mice dead upon the same day.

Jess Squirrel sat with her head between her paws. Mr. Squirrel
had taken the inconsolable Silent Sam off to bed. Jess had explained fully to the Abbot and the Council how she had witnessed Matthias's fall from the roof with the sparrow. Instead
of falling straight down, both creatures had been swept out of
Jess's line of vision by huge gusts of wind. Where Matthias's
body lay now nobody knew.

As soon as her feet touched ground the squirrel had gone
about organizing search parties. They had scoured the area until
the light became too bad to continue, returning after fruitless
hours spent searching Redwall grounds and Mossflower Wood.

The compassionate Father Abbot consoled the sad squirrel:
"Jess, it's no fault of yours. There was not a thing that you
could have done, my friend. The fall was so great that no creature could have survived it. Tomorrow we will search again,
then we must bury my old companion Methuselah. Poor mouse,
he never did anything to deserve such a cruel fate."

The Abbot pointed to the tapestry, shaking his head. "See,
my old gatehouse-keeper's last good work. He restored Martin
to his place of honor. Methuselah was the gentlest mouse I ever
knew. Oh what a tragic waste of two lives: one who spent his
years in search of knowledge, the other cut down before his tree
of youth had chance to blossom!"

Cornflower spoke up. She was dry-eyed and pale, her paws
tightly clenched. "Father Abbot, the loss of Matthias's life was
not a waste. It was a tremendous act of bravery and self-
sacrifice. He died trying to aid Redwall and all of us in the
struggle against the forces of evil, as did his friend Methuselah.
I am sure that this is the way they would wish to be remembered
in our hearts, as warriors and heroes."

There was an instant murmur of approval from all present. Overcome by the sad events, the defenders left the hall, some to do guard duty, others to their beds.

Constance remained sitting upon the floor, her face expressionless, the mighty paws clenching and unclenching. Brother Alf rose and stretched.

"You'd best get some sleep, Constance."

The badger stood up wearily and rubbed her eyes.

"No thank you, Brother. I couldn't sleep a wink at a time like this. You know how it is."

Brother Alf sighed deeply. He knew, having watched Matthias since the first day he arrived at the Abbey gates, a woodland orphan, always polite, willing and cheerful. But now . . .

"Come with me then," said Alf. "I've got work to do. There's all the fishing nets to be laid for the night. Perhaps you'd like to come along and help me?"

Glad of the chance to do something, the badger agreed. She and Alf strode off, talking of old times.

"D'you remember that big grayling that you and Matthias caught?" Constance said.

Brother Alf chuckled. "Do I! Matthias wouldn't be satisfied until that fish was landed on the bank. I was all for giving up, but not him."

Constance nodded admiringly. "Aye, that fish fed the whole Abbey! I remember, because I had three helpings, two less than that spiky wastebin Ambrose."

Strolling leisurely around the bank of the Abbey pond, the two companions gathered up the nets preparatory to spreading them upon the water. Brother Alf went farther along the bank, looking for floats. Constance was about to sit down at the water's edge when she heard Alf calling, "Constance, look! Down here! There's a sparrow!"

The badger ran and joined the mouse, looking to where he pointed. Sure enough, half in and half out of the water was the body of King Bull Sparra. With a great splash Constance waded into the shallows and dragged the corpse up on to the mossy bank.

"It looks as if he's been drowned, Brother. Quick, get some help and bring lanterns. Hurry!"

The badger thrashed about in the water. Why, oh why, hadn't

the search party thought of looking in the Abbey pond?

Help arrived swiftly.

"Out of the way, Constance! The rest of you keep those lanterns high." With hardly a ripple, Winifred and three of her otters slid into the water. As she swam Winifred issued orders. "Spread out and dive deep. We'll quarter the pond between us. I'll take the south corner."

Tense moments ticked by. A crowd of creatures lined the banks. All that could be seen was the still, dark water, broken at intervals as the sleek form of an otter surfaced and dived again.

A cry went up as Winifred appeared, towing a still shape. Willing paws dragged the otter's burden up on to the bank.

Shaking herself like a dog, Winifred panted, "Look what I found half-sunk in the water over there. It's a good job the rushes held him up."

Creatures crowded around, all asking the same questions.

"Is it Matthias?"

"Is he dead or alive?"

Constance pushed her way through to the limp sodden figure. The Abbot and Cornflower were close behind her.

Abbot Mortimer appealed to the onlookers, "Give us room there! If you really want to help, then stand back, please. Someone give Cornflower a lantern. Good mouse, hold it up."

Obediently the crowd fell back. More lanterns were brought forward. The Abbot worked feverishly, resuscitating, levering and pounding the prone form of Matthias.

Cornflower voiced the question that was on the mind of every creature there. "Oh Father Abbot! Is he alive? He doesn't seem to be moving."

The otter clamped a damp paw about her shoulders. "Hush now, the Abbot is doing everything in his power. We will know soon enough."

Brother Alf pushed through, carrying something. "Winifred, one of your otters has just come up with this sword belt and scabbard. He found them near where Matthias was."

"Bring them forward," said Constance. "They may be of some help if Matthias opens his eyes. You never know."

The Abbot beckoned urgently. "Cornflower, give me that lantern, child. Quickly!"

Holding the lantern-glass close to Matthias's nose and mouth, the Abbot was rewarded by the sight of the faint mist that appeared on it. "He lives! Cornflower, Matthias is alive! Bring blankets, get a stretcher, we must get him inside the Abbey. . . ."

Without a word to anyone, Constance lifted Matthias gently as if he weighed no more than a feather. Carefully the big badger clasped the young mouse close into the warmth of her rough coat. The crowd formed an aisle either side of her as she strode swiftly to the Abbey. Lanterns bobbed about in the darkness like fireflies as the great Joseph Bell tolled out a message of joy and hope to Mossflower.

CHAPTER

20

The new day dawned in a haze of soft sunlight. It crept across the countryside suddenly to expand and burst forth over all the peaceful woods and meadowland. Blue-gold tinged with pink, each dewdrop turned into a scintillating jewel, spiders' webs became glittering filigree, birdsong rang out as if there had never been a day as fresh and beautiful as this one.

The extravaganza of nature's glory was completely lost upon Cluny the Scourge. His one good eye squinted upwards through the smoke of the morning campfires.

"Huh, it's going to be as hot as the hell's furnace, but at least it won't rain," he muttered aloud to himself.

Under the impatient eye of the Warlord, Cluny's horde gulped down a hasty meal and scurried about picking up weapons. Suitably geared for battle, they quickly fell into ranks.

Cluny's personal armorer put the final touches to his Chief's war apparel. With the tip of the standard Cluny signaled his captains. Darkclaw, Frogblood, Fangburn, Cheesethief, Scumnose and Mangefur scrambled into their positions.

As yet Cluny had not chosen a new second-in-command, though he had let it be known that any of his followers who distinguished himself in the coming battle would receive immediate promotion in the field. Killconey the ferret stood alongside his Chief with a drum that he had made from an old water butt. He had unofficially appointed himself drummer-cum-soothsayer. The ferret watched Cluny intently. The Chief was going to speak. He banged the drum, calling the horde to silence. Cluny lifted the visor of his war helmet and stared out across the waiting horde.

"This time there will be no mistakes!" he yelled. "And there will be no retreat! We stay, even if it means putting Redwall to siege. We stand firm! Anyone who takes one backward step is dead. Anyone who disobeys orders is dead. Anyone who does not fight tooth and claw with all of his might is also dead.

"That is my promise, and Cluny always keeps his word. Hear me! All we face is a lot of peaceful mice and some local wood-land creatures. Defeat them and I will give you rewards you never dreamed of. The enemy are not trained fighters like we are, not natural killers. There is not one among them who can lead as I lead you."

At the center of the front rank stood a rat who had been wounded in the first encounter at the Abbey. He whispered out of the corner of his mouth to his comrade-in-arms alongside him, "Huh, leads us, my foot! Last time we attacked he stood well out of the way, back in some meadow."

The sharp ears of Cluny had caught what the unfortunate soldier had said. The Warlord leaped down from his rostrum and seized the trembling miscreant, booting him forward into plain view of the army.

"See this traitor?" Cluny shouted. "Here's a rat who doesn't think I lead my horde. Cluny the Scourge sees and hears all. Watch now, and let this be a lesson to anyone that dares doubt me."

The wretched rat soldier lay shaking on the churchyard path. A hush fell across the entire horde. He stared beseechingly into the merciless eye of Cluny.

"Oh please, Chief, it was only a joke, I didn't mean to—"
Crack!
The powerful tail whipped expertly out, slashing across the rat's face with its poisoned metal war barb. The army looked on in horror as the stricken victim shuddered and lay dead at Cluny's feet. Ignoring the slain soldier, Cluny the Scourge pushed his way roughly through the horde until he reached the cemetery gates. It was going to be a long march to Redwall,

burdened as they were with the battering ram and all the para-
phernalia of destruction. They would have to camp overnight
by the roadside, and the great attack upon Redwall would take
place early the next day. There was to be no secrecy. For maximum effect the army must be seen marching boldly up to the
very gates of the Abbey in full array.

Cluny shook his standard. As the ferret's drum thundered out
he roared madly, "On to Redwall! Smash the gates! Kill, kill!"

The shimmering heat waves from the road reverberated to the
shouts of the horde: "Cluny, Cluny, kill, kill, kill!"

CHAPTER

21

In his fevered dreams the young mouse wandered through dark caverns. Somewhere a voice was calling out to him.

"Matthias, Matthias."

It sounded vaguely familiar, but he had other things to do than identify the voice. He must find the sword. In the stygian gloom he saw the late rose. It was bathed in a pale blue light. What was it doing here in this dark netherworld?

Matthias saw that all the tiny thorns on the rose stems resembled small swords. He felt he should speak to the rose.

"Please tell me, late rose, where will I find the sword?"

The topmost rose quivered. He watched it blossom before his eyes. At the center of the blooming petals was the face of Methuselah. "Matthias, my friend, I can help you no more. Seek out the aid of Martin. I must go now."

The face of the old gatehouse-keeper faded. Slowly, his feet hardly touching the floor, Matthias traveled a long corridor. At its end were two figures. He halted by the first figure, unable to distinguish who it was, but feeling an aura of friendly kinship emanating from it. Matthias looked to the second figure. Here was something he had never before encountered. It had neither arms nor legs. With a hissing sound the spectral thing opened wide its mouth. Inside there were two sharp fangs and a flickering tongue which quivered and turned into a sword. With a cry of joy the young mouse started running forward, only to be restrained by the phantom figure of the first apparition. Matthias was not surprised to see that it was Martin the Warrior.

"Martin, why do you stop me from getting the sword?" he asked.

Martin's voice was warm and friendly. "Matthias, I am that is. Stay! Beware of Asmodeus."

Martin took hold of Matthias's shoulder. The young mouse tried to wrench himself free.

"Let me go, Martin! I fear no creature that lives."

Martin tightened his hold relentlessly upon Matthias's shoulder. Pain shot through him like a red-hot lance. Martin cried out, "Hold him still now, hold him still!"

The agony increased. Matthias's eyes snapped open.

"Hold him still now, hold him still!"

It was the Father Abbot. He was saying the same words as Martin had said. Brother Alf held tight to Matthias's shoulder as the Abbot dug deep with a probe. He extracted a dark pointed object which he tossed into a bowl that Cornflower was holding.

"Ouch! That hurt, Father," Matthias said weakly.

The Abbot wiped his paws upon a clean cloth.

"Well, my son, you are back with us at last," he said. "That must have hurt. There was half of a sparrow's beak lodged in your shoulder."

Matthias blinked and looked about. "Hello, Cornflower. You see, I got back in one piece. Oh hello, Brother Alf. I say, is that Basil in the next bed?"

"Hush now, Matthias, and lie still," Cornflower chided him. "You're lucky to be alive. It was touch and go right through the night."

Abbot Mortimer pointed at the first rays of sun streaming in through the window. "Yes, but you are back now; and see, you've brought with you a magnificent June summer morning."

The young mouse lay back upon the crisp white pillows. Aside from a bursting headache and the pain in his shoulder it felt good to be alive.

"But what's Basil doing asleep in the next bed?" he persisted.

"Oh him," Cornflower chuckled. "He says that he has an honorable war wound that requires a lot of food and rest, the old rogue."

"That may be," replied the Abbot. "But it would be churlish

to begrudge Basil's requests. After all, he did recapture our tapestry from Cluny. It was a very daring deed.''

Matthias was delighted. ''Martin's tapestry, back here at the Abbey? How marvelous! I'll bet old Methuselah is over the moon to have it back once more.''

There was a moment's silence. The Abbot turned to Brother Alf and Cornflower. ''Please, would you leave us alone for now? I have something to tell Matthias. You may visit him tomorrow. He still needs a lot of rest.''

The two mice nodded understandingly and left.

Half an hour later, after unfolding the sad tale of Methuselah, the Abbot also took his leave.

Matthias turned his face to the wall, bereft of any tears or lamentation after the stresses of the experience he had recently come through. The death of his old and valued friend left a feeling like a large leaden lump inside his chest. He curled up and tried to hide within himself.

How long he lay there, racked by grief and misery, he had no way of knowing. But one morning, Basil Stag Hare awakened and called across, ''What ho! Well, bless me medals, if it ain't young Matthias! How are you, laddie buck?''

Matthias replied in a small sad voice, ''Please, Basil, leave me alone. I've lost Methuselah. I don't want to speak to anyone.''

Basil hopped nimbly across and perched on Matthias's bed. ''There, there, young feller m'lad. Don't you think I know how you feel? Good grief, an old campaigner like me? When I think of the chums I lost in bygone battles . . . Good and true friends they were, but I taught meself to keep a stiff upper whisker, y'know.''

Matthias remained with his back turned upon the hare.

''But you don't understand, Basil.''

The soldierly hare snorted. He grabbed Matthias and turned him over so they were face to face.

''Don't understand? I'll tell you what I don't understand, young chip. I don't understand how a chappie like yourself who is supposed to be a great warrior can lie there moping any longer. You're like an old lady otter who's just lost a fish. If old Methuselah were here now, he'd chuck a jug of water over you and turf you right out of that bed on your fat little head!''

Matthias sat up and sniffed.

"D'you think so, Basil?"

The hare slapped his "injured" leg, winced, then laughed aloud. "Think so? I know so! Do you imagine that old mouse sacrificed his life so that you could lie about feeling sorry for yourself? Huh, he'd have told you himself. That's not the way of a warrior. Get up, sir, stir yourself, make Methuselah proud of you!"

Matthias's eyes gleamed with a new determination.

"By golly, you're right, Basil! That's exactly what my old friend would have wanted! I'm sorry. You must think I've behaved like a dreadful young fool."

The hare's ears flopped comically as he shook his head.

"Not at all, m'dear feller; think nothing of it. I must confess that I was a bit like you when I was a leveret, y'know. Now, what d'you say we get about the business of living properly again? I say, I'm positively famished. What about you?"

Matthias could not help laughing at the irrepressible hare.

"Well, I am a bit hungry, now you come to mention it."

"Capital," cried Basil. "I could eat a stag, antlers and all. I say, they do a wonderful nosebag for us wounded heroes, y'know. Just watch this, m'lad."

The hare tinkled a small brass bell on the bedside table. Within seconds Friar Hugo and Cornflower appeared.

"Ah yes, the catering staff," said Basil. "Er, harrumph! The other injured warrior here and myself would be greatly obliged for a little sustenance. Nothing too grand, y'know; just something for our poor wounded teeth to nibble on. Got to keep body and fur together, what, what?"

Cornflower was pleased to see Matthias looking so much better. She exchanged winks with him and Friar Hugo. The fat friar bowed in a servile manner as he answered the hare. "Very good, Mr. Stag, sir. Two bowls of gruel coming up."

Matthias and Cornflower struggled not to laugh aloud. Basil exploded. "Gruel! What the devil do you mean by gruel? What sort of slop is that to give renowned warriors, eh? We want to be cured, not killed! Now listen to me, you pair of scullery fusiliers, I want a decent brunch: half a dozen boiled eggs, some crisp summer salad, two loaves of hot bread, two hazelnut cream junkets, two—no, better make it four—oven-baked apple pies, oh, and chuck in some of those medium-sized quince tarts if you see any lying about. Well, don't stand there with your great jaw flapping! Cut along now, quick as y'like."

Cornflower curtsied with mock solemnity. Friar Hugo held up a paw. "You forgot the October nutbrown ale, sir."

Basil thumped the bed. "Good Lord, so I did! Er, just four flagons, thank you, my good mouse."

Cornflower and Friar Hugo exited leaning upon each other, their faces crimson with suppressed laughter.

"Strange creatures," Basil mused. "Blowed if I can see anything funny about a couple of heroes wanting to be fed so that they can stay alive. Takes all kinds to make a world, young feller, other ranks included."

Later, as they made a hearty meal, Matthias set about pumping the hare for information.

"Basil, what's a viper?"

"Hmm, a viper? Well, it's an old poisonteeth snake y'know, an adder. Never had a lot of truck with the slimy fellers meself. You'd do best to stay away from them, old chum."

Matthias continued probing the hare's knowledge. "Are there any adders around the Mossflower region, Basil? I mean, if there were, then you'd be the very creature to know about them, being an expert and all that."

Basil puffed out his narrow chest as he absentmindedly ate one of Matthias's quince tarts. "Adders in Mossflower? Now let me see. No, I don't suppose there are nowadays. There was talk of one a long time back, but I shouldn't think he's around anymore. Filthy reptiles, adders. Nothing like stags, y'know. Now what the devil was that adder chap's name? No, I can't remember it for the life of me."

"Could it be Asmodeus?" Matthias inquired innocently.

Basil Stag Hare dropped a half-eaten apple pie on the bedside table. He was suddenly very serious.

"Asmodeus? Where did you hear that name?"

"A little bird told me," Matthias replied.

Basil retrieved his apple pie. He munched thoughtfully.

"Your sparrows, eh? Savage little creatures. No discipline, of course. Darn good fighters, though. But tell me, what do jolly old sparrows know about Asmodeus?"

"It all has to do with Martin's sword," Matthias explained. "You see, one of their kings stole the sword from the north point of the vane on the Abbey roof. That was many years ago. From there the sword has been passed down through sparrow kings until it came into the claws of the late King Bull Sparra.''

"Not the silly ass who managed to get himself drowned yesterday?" said Basil through a mouthful of hazelnut junket.

"The same one," Matthias replied. "But to cut a long story short, the adder stole the sword from him. That's why I want to know about Asmodeus, you see."

"Play with fire, you'll get yourself burned," warned the hare.

Matthias knew Basil could be manipulated. He was insistent: "Oh please, Basil, you must tell me all you know. It was Methuselah's life-work trying to find that sword. I must continue for his sake."

The hare gnawed thoughtfully on some bread and salad. "Well, if you put it that way, young feller, anything I can do to help I will. You'll need a good guide—"

Matthias interrupted: "I must find the sword by myself, Basil. Just tell me all you know about the adder called Asmodeus."

The hare lay back on his bed. He took a long draught of October ale before answering. "Quite frankly, old chap, I know nothing about the bally snake. I thought the blighter had died years ago."

Matthias groaned aloud, but Basil cut him short. "Mind you, having said that, I think I have a pretty fair idea who *will* know. Listen, if you strike out north-east across Mossflower Wood, you'll find a deserted farmhouse beyond the far edge. Now, the chap you want to see is a whopping great snowy owl that patrols between the fringes of the wood and the old sandstone quarry. His name is Captain Snow. Bear in mind, though, he'll eat you on sight if he gets the chance! Military bird, but a real bounder."

"Then how do I get to talk with him?" asked Matthias abruptly.

"Temper, temper, m'lad," Basil chuckled. Reaching down to his bedside locker he dug out his dress tunic. It was covered in medals and decorations from a hundred campaigns. The hare selected a medal. Detaching it from the jacket, he tossed it across to Matthias.

"Here, catch! That's a medal, doncha know. Captain Snow gave it to me for saving his life."

"You saved the owl's life?" said Matthias.

"I should say I did," Basil laughed at the memory. "Feathery old fool went to sleep in a rotten dead tree. It got blown down in a gale and trapped the blighter underneath. He'd have died if I hadn't come along, dug under the thing and pulled him out. Popped out like a shuttlecock under a door. Fellow officer, you understand. Couldn't leave him there to get flattened. His face is flat enough as it is.''

"So all I do is show him this medal?'' asked the young mouse.

Basil laughed at his friend's naïveté. "Yes, that's all, but if you don't want to be scoffed, make sure he sees the medal before he sees you. Tell the old buffer that Basil Stag Hare sent you. And mind your manners! Make sure you call him by his proper rank, 'Cap'n.' Oh, and I'd like that medal back sometime. Spoils the look of me number-one dress tunic, missing decoration.''

Matthias studied the medal. It was a silver cross embellished with a spread-winged owl. The ribbon was of faded white silk. Though it was old, it shone bright in the sunlight.

"Thank you, Basil,'' he said. "I'll see you get it back. Is there anything else I should know?''

"Not much. Just remember what I've said, old chap. This Captain Snow is a night hunter, by the way. He probably sleeps in some old tree all day with one eye open. You mark my words, laddie, old Snow doesn't miss a thing. He knows all the creatures in his territory, where they live, what trails they use and so on. Ha, they don't call owls wise for nothing. Bit of a duffer all the same, letting a tree fall on him. Keep your eye on him, though. If he catches you napping he'll chomp you up, medal and all.''

Basil finished his ale and yawned. "Now get some sleep, Matthias. I'm fagged out after that snack. My old honorable war wound is beginning to play me up. I must have a bit of a snooze.''

With that Basil closed his eyes. He was soon snoring gently. Matthias realized there was no more to be said, so he decided to have a rest too. Basil Stag Hare: what an amazing old campaigner, the young mouse thought, as he drifted off to sleep.

Shortly after twelve o'clock Matthias awakened. The noontime sunlight flooded the room. Basil was flat on his back snoring stentoriously. Although his shoulder still throbbed, Matthias felt fit and refreshed—well enough to travel. He knew, however, that he must act with stealth and secrecy. If the Abbot or Cornflower or any of his friends knew of his scheme he would have no chance at all. They would make certain he was confined to bed until further notice.

Quietly he arose and dressed himself, hanging his sandals around his neck by their thongs. Taking a clean pillowslip, he stocked it with the remainder of the food from the table. Someone had thoughtfully placed his dagger in the bedside locker. It must have been found on the floor of Great Hall. Searching around, Matthias came upon a good stout pole, probably used as a window or curtain opener. He decided it would come in handy.

Carefully he inched the door open, closing it again swiftly as the Abbot and Brother Alf padded by. Matthias listened to Alf's voice. "I looked in on them about ten minutes ago, Father. They're both sleeping like hibernating squirrels. It's not likely that they'll wake until evening."

The footsteps receded down the passage. Matthias crept from the room, and stole off in the opposite direction.

He was surprised at the ease with which he left the Abbey, slipping off into Mossflower through the side door in the wall, where unknown to him Methuselah's murderer had also passed on the previous day.

Alone in the woods, Matthias felt a bit wobbly upon his legs. He sat down against a beech tree until the feeling passed. Tying the pillowcase bundle to his pole, he hefted it across his good shoulder and struck off boldly through Mossflower towards the north-east.

CHAPTER

22

Matthias judged by the sun that it was past mid-afternoon. He had made steady progress through the woods. Nothing untoward had occurred. He had stopped and had a light snack, gained his second wind and pressed forward, taking care not to create too much noise lest he disturb any predators. The young mouse had discovered a path of sorts, skirting the dense underbrush and avoiding patches of marshland. Always keeping the tree moss on his left, he continued eastwards.

Matthias pinned the medal to his habit, telling himself that he might stumble into Captain Snow's territory at any moment. Lulled by the warm sun, cool shade, and birdsong, he trekked onwards, thinking of nothing in particular and enjoying the sense of freedom amid so much beauty.

Seemingly from out of nowhere a mouse leaped, barring Matthias's path! He halted, sizing the strange mouse up. It was an odd-looking wild thing. Matthias was not even too sure it really was a mouse.

The creature had spiky fur which stuck out at odd angles all over. Around its brow was bound a brightly-colored scarf. The stranger was fully a head shorter than Matthias. It stood defiantly blocking his way, glaring at him with the maddest-looking eyes he had ever encountered.

Matthias smiled politely and addressed the odd mouse, "Hello there! Beautiful afternoon, isn't it?"

"Never mind that nonsense," it replied in a gruff voice. "Who are you? Why are you trespassing on shrew land?"

Matthias paused. So this was what a shrew looked like? He had never seen one before, but he had been told of their bad tempers.

The young mouse decided to fight fire with fire. No point being good mannered with this little hooligan. He snarled in what he hoped was an aggressive manner, "Never mind who I am! Who do you think you are, you little rag-head?"

The shrew seemed uncertain for a moment, then she stormed back in her low gruff voice, "I am Guosim, and you still haven't told me what you want in shrew territory."

"Guosim," echoed Matthias. "What sort of a name is that? And anyhow, if you don't want creatures coming across your land, then you should put signs up. As far as I'm concerned Mossflower has always been free to all."

"Except this part," snapped the shrew. "Don't you know anything? Guosim stands for Guerrilla Union of Shrews in Mossflower."

Matthias laughed scornfully, "I couldn't care less what it stands for! Make way for a Redwall Abbey Warrior. I'm coming through!"

Immediately Matthias took a step forward. Guosim stuck her paws between her lips and emitted a sharp whistle. There was a swift rustle in the undergrowth. Matthias found himself surrounded by at least fifty shrews.

They packed around him, creating an angry hubbub in their deep rough tones. All of them wore colored headbands, all carried short, rapier-like swords. Guosim had difficulty in calling them to order.

"Comrades," she shouted. "Tell this mouse what happens to a trespasser."

The replies that came back were varied.

"Break his paws."

"Skin him alive."

"Chop off his nose."

"Hang him by the tail."

"Stuff his whiskers down his ears."

A stern-looking old shrew barged Guosim out of the way and whistled sharply. He produced a round, black pebble and held it up.

"Any comrade who wants to speak must hold the pebble. Otherwise, shut up!"

Complete silence fell. He handed the pebble to Matthias.

"Now, explain yourself, mouse."

There were one or two murmurs of dissent, that a stranger who was not a shrew should have first say. The old shrew danced with rage. "Will you lot shut up? The mouse has the stone."

Silence fell once more. Matthias cleared his throat. "Er, ahem. Guerrilla Union of Shrews in Mossflower, forgive me: as you see, I am a stranger in these parts. I do not intentionally trespass on your land. Had I known I would have taken a different route. You have probably noticed by my habit that I come from Redwall Abbey. Though I am a warrior, we are a healing and helping order. It is usual for all creatures to allow a Redwall mouse to pass in peace. This is the unwritten law."

The older shrew (whose name was Log-a-Log) took the pebble from Matthias and addressed the others. "Right, comrades. Now we know a bit more about things, let's have a show of paws. All those in favor of letting the mouse go free."

Paws went up: Log-a-Log counted them. Exactly half of those present. He called for those against, and took another count.

"Half one way, half the other. The casting vote is mine. Now let me tell you, I know we take care of our own, but the Redwall mice are a legend in Mossflower. They do no harm to any creature. In fact they do a lot of good." Log-a-Log raised his paw. "Therefore, comrades, I vote that the mouse goes free!"

There followed an equal number of cheers and boos, a squabble ensued and fighting broke out. Guosim snatched the stone from Log-a-Log and waved it about.

"Listen to me," she roared. "I know that Log-a-Log is a wise elder, but I am president of our union, comrades. The mouse hasn't told us where he is going."

There was a brief silence. Another shrew snatched hold of the stone. "Aye, that's right! Where are you off to, mouse?"

The stone was thrust at Matthias.

"I'll tell you," he said. "But my name is not 'mouse.' It's Matthias. Redwall Abbey is in danger from Cluny the Scourge and his horde—"

There was immediate shouting and gruff oaths. Matthias knew the drill; it was surprising how the stone-holder could gain quiet among such a noisy, quarrelsome gathering. Matthias continued, "As I was saying before I was so rudely interrupted, we at Redwall are under attack by Cluny and his horde. Evidently you have heard his name before. Well, I believe that I have the solution to Cluny. It is an ancient sword that once belonged to a great mouse named Martin the Warrior. To find the sword I must ask Captain Snow the whereabouts of Asmodeus."

The shrews made a frenzied rush into the undergrowth; Matthias found he was standing alone. After a few minutes Log-a-Log and Guosim ventured stealthily out again. Forgetting the stone, Guosim spoke in an awed voice, "D'you mean you actually intend to walk right up and speak to Snow?"

Matthias nodded. Log-a-Log continued where his comrade had left off: "You're going to ask the Cap'n where you can find Giant Poisonteeth, mouse? Er, I mean, Matthias. You are either very brave or raving mad."

"A little bit of both, I suppose," said the young mouse. "Do you know much about Captain Snow and Asmodeus?"

Both shrews trembled visibly. Guosim's voice had risen an octave. "Matthias, you must be crazy! Don't you know what you're walking into? Captain Snow . . . why, you'd be just a snack to him. And as for the other one—Giant Ice Eyes—who could even go near him? He eats as many shrews as he wants. No living creature can stop the poisonteeth!"

A heart-rending moan arose from the shrews in the undergrowth.

Matthias still had the stone. He held it up and addressed them boldly. "Guerrilla Shrew comrades, I do not ask you to do my fighting. Merely point me in the direction of Captain Snow. Who knows? If I finally get the sword I may be able to liberate you."

Log-a-Log took the stone. "Matthias of Redwall, you are on our land. We will escort you. The Guerrilla Union of Shrews in Mossflower would never live down the shame of having a stranger fight their battles for them. You may not always see us, but we will be close by. Come now."

Matthias moved north-eastwards with the company of shrews, whose numbers seemed to swell as they went along. At nightfall there were upwards of four hundred members of the Shrew Union seated around the campfire, breaking bread with the warrior from Redwall. That night Matthias slept inside a long hollow log with both ends disguised to make it appear solid.

Like Basil, the shrews were masters of camouflage. Their very survival depended upon it.

Half an hour before dawn the young mouse was roused by a shrew who gave him an acorn cup full of sweet berry juice, a loaf of rough nutbread and some tasty fresh roots that he could not identify. By dawn's first light they were on the move again, marching until mid-morning. Matthias saw the edge of Moss-flower Wood. The tall trees thinned out, bush and undergrowth were sparse. Before them lay an open field of long, lush grass dotted with buttercup and sorrel. In the distance he could see the abandoned farmhouse that Basil had spoken of. All the shrews had disappeared with the exception of Guosim and Log-a-Log. The latter pointed to the barn adjoining the farmhouse.

"You might find Captain Snow in there taking a nap. Now is the best time to approach him, after he has a full stomach from the night hunt."

The two guerrilla shrews melted back into the woods. Alone now, Matthias crossed the sunny field leading to the barn, just as Basil had taught him: zig-zag, crouch, wriggle and weave.

He tiptoed into the barn. There was no sign of an owl. In the semi-darkness Matthias could make out various old farming implements rusted with disuse. On one wall there was a huge stack of musty, dry straw bales. He decided to climb up the bales, in the hope of getting near Captain Snow, who most probably would be sleeping perched in the rafters.

Matthias scaled the packed straw. He stood on top and looked about. Nothing. He ventured forwards, and suddenly slipped and fell down a hidden gap between the bales. Scrambling and clutching, he plunged down to the floor.

Matthias's feet never touched the earth. He landed clean in the gaping mouth of a huge marmalade cat!

CHAPTER

23

Constance stood on the parapet overlooking the road. Dawn was breaking behind her, in the east. However, more important things troubled the badger's mind. The Abbot came bustling up with Basil limping in the rear. Both creatures looked extremely concerned.

"Have you seen Matthias?" the Abbot asked. "He's been missing from his room since yesterday afternoon."

Basil looked rather shamefaced. "All my fault, I'm afraid. Should have kept my eye on the little rascal. We'll have to organize another search party."

"No time for that," snapped the badger. "Look!"

Down the road in the distance, a long column of dust was rising. The three creatures sniffed the faint breeze. It was unmistakable. Cluny's army was coming to Redwall!

"We'll need every available defender," Constance murmured. "No need to cause a panic, but this looks like a full-scale assault. The fox's warning was true."

Jess, Winifred, Foremole and Ambrose were sent for. Together they leaned over the parapet, watching the dust-cloud draw nearer. The beat of a drum was audible, and individual rats could be picked out.

"They're heading right for us," said Jess grimly. "Better get all defenders to battle stations."

At a given signal, John Churchmouse began tolling the attack warning upon the Joseph Bell. All through the Abbey and its grounds creatures stopped what they were doing. Picking up weapons that lay close to paw they assembled at their appointed posts to await further orders.

Cluny waved his standard above the sun-flecked dust rising from the road. Gradually the horde ground to a halt.

Shading his eye against the sun, he stared up at the walls.

"Surrender to Cluny the Scourge," he bellowed harshly.

"Go and boil your head, rat!" came Constance's gruff reply.

Cluny took a pace back, letting his standard dip low. Two score of sling-rats ran forward, whirling their stone-laden weapons. They let fly a volley at the ramparts, shouting bloodcurdling war cries. The stones clattered harmlessly off the wall and fell back to the road.

Cluny cursed inwardly. For all his show of force and arrogance, he had made a strategical error.

The sun was in his army's eyes!

The defenders had the advantage. This soon became clear when a platoon of otters on the ramparts unloosed a rattling fusillade of heavy pebbles. Pandemonium broke out in the vanguard of Cluny's horde, with cries of agony as the pebbles found their marks. One stone actually struck Cluny's helmet.

"Back to the ditch and the meadow! Stay out of their range!" Cluny did his best to keep his voice even. As the army retreated to safety he was the last to go, willing himself to walk slowly as if that were the way he had planned it.

Four rats lay dead near the wall, and Killconey's drum stood unattended in the road. Basil Stag Hare sniffed dryly.

"Not a very well organized initial sortie for the invincible horde. Our chaps took the wind out of their sails, what?"

"Hurr, they do 'ave to wait 'til sun moves round," commented Foremole.

"But we don't," cried Jess. "Bring the archers! Keep the slings going! Let's give that mob in the ditch something to think about."

Out in the safety of the meadow, Killconey attempted to soothe Cluny's ego. "Ah, what a sly ould move of yours, sir, lullin' them into a false sense of security! Make 'em think they're winnin', that's the game.''

Unexpectedly Killconey received his reward for flattery at the wrong time—a thwack over his head from the standard.

"Shut your mouth, ferret," Cluny said sourly. "Get me some sort of a command post rigged up here. Cheesethief, where are the gangs with that battering ram?"

"Coming up right away, Chief," called Cheesethief as he trotted off to find where the ram-carriers had got to.

It was not long before the tiny harvestmouse archers were bending their bows, sending small pointed shafts darting into the ditch. These, supplemented by the stouter arrows of the field-mice and the otter slingers, caused many wounds and great discomfort to the would-be attackers, pinning a good number of them down. Morale was low because Cluny had ordered no retaliation until after midday.

Jess Squirrel rappelled swiftly down to the road on a rope. Looping the rope's end around the old water-butt that had been the ferret's drum, she sprang inside, calling up to the parapet, "Haul away, Constance."

The barrel fairly flew up under the badger's strong paws. Jess was quite pleased with herself. She had plans for the drum to beat the rats! Basil Stag Hare strode the parapet with a swagger-stick tucked beneath his arm. He dodged around the squirrel, who was rolling the barrel along. Retaining the dignity befitting his rank, Basil kept up a constant stream of orders, "Fire at will, you mouse types! Otters, pick out your targets! Any moles here? Report to Foremole down in the grounds right away."

The hare had cast off his leg bandage. Now that he was back in active service the "honorable war wound" was completely forgotten.

Meanwhile, back at the meadow Cluny sat brooding under a makeshift tent. At least the ferret was good for something.

Cheesethief came hurrying up, urging on the contingent of battering-ram carriers. Hoping to find favor with Cluny he had put himself at the head of the party, helping them to carry the cumbersome object.

"Come on, mates," he cried. "Let's knock on the Abbey door!"

Having negotiated the ditch, they charged across the road. Once they had passed a certain point it created a difficult angle for the defenders on the wall to fire at them.

The massive ram shuddered as it smashed against the gatehouse door. With Cheesethief shouting encouragement, the ram-carriers took a short run back and battered the door again.

Cluny was heartened to see things going right for a change. There was more to Cheesethief than he had at first thought.

The door was rammed a third time. Now creatures on the wall stood up in full view as they retaliated by firing down on the ram-carriers. Cluny called up his best slingers and archers, ordering them to pick off the defenders. Fortunately for him, the sun was starting to move southwards, and the otters and mice on the ramparts were clearly visible. Cluny's archers caused numerous casualties, forcing the defenders to drop below the parapet. The battering ram continued, although as yet it had made no lasting impression upon the solid construction.

Missiles from the wall had slackened off, giving Cluny's horde a chance to desert the ditch for the relative safety of the meadows. Cluny appeared well satisfied for the moment. He called Killconey to his side.

"This is more like it, ferret. Right, get the tunnel gangs! Gather your weasels, stoats and ferrets. Take them back along the ditch to the south-east corner of the Abbey wall. When it is dark I'll send you a signal, then you can start tunneling through the ditch wall, across the road and under the Abbey wall. Is that clear?"

Killconey threw an elaborate salute. "Sure, it's clear as the mornin' dew, yer honor!"

Cluny closed his eyes, intent upon keeping his present good mood. "Then get going, and try to get it right this time."

The battle continued sporadically all day and into the evening. The ram-carriers kept up their attack, but somehow the great door withstood them. When the last vestiges of twilight were gone, Constance called the captains together. They squatted beneath the parapet in darkness as the badger outlined the situation.

"Listen, we're all right for the moment, but sooner or later something will have to be done about the battering ram. Has anyone got a good idea? I'm open to sensible suggestions.''

Below them the ram kept up its remorseless battering. Ambrose Spike had reported some minor splintering at the top inside edges of the door, but the shoring of earthworks was holding out. Foremole had assured them that any attempted tunneling would take at least a few days before signs showed. Meanwhile, he and his moles were carefully monitoring the earth in the Abbey grounds.

Throughout the day-long battle, the animals not directly involved in the fighting had been busy too. Father Abbot was tending the wounded in Great Hall, Friar Hugo was constantly sending Cornflower and her helpers back and forth to the ramparts with food and drink. Mrs. Churchmouse and Mrs. Vole were making bandages from old clean sheets. Silent Sam had been left with Tim and Tess, the Churchmouse twins. He had played with the infants until they fell asleep in a heap of bandages.

Sam wanted to go up on the wall, but his parents had forbidden it. Slipping out of Great Hall, he passed the time for a bit, listening with an ear to the ground in the company of the moles. But Sam soon became bored. He stabbed at the earth with his tiny dagger, imagining that rats were popping up from make-believe tunnels. After a while he wandered over to the foot of the wall and sat sharing some food with Jess. The little squirrel signaled to his parent, asking her what she wanted the big barrel for.

Jess Squirrel took her little son upon her knee and explained. She had an idea that the barrel, filled with something or other, could be dropped down upon the ram-carriers. But she was not too sure what it would be best to fill the barrel with.

Sam jumped down from his mother's knee. The barrel was lying on its side. He sprang up on it and walked it about, rolling it very skillfully under his feet. All the time he was sucking hard on his paw, trying to think how he could help.

The tunnel gangs lounged about, leaning on the sides of the ditch. Killconey stretched full length on a mossy patch.

"Ah, I tell you, this is the life! Better than gettin' shot at! Me ould mother always said, get a good job and keep yer head down.''

Scumnose came creeping along in the darkness. He nudged the ferret. "Cluny says you can begin tunneling now."

Killconey marked a cross on the ditch wall with his claw. "Right you are! We'll start about here, buckoes. Come on now, dig for victory."

BOOK THREE

The Warrior

CHAPTER

I

The invasion at Redwall continued throughout the night, the whole scene illuminated by a bright summer moon. Neither side gave the other any quarter. When the main action went into a lull, sporadic sniping would break out: bow, lance, sling and spear all coming into play with deadly effect. One thing that remained constant throughout the battle was the sound of the battering ram pounding away remorselessly at the Abbey gatehouse.

Cluny made it his duty to assess personally the progress at the tunnel workings. He was scathingly critical of the small hole that had been gouged into the side of the ditch, roundly cursing any creature who dared to complain of difficult obstacles.

"Can't get past the rocks and tree roots, my eye!" he snarled. "Idle stupid laziness, that's what is holding up the progress of this tunnel! I'll be around first thing tomorrow to see how much farther you lot have dug, and if it's not to my liking, I'll cave it in and bury the whole shirking crowd of you!"

However, the battering ram pleased Cluny much more. He knew it was worrying the Abbey defenders. The rat crews that manned the heavy object were changed every hour by Cheesethief, who stayed with the ram the whole time, encouraging the carriers on to greater efforts.

Cluny had gained a new respect for Cheesethief. Mentally, he had already promoted him to second-in-command. Sensing this had made Cheesethief redouble his efforts. He worked the rat crews like a slave driver. No rodent dared complain about one whom the Chief held in such high regard.

Constance stood on the wall with her captains. The badger's brow was furrowed with anxiety. Basil Stag Hare, the most seasoned campaigner among them, was the only one who apparently took it all quite lightly.

" 'Pon my word," he chuckled, "the way those blighters down there are carrying on with the jolly old ram, they won't need to tunnel in soon. I'll give it half a day at most, then we'll have rats piling in over the shoring, what!"

Ambrose Spike positively bristled at the nonchalant hare. "Well, I must say that *is* a comforting thing to know! Any more little gems of information to cheer us up, eh?"

Basil strode off in high dudgeon, re-emphasizing his previously forgotten limp. "Dearie me, old lad, no need to be so touchy! Merely making a military observation, y'know."

Constance called the two old friends together. "Look, it's no use quarreling among ourselves. We should be thinking of a solution. Come on, you two, stop sulking and be pals again."

Smiling sheepishly, Basil and Ambrose shook paws. Winifred the otter pounded the stones of the parapet in frustration.

"I say there's got to be a way to stop that confounded ram! We've lost far too many defenders. They get picked off every time they stand up to retaliate. It's got to be a very simple solution, a small obvious thing that we've all missed."

Jess Squirrel, aided by Silent Sam, maneuvered the barrel up on to the ramparts. She patted it. "Something simple—like this!"

The captains gathered around the barrel, examining it. The top had been covered over with gauze. A strange noise issued from within.

"Well, Jess. Don't keep us in suspense. What's in the barrel?" the badger growled.

"Shall we tell them, Sam?" grinned Jess.

Silent Sam gave a broad wink and tapped a well-sucked paw against his nose. He and his mother were enjoying this.

"What we have here, my good comrades in arms," said Jess grandly, "is stage one of our anti-battering-ram scheme, thanks to my small offspring here who found the hornets' nest.''

Basil clapped the two squirrels soundly upon their backs. ''Of course, that's the ticket! A hornets' nest in a barrel. Just chuck it down on the beastly old enemy, what?''

Jess and Sam smiled with wicked delight.

''Ha, but that's only the first stage,'' said Jess. ''Here's the second.''

She and Sam ducked out of sight. A moment later they were back with two buckets.

''Two pails of good, fine, slick vegetable oil,'' Jess announced. ''The minute they drop the battering ram, we'll tip this down all over it. Let's see them try to break a door with it then!''

Jess and Sam were congratulated heartily by all. Smiles appeared on faces that had been gloomy shortly before. Sam bowed graciously each time he was thanked. Nobody was refusing him permission to be up on the wall now.

Down below, the scrabbling of rats' feet and the monotonous thud of the ram continued. Winifred and Constance lifted the barrel on to the parapet edge. They angled and tipped it until a fine delicate balance had been achieved. The badger peeped over at the activity below, waiting for the best moment. She beckoned Silent Sam to her. The time was exactly right.

''Pray, would you do us the honor, Master Samuel?'' said Constance with mock courtliness.

Feigning an equal gravity, Sam made an elegant leg, and delivered a short, sharp kick to the barrel. Buzzing angrily, it dropped out of sight over the edge of the Abbey wall.

There was a crash and a yell, followed by the shocked screams of agonized rats. They milled about in the roadway, dancing in pain as myriads of maddened hornets attacked furiously. Some rats ran off down the road, others hurled themselves into the ditch, pursued by the relentless, stinging insects.

The long battering ram lay unguarded, conveniently spotlighted by the rats' abandoned torches. Two well-aimed buckets full of vegetable oil were hurled down. They smashed directly on target, saturating the entire length of the ram.

Before the hornets could seek out new victims, Basil ordered the defenders down to the gatehouse study, where they had a celebration snack.

*   *   *

Cluny stooped inside the tunnel workings, surrounded by as many of his followers as could pack in without causing mass suffocation. Killconey held Cluny's cloak over the entrance hole. Outside the air resounded with buzzing and pitiful screams.

The ferret gingerly touched the tip of his swollen nose.

Cluny stooped in stony silence. He did not sit or attempt to touch his own injuries. The others might laugh. Dumbly, he endured the pain of the fiery stings. Farther across the meadows there was a mass scramble of bodies into a small pond. The hornets zinged about waiting for snouts to break the surface.

Dawn revealed a sadly-disorganized horde. Cluny wisely held back his temper. Many of his soldiers looked so demoralized that they were liable to make a run for it and desert. He reasoned that there was little to be gained by adding insult to injury. Seven rats, two ferrets and a stoat lay dead in the ditch. Unable to escape the main body of hornets, they had been stung so many times it had proved fatal.

Cheesethief limped slowly up, covered in ugly lumps. "Chief, they've poured some stuff over the battering ram! We can't hold on to it. We tried, but it's like trying to pick up a wet eel. The blasted thing slid right out of our claws. One of the bearers had both legs broken when it slipped and fell. Sorry, Chief, but we didn't expect them to think anything up like that. Hornets and slippery stuff: it's not fair!"

Cluny pointed across the meadow. "Regroup the army over there. Let them feed and rest. Send someone scouting for dock leaves to rub on those stings. I'm going into my tent to do some serious planning. We're not beaten yet, not by a long chalk. They can't produce a hornets' nest every day."

Cluny stumped off dejectedly, rubbing his backside with one claw.

There were one or two insect-sting casualties to be treated at the Abbey Infirmary. Fortunately, Brother Rufus had a specific compound that he had invented some years back to deal with such emergencies as summer stings.

Silent Sam was re-enacting the entire episode in pantomime for the benefit of Tim and Tess and some other infant creatures. They were in tucks of laughter at his antics as Sam slapped at his fur and performed somersaults with a comical expression on his face.

Constance and the captains assembled back on the wall after a few hours' rest. They could see no immediate threat from the horde licking their wounds across the meadow. This gave ample opportunity to assess the damage caused to the gatehouse door.

Jess Squirrel was lowered over the ramparts on a rope. She went swiftly down and inspected the door. In a short while she was back up again to report that although there were many deep dents and at least two long cracks, the old gatehouse door was still holding well.

Constance decided that later on they could lower some carpenters and smiths to deal with the repairs. Of late the badger had become preoccupied with an idea that was rapidly turning into an obsession. Cut off the head and the body would die. By some means she must kill Cluny the Scourge!

Out across the meadow she could plainly see the Warlord's tent. In the strong sunlight the badger watched the silhouette of the big rat moving about behind the canvas. The main problem was that the tent had been pitched too far out of range for sling or bow. Unless the weapon was big and powerful enough to reach that far . . . That was it!

A large powerful bow, something along the lines of a crossbow. What if it could be mounted upon the ramparts unknown to Cluny and his horde? At a given time, say mid-afternoon, Cluny's shadow would be clearly visible through the tent fabric in the bright June sunlight. A big arrow or bolt properly aimed from the bow, and *twang!*

Exit Cluny.

Delighted with the plan, Constance shared her knowledge with only one other creature, the solitary beaver. Enlisting the aid of the beaver's highly capable molars, the badger left him gnawing away at a yew sapling in the orchard while she went off to find an arrow that would fit her brainchild. An ash staff that had seen service as a candle-snuffer proved to be ideal. With a heavy stone Constance flattened the conical brass extinguisher fitted to the top of the staff until it resembled a vicious-looking spear. She flighted it with duck feathers. A thin plaited climbing rope rubbed with beeswax made an excellent bowstring. With the help of the beaver, Constance bent the yew sapling against the Abbey wall and strung it to the right tension.

Together they mounted it upon a dining table with nails and strapping, and bore it up to the ramparts. Constance would only grunt brusquely at anyone inquiring what the strange contraption was for; only she and the beaver needed to know that. The two creatures sat out upon the ramparts sharing lunch, conversing in low secretive tones.

"That should do the trick!"

"Aye, let's keep our paws crossed that it does. We'll only get one shot."

"Ha, one shot is all we'll need."

"Shall we wait until the sun has passed its zenith? That way we can see him clearer."

"Good idea. When the Joseph Bell tolls mid-afternoon should be best."

Having finished lunch, the pair lay out like old watchdogs on the sun-warmed stones.

Half an hour later they were snoring.

Cluny was a resourceful rat. He often wished that his army thought as he did instead of being just a mob of incompetents. But then, if the horde were as clever as he was, there would be no need of a leader. Such was life, he reflected. Nobody could think up a new strategy as he could.

And this time Cluny reckoned that he had hit upon a foolproof plan! He strode across the meadow and hand-picked thirty-odd rats.

"Follow me," Cluny rapped. "Cheesethief, I'm leaving you in charge until I get back."

Without another word Cluny marched off with his selected rodents, first to the upturned hay cart in the ditch down the road, then a quick circle around into Mossflower Wood.

Like his predecessor Redtooth, Cheesethief was ambitious. He interpreted Cluny's order as the much-coveted promotion to second-in-command. The Chief had not even acknowledged Darkclaw. In his elation, Cheesethief even forgot the painful hornet stings. He strutted about asserting his newfound authority.

"Darkclaw, send those ferrets out for more dock leaves, will you?" he ordered. "Oh, and see that no one else strays too far.

I'll be in the tent if you need me for anything, but try not to disturb me.''

Darkclaw scowled resentfully. Nevertheless he carried out the orders. If he didn't, he was certain that Cheesethief would report him to Cluny for insubordination.

Cheesethief swaggered into the tent and glanced around. Cluny had left the better part of a wood pigeon, some cheese, and there was still a handsome measure of the best St. Ninian barley wine in the Chief's canteen.

Cheesethief tucked in with satisfaction. Redtooth used to, so why not he? It was his entitlement as Cluny's second-in-command. He sprawled languidly in the Warlord's chair, tilting it and resting his feet on the map-strewn camp table, happy in the knowledge that his destiny was being fulfilled. He secretly hoped that it would start raining heavily, then the rest of the army would recognize his exalted position when they were outside getting soaked, while he was snug and dry inside the tent.

Cheesethief tried studying the maps. He could not make head or tail of them and soon grew restless.

There was Cluny's poisoned tail-barb which he wore in battle. Careful not to pierce his claws by accident, he fitted it to his own tail. Next he draped the Warlord's cloak about him. It was a bit long, but what a dashing figure he must cut. For a while he contemplated the massive war helmet. Peeping around the tent flap he checked that there was no sign of the Chief returning. Good! Cluny would probably be gone for another hour or two yet.

The Joseph Bell tolled for mid-afternoon.

Constance shook the beaver into wakefulness.

''Look, what a golden opportunity! There's the Scourge himself, all dressed up to kill. We'll never get another chance like this.''

The giant bow worked perfectly. Cheesethief's latest promotion was swift but brief. He never knew what it was that snuffed his life out!

CHAPTER

2

Matthias screamed aloud with fright inside the cat's mouth. It was sloppy and hot, pink and black, smelling indescribably and seemingly full of huge yellowed teeth.

"Phut!"

The marmalade cat spat the young mouse out upon the barn floor. He lay wet and sticky, quivering all over, dust and straw clinging to his fur. Instinct warned Matthias to lie inert and play dead. He had no chance to make a run for it, surrounded as he was by the cat's paws. He could not stop his body from quaking badly. He lay staring into the feline eyes, great twin pools of turquoise flecked with gold.

The cat stared back at Matthias in disgust. Disdainfully it wiped a fastidious paw across its soiled tongue and spat as if trying to rid itself of a horrible taste.

"Ugh! I simply cannot abide the taste of mouse. Filthy little vermin, one can never tell where they've been."

The cat's voice, though cultured, was a high reedy tenor. It would have sounded comical under different circumstances. Matthias lay as still as possible.

The marmalade cat prodded him with an indolent paw. "Oh get up, you disgusting little beast! I know you're not dead."

Slowly the young mouse rose to his feet. The cat seemed uninterested in him as a possible food source. Matthias's legs were shaking so much that he had to sit down again.

They stared at each other. Matthias could think of nothing to say. The cat spoke again. This time its voice was indignant. "Well, have you nothing to say for yourself, mouse? Where are your manners? Don't you think you should apologize for leaping into my mouth like that?"

Matthias managed to stand again. He bowed shakily. "I beg your pardon, sir. It was purely accidental. I fell, you see. Please accept my humble apologies. I am Matthias of Redwall and I sincerely hope I have not disturbed you in any way."

The cat sniffed distantly. "Yes, at least you seem to have some sort of decent upbringing, Matthias of Redwall. I accept your apology. Allow me to introduce myself. I am Squire Julian Gingivere."

"Pleased to meet you, Squire Julian," said Matthias politely.

The cat yawned regally. "You may call me Julian. The title is hereditary. I never wanted it. Squire of what? A broken-down ramshackle farm building and a stretch of river over yonder! One has no real friends, no trusty servants, not even a mate for that matter. Hmmm, I suppose the Gingivere line will become extinct when I die."

Matthias could not help feeling a certain amount of sympathy for the lonely aristocrat.

"At least you seem to lead a peaceful life," he said hopefully.

"Oh, spare me your platitudes, mouse," Julian replied in a world-weary voice. "What would you know about loneliness and trying to preserve one's standards in a decaying world. I say, do you think you could manage to clean yourself up a bit? You look an absolute fright, standing there all covered in dust and straw. And while you're doing that maybe you'd like to explain how you came to be sneaking around my barn."

As Matthias brushed himself down, he related the object of his mission. Julian looked down at him in surprise.

"Captain Snow, eh? That old maniac! I've forbidden him the use of my barn, you know. What a thoroughly dreadful bird! He eats anything that moves or crawls. Atrocious table manners, too. All that regurgitating of bone and fur. Ugh!"

"Could you tell me where I might find him, please?" Matthias asked.

"Certainly," replied Julian. "Snow lives in a hollow tree these days. I'll stretch a point and take you there. But please don't expect me to introduce you or even talk to him. When I barred Snow from here we had a dreadful quarrel. Things were said that cannot be rescinded. I vowed that day never to speak to that old owl for as long as I live.''

Matthias sensed that Julian and Snow had once been good friends. Maybe the rift in their relationship was the cause of Julian's present state of fatalism and gloom. He decided wisely not to pursue the matter further at the moment.

Riding upon a cat's back was a new and unusual experience for Matthias. Although he took great care to disguise it, Julian was quite an observant creature. As he strode with an easy grace across the farmyard, he remarked idly, ''Your friends the shrews are out in force today. Ignorant little things! They think I can't see them. Give Log-a-Log and Guosim a message from me, will you? Tell them it is quite safe to come into the barn for hay and other items. Snow doesn't roost there any more. Goodness knows, I certainly won't hurt them. My diet consists of herbs, grasses and an occasional fish from the river. I gave up red meat years ago. You might also mention that if they must come to my barn, would they please desist from arguing and fighting so much? There's nothing quite as upsetting as quarrelsome little shrews disturbing one's meditations.''

Matthias agreed to convey the message to the Guerrilla Shrews. They had arrived at a small overgrown orchard. Julian halted within twenty paces of a stunted oak. As he bade Matthias ~~~~ down he cautioned him, ''You probably can't see Captain Snow, but he's watching us. I can tell when he's at home. Be extra careful, Matthias. The old glutton will more than likely eat you on sight—typical of an owl. Well, I'm off now. If you get the chance, say Squire Gingivere said that he must surely admit he was in the wrong and apologize. Only then can we resume our friendship and live together in the barn. Goodbye, Matthias, and do take care.''

''Goodbye, Julian, and thank you!'' Matthias called after the retreating figure of the last survivor in the Gingivere dynasty.

The young mouse unpinned Basil's medal from his tunic. He ventured cautiously forwards, holding it aloft. If Julian said that Captain Snow was about, then it must be so.

An unearthly screech shattered the silence, followed by a rush of wings. The owl swooped out of nowhere straight for Matthias.

Ducking and weaving as Basil had taught him, Matthias waved the medal and yelled at the top of his voice, "Truce! Basil Stag Hare sent me here. I claim a truce!"

He was knocked flat upon his back. Massive needle-pointed talons tore the medal from his grasp. Captain Snow landed in front of Matthias, raising the dust with his vast wings. The young mouse found it hard to believe that such an awesome and impressive bird existed.

Captain Snow stood hugely tall with an incredible wingspan. The owl's pure-white plumage was broken only by a few brown bars on the wing and some dark spots on the crown. He had six dangerous talons in front, two at the back of his legs and a sharp heavily-curved beak. His eyes were colossal: twin golden orbs with circular black centers.

Matthias continued ducking and weaving, conscious that his life hung by a thread. Captain Snow flicked out a talon. Matthias dodged nimbly aside.

"State your name and rank. Who gave you my medal?" snapped the owl in a flat hard voice.

Still moving quickly, and panting for breath, the young mouse gasped, "Matthias mouse, Warrior of Redwall Abbey. The medal belongs to my friend Basil Stag Hare. He sends his compliments, Cap'n, sir."

"Stand fast," snapped the Captain.

Matthias stood rigid. The owl's talons started to inch forwards as if they had a life of their own. The young mouse m steadily backwards away from the talons. Captain Snow licked saliva from the edges of his beak. It was plain that he desperately wanted to eat Matthias.

"What did the cat say to you, mouse?" he rasped. "Did he mention me?"

Matthias repeated the message from Julian. "Squire Gingivere says, sir, that if you were to admit yourself in the wrong and apologize to him, then you could both be friends and live in the barn again."

As he spoke, Matthias had been moving away from the seeking talons. On a sudden instinct he dived to one side as the owl pounced. He skipped and ran on a zig-zag course, away from the murderous bird. Bilked of his target, Captain Snow madly tore at the grass and scattered dust. All at once he wheeled about and flew upwards, perching at the entrance to his nest-hole in the stunted oak. "All right, you can stop running away now, little warrior. Come back here. I want to talk to you."

Matthias stood a safe distance away from the tree. Captain Snow shifted from one foot to the other, muttering huffily, "Me, in the wrong? Never. I won't apologize to that cat! I refuse to!"

When the owl had finished arguing with himself, Matthias called out, "Cap'n Snow, sir, there is a question that I must ask you."

The great snowy owl beckoned towards his hole with a sweeping wing. "Listen, mouse, you can't stand down there shouting up at me. Why not come into my lair, er, nest. Then we can chat together in comfort."

Standing on tiptoe Matthias could catch a glimpse of the "nest." The walls were lined with all types of fur, shrew, mouse, vole, even rat. The skulls and bones of small creatures were hung up as macabre decorations. Matthias smiled nervously. "Er, if you don't mind, Cap'n, I think I'd prefer to stay where I am."

The Captain cackled raucously and pointed a talon. "So, you'd prefer to stay where you are, sir? Well, I don't blame you. Right, out with it. What's this question you want to ask me?"

"Do you know of Asmodeus the giant adder, and where might I find him, sir?" Matthias called boldly.

The owl preened his breast feathers. He cocked his head on ▬▬ side. "I know of everything that moves within my territory, mouse. Yes, I do know of Asmodeus. I also know where he calls home. Why do you ask?"

"Because the adder has something that belongs to our Abbey, an ancient sword, sir," Matthias replied.

"Ah, the sword," said the owl. "I remember the night he passed here carrying it. You'll never get that sword from Asmodeus, a puny little mouse like you! The adder has magic in his eye that would freeze you like a statue. Huh, I wish mine could."

Matthias felt his temper rising. He shouted angrily at the self-opinionated bird, "I don't care if he's got magic eyes, poison teeth, coils of steel, or whatever! I mean to have that sword! I'll steal it from the snake or fight him for it. If I have to I'll—"

The rest of Matthias's words were drowned out by the hysterical screeching laughter of the owl, who nearly fell from his perch with merriment. He blinked tears from his huge eyes.

"You'll what? Did I hear you say that you'd fight Asmodeus? You! Oh little mouse, run away and play before I crack a wing laughing. Ha ha ha hee hee oh hohohoho! Oh, dearie me! Are you sure you haven't been drinking old apple brandy? A mouse fighting an adder! Oh my, now I've heard everything!"

Captain Snow laughed helplessly. Matthias yelled up challengingly, "Ha, I'll bet *you* couldn't fight Asmodeus!"

The owl wiped tears from his eyes with a snowy wing as he hooted. "I've never tried. And I wouldn't relish the prospect, little one! The snake and I would probably both end up dead."

Matthias called mockingly, "That's because you're afraid. Look, I bet I'll fight Asmodeus and win too."

"Bet you won't."

"Bet I will."

"Bet you anything you won't."

Matthias pointed at the medal in Captain Snow's talons. "Bet you that medal that I will!"

The Captain flung the medal backwards into his nest. "Done!"

"Hold on, owl," Matthias shouted. "What are you putting up as a wager? The medal is not yours. You gave it to Basil Stag Hare."

Spreading his wings to their incredible length, Snow screeched, "I'll bet anything. Whatever you say, mouse."

Matthias nodded cunningly. "Oh, I don't want to take everything you own. Let's just say that you guarantee to return my medal and make a few little promises."

Again the owl had difficulty in controlling his unbridled hilarity. "Ha ha ha! The nerve of him! All right, my little warrior! It's a bet. Name your promises."

"Right," said Matthias solemnly. "You must promise on your oath that if I win you will never eat another mouse or shrew of any type."

"Agreed," chortled the owl. "In fact I'll go even further. I promise you that if you defeat the snake, I'll admit I was wrong to that stuffy old cat. I'll even apologize to him on bended knees, so there!"

"On your word as a captain," Matthias pressed.

The owl held out a wing and a leg as he recited: "I swear

by my captaincy and by my illustrious ancestors Nyctea and
Glacier, that I, Captain Snow, will return the medal and cleave
to my oath if you should win against Asmodeus." The owl
broke into laughter again: "Oh, hahahaheeheeheehohoho! This
is the easiest bet I ever made! It'll be like taking the wings off
a dead butterfly."

"Maybe to you, sir, but not to me," Matthias countered.
"Now, tell me where I may find Asmodeus, Cap'n."

"In the old sandstone quarry," the owl replied. "You'll have
to cross the river. There are caves in the quarry, passages too.
Explore them. You won't find Asmodeus until you are least
expecting him. By then it will be too late. You'll be deader than
an icicle in hell. Goodbye, mouse."

Matthias turned his back upon the snowy owl and strode off
with a string of taunts ringing in his ears.

"Nice to have my silver medal back!" jeered the owl. "I'll
think of you when I wear it. You should have let me eat you.
It'd save you a journey to the quarry. . . . Oh, I almost forgot.
You won't be able to give the hare my best wishes. . . . You'll
be snug inside the snake!"

Matthias walked onwards, ignoring the cruel jibes of the owl,
through the farmyard and across the grassland, not stopping until
he arrived at the fringe of Mossflower Wood. The shrews broke
cover and milled about noisily with their endless questions.

"Ha, so you got back then?"

"Why didn't Snow eat you?"

"Bet you've never seen an owl that size before, eh?"

"What news of Poisonteeth?"

"Did you find out where he is?"

"Don't just stand there! Tell us, tell us!"

Fierce quarreling broke out. Swords were being drawn as
Matthias sought out Log-a-Log and took the black stone from
him.

"Shut up and stop fighting, you hooligans, or you'll get to
know nothing!" Matthias bellowed.

An expectant hush descended upon the union members of the
Guerrilla Shrews of Mossflower. Matthias found it hard to keep
the contempt out of his voice. "I found Captain Snow. Actually
I was led to him by Squire Julian Gingivere. Does that name
ring any bells?"

There was an embarrassed shuffling in the ranks of the listeners. Many turned their eyes to the ground, particularly Guosim and Log-a-Log.

Matthias folded his paws. He stared about in disgust. "Oh, yes. I'd just like to thank you all! Especially you, Guosim, and Log-a-Log. What a sly, nasty, despicable thing to do, sending me into that barn without a single word of warning about the cat."

Log-a-Log ripped the cloth band from his brow and flung it down. He took the stone up in his paw. "Matthias, I speak not only for myself but for all the Guerrilla Union. We are very sorry, you must believe that. It completely slipped our minds. We forgot about the cat. You see, we are shrews, not only by name but also by nature. We argue, quarrel, bicker and fight so much among ourselves that we lose sight of the important issues. That is the way it is with us. Please accept our apologies, friend."

Matthias retrieved the stone. "I forgive you this once. You say you are shrews and you call me friend. You tell me that you forget. Let me tell you, I am a Redwall warrior. I always remember who my friends are, and I never forget an injury done to me! However, we will say no more of this. You must listen to me now. What I have to tell you is of great importance. It can change the life of every shrew here. Captain Snow has told me that Asmodeus lives in the old sandstone quarry across the river. He has given me his promise on oath: if I defeat Asmodeus, the owl will never again take the life of a shrew."

When the astonished hubbub had died down the young mouse continued, "Think about it, Guerrilla Shrews! It would be a double blessing for you. With Asmodeus dead and Captain Snow held to his oath you could live in safety from both. And while I'm on the subject, my friend Julian the cat is quite harmless. He will not hunt you. Any time you need something from the barn, you have his permission to take it, providing you do so quietly, with no fighting or arguing. That is all I have to say to you, save for one thing. Lead me to the quarry."

Matthias stood patiently waiting as subdued conversation went on all about him. Surely they could not refuse so generous an offer? He tried hard to pick up the threads of talk. Some seemed all for it but others were apparently reluctant to trust his word.

Finally, a small militant-looking shrew came forward and picked up the stone. He addressed Matthias in a very official manner. "Our rules say that the quarry across the river is not in shrew territory, mouse. Therefore, we cannot go with you!"

Log-a-Log sprang forward and dealt the speaker a mighty blow, laying him flat out on his back.

"You cowardly, ungrateful little fool!" cried Log-a-Log. "How can you say such a thing after all this warrior is trying to do for us?"

Guosim grabbed the stone from the ground. "Stop, Log-a-Log! You have no right to strike a comrade! He was only stating the facts. Our Guerrilla Union rules clearly state that no member can be forced to venture beyond official shrew boundaries."

Before Log-a-Log had a chance to reply, a riot broke out. Shrews began kicking, punching, arguing, screaming, wrestling and shouting. The edge of Mossflower Wood was in pandemonium.

Matthias held up the stone and tried shouting above the mêlée. His voice was lost in the uproar. Angrily, he grabbed the nearest shrew and shouted at him, "Listen, you! Tell me which direction the river is in, or else—"

The struggling creature pointed a paw to the north-east before wriggling from Matthias's grasp to dive headlong into the fray.

Fury took hold of the young mouse. He waved the stone and cried out, "Go on, fight, then, little fools, you and your bossy little union. I don't need any of you! I'll go it alone," and he hurled the stone with a mighty effort. It flew off over the heads of the rioters, disappearing into the wood.

Matthias turned on his heel and stormed off towards the river.

CHAPTER

3

An air of apprehension lay across the camp in the meadow. Cheesethief was dead. Pierced by an immense arrow and dressed in Cluny's best battle armor, he lay amid the wreckage of the leader's tent. Not one of the horde dared go near the gruesome scene lest they be found in a position of blame upon Cluny's return.

Constance peered agitatedly over the parapet. Something was not quite right, she felt it in her nostrils. The badger's worst suspicions were confirmed by the sight of Cluny crossing the road and heading back into the meadow. Constance watched him leap across the ditch. There could be no doubt about it, that rat was definitely Cluny the Scourge. She had killed the wrong rat!

Cluny had left his picked band back in the woodlands. They knew what they had to do. It would take a bit of time, but it was a sound, workable plan. Striding swiftly over the meadow, some sixth sense told Cluny that all was not right. His one eye scoured the area. There was the horde, gathered together at the far end, but what had happened to his tent?

Cluny could vaguely discern a huddled figure tangled in the wreckage. Speculation was useless; he speeded up his pace.

Fangburn met him halfway. Cluny held up a claw, silencing him. He would get to the bottom of things without stuttering excuses. He kicked the tent folds aside, revealing Cheesethief's stricken face. The great arrow-shaft protruded from the ruined armor, his war gear.

Cluny glanced backwards and forwards from the Abbey to the body. He took in at a quick rate all that had happened. The big badger was peering over the wall. It was her doing!

Cluny's brain raced ahead. On the far edge of the meadow the horde were looking decidedly uneasy. A mistake had been made, the arrow was meant for him. The Warlord's fertile mind suddenly came up with an idea of how to turn the situation to his own advantage.

Fangburn was, to say the least, surprised. Cluny clapped him heartily on the back and led him across to where the rest of the horde waited apprehensively. Cluny laughed aloud to put them at their ease. He winked his eye roguishly.

"Well, I see my little scheme worked out just fine. We got the dirty traitor, didn't we, Fangburn, my old mate?"

Fangburn was completely baffled, but he knew better than to disagree.

"What? Oh, er, of course we did, Chief."

Cluny nodded over at where the body lay.

"Do you see that? Well, let it be a warning to you all. Ha, I knew what was going on with Cheesethief. Didn't anyone see him at the battering ram last night acting all high and mighty?"

There was a general murmur of agreement. Most of the rats had been pressed into volunteering as ram carriers by the ambitious Cheesethief.

"Aye, we saw him, Chief."

"Chucking his weight about, shouting orders."

"He kept me on that ram for two hours."

"Yes, you'd have thought that he was the commander of the horde."

"Exactly!" Cluny shouted. "I'd had my eye on Cheesethief for quite a while! He was doing a fair piece of ordering about without my permission. Why, I bet he ordered some of you lads around while I was gone."

"He started shoving me around, Chief," volunteered Darkclaw indignantly. "It was 'do this,' 'fetch that,' 'jump to it,' 'I'm using the Chief's tent.' I think Cheesethief was getting too big for his boots, Chief."

Cluny threw a claw around the speaker's shoulder. "Thank you, Darkclaw. You're an intelligent Captain. You could see as well as I did that Cheesethief was planning to take control of my trusted horde. Why else would he start using my tent and dressing up in my battle armor?"

The soldiers nodded sagely to each other. Cluny was right. There was no fondness in the ranks for the dead, power-hungry bully.

Cluny continued, "You see, I knew the badger and her friends were planning to kill me, so I thought I'd kill two birds with one stone: fool them, and save myself the trouble of having to execute Cheesethief. In fact I let the Redwall crowd do the dirty work for me. I didn't want any of my loyal soldiers put to any trouble. I gave the traitor enough rope and let our enemies hang him!"

Cluny slapped his thigh and burst out laughing. The horde joined him, falling about with merriment at their Chief's black joke. What a cunning idea! There was no doubt about it, the Scourge didn't miss a single trick.

Cluny waved cheerfully to the distant figure of Constance on the wall.

"My thanks to you, badger!" he shouted. "You did a fine job!"

Constance could not hear a thing from the distance of the ramparts, which was just as well in the circumstances.

Cluny was almost jovial as he turned to the horde. "Well, my good warriors. Has anything else happened while I was away?"

Killconey performed one of his most elaborate salutes. "The tunnel is goin' very well, yer honor."

"Good, good," said Cluny. "Anything else to report?"

Mangefur and Scumnose piped up jointly. "We was out searching for dock leaves, Chief, way out across those fields over there—"

Cluny halted them. He nodded to Scumnose.

"You tell me."

"Well, we was rootin' about by some hedges, Chief," said Scumnose, "and we found a whole tribe of dormice fast asleep. So we pounced on 'em and tied them up in a bunch. Nice big fat ones they are, Chief."

Cluny interrupted. "Dormice, eh? You haven't killed them yet, I hope?"

Scumnose shook his head vigorously. "Oh no, Chief. We're keeping 'em nice and fresh in the ditch there. D'you want to see 'em? I think there's about twenty, all told."

"Good. You did well. I want them kept alive," muttered Cluny as he walked across to the ditch and peered down at the captives.

The dormice were huddled miserably together, their necks looped cruelly together on a rope. They whimpered fearfully at the sinister sight of Cluny the Scourge.

"Which one of you is the leader?" he snarled.

A bedraggled youngish mouse held up a timid paw. "I am, sir. My name is Plumpen. Please let us go free. We have done no harm to any living creature. Violence is against our nature. We—"

"Silence," Cluny snapped. "Or I'll teach you what violence means."

An anguished moan arose from the dormice lying in the ditch. Cluny cracked his tail.

"Cut out that cringing," he said contemptuously. "You are my prisoners to do with as I like. Oh, don't worry. I won't let them kill you yet. I've got other more useful things in mind. You, Plumpen, or whatever your name is, tell your tribe that they won't be harmed as long as you do what I say. For the present you are to stay down there under guard. Scumnose, Mangefur!"

"Yes, Chief?"

"You two are responsible for these prisoners," said Cluny. "See that no creature goes near them. Stand guard night and day. If just one of these dormice is missing, you'll both end up on a roasting spit. Is that clear?"

After Cheesethief's carcass had been disposed of, Cluny sat beneath an awning that had been improvised from the damaged tent. He watched the armorer diligently repairing his prized war gear and fumed inwardly. His equipment had been battered—and he had lost a valuable Captain. The Redwall contingent had stolen a march upon him, and the battering ram had failed miserably. Once again the thinking was left to him. The horde were more concerned with licking wounds and feeding their stomachs. Strategy was not their responsibility. However, on reflection the balance was beginning to swing in his favor again. He now had three possible keys to the Abbey. One was the tunnel; the rats in Mossflower Wood were attending to his second scheme; and the third—Cluny glanced over to the ditch. The capture of the dormice would prove an even more devious avenue to the conquest of Redwall, provided he played his cards right.

Early evening saw the attack upon the Abbey get under way once more. Jess Squirrel and Ambrose Spike had joined the ranks of archers. They popped up and down selecting random targets.

"I don't like it," Jess remarked.

Ambrose grunted as he released a feathered shaft at the ditch. "Don't like what, Jess?"

The squirrel put aside her bow and sat down under cover of the parapet. "They seem to have slackened off somehow, and we haven't seen much of Cluny lately. It's not like the horde to behave in this way. Personally, I think there's something afoot that we don't know about."

Winifred the otter was standing nearby. She slung a stone hard, nodded in satisfaction at the resultant scream, and joined the two friends. "Aye, I'm inclined to agree with you, Jess. The Scourge has probably figured some new move. This attack may only be a cover. By the way, is there any word from Foremole and his crew?"

"Oh, they've still got their ears to the ground," Ambrose said gruffly. "Foremole says they've heard the odd echo, nothing definite though. South-west corner is where he thinks they might surface eventually."

"Yes, I've heard that, too," Jess agreed. "We'll have to arrange a warm reception for those filthy vermin when they show up!"

"What baffles me," Winifred mused, "is where young Matthias has got to. It's not like him to miss the chance of a battle."

Abbot Mortimer was on his rounds with food. He had been eavesdropping on the conversation and could not help commenting, "D'you know, I was just thinking that same thing myself, but we must give Matthias the benefit of the doubt and trust in his judgment. I've a feeling that he could be the salvation of us all. One thing you may rest assured of, wherever that young mouse is he'll be concerned with the survival of Redwall in one way or another, I'm sure.''

''Ah, well,'' Jess sighed as she picked up her bow and notched an arrow to it. ''We'd better make sure he has a home to come back to. On with the war, friends.''

The squirrel drew the bow full stretch and stood up. She paused a moment, peering along the yew shaft, then released the string with a vibrant twang. Below, on the edge of the meadow, a creature fell transfixed. One stoat less to carry out Cluny's commands!

CHAPTER

4

Matthias set up a solitary makeshift camp that night. After a frugal meal he wrapped his habit tight about his body to ward off the chill breeze and settled down to sleep. Alone with his bitter thoughts about the ungrateful shrews, the young mouse finally dozed off.

Sometime before dawn he became aware of movement and sound nearby. Carefully, Matthias slitted one eyelid open. His feet were warm. He felt the extra weight of a blanket that had been draped over him while he was asleep.

The Guerrilla Union of Shrews in Mossflower had returned! Small campfires had been lighted, and breakfast was being prepared. Matthias decided that it must be nearly daybreak. Turning on his side he kept up the pretense of sleep. Ignoring the presence of the shrews he drifted back into a warm slumber.

It was fully daylight when he reawakened. The sun beat down through the trees, mixing its rays in the pale blue smoke of the cooking fires. Log-a-Log brought toasted wheatcake and a bowl of herb tea. Sitting up, Matthias accepted them noncommittally. He ate and drank in silence while Log-a-Log folded the blanket and packed it away. The shrew stood beside him and gave a short, nervous cough.

"Ahem, er, Matthias; I'm sorry about what happened yesterday. As you can see, we've decided by majority vote to come along with you."

The young mouse continued to ignore him. Log-a-Log slumped down.

"Matthias, listen. We shrews of the union try to run our lives along democratic lines. You must not think too harshly of us. The shrew who spoke out against accompanying you was only stating chapter and verse of the act. I was wrong to hit him. Guosim did right to uphold his argument."

Matthias arose and shouldered his bundle. "Look, Log-a-Log. Don't talk to me about your silly rules: subsection three, paragraph four, and all that nonsense. You are either with me or against me. I haven't got valuable time to waste on a lot of Shrew Union rules and disputes."

Log-a-Log picked up his pack and smiled broadly at the young mouse. "Matthias, my friend, we are with you to a shrew. Tooth, claw and nail! Lead on, bold warrior."

Matthias laughed in open relief. "Well, let's get started, friend Log-a-Log. We've got an adder to fight and a sword to win!"

Surrounded by a band of shrews that had started quarreling over the best route to the quarry, Matthias marched stolidly forward. They trekked through the trees, leaving Mossflower Wood far behind, across open ground, giving the farmhouse a carefully wide berth, breeching hawthorn hedges and spanning dried-out ditches, through several fields that lay fallow in the summer stillness.

A halt was called at lunchtime on the banks of a slow, broad river.

Matthias sat next to Guosim during the midday meal. It would be the last cooked food they would get. Stealth and secrecy would be the order of the day upon the other side of the river. No fires, no noise. Matthias flicked a pebble into the water.

"How are we supposed to cross this lot?" he asked.

Guosim spoke through a mouthful of bread. "Log-a-Log. How else? That's how he got his name, you know. His father and his father's father before him were all called Log-a-Log. The whole family were all ferryshrews on this river. If you needed to cross the water you stood on the bank and shouted 'Log-a-Log'. Here, let's see if it still works."

Guosim walked to the river's edge. Cupping her paws around her mouth she called in a ululating voice: "Logalogalogalo-galog!"

The older shrew appeared out of a reed bed, balanced upon a large floating tree trunk which he propelled skillfully with a long pole into the side of the bank. Angrily he sprang ashore, upbraiding Guosim. "Puddenheaded shrew! D'you have to broadcast the fact we're here? Shouting out like a great foghorn! We'd better strike camp and get across now, before someone comes."

"I was only showing Matthias how to call for the ferry-shrew," Guosim muttered surlily.

"Is that all!" said Log-a-Log heatedly. "Then why don't you show him the snake tracks in the mud there? Or didn't you notice them? Asmodeus passed through here not four hours ago. He's probably gone hunting in Mossflower Wood. It's a mercy we didn't bump into him. He might come back this way before the day is through."

Matthias stared in horrified fascination at the broad slimy path that had been left in the mud by the snake. The shrews had all clambered hastily aboard the strange craft.

"Hurry along, Matthias! All hands on deck!" Log-a-Log hissed.

Despite the danger of the enterprise, the young mouse actually enjoyed the ride across the river on the tree trunk. Several of the shrews dug lines out of their packs and fished successfully, amassing quite a tidy little catch before the ferry nosed into the opposite bank with a gentle bump. The shrews disembarked and Matthias helped Log-a-Log to conceal the ferry in some bul-rushes.

"I was thinking," Matthias mused. "Do you suppose we could all hide somewhere? That way we might see Asmodeus return and track him to his lair."

"That's exactly what I had planned myself," the shrew replied. "If we spread out along the bank and remain hidden, then we'll stand a good chance of spotting Poisonteeth. It's a good idea, but I can see a drawback. Supposing the adder catches the scent of shrews? There's so many of us that it's a distinct danger."

"Then again," Matthias argued, "would it not be better if

we made our way to the quarry and waited there? Asmodeus is bound to head for home."

"I wish it were that simple, my friend," Log-a-Log replied. "The land around the quarry offers no concealment; too flat and bare. Poisonteeth is full of ancient cunning too. He may have a secret entrance outside the quarry itself. I think it is best we wait here. I'll spread the comrades out in a line. We'll all keep watch."

Throughout the long afternoon, Matthias lay hidden at the base of a lilac bush. He was within calling distance of shrews secreted a short distance away, as they were of their neighbors farther along. Fully a half mile of the bank was covered in this fashion. Whoever spotted Asmodeus was to report, after letting one minute elapse, to Matthias, who was positioned roughly at the center of the line. Guosim and Log-a-Log were stationed on either flank.

The blazing sun hung over the watchers like a fiery disc. Matthias kept his sights on the river and the ground in front of him, not daring to move, whether to eat, drink or scratch. He was forced to endure the unwelcome attention of inquisitive flies and insects that buzzed about and walked across him at their leisure. Often he would focus so hard that his imagination played tricks. A slight ripple upon the water, or a vagrant breeze through the grass, became Asmodeus. He would blink and reassure himself that it was only a product of his tensed mind.

The young mouse lost track of time until he became aware of the sun starting to sink in a reddening sky heralding the twilight. Surely the snake must pass this way soon!

As complete darkness descended, a shrew sneaked up through the grass and tapped Matthias's shoulder.

"What's the matter? Has Asmodeus been sighted?" Matthias asked.

The shrew pointed out along the flank that Guosim headed. "I don't know, mouse. You'd better come and see for yourself. I'll go and get Log-a-Log."

Matthias scrambled out from beneath the lilac. Something must have gone wrong! Throwing caution to the winds, he dashed along the river bank. Other shrews left their hiding places and followed him.

Guosim was seated upon the open ground, her eyes wide with

fright, teeth chattering madly, her whole body trembling like a leaf.

Log-a-Log came racing up. Matthias shouted to him, "Guosim's in a state of shock! Help me, let's get her into the water."

Grabbing Guosim between them they rushed her into the shallows and ducked her under the surface of the river. She came up spluttering but coherent.

"Giant Poisonteeth, the snake, Asmodeus, he was here! I didn't spot him until it was too late. He's taken Mingo. Gave him the magic eyes, then bit him and dragged him off! Poor Mingo. Ugh! It was horrible, horrible, I tell you, the rotten filthy reptile!" Guosim flung herself down sobbing into the grass.

Log-a-Log pulled her roughly to her feet. "Come on, don't lie there crying, shrew! The adder probably left a good wet trail for us to follow. Where did it happen?"

Guosim ran shakily some distance to the left. She pointed to the ground. "Right here! You can see the great slithering marks! Look!"

The evidence was quite clear. The wet path in the dry grass gleamed in the dark.

They followed the trail with Matthias and Log-a-Log in the lead. It twisted and turned tortuously, over small hillocks, through hedges and across fields. Even when the wetness stopped there was the musty odor of death clinging to the ground.

At the top of a small rise Matthias dropped into a crouch. Signaling everyone to do likewise, he pointed downwards.

"Look, Log-a-Log! There!"

Spread out beneath them was a vast disused quarry. It was as if some gigantic hand had scooped a great hole in the landscape. The shape was roughly oval. The steep, red sandstone sides were terraced halfway around into long flat shelves. Piles of fallen stone were dotted about amid the defunct workings. The scant vegetation lent the quarry an air of stark desolation.

They lay on the edge of the pit, straining their eyes into the dark floor area below. Steadily, Log-a-Log gave orders to the Guerrilla shrews to retire back across the field where they could rest up and eat a much-needed meal. Only he and Guosim remained at the edge of the quarry with Matthias, who settled any further debate by saying, "I'm going down there for a look around as soon as it's light."

"If you must go, then we will come with you," murmured Log-a-Log.

Matthias shook his head. "No, I cannot allow it. It's far too dangerous."

Guosim, who was fully recovered, spoke out courageously, "You cannot stop us, Matthias. You are not a union member; therefore we are not under your command. The rules clearly state this, so the decision is out of your paws. We go! You and Log-a-Log get some sleep. I'll take first sentry duty."

The three friends slept in turns, relieving one another through the long watches of the night hours. Matthias was on duty when the first fingers of dawn probed the quarry. What a difference daylight made to the sinister nighttime appearance of the scene below!

The sandstone ranged through a spectrum of pale sunlight gold, banded through every shade of yellow, fawn, umber, brown, down to the dusty red sandstone that must have been hewn out in distant ages to provide the masons with material to build Redwall Abbey.

He roused his companions to view the awesome spectacle.

"To think that all this peaceful beauty should hide such cold evil," he breathed wonderingly.

In silent Indian file they began the descent. The going was not too hard. There were lots of handholds and steps and the sandy rock was quite firm, not at all slippery. It took less than an hour for the three friends to climb down. They stood together on the flat quarry floor gazing around.

"Supposing Poisonteeth decides to hunt today," whispered Guosim.

"I have a feeling he won't," Log-a-Log replied. "Asmodeus got a full day's hunt in yesterday. With the unexpected bonus of poor old Mingo on his way home he'll probably sleep through today and go out to hunt tonight."

"So that gives us all day to find out where he is," added Matthias. "Shall we look together, or split up?"

"Stick together," said Guosim as she and Log-a-Log drew their short rapiers. Matthias took out his dagger. They started searching the quarry for a possible hole or concealed entrance.

The trio scoured the lower slopes, poking and probing. They inspected underneath stunted bushes, turned over chunks of rock, crawled beneath huge slabs, always watching keenly for the telltale single winding track of the adder. The silence was oppressive. There was neither birdsong nor the hum of insects inside the sunken arena. Having crisscrossed the floor, they progressed to the middle terraces, but the results were equally disappointing. All morning they had searched the quarry without any success.

At midday Log-a-Log called a halt. They sat on a flat table-shaped rock halfway up and shared a hardtack lunch followed by a canteen of water. It was not a cheerful meal. They each sat with their own thoughts. Finally Guosim stood up, dusting her fur off. She clapped her paws together in a brisk manner, urging her companions to resume the task.

"Right, come on, you two, we've only got half a day left."

Matthias and Log-a-Log gathered up their packs and weapons as Guosim leaned on the side of a narrow slab and continued her summary.

"If we search around the top lip this afternoon, that only leaves us the heeeeeeeee . . . !"

The echo of the cry hung upon the still air. Guosim was gone. The narrow slab she had been leaning against swung loosely on a pivot. They had found the entrance to the lair of Asmodeus Poisonteeth.

CHAPTER

5

Cluny the Scourge anxiously awaited the arrival of darkness. One of his three plans had reached fruition a lot earlier than he had expected.

Killconey had proved an invaluable help. He had been across to the woods to satisfy his curiosity about what the rats were doing there. It came as no surprise to the ferret to see a large siege tower under construction. However, there was a problem. The cart still lay upturned in the ditch. Try as they would, the rats had not been able to remove a set of wheels and an axle from it.

Killconey had a word with Cluny and was immediately sent down to supervise the operation. The garrulous ferret showed the rats that he possessed a sound knowledge of the principles of fulcrum and leverage. He rigged a block and tackle to supplement a dead tree limb that they were using as a lever. Ignoring wheels and axles he roped the cart to the block. With all the rats, and a great deal of luck, he managed to lift the hay cart until it was halfway out of the ditch. Further pressure on the lever sent the hay cart past its own point of balance. The block and tackle parted under the strain, sending the ferret and the rats on the level shooting down into the ditch. By mistake it did the trick. With a crash the cart landed upright in the road.

They pushed it into the woods. Killconey oversaw the lifting of the tower on to the bed of the cart. Delighted by his own ingenuity he added the final touches. In a short time the siege tower, its wheels muffled with sacking, stood completed, ready for use.

Cluny gathered his captains about him and outlined his strategy. Tonight, when it was dark, Fangburn would step up the attack on the gatehouse wall as a diversionary measure. Cluny would command a picked band of the best fighters. They would bring the siege tower from out of the cover of Mossflower Wood and wheel it to a part of the wall where the defense appeared weakest. Under cover of darkness they would filter from the top of the tower on to the ramparts. A quick slaughter of the defenders would leave Redwall wide open to them.

Cluny watched the evening sky anxiously. It would not be long now. He signaled Fangburn to begin the diversionary assault.

Yelling and shouting fearsome war cries, the attackers leaped from the ditch, peppering the ramparts with a hail of arrows, spears and stones.

"Redwall to me! Come on, mice!" cried Constance. "Let's give better than we get. Redwall to me!"

Basil Stag Hare had formed three lines of bowmice on top of the wall. They worked with military efficiency as the hare rapped out orders.

"First rank, fire! Drop back, kneel and reload!"

"Second rank, fire! Drop back, kneel and reload!"

"Third rank, fire! Drop back, kneel and reload!"

"First rank, forward again. Fire!"

The commands continued unabated. Enemy soldiers fell stricken on the road, Darkclaw rushed about bringing up reinforcements.

"Keep those slings throwing! Bring up extra spears! Close up that line! Don't fire until you see them stand!"

John Churchmouse, Mr. Vole and Friar Hugo ran about bending low. They collected up all the arrows, spears and stones hurled by the horde, issuing them to the defenders.

"Come on, otters! Give them back a taste of their own medicine!" Winifred urged her slingers on while directing fresh archers into the ranks of the bowmice.

Constance and the beaver shared a stack of enemy spears.

They returned them with frightening power and devastating aim.

Ferret archers at the edge of the meadow found the range of Basil's bowmice. Several were felled before Jess Squirrel and Winifred, along with some crack otter slingers, sent down a barrage so swift and accurate that it decimated the ferrets within minutes.

While the battle went ahead, ranging from the heights of the parapet to the depths of the ditch, the Joseph Bell rang out over the carnage.

Cluny snapped the battered visor down on his war helmet. He rapped Killconey on his shoulder.

"Good! Now is the time! Come on, ferret!"

Together they slunk off down the ditch, running crouched over to the south-east corner of the wall where it was relatively quiet. Keeping noise down to a minimum, Cluny ordered his troops to bring forward the siege tower. Straining and pushing, the rat soldiers trundled the tall contraption from its woodland hiding place. The going was even harder across the short space of soft meadow ground. Cluny himself lent a claw, pulling on one of the lead ropes. He tugged mightily, causing the cumbersome tower to sway dangerously as it bumped over grassy hillocks.

"Bring it up close to the wall," he whispered urgently. "That's it! Now make sure it's on an even keel! I don't want the top wobbling all over the place."

Stones and soil were tamped around the wheels, wedging them still. The great tower stood ready for use.

When Friar Hugo hurried off to join the defenders he left Cornflower in charge of the kitchens. She had busied herself with setting pans of oatmeal and oven bread ready for the next morning's breakfast. Cornflower then thought of the sentries up on the wall, and she set about making a large pan of vegetable soup. It was a great favorite with the defenders at nighttime, especially when she made it to her own recipe.

Helped by Mrs. Vole and Mr. Squirrel, she ladled it into three big earthenware jugs. Taking up a jug each, with a small basket of fresh loaves and some goat cheese, they set off, with Cornflower in the lead carrying a lantern. The first stop was the south-east corner, where Foremole and his crew had a monotonous task: night and day they monitored the grounds for sounds of tunneling. They were glad of a short respite and some hot food while they chatted to the caterers in their gruff polite tones.

Cornflower was never quite sure of what Foremole was saying, but she loved listening to his funny, countrified-mole dialect.

"Yurr, missie, they ratten varments be a-comin' up'n two days, oi'll reckern. Gar! We'm give em owd 'arry if'n they shows thurr 'eads."

Cornflower was only picking up one word in three, but by the fierce scowl on Foremole's face, she was certain that the rats would not find it a pleasant experience being given "owd 'arry."

Foremole tugged his nose graciously at her. "Wurr! Thankee kindly. Nought loik vedgible soop to keep'n loif in uz moles."

Mr. Squirrel chuckled to Cornflower and Mrs. Vole. "Well, I take it the moles are quite fond of homemade vegetable soup. I know my Jess'll be ready for some."

"Yes, and so would Sam if he weren't fast asleep in bed," Cornflower replied. "Look, you and Mrs. Vole start serving along by the gatehouse. Keep your heads low and be careful. I'll start up here at the corner and see you back at the kitchen later."

With the lantern and basket in one paw and the jug in the other, Cornflower ascended the steps at the south-east corner of the wall. Brother Rufus assisted her up on to the ramparts.

"Ah, the young fieldmouse with the magic soup! Nice to see you, Cornflower. It gets lonely up this end where there's no action."

Brother Rufus held out his mug. He watched gratefully through the cloud of steam that arose from the jug. "Mmm, that smells good! Vegetable soup, my favorite!"

Cornflower was not listening. She was staring open-mouthed across Brother Rufus's shoulder. The soup was overflowing from the mug and spattering on the stones as she continued to pour.

Across the top of the parapet a ramshackle wooden platform had appeared as if from nowhere. Perched on top of it, ready to spring, was a villainous-looking rat with a cutlass clenched between his teeth.

Cornflower shrieked aloud.

More by accident than design, Brother Rufus spun around and sent the scalding contents of his mug splashing full into the rat's eyes. With a piercing wail of agony the rat fell from the top of the platform. Scarcely aware of what she was doing, Cornflower threw the lantern. It shattered on top of the siege tower, drenching the dead wood in lamp oil. Instantly the flames licked hungrily over the platform, turning it into an inferno.

Attracted by the flaring blaze that lit the night, defenders rushed from all quarters to see what was happening. Over thirty rats were in the high reaches of the burning tower. Many more were in the middle and still more on the lower frames. Rats were kicking and fighting each other to get down from the blazing tower. They bit and trampled and slashed. Some jumped while others were pushed, screaming as they fell to the field far below.

Cluny ran about in a berserk rage. Temporarily bereft of his senses, he seized hold of smoldering, injured rats, some with their fur alight.

"Get back up there, you cowards! Jump on to the wall!" he screamed in his madness.

The rats who had been attacking the gatehouse left off fighting and ran down the road to the fiery holocaust. Sparks crackled and shot off into the night sky. Cluny lashed out at all and sundry with his tail, foaming at the mouth and cursing wildly, his face a terrifying mask of insanity in the glare from the tower.

"It's only a bit of fire! Get back up there, you blundering fools! Kill the mice!"

Darkclaw and Fangburn grabbed hold of Cluny's smoldering cloak. They dragged him backwards.

"Get out of the way, Chief! It's starting to fall!"

With a roaring crackle and snap of blazing timber the siege tower leaned crazily to one side. It tottered, then collapsed in a flaring sheet of flame and sparks. The hay wagon listed drunkenly and was pulled over on to its side where it lay burning furiously.

*   *   *

The incident put an end to that night's fighting. On top of the wall cheering broke out. Cornflower was the heroine of the hour. She blushed as Foremole nodded admiringly.

"Arr, you'm looken more 'andsome in this loight, missy! Yurr, you gotten any vedgible soop left? Didn't give it all to those varments, did ye?"

Below the wall was a scene of mass carnage. The ground was littered with the bodies of attackers who had fallen prey to the flames in the ill-starred venture of the siege tower. Surrounded by his captains, Cluny was led down to the safety of the ditch. Apparently unaware of anything about him, he muttered dark words to himself, strange things that others could not comprehend.

Behind the Warlord's back the captains looked at each other in a puzzled fashion.

Had the mind of Cluny the Scourge finally snapped?

The fire had dwindled to smoldering embers by the next morning. Constance and the Abbot looked at the results from the ramparts. A wide area of the meadowland was burned black and scorched flat. Even now parts of it sizzled in the morning dew.

"Thank goodness it did not spread to the woods," said the Abbot, "otherwise all of Mossflower might have gone up in flames."

The badger stared sadly at the scorched earth. "True, no side uses fire as a weapon, not even Cluny. It is the one thing that spells certain death to creatures on both sides. We must look on it as an accident, Father Abbot."

"Accident or not, we owe Cornflower a debt of gratitude," replied the Abbot. "She is a very brave young fieldmouse. But for her swift action we would all have been under the heel of the tyrant today."

In the Abbey kitchens Cornflower stirred the oatmeal and checked on the bread baking in the oven. She smiled to herself. What would Matthias have thought of it all?

Last night's heroine. This morning's cook!

CHAPTER

6

While Log-a-Log held the rock from closing, Matthias peered into the hole. It was a long dark tunnel sloping down the side of the quarrystone.

There was neither sight nor sound of Guosim.

They called her name in loud whispers, not wanting to shout for fear of disturbing the snake. Matthias became impatient.

"Come on, Log-a-Log. We'll have to go in there. Be as quiet as you can."

"Wait a tick," the shrew replied. Taking a small boulder, he jammed the entrance slab from swinging shut. "I'm ready now. Lead on, Matthias."

They ventured cautiously into the long sloping passage, digging in their heels to prevent themselves sliding right down as Guosim probably had done. On reaching the bottom they stood awhile to let their eyes become accustomed to the gloom. The floor leveled out. The tunnel was high and broad enough to allow them to walk side by side without stooping. As they walked further, Log-a-Log pointed at strange symbols and weird signs that had been scraped into the surface of the soft stone. Though the quarry tunnels were natural, they had obviously been the lairs of generations of serpents; most of the signs were of a reptilian nature. The friends pressed onwards until the passage broadened out into a small chamber with two more tunnels leading from it.

"You take the left and I'll take the right," Matthias whispered. "Mark an arrow on the wall with your sword at intervals. I'll do the same with my dagger. That way we won't get lost. Should you find Asmodeus, come straight back to this chamber. If he finds you, then the best thing to do is run as fast as you can and shout like mad."

"Take care, warrior. I'll see you later," said Log-a-Log.

Gripping his dagger in readiness, Matthias crept into the right-hand tunnel. It was slightly narrower than the first, but just as high. The walls were yellow stone, so soft that it was almost like damp sand. Scarcely daring to breathe and glad that his feet made no sound on the sandy floor, Matthias went ahead, remembering to mark an arrow every few yards. From somewhere up ahead the young mouse could hear the sound of dripping water; the musical echoing plops made an eerie noise in the sinister stillness of the passage.

His paw encountered a space in the left wall. It turned out to be a rectangular anteroom. Matthias was horrified to discover that it was full of cast-off snake skins. They lay about on the floor, dry and withered. He shuddered at the thought of their former occupants, the hairs rising on the nape of his neck as he swiftly abandoned the repulsive scene and hurried along the passage.

It was more than twice as long as the entrance tunnel. As Matthias cut another arrow into the wall, he noticed that the carved symbols looked older, more primitive. This place had been a serpent's den long before it had been a quarry. The passage ended abruptly. Matthias walked out into an immense cavern.

Great Hall of Redwall would have fitted into a corner of this colossal structure. At its center was a vast shimmering lake that glowed with a pale phosphorescent light. The droplets of water came from somewhere high up in the dark recesses of the roof; they dripped steadily down and broke the surface of the subterranean lake, causing a continuous ripple. Matthias noticed that there were numerous other caverns and tunnels leading from this large cave.

"Asmodeusssssssss!"

The sound froze the very blood in his veins. The adder was close by: where he could not tell. The deadly hiss echoed all around him.

"Asmodeussssssssssssss!"

Matthias bravely tried to quell the panic that welled up inside him.

"If the snake knew where I was, he wouldn't waste his time trying to scare me," he reasoned. "He would have got me by now."

Feeling slightly reassured, but still very uneasy, Matthias circled the pool, trying hard to ignore the loathsome hissing sound.

"Asmodeussssssssssssss!"

Summoning up his courage, he stole silently into the nearest cave. In the glow that reflected from the pool, Matthias saw a sight that gladdened his heart.

There was Guosim seated with her back against the wall!

Matthias ran across and seized the Guerrilla Shrew by her paw. "Guosim, how did you get here, you little nuisance? We've been sear—"

Guosim toppled on her side, dead!

With a strangled sob the young mouse recoiled. He could see the poison-fang marks clearly upon the shrew's chest. Guosim's face was bloated, the eyes screwed shut, the lips blackened.

"Asmodeussssssssssssssss!"

Matthias stumbled from the gruesome death-larder of the adder, out into the main cavern. He sat for a while shuddering with horror at what he had seen, hardly believing that the still body had been a warm, living, breathing creature not long ago. Forcing himself to rise and carry on, Matthias continued his explorations.

The next entrance was a tiny hole in the wall, scarcely worth bothering about. Nevertheless, he decided to investigate it. Crouching on all fours, Matthias forced his way into the hole which proved to be another tunnel. He began forcing his way along its narrow length.

"Asmodeussssssssssssssss!"

The dreadful sound was much closer now! Struggling and pushing forward, he came to the end of the tunnel.

Suddenly Matthias was face to face with the giant adder.

"Asmodeussssssssssssssssss!"

The huge reptile was sleeping. With every breath it expelled, the snake's tongue flickered out, repeating the vile name: "Asmodeussssssssssssss!"

Matthias stared in mute fascination. The snake's eyes were

not shut but filmed over in sleep. It was breathing slowly and regularly. The huge muscular scaly body was coiled in no recognizable pattern. At odd intervals the immense coils would shift lazily with a dry scaly rustle; the head, however, remained fixed in the same position. Across the jumble of banded coils Matthias thought he could catch a glimpse of the tapering tail.

There were other things in the lair of the snake: a fox's tail, wood-pigeon wings, the head of a big fish, and fur pelts of many species of creatures.

But Matthias saw only the sword of Martin the Warrior!

It hung from the fork of a tree root at the back of the viper's den. A large red pommel-stone was set into the top of the hilt. The handle was of black leather and silver to match the belt and scabbard. Below a heavy silver crosspiece was the blade. Made from the finest steel, its double edges tapered to a ruthlessly-sharp tip. Down the center of the blade ran a blood channel, either side of which there were symbols which Matthias could not make out.

This was truly the Sword of Redwall Abbey! It was his duty to get it. Matthias moved more stealthily than he had ever done in all his life. Inch by careful inch, paw by whisker, slowly, painstakingly trying to make his body as small as possible, he flattened himself against the wall to get by the huge spadelike head. The tongue almost slithered across his face as it slid in and out, constantly repeating the dreaded name.

"Asmodeussssssssssssssssss!"

He felt the adder breathing, its cold exhalations carrying the sweet musty odor of death stirring his whiskers. A coil moved and faintly touched his leg. Matthias sucked in his breath and squeezed closer to the wall. The snake blinked, sending the opaque tissue upwards. The young mouse was confronted by the wide-open eye of the monster staring directly at him.

"Asmodeussssssssssssssssss!"

The eye filmed over again as the snake carried on with whatever evil vision it was dreaming. Sweat like ice water drenched Matthias's fur. Asmodeus had opened his eye while still remaining asleep. There was no other explanation possible.

The moments of suspense ticked by for what seemed ages until Matthias managed to squeeze past the serpent's head. Avoiding the gigantic coils, he walked quickly and quietly over to where the sword hung from the tree roots on the cave wall.

Matthias lifted the ancient sword down. Reverently he placed both paws around the handle. Tighter and tighter he gripped it until the point lifted from the floor and the bright blade stood out level in front of him. He sensed how Martin must have felt each time he had held this beautiful weapon. The young mouse knew that he had been born for this moment, his grip causing the tremor of the steel to run through his entire body. It was part of him!

Matthias's main concern was to get safely away with the sword. In the confined space of the snake's den there was no room to wield the fabled blade. If he struck at Asmodeus, he would be crushed to death against the walls by the powerful lashing coils of the adder in its death throes. Nothing would be accomplished by such a foolhardy action. Like a seasoned fighter, the young mouse chose to nominate the time and place of combat. He looked around the den. The hole he had come through was obviously too small for the adder to have used for the same purpose. It served as a breathing hole for Asmodeus, also as amplification to echo the dreaded name through the caves and tunnels as a warning to intruders.

Near the snake's tail which lay directly across his path, he saw the skins and pelts on the cave wall tremble slightly. They were covering the only possible entrance and exit for a reptile of such enormous girth. Emboldened by his ownership of Martin's weapon, Matthias tickled the tail lightly with the sword point. It had the desired effect. The long, scale-encrusted coils rippled as the serpent changed position in its sleep. Speedily he slipped through the curtain of skins into the passage. It curved in a crescent-shaped arc, bringing Matthias back into the main cavern with its luminous lake.

Log-a-Log came dashing, pale-faced, out of the cave that contained Guosim's body. Eyes wide with terror, he ran straight into the paws of his mouse friend, narrowly missing injury on the sword blade.

Before he could be silenced he yelled out in a panic-stricken shout, "Matthias, Guosim's dead! I've just seen her in that cave! She's dead! Guosim is dead!"

In his den down the tunnel, Asmodeus came awake.

CHAPTER
7

The captains of Redwall looked to Constance for guidance.
There was no question of overriding her commands. Of all the
woodlanders she was the oldest and wisest creature within the
walls. The badger was slow-thinking and deliberate, but straight
as a die. Her knowledge was born of vast experience, the natural
cunning of a survivor.

Jess, Winifred and Basil stood solidly behind Constance.
They had just related to her the latest piece of intelligence received. The attackers would emerge from their completed tunnel
sometime around mid-afternoon.

The badger thanked them and shook her striped head knowingly. She had not been caught off guard, thanks to Foremole.
Now she would need the aid and specialized knowhow of the
mole leader to stave off this latest threat to the Abbey.

Cluny the Scourge was still acting strangely. He sat in his
patched-up tent at the far edge of the meadow and said nothing.
Even when Killconey marched jubilantly up with the news that
the tunnel was within a fraction of being completed, Cluny sat
and stared at the ground. He did not appear in the least moved
by the good tidings.

The ferret stood awkwardly, ill at ease, awaiting orders. Cluny
sat unmoving, as if he had forgotten Killconey's presence. The
ferret tried once more.

"It's the tunnel, Chief. We'll have it ready by this after-noon!"

The Warlord looked up blankly.

"Oh yes, the tunnel! Well, carry on. Er, you know what to do. I've got things to think about," he muttered absently.

Outside in the meadow, Fangburn and Darkclaw listened in disbelief to the ferret.

"I tell you, he's off his rocker," said Killconey. "Sittin' there like a stuffed dummy, ha! Things to think about, if you please! Meanwhile, we've got the whole horde ready to go through that there tunnel and take the Abbey. What're we supposed to do?"

"There's only one thing we can do," replied the stolid Dark-claw. "We've got to carry it through ourselves while the Chief's not well."

"Darkclaw's right," agreed Fangburn. "The three of us will take charge of the whole business."

They both looked at the ferret, waiting for him to express an opinion.

"I suppose you're right," Killconey said. "But listen. The rest of the army mustn't get to know about the Chief, otherwise they'll desert. Y'know, I can't seriously believe that Cluny's out of his mind. Just you wait and see. It's probably just another grand ould plan he's thinking up."

The trio of self-appointed generals marched down to the tunnel. They climbed inside to check upon progress. It was long, dark and smelly. Weasels and stoats jostled past them carrying baskets of earth or dragging rocks and roots. Killconey pointed out the finer details to his fellow commanders.

"Sure, we're right underneath the road now. The ground is good and hard. It didn't need any shoring at all. Now, see the footings of the wall! Mind your heads! From here I've had some props put in to hold the weight. Farther on the going gets really soft, but we've run out of decent timber. Still, I don't reckon it'll make a great deal of difference. If we move the army along fast enough we should all be inside the Abbey before they know what's hit them."

Above ground, a mole leaning his ear against a thinly-beaten copper basin that was upturned on the earth listened carefully to every word the ferret was saying. He repeated it to Brother

Walter, who wrote everything down word for word.

Constance scanned the report and picked up her heavy cudgel.
"Before we know what's hit us, eh?" she growled. "We'll
be doing some hitting of our own before the day is through!"

From the south-west corner of the wall, moles had marked the
exact run of the tunnel with two lines of cord and pegs. Foremole and his team knew all there was to know about the dig-
gings: depth, approximate dimensions, the placement of shoring,
even where the first rat's head was likely to break ground. The
plan that Constance and Foremole had jointly worked out would
require very little hand-to-hand combat, much to the badger's
displeasure.

Two oversized cauldrons of boiling water stood ready on tri-
pods with slow fires burning beneath them to keep up the temperature. Constance and the beaver positioned themselves
behind these, tipstaves at the ready. All available mice and
woodland defenders were gathered in two groups, on either side
of the cord-marked aisle. They waited, looking to the badger for
further instructions. To a passing stranger it might have looked
like some strange Abbey ritual: two fires, two parallel cords,
and all the serious-faced creatures gathered in two groups on
the grass in the hot June afternoon, waiting silently.

The armed ranks of the horde were formed up in the ditch.
Fangburn marched up and down, issuing final instructions. It
had not been an easy task getting them in line without Cluny
there, but the persuasive tongue of Killconey had assured them
that the Chief was aware of their every move and would deal
with malcontents and troublemakers later on.

"Pay attention now," Fangburn called. "Darkclaw is up at
the end of the tunnel. When the diggers break through he will
leap up into the Abbey grounds. Four soldiers are with him.
They'll hold off any attack while the rest of us get above
ground. Now, once you are up don't hang about. Make straight
for the Abbey building. Try to capture the mouse Abbot. Darkclaw won't be with you; he'll take some warriors and fight his
way through to the gate. Once it's open the others will be able
to get in. I don't need to tell you, these are not peaceful creatures
we are up against. You've seen for yourselves; they've had a
certain amount of luck to date, but they are determined fighters,

so when you get up there Cluny wants you to show them what a horde of trained soldiers can really do! Don't forget, the Chief knows how to reward good fighters when it comes to splitting up plunder.''

Cluny had fallen asleep in his tent. He needed peace to clear his troubled mind. But peace was not easy to come by when the mouse warrior visited his dreams once more.

Try as he would, Cluny could not evade the grim avenger with the sword. Shades of creatures that he had slain through the years came back to mock him. They got in his way, tripping him so that he stumbled and fell. Each time he would rise wearily and start to run again, the nemesis at his back, pursuing, striding unhurriedly, never changing pace as the wraiths of his dead captains, Skullface, Redtooth, Ragear, and Cheesethief, hovered about, urging him to turn and face the warrior mouse. But he dared not turn. He kept running.

The two weasel diggers thrust upwards in the narrow confines of the tunnel. They sprang aside as earth showered down and daylight poured in. With a seething press of soldiers behind him, Darkclaw stepped up to the waiting diggers. They boosted him upwards. He grabbed at the grass, his spear tucked under one claw. He stopped suddenly, his body halfway out of the hole.

The first things he saw were two huddled crowds of small creatures. They stood either side of a double line of pegs and rope. Darkclaw grinned wolfishly. They were obviously playing some kind of silly little country game. He had caught them unarmed.

A noise from behind distracted the rat. He swiveled around. He found himself facing two huge cauldrons which bubbled and simmered ominously over twin fires. Behind them stood the big badger and another strange-looking creature, equally well built.

Darkclaw set his claws against the ground to lever his body out of the hole. Before he could do anything to stop them the badger and her companion tipped the bulky pots over.

Darkclaw did not even get a chance to scream out a death cry. Boiling water cascaded down over his head in a hissing, steaming deluge. The force of the rushing water sent his body plummeting back down the hole. Endless gallons of scalding water hit the rats in the tunnel like a hellish tidal wave. The tightly packed rodents were instantly slain.

On the surface, Constance cried out to the waiting defenders. "Jump in between the ropes. Now!"

The weight of combined bodies hit the ground between the lines.

Constance began a steady chant: "Jump-two-three! Jump-two-three! Jump-two-three!"

Under the constant pounding of countless feet the whole area that had been marked out by the moles suddenly sank into a trench. The tunnel had collapsed.

The defenders stood and cheered in the depression directly above what had once been Killconey's tunnel. The badger gave the order to stop. Foremole and his crew moved in to block off the hole with rocks and rubble. Friar Hugo ordered the cauldrons to be carried back inside to his kitchens. The Abbey creatures fell silent and drifted away from the heap of stones which blocked the hole, a fitting headstone for a mass grave of the enemy.

At the tunnel entrance in the ditch, Fangburn and Killconey were madly thrust aside as rats, weasels, ferrets and stoats fought their way out of the tunnel.

"Hey, what's happened?" Fangburn shouted. "Come back here this minute! Where d'you think you're all going?"

The defeated warriors ignored him. Caked with filthy mud and trailing broken spears, they dashed off along the ditch.

Killconey peered into the tunnel. All he saw was the battered body of a stoat being borne towards him on what appeared to be a boiling wave of ooze. The ferret jumped backwards as the shoring burst and the tunnel workings caved in with a dull rumble of earth.

As Cluny ran, another specter appeared in his fevered dream, it was a hideous-looking thing covered in a dark steaming substance. It stood barring his way with its arms stretched wide as if to embrace him. Cluny pushed it savagely from him. It moaned piteously: "Chief, it's me, Darkclaw. Look what they did to me."

Outside the tent Killconey and Fangburn exchanged uneasy glances.

"You dug the tunnel, so you go in first."

"No fear, I'm only a ferret. You're a naturally superior rat. You'd better go first."

"Shall we go in together, then?"

"Better not. It looks like the Chief's asleep. He might not thank us for waking him up out of a nice dream."

"Aye, that's true. Let's leave it until later."

CHAPTER
8

Asmodeus's eyes glared through the narrow hole in front of him. There were two creatures standing together in the big cavern, a shrew and a mouse. He hissed in anger. The mouse was holding his sword, his own beautiful sword!

The adder bunched his sinewy coils and shot through the skin-hung opening. He bared his evil poisoned fangs. No mouse was going to steal the sword of the serpent.

Matthias seized the frightened Guerrilla Shrew by his paw, pulling him along at a swift run.

"Asmodeus must know we're here by now. Come on, Log-a-Log! Let's get out of this place, quick!"

They hurried down the nearest opening, immediately spinning around and racing back. Asmodeus was in the passage sliding towards them. They paused momentarily in the big cavern. With the shrew on one paw and the sword in the other, Matthias looked wildly about.

"Over there, Log-a-Log! Move!"

Skirting the edges of the shimmering pool, the two friends dashed into a smallish tunnel at the other side.

Behind them in the cavern the giant adder settled down to a leisurely slither, his tongue flickered wickedly.

"Asmodeussssssss! No hurry now, they are not going anywhere!"

With a cry of dismay the fleeing pair saw the blank wall ahead. They had run into a cul-de-sac!

Log-a-Log had stopped. His teeth were beginning to chatter. "Th . . . th . . . th . . . there's no way out! We're trapped!"

Matthias continued running to the dead end. He felt the surface of the wall, and ran his paws up and down it.

"We must do something," he panted. "There must be some way to escape the snake. Get hold of yourself, shrew. Think!"

Asmodeus poked his head into the entrance. His sibilant voice called in to them: "Stay where you are, little ones. I will come to you, Asmodeussss!"

Log-a-Log had gone rigid with fright. He stood petrified. Matthias had begun digging furiously at the wall with his sword point. He gouged and thrusted, muttering to himself. "At least we've got nothing to lose but a sword and our lives. There might be something on the other side."

The sword struck a tree root. He dug around it, probing, probing busily until the soft half-formed sandstone gave beneath the blade. Frantically, Matthias redoubled his efforts.

Log-a-Log gave a strangled sob. In the dim distance of the tunnel, Asmodeus could be seen advancing slowly but surely towards them.

Matthias felt the sword of Martin break through the stone. He looked back over his shoulder. The giant adder was slithering closer with each passing second. He hacked madly to widen the opening he had made. Sticking the sword in the ground, he grabbed Log-a-Log and shook him soundly.

"Here, shrew! You are smaller than I am! Climb through, then see if you can tug me backwards by my feet. Come on, move yourself if you want to live!"

Log-a-Log came out of his trance. Leaping quickly into the hole, he scratched the damp sandy grit left and right. Ducking beneath the tree root, he scrabbled awkwardly through into a tiny cell-like space on the other side.

Asmodeus was close to Matthias now. Wielding the sword, the young mouse backed off. He felt the hole behind him and scrambled into it sideways, still facing his enemy. Taking care not to let the sword-point drop, he shouted to his companion, "Log-a-Log, can you see my feet? Grab hold of them, pull me through."

Matthias hung uncomfortably. He tightened his paws on the

sword-handle and moved it from side to side with the sway of the big viper's head. Suddenly he felt the shrew pulling on his feet. Wriggling his body, Matthias started to move backwards. Asmodeus bared his fangs. He moved forward at the struggling mouse. Matthias swung the blade at the snake's open mouth. It hissed and recoiled. As Matthias contorted himself to negotiate the tree root, he poked the point of the blade at his enemy's head.

"Stay back, evil one, or I'll kill you!" he shouted.

Asmodeus gave a low, soothing, hiss. "Come to me, little mouse. Let me wrap myself around you. I will give you the kiss of eternal sleep."

With a triumphant shout the young mouse disappeared completely into the hole. He fell on top of Log-a-Log at the other side. Forcefully the snake launched his great body at the opening, crumbling earth and rock as he pushed his coils through the aperture.

"He's coming!" Log-a-Log screamed in terror.

Matthias shoved his friend behind him. Planting his feet wide apart he hefted the great sword in both paws.

"Stay out of the way, shrew. There's no more retreating. All ends here!"

The gigantic spadelike head of the snake thrust itself through into the small space.

"Give me my sword, mouse, and I will make your dying easy!" he hissed.

Matthias laughed in the face of the adder. "Come and get it, Poisonteeth."

Asmodeus tried forcing his body through with one swift thrust. He found his bunched coils jammed firmly in the tree root. Relaxing, he allowed his head to wave from side to side.

"Look at me, my little friend. I can see that you are a great warrior. You are not afraid to gaze into my eyes. Look at me."

The eyes seemed to expand and dilate until they filled the whole of Matthias's vision. They dominated him. He could not tear his gaze away. Asmodeus continued in a persuasive undertone.

"See, they are the twin pools of eternity. Sink into them, and you will find darkness and rest."

Log-a-Log was completely hypnotized. Matthias, too, felt overcome by an immense lethargy. The adder's voice was a

cold, dark, green velvet fog that threatened to envelop him. He
stared deep into the deadly eyes, his lids began to droop heavily. . . .

Martin the Warrior strode boldly up through the dark mist.

*"I am that is! Matthias, why do you sleep! There is a war-
rior's work to be done here! Pick up your sword, Matthias! The
evil one shall not have it. Strike out for me now, my brave young
champion!"*

Asmodeus was working his body free, pushing forward.

Matthias's eyes were shut, his lips moved with one word.
"Strike."

Suddenly the spell of the snake was broken. The young
mouse's eyes snapped open, clear and bright. He swung the
ancient sword high and struck at the giant adder.

He struck for Redwall!

He struck against evil!

He struck for Martin!

He struck for Log-a-Log and his shrews!

He struck for dead Guosim!

He struck as Methuselah would have wanted him to!

He struck against Cluny the Scourge and tyranny!

He struck out against Captain Snow's ridicule!

He struck for the world of light and freedom!

He struck until his paws ached and the sword fell from them!

When Log-a-Log awoke from out of the trance he saw his friend
Matthias the Warrior.

He stood shaking. His chest heaved with exertion. His paws
hung limp at his sides. The great sword lay against the warrior's
blood-flecked habit, its long, deadly blade crimsoned in victory.

And the head of Asmodeus Poisonteeth, the giant adder, lay
severed upon the ground, its eyes dulled in death, never again
to hypnotize another living creature!

CHAPTER

9

It was the afternoon of the following day. Matthias marched into the farmyard at the head of all the Guerrilla Union of Shrews in Mossflower. He halted the entire regiment outside the barn and turned to Log-a-Log.

"Wait here, my friend. There's someone I have to see."

The young mouse stood in the gloom of the barn, knowing he was being watched. Without turning or looking around he addressed the cat.

"Julian, it is Matthias. I have returned."

The marmalade cat loomed up out of the half-light. "So I see. Welcome, little friend! Is that the sword you told me of?"

Matthias proffered the blade for inspection. "It is indeed. Asmodeus the snake lies dead. I slew him with this very weapon. It is the great sword of Martin the Warrior!"

Squire Julian Gingivere handled the sword with care. He laid it on a hay bale. Sitting next to it, he folded his paws under him and half shut his eyes.

"Matthias, let me give you some good advice. I am much older than you and have seen far more of life. There are not many illusions left to me, and I do not want to shatter your dreams or blight your ambitions, my friend, but I must say what I have to.

"We Squires of Gingivere are an ancient line. In the past I have seen many such tokens as this weapon. My grandsires

305

owned a vast armory full of magnificent and valued battle equipment. No doubt your sword is indeed a beautiful thing. It is a tribute to whoever forged it in bygone ages. There are very few such swords as this one left in the world, but remember, it is only a sword, Matthias!

"It contains no secret spell, nor holds within its blade any magical power. This sword is made for only one purpose, to kill. It will only be as good or evil as the one who wields it. I know that you intend to use it only for the good of your Abbey, Matthias; do so, but never allow yourself to be tempted into using it in a careless or idle way. It would inevitably cost you your life, or that of your dear ones.

"Martin the Warrior used the sword only for right and good. This is why it has become a symbol of power to Redwall. Knowledge is gained through wisdom, my friend. Use the sword wisely."

Matthias picked up his weapon. He was surprised at Julian's words. They were an echo of something that his old companion Methuselah had once said to him.

"Thank you, Julian," he said. "I will remember your lesson well. Now I must ask a favor of you. Would you come with me? I want you to be present when I speak to Captain Snow."

The cat sniffed disdainfully. "You ask quite a lot. I wouldn't do this for anyone else, you know."

Reluctantly Julian stalked out into the sunlight with Matthias. There was an immediate spate of loud, frightened chatter from the regiment of Guerrilla Shrews. Squire Julian Gingivere merely nodded, and addressed them in a regal but distant manner: "Good afternoon. Very clement weather for the time of year, don't you think?"

For the first time since the formation of their union, the shrews stood in slack-jawed silence, completely lost for an answer!

As they strolled along, Julian protested to his companion, "Really, Matthias, I think you are asking a bit much of one. Does one have to stand around listening to that befeathered regimental bore giving air to his hide-bound militaristic views? Oh, it's too much!"

Matthias stroked the sulky cat's forepaw. "Come on, Julian. I think you'll be pleasantly surprised."

The marmalade cat stifled a yawn. "You don't say. Has another tree fallen upon the pompous old fool?"

Captain Snow paced around the base of his nest tree. He glared at the cat, then at the mouse holding the sword. He snorted, hunching his neck into ruffles and folding his wings behind him.

"Listen, mouse. I don't want to hear how you did it. Probably wouldn't believe you anyhow. But here you are, and I suppose that's that?"

Matthias hid a smile; he tapped his foot in mock impatience. "I'm waiting, Cap'n Snow, sir. Remember your promises on oath?"

The owl's eyes bulged with ill temper. He flung Basil's medal at the young mouse's feet.

"There! Take your medal back, you insolent little pup. I'm not saying another word while that salad-eating cat is within hearing range."

Matthias traced patterns in the dust with the sword-point and spoke civilly to the owl. "Well, Cap'n Snow, sir. I never took you for a bad sport. Besides, I've got an entire regiment of shrews hidden all about. They're waiting to hear you honor your wager."

The owl spread his wide, snowy wings and flapped upwards to perch on the edge of his den. Folding the wings and shutting his eyes tightly, he shouted out with bad grace, "I promise never to kill or eat another mouse or shrew of any type as long as I live, so there!"

He hooted and vanished swiftly into his den.

Instantly the shrews broke cover, dancing and whooping with delight.

Captain Snow popped his head out of the nest. "Go away! Begone! I can't stand it, all those little dinners dancing around. It's too much, I tell you!"

"Excuse my mentioning it, sir," Matthias shouted over the hubbub. "But what about your promise regarding our friend the Squire?"

The owl emerged grumpy and ruffled. Thoroughly humiliated, he called out to his former friend the cat, "It was all my fault. I apologize to you, Squire Julian."

He was completely taken aback by the cat's reply. "Not at all, my dear friend. It is I that must apologize to you. The whole incident was entirely due to my priggishness and lack of manners.''

Captain Snow swooped down and perched near the cat. ''D'you really think so? Oh, come on, Julian, old chap. I must share the blame. It was my barrack-room feeding habits that started the whole thing. You mustn't blame yourself, old friend.''

A rare smile covered the features of the normally laconic Julian. He purred comfortably. ''No, no. I insist that we share the blame fifty-fifty. Besides, the question won't arise now that you've sworn off shrews and mice. I say, have you ever tried a fresh trout salad with mustard and cress? Why don't you come over to the barn? I'm sure there'll be enough for two. I mean, trout's not exactly a vegetable, is it?''

Wing in paw, the reunited comrades strolled off to the barn, chatting amiably as if there had never been a cross word between them. Julian was last to enter the barn. He gave Matthias a broad wink.

''Who knows, my friend? Maybe the sword does possess some magic. Personally, I think it's the warrior who wields it.''

For the first time in many days, Matthias laughed heartily. He felt so good within himself. After all the action and mental strain, travel and grief, he felt suddenly reborn, larger than life and brimming with new-found self-confidence. Certainly there were great difficulties and hard tasks ahead of him; when the time came he would handle them. For the present he was satisfied with this feeling of immense happiness.

Holding the sword lightly, he balanced its point against the earth and laughed freely. It was infectious: Log-a-Log joined in; then one Guerilla Shrew; then another, and still yet more, until the whole regiment and their warrior mouse friend set the countryside ringing from river to woods to farm and field with the happy sounds of their honest joy.

CHAPTER

10

The Cluny that emerged from the ragged tent in the meadow
was far from being sick in the head.

The members of the horde watched the way he strode pur-
posefully about. The old glint was back in his single eye. His
orders were crisp and concise. Even the long tail had a fresh
crack about it. The Chief seemed sharper than he had been before.

In the aftermath of the tunnel disaster, Cluny had called off
the attack for a full day, withdrawing all his followers well back
across the meadow. The Warlord gave his horde time to recu-
perate from the fiasco: a whole day's leisure, with no recrimi-
nations and hardly any orders.

The captains of Redwall wasted no time in making use of the
temporary respite. Repairs were started upon the gatehouse door.
Teams of woodland carpenters, Abbey smiths and laborers, plus
any creatures that felt the need to help were lowered down to
the road in large wickerwork baskets. Should the enemy in the
meadow decide to make any sudden move, the workmen could
be speedily hauled back up to the ramparts. All that day the
rope gangs were kept busy sending down wood, spikes, cordage,
tools and repair materials.

Cluny sat and watched them from the distance as he talked
aloud to himself. "Good work, mice, strengthen my gates. I

wouldn't want to rule a fortress with broken doors.''

Fangburn was passing. He overheard Cluny conversing with himself. Not sure whether the remarks were addressed to him, he stopped.

"Er, are you feeling all right, Chief?"

"Never better!" Cluny replied. He pointed at the repair crews. "See that, Fangburn? Honest industrious work, and what for, eh?"

Fangburn hazarded a guess. "To keep us out, Chief?"

"No, to stop us getting in," Cluny chuckled. "Get some soldiers and light a fire down in the ditch. Make it a proper blaze, good and hot."

Fangburn knew better than to question the reason for his Chief's order, no matter how strange it sounded.

"A big fire? Right you are, Chief. I'll get them going right away."

Fangburn hurried off, aware that Cluny was watching him.

Shortly after there was a huge fire burning in the ditch. The horde gathered close by to see what Cluny was up to. The crackling flames gave off waves of heat, causing everyone to step back. Above the ditch the air shimmered and danced.

Cluny stood in the ditch, claws on hips. He cracked his tail. "Scumnose, Mangefur! Bring up those dormice prisoners!"

The twenty dormice were dragged forward in a pitiable condition. They cowered on the ground in front of the Warlord, half starved and dull-eyed.

Cluny pointed. "You, leader mouse! What's your name again?"

"Plumpen, sir," the bedraggled mouse replied.

Cluny grabbed Plumpen roughly, dragging him away from his fellow captives on the ground.

"What are these other miserable creatures to you, Plumpen?" he snapped.

The dormouse explained in a shaky voice: "My family, sir. My mother, father, brothers, sisters, and my wife and two little ones. Oh please, sir, spare them, I beg you!"

Cluny laughed cruelly. His eye was devoid of pity. He leaned close to Plumpen and whispered harshly, "What would you do to save them?"

The dormouse watched Cluny's eye rove lazily from his family to the blazing inferno.

"Anything! Anything you say! What do you want of me?" he screamed in his fear and anxiety.

Cluny cracked his tail triumphantly, pulling Plumpen forward until their noses touched. The big rat's voice was as foul and evil as his breath.

"Listen carefully. You are going to open the Abbey door for me, my friend. If you fail, your precious little family will pay the penalty! Now, here is what you must do."

Constance hauled upon her rope. It was no hard task for a fully-grown badger. On the other ropes there were creatures that could not compare with her for strength, but they hauled and pulled with an equally good will. Cornflower and Silent Sam kept busy supplying cool drinks and sweat cloths. The repair work went ahead at a steady pace.

No one noticed that there was an extra mouse laboring among the workers in the roadway.

Plumpen!

Cluny had supplied him with a habit taken from the body of one who had fallen slain from the ramparts. Plumpen had concealed himself in the ditch and traveled under cover until he was level with the gatehouse. At the appropriate moment he slipped out with a plank upon his shoulder and joined the work force. They toiled away industriously until Jess Squirrel, who was acting as overseer, decided that the work was completed, as indeed it was. The old gatehouse door looked as good as new. All the tools and spare timber were gathered up and the roadway was swept. Satisfied with a job well done, the work crews stacked up their materials, and were hauled up to the ramparts in the large grain baskets. Plumpen sat between Brother Alf and Brother Rufus. Across the meadow he could see Cluny, watching, always watching.

Plumpen cursed the fate that had put him and his family in the hands of the rats. What a happy, friendly lot the Redwall creatures were. He was served afternoon tea sitting on the grass in the cloisters. The dormouse felt the good food turn to ashes in his mouth at the thought of his betrayal of fellow mice, but there was no alternative if he wanted to save his family. After tea he

wandered off on the pretense of carrying out some fictitious task.
When there was nobody about, he hid himself in the old gatehouse den which had once been Methuselah's study. Locking
the door, Plumpen lay down lonely and miserable to await nightfall.

Inside Cavern Hole the Father Abbot addressed a morale-
boosting speech to his captains.

"Friends, it will avail Cluny little to put the Abbey under
state of siege. As you know, Redwall is virtually self-supporting.
All we require to sustain life and comfort is here within these
walls. Therefore, I suggest we carry on as normally as possible.

"However, the walls must always be guarded. I leave it to
you, my captains. Stay ever vigilant against Cluny and his horde.
I know that with your counsel and good judgment, we will soon
see the day when the enemy are forced to go elsewhere and
leave Redwall in peace."

There was loud applause for the Abbot's heartening words,
but Constance was not convinced. She whispered her thoughts
to Basil and Jess. "Never. Cluny won't leave us alone until
either we are dead, or he is!"

Basil Stag Hare nodded in agreement. "I know, old scout.
But the Abbot's such a decent old buffer that he believes there's
good in everyone, even Cluny. What?"

"And so do I," Jess muttered. "I believe Cluny *will* be good
someday. Good and dead!"

Gradually the day drew to a close. Lights dimmed as Redwall
prepared for a well-deserved night's rest. The meadowland and
woods grew quiet and peaceful. On top of the walls, sentries
leaned on the parapet listening to the evening bird-songs. Across
the meadows the enemy campfires burned low into the soft June
night.

Plumpen waited another hour as Cluny had instructed: then it
was time to make his move. Stealing quietly out of the gatehouse study the dormouse headed north, staying well within the
deep shadow of the wall. At the small north wall gate, Plumpen
drew a scarlet cloth from his habit. Smearing the bolts with
grease from the cloth, he silently worked them loose.

Killconey lay watching the gate from behind a sycamore in

the woods. Near to every other entrance one of Cluny's most
trusted soldiers was concealed, awaiting the signal. It was the
ferret who was rewarded by the sight of the scarlet cloth being
shoved through the doorjamb. He hurried away to tell Cluny.

It was dead of night when Cluny's horde moved out of the
meadow. Around the embers of each campfire, bundles of grass
and twigs had been wrapped in blankets. To the unsuspecting
sentries on the wall the bundles looked like sleeping forms: they
sensed nothing amiss. The horde circled northwards through the
meadowlands until Cluny judged they were far enough from
Redwall to escape detection. He crossed the road at the head of
his army.

They filtered back through the leafy cover of nighttime Mossflower towards the Abbey. Now that his goal was in sight, Cluny
used all the stealth of a stalking hunter, waiting until the entire
horde was in position. Each soldier crouching quietly among the
ferns and bushes knew the penalty for making any sound that
would betray their presence; not death from the defenders, but
death at the claws of their own Chieftain.

Cluny could wait. He gave it another half-hour, until he could
actually see some of the guards on top of the wall nodding off
at their posts. What was thirty minutes, after he had waited so
long for this moment? With practiced skill he slid from his hiding place and crossed to the wall door. One gentle push and the
small iron door swung slowly open on its greased hinges. Cluny
stood in the doorway as his soldiers filed past him on their way
to the Abbey building. There was little need to worry about the
wall guards. Those who were awake would be watching the road
or the enemy camp, their backs turned on the secret invaders.

Plumpen stood by, anxiously watching the Warlord. At least
his family would be safe now. The dormouse had faithfully carried out his part in the dreadful scheme; Cluny must surely keep
to his word. He did not see the look that passed between Cluny
and Fangburn.

Fangburn swung the heavy club and brought it crashing down
on the back of Plumpen's head from behind. The unlucky dormouse crumpled to the ground without a sound.

Cluny the Scourge bared his fangs, grinning wickedly into
the dark. He had finally brought his horde into Redwall!

CHAPTER

11

The last rays of the sinking sun streamed through the open barn doorway, lighting up formerly darkened corners. Matthias lay on the hay amid the remnants of an epic celebration feast. The Guerrilla Union of Shrews in Mossflower had really outdone themselves laying out this spread. He picked up a truffle and tossed it away with a sigh of satisfaction, fearing he might burst if he forced another bite into his mouth.

On one side of the young mouse the gifts from Squire Julian Gingivere, Captain Snow and the shrews were piled high; on the other was his sword, reflecting the rays of the afternoon sun. The Guerrilla Shrew regiment had chosen to sleep off the effects of the party outside in the sun. They lay about the farmyard, too full even to argue.

Log-a-Log shuffled lazily in and flopped down beside his mouse friend.

"Greetings, oh mighty warrior," he giggled. "Savior of the shrews, slayer of Poisonteeth; he who speaks with cats, friend-maker of owls and uniter of—"

"Oh shut up, you noisy little devil!" Matthias chuckled as he kicked Log-a-Log off the hay into the dust.

"D'you know much about birds?" Log-a-Log said. "What about sparrows?"

Matthias yawned. "Well, what about sparrows? I've had some dealings with 'em. What do you need to know?"

"Nothing really," the shrew murmured sleepily. "But there's been one reported over at the edge of the woods. Of course, no one can understand a single word that the savage heathen is saying. She's screeching away back there, hopping and dancing about, working herself up into a right old tizz-wozz, or so I've been told."

Matthias sprang up, grabbing his sword. "Come on, Log-a-Log. I speak the Sparra language. We'd best get over there and find out what's upsetting her."

With a score of Guerrilla Shrews in their wake the two companions set off for Mossflower on the double.

Above the long grass in front of the woods the Sparra warrior could be seen. She fluttered up and down creating a raucous din. Log-a-Log and the shrews were taken aback when Matthias ran ahead of them, shouting at the top of his voice, "Warbeak Sparra, thatta you, old worm warrior!"

Joyfully the two friends reunited. They rolled about in the grass like a pair of mad creatures, pounding each other on the back.

"Matthias mouse! Old wormfriend! Big fat warrior now! How are you?"

The shrews were completely baffled. They sat about scratching their heads at the strange behavior of the sparrow and the mouse. Matthias chattered to Warbeak in the rapid Sparra tongue, telling of all that had happened since they last parted. Warbeak for her part told Matthias of her fortunes to date.

Upon the death of King Bull Sparra, Warbeak had been crowned Queen. Dunwing, her mother, had wished it to be so. The tribe was happy under the wise rule of its youngest-ever Queen. No more would sparrows have to live under the claw of an unpredictable maniac.

After Warbeak had related her story she became grave. "Matthias, Redwall have big trouble. We watch, see from roof. Ratworm make lotta plans, mice brave warriors. Alla time fight back, beat ratworms plenty. But Warbeak watch ratworm King. He badworse than King Bull. Him make bad plan, catch Abbey. Ratworm soon be inside Redwall. Matthias mouse come quick. Bring sword."

An icy claw of fear gripped Matthias's stomach. He sat down hard in the grass.

Log-a-Log shook his friend. "What's she saying, Matthias? You look as if you've seen the ghost of Poisonteeth. For goodness' sake, what's going on?"

"It's my home, Redwall," Matthias said in a hollow voice. "Cluny the Scourge is about to capture it!"

Log-a-Log spoke urgently to the shrews. "Quick, get the regiment ready as fast as you can. We're off to the Abbey at Redwall. Tell them to catch us up. I want no argument or votes! Tell every shrew to be fully armed. We must march night and day if we are to save Matthias's friends."

Matthias picked up the sword of Martin. "By thunder, Log-a-Log! You're right! I fought hard for this sword in order to save Redwall! Come on!"

"Shrewmouse help you. How many warrior him got?" Warbeak chimed.

"A full complement," Log-a-Log answered. "About five hundred shrews."

Warbeak spread her wings. "I bring alla tribe Sparra warrior. We come, help."

Matthias shook Warbeak's claw warmly. "Thank you, Queen Warbeak, my friend. Now we must go. A strategy can be worked out on the way to the Abbey. Let's hurry. There's no time to lose. It's do or die now!"

The mouse, the shrew and the sparrow plunged off into the green wooded world of Mossflower together.

One thing Matthias was certain of as he strode swiftly through the trees: it would be he and he alone who faced Cluny the Scourge at the bitter end.

CHAPTER

12

The Father Abbot was awakened by a sword-point at his throat. He was completely surrounded by snarling rats. Jess, Basil, Winifred and Foremole all found themselves in similar situations. The iron claw of Cluny's discipline was strongly evident throughout the maneuver. Complete silence had been observed. Only those held captive were aware of the horde's presence.

The main danger to the attackers was Constance. As always, she slept out upon the grass in the Abbey grounds. More than two score of rodents carrying a strong rope net between them had stolen up on the sleeping badger. They threw the net over Constance, fixing it into the ground with long stakes and bludgeoning her senseless before she was properly awake. Cluny watched the proceedings with grim satisfaction. Redwall was his!

Small creatures rubbing sleep from their eyes in confusion were dragged out into the Abbey grounds. Woodland infants wept fitfully as they clung to their parents. Bullying rats pushed and harried everyone out into the open where they made them sit on the grass. Abbot Mortimer in his homespun nightshirt was kept to one side with his captains. Their paws were cruelly bound behind them. They stood in stolid silence as sniggering rats referred to them as "The Ringleaders."

*   *   *

Cluny the Scourge stood in Great Hall, surveying the marvelous tapestry. He did not need to steal scraps of it now. It belonged solely to him. Fangburn, Frogblood, Scumnose, Mangefur and Killconey came marching smartly up. They saluted him.

"The Abbey is yours now, Chief."

"We've got all hands outside, Chief."

"Any further orders, Chief?"

Cluny ran his tail reflectively through his long claws. "Yes. Bring the Abbot's chair out of the place they call Cavern Hole. Have it set up for me on a platform by the gatehouse. I've got some judgments to deliver."

The horde captains swaggered off jauntily. Cluny addressed the picture of Martin upon the tapestry.

"Well, warrior mouse. What do you think of your brave Redwall defenders now? Huh, not much, I imagine! I'm going to let you stay up there and witness some drastic changes."

Cluny jabbed a claw at Martin, his voice laden with menace, "No more will you haunt my dreams! A voice inside me spoke as I waited in the woods tonight outside your precious Redwall. It said that before sunset this day I would be free of my nightmares forever. What do you think of that?"

Martin continued to smile fearlessly down upon Cluny. The Warlord cracked his tail, shattering the silence of Great Hall. He seemed driven to great anger by the apparent unconcern of the Warrior.

"Henceforth this place shall be known as Hall of the Scourge," he shouted insanely. "No more will the Abbey be known as Redwall, it shall be called Cluny's Castle! Everything will change!"

The Warlord went off into a berserk rage, stamping about the Hall, slashing and whipping at the shadows with his tail as he invented new titles, screaming them out as the echoes bounced back off the walls at him.

"The Great Rodent Wall!"

"The Lake of Drowning!"

"The Field of Dead Mice!"

"Ferret Gate, Stoat Orchard, Weasel Bell. Hahahahahahaha!"

Outside upon the grass the woodland captives heard Cluny's crazed laughter ringing from the Abbey. They shivered at the thought of their inevitable fate. He was making them wait, drawing out the tension, reveling in their misery, savoring his evil victory.

Abbot Mortimer looked up at the sky.

"It will soon be dawn," he said sadly.

A rat pushed him heavily to the ground.

"Shut your doddering mouth, old one," he snarled nastily.

Jess Squirrel knocked the rat flat with both her feet. She sank her teeth into the bully's back. A pack of rats leaped upon Jess. They dragged her off their screaming companion and beat at her with their spear butts and cutlass handles.

"Leave her alone, you cowards!" Mr. Squirrel shouted as he struggled to hold back Silent Sam. "You're very brave in a gang, but you wouldn't face my Jess if her paws were free, you scum, not if there were twice as many of you!"

Father Abbot struggled to his knees. "Please, I beg of you, do not fight on my account. They have the advantage. You'll only get hurt."

"Aye, sensible words, yer honor," Killconey said, as he made way for the Abbot's chair to be carried through. "Take my tip and sit quiet until the Chief comes out. Don't make it harder on yourselves than it's going to be. That's what me ould mother always used to say."

"Good grief, shouldn't think a blaggard like you ever had a mother," Basil sniffed disdainfully.

Killconey cackled and slapped his thigh. "Well now, aren't you the big comical rabbit? Let me tell you, my fine gentleman bucko, you won't be half so funny when the Scourge is done with you. No sir!"

The prisoners slumped dejectedly upon the Abbey grass, awaiting the break of dawn and the coming of Cluny the Scourge.

CHAPTER

13

Warbeak and Log-a-Log had to force Matthias to take a rest.
The young mouse had set a scorching pace, marching through
the night from the far borders of Mossflower Wood. The Guerrilla Shrew had trouble keeping up. He was smaller than Matthias and did not have the advantage of flight like the sparrow.
Always several yards behind, he panted for breath as he stumbled gamely on. Even Warbeak was beginning to feel the effects
of prolonged low nighttime fluttering, through the woodlands,
around trees, over bushes; it was not the same as a clear, clean
flight through the upper atmosphere. Only Matthias kept going
at a dogged headlong dash. He stopped for nothing. The heavy
sword hanging from his shoulders by a length of cord thumped
against him as he urged his legs forward: the breath rose ragged
in his throat. His companions realized the urgency of the situation, but they saw that if Matthias continued to drive himself
at this rate, he would soon collapse.

The matter was solved when Matthias tripped upon a tree root
and went sprawling flat. His two friends pinned him down and
held on while they tried to talk sense to him.

Finally convinced, Matthias sat among the ferns with his allies. It was not wasted time: they held a council of war.

''You carry on to Redwall, Matthias,'' Log-a-Log said. ''I
will wait here for my band. We'll force march most of the way,

don't worry. The Guerrilla Shrews won't be far behind you. We'll make good time in this cool night air."

The young mouse was assailed by gnawing doubts. "That's all very well, but how are we going to scale the wall into the Abbey grounds? If Cluny has captured Redwall, he's bound to have sentries posted upon the ramparts."

"What for ratworm want sentry?" Warbeak shrugged her wings. "Him catch Abbey, not know we come to catch back."

"Warbeak, you're right! But it still doesn't solve the problem of how we get in," Matthias replied.

The young Sparra Queen winked cheekily. "Is easy. Me get Sparras to open little wormdoors in wall: east, south, north. You see, they do good. Warbeak go now, see friend Matthias mouse at Redwall."

The Sparra Queen shot off into the air like an arrow from a bow. Matthias arose to continue his journey. Log-a-Log stayed behind and waited for his warriors to catch up.

Beside the north wall gate, Plumpen stirred. He groaned and rolled over. There was a bad wound on the back of his head, but he was still very much alive. The first sight that greeted the dormouse's hazy vision was three sparrows standing over him. They were Dunwing, Battlehawk and Windplume. Silently they slid Plumpen out of the open door into the woods.

Dunwing gave orders to the two Sparra warriors: "Take red rag and grease. Bring many Sparra. Fly quiet, grease other little wormdoors. Wait 'til Queen Warbeak come. No let ratworms see warriors, go now."

Throughout the night hours many sparrows worked secretly on the locks, bolts and hinges of the small wallgates.

Somewhere in Mossflower, Matthias was still pressing on to Redwall. Log-a-Log and the regiment of Guerrilla Shrews were hot on his trail. A thousand Sparra warriors perched in the branches of trees all around the Abbey, waiting.

CHAPTER

14

The light of dawn began to appear in the sky. The sun's rays tinged the sandstone walls to a dull pink and clouded red. Dew was upon the late rose.

Despite the blessing of a glorious summer day, the whole of Mossflower was doom-laden with an awful tension that threatened to burst upon the captives seated on the grass.

Horde captains came stamping out of the Abbey. They prodded the prisoners with cutlass points and slapped out with flat blades at the helpless defenders.

"Come on, you lot! On your feet! Stand up straight, you mice! Step aside there! Make way for Cluny the Scourge!"

Reluctantly the Redwall contingent complied. They turned. All eyes were on the door of Great Hall.

The silence was broken as the door slammed back upon its hinges. Cluny strode out. Behind him, bearing the horde standard and a lighted torch, came Fangburn and Killconey. The victorious horde soldiers cheered wildly. Cluny was the picture of barbaric power, geared for war from his poison tail tip to the frightening battle helmet. He looked every inch the conqueror.

Regally he swept through the ranks of both sides, looking neither to right nor left. Mounting the dais which had been set up for his use, he swirled the sinister cloak about him and sat down in the Abbot's chair. All that could be heard was the crackle of the torch and the unhappy whimper of one of the infant captives. He sat impassively, claws gripping the chair arms, visor lowered.

Slowly lifting the visor, Cluny allowed his single eye to rove around. It came to rest on the Abbey leader.

"You, Abbot Mouse, come here!"

With two rats flanking him, the Father Abbot stepped forward in a slow, dignified manner. Even clad in his nightwear he radiated calm and fortitude. Cluny sat back, sneering openly.

"Ha! So this is your leader? A little fat mouse in his nightshirt! What a fearsome warrior he looks! Well, what now, mouse? Are you going to go down on your knees and beg for your life, old one?"

Abbot Mortimer stared calmly into Cluny's savage eye. "I will never bend my knee on my own behalf. However, if I thought I could save the life of one of my friends I would gladly fall down on both knees. But I know you, Cluny, better than you know yourself. There is not a scrap of pity or mercy in your heart, only a burning desire for vengeance. Therefore, I will not kneel to one who is consumed by evil."

Cluny sprang to his feet trembling with rage.

"Kneel to me, mouse! Kneel or I will kill you," he stormed.

Angry growls and the rending of grass from beneath the net on the ground heralded Constance's awakening. She began to heave and push. The net started to work loose. She called out to Cluny in a gruff, insulting voice. "Hey, you! You scruffy, one-eyed vermin! Remove this net and face me alone! We'll see who ends up on their knees!"

At a signal from the Warlord, a gang of rats leaped upon Constance and beat her back into unconsciousness with their weapons. They drove the securing stakes deeper around the net.

Basil Stag Hare kicked out at them. When he had driven the rats off, he faced Cluny boldly.

"You, sir, are not fit to command any creature! You are a coward and an evil maniac. Even if my paws were not tied I would think twice before soiling them upon the likes of you. Tcha! You are beneath contempt, you . . . you . . . Rat!"

A stinging blow from a weasel's club sent Basil limping and tripping to the ground. The weasel struck him again and again upon the legs. He doubled up in pain as the horde jeered and laughed.

Cluny pointed at the hare. "Remember your tricks on the

common behind the church? Before this day is done you'll never run and dodge again!''

His eyes blazing with madness, Cluny flung his claws wide. ''All of you, defenders of Redwall, listen to me! When I first came to the Abbey I gave you a choice: surrender or die. You chose to fight me. Me, Cluny the Scourge! I lost battles, I lost skirmishes, I lost soldiers, but I have won the war. You are the losers. Now you must pay with your lives!''

As the Warlord spoke, something seemed to snap deep within the Abbot. He rushed forward and tried to grasp Cluny.

''No, no, you dare not harm these creatures!'' he cried. ''It would be murder.''

Cluny grabbed the Father Abbot and threw him to the ground. Lashing the frail figure with his poison-barbed tail, he shouted, ''Who are you to tell me what to do? There is only one law, my word! There is none to stop me, not badgers or hares or otters or mice. I will kill you all. Kill, kill, kill!''

Suddenly a thunderous voice was heard. ''Cluny the Scourge, I have come to settle with you!''

A gasp arose from the crowd. Cluny's tail fell from his grasp as both victors and vanquished turned towards the Abbey whence the voice had issued.

There in the open doorway of Great Hall stood the Warrior Mouse!

It was as if he had stepped out of the tapestry upon the wall. On his arm was a burnished shield, at his waist was a sword belt of black leather and silver. From the scabbard at his side he drew forth a mighty sword.

Cluny's voice shook as he addressed the nightmare visitor. ''Who are you?''

The Warrior stepped forward into the daylight. Sunrays glinted diamond-like off his sword.

''I am that is!''

Unable to take his eyes from the Warrior, Cluny stumbled backwards.

He cowered behind the Abbot's chair, his mouth working convulsively. ''You are something out of my dreams. Go away, I'm not asleep!''

The Warrior Mouse strode out into the crowd. He pointed his blade at the quivering Warlord.

''I am that is! Martin, Matthias, call me what you will. It was long ago written that you and I would meet, rat.''

"Seize him!" Cluny screamed.

Frogblood sprang forward, brandishing a spear. Before he could raise it, the ancient sword flashed in the warrior's grip and hewed him lifeless to the ground.

"I will slay any invader that moves," Matthias shouted. "Cluny, this is between you and me. Your army will not interfere.''

Suddenly the Joseph Bell began tolling. Sparra warriors appeared in swarms that almost obscured the sky above the Abbey. They landed in droves around the parapet edges. The grounds came to life with teeming swarms of Guerrilla Shrews armed to the teeth with rapiers, cudgels and slings. Matthias whirled the sword above his head as he roared out his battle cry.

"Redwall, Redwall. Strike for Redwall!''

The final conflict had begun.

Shrews struck down the enemy guards as Sparra braves released the prisoners' bonds with short slashes of their sharp beaks. The freed defenders grabbed up anything that would serve as weapons. They hurled themselves upon the enemy, sparrows and shrews siding them against their larger adversaries. Rats, ferrets, weasels and stoats fought with the ferocity born of desperation. Their very lives depended on the outcome.

Cluny plucked the blazing torch from Killconey's grasp. He flung it at the face of the oncoming warrior. Matthias deflected it with his shield in a cascade of sparks and went after the horde leader. To gain a brief respite, Cluny pushed Killconey into Matthias. The ferret grappled vainly but was cloven in two with one swift stroke. Matthias stepped over the slain ferret, whirling his sword expertly as he pursued Cluny.

Ignoring his unprotected back, Matthias failed to see Fangburn stealing up behind him. The rat raised his cutlass in both claws, but, before he could strike, Constance had hurled the net over him. Fangburn struggled like a landed fish as the big badger picked up the net and swung it several times against the gatehouse wall. Dropping the lifeless thing, Constance plunged with a terrifying roar into a pack of weasels.

The thick tail of the Warlord flicked out venomously at Matthias's face. He covered swiftly with his shield as the poisoned metal barb clanged harmlessly off it. Cluny tried again, this time whipping the tail speedily at the young mouse's unprotected legs. Matthias leaped nimbly to one side and swung the sword in a flashing arc. Cluny roared with pain as it severed the tip of his tail. The bloodied stub lay on the grass with the barb still attached. Hurling the Abbot's chair at his adversary, the rat seized an iron spike. Metal clashed on metal as the Warrior Mouse parried Cluny's thrusts.

They battled across the green Abbey lawns, right through the center of the maelstrom of warring creatures. Oblivious to the fighting around them they sought to destroy each other, hacking, stabbing, lunging and swinging in mortal combat.

Meanwhile, teams of Sparra warriors were jointly lifting struggling rats and flying high to drop them into the middle of the Abbey pond. Ferrets had cornered a band of shrews and were threatening to massacre them when a column of otters sprang to the rescue. Keeping heavy pebbles locked in their slings, they battered continuously at the ferrets. Besieged by fierce sparrows, rat sentries leaped in panic from the top of the ramparts; those who stayed were dealt with by Jess Squirrel who swung a heavy iron chain around like a deadly flail. Down below, Ambrose Spike was rolling about like a whirling ball of needles. Silent Sam acted as his eyes, propelling him into each fresh bunch of rats with a long stick.

Matthias and Cluny continued battling savagely. Iron smashed upon steel as Cluny called up reserves from his vast strength and cunning to defeat his opponent. Twice he had hurled clawfuls of soil at Matthias's eyes, but each time the shield rose swiftly and deflected them. The Warrior Mouse hacked away stoically. He was beginning to feel his paws numbed by the jarring blows of the hefty iron railing against the sword blade. Cluny too felt the vibrations each time the sword clanged upon his weapon. The pain shot right through him, down to the tip of his injured tail. Along the ramparts they fought, blinded by sweat, panting and blowing, neither asking nor giving quarter; down the stairs and across the grass once more, they slashed and struck at each other, right up to the entrance of Great Hall.

Cluny dodged behind the half-open Abbey door and hit out at his attacker. Matthias's sword-point lodged deep in the wood. Seizing his chance, the rat dodged nimbly into the open, and battered madly at Matthias's upheld shield until he was forced to drop it. Cluny's iron spike drove cruelly into the mouse's unguarded paw. Matthias cried out and instinctively kicked the shield upwards at his adversary. It struck Cluny squarely under the chin, the sharp metal edge causing a long slash.

As the rat reeled away clutching at his throat, Matthias freed the sword from the door. Ignoring their wounds, they immediately clashed again, going at it hammer and tongs. Cluny lashed out with his bleeding tail and tripped Matthias. As the Warrior Mouse lay upon the ground, the rat roared and stabbed downwards with the spiked railing. Matthias rolled to one side; the point sank deep into the earth. He struggled to his feet, striking out and scoring Cluny heavily down the side. But the long tail whipped out, lashing the Warrior Mouse several times across the face.

Cluny staggered into the entrance to the bell tower, where Friar Hugo had been tolling the Joseph Bell. At the sight of the rat Warlord, he released the rope and scuttled underneath the stairs, where he hid trembling. Matthias came thundering in. Cluny dodged around him and slammed the door, locking them in together. If only he could get the mouse at close quarters and stop him from using the sword, Cluny thought, then he could win with his superior strength.

They locked in combat again. Cluny barred the railing across the sword blade. Pushing with both claws he drove Matthias backwards. Now he could see victory in sight. If only he could pin the Warrior Mouse against the wall, he would be able to throttle him with the edge of the railing. Cluny braced his feet and strained. He could feel the breath laboring raggedly within his chest; he must win! The voices had told him he would never again see the warrior after the sun set upon this day. The prophecy had to be fulfilled once and for all.

Remorselessly he used his greater strength to drive the young mouse backwards. They were only inches from the wall now. Matthias realized what Cluny was doing. He would be finished once he was pinned against the wall. There was only one thing to do. Matthias suddenly swerved aside and collapsed on his back. Kicking his legs out rigid, he sent Cluny crashing into the wall. Matthias leaped over Cluny, and bounded up the spiral stairs into the darkness of the belfry.

Cluny lay against the wall, panting heavily. He managed an evil, wheezing laugh.

"There's no way out up there, mouse," he called. "I'm coming up after you. You're as good as dead now."

Matthias didn't reply. He sat exhausted up in the dark belfry with his legs dangling over the stout timber bell axle. Down below, Cluny squatted against the wall, glad of the chance to take a breather. Beneath the dusty stairs, Friar Hugo sneezed.

Laughing triumphantly, Cluny seized the little fat friar by his tail and dragged him from his hiding place.

"Look, mouse!" he called. "See, I've got your little fat friend. Ha, I won't have to climb those stairs after all. Throw the sword down or I'll spike him like a lollipop."

From his vantage point Matthias looked down. Far below him on the floor he could see Cluny holding the spike under Friar Hugo's chin.

Cluny gave the point a light jab. Hugo gurgled unhappily. "You see? All it takes is a little harder push and he's dead. Now throw down your sword and get down here yourself, quick."

Matthias peered over the rim of the Joseph Bell.

"All right, rat, you win. But how do I know you'll keep your word? First let the friar go, then I promise on my honor as a warrior that I'll come down."

Cluny grinned wickedly. There it was again, that stupid thing called honor, the code of the warrior! But it was not his code: he had won!

"Get out of my sight, you sniveling little wretch," he grated, thrusting Friar Hugo away from him. The frightened mouse dived back underneath the stairs. Cluny stood in the center of the room, his one eye straining to catch sight of Matthias in the belfry. Blood dripped from the dozen wounds the mouse warrior had inflicted upon him during the course of their battle. But now he knew he had won; the voices had been right; he would soon see the last of the mouse warrior.

"Come on down, mouse, Cluny the Scourge is waiting for you," he cried.

Matthias stood up on the wooden beam. With one mighty blow from the blade of the ancient battle-scarred sword he severed the rope holding the Joseph Bell.

It appeared to hang in space for a second, then it dropped like a massive stone.

Cluny remained riveted to the spot, his eye staring upwards. Before he had time to think it was too late. . . .

CLANG!!!

The Joseph Bell tolled its last, huge knell. The colossal weight of metal smashed Cluny the Scourge flat upon the stone floor of the bell tower.

Wearily Matthias the Warrior descended the spiral stairs, sword in hand. He led the sobbing little friar out of his hiding place. Together they stood and stared at the Joseph Bell where it lay, cracked clean through the center. From beneath it there protruded a bloodied claw and a smashed tail.

Matthias spoke, "I kept my promise to you, Cluny. I came down. Hush now, Friar Hugo. It's all over now. Wipe your eyes."

Together the friends opened the door and walked out into the sunlight of a summer morning.

Redwall had won the final battle.

The bodies of both armies lay scattered thick upon the grass and stones where they had fallen. Many were sparrows, shrews and woodland defenders, but they were far outnumbered by the slain rats, ferrets, weasels and stoats. Nowhere was there one of Cluny's infamous horde left alive.

Constance ambled up, her big flanks heaving, covered in wounds. She pointed to the bell tower and uttered a single word.

"Cluny?"

"Dead!" Matthias replied. "Were all the horde slain? Did we take no prisoners at all?"

The badger shrugged wearily. "A lot of them tried to escape. We didn't really stop them. They managed to unbar the main gate and ran out into the road. There were a big ginger cat and a white owl waiting for them. Hell's whiskers! I've never seen anything like it!"

Basil Stag Hare limped up and threw Matthias a wobbly salute. "Squire Julian and Cap'n Snow. You can talk to them later on, young feller. Right now you're needed over in the cloisters. It's the Abbot. Better hurry."

As fast as their tired limbs would allow them, Matthias, Constance and Hugo went together.

Abbot Mortimer lay in the cloister gardens surrounded by his mice and woodland friends. Everyone was there, from Queen Warbeak and Log-a-Log to Cornflower and Silent Sam, down to the humblest mouse. The poison barb on Cluny's tail had done its deadly work. The Father Abbot was dying.

Respectfully the ranks opened to allow Matthias and his companions through. Constance knelt to cradle her old friend's head, and Matthias gently clasped the wrinkled careworn paw. The Abbot smiled fondly at his young mouse.

"Matthias, my son, I see you have restored the sword of Martin to our Abbey. Is your mission completed then?"

Matthias rested his forehead against his Abbot's paw. "Yes, Father, Cluny the Scourge is dead. I have done my task."

The Abbot nodded slowly. "So have I, my son, so have I."

"Father Abbot, you must live," said Constance in a gruff choking voice.

The Abbot's old face broke into a weak smile. "My old friend, I am not like the seasons. I cannot go on forever. It has to finish sometime."

The tears rolled down Matthias's cheeks. He could not stop them. The Abbot patted his paw kindly.

"Ah, Matthias, Matthias, the brave one. Wipe away your tears, my son. Death is only part of life. Tell me, can you see the late rose?"

Matthias dried his eyes on the Abbot's wide sleeve. "Yes, Father. It is in full bloom now."

"And are all the little roses as red as blood?" said the Abbot.

"They are, Father," Matthias answered.

The Abbot sighed. "It is as it was meant to be. Is Brother Alf nearby?"

Brother Alf knelt before the Abbot.

"Ah, Brother Alf, my old and valued companion. When I am gone to my rest you will take my place as Abbot. You are a wise and compassionate mouse. I know you will look after my creatures for me."

Abbot Mortimer closed his eyes for a moment before carrying on with his final instructions.

"What a great pity that it took so much bloodshed to unite

us all. Henceforth the sparrows may come and go as they wish. They must share our food and use our Abbey, not only the roof but all of it. These good Guerrilla Shrews also—no longer will they be as gypsies roaming the woods: they will have a proper home here at Redwall as long as they wish. And now, Matthias my son, I must tell you my decision regarding you. It is my wish that you do not enter our Order as a brother!''

A gasp of surprise arose from all those within hearing range. Matthias bowed his head. He was stunned by his Father Abbot's words.

The Abbot continued. ''No, my son. Your heart is far too brave. This Abbey needs you, but not as a brother. Therefore, I name you Matthias, the Warrior Mouse of Redwall, champion of our Order. From this day you will defend this Abbey and all of its creatures from evil and wrong. Your sword shall be known far and wide as 'Ratdeath.' Now, Cornflower. Where is little Cornflower?''

The young fieldmouse came. She stood by the Abbot waiting upon his word.

''There you are, dear Cornflower,'' the Abbot smiled. ''A warrior needs a good wife. You are the beauty that will grace Redwall and rule the heart of our Matthias. The old gatehouse will be extended into a proper home. It belongs to you both. Guard our threshold wisely and well.''

There were no words to express the feelings of Matthias and Cornflower. They could feel the joy and pride singing from their hearts.

The Abbot looked up at Constance. ''And you, my oldest friend. Do me one last service. Lift my head a little and I will tell you what my failing eyes can see before I leave you.''

Obediently the badger raised the Abbot's head.

''Ah yes, I see the most beautiful summer morning of my life. The friends I know and love are all about me. Redwall, our home, is safe. The sun shines warmly upon us. Nature is ready to yield her bounty again in plenty this autumn. I have seen it all before, many times, and yet I never cease to wonder. Life is good, my friends. I leave it to you. Do not be sad, for mine is a peaceful rest.''

Thus did Mortimer, the Father Abbot of Redwall, die.

CHAPTER

15

One year later.

The following is an extract from the annals of Redwall by John Churchmouse. It was he who took over as recorder from Methuselah. Here is part of his written record:

> *It is the Summer of the Talking Squirrel!*
>
> *Only yesterday the young one known as Silent Sam was heard to speak. He was heard conversing with the son of Matthias and Cornflower. The young squirrel suddenly began to relate the saga of the Late Rose Summer Wars to the baby mouse. I fear that we will not be able to stop him from talking, or his parents from laughing with delight. The son of our warrior is a strong chubby little fellow. Everyone calls him Mattimeo because 'Matthias Methuselah Mortimer' is too big a mouthful, but that was what his parents wished his name to be. Even now he tries long and often to lift the great sword Ratdeath. I think one day he is sure to succeed his father as Abbey Champion. Our Abbot, Mordalfus (no wonder he always preferred the name Alf, I mean, Mordalfus?), has declared that his first anniversary shall be marked by a huge feast. We are all invited. Constance has been pulling her cart around the woodland and meadows far and wide, bringing in guests.*
>
> *The Guerrilla Shrews are out collecting honey from the*

bee folk; they have struck up a great friendship with the bees, even learning their language so that they can argue with them.

The Sparra Queen Warbeak has appointed herself deputy to Friar Hugo. She shows a great interest in the culinary arts, though I fear she will grow quite fat before too long. Lady Cornflower is out in the meadows with Mrs. Churchmouse, my wife, and Dunwing, the Sparra Queen Mother. They are gathering flowers for the tables. All about me the June sunshine is like liquid gold!

Basil Stag Hare has gone off on a journey to bring his friends Captain Snow and Squire Julian Gingivere back to the Abbey with him. Basil is ignoring the fact that it is the Abbot's anniversary. He constantly refers to it as 'A Regimental Reunion Dinner.' Winifred the otter, and the beaver, in company with that reprobate Ambrose Spike, are testing the quality of the October nutbrown ale. It must be particularly fine this year, judging from the sound of many rowdy ballads issuing from the wine cellars. Plumpen and his family of dormice are helping Foremole and his crew dig a roasting pit. Early this morning our Father Abbot went out fishing with Matthias the Warrior. They consider it no less than their bounden duty to bring back a larger fish than last year. The Joseph Bell which was broken has been recast into two smaller bells. I can hear them now. They are named Matthias and Methuselah. My twin Churchmice, Tim and Tess, are grown quite sturdy over the past year. They are our Abbey bellringers, and a splendid job they make of it too!

The crops are growing well. The fruit trees and bushes in the orchard show much promise. The old gatehouse is now a beautiful rambling cottage. The grass is green, the sky is blue, and the honey sweeter than ever before. I will finish my writing now and go to prepare myself for tonight's festivities, which will be held in their usual place, at Cavern Hole in Redwall Abbey. Please be sure to visit us if ever you are passing.

John Churchmouse (Recorder, formerly of St. Ninian's)

Here ends the story.

The book that inspired a legend—the first novel in the bestselling saga of Redwall

Welcome to Mossflower Wood, where the gentle mice have gathered to celebrate a year of peace and abundance. All is well . . . until a sinister shadow falls across the ancient stone abbey of Redwall. It is rumored that Cluny is coming—Cluny, the terrible one-eyed rat and his savage horde—Cluny, who has vowed to conquer Redwall Abbey! The only hope for the besieged mice lies in the lost sword of the legendary Martin the Warrior. And so begins the epic quest of a bumbling young apprentice—a courageous mouse who would rise up, fight back . . . and become a legend himself.

"Charming . . . rollicking good adventure."

—*Fantasy Review*

"Good, absorbing fantasy."

—*Philadelphia Inquirer*

"*Redwall* is both a credible and ingratiating place, one to which many young readers will doubtless cheerfully return."
—*New York Times Book Review*

"Reminiscent of *Watership Down* . . . *Redwall* is a thrilling tale of danger and adventure . . . an edge-of-the-seat, can't-put-it-down book with the potential for classic status."
—*Parents' Choice*

"*Redwall* is a fine work, literate, witty, filled with the excitement of genuine storytelling . . . extraordinary."
—Lloyd Alexander, author of
the Newbery Award winner, *The High King*

"Provocative and enticing. From start to finish, readers and listeners will cheer the dwellers of Redwall."

—*Booklist*

"Rich and thought-provoking."

—*School Library Journal*

"An exciting tale."

—*Cleveland Plain Dealer*

continued . . .

DON'T MISS THESE
OTHER NOVELS OF REDWALL

The Pearls of Lutra

A young hedgehog maid sets out to solve the riddle
of the missing pearls of legend—and faces an evil
emperor and his reptilian warriors . . .

"Plenty of adventure."

—Publishers Weekly

"The Redwall books . . . add a touch of chivalry and adventure
reminiscent of the King Arthur stories."

—Arkansas Democrat Gazette

The Outcast of Redwall

The abandoned son of a ferret warlord must choose
his destiny beyond the walls of Redwall
Abbey . . .

"Grand exploits . . . another rousing saga."

—Booklist

"Strongly plotted and spiced with a variety of secondary
characters."

—Publishers Weekly

The Bellmaker

The epic quest of Joseph the Bellmaker to join his
daughter, Mariel the Warriormouse, in a
heroic battle against a vicious Foxwolf . . .

"Filled with rousing adventure, strong characters, and vibrant
settings."

—Boston Sunday Globe

"Jacques spins another irresistible tale."

—Booklist

Martin the Warrior

The triumphant saga of a young mouse destined to become Redwall's most glorious hero . . .

"Wonderfully imaginative."

—New York Times Book Review

"Readers will rejoice."

—Los Angeles Times

"An excellent adventure with an enlightened conscience. . . . With vibrant and distinct animal characters, Jacques's classically inspired plot-weaving achieves virtuosity."

—Publishers Weekly

Salamandastron

When the mountain stronghold of Salamandastron comes under attack, only the bold badger lord Urthstripe stands able to protect the creatures of Redwall . . .

"A good yarn . . . grand climax . . . Jacques charms readers . . . another winner."

—Booklist

"Swashbuckling adventures told with great gusto in rousing words."

—Chicago Tribune

"The medieval world of Redwall Abbey—where gallant mouse warriors triumph over evil invaders . . . has truly become the stuff of legend."

—Seattle Post-Intelligencer

Imagine walking into a room occupied by thirty-five tiny and very sick premature newborn babies. For the next twelve hours their well-being, their very survival is your responsibility. That was how my internship year began. It was definitely one of the most terrifying days of my life.

I somehow survived that year in spite of the fact that I and the other interns in my group received negligible guidance from the senior people in the program. I was overworked, overtired, lonely and insecure, often depressed, and conflicted by my own responsibilities, whether admitting an infant with a dangerously high fever or coping with the psychological and physical stresses of dealing with AIDS patients.

From July 1985 through June 1986, I worked with three interns: Amy, Andy, and Mark. Together, we've collected very personal notes—often recorded after a grueling night on call—about what it's really like, day by day, to spend a year as an intern, meeting too often with frustrations and not enough encouragement.

The Intern Blues is the product of those notes.

ROBERT MARION, M.D.

Also by Robert Marion:

BORN TOO SOON

THE
INTERN
BLUES

The Private Ordeals
of Three Young Doctors

Robert Marion, M.D.

FAWCETT CREST • NEW YORK

PREFACE

All of the events described within this book actually occurred. Not all of them, however, involved the intern to whom they have been assigned here. In order to provide the doctors, patients, and staff with anonymity, some of the occurrences, patient contacts, and reactions have been altered or switched. As a result, some of the characterizations that emerge represent composites rather than actual portraits.

Additionally, the names of the hospitals, physicians, staff members, and patients have been changed. To render the interns even less identifiable, their physical characteristics have been appreciably altered. In spite of these changes, however, this is a work of nonfiction; the events and experiences described are all true.

This book would not have been possible without the cooperation of a large number of people. I'd like to take this opportunity to thank the faculty and administration of our pediatric program, the administrations of both the hospitals through which our interns and residents rotate and the medical school affiliated with those hospitals, the house staff who make up our program, and especially the interns who allowed me to just about live inside their heads during that very difficult year.

Finally, I'd especially like to thank the following people: my wife, Beth, and my children, Isadora, Davida, and Jonah, for putting up with the long hours I spent playing with my computer rather than playing with them; Pamela Altschul, editorial assistant at William Morrow, for her help and sharp insights; Diana Finch, my literary agent, for her encouragement; and Adrian Zackheim, senior editor at William Morrow and self-proclaimed "medical junkie," who has been there to guide me through every step in the writing of this book.

INTRODUCTION

The stretchers arrived at the emergency room about fifteen minutes after I started my shift. I had barely had enough time to say hello to the residents and nurses on call when suddenly, out of the clear blue, three critically ill brothers were being wheeled into the trauma area.

We all immediately went running to the back to meet them. One of the Emergency Medical Service workers yelled out an abbreviated version of their story: "It's an apartment fire. The FD [Fire Department] pulled them out of the bedroom. We loaded them onto the stretchers and transported." He further explained that the boys' mother was at that moment being wheeled into the adult emergency room. She was near death.

Apartment fires were unusual in May; they're usually winter events, when everyone's using space heaters to try to keep warm. But unusual or not, we swung into action. With very little discussion, we triaged them: The senior resident took the eight-year-old, who was semiconscious. The junior resident began to work on the six-year-old, who was the best off of the three: His vital signs were stable and he was awake enough to answer questions. And the two interns and I moved straight toward the ten-year-old, who was comatose; he wasn't breathing on his own, and his fingers and lips were beginning to turn purple. We knew we had to act fast.

By reflex, Amy, one of the interns, grabbed the black rubber ambubag and began to force oxygen into the boy's lungs while I went about gathering the supplies needed for intubation. I got a pediatric laryngoscope (a light source with a metal blade at its end, designed to push away the tongue and illuminate the back of the throat) and an endotracheal tube from the code cart.

Meanwhile, Andy, the other intern, after listening with his stethoscope, had determined that the boy's heart wasn't beating. Without a word, he immediately begun pumping the chest about a hundred times a minute. At that point I heard the announcement over the loudspeaker: "Attention, attention: CAC in the pediatric emergency room. Attention attention: CAC in the pediatric emergency room." I was relieved to hear it: It meant that help was on the way.

After Amy had bagged the kid for maybe a minute, I nudged her away and got ready to do the intubation. I concentrated all my efforts on the back of that boy's throat. Holding the laryngoscope in my left hand, I placed the instrument into the patient's mouth and shifted it around until I could clearly see the vocal cords. Then I began to push the endotracheal tube through those cords. At first the tube slipped backward, falling down into the esophagus. I repositioned it and tried again. This time the tube slipped right through the cords and slid down into the trachea.

I was sure it was in, so I began to call for a piece of tape, but before I could get the words out, a healthy piece of the stuff was being dangled before my eyes. Anticipating my need, Amy had torn a supply and now all that needed to be done was to apply one end to the skin of the boy's upper lip and wrap the other end around the tube so it would remain steadily in place. It took me about a minute to secure the tube, and when I finished, I hooked up the ambubag and began to force oxygen directly into the boy's lungs.

As I compressed the ambubag, I began to take stock of the situation. The trauma area was now packed with medical personnel who, thanks to the loudspeaker announcement, had come running from all corners of the hospital. It was then that I realized that for the first time all year, Amy Horowitz, Andy Baron, and Mark Greenberg, who had answered the call for help, were all working together on a single patient.

Amy grabbed the ambubag and relieved me. Andy was continuing the chest compressions, while Mark was working on getting an IV into the boy's arm. He succeeded on the first try and was simultaneously hooking up the IV drip and asking one of the nurses for a shot of epinephrine, a drug that hopefully would help start the boy's heart beating again. Meanwhile, I began to attach the leads from an electrocardiograph machine to the boy's wrists and ankles, in an attempt to monitor the activity of his heart better. All this was being carried out without a word of direction from me. Each of us knew what had to be done and were doing it without any prompting.

It took nearly fifteen minutes to get that kid's heart started again, but after Mark had pushed in the second round of medications, electrical activity began to appear on the cardiograph paper. "We've got complexes," I said when I saw them. "It looks like a normal rhythm." The interns breathed a sigh of relief when they heard my words. Now comes Miller Time!

In another minute, the boy began breathing on his own. He was reasonably stable now, so we pulled back and took stock of what needed to be done. Amy volunteered to take charge of the boy until the intern from the ICU [intensive-care unit] upstairs came down to get him. His brothers, now also stable, and our patient went up to Jonas Bronck's pediatric ICU about a half hour later. After prolonged hospital stays, they each recovered and were discharged home. Their mother, however, wasn't as fortunate. She never regained consciousness and died later that night in the adult ICU.

Watching those three interns working together on that boy in such perfect harmony, with such confidence in their judgment and their technical ability, it was hard for me to believe that only eleven months earlier they had begun this internship. It seemed incredible that they were the same people who, when I had talked with them out on the lawn of Peter Anderson's house in Westchester County at orientation, had seemed so tense and uncertain and downright scared to death.

I had met Amy, Mark, and Andy at that orientation retreat at the house of the chairman of the Department of Pediatrics on June 26, 1985. All around us on the lawn, the exact same scene was being played out: Stretched out on the grass were groups of three or four new interns, each looking well rested and tanned from their month of vacation and each as tense as a turkey around Thanksgiving because of the year of torture that loomed ahead. Sitting with each group of interns was an attending physician, one of the senior doctors affiliated with the pediatric program, who would serve as teacher, mentor, and at times taskmaster to the new interns. We attendings were trying our best to convince these guys that the next twelve months weren't going to be as bad as they had been led to believe. In other words, we were lying through our teeth.

Over the past seven years, it had become traditional in the Albert Schweitzer School of Medicine's pediatric residency training program that the internship year begin with this orientation retreat. Regardless of what the day accomplishes, it's a nice idea, an opportunity for the thirty-five new interns to get to know each other in a relaxed atmosphere, to make friends with the people with whom they'll be spending every day and every third night over the next twelve months. The retreat also gives the interns a chance to meet the chief residents, the four physicians who are directly in charge of them, the people they'd have to turn to in times of crisis.

My first meeting with Amy, Mark, and Andy started out pretty disappointingly. I'd led small groups at these retreats for the past three years, and this one was definitely the hardest to get off the ground. The idea was to get the interns talking about their concerns so that they'd discover these concerns weren't unique, that the same fears were shared by each of their classmates. But for that to happen the interns had to talk, and so far they were keeping their mouths tightly shut.

I decided to cut through the small talk and take a more direct approach. "Look," I began, "I know you guys must be scared to death. You're so nervous, I'm getting jumpy just sitting here. What are you so worried about?"

There was silence again for what seemed like hours, but it was probably no more than a minute. I was thinking I'd have to come up with some other tactic when Andy Baron suddenly spoke up. "I'll tell you what I'm worried about," he said just loud enough to be heard. "I'm worried I don't know enough."

"Don't know enough about what?" I immediately asked, overjoyed that somebody had actually said something.

Andy thought for a few seconds. "I'm worried that I'm going to get out there on the wards and be expected to know certain things that I just don't know. I don't know the kinds of things doctors are supposed to know."

"What are doctors supposed to know?" I asked.

"They're supposed to know everything," Andy replied without hesitation. "They're supposed to know what to do in an emergency; they're supposed to know what's going wrong when it goes wrong and what to do to make it better. I don't know any of those things. I never had to know anything that important when I was a medical student.''

''Doctors are also supposed to be able to do things like start IVs and do spinal taps,'' Mark Greenberg said next. ''I don't know about you guys, but if I were to go into a hospital today and do a spinal tap on a baby, I could be charged with assault with a deadly weapon. I'm not sure, but I don't think a criminal record is exactly what we're trying to accomplish here.''

''So you're worried that you don't know enough and that even if you did know enough, you couldn't do anything to help the patients because you don't have the technical skills,'' I said. ''Is that about right?'' The three of them nodded yes. I wrote this down on a piece of paper. As group leader, I was supposed to act as a kind of anxiety scorekeeper.

''Look,'' I began to explain, ''if you think we'd expect you to come into this knowing how to start IV's and do spinal taps, and knowing what to do in a cardiac arrest, you're out of your minds.'' Meeting blank stares, I went on: ''All of us were interns once and we know how completely hopeless you are at this point. We know that all four years of medical school gives you is a basic foundation on which to build. Every medical school graduate knows a bunch of facts but very little practical information. You know all the complex physiologic mechanisms that are necessary for the digestion of food by the intestine, but you've never actually taken care of a patient with a malabsorption syndrome; you know how the glomeruli of the kidneys filter impurities out of the blood, but you've never had to manage fluids and electrolytes in a patient whose kidneys have failed. That's what you're going to do in this internship: learn how to put all these principles into practice. And while you're learning this stuff, we're not going to let you do anything that might even come close to hurting the patients. The only thing we'll ask of you over the next few days is that you somehow figure out how to get yourselves onto the wards without getting too lost. Anything more than that is extra credit. Now I'm sure that made you all feel a lot better, right?''

It obviously didn't, and they all fell silent again. ''So what else are you worried about?'' I finally asked. ''Or is that it?''

''Well, okay, so maybe you don't expect us to be able to make decisions on our own, but there are a lot of other things we're going to be responsible for,'' Andy responded after a bit more silence. I liked Andy right away. "I mean, starting Saturday, parents are going to be trusting us with their sick kids. They're going to expect us to take care of them and make them well. I'm worried I'm going to wind up betraying that trust."

The other two considered this. "That's certainly a frightening thought for society," Mark added. "People trusting me with anything."

I added "Anxiety about responsibility" to my list.

"I don't know about you guys, but I'm worried about my home life," Amy Horowitz said next. "I can understand worrying about doing a good job, but I've got a two-month-old baby at home. If I'm on call every third night and I'm exhausted the next night, that means I'm only going to have one night out of every three to spend with her and just about no days."

I knew Amy from her days as a medical student, and of all the interns in the incoming group, she was the one about whom I was most concerned. "Who's going to be taking care of the baby while you're at work?" I asked.

"We have a baby-sitter during the day and my husband will be home every night," she replied. "I've been on vacation since I delivered, and I've spent a lot of time with her. It's really going to be hard."

The others considered this and were silent for a few moments. "Yeah, outside life, that's a problem for me, too," Andy finally added. "I've seen what happens to interns. They don't have time for anything. They turn into boring, out-of-shape slobs, and I don't want that to happen to me."

And I added "Anxieties about home life: No time for families, hobbies, or exercise" to my list.

We spent about an hour talking. Even though it started out slowly, our discussion rapidly picked up steam. The interns had some kind of chemistry that made them work well together. By the time Mike Miller, the department's director of education, finally called us to lunch, our list of anxieties covered nearly two pages.

Things had gone so well during the second half of that hour that at the end of our session I told Amy, Andy, and Mark about a project I'd been thinking about for some time. "I've thought about trying to write a book about internship," I told them, "and I'd like you guys to help me with it. All you'd have to do is keep a diary and meet with me for dinner every once in a while." After some discussion, the interns agreed that they'd like to give it a try. Since one of their anxieties was that they'd lose touch with their nonphysician friends who had no understanding of what it was like to work a hundred hours a week and who therefore could not possibly sympathize with this life-style, they thought that a book about what an intern's life was like might be helpful to future interns. They decided that tape-recording their experiences would be the best method of keeping a diary.

And so what follows is the edited, collected diaries that resulted from the suggestion I made on the lawn of Peter Anderson's house. As witnessed on that evening in the emergency room in May, Andy, Mark, and Amy came a long way during that short year: They were transformed from medical students into competent doctors. And each survived their year of internship with their lives largely intact.

But what happened between that day in June 1985 in Westchester and the day one year later when it was all over is an amazing story, a story that, for people who have not lived through an internship, might seem more fictional than real. But all that follows is true. Although the names of people and the hospitals have been changed and certain features of the patients have been altered to protect their identity, all of this really happened.

To live by medicine is to live horribly.
                    —*Linnaeus*

ANDY

July 1985

Sunday, June 30, 1985*

I suppose I should have started this diary forty-eight hours ago, before I'd actually started my internship, but I only got this tape recorder today. So now I've actually had a day and part of a night of call. I think I'll start by talking about what I think about being an intern.

The fact that this was going to be starting didn't really hit me until I began packing up my stuff last week. The last couple of months have been the best time of my life. I finished all my medical school requirements back in March, and after that, Karen and I took off for Asia. We traveled around for two months, having a great time and then got back to Boston near the end of May. I loved that time we spent traveling. It gave me time to think about the future. But then a couple of weeks ago, I started getting ready to move, and that's when I really began to think about being an intern. I've had some pretty weird feelings about all this, and I guess I should try to put them into words.

Leaving Boston has been very traumatic for me. Except for the time I spent at college, I've lived around Boston since I was ten years old. It's a great city; I really got to know the place like the back of my hand. I met Karen a couple years ago; she's a fourth-year medical student now, and we lived together this past year. To leave all that, the city, my friends, my girlfriend, our

*Like everything else, the interns' months are different from other people's months. In order to allow continuity of care, the interns switch to new rotations a few days before the calendar month begins.

1

apartment, my family, it's been really a difficult, dramatic thing. It's going to be a big adjustment. The only thing that's making it a little easier is that Karen came out with me; she'll be around for another week or so, just until I've had a chance to get myself settled. But after that, she'll be gone, too. I don't know what I'm going to do after that.

I've felt kind of lost since getting to the Bronx. I moved in last Sunday night, and Monday and Tuesday, the first days of orientation, were really stressful. I came home on Tuesday after the lectures on management of emergencies and cardiac arrests and I just fell into Karen's arms and cried for a while. I've never done that before; it kind of scared me. I felt so wound up about these new responsibilities that were looming larger and more threatening every second. I felt terrible. I just thought, "What am I doing here? I can't do this, I'm not good enough to know how to rush in there and save people's lives when they're dying all over the place, when they are bleeding and not breathing."

Something about those lectures scared the shit out of me. It wasn't that I hadn't heard the stuff a million times before; it was the way the lecturers were saying it. "Well, *you'll* want to do this and *you'll* have to know this, because *you'll* be the intern." They weren't talking *at* us, like they did in medical school, they were talking *to* us. That was scary. I really didn't sleep well those first couple of nights, mostly because there was so much to think about.

I guess one of the things I'm worried about is how much this internship means. When I started medical school, I had great expectations about how much I'd know and how skilled I'd be when I graduated. I thought I was going to be a doctor with a capital "D." Now that I've finished medical school and I've been through all the disillusionment about the capabilities of twentieth-century technological medicine, I feel like I don't even deserve to be called doctor with a small "d." Medical school turned out to be a very negative experience, a real grind for the first two years, sitting in lecture halls day after day, week after week, being bored to death by people who don't seem to care about anything except what's happened in their research lab over the past ten years, and a mixture of wasted time, humiliation, and feeling intimidated the last two years. As a third- and fourth-year medical student, you get to realize how unimportant you are, how things go on whether you're there or not; you're only there to get yelled at by the attendings for doing stupid things, or to get abused by the house staff, who treat you like a slave. You don't really learn how to be a doctor in medical school. So I'm coming into this internship hoping and praying it's everything medical school wasn't. I'm hoping again that when I finish this part of my training, I'll be that doctor with a capital "D," but this time there's more pressure on me: This has got to be it. When I leave here, I've got to be a doctor.

And I'm entering with expectations that this'll be an exciting and interesting time in my life, with memories I'll always cherish. I know it's not going to be easy, and it's not going to be a lot of fun. I'm going to feel lousy a lot. But I hope when I'm all done, I'll be able to look back at these years and be able to say that the time was better spent as an intern than in almost any other way I could have spent it. I've invested four years in this already; if I invest another three years and wind up realizing I hate being a doctor, well, that's seven years of my life completely wasted. I'm twenty-seven, I'm still a young guy, but seven years of wasted time, that's pretty sad.

And finally, after all these emotions and worries, it started. I was on call on Saturday in the Mount Scopus emergency room. Once the day began, it really wasn't so bad. There was just a resident and me. My first case was a little eight-month-old with a really bad case of cervical adenitis [swelling of the lymph nodes in the neck due to infection], and I thought, wow, here I am, a real doctor, with real pathology. I wound up having to admit the kid for IV antibiotics.

I did pretty good during the day, I was really enjoying it. I wasn't scared, I wasn't freaked out and I don't think I made any really horrible mistakes. I went at my own pace, which was about half the speed of the second year residents but I felt good about it. I did an LP [a lumbar puncture, commonly called a spinal tap, a test in which a needle is inserted through the back and into the spinal canal, so that a sample of spinal fluid can be obtained for analysis] on an 18 month on whom we had a suspicion of meningitis, and it went perfectly. I got the spinal fluid and I started an IV without any problem at all. I did a CSF cell count [counting the number of white and red blood cells in the spinal fluid specimen in order to diagnose meningitis], and I learned a bunch of good bench lab stuff that I never knew how to do before. Hell, it was a good day and we even got a chance to eat dinner. I got out of there at 12:30 A.M., which isn't bad. I have to say my first night on call was a positive experience, which gave me a good feeling about coming to this program in the first place.

Sunday, July 7, 1985

Karen went back to Boston today. Even though she'll be back in three weeks to visit for a weekend, I know things are not going to be the same as they were for at least this whole year. I took her to the airport, she went through the gate, and I stood there waving and she waved back until all I could see was her arm. Then that disappeared and she was finally gone.

I got back from the airport and putzed around the apartment for a while, feeling aimless. I dropped off Ellen O'Hara's [one of the other interns] car keys—she had loaned me her car for the weekend—and Ellen and I talked for a while. She was a little spacey; she'd been on in the NICU [neonatal intensive-care unit] last night and didn't get any sleep. Then I went out shopping.

I was in the vegetable store and I had this really funny feeling, like I couldn't think clearly for a minute. I couldn't figure out what was wrong at first, but then I realized that I was shopping for myself. I started feeling really bad because I'd be the only person in the apartment eating this stuff. When I got back from the store, I called Karen right away. She was home already. I told her how much I missed her and how lonely I felt. She told me she felt the same way. We talked for a while and when we got off the phone, I felt real down, real down, and I didn't know what to do. I just walked around the apartment, feeling very empty. I felt like I wanted to cry, so I sat down at my desk but the tears wouldn't come. I had to talk to someone; the only person I knew was Ellen, so I called her and told her I'd like to come and talk for a while and she said sure. I went up to her apartment, she opened the door and asked what was wrong, and I told her I was feeling real low. We sat down on her couch and I started crying. I kind of fell onto her shoulder and cried for ten, fifteen minutes, really crying, soaking her blouse. She held me and I held on to her. I felt a lot better after that. We talked about getting together for dinner, and so I went back down to the store to get more food.

That was amazing! That kind of thing, crying on a total stranger's shoulder, is not something I've ever done before. I was feeling bad, really bad, and she was the only person I even knew here. All I can say is, I'm glad there are people like Ellen in this program.

But all is not lost. When I went out for food the second time, I found a store that sold Häagen-Dazs ice cream! Häagen-Dazs in the Bronx! Amazing! [**Häagen-Dazs ice cream has always been manufactured in the South Bronx.**] There's hope for this place after all!

Work is good. I've finished my first week as an intern, and it's shown me that I actually like being a doctor. I enjoy the people I'm working with, I like the kids . . . I'm rediscovering some of the things that made me go into pediatrics in the first place. This week, working in the ER [**emergency room**] and the clinics, I saw more kids than I had seen during the entire six-week rotation I spent in pediatrics in medical school. I love the kids, but I can see that the adolescents can drive you nuts!

There are a lot of things I don't understand about adolescents. Do you examine them with their parents in the room? Do you throw the parents out, and if so, when do you throw them out? And there are all these hidden agendas going on between the parents and the kids. The other day, I saw a fifteen-year-old girl with a vaginal discharge. Her mother insisted on staying in the room the whole time. I felt pretty uncomfortable asking the girl whether she was sexually active or not with her mother standing right there next to her, but the woman just wouldn't leave. So I wound up doing a pelvic exam and getting all the cultures and stuff without even knowing what I was looking for. I guess when I get some of these issues sorted out, I'll feel better about them, but as of now, give me those toddlers and little kids anytime!

I'm starting to feel more confident and more willing and able to see patients without supervision. [**In the beginning of the year, interns working in the emergency room are supposed to check with the attending on duty before discharging any patient.**] It was so busy the other day, I didn't have time to check everything out. We were about four hours backed up most of the time and I was just running from one thing to another without any time even to think, let alone consult an attending. Occasionally I asked for advice just to check myself, and the attending who was on call in the ER always agreed with what I wanted to do. That felt good; it was a real boost to my ego.

There is one thing about work that's starting to bother me, though. When I was in medical school, one of the things I liked best about pediatrics was dealing with the parents. Over the past few days, though, I've found myself getting really annoyed with some of the parents who bring their kids to the emergency room. For instance, this mother brought her two-year-old in the other night. When I asked her why she was there, she said, ''My kid hasn't gone to the bathroom for two days.'' All she had was minor constipation, for God's sake! And the woman hadn't even tried anything. Here it is, twelve-thirty in the morning, and there's an eight-year-old boy in the other room who just got his eye blown out by a firecracker. And there's a five-year-old sickler with a fever in painful crisis [a child with sickle-cell anemia, a common inherited disorder mainly occurring in blacks and Hispanics, in which the red blood cells collapse when the blood oxygen is low; the collapsed, or sickled red blood cells clog up the smaller blood vessels, leading to obstruction and further lack of oxygen, which results in pain in the hands and feet; in a patient with sickle-cell disease, fever can be a sign of serious, possibly overwhelming infection.], it's time for me to get home, and this woman brings her child in for minor constipation. I wanted to strangle her, just put my hands around her neck and strangle her! And this kind of thing isn't unusual. It happens all the time, every night, that's why there's always a three- or four-hour wait to be seen. I tried to be nice to her, but I can't help getting really pissed.

Occasionally there'll be parents who seem really weird. The other day, this woman came in with her two kids who had colds. She was like a street person, she was carrying around all her possessions in shopping bags and she was dirty and her hair was all matted. The kids seemed perfectly okay though. There wasn't much I could do; just examine them, tell her to give them Tylenol, and send them on their way. But it bothers me; there has to be something wrong there. I've tried to figure out a way to get kids like that away from the parents, to protect them, but it seems to be impossible to do unless the parent actually harms the kid. You can't call the BCW [the Bureau of Child Welfare, the state-run agency that investigates physical and sexual abuse of children] just because a mother looks and acts a little funny. Even when the parent actually does harm the kid, like when they beat the kid with a strap because he or she misbehaves or acts up, it's sometimes difficult to do anything to prevent it from happening again.

Tuesday, July 9, 1985, 3:00 A.M.

Must internship really be like this? Must it really have hours like this? Today was just one of those long, zooish days. I had clinic this morning, had about three seconds for lunch, went to the emergency room where there was already a big pile of charts in the triage box, and that's how it stayed until a little while ago. There wasn't even a minute to get some dinner; I was starving, but there just wasn't any time to stop. We kept working and working and the triage box of charts of patients waiting to be seen just kept getting bigger and bigger.

I've noticed I'm not nervous anymore. I did another spinal tap today, on a little one-year-old with a fever who had had a seizure. It went fine, the kid didn't have meningitis, it must have just been a febrile seizure [a convulsion that occurs with fever and having no adverse long-term effects]. I admitted a kid with anemia, the second kid I've admitted since starting. I used to sweat like a pig when I had to do procedures and stuff; I don't seem to be sweating much anymore. It happened very suddenly. So far, internship has been a period of exponential learning. I just hope all I'm picking up sticks.

I still can't believe I'm getting paid for this. But I'll tell you, I don't think it'll be long before I start thinking I'd damned well better be getting paid for this. I think that happens when you start to respect your skills. I'm not there yet; but I'm getting there, I think.

But I do get really pissed off about working in the West Bronx emergency room [West Bronx, also referred to as WBH, is a municipal hospital adjacent to Mount Scopus]. I was drawing blood today from a four-year-old and I had to stick him three times because he kept pulling his arm away and pulling out the needle. The reason he kept pulling his arm away was because the nurse wasn't holding him tightly enough. When I told her, she said, "I don't care, I don't give a damn!" Oh, really! She just didn't give a shit about the kid! Here's a woman who must really love her job.

I forgot to talk about something I can't believe I haven't mentioned yet. Something really significant happened tonight, something horrible, and I guess I blocked it out of my mind for a while. As the triage box was filling higher and higher with charts and we were getting farther and farther behind, we were called by a frantic clerk to come over to the critical care room. He said there was a pediatric cardiac arrest going on.

So we tore over there to see what was happening. I got there first. I found the place jammed with doctors and nurses working on what looked like a pretty big adolescent. They were pumping on his chest, they had him hooked up to the cardiac monitor, they were sticking him for blood and starting big IVs in his groin. I had no idea what to do. The resident showed up a few seconds after I got there and we stood around for a couple of minutes until they just told us that we could leave unless we wanted to run the code. "No," we said (laugh), "it looks like you guys are doing just fine." But no one had taken a history yet, or even talked to the mother, so the resident told me to go out there and get the story. I found the woman; she was perched outside the critical care room looking scared to death. I took her over to the social work office and started talking to her.

Briefly she told me the kid was a fifteen-year-old asthmatic who'd been in the middle of a bad asthma attack when it sounded like he had become obstructed [**the main breathing tube, the trachea or one of the mainstem bronchi, the tubes leading from the trachea to the lung, became blocked**]. He stopped breathing and they loaded him into a car and sped off to the hospital. They were headed for Jonas Bronck but on the way the kid was snatched up by a passing EMS team and brought to West Bronx. He had been pulseless, breathless, and unresponsive for God knows how long. When he got in the ambulance, he had vomited and aspirated [**leaked stomach contents into his lungs**] and gone into arrest.

So he was kind of dead when they brought him in, but I don't think I really believed it. His first pH was 6.9 [**indicating severe buildup of acid in the blood, a condition resulting from lack of oxygen delivery to the tissue and not consistent with life for longer than a few minutes**], which isn't great. His heart was beating only about eight times a minute, but he was a kid, and kids just don't die like this. Not the ones I'd known anyway.

When I was getting the history, the mother asked me, "How

is he, Doctor?'' and I was about to say . . . I don't know exactly what I was about to say, but then the clerk opened the door and took the mother away because he had to register the kid or something administrative like that, and I left, after telling her I'd come back to talk to her again when she was done.

Next thing I knew, that clerk came back to me, not as excited this time, and he said, ''The kid died; he's dead.'' I couldn't believe it. I knew he hadn't been doing well and that they were doing everything they could for him, but dead? I just couldn't believe it. I had to walk in and see him myself.

In the critical care room, the crowd was gone; there were just a couple of nurses, removing all the lines and stuff, cleaning him up, getting ready to bag him, and there he was with his glazed corneas—yeah, he looked dead, all right. The medical resident came in and we talked about it for a minute. No one had said anything to the family yet. I told him I'd gotten the history from the mother. ''Well, I guess you're the only one who's established rapport . . .'' he said. Rapport? I spoke with the woman for five lousy minutes; that's not exactly what I'd call establishing rapport.

But I was elected. Other than me, nobody had even laid eyes on the woman. The medical resident said he'd come along with me. On the way back to the social work office, I stopped myself and thought, What the hell am I going to say to this woman? I knew she was totally unprepared for this. When I had talked with her earlier, I got the impression she thought everything was going to be okay. I knew things weren't okay. I had seen him getting his chest pumped, being a full code. I should have said, ''Your son is in critical condition. There's a chance he won't make it.'' I wish I had said it when I'd had the chance, but then that damned clerk had come in and had taken her out to register her. I should have booted him out, told him I was talking and that it was important, but I didn't think to do that, so I didn't get to prepare her in any way. Ah, maybe she didn't want to know, maybe she would have been worse off had I tipped her off beforehand. Who knows?

Anyway, there I was, sitting in front of her in the social work office, and the medical resident was standing behind me and there she was, looking at me, not having a clue what was going on. All I could think to say was, ''I'm sorry, but I have to tell you, your son is dead.''

She looked at me, her eyes bugged out, and she became completely hysterical. And the woman who was there with her also became completely hysterical. They began screaming in Spanish and wailing and throwing themselves around. I didn't understand a fucking word they were saying, I didn't know what was going on, they were making a tremendous ruckus and I just . . . I just didn't know what to do. It was a terrible moment. I felt completely powerless. I couldn't think of anything to make her feel better. It was probably the most horrible moment in her life.

As we were walking to that room and I knew I was going to be the one to tell her about her son, I remembered hearing about situations like this, when you have to tell a mother that her child has died, and you don't even know her; you're just on call and it's not your patient and you just kind of get signed out to take care of the dying person. I expected it to happen sooner or later; I'm just kind of surprised it happened so soon in my internship, in virtually the first week.

Wednesday, July 10, 1985

I spent the afternoon in the West Bronx ER, where I had a great case. We had this kid I saw a couple days ago, the one-year-old who came in with a febrile seizure. I tapped him and found he didn't have meningitis, but today the blood cultures I'd sent came back positive, with gram negative rods [meaning that there was a bacterial infection in the blood with a bacteria called E. *coli*, a potentially serious infection]. We called the kid back in and he still had fever on the antibiotics I had prescribed, so we admitted him for treatment of sepsis [infection of the blood].

Then later in the day, a little five-month-old came in with a high fever. I did another spinal tap and did the cell count and this time, yes, lots of white cells; this kid did have meningitis and was admitted. That's routine pediatrics, very routine, I know, but for me it was a very exciting thing. I was able to do everything from start to finish, and that was all stuff I learned here, stuff I didn't know how to do in med school, and that's very exciting. I'm now able to do some things that doctors are supposed to do.

I told the mother we'd have to admit the baby and take more

blood and she said "No way." She was frightened to death. I knew there was no way that I, with my vast two-week experience as an intern, was going to be able to convince her to let us do what we needed to do, so I called the attending and he came over and sat and explained the whole thing to her, telling her how important it was that we start an IV and begin antibiotics as soon as possible so that the baby would have the best chance possible of surviving and she listened carefully but it was clear she was so frightened she couldn't think straight. She finally said, "I don't know what to do anymore. Call my husband and ask him." We called the father and he said, "Do whatever you have to," and he came in. It was very sad: Here's this beautiful, normal baby with this terrible infection and the real possibility that he'll wind up retarded, and I was excited because I had been able to do the workup from start to finish. It's like I'm less interested in the patients and more interested in what I can and cannot do.

I've been here a week and a half and I've done more spinal taps than I'd done in all of med school. You see a lot in this place, it's a great program, but I can see how I could get burned out. It's a real danger in a place like this, with call relentlessly every third night and the ancillary staff somewhat less than helpful. I can see I'm going to have to watch out; down the road when it's the winter and my vacation is a month or two away, I can see how I could possibly come to hate this, how what seems like fun and is exciting now could turn into a real drag later.

Monday, July 15, 1985

Time seems both to drag and to race onward. It seems like forever since I last saw Karen; it's only been a week and a half. I really miss her.

Last night I was on call in the West Bronx ER again, and from the word go, it was crazy, packed from the start until about two o'clock. I didn't have even a second to catch my breath. This is getting to be a very disturbing routine.

I spent Friday and Saturday down in Manhattan with some of my friends from college, Gary and Maura. They live in the city; it was nice to get out of here and see some people outside of medicine. I tried to explain to them about some of the stuff I've been doing and seeing. They say they understand, but I get the feeling they only believe about half the things I tell them.

Today I acted as the supervising physician for IV sedation in a kid who was getting a radioulnar fracture [**a fracture of the two bones of the forearm**] reduced by the orthopods [**internese for orthopedic surgeon**]. Although the attending popped his head in a few times to make sure everything was all right, I basically just did it on my own. Even though nothing really happened, it's still kind of a nerve-racking experience.

Thursday, July 18, 1985, 2:00 A.M.

Just finished another call in the West Bronx ER. The past few days have been mixed. Today was pretty good, but the two days before pretty much sucked. I had a couple of aggravating days in clinic [**all pediatric house officers are assigned to a "well-child clinic" in one of the hospitals; interns and residents have office hours once or twice a week in clinic during which they usually see six or seven of their own patients**], where I just felt overwhelmed and disorganized; it was driving me crazy. The problems were pretty boring, but I'm picking up lots of new patients, slowly but surely drumming up my clinic. I have the feeling it's going to be a booming clinic pretty soon. It seems like every walk-in [**a patient who comes to the emergency room**] needs a regular doctor. They ask me if I'd be their doctor, I say sure and give them the clinic's number. I have a feeling this is going to be a mixed blessing in the long run, but anyway . . .

I was really tired most of today. I just don't seem to have any pep. It's this every-third-night-on-call business, the inevitability of it, it's just dreadful. Even though this is the easiest rotation I'll have and I get to go home every night (even though it might be at three or four in the morning), these hours just get very tiring. Is it possible that I'm really starting to get tired this early into the year? I'm worrying about everything; I've even started to have trouble sleeping on the nights I'm not on call. I didn't sleep well last night—I woke up three times before my alarm went off.

Well, it's time to go to sleep, my favorite pastime.

Saturday, July 20, 1985, 3:30 A.M.

Today was my worst day of internship so far, because of two incidents I had with orthopedics. First, there was a kid with a dislocated elbow. I was doing the IV sedation and the prick ortho resident didn't like the amount of sedative I was giving, he wanted the patient to get more and at one point he actually put his hand on the syringe full of morphine I was holding and started to squeeze. I had to shake his hand off and tell him, "No, you're not supposed to do that." The rest of the procedure was punctuated by him cursing at me for not wanting to give enough sedation. The jerk!

Later there was another kid who needed sedation, so this same resident and I decided together to give him a DPT [a **cocktail of three sedatives: Demerol, Phenergan, and Thorazine, given through an intramuscular injection**], but the nurses wouldn't do it. They have this rule that DPT is not allowed to be used. So this started a big stink and things were getting more and more hairy. The pediatric resident who was on got pissed off at the nurses and they got pissed off at us, and the ortho resident's yelling, "Hey come on, guys, hurry up!" Finally we decided to give IM [**intramuscular**] morphine but I wrote the order on the wrong part of the chart and the nurses didn't see it and they didn't give the medication and before you know it, the ortho resident was back, pissed as hell because we were taking so much time, and he started yelling at me for being so incompetent and then I started yelling back at him and I could feel the blood rising in my face. I've never felt that angry at anybody before. It was making me crazy that I had no way to get back at him, so I just kept yelling at the fucking guy, telling him he was a jerkoff and a dickface. It was a very uncool thing to do.

Right after this, I grabbed a chart and went into an examining room but I was still so angry, I couldn't concentrate. So I told the senior I needed two minutes to cool off, and I went down to the vending area to get a Coke. I put my money in the machine, and what came out? A nice, warm Pepsi! No ice! No refrigeration! Oh, God, how I love West Bronx!

I went to a corner, sat down, and tried to cool out for a while. Then I went back to the ER, got some ice, and drank my fucking Pepsi. I apologized to the nurse I yelled at; I even apologized to the ortho resident, even though I think I'd still like to break his arm.

A few of us 'terns got together the other night and went out. We had dinner at an Indian restaurant in Manhattan, then went to get some ice cream and roamed around for a while in the rain. It was pretty good, but we were all so damned tired. Everyone was either postcall or precall. Shit! It's just amazing how often call comes around. It's like you feel you just got off and it's your night again.

Wednesday, July 24, 1985, 12:20 A.M.

The month's almost over and I'm looking at the end with mixed feelings. On the one hand, this ER stuff is starting to get pretty old. It gets repetitive and frustrating after a while. But on the other hand, I can't say I'm looking forward with any great excitement to being in the NICU next month. I basically like to work decent hours; I don't like staying up all night, which is what you have to do in the NICU. Thank God there're caffeine and other stimulants.

Actually, I've never taken other stimulants. I never liked the idea of speed. Of course, I've never had to go for more than twenty hours without sleep. Being exhausted and having a little twelve-hundred-gram baby crumping [trying to die; deteriorating] in front of you, that kind of gets you worried.

Sunday, July 28, 1985

I had a really wonderful weekend. I was on call Friday night and it was really quiet. I got home at twelve-thirty and Karen was here. She had just gotten in. We stayed up and talked until I was too tired to stay awake and then we went to sleep. It was restful, relaxing, and wonderful. Then today we were down in Manhattan and I saw Karen off to her bus to the airport and I started feeling very sad again. I've felt kind of sad and kind of nervous and lonely all day.

I took the train back home. That's the worst part for me: coming home to an empty apartment, knowing no one's going to come home after me, that I'm not waiting for anybody, I'm home and that's it. I called a couple of people; I called my friend Anne from medical school. She's an intern in Boston. We had a nice talk. Then I called my mom, who had just gotten home from England, and we talked for a long time. Then I got ahold of my intern friends Ellen and Ron, and we went out for some dinner. That was nice; I needed the companionship, I needed to be with people I felt close to.

And tomorrow morning I start my new rotation in the neonatal intensive-care unit, and I'm on call the first night. I've heard all sorts of horror stories about being an intern in the NICU.

It's only been a month since I started, and I can already see a big change in myself. I don't think anyone outside of medicine really understands what this whole thing is about. I've had trouble explaining my life this month to people, and I'm sure next month is going to be even more impossible to explain. I'm starting to think that it probably isn't even worth the effort for me to try. Most people in the nonmedical public, they have their own ideas about what doctors should be like, and I don't think they want to have those ideas shattered. They don't want to know about the long hours and the lack of sleep and everything else. They have these myths that we're all like Dr. Kildare or Marcus Welby. I hate to disappoint them by telling them the truth.

AMY

July 1985

Tuesday, July 2, 1985

The hardest part of this year is definitely going to be leaving Sarah. There's no question about it. I'm not sure yet what being an intern is going to be like, but I am sure of one thing: There's nothing they can make me do that could possibly be any harder than saying good-bye to the baby was for me yesterday morning.

Some people might think it a little strange to have a child two months before you start an internship. Well, there are a lot of things that went into our decision. First and foremost, Larry and I have wanted a baby ever since we got married. We both love children; that's really the main reason I decided to go into pediatrics in the first place.

Another reason has to do with my family. My mother died when I was in college. I still haven't gotten over it. Ever since, I've wanted to have a baby, a girl, and name her for my mother. That's been very important to me. That's why our baby is named Sarah.

I guess the third reason has to do with my miscarriage. I was pregnant when I was a third-year student. That one wasn't planned; I just got pregnant. Larry and I were both happy about it. I went to my obstetrician's office when I was about ten weeks and he heard the fetal heart. Everything seemed to be going fine, but then two days later, I started to have some pains and Larry had to take me over to the Jonas Bronck emergency room, where the miscarriage was diagnosed. They did a D and C and sent me home. If I hadn't lost that pregnancy, I'd have had the baby in the beginning of my fourth year of med school, which would have been perfect: I would have been able to take some time off then; things aren't too hectic in the fourth year. And I'd have had a one-year-old at this point, and leaving a one-year-old all day with a sitter isn't as bad as leaving a two-month-old. But having had that miscarriage, I started to wonder whether there was something wrong with me. I thought I'd never be able to have a baby. I guess I became obsessed with it.

Well, all of these are reasons for having a baby, but they don't explain why I decided to have one two months before I started internship. I guess the reason I didn't want to wait until after I finished my internship and residency was that you can't tell what might happen; there are people who wait and something happens to them medically and they find out that they can't have a baby. I didn't want to take a chance. I had thought for a while that maybe I'd take this year off and spend my time just being a mother and wait until next year to do my internship. A lot of people advised me against that. I was told it would be hard to get back into medicine after I'd been away from it for a whole year. And Larry encouraged me to go ahead with my internship; he told me he could manage the baby when I was on call. So here I am.

But I didn't think it was going to be this hard to be away from her. From the day Sarah was born until orientation started last week, I spent every minute with her. I took May off as vacation time. In the beginning of May, we put an ad in the paper for a full-time baby-sitter. We chose the woman we finally hired because she seemed really nice and she had great references. Her name is Marie; she's a Jamaican woman who's about forty. She has full-grown children of her own. She started two weeks ago, while I was still around. She's going to come every morning, Monday to Friday, at seven-thirty and stay until Larry or I get home at night. Larry and I will be alone with Sarah on weekends. Marie seems to like the baby a lot, but then again what's not to like? There are a couple of little problems, though: She spends all day carrying Sarah around, she feeds her every two hours because she says she's afraid the baby will cry and get colic. I guess I'll eventually have to talk with her; I'll have to be more assertive. I know Marie'll do a great job and everything'll turn out okay. It's just that . . . I'm worried she might turn Sarah into a wimp!

So far, being an intern isn't any worse than being a medical student. I'm in the OPD [**Outpatient Department**] at Jonas

Bronck this month. I was on call last night for the first time and I got out of the ER at about a quarter to three. There was a lot of trauma, plenty of lacerations and head wounds, but since I don't know how to do anything yet, I wound up seeing the more basic medical problems. For some reason, most of the kids I saw were four-month-olds with fevers. There's something going around, I guess. I felt bad for Evan [**the senior resident who had been on call that night**]. He was the only person on who knew how to suture, so he wound up spending the entire night sewing lacerations. Since the attending went home at ten o'clock, the other interns and I had to keep interrupting him every five minutes to discuss patients with him. I felt bad doing it, but I wasn't about to send anybody home without clearing it with a senior first!

When I got home, something weird happened. I went to bed and I must have fallen into a deep sleep because Sarah started crying at around four and I thought I was still in the ER getting ready to see another screaming kid. Larry told me he heard me say, "Please God, let me go home."

Monday, July 8, 1985

I've been on call three times now. Last Friday was the worst so far. Everything had been going pretty well until about eight o'clock, when a thirteen-year-old girl who had been raped came in. I wound up seeing her.

She was a young thirteen; she looked more like eleven or ten. She was really broken up, but I got her to tell me what had happened. She had been alone in her family's apartment when a knock came on the door. She looked through the peephole and saw her fifteen-year-old brother's friend. He told her he had left a book in the apartment, and she let him in. They went into the brother's bedroom and started looking around. Suddenly the girl felt something around her neck. The boy had pulled out an electrical cord and he kept pulling it tighter until she got down on the bed and took off her clothes. He then proceeded to rape her.

He was there a total of about an hour. A little while later the girl's family came home and found her hysterical. They immediately brought her to the ER.

The attending and I went over what had to be done. I did a

complete exam and got all the samples that would be needed as evidence when the case went to court. There's something called a rape kit that has to be used, with directions that have to be followed exactly or the whole thing can be thrown out of court. I made sure I did everything right. I was working like a robot all through it, trying not to think about anything except getting the job done. After I finished, I handed the rape kit over to the cop. The social worker came in to talk to the girl and her parents, who were crazy at that point. The father wanted to go out and kill the kid slowly, really make him suffer. The mother just cried. The girl didn't speak much, she was in shock. The cop called a little while later to say the boy had been caught. The parents took the girl home at about midnight. As soon as they left the ER, I just fell apart. I spent the next hour crying. We were still busy, so when I pulled myself back together I had to start seeing patients again. We didn't get out until nearly five in the morning. It was a terrible night. Terrible.

Yesterday was busy, too, but it wasn't nearly as bad as Friday. Yesterday's specialty was trauma. We had all kinds of trauma, kids falling out of windows onto their heads, firecrackers blowing off fingers, and the basic foot laceration from Orchard Beach [a beach on Long Island Sound]. Since I still haven't learned how to suture, I spent most of the day seeing kids with head trauma. Most of them were okay; I just examined them, found nothing wrong, and sent them home with a head trauma sheet [the emergency room provides instruction sheets in English and Spanish covering most of the common pediatric problems]. At about 3:00 A.M. we had finally cleared out the triage box and I picked up one of the last charts, a six-year-old who had hit his head on a coffee table. The nurse who had seen him when the mother first registered at about eleven thought he looked all right and put him at the bottom of the pile. [The nurses triage each patient according to his or her symptoms: Patients who require real emergency care are "up-triaged" and their charts are placed near the top of the pile; patients who are judged to be stable are triaged to the bottom of the pile. On exceptionally busy days, the wait to be seen by a physician may be as long as six hours.]

The mother told me the boy was running around the apartment and had fallen and hit the back of his head on the coffee table. He hadn't blacked out but had become very sleepy. I examined him: He *was* sleepy, but then again, so was I. There were no focal findings. **[A focal neurologic exam, one in which there is weakness, paralysis, or abnormal reflexes on one side of the body, indicates a neurologic deficit. A negative neurologic exam following head trauma is a fairly good indication that the brain hasn't been harmed.]** The senior resident told me it was okay to send the kid home, but when I went to give the mother a head trauma sheet, the kid suddenly couldn't remember anything that had happened over the past few hours. So the senior told me to check the kid out with the neuro fellow **[the pediatric neurology department trains a group of fellows, individuals who have completed two years of residency and have gone on to do another three years in neurology]**. It took him twenty minutes to answer his page, and when he did and I told him the story, he told me he had to check with his attending **[the senior doctor on call for neurology that night]** before deciding what to do.

It took him another forty minutes to get in touch with the attending! There I was in the ER in the middle of the night with nothing to do but wait. I could have been home sleeping! But I couldn't sign this out to the night float. I had to stay.

When he finally called back, he said the kid needed a CT **[CT scan: a computerized X ray of the brain]** and that he had to be admitted. I had to bring him up to the fourth floor and help the technician get him settled on the CT table. Finally, the intern from the ward showed up and I got out of there. I didn't get home until four-thirty. If I hadn't picked up that last chart, I would have gotten about two hours' more sleep.

Thursday was July 4 and I had the day off. It was great: just me and Larry and Sarah. We went swimming in the pool at our apartment complex; Sarah seems to love the water. It was like getting reacquainted.

I had another run-in with Marie on Friday. I'm still having trouble with her. Even though we had a talk, she still carries Sarah around all the time and feeds her every two hours, as soon as she opens her mouth and lets out a peep. We got into a fight last Monday. I came home for lunch after clinic ended at about eleven-thirty. When I came into the apartment, Marie was holding the baby. I tried to take Sarah, but Marie wouldn't let go of her. I just about had to pry them apart. I said a few things I probably shouldn't have said. I don't know what's going to happen with her.

I think having a baby at home is making me into a more efficient intern. I find myself trying to get my work done as quickly as possible and running home. Sarah gives me a lot of motivation to work fast.

Friday, July 12, 1985

I feel bad talking about this, but I think I should anyway. Maybe it'll make me feel better to get it off my chest; I don't know. I feel terrible and it isn't my fault, it just isn't my fault. I did what I was supposed to do, that's all I know, and somehow I got into trouble.

Last week, this adolescent girl came in complaining of rectal bleeding. I recognized her from my subinternship [**a two-month rotation in the fourth year of a medical student in which the student works as an intern, taking night call and admitting and following patients**]. She was on the ward for some psych problem, I don't remember exactly what. I examined her and did a rectal exam; I didn't find anything wrong, and the stuff I smeared from the glove onto the guaiac card was negative [**the guaiac test is for hidden blood in the stool**]. So I thought she was a crock [**a patient who has nothing wrong and is faking symptoms; short for a "crock of shit"; sometimes referred to as a "turkey"**]. I presented her case to Tom Kelly, who was the attending, and I told him . . . I told him . . . I'm sorry, I have to stop for a minute and pull myself together. Crying is not the answer.

Sorry. Anyway, I told Tom I thought the girl was lying. He told me that very well might be the case, but that I should draw some blood for a CBC [**complete blood count: a blood test that measures anemia**] and a sed rate [**erythrocyte sedimentation rate, a test for inflammation or infection, in this case used to rule out inflammatory bowel disease, which is a cause of rectal bleeding**] anyway, to rule out any real problem. I agreed with him and I went back and got the blood. I sent the CBC to the lab and spun a hematocrit [**a direct test for anemia**] myself. It was fine—37 or something like that. I forgot to get the sed rate, though. I just . . . it slipped my mind. The girl . . . she was making me crazy while I was taking the blood and

I just forgot about it. I did it, I don't know why they don't believe me. . . . I'm sorry, please forgive my outburst.

A few hours later, Tom got it in his head that I hadn't taken the blood. I don't know why. He didn't come to me directly and ask. He checked with the clerk and she told him she didn't remember sending anything off to the lab. Then he called the lab and they denied ever getting a CBC on the patient. Then he called the girl at home and asked her if anyone had taken blood from her and she denied it. And then he came and confronted me with all this and accused me of having lied about the whole thing. I don't know . . . I did it, that's all I can say. I don't know why the lab didn't get it. The girl's crazy, so I can understand her saying I didn't take it. I don't know. . . .

The worst part of this is that now everyone knows. I didn't do anything wrong, I swear it, but all the ER attendings are talking about it. Some of the residents know. Nobody's going to trust me, I know it. I've been crying for the past three days. I'm on tomorrow and I can't let this affect me. I have to go on and just ignore this. But how can I do that?

Wednesday, July 17, 1985

Things are a little better today. On Monday, Jon Golden [one of the pediatric chief residents; the chief residents are responsible for the house officers; they directly manage the patients, make up the on-call schedules, and look after house staff morale] came to talk to me. He told me he had heard about what had happened in the emergency room and he assured me he didn't believe it and that I shouldn't let it bother me or interfere with my work. It was nice to talk to him, it made me feel much better, but it's sad to think it had reached the higher-ups that fast. Even though we've got so many interns and residents, this is a small department in terms of gossip. You have to be really careful what you tell people.

Then yesterday, Tom Kelly talked to me in the ER. We cleared the air. He apologized for the story getting around. I understand it in a way; the ER attendings at Jonas Bronck are all close friends and they have to talk to each other about something! Anyway, it looks like this storm has passed. Now if I could only straighten things out with my baby-sitter.

I'm still having trouble with Marie. I don't know what to do about her; she's very good but she's got her own ideas about things and there isn't anything I can do to change her. It comes down to two options: Either I try to live with the way things are, or I let her go and try to find someone else. I don't think it would be very easy to find a replacement for her right now. I barely have enough time to eat; I don't think I can afford to go through another round of interviewing. So, I guess I'll have to keep her. It could be worse.

I wonder what the other interns are doing with their free time. I mean, I spend all my time away from the hospital with Sarah. I never talk to anybody outside of work.

Friday, July 26, 1985

Yesterday was a terrible day. I was on call. I seem to be on call every night! But yesterday was worse than usual because it was Sarah's birthday. She was three months old and I wasn't there to see her. In the last couple of weeks, she changed into a real person. She doesn't just lay in her crib anymore: She can lift up her head and look around and she smiles when she sees me. She's got a beautiful smile. It's great coming home to see her. I just wish I could spend more time with her!

We were really busy all day and I couldn't seem to do anything right. In the afternoon, I had this four-year-old who came in with a high fever and chest pain. She was coughing and congested and I was sure she had pneumonia. I listened, and sure enough, I heard rales [a crackling sound in the lung fields, usually associated with pneumonia] in the area of the right lower lobe. I sent her for an X ray but it turned out normal, no evidence of pneumonia. I went to the attending, Harvey Abelson, for help. He examined her and said he didn't hear any rales but he found that she had right CVA tenderness [tenderness over the costovertebral angle, the area of the back that overlies the kidneys] and told me to check the urine. Sure enough, the urine was loaded with bugs [bacteria] and white cells. I gram-stained it [a test to identify the type of bacteria causing the infection] and found E. *coli* [the most common bacterial cause of urinary tract infections]. She had pyelonephritis [an infection of the kidney], not pneumonia. She needed to be admitted, and I had almost sent her home! I'm just about finished with my first month of internship, and I think I know less now than I did when I started.

I didn't get home this morning until after four and I didn't get much sleep. I'm exhausted. But what can I do? This is the way internship is, and I've just got to survive it. At least I've got tomorrow off. Then I'm on again on Sunday for the last time this month. Larry's team has a softball game on Sunday, so he's going to take Sarah with him. Thank God he's so good with her! He takes her everywhere he goes when I'm on. I don't know what I'd do if he weren't so understanding or helpful. If I do make it through this year, it's because of Larry.

I start at University Hospital on Monday. I don't know what that's going to be like. I've heard bad things about it. I don't care if it's hard or boring or whatever. All I care about is getting out at a reasonable hour.

MARK

July 1985

Friday, June 28, 1985

My internship officially starts tomorrow. I've waited for this day a long time, years, the way people wait for their arteries to clog up enough for them to have a heart attack. I'm starting on 6A, the ward at West Bronx. I talked to some of the old interns and they told me that 6A was a pretty horrible place to work, that the nursing stinks, the lab technicians were impossible, and, on a good day, the clerical staff mostly just ignored you. Sounds like my kind of place! I like a challenge like that. It's just what I need, a little more aggravation. And of course I'm on tomorrow night, the first day of the year. Just my luck; I'll probably also be on call every holiday and the last day of the year as well.

At least orientation's over. It was a lot of fun, if your idea of fun is hanging around a bunch of terrified lunatics who are just figuring out that they've made a terrible mistake in their career choice and have ruined their entire lives. It really wasn't that bad; at least the food was good.

It's funny, my coming here to Schweitzer. I worked with AIDS patients in New Jersey during med school and I became pretty convinced it was a disease I didn't want to experience personally. So I was looking for a program that didn't have a lot of AIDS patients, and Schweitzer didn't exactly top the list of places meeting that criterion. I went on some other interviews and got a look at some of the other programs and suddenly the Bronx didn't look all that bad to me. So whatever happens during this internship, I can't blame anybody but myself; it's all my fault.

Carole wasn't all that happy about my coming here. I guess I should mention Carole. We've been going out off and on since we were seniors in college. She's an accountant in Manhattan and she lives in New Jersey, so my being in the Bronx is probably the worst thing that could happen to our relationship. We'll probably never get to see each other over the next year. Not that it would be much better if I were working in Manhattan. It's pretty hard to keep up a reputation as Mr. Romance when you're working a hundred hours a week. Oh, well; being an intern is probably going to be like becoming a monk; except monks have a stronger union, I think.

Well, I'm going to try to get some sleep now. I'm sure I'll wind up walking around the apartment half the night. I've got all these butterflies in my stomach, and it feels like they've just organized a softball game.

Monday, July 1, 1985

What a great idea it is to start new interns on Saturday! What better way to greet someone who's not only completely new to the hospital and doesn't even know where the bathrooms are, but also who has never worked as an intern before, than to have him cover a ward filled with twenty-five sick patients, none of whom he's ever even seen. I wonder who came up with that brilliant stroke of genius?

Needless to say, Saturday was a complete disaster. I started off the day just nervous, but by the time we finished work rounds at about ten, I was completely petrified. I mean, they had kids with meningitis who could die without batting an eyelash, kids with asthma who were on oxygen, and they were telling me to do things like "Get a blood gas on that kid" [**blood gas: an analysis of the acid, oxygen, and carbon dioxide levels in the blood; usually performed on patients in respiratory distress**]. "Check the X ray on that kid," "That other kid needs a new IV," etc., etc. I had to sit down for an hour after rounds, just to talk myself out of quitting right then!

I have to admit, the technical stuff is about the only thing I can do. So I started off by drawing all the bloods and starting the IVs that were needed. Then I was heading for the lab, wherever the hell that was, when I got called down to the emergency room to pick up a patient. And that was the first time I got lost. I couldn't believe it, I wound up wandering around in the basement of the hospital for twenty minutes, having no idea where

I was. I found the morgue, I found the Engineering Department, but the ER seemed to be missing. I had this medical student with me, but he wasn't much help; this was the second week of his first rotation and he was more confused than I was, if such a thing was possible. We finally found a guy down there who spoke English and I asked him where the ER was. He laughed at me for a few minutes and then told me I was on the wrong floor, it was one flight up.

Anyway, my first admission was a six-year-old with asthma. My first admission. What a moment! I wanted to have the kid bronzed so I could hang him from my car's rearview mirror, but his parents wouldn't give their consent. I managed to find my way back to the ward with the kid, who didn't seem all that sick, and then I got yelled at by the head nurse: "You have an admission? Nobody told me about any admission! We're not ready for an admission!" So I made a mistake, but she stood there, blocking the door to the treatment room like she wasn't going to let us in. What'd she expect me to do, bring the kid back down to the ER and call and tell her I was coming up with him? The way things were going, I probably would have screwed up, gotten off on the wrong floor again, and wound up bringing the kid straight to the morgue (at least I knew where that was).

Well, I finally apologized, told her I wouldn't let it happen again, and she let us into the treatment room. There really wasn't much to do for the kid except take a history, do a physical, and write an order for aminophylline [an asthma medication]. Even I could do that! So it only took me about an hour to finish, and then I tried to get up to the lab but I got called back to the emergency room for another admission.

This went on all day. I got one admission after the other from about noon until after seven at night—six admissions in all. By that point I had a lot more lab tests to check and finally made it up to the thirteenth floor [the laboratory floor at West Bronx] at about eight. It took me an hour to check all those labs. Then I came down and had to show them to the senior resident and he told me what to do next. So it was about nine o'clock, I had gotten six new patients, I had done most of the scut that had been signed out to me, but I had missed three complete meals, I hadn't even had a chance to pee (it was about then that I felt the top of my bladder hitting my rib cage). And that's when all the IVs started falling out.

I don't know what it was, but all of a sudden three nurses came up to me at once and told me that an IV had come out on one of her patients. Three IVs at once! It seemed to be to much of a coincidence. I went to find the senior resident to ask him if it was possible that the nurses were pulling them out to torture me. He said it definitely was a possibility but there was nothing I could really do about it and, no matter what happened or what I was thinking, I'd better not get into a fight with any of the nurses or my life would be ruined. I told him about what had happened when I had brought up my first patient and he just sighed and shook his head.

I got two more admissions in the middle of the night and more IV's fell out and there was more scut to do and I didn't get a chance even to lie down but somehow I made it through and nobody died. So I guess, all in all, I'd have to say it was a successful night. My only problem is, I don't ever want to be on call again!

Well, after a night like that, at least today was pretty good. I met our team's senior resident, and he seems great. His name is Eric Keyes and he's got a weird sense of humor. Then I met our attending, Alan Morris, who's director of pediatrics at West Bronx. He's very serious and kind of stiff, but he also knows a lot and I've heard he's great.

I didn't get out tonight until after nine. I was trying to get my work done, but I kept getting lost around the hospital. I'm really hopeless. I'm going to have to get better organized.

Saturday, July 6, 1985

I am definitely on the chief residents' hit list. I've been on 6A for a week now, and everything seems to have settled down. I've finally figured out where everything is; I know where the admission forms are kept and where the lab slips are stored. I've found the ER three straight times without getting lost. I liked the people I was working with. I even made up with the nurses; I brought them a box of cookies on Tuesday, and amazingly, no IVs fell out when I was on call Tuesday night. Everything was going fine and then, yesterday, just when I was really beginning to feel comfortable, one of the chief residents came up to me and said they'd decided to transfer me to the Children's ward at Mount Scopus. I told her I didn't want to go, that I was having a really good time on 6A. She said she was sorry but they were a body short on Children's and there was an extra person on 6A that month (because we had a subintern) and there was nobody else who could be pulled. I argued a little more, but I could see there was no way I was going to change her mind. Finally I just gave up. So after figuring out 6A, I had to move over to a completely different ward in a completely different hospital, pick up a whole new group of patients, learn where the Mount Scopus labs are and where the forms are kept, and I have to meet a whole new group of nurses and probably go through another night of IVs falling out. Terrific!

Children's isn't so bad, though. First of all, Elizabeth is there this month [**Elizabeth Hunter, one of the other interns, went to medical school with Mark**], and it's nice to be together with her. And the other intern, Peter Carson, seems like a nice guy. And everybody tells me that Children's is much easier than 6A. I can see that that may be true: I was on last night and actually got three hours of sleep. Three hours of sleep! It was the first time I've even seen an on-call room since I got here. There are fewer admissions, and the patients aren't as sick. The chiefs have promised me that they'll still give me the month of Children's I'm scheduled for later in the year, so maybe this will work out well. I doubt it, though; in internship, nothing is supposed to work out well.

I spoke with Carole a little while ago and told her I missed her. I think she was surprised to hear me say that. I'm not what you'd call the most demonstrative person around, but I really do miss her. I miss everybody! All I've done since starting this internship is work or go home and fall asleep. I don't know if it's possible to survive a year like this.

I'm going to sleep now. Maybe I'll dream that it's next June and all this is finished.

Thursday, July 11, 1985

Yesterday was my third night on call on Children's. When I was on last Thursday and Sunday, I didn't have any trouble. I didn't get a single admission, and I slept three or four hours each night. I was thinking maybe I'd try to arrange to go to Children's for my vacation this year. So I wasn't at all prepared for what happened last night.

I got five admissions. There was one every hour or two. I'd just have time to finish working up one when the next one would show up. They weren't really very sick: an eight-year-old who came in to have a repair done on his cleft lip that had originally been repaired when he had been a baby; a kid who had developed an infection in his leg after he had been bitten by a dog and needed IV antibiotics; another kid who had periorbital cellulitis [an infection of the tissue surrounding the eye; dangerous because it can lead to infection of the eye itself and, occasionally, of the brain] and who needed IV antibiotics; and an asthmatic. The sickest kid was also the most interesting; it was a four-year-old with a week's worth of facial swelling.

He had kind of an interesting story: His mother noticed the swelling around July 1 and brought him to their local doctor. The LMD [local M.D.] sounds like he graduated from a medical correspondence school. He brilliantly decided the kid was allergic to trees and started him on Benadryl [an antihistamine used to reverse effects of allergic reactions]. The mother was back at the guy's office in two days: Not only didn't the Benadryl work, it also seemed to make the swelling worse. Now not only was the kid's face swollen, but also his hands and feet were puffy. The LMD told the mother that sometimes it takes a while for the allergy to get better, especially since there are so many trees around, and that she should give the medicine more time to work.

Well, she gave the medicine as long as it took for the kid's belly and scrotum to get swollen and then she brought him to our ER, where one of the residents made the diagnosis in less than a minute. The kid, of course, had nephrotic syndrome. [This is a disorder in which the urine contains large amounts of protein and, as a result, the body becomes protein depleted, leading to swelling of the body. The face, especially the area around the eyes, is typically the first area affected in children. The disorder usually is self-limited; it is treated with steroids and usually resolves in weeks.] For God's sake, even I could've made the diagnosis! So we admitted him, I called a renal consult, and we started him on 'roids [internese for steroids].

One of Elizabeth's patients almost got kidnapped two days ago. This three-year-old had been brought to the hospital by her aunt last week. The kid had had a couple of episodes of blacking out while the aunt was baby-sitting for him. A whole workup was done and everything was negative except the tox screen [toxicology screen, a blood and urine test looking for toxic substances in the system], which was positive for alcohol. So social service started an investigation. The mother and her boyfriend showed up on Tuesday at noon, and after visiting with the kid for a while, asked to speak to the doctor. Elizabeth showed up and they asked her how the baby was doing. Elizabeth said that he was fine, and before she could say another word, the mother said, "If he's fine, I want to take him home."

So Elizabeth told her he couldn't leave yet, that tests were still pending and that, for the sake of the child's health, he'd have to stay at least one more night. Then the mother started yelling that if her baby was fine, the only thing that could happen to him in the hospital is that he could get sick, which was actually a good point, and she picked the kid up and started moving toward the elevator.

At that point, we all moved in. Someone called security stat [immediately], and within a minute a phalanx of Mount Scopus's finest emerged from the elevator bank and we had a standoff. The mother held on to the kid tight and shouted, "I don't want my baby in this fucking hospital!" at the top of her lungs, which went a long way to put most of the other parents on the floor at ease. Next she yelled, "I know what's best for my own fucking kid! If he's fine, I'm taking him home! Just try to stop me!"

Attendings, house staff, administrators, and more security guards started to show up. The mother and her boyfriend got madder and madder. The boyfriend finally said, "We're taking the kid out of here! If you don't like it, you might as well shoot us in the back, 'cause we're going!" The kid was screaming at the top of his lungs while this was going on.

The whole thing lasted about a half hour. It ended when an administrator, obviously someone who had majored in psychology and guerrilla warfare in administrator school, showed up and firmly told them that maybe they'd like to talk the whole thing over in the conference room. For some reason, the mother agreed and she, the baby, and the boyfriend headed off with him. I think our suspicions about the parents were correct. The BCW [Bureau of Child Welfare, the state agency charged

with investigating child abuse] probably will be interested in doing an investigation.

I've nodded off to sleep three times while recording this. I think it's time to stop.

Wednesday, July 17, 1985

I'm a little more coherent tonight, I think. Nothing much is happening. Elizabeth's patient whose parents tried to kidnap him got sent home by Social Service last Friday. In their infinite wisdom, they cleared the family in two days. I've got a bad feeling about this family. I hope I'm wrong.

My patient with nephrotic syndrome is doing much better. Most of the swelling is gone, and he doesn't look so much like Buddha anymore. Those steroids are amazing! We're going to send him home in a few days; renal will follow him as an outpatient. They say his prognosis is excellent. The mother asked me if all this means he's not allergic to trees. I told her I thought it probably would be a good idea not to go back to that LMD anymore.

Last night was pretty easy. I got four hours of sleep, and that's been pretty much the pattern on Children's. I guess I did kind of luck out when they switched me from 6A. Those guys have been getting killed. As far as I know, none of them have gotten any sleep on any night they've been on call.

Wednesday, July 24, 1985

I'm about ready to die. I thought I was bad that night earlier in the month when I was up all night, but this is ten times worse. I haven't gotten any sleep for the past two nights, and I'm pretty worried about my grandmother.

I haven't mentioned my grandmother yet. She's my mother's mother. She's over eighty and she lives in New Rochelle by herself. I try to get over to her apartment for dinner at least once a week, usually on Tuesdays, if I'm not on call or too tired. I went last night and I found out she was really sick.

She's got a bad cellulitis on her leg. She cut herself with a knife about a week ago. When I showed up yesterday, she was febrile and looked terrible; she could barely get out of bed. She showed me the cut; it was all red and swollen with lots of pus.

Her temperature was 102.5, and I told her she had to go to the hospital for IV antibiotics. She said I was crazy. She's a little on the stoic side. I argued with her for about an hour and finally convinced her to let me take her to the Mt. Scopus ER to at least get a third opinion. I got her seen without any wait. A medical intern looked at her and said, "You've got to come into the hospital for IV antibiotics." She started to tell him he was crazy, but I guess maybe she really wasn't feeling so well because she finally said, "All right."

She's on one of the medical floors. They put in an IV and started her on megadoses of pen and Naf [**penicillin and naf-cillin, two antibiotics**]. They didn't get her settled until after two in the morning. I stayed with her until six and then went home to change my clothes and take a shower. I might as well just move my stuff over to the hospital. As it is, at this point I'm only just occasionally visiting my apartment.

Anyway, I don't know how I got through work today. I've got seven patients, and I don't remember what happened to any of them. I was like in outer space for most of the day. My mother showed up this afternoon to stay with my grandmother, and I came home. I'm going to sleep now. I remember sleep; I think it's something that feels really good.

Friday, July 26, 1985

The past few days have been nothing but a blur. I was on last night and I managed to get some important sleep. My grand-mother's much better; they're probably going to send her home over the weekend. And my time on Children's is coming to an end. Of course, I'm on the last day of the month. You can almost set your calendar by my on-call schedule. And then on Monday, I start on Infants'. I have the feeling the shit's about to hit the proverbial fan. Infants' is a bitch!

The only good thing about all this is that I know I'm not going to be on the first night. The chiefs may have decided they don't like me for some reason, but they're not crazy. They couldn't make me work two nights in a row. But actually, since I'm on Tuesday, I get a weekend off next week. Weekends off, I re-member those; that's when you get to visit your apartment for two whole days.

BOB

July 1985

You might wonder how these three interns wound up coming to our little corner of the world. It is not fate or destiny that brought them here, but rather the bizarre intern mating ritual known as "the Match."

All of medical school—in fact all of life—is nothing but preparation for the Match. It's the first of many horrendous and inhuman experiences to which house officers are exposed. In other professions, a person who wants a particular job submits an application and a résumé; the person goes on interviews, trying to convince the employer that he or she is right for the job; if the job is offered, the person has the right to accept it and begin work, or to reject it. But this system, good enough for American business, apparently is too simple for medical residency training. After all, there's no torture involved.

The search for the perfect internship begins early in the summer before the medical student's fourth and final year of school. The student interested in pediatrics or internal medicine fills out as many as twenty applications for residency programs. He or she then spends a month interviewing at hospitals around the country, asking numerous questions of the house staff and attendings, trying to get a feel for the place. After narrowing the field down to a few top choices, the senior arranges to do "high profile" rotations at these hospitals. These rotations, often a subinternship in an ICU setting, give the student the opportunity to work himself or herself sick, taking call every third night, in hopes that somehow the director of the program will notice and think highly of him or her and possibly place the person near the top of the match list. But I'm getting ahead of myself.

Here in the Bronx, a committee of pediatric faculty members is attempting to select an outstanding group of interns from a pool of hundreds of applicants. For our entering group of thirty-five, more than 225 senior medical students were interviewed in the fall of 1984. This interviewed group was ranked from one to 225 on the basis of grades, letters of recommendation, the impression made during the applicant's interview, and performance during these elective rotations spent at one of our hospitals.

The fun of the Match actually begins in January. Each applicant sends off a list of programs to which he or she has applied, ranked from first choice to last, to the National Intern and Resident Matching Program (NIRMP) in Illinois. Simultaneously, the director of each program submits a list ranking all senior students who have applied for a position. All this information is fed into a computer and the machine grinds out the Match, coupling applicants and programs. One might think that this chapter of the matching procedure would end with a friendly letter mailed from NIRMP and received anonymously and privately in a mailbox some days later. But no; nothing in an intern's life is that simple!

The results of the computer's work are stored in a vault and released in the middle of March. The senior students from each school are assembled in a centralized location, one usually designed to maximize feelings of anxiety and hopelessness, and the envelopes are distributed one by one by the person, usually a dean of the medical school, charged with guarding the secrecy of the Match. A name is called, the student rises and slowly approaches the front of the room; the envelope is handed over, it's cautiously opened, and the student either sighs a sigh of great relief because his dream has actually come true, he's matched at his first choice program and as a result his future is assured, or he lapses into an immediate and frightening anxiety attack, often complete with hyperventilation, because he's gotten his third, or fourth, or, God forbid, fifth choice and is going to have to work at a hospital with a bad reputation or, worse yet, at a place that's considered "anti-academic" and no matter how hard he works in his internship, his residency, or his fellowship, he truly believes that he will never be able to become a true success.

Those anxiety attacks are fueled by a fact known to all subscribers of the Match. Unlike normal job offers, the Match assignments are binding. Unless there are major extenuating circumstances, there's no chance of changing once an assignment to a hospital has been made.

Why fourth-year medical students put up with this system has something to do with the whole mentality that supports internship. "It's the way it's always been done," "it's accepted," "there's nothing we can do about it," are the usual responses when the question of why it continues to be done this way is raised.

Well, that explains how the interns got into our program. I probably should next explain a little about the composition of our program.

The Schweitzer School of Medicine's pediatric training program is made up of two campuses. The one that's presently referred to as "the east campus" is composed of two hospitals: Jonas Bronck, a part of New York City's municipal hospital chain that provides primary care to the poor and not-so-poor of the northern reaches of the South Bronx, and University Hospital, a voluntary facility that mainly acts as a tertiary-care center for patients referred for consultation to the school's subspecialists by private physicians in the North Bronx and in lower Westchester County. University Hospital is located about a half mile south of Jonas Bronck.

"The west campus" is also made up of two hospitals: the Mount Scopus Medical Center, a huge voluntary hospital that, like University Hospital, serves as a base for subspecialists; and the West Bronx Hospital, sometimes referred to as WBH, another municipal facility that, like Jonas Bronck, provides all medical services for the indigent families of the western region of the borough. Mount Scopus and West Bronx are literally attached to each other. Although the Mount Scopus-WBH complex is immense, filling four square city blocks, the pediatric services in the two hospitals are adjacent to each other and conveniently connected by a bridge. The east and west campus hospitals are separated from each other by about five miles.

The program, with over a hundred house officers, 120 full-time faculty members, four chief residents, and over two hundred inpatient beds spread over the four hospitals, is one of the largest pediatric training programs in the country. Our interns rotate through three emergency rooms, six primary-care clinics, seven general pediatric wards, two pediatric intensive-care units, three neonatal intensive-care units, and three well-baby nurseries. If you're confused reading this, just think what it must be like for the interns who have to become familiar and comfortable with the nursing staffs, ancillary services, medical forms, and peculiar habits of the laboratory personnel in all these different hospitals before they can even think about taking care of patients.

So the question naturally must be asked, why would anyone electively want even to attempt to deal with all this? Internship is difficult enough, what with the long hours and the frequently depressing subject matter; what would possibly motivate someone to want to come to our program, where the difficulty seems to be compounded by the massive size and complexity of the place? Well, probably the main reason medical students want to train at the Schweitzer program is because of the amazing variety of experiences to which they will ultimately be exposed. Our residents see asthma and pneumonia, ear infections and lead poisoning, the mundane, "bread and butter" of pediatrics at West Bronx and Jonas Bronck, the municipal hospitals; but they also see the congenital heart disease and the renal transplant patients, the craniofacial cases and the weird metabolic diseases, all of the rarer medical and surgical problem patients who wind up being referred to Mount Scopus and University Hospital, the voluntary hospitals in which the subspecialists lurk. So when a resident finishes three years in the Bronx, it can safely be said that he or she will have seen every kind of pediatric patient who exists. Our graduates know that nothing will ever surprise them; they'll have had experience with anything that might darken the threshold of their medical offices.

That's why Mark Greenberg came to the Bronx. He told me he wanted to get as much experience with as many types of patients as possible during his training. After meeting him for the first time at orientation, I got to know Mark a little better this month. He told me he had chosen pediatrics because it was the third year clerkship he had enjoyed the most. He had liked it for the same reason most people are attracted to the specialty: He said it seemed to make more sense to watch sick children get well than it did to watch sick adults get sicker and die.

Mark told me his biggest problem with being an intern is that his brain is always tending toward entropy. Unless he tries very hard to keep his life controlled, he becomes exceedingly disorganized. Disorganized is not a great way to be during internship. All interns share a common short-term goal in life: to get out of the hospital as soon as possible. One must be very organized to accomplish that. If Mark continues to be disorganized, he might have to consider permanently moving into an on-call room.

There's something about Mark I noticed very early in the month. It's a funny thing: There are some people who look great after a night on call. No matter how many admissions come in and how little sleep they get, these people look unbelievably good the next day. Mark is definitely not one of these people. He had a couple of bad nights during July, and this was readily apparent in his appearance the next morning: His eyes were very droopy; his reddish-blond hair was uncombed and shot straight up in the air in all directions; and his clothes looked as if they'd been slept in, which obviously was not the case because Mark always claimed that he hadn't gotten any sleep at all.

Amy Horowitz didn't really decide to come to Schweitzer; she decided to stay here. She had been a medical student in the Bronx and had stayed on because she liked the program and felt comfortable with the people. She's always lived in the New York metropolitan area. Born in Morristown, New Jersey, she was her parents' only child. Her father owns an office supply business.

I've known Amy for a little over a year. In March, when she was in the ninth month of pregnancy, she told me that she'd thought a lot about being an intern and having a young baby but was somewhat concerned that she wouldn't have time to be both a good intern and a good mother. But she's convinced she can do it. It's because of this conflict that Amy's the one intern in the entire incoming group about whom I'm truly worried.

Early in the month, a crisis developed involving Amy. While working in the emergency room at Jonas Bronck, she was told by one of the attendings to get some blood tests on a patient. Amy swears that she drew the blood and sent it off to the lab. The attending, in checking on the situation a little later, could find no evidence that the lab had received the specimen or even that the blood had been drawn. He confronted Amy and, when she affirmed that she had done what was requested, he accused her of lying.

Whether this is true or not, lying about lab results is about the worst sin a house officer can commit. The implications are far-reaching. First, although our department is immense, word of mouth travels like wildfire, and within three days of this incident, rumors about Amy had already reached every member of the outpatient faculty. Second, and more importantly, whether she was guilty or not, Amy has lost a great deal of credibility. Interns have to be trusted. Although life-and-death decisions are always made by more senior physicians, such as attendings or chief residents, interns must be expected to function fairly independently with only occasional supervision when it comes to performing the more mundane, everyday types of activities, such as drawing blood, checking lab results, ordering tests, or making appointments for their patients. Amy's ability to function independently has been called into question. Whether she drew that blood or not, Amy probably will have an attending or senior resident perched over her shoulder at all times to make sure she does what she's supposed to do, at least for the immediate future. Amy is smart and a reasonably good worker, and within a month or so she'll probably make everyone forget that this happened. But if she screws up just one time, she's going to get nailed. And that could be it for her for the rest of this year.

I'm pretty sure Andy Baron doesn't want to be in the Bronx. I think he was one of those people who had a major anxiety attack when he opened his Match envelope last March and found out he was coming here. I don't think he objected because of our program. It's just that he never thought he would actually have to leave Boston.

Except for college at Princeton, Andy's spent his whole life around the Boston area. He returned to that city after college, attended medical school at Tufts University, and vowed that he'd never leave again. He told me he ranked Boston Children's Hospital first on his list, and he'd been led to believe that getting in there wouldn't be a problem. So you might say he was more than a little surprised when he found out he hadn't matched there.

I think leaving Boston will have a major impact on Andy. Back home he had a very structured and broad-based support network. His family and friends are there, and, most importantly, so is Karen.

Karen Knight is the woman Andy's lived with for the past

year. Karen is a fourth-year medical student at Tufts; she's going to have to spend a good portion of the year there. Andy has told me repeatedly that their relationship is strong, that it had lasted through a lot of adversity in the past, and that he feels it will easily be able to weather this year of separation. It sounds almost as if he were willing it to be that way.

And what was waiting for Andy here in New York? Almost nothing; there are a few friends who attended college with him, but nobody close who would understand or be there when things start getting rough. Internship is hard enough when you have a lot of love and support to help you through; it's nearly impossible when you have to go it alone.

ANDY

August 1985

Thursday, August 1, 1985, 12:40 A.M.

I just got off the phone with Karen, the only nice thing in the entire day. Three days of the NICU done, three and a half more weeks to go. What can I say? It's another planet.

Saturday, August 3, 1985, 7:00 A.M.

I just woke up. I'm thinking about going back to sleep again, but I've got to get to work. Internship is turning out to be so much harder than I thought it would. The NICU is amazing; it's only about twenty-five yards from one end to the other, and there are four little rooms off the central nursing station. In each of the rooms, which are about ten feet by ten feet, they have five or six tiny babies arranged with all this massive equipment around them. It's claustrophobic and frightening because each of the kids is so sick. Being in the NICU so far has been a total shock.

I was on call the first day (Monday) and I actually got a couple of hours of sleep. I was on call again on Thursday and it was a horrible, horrible night. We didn't get any sleep at all. And there were these three kids who kept trying to crump [deteriorating; trying to die] on us. We seemed to be doing a good job of stopping them, but then at about five in the morning, little baby Cortes decided to really crump. Cortes was one of the "ageless" preemies who live in the ICU. She was born fourteen weeks prematurely, weighing about a pound and a half, and she'd lived for four months right on the edge between life and death. We called a CAC [West Bronx's and Mount Scopus's

41

term for cardiac arrest; literally, "clear all corridors"; also called a "code"]. I pumped on her little chest for about half an hour while everybody tried to put in IVs and get access. We called for epinephrine [a drug that stimulates the heart to beat], and we called for more epinephrine and we called for bicarbonate [a drug that reverses the buildup of acid that occurs any time blood stops circulating], and we tried to give bicarb intraosseously [through a needle directly into a bone, usually in the lower leg; intraosseous meds are given only in dire emergencies, when an intravenous line cannot be established] and we got a blood gas and the pH was 6.6 [indicating that there's so much acidity in the blood that life is not possible], and then the heart rate kept slowing down and we gave intracardiac bicarb [through a needle passed through the chest directly into the heart; used as a last-ditch attempt]. And the heart rate came up again. Unbelievable! It looked like she was going to make it, but her color still was really bad. We bagged her [blew oxygen through an ambubag through an endotracheal tube and directly into the lungs] and we pumped her heart, but then she went into V-tach [ventricular tachycardia, a preterminal heart rhythm] and we gave her some lidocaine [an anti-arrhythmic drug, used to reverse an abnormal heart rhythm], and then the surgeons came and did a cut-down [a surgical procedure in which a vein is found and a catheter is placed into it, ensuring direct intravenous access], and we pumped some albumin into the femoral artery. We got another blood gas; it was still 6.6 and the kid had deteriorated into an agonal rhythm [a heart rhythm signifying impending death].

So we stopped the resuscitation. We had been working on her for about an hour, I guess. There was nothing more to do. I left the room and went back to try to finish up the evening scut before the morning shift came on. The baby died. And I felt really, really shocked. I felt stunned, like somebody had hit me over the head with a two-by-four. I had gotten so close to that little baby. She was so sick and so tiny. She was the first patient I ever did CPR [cardiopulmonary resuscitation] on. It's a strange thing doing CPR on a baby that small. It's kind of an intimate act. You've got your hands all the way around the chest and you're trying to pump her life back into her. You're trying to prevent her life from ebbing out of her. It doesn't matter that the kid's got snot running out of her nose onto your hands, it doesn't matter that she looks like shit, you just want her to live so badly! It was terrible when she died.

Laura Kenyon, our attending, came in at about eight. She took a look at me and asked if I was okay. I told her I was fine, and she took me into the on-call room and kicked everybody else out. "Are you really okay?" she asked. At first I told her yeah, but then I said I was really upset and I started crying. I was crying for that little baby whose life we couldn't save. I told her how much I liked that little baby even though I hardly knew her. I told her how I thought we were going to bring her back to life and keep her from dying. I told her I'd seen other people die when I was in medical school, but this was completely different. It's different when it's a baby. She told me it was okay to cry, it was okay to feel bad because it meant you really care about people, about your patients. She said that eventually you're able not to feel so bad, you can internalize it, but that you always feel something, because each death reminds us of all the others that preceded it.

She was really good. She let me get that baby's death out of my system. She told me I could go take a shower and have some breakfast. That was nice of her, but I didn't do it because I knew if I left the NICU, I'd get horribly behind in my work, and I knew that once that happened, I'd never get out of there.

After she talked with me, Laura had to go deal with the parents. She told the mother what had happened, and the woman started wailing. I turned around and saw Laura walk out of the unit. She had this expression on her face; I could tell she was really upset. She put her hand over her mouth; she was fighting off tears. For a second or two she looked really different, she almost looked like a little girl. And then she began to regain her composure and her face returned to normal. I listened to the mother's wailing for a while, but then I had to get back to work.

A little while later, I had to go back into the room where the baby died to draw blood from another patient, and there was Laura with the parents looking at the poor little dead baby, all swaddled and wrapped up. All day, I felt really down. Any time I'd think about it, I felt bad . . . really bad.

During the day, I was completely drained. The night had been such an emotionally exhausting experience for me, I was completely wiped out. It was so bad, any time I sat down, I'd start to fall asleep. Laura gave a really good lecture on physiology that I wanted to hear, but I just kept falling asleep. It was embarrassing; at one point, in front of everybody, she said to me, "You can go to sleep if you want, Andy." I wanted to pay attention, but I just couldn't.

Laura's the most amazing attending I've met here. She's tough, but I think she really cares. I think she loves her work and she wants everything to work well, so she's willing to put in the effort to make everything work on all levels. It's really exceptional, having someone around like that. I'm lucky to have her as my attending.

I got out of there around seven. I was too tired to do anything. I went out and got some food and ate dinner. By seven-thirty, I was ready to go to sleep. Karen called at about ten. We spoke for over an hour. I kept telling her how much I missed her. We didn't want to get off the phone; we kept thinking of something else to talk about. It's really hard being away from her this long. It's another four weeks until we get to spend any real time together again.

So anyway, the NICU is a very strange place. It's very exciting, physiology in medicine brought to its highest application. But when you think about it, it's also a very sad place because there's life and death involved; you take these little babies, most of whom would have been dead ten years ago, and there they are, just sort of cruising along. I think the best workers for a place like the NICU would be robots, or people who can blot out all their emotions and just do the work that has to be done.

The technical work you do in the NICU is pretty straightforward; once you've had some experience, you get very good at it. But the technical stuff is really the easiest part of the job. It's the decision-making that's the hard part. Almost every day in there, we're called on to decide whether to keep a baby alive or to let him or her die. I don't have any of the tools necessary to make those kinds of decisions. I don't have any experience with preemies, I don't know which babies might have a reasonable chance of surviving and which babies don't. All I can do is what somebody else tells me.

A lot of these babies don't even look human. They're really fetuses. Take poor baby Cortes, for instance; she weighed about a pound and a half at birth. I don't know, it doesn't seem to me like we're doing anyone any favors by working so hard to keep a baby like that going. We're just delaying the time when the parents'll have to mourn their baby's death.

Saturday, August 3, 1985, 8:00 P.M.

I thought I'd make a little list here, not necessarily in order of importance:

What's Right with My Life

1. I'm in an excellent training program and basically enjoying my work, despite the fact that I complain a lot.
2. When I'm at work, where I spend most of my waking hours, I'm with people who, for the most part, I like, some of whom I'm becoming friendly with, people like Ellen O'Hara and Ron Furman.
3. In my nonwaking hours, I'm in an apartment that I basically like. It's not great, but it's sufficient, and I tend to sleep pretty well because I'm not overly anxious, even though I have lots of reason to be.
4. When I'm not working, I have some old friends around whom I get to see.
5. New York City is a great place to live with tons to do, and I'm taking a lot of advantage of being here. I went down to Manhattan today, my only day off for the next two weeks. Oh, well.
6. I'm not depressed, something about which I worried when I came out here.

What's Wrong with My Life

1. I'm not with Karen, and I miss her a lot.
2. Even though I've made a few friends, I don't have any really good friends here. I miss having good friends around whom I can call and talk to about the things that are troubling me.
3. I'm not wild about this neighborhood. As time goes by I find more and more that I do like, but basically it's a kind of boring neighborhood that tends to roll up its sidewalks at about eight o'clock.

4. I miss my family—my parents, my brother, his girl-friend, they're all back in Boston. I used to see all of them very often; they were a source of great support, of great enjoyment.

5. I miss Boston. I really like it. It's much more hassle-free than New York, a more sane and easy place to live, and far less crazy and bizarre.

6. Sometimes I wonder if I'm in a program that has just too goddamned much scut and is too goddamned big. Some-times I wonder if the great downfall of this program is the fact that we rotate through too many fucking hospitals and we have to spend so much time and energy on just learning the mechanics of survival on all the different wards that there's almost no time and energy left for stuff like relaxing, socializing, reading, sleeping, and just thinking constructively and thoughtfully about the pa-tients.

So, those are my lists. Now that I think about it, they are basically arranged in order of importance.

Tuesday, August 6, 1985

Things are going all right, I guess. I got rid of a couple of patients. I have only three right now, and they're pretty stable. And I got a decent night's sleep last night. I really needed it; I basically collapsed at nine-thirty after I got home totally wiped out from another all-nighter without any sleep. So right now, things are looking up.

But Sunday night was one of the worst possible nights I could imagine. I was on with Larry, the senior resident, and we were both working our butts off. I spent most of the afternoon and evening doing shitloads of scut. At about one in the morning, I finished most of my work and went up to the well-baby nursery [the well-baby nursery, maternity ward, and labor and de-livery suites are on the seventh floor of WBH] to try to finish all the physsies [physical exams; all well newborns must be examined within twelve hours of birth]. There were a lot of new babies, and I was plowing through them all. At about 3:00 A.M. I realized that the chart of the baby I had just examined was still over in labor and delivery, so I went over there to get it. Just as I got through the door, a nurse came running out of one of the labor rooms, yelling, "Get peds! Get peds stat!" She saw me and asked if I was from peds. I told her I was and she said, "There's a little preemie just delivered right in this room."

Great! This was just what I needed at three o'clock in the morning. I thought, Oh, my fucking God, what am I going to do? I had never been alone with a new preemie. So I turned to the unit secretary, yelled at her to call Larry stat, and then I ran into the labor room.

Lying at the foot of the labor bed was this little fetus. The midwife said, "I measured him. He's twelve inches long." [A baby's gestational age in weeks is roughly equal to two times its length in inches. Therefore, this baby was probably at about twenty-four weeks of gestation.] The baby was tiny but he was moving and I didn't know what the hell to do.

Last week I had gone to the delivery room with the neonatal fellow to see a micropreemie who had just been born. We knew about that baby in advance and we knew that it wasn't going to be viable, but the fellow had taken me to teach me about what's viable and what's not. That baby had no breast buds, his skin was gelatinous, his eyelids were sealed shut, and he was only ten inches long [all signs of extreme prematurity]. And the fellow said, "This baby is clearly not even twenty-four weeks; he's not viable. There's nothing to do for this baby." So we didn't do anything, and he died. And that had been my one experience with extreme prematurity.

Well, I checked all those things out in this kid. I measured him, and sure enough, he was twelve inches long. I looked at the eyes and they were sealed and there were no breast buds and the skin was gelatinous and I thought that this kid couldn't possibly be viable. Then I listened to his chest; he had a strong heartbeat, so I rethought the situation and figured maybe I was wrong. I didn't know what to think.

I decided to take the baby over to the warming table in the DR [delivery room; all delivery rooms are outfitted with resuscitation equipment for preemies] to see what I could do. Everything I knew was telling me that this baby could not possibly survive, but I just hadn't had enough experience and I was all alone. I ran into the delivery room with the baby and I laid him down on the warming table. I realized I didn't have any idea what to do next. I figured I'd try some oxygen: I grabbed the oxygen mask, turned the oxygen on and started to try to bag the baby, but the face mask was too big; it went over his whole head. I wasn't having any success.

Just then the baby kicked a couple of times so I listened to the heart again with my stethoscope. It was still beating pretty strongly. I decided that weighing the kid might help decide whether he was viable or not, so I asked the nurse to get a scale. And just then, as my panic was reaching its peak, Larry came walking in. Thank fucking God! I think I had been out of the labor room for maybe a minute by that point, but it had definitely been the worst minute of my life.

I told Larry everything that had happened. He took one look at the baby and said, "Forget it. This kid's not viable. Don't do anything." I was pretty relieved. I still felt bad because I didn't even have a clue about what I was supposed to do, but at least I realized I hadn't done anything that was harmful.

Then the nurse came back with this rickety old scale; it looked like something out of the nineteenth century. We put the baby on it and it read twelve hundred grams. No way that baby weighed twelve hundred grams! She said, "Well, this is the scale we use to weigh all the babies." Larry said, "Well, it's wrong."

We wrapped the baby up in a towel and brought him back into the labor room. Larry explained to the mother that the baby was too small to survive but since he still had a heart rate, we were going to have to take him down to the NICU. The midwife started throwing a shit fit. She said, "You can't take the baby downstairs! This baby belongs with his mother! You have no right to take the baby out of this room!" Larry told her that he wished he could leave the baby, but it was hospital policy that any infant with a heartbeat had to be brought to the NICU.

Then Larry and the midwife started fighting about where the baby should be kept while we waited for him to die. I stayed out of it; I agreed with the midwife, but I wasn't going to argue with the resident who had just rescued me. Finally Larry called the hospital administrator. She showed up, heard the story, and agreed with Larry. The midwife argued with her for a while but finally she backed down and we took the baby downstairs.

When we got down to the NICU, we reweighed him; he really weighed only 460 grams. We put him in an isolette [also called an incubator—a Plexiglas box with a mattress and a heating element, used to house sick newborns] to keep him warm. I checked his heart rate about every ten minutes. Finally, after an hour, the heart stopped and I declared him dead. Then I went upstairs and told the mother that the baby had died. We brought him back up and gave him to her to hold for a while. She was exceedingly sad.

Then I went downstairs and started doing more scut. At about seven o'clock all the new nurses came on, and they started yelling at me. They wanted to know why I hadn't filled out the death certificate and gotten permission for an autopsy. They were being really hostile. I was exhausted and I'd had a horrible night; all I wanted to do was be left alone. I didn't even know I was supposed to fill out the damned death certificate and get consent for the autopsy. Nobody told me I had to do those things.

Finally, one of the nurses came up to me, and she was really nice. She knew I hadn't done any of this stuff before so she showed me exactly what had to be done. She gave me the death certificate and the autopsy form and the form for burial. She told me that I should go up and talk to the mother and tell her that if she wanted a private funeral, it'd cost $600, and if she didn't have the money, the city would bury the baby free.

So I went back upstairs and talked to the mom, told her how sorry I was. I didn't know what to say; I don't have a lot of experience with this. I asked her if she wanted us to do an autopsy and she said no. She was really broken up.

So I was up all night working pretty hard. Then today we rounded nonstop until one-thirty and then I had to go to my outpatient clinic. I signed out all my work. I saw five patients in clinic and that went pretty well. I got done by four o'clock or so and then I sat around and talked with my clinic preceptor, Ann Covington, for a while. I like Ann a lot. It's nice to have someone calming like her to talk to.

I went back to the NICU after clinic to finish my work. I got out at about eight and had to go to the bank and to the supermarket. The A&P closes at eight, so I missed it and now I can't go shopping again for another three days. I'm totally out of food. I have to bring stuff home from the deli down the street if I want to eat dinner. It's either that or going out every night. Fuck!

Karen called last night; I guess it was after I had gone to sleep. I don't even remember what we talked about. I don't remember a word I said. We talked for quite a while, I think.

It's ridiculous. I hope she's home tonight so I can find out what's happening.

ˉSo here it is, eight twenty-five on my good night, my one night out of three that I'm not either on call or postcall and I have nothing to do and I have to go to sleep in an hour, so I can get a good night's rest before I'm on call tomorrow. I hate this! I think I'd really like the NICU if I weren't so tired, but I'm tired all the time. And you just don't get any normal human contact in your free time unless you're married or living with somebody. Even though I've made a couple of friends, they're all interns and they're either on call or tired. I really should be doing some reading about neonatology tonight, but screw it! I've got to get out of here!

Friday, August 9, 1985

I have a pretty nice white cloud right now [**white cloud: good luck on call; black cloud: bad luck on call**]. I still have only three patients. One's just a grower [**a preemie who has no medical problems except that he weighs less than two kilograms, the necessary weight for discharge from the NICU**], and the others are pretty easy also. Poor Dina, the junior resident, she's got five patients, three of whom are pretty sick, two of whom are *really* sick, both with NEC [**necrotizing enterocolitis, a serious disorder of the intestinal tract**]. I offered to take one of them but she didn't want to give them up, I guess. I'm on tomorrow, so I know I'll be picking up a sick kid who was born this afternoon, and I heard there's another preemie on the way, so I'll have at least two new ones to pick up. That'll fill out my service to five. Not exactly a piece of cake, but still pretty easy.

Boy, was I *dumb* on rounds today! Laura asked me a simple question about how much glucose I was giving one of my kids. Shit! I couldn't remember how to calculate it; everyone was standing there staring at me. I felt like an idiot. Later on I finally figured it out. Rounds are generally good, Laura's a great teacher, and except for when I'm making a dope of myself, I really enjoy it. Well, I've got to stop now, Ron's here, and we're going out to dinner.

Thursday, August 15, 1985

Being cooped up inside the NICU, you miss things and you don't even know it. I was riding down to Manhattan in the train this evening, you know, there's always something to look at, there's always guys coming through, telling you their life stories, begging for money, never fails. Walking around Manhattan on the way to the theater, I was just looking at all the people. They were all well-dressed, there were some very pretty women, something I almost never get to see in the Bronx. I realized that after only two weeks, I already missed the excitement that exists in Manhattan.

Today I got a call from Nelly Kahn, one of the social workers who works in the outpatient clinic. She told me she thinks I should report one of my clinic patients to the BCW. It was a mother who told me that she beats her kids with a strap when they act up. Ann Covington was right there, so I talked it over with her and she thought I should, too. So I had to call the mother and tell her I was reporting them. It really surprised me, she took it pretty well. Maybe it was like Nelly said, maybe letting us know she hit the kids was like her cry for help. I'll never figure these mothers out.

Then I called up the BCW, and they put me on hold for about twenty-five minutes! Twenty-five minutes, and I finally only got to speak to someone for five minutes. I was kind of surprised, the worker seemed really nice and friendly. I thought they'd be boring bureaucrats. All they wanted to know about was whether there were marks on the child. I told them there were and that we'd taken Polaroids of them. They said that was enough, they were going to start an investigation.

Sunday, August 18, 1985, 2:00 A.M.

I've been in the NICU every day now for two weeks solid (having been on call last Saturday) and I finally have a whole day off. The sick thing is, I'm thinking I should go in today for about an hour because there's a workup I didn't quite finish. It wasn't really clear that I was supposed to be taking this one patient. It was one of those situations, I thought the resident was picking the patient up, then it turned out she wasn't . . . I don't know. So I may actually go in for an hour, just to finish that up, then

I'll split before anybody catches me there and asks me to do something else.

It looked like Friday night was going to be really easy. All my notes were written early, and I was ready. It looked like I was going to get to bed by two in the morning, then things got complicated and then, around four o'clock, the deliveries started. Shit! Then it was just one delivery after the next. What do they do, wait until four in the morning to have all the deliveries? It's always like that! So the bottom line is I didn't get any sleep.

Truthfully, I've only actually gotten the chance to lie down in the bed in the on-call room once since the first night of the month, and that was only for about fifteen minutes or so. It was last week, at about five in the morning. The bed was unmade, the room was a mess, but it felt great! I fell asleep right away but I got woken up about fifteen minutes later: This weird guy who must have been high or something was in the room with me. He was opening and closing the door and doing all kinds of weird things. I lifted my head up and yelled, "Who the fuck is that?" and he ran away. I got up and locked the door, but my beeper went off and that was it for dreamland. Oh, well.

There were a couple of exciting things that happened the other day. There was a twenty-nine-weeker [**born eleven weeks prematurely**] who was an extramural delivery [**born outside the walls of the hospital**]. We got stat paged to the ER, so we went running down the stairs, and there's one of the pediatric residents holding this tiny, tiny baby. The guy looked uncertain about what to do. So we took the kid, who was doing fine at that moment, and we whipped him upstairs and wound up intubating him [**placing an endotracheal tube into his trachea so that direct ventilation of the lungs could be accomplished**] and so on and so forth. And it turns out the mom's a drug abuser. She claims not to use them intravenously, but who knows? So I might have gotten my first AIDS patient, although it's a little too early to tell, but who knows?

I went and talked to the mom later in the day. She doesn't want the baby at all. It's really sad. The father is nowhere to be found; when she was telling me this she got really teary-eyed.

So I didn't get out of there until six last night and I was just delirious. I'm not as good a doctor postcall as I am precall; I don't think anybody is. You just can't make as good decisions when you're that tired. I think postcall, I function at about 80 percent, which is not bad, but that extra 20 percent, that's got to be important sometimes. I think it's really stupid, I just think this whole unbelievable call system is stupid because it really makes you . . . you're just not as good! Don't misunderstand me, I'm not so much complaining that I'm unhappy about having to take the abuse of being up all night every third night, I don't like that, I don't like the way it makes me feel, but the thing that *really* bothers me is I don't think I can give as good care. If you're trying to give the best care in the world, you should be able to work out a system where doctors can function at their best. Anyway, I'm sure this won't be the last time I tirade about the evils of call.

Monday, August 19, 1985, 6:45 A.M.

I can talk only for a minute or two because I have to go back to work. I'm glad that I have only another nine days to go in the NICU and that I have only three more calls (one of which is tonight), because I don't think I'm wild about neonatology. I can't say it's been a horrible experience, but I wouldn't want to spend my life with tiny babies. There're much more interesting things in pediatrics than little tiny critters.

This morning I've been feeling kind of low; I've been missing Karen a lot. I talked to her yesterday morning, but she could talk for only a minute. I tried to call her last night, but she wasn't home. I really feel cut off. I fell asleep thinking about her and missing her and I woke up this morning feeling kind of low and lonely. I never want to do this again, be apart from her for so long, never, never. I never want to feel this homesick for Boston again either. It's eleven more days until Karen will be here, and she's coming for a month. It's going to be great, really great.

In the meantime, nine of those days I've got to bust my butt. So that's what I've got to do. I'm on call tonight with Larry, the third-year resident in the NICU; I'm kind of glad about that. There's a definite difference between the second-year resident and the third year; the third years let you do things on your own; the second years hog all the procedures. So with the second year, all you do is scut, but when you're on with the third year at least you get to feel a little bit like you're doing something. And Larry's a good guy; he's a really fun guy, I'm sure we'll have a good time.

Well, I guess I gotta go. I'd rather go back to bed. But I gotta go . . . I know I'll feel better about it when I get there; it's always hard just getting there, though.

Friday, August 23, 1985, 7:20 P.M.

I'm in bed, and I'm going to go to sleep because I was on call last night and I didn't get any sleep, and I'm really tired because I worked my butt off. It's really ridiculous, this every fourth is crazy . . . I mean every third. I suppose I should have a lot to talk about . . . it's all so much of the same shit . . . you know . . . creatinine, BUN, all that shit . . . it's all gobbledygook. I'm going to sleep. . . .

Saturday, August 24, 1985, 8:00 P.M.

In another couple of days I'll have finished my second rotation. Two down out of twelve and already, so early on, I feel tired. I'm not worn out, I'm not whipped yet, but I feel tired. I feel the effects of this every third night, it's already wearing on me. And I already hate the system; I think it's a stupid and foolish system that rules your life and hurts your patients. And already I'm losing some sensitivity toward people—you know, as hurting, suffering human beings.

This morning when I woke up, I thought, What will I do with myself today? I got this fantasy; I thought about going back to my college, Princeton in New Jersey, and just spending the day down there. I figured I'd look up a couple of my professors and try to go see them. And then I got into the shower and the more I thought about it, the more appealing it got. I had it all planned: I'd go into the city and catch the train down to Princeton. I thought of all the beautiful green lawns and the tall trees reaching way up over the buildings, and about the flowers that would be in bloom, and the serenity and peacefulness of the place since there wouldn't be any students there yet. I became entranced with the whole idea, how quiet and pretty and pastoral it would be.

Then I got out of the shower and as I sat around thinking, I realized that I wasn't going to go to Princeton, it was all just a fantasy. My professors weren't going to be around, they were going to be out of town on vacation. And I couldn't just go and hang around there. I just wanted to escape from the difficult times I'm having right now into the past, when life was easier, when I didn't have to worry about all the diseases and falling asleep on attending rounds, the jaded attitude of some of the residents, the oppressed lives my patients and their mothers lead, the crummy neighborhood I live in and the fact that I'm far away from my loved ones. I think this'll blow over. When I finish this year and my residency and I'm just a practicing doctor when my hours are more regular and I'm more used to the responsibilities, it won't be so bad. I don't have any control over my life now, and that's very difficult.

I know I'm just saying this stuff over and over again, but it's just so difficult! I knew internship was going to be hard, everybody tells you that, you see the interns work their butts off, you know it's hard! But somehow you don't believe it. I was trying to tell my friend Maura about being an intern tonight, she really wanted to know. I told her a little bit, I told her a story, and then I just shook my head and all I could say to her was, "It's just really hard." I was thinking, Why am I trying to explain? I don't want to explain anymore, I don't want to tell anybody about this, it's just too crazed.

AMY

August 1985

Tuesday, July 30, 1985

University Hospital is a strange place. I'm not really sure what I'm supposed to be doing there. I've got about eight patients, but none of them is really mine. Everyone has a private pediatrician, and the attendings are the ones who run the show. So we make rounds in the morning and decide what we'd like to do on each patient and then the attendings come around and tell us what we're *really* going to do. Having us there seems pointless. It doesn't make any sense.

We started yesterday and I got out at about three in the afternoon. Then today, I got home at three-thirty. All you do is eat lunch, write progress notes, and leave. My patients don't keep me very busy. I've got this eight-year-old named Oscar who was in a car accident or something last year. He had a really bad head injury and was in a coma for months. They had to trach him [**perform a tracheostomy: create an opening into the trachea, or windpipe**] because he was on a ventilator for three months. He's much better now, although he still needs a wheelchair, and ENT [**the ear, nose, and throat service**] admitted him to take out his trach tube. He's been in the hospital for two days so we can watch him breathe, and he'll have to stay for another day or two. Very exciting!

My only really sick patient is this six-year-old renal transplant kid. He was born with dysplastic kidneys [**abnormally formed and nonfunctional kidneys**], and he's been in renal failure his whole life. They did the transplant yesterday morning using his mother as the donor. He was sick as a dog all last night and most of today but I couldn't even get near him! The renal service

56

is running the whole show. Occasionally one of them will talk to me, to tell me what scut they want me to run. I probably could be learning a lot, but I can barely squeeze myself into the room!

This whole place is depressing! My patient is the newest of four transplant patients on the floor. The other three are all in some phase of rejection [rejecting the transplanted kidneys]. It's a real pleasure to go into their rooms; they all want to die because they know that if they continue to reject, sooner or later they're going to wind up back on dialysis.

Of my eight patients, there's only one who's anything like a regular pediatric patient. It's a three-week-old FIB [fever in baby; all infants under two months of age who are found to have a temperature of 100.6° or greater are admitted to the hospital, have blood work and a spinal tap, and are treated with antibiotics]. When she came in, I tried to do the workup but I had trouble getting the blood; I stuck her three times and I couldn't get a drop. I know I'm not great at drawing blood so it didn't bother me but then I called Diane Rogers [the senior resident assigned to the ward that month] and she tried five or six times and couldn't get anything either. Diane got very angry, as if not getting the blood was a personal insult. Finally Dr. Windom, the baby's private, came in and tried and he couldn't get it either. We wound up just treating her as if she were septic [had an infection in her blood]. Windom told me to send off urine for viral cultures [a method of determining whether a viral infection is present]. What a waste of time and money! There's nothing you can do if it's viral, and besides, those cultures take at least two weeks. The baby will be completely better by the time we get the results back. But if that's what he wants, then that's what he'll get. I had enough trouble last month with attendings. From now on I'm just going to do whatever anybody says and not protest at all.

I was on in the ER for the last time Sunday night and it was pretty quiet. Larry took Sarah with him to his team's last softball game. They made it into the league's semifinals but they got beaten and Larry's depressed about it. I can't get over how good he is with Sarah. But Sarah is a good baby. She really has developed a personality. And she's growing like a moose! I took her to see Alan Cozza [the chief of pediatrics at Jonas Bronck Hospital; he also is Sarah's pediatrician] yesterday for her three-month checkup; she weighed twelve pounds, two ounces. She's gained over five pounds in three months. Alan said everything was fine. He told me we were doing a good job with her, that she seemed like a happy, contented kid. I think she is, too. I'm happy that my internship doesn't seem to be doing her too much harm.

Monday, August 5, 1985

I could take a whole year of University Hospital. It's almost like being on vacation. I've been on call twice so far and I got about six hours of sleep both nights. That's more than I usually get at home. And things have been quiet enough for Larry and Sarah to come visit me while I'm working. They spent most of Saturday afternoon at the hospital and they even had dinner with me in the cafeteria. There are almost never emergency admissions at night, and on days I'm not on call, I've been getting out by three in the afternoon.

The other two interns have been having a pretty easy time, too, but they haven't been leaving as early as I have. They stay until at least five. They don't have more work than I do, they've just been hanging around, spending time teaching their medical students and basically just looking for things to do. When I'm on call, I tell them just to sign out and go home but they won't do it. I think they feel guilty about leaving early, like it's a sign that they're goofing off. It's not goofing off; it's more like survival.

I'll tell you, even if I didn't have a baby to get home to, I wouldn't want to stay at that hospital any longer than I have to. The place is so depressing! My patient Ricky, the six-year-old boy who got his mother's kidney, stabilized last week and the renal team finally let me into his room. He's a nice kid; he's very small [**the effect of his chronic renal failure**], maybe the size of a three-year-old, but he's smart and he's got a good sense of humor. I talked with his mother who was discharged from the hospital on Thursday [**she had been hospitalized for removal of her kidney**]. She and her husband have been through hell since Ricky was born. Now, because of the transplant, they were hoping their lives might finally get back to normal again. But then over the weekend, Ricky's BUN [**blood urea nitrogen**] and creatinine started to rise. [**BUN and creatinine are mea-**

sures of renal function. Elevations imply that the transplanted kidney may not be functioning well.] Renal decided today that he was in acute rejection; they had me order a renal ultrasound and started him on ATG [**Antithymocyte globulin, a drug designed to prevent the immune system from making antibodies against the foreign kidney**]. The renal attending told Ricky's mother this afternoon and she started to cry and of course then Ricky started to cry. The whole thing really upset me, so I was glad I was finished with my work. I just packed up and came home.

One of my other renal patients is a twenty-year-old with Down syndrome [**a condition caused by an extra chromosome that leads to mental retardation and other abnormalities**] who also happens to have chronic renal failure. He's extremely high-functioning for a Down's patient and he understands everything that's happening. He came into the hospital last week because his BUN and creatinine were going up. He had had a cadaveric transplant [**his transplanted kidney had come from a dead donor**] a year ago, and they thought he was in rejection. They scheduled a biopsy [**a procedure in which a needle is passed into the donor kidney and some tissue is removed; the biopsied material is analyzed under a microscope for signs of rejection**] for Friday and told me to make him NPO [**nothing by mouth**] starting at midnight the night before. Well, of course they didn't say a word to him about the biopsy, and when the breakfast trays showed up on Friday morning and he didn't have one, he started to yell. I had to tell him they were going to do a biopsy. Nobody from the renal team had the decency even to talk to him about it!

The biopsy was done and it did show signs of rejection, so they rolled him back to the ward and started him on ATG, too. I've got five patients on ATG now. The drug doesn't seem to cause any harm, so having all those patients on it isn't making my work any harder, but since it's only given to patients who are in the process of rejecting their transplant, there's a lot of misery attached to giving it. This ward is filled with gloom and doom.

Things with Marie have calmed down. She and I have been on good terms since I changed services last week. I think she's relieved I'm not coming home for lunch anymore. And I don't think she minds very much that I've been sending her home early two out of every three days. So, all in all, if things keep up like this, I don't think I'll mind the rest of my internship. Of course, I doubt that it'll keep up like this!

Tuesday, August 13, 1985

I was on call last night and I'm tired. It was my hardest night so far this month and I got only an hour and a half of sleep. Ricky's been really sick. He had to go back to the operating room yesterday because of complications. I really thought he was going to die.

I guess he started to go bad last Thursday night. He started complaining of belly pain. His mother told me about it when we were on rounds on Friday morning and I told her I'd check with renal but I forgot to mention it to them. I was on Friday night and he seemed to be in pretty good spirits even though his BUN and creatinine had gone up a little. He did complain that his belly was hurting a few times but whenever I examined him, I couldn't find anything wrong. He slept well and didn't get a fever or anything, so I just forgot about it. But I guess the pain got worse on Saturday afternoon and his mother told Margaret Hasson, the intern who was on call, about it and she examined him and found that he was tender all over the place and that his belly was distended. She called the renal fellow and he told Margaret to get a CBC and a sed rate and another BUN and creatinine and that he'd call ultrasound and try to arrange an emergency renal scan. Margaret said he seemed to be a little better when she went back to draw his blood, so the renal fellow wasn't as concerned when it turned out he couldn't get the scan done because there wasn't a technician available during the weekend.

Things got worse again on Sunday afternoon when the third intern, Janet, was on call. Ricky's belly became very distended again, he was complaining of more pain; now he had pain shooting down his leg. The renal fellow came in and got all the information together. He found out that Ricky's urine output had steadily dropped over the past couple of days, so he called Dr. White [the renal attending] at home and discussed the whole thing with him. Dr. White must have called the radiology attending at home because within an hour there was somebody there to do an ultrasound exam. They found that the kidney looked fine but that there was some problem with the ureter [**the tube connecting the kidney with the bladder**]. Dr. White thought that Ricky's ureter had detached itself from his mother's kidney and that the kidney was making urine that was slowly leaking into the abdominal cavity and causing the pain.

This was an emergency, so Janet called the urology resident and he came to see Ricky and agreed with what Dr. White had said. The resident called the urology attending at home and the urologist refused to come in! He just refused to come in; he said it wasn't such an emergency that it needed to be fixed on a Sunday night and that he'd be in the next morning to assess the situation and, by the way, that it probably would be a good idea to keep Ricky NPO and pre-op him [**do everything necessary for surgery**]. By this point, Ricky was in intense pain and his temperature went up to 102, so Dr. White was called and he went nuts! He called the urologist at home and they yelled at each other for a while, but the result was still the same, the guy wasn't going to come in until the next day. Since there was nothing he could do about it, Dr. White called Janet, told her to start Ricky on broad-spectrum coverage [**antibiotics to cover a wide range of possible bacteria**] and pain medication. It was terrible; his mother and Janet and Ricky's nurse were up all night with him.

Then finally, yesterday morning, the urology attending showed up. By the time we started work rounds on the floor at eight o'clock, Ricky was on his way to the operating room. I saw him before he left; he looked terrible. His belly and his right leg were tense and swollen. It turned out he had so much urine in his abdomen that some of it had worked its way down into his leg. It was a real mess. He was in the OR four or five hours. First they had to clean out all that urine. Then they had to reattach the ureter to the kidney and make sure it was working okay. He spent another three hours in the recovery room and he didn't get back to the ward until after four in the afternoon. The renal fellow and I were with him all night. Plus I had four new admissions to work up, nothing serious, just more pre-ops for tomorrow. It was far and away the worst night for me at University Hospital, and now I'm exhausted. I couldn't even eat dinner. Larry fed the baby and took her out for a walk and I've just been lying here, not able to get out of bed.

I don't think I've ever seen anybody as angry as Ricky's

mother. Most of the parents at University Hospital are weird. They're very private, and they protect their privacy and that of their children. I guess it's understandable, since so many of them are chronically sick and wind up spending so much time in the hospital with all these doctors and nurses and medical students and other people constantly going in and out of their rooms. So they give you a really hard time when you have to do something and it makes you feel as if you're intruding into their space. Ricky's mother is different. She's friendly and she likes to have company in the room. But she's been seething since she found out the urologist refused to come in Sunday night. She's sure the delay in getting Ricky to the operating room is going to cause permanent damage to the kidney, her kidney, the only kidney she can give to her son. Dr. White told her he didn't know what effect this would have, that only after everything's back to normal will we be able to figure out what's what. She was still livid when I left the hospital this afternoon. I hope everything works out all right. But in the meantime, Ricky's on about a hundred medications, he's still NPO, and he's still really sick. There is at least one good sign: His BUN and creatinine from this afternoon were down.

I can't stay awake any longer. I'm going to sleep.

Monday, August 19, 1985

It's been a good week. I've been getting sleep, I've been coming home early, I've been spending time with Sarah and Larry. I can't complain.

The other interns on the team seem depressed, and I can understand why. There just aren't any normal children on this ward. Very few of these patients wind up being normal at any time during their lives. There's almost no hope here. On rounds yesterday, Janet said there were two kinds of patients at University Hospital: the ones who cry when you stick them for blood and the ones who don't. She said the ones who cry are bad because they make you feel guilty when you stick them. But the ones who don't cry are much worse because they're the ones who know that crying isn't going to do them any good.

I know what she meant and I know that if I were to hang around the hospital as much as she and Margaret do, I'd be depressed, too. But I can escape; I've got Sarah to run home to. And that makes everything a lot better.

Here's an example of what we have coming into this place: When I was on last Thursday, I got a five-year-old girl with intractable seizures who was coming in to have her anticonvulsant medication manipulated. She had metachromatic leukodystrophy [a rare inborn error of metabolism caused by deficiency of the enzyme arylsulfatase; the disease leads to severe neurological abnormalities]. Metachromatic leukodystrophy: You know how many of those there are in the world? Maybe a dozen. And one of them comes waltzing into University Hospital to have her seizure medication changed. She's still on the ward. She's on five separate anticonvulsants and we're raising one and lowering another. So far I haven't seen any real change in her. She could wind up staying in the hospital for months.

Her story's frightening. She was completely normal for the first year and a half of her life, and then her mother noticed she was getting clumsy. She started falling down a lot and losing her balance. She took her from doctor to doctor until she saw Dr. Rustin [a pediatric neurology attending] who made the diagnosis immediately. And now she's a GORK [an acronym for "God only really knows"] with an intractable seizure disorder.

The first thing I thought about when the mother told me the story was, Can something like that happen to Sarah? I mean, she seems completely normal now, but who knows what might happen next year or next month or next week? Who knows? Thinking about things like this can drive me crazy! I find myself doing it a lot. Every time I admit someone with something strange I think, Can Sarah get this? It usually doesn't stay with me for long, I can shake it pretty fast, but when it happens, it's like a wave of terror passing through me. I don't even want to think about it.

Ricky's much better. He had a pretty rough time last week but by Friday he was about back to normal. His kidney seems to be functioning well, and his BUN and creatinine came down to all-time lows today. He's been out of bed and walking around the ward, playing with some of the other patients. His mother's also calmed down a lot. Dr. White is pretty sure that no harm was done to the kidney but he says we'll still have to see what the future holds. He plans to send Ricky home either tomorrow or the next day.

Sunday, August 25, 1985

Today is Sarah's four-month birthday and we had a little party. My father came and so did Larry's parents. It was the first time we'd all been together since Sarah was born. My father was doing pretty well; he looked good and he seemed happy. Everyone was worried about me. They thought I looked pale and tired. I should look pale and tired; I'm working hard and I haven't exactly had a lot of time to go sunbathing, but I told them I think I'm doing okay. I think I am. I think I'm doing better than most of the other interns I've seen around.

Sarah rolled over for the first time last week. She did it first for Marie. Marie said she put her down in the crib on her belly and when she came back a few minutes later, she was lying on her back. So she put her back on her belly again and watched her, and sure enough, she flipped right over again.

I've been getting along very well with Marie. She really does love Sarah. I think she's been holding back on the feedings a little and not carrying her around as much. At least that's what she's been telling me. So things are going well on that front.

The renal team discharged Ricky on Friday. The nurses had a little going-away party for him. It was really nice. He was definitely my favorite patient of the month.

I finish this rotation on Tuesday. I'm on tomorrow night, the last night of the month, and then I start on 8 West [one of the general pediatric wards at Jonas Bronck]. Going to 8 West'll be like coming home. I did my subinternship and my third-year rotation there. I'm looking forward to it. But I know I'll never beat the hours I've been able to keep at University Hospital.

MARK

August 1985

Sunday, August 4, 1985

I started on Infants' [a ward at Mount Scopus Hospital] last Monday and so far this place makes Children's look like an amusement park! I was on yesterday; I worked my ass off all day long, running from one thing another; and at no time did I have any idea what the hell I was supposed to be doing. Usually, when you're on call on the weekend, you start with work rounds where you and the resident decide what needs to be done on each patient. It doesn't work quite that way on Infants'. First of all, when I got to work at eight o'clock, the resident who gave us sign-out was a cross-coverer [a resident who works in another part of the hospital during the day and covers the particular ward at night only], and she didn't have much of an idea of what was going on with the patients. We didn't get any kind of intelligible sign-out, so we started off with one strike against us. And then when we finally got everything sorted out and came up with a plan of what we wanted to do for each kid, the private attendings starting calling to tell us what actually was going to be done. And then there were all these admissions coming in. I just wanted to say, "Okay, I'm going to go outside now and come back, and then we'll start the whole damned day over again."

I picked up some real terrific patients when I came over to Infants'. I've got this incredible specimen named Hanson, who's four months old and has never been out of the hospital. When we went into his room on Monday morning, he was lying there in his crib, weighing all of about two pounds, with these wasted, shriveled arms and legs that were stiff as boards. He wasn't able to suck on a pacifier, and it seemed like he was having these little seizures. He looked like warmed-over death, and the senior actually said he was looking good that day compared to how he looked last week. My God, he must have looked like rotting hamburger the week before! It turned out he had crumped before we changed services and when they worked him up [in this case, the workup consisted of blood cultures, a spinal tap, and urine cultures] they found he had a disseminated fungal infection. A fungal infection! Now, there's a common cause of a crump. But I guess it wasn't so strange in this kid: He's had chronic diarrhea for the past two months and he hasn't gained an ounce in all that time. Since his mother's an IVDA [intravenous drug abuser], we're sure he'll be a candidate for admission to the AIDS clinic.

Anyway, he's being treated with amphotericin [a drug for systemic fungal infection], which is so toxic that even if the infection doesn't kill him, there's a good chance the treatment will. It's got to be given by IV. He has a central line [an indwelling catheter passed through the skin into one of the major veins in the chest], but we're giving him his TPN [total parenteral nutrition, a treatment in which a large number of calories are provided by vein] through that, so we have to give him the amphotericin through peripheral lines [normal IVs]. His IVs usually last only about twenty minutes, and most of the veins in his arms and legs are already blown, so I can see this kid is going to take up a lot of my precious time this month.

The people on my team seem pretty good. There's Elizabeth, of course. She already told me she doesn't like Infants' and that if it were all the same to the chiefs, she'd rather be back on Children's. And then there's the other intern, Valerie Saunders. I don't know about her, she seems kind of depressed. Our resident is Rhonda Bennett. She's smart, but she treats us like we're real morons. I mean, on rounds in the morning, she makes sure to go over every little detail two or three times, and then makes us repeat what she says and write it all down. It's like being in first grade or something. Elizabeth said something to her like, "C'mon, Rhonda, we promise we won't forget, cross our hearts and hope to die," and she got real defensive and said she was just trying to help us and make it easy for us. Well, I'll tell you, if she keeps it easy for us, I might have to murder her.

Wednesday, August 7, 1985

I'm going to kill them, I'm going to kill them all! I was on last night and today was the worst day of my internship. It's bad enough spending the night running from room to room trying to keep twenty-eight babies from dying, but to do that and to have to spend the next day being nice to Rhonda *and* putting up with all the shit the chief residents are handing us, that's a little too much. So it looks like I'm going to have to kill everybody to get any peace.

The first one I'm going to kill is that Hanson. He crumped again last night. He stooled out [**developed diarrhea**] and got acidotic [**built up acid in his blood, a sign of deterioration**] and shocky. I had to do a whole sepsis workup including a spinal tap and pull out his old IV and start a new one; the whole thing took over four hours. And then I had to call the ID fellow [**the fellow covering the infectious disease service**] and argue with him about what antibiotics to start him on. He told me to use three drugs, two of which I'd never even heard of before!

The second one I'm going after is Rhonda. She's so damned cheerful all the time, it's disgusting! At two o'clock in the morning, after I got off the phone with the ID fellow, I went to tell her what antibiotics he had suggested and she smiled and said, "Well I don't know about that, Mark, I don't know if those antibiotics give adequate coverage against enteric gram negatives [**bacteria that normally inhabit the intestinal tract**]. You did tell him that Hanson had chronic diarrhea, didn't you?" Of course I hadn't mentioned the kid's diarrhea. It was late and the kid had been trying to die on me all night and I can't be expected to think of everything! So, still smiling, she ordered me to call the ID fellow back and rediscuss the case with him. Of course the guy knew Hanson had diarrhea; he had suggested the drugs just for that reason.

The thing about Rhonda is if you go and tell her she's a pain in the ass and that she's making your life miserable, she takes it personally and starts to get teary-eyed. So even though she is a pain in the ass who's making my life miserable, I have to be nice to her anyway. I don't think I can take this for a whole month. So I'm pretty sure I'm going to have to kill her.

And the third one I'm going to have to kill is Arlene, the chief resident. There I was, sitting in the residents' room at noon today, minding my own business, trying to catch my breath; I'd made it through the night; I'd worked up six admissions. I had managed to keep Hanson and all the rest of them alive; I had even managed to make it through work rounds and attending rounds without falling asleep or complaining much. All I wanted to do was finish my scut, write my progress notes, and get my ass out of there. But could I do that? No! Arlene came in, saw us interns sitting there, and she said, "Aren't you guys going to the noon conference?" Well, Elizabeth said she had to start an IV on a kid who was supposed to go to the OR at one and Valerie said she had something else to do, and I just sat there unable to move. So Arlene said, "You know, these conferences are for you guys, not for us. It's just more work for me to schedule them. If you interns don't want to come to them, maybe we shouldn't schedule them anymore." None of us said anything back to her. I just glared. Here I was, having killed myself all night, having killed myself for over a month now. Maybe you'd think the chief resident ought to come up to us and compliment us every once in a while, tell us we're doing a good job and that we should keep it up, but no, all we get told is that if we don't come to conferences, they're going to cut them out! So if she ever says anything like that to me again, I'm definitely going to kill her.

I'm worried about all of us, but I think Val's in a lot more trouble than Elizabeth or me. She's really depressed. She says she'd rather be hiding under her bed than working in the hospital. Now I'm no psychiatrist, but that sounds pretty abnormal to me. She was on Sunday and spent the whole day trying to start an IV in Hanson and doing a lot of other technical scut. To hear her tell it, she missed every single time. And then the senior resident would come along and plop a needle in and get it on the first stick. Val got so frustrated that by Monday morning she couldn't even get blood from the veins of the easy kids. She walked around like a zombie most of the day. Rhonda had to tell her to go home in the early afternoon because she wasn't doing anybody any good. I think Rhonda felt better about Val leaving. I get the feeling Rhonda would be happiest if we all would leave. That way, she'd just take care of all the patients herself without anybody to bother her. Have I mentioned yet that I'm going to have to kill her?

Well, all this may not make much sense, but it sure as hell

made me feel better to get it off my chest. I can now go to sleep without worrying about tearing my pillow to shreds.

Thursday, August 8, 1985

Maybe Rhonda isn't so bad after all. At the end of attending rounds today, Claire, the other chief resident, came into the residents' room and said, "It's come to my attention that maybe we haven't been paying enough attention to you guys." That's an understatement! She told us how sorry she was about it and that she wanted to find out what the chiefs could do to make our lives easier. And before anyone could say anything else, Rhonda yelled, "This makes me so damned mad!" and immediately broke into tears. She caught her breath and said, "Here we are, working our rumps off. I had eleven admissions the other night [on nights on call, Rhonda was responsible for all patients admitted to both the Infants' and the Children's wards] and Arlene knew it but not once did I get a 'You did a good job last night, Rhonda' or anything. All she gave me was, 'If you can't get your interns to conferences, we just won't have them anymore.' "

Then Claire got a real concerned look on her face and asked, "Rhonda, what's wrong?" and Rhonda yelled back, "You want to know what's wrong? You treat us like dirt! It wasn't so long ago that you were doing this! You can't tell me you don't remember what it's like to be the senior on Infants' with all these sick kids and all these admissions and all the attendings coming around to bombard you with demands every second of the day! But neither of you seem very sympathetic. All you can do is complain that we're not coming to conferences. You know I'd love to be able to go to the conferences, I'd like to learn something. But I don't see you or Arlene volunteering to cover the ward for me so I can go!"

I wouldn't have believed it if I hadn't seen it. Elizabeth felt the same way. Neither of us thought Rhonda had it in her to stand up for herself like that. She seems like too much of a robot to show that much emotion. I mean, she's feeling as rotten about working on this ward as we are.

The rest of the exchange was pretty amazing, too. After Rhonda finished yelling, Claire said, "Rhonda, you know what we think of you. We might not always say it, but you're the best we've got. Whenever I see your name on the schedule, I breathe a sigh of relief because I know you're never going to do the wrong thing." And then Rhonda said, "You sure have a strange way of showing it. I don't expect a pat on the head just for taking night call, but I don't expect to be yelled at either." They talked a while longer after that, but it wasn't as good as this first part. It was pretty amazing. It made me feel a little better about working with Rhonda. Who knows? Maybe I won't have to kill her after all.

Tuesday, August 13, 1985

What a calm, relaxing night last night was! I got four admissions, all of them in the middle of the night, all real simple: a kid with congenital heart disease that's so complicated I need a medical dictionary, an anatomy textbook, and a road map just to get through the old chart; I also got a ten-month-old who had GE reflux [**gastroesophageal reflux, the reflux of acidic stomach contents back into the esophagus**] that was corrected surgically when he was a couple of months old, who got diarrhea over the weekend and got himself pretty dehydrated; a straightforward meningitic who happened to be seizing; and a three-year-old with meningomyelocoele [**a congenital defect of the spine that causes paralysis of the legs, bowel and bladder incontinence, and hydrocephalus; also called spina bifida**] who came in with a high fever and looked like shit. We thought he probably had meningitis, too, but it turned out he probably only has a UTI [**urinary tract infection, a common problem in children with bladder incontinence**]. I managed not to get any sleep again. And then today my pal Hanson, who was getting better, decided to get a fever. He looked pretty good so I didn't make too much out of it. I figured he had the virus that's going around but then Rhonda heard about it and took a look at him and said, "Well, it may be the virus, but I don't like the look of those IVs" [**fever in a child with IVs can be caused by infection of those IVs**]. I was planning to spend the day writing my notes and getting the hell out of there. But did I do that? Of course not! I wound up spending the afternoon sticking needles into Hanson's body, trying to start new IVs. I must have stuck him ten times before I got one in. The kid's totally aveinic [**internese for "without veins"**].

My new diarrhea patient has a strange story. He came in with his grandmother, who said he got all his care at another hospital but she doesn't remember the name of either the hospital or the doctor. She said she came to Mount Scopus this time because that other place had the kid for all those months and they couldn't do anything to make him better, so she was coming to give us a chance to cure him. To tell the truth, he didn't look that bad to me, but to hear his grandmother tell it, he's at death's door. I'm going to have to figure out what's going on with him, but I sure as hell wasn't going to do it today.

So finally I sat down to write my notes and got out of the hospital at about four-thirty. My progress notes have gotten worse and worse. It's gotten to the point now where I can't even read my own handwriting. An attending came up to me yesterday and asked me what I had written on his patient's chart and I simply could not read the thing. I'm pretty sure I'm going to get yelled at about my handwriting sooner or later. But what can I do? If I decided to take my time and write neatly, I'd never make it back to my apartment. It's kind of a shortcut I've got to take to keep my sanity at this point. Maybe this is how the doctors' handwriting myth began.

Monday, August 19, 1985

Things are looking up. Really! Last night wasn't bad, I only got one hit [hit=admission], and for the first time this month I actually got into the bed in the on-call room and fell asleep for a while. And Hanson is better. His fever went away without any change in his antibiotics, so either it was the virus that was going around or maybe one of his IVs actually was infected. We started feeding him formula again last weekend [he had been NPO for a few days following his most recent episode of diarrhea], and he's tolerating it pretty well. He hasn't had any diarrhea and he actually gained a few ounces. He's a pretty cute kid, actually. I'm getting to the point where I actually like him. If he behaves himself and doesn't crump or do anything stupid like that, he may become one of my favorite patients. We're even starting to think about sending him home. The only problem is, his mother, who's an IVDA, has never come to see him. I've never met her or even spoken to her on the phone. So it looks like he's going to turn into a social hold. I've got to start talking to the social worker about placing him somewhere. Oh, well, he'll probably wind up staying on Infants' until I'm a senior resident.

And that patient with the meningomyelocoele I admitted last week turned out to be a great kid. It's a funny thing about him, he turned out to be kind of cute. He'd sit in his little stroller and make this weird clicking sound with his cheek to get your attention, and when you'd look over at him, he'd smile at you. I liked that kid a lot and I really miss him since he went home. He was the only kid I've taken care of this month who's old enough to actually be sociable.

So far, the weirdest story of the month has to do with Fenton, that GE reflux kid I admitted on Monday. I sat down and talked to his grandmother on Wednesday. She's the kid's caretaker; his mother's about fourteen and is treated more like an older sister. Anyway, the grandmother told me this real bizarre story. She said he vomited everything they fed him when he was a little baby and she brought him to some hospital in Westchester, which we all finally figured out had to be Westchester County Medical Center [a teaching hospital affiliated with New York Medical College, in Valhalla, New York]. They worked him up, diagnosed the reflux, and did a fundoplication and a feeding gastrostomy [placing of a tube directly through the abdominal wall and into the stomach, to facilitate feeding while the esophagus is healing]. But he never seemed to get any better after the operation. The grandmother took him home but he kept vomiting whenever they fed him anything by mouth and got diarrhea when they gave him anything through the g-tube [gastrostomy tube]. She kept bringing him back to the hospital and they finally started him on continuous gastrostomy drip feedings [sort of like an IV, delivering small amounts of fluid throughout the day and night, into the stomach]. She told me that that was the only thing that seemed to work.

Well, none of this made any sense to any of us, including Dr. Gordon [the pediatric gastroenterologist]. There's no way this kid could have so many problems and look so healthy. And the grandmother is a pretty suspicious character; she knows all the medical terms and the names of all the procedures. So yesterday we called the gastroenterologist at Westchester County Medical Center and he told us what really was going on. He said that the grandmother kept bringing him to the ER there with a history of diarrhea and vomiting but the kid never looked dehydrated.

They admitted him a few times and he did have loose stools but for a long time they couldn't figure out what was happening. Finally, during an admission about a month ago, one of the nurses found a bottle of laxative in the grandmother's possession. They couldn't prove it, but they're convinced she was giving the kid the laxative in his bottle to make him have diarrhea. Amazing!

So today, while the grandmother was off the ward, we started the kid on regular feeds and he took it like a normal child. When the grandmother showed up, she got really angry and tried to sign him out of the hospital AMA [against medical advice], but we stopped her and slapped a BCW hold on the kid [the Bureau of Child Welfare can order a child retained in the hospital if the child's well-being is endangered]. The grandmother went crazy but the social worker talked her down; the social worker handled the whole situation pretty damned well.

Well, there's only about another week of this insanity left. I can't wait. I've had about enough of this Infants' nonsense!

Friday, August 23, 1985

I meant to record this yesterday, but I fell asleep as soon as I got home and I couldn't do it. Wednesday was another classic night on Infants'. I'm beginning to lose my sense of humor about all this, which is a pretty serious problem. It's definitely time to get off this ward. I'm going to OPD [Outpatient Department—the ER and Clinics] for two weeks and then I've got vacation.

Well, Hanson crumped again yesterday morning. He started stooling out again and got acidotic, and while we were trying to start an IV his heart rate dropped and we had to call a CAC [resuscitation for cardiac arrest]. We got him back but the chiefs decided he was sick enough to be transferred to the ICU, so we shipped him up to the sixth floor. Just like that! I don't know, he's fine as long as he doesn't do anything to bother you. But the kid crumps at least once a week! He's got to learn a lesson if he expects anyone ever to like him.

And Fenton is fine, absolutely fine. His grandmother has become a basket case, though; she simply can't cope with the fact that he has no medical problem. It's really weird. The grandmother told one of the nurses that she herself has had over twenty operations; she even had a CAT scan last week while the baby was in the hospital because she's afraid she's got a brain tumor. The nurse pointed out to us that she wears one of those plastic hospital bracelets as jewelry! The social worker has been trying to get her into some sort of therapy but the woman is resistant. I'm not sure, but I think it's going to come down to either the woman gets some form of help or the baby is going to be placed in a foster home.

I'm on tomorrow for the last time on Infants'. I can't wait to get it over with. Carole and I are going to go out for dinner Sunday night to celebrate. I'm really afraid I won't find anything funny anymore. I really think I've lost my sense of humor on Infants'.

BOB

August 1985

Although I was a medical student at Schweitzer and did my residency at Jonas Bronck and the Schweitzer University Hospital, I was an intern at a medical center in Boston. I left the Bronx because it was suggested that I should see how medicine was handled at places other than those associated with the Albert Schweitzer School of Medicine. So I spent a year in Boston; I'm still recovering from it.

I did my first month of internship in the neonatal intensive-care unit of a maternity hospital that was affiliated with the program's main teaching hospital. I arrived at work on the first day, a Saturday, and took sign-out from the old intern who had been on call the night before. After he left for home that morning, I was pretty much left on my own with thirty-five of the sickest premature babies you could possibly imagine. That first day of internship was definitely in the top ten of the most frightening days of my life.

When I started in that NICU, I knew absolutely nothing; the intern who signed out to me communicated in what seemed to be a foreign language. He spoke a hodgepodge of medical terms, slang, and numbers all mixed together. I just wasn't ready for: "That's a forty-five-hundred-gram IDM who aspirated mec and got PFC. We tubed him and put him on the vent with settings of twenty-five over five, 100 percent, and forty, and his last gas was seven point thirty, forty-four, and forty-five. He blew two pneumos so we put in tubes. He's on DIOW at eighty per kilo per day." I had absolutely no idea what any of this meant; I just wrote as much of it as I could on my clipboard, nodded my head to make him think I understood what he was saying, and hoped to God that the nurses knew what the hell was going on.

I eventually figured it all out. It didn't take long before I could translate even the most complex of these monologues into English. (By the way, the intern was talking about a nearly ten-pound newborn whose mother was a diabetic. The baby had passed a bowel movement while still in the womb and had breathed in the contents of the bowel movement, causing severe respiratory and cardiac problems. He was being breathed for by machine, had too much acid and not enough oxygen in his blood, had had two episodes of collapsed lung, and was being given intravenous sugar water. That baby, one of my first patients, survived and did fairly well in spite of me.) And eventually I even became comfortable with the preemies. But that Saturday was terrifying for both me and my patients.

I spent August back at the medical center, working in their NICU. Although I was feeling more comfortable with preemies after my month at the maternity hospital, I encountered many other problems. First, two months in a row in a NICU is cruel and unusual punishment. Preemies, unlike older children and adults, don't seem to understand the difference between day and night. They didn't discriminate: they'd crump at any moment, morning, afternoon, evening, and in the middle of the night. As a result, when working in a NICU, it's almost impossible to get any sleep during nights on call; you usually don't even get a chance to see the inside of the interns' on-call room.

Second, although the neonatologists will tell you that saving preemies is an exciting and exhilarating experience, to me the unit was an unbelievably depressing place to work. There were a lot of deaths, and although dealing with the parents of the babies who died was sad and difficult, it was even harder to care for some of the very tiny and extremely sick infants who didn't die. These survivors often didn't have a snowball's chance in hell of leading anything resembling a normal life. Yet we were ordered to do everything possible to keep them going, and their parents were often given unrealistic expectations about how their infant would turn out. That conflict between what was medically demanded and what seemed ethically correct took a toll on me and on a number of my fellow interns.

The third problem that struck me when I made it back to the medical center was that I felt alone. There were two reasons for this. First, all the other interns had met and become friends during July. By being farmed out to the maternity hospital, I had become "odd man out." It took me months to make inroads into the cliques that had formed.

The other reason I felt alone was because my wife and the rest of my family were back in New York. In a situation almost parallel to Andy Baron's, while I was off in Boston, my wife was a graduate student in New York. We would see each other only on those weekends when I had at least a full day off. Since that happened only two of every three weeks, there were long stretches of time when I was completely alone. Without friends and family, my life was miserable.

And miserable was the tone set for the entire year. I felt overworked, dead tired, conflicted by what I was being called on to do, and uncared for by the senior people in the program. And even though I had originally planned to stay in Boston for the three years of my training, I decided to leave the medical center after my internship. I made my first call to Alan Cozza, the chief of service at Jonas Bronck Hospital, asking for a job as a junior resident toward the end of August. By September I informed my chief resident in Boston that come the following July 1, I'd be moving back to the Bronx.

In retrospect, my experiences in Boston were not unique. All interns suffer during their internships. Although there might be some variations, the issues are pretty much the same for everyone. The main issue is the hours: Being on call every third night all year long makes it impossible to lead anything like a normal life. Regardless of how caring the people who run the program are, or how nice the city in which it's placed is, or how much support is available from family and friends, interns usually spend a hundred hours or more per week in the hospital. And anytime someone spends that much time at their place of work, there are going to be problems.

But why do house officers have to spend so much time in the hospital? What do interns do all day long? To explain this, I should outline what a typical intern's day it like.

On a typical day, most of the interns show up for work at about 7:30 A.M. They briefly walk around the ward, making sure that all their patients have literally survived the night. They check the vital-sign records kept by the nurses to see if the patients have had fevers or any other complications. Then, at about eight, work rounds begin. The ward team, made up of three interns, a resident, the head nurse, and the third-year medical students who are assigned to pediatrics that month, walks past each patient, reviews his or her progress and decides on a plan of action for the day. The interns must carefully note the plans for each of their patients; it is their job to make sure the plans are carried out, to order the tests, schedule the appointments, send off the lab specimens, and check on their results. It is at work rounds, which last until approximately nine o'clock, that the interns generate the "scut lists" that will occupy them for most of the rest of the day.

At nine, an intake conference occurs. At intake, all patients admitted the night before are reviewed with the chief of the service. This is a teaching conference, and a large portion of the house staff usually is present. The interns are expected to present their own patients briefly and, if recommendations regarding management are made, to add these to their usually already burgeoning scut lists.

Intake lasts until about nine-thirty, at which time an X-ray conference begins. At this conference, all X rays taken the day before are reviewed with the radiologists. This X-ray conference usually lasts until ten o'clock.

Then comes attending rounds, when the ward team meets with a member of the faculty. During attending rounds, admissions from the night before are focused upon, the presenting symptoms dissected, and the patients' diagnoses discussed at length. The ward attending is the person who is ultimately responsible for the care that's delivered, and so in addition to teaching about the conditions that afflict the patients, the attending must make sure that the proper things are being done in a timely fashion. Depending on how many patients were admitted the day before and how long-winded the attending is, rounds can go on until between eleven o'clock and noon. Every day at noon there is a didactic lecture on a pertinent topic in pediatric medicine. So, the average intern may not get down to attacking the scut list until after one o'clock in the afternoon.

Most interns will tell you that scut is the sole reason for their existence. Scut includes blood drawing, IV starting, the tracking down of lab results, the ordering of diagnostic tests, the calling of consulting services, and finally the writing of progress notes. Most of this stuff is sheer frustration and takes hours and hours to complete. While "running the scut" the intern also is responsible for teaching his medical student about pediatrics. Depending on how many patients he's following, how efficient he is, and how many questions his medical student asks, the intern who's not on call may get out of the hospital anywhere between three in the afternoon and nine o'clock at night, with the average being around six.

When they're on call, of course, they don't go anywhere. They stay all night, managing any complication that may arise in any of the patients on the ward and admitting all new patients who are sent up from the emergency room. Sometimes, when the emergency room is quiet and the patients on the ward are stable, the intern might be able to retire to the on-call room to get some sleep; at other times, when things are hectic, he or she might not even have enough free time to go to the bathroom. And the daily routine begins again at seven-thirty the next morning; even if the intern has gotten no sleep during a night on call, he or she is expected to participate in all the activities that occur during the entire postcall day.

This cycle is repeated every third night. Interns spend the first night in the hospital. The next night, when they're postcall, they usually are unable to do anything other than go home and hit the sack. The final night in the cycle, the precall night, is the only one in which most interns feel alive enough to go out and have a little fun. But very often, the precall night is ruined by anxiety; lurking in the back of the intern's mind when they're precall is the fact that the following night may be a complete and utter disaster. And so, in a sense, even when they're out of the hospital, there's no escape.

The interns are also expected to carry out certain tasks that are not all that difficult when well rested but may prove to be impossible after a night spent on call without any sleep. Without sleep, an intern can lose track of the subtle social skills that are necessary for communication; as a result, talking to patients and their families can become torture. The intern also is expected to present orally, during attending rounds the next day, all the patients who were admitted during his or her shift. Keeping track of names, symptoms, physical findings, lab results, and treatments can become an insurmountable task when you're having trouble just keeping awake. And screwing up a presentation can bring on the wrath of the attending, who is relying on the intern's information, and a lowering of the intern's own self-esteem.

This system of night call has come under a great deal of scrutiny in recent years. Public awareness, however, has not been focused on the toll that these long shifts are taking on the interns and residents, but rather on the toll that they're taking on the patients. It's been argued that a house officer who's been up all night can't possibly provide adequate care for critically ill patients. So, over the past few months, some alternatives to the current system have been proposed. The most popular of these would limit both the number of hours an intern or resident could work during a single stretch to twenty-four, and the number of hours worked within a single week to eighty.

On the surface, this seems as if it would be a good situation, but some house staff members have expressed fear that new regulations such as these would actually make their lives more miserable. These house officers recognize the fact that to provide staffing of the wards and emergency rooms on a twenty-four-hour basis, hospitals would have two choices: Either hire 25 percent more interns, or have the existing interns work twelve-hour shifts seven days a week. Because of the lack of availability of funds to pay for a whole crop of new house officers, as well as the problem of finding qualified medical school graduates to fill these positions, people are worried that the second choice is the one that would be instituted. And almost everyone agrees that they'd much rather work thirty-six hours at a stretch and have a day off every week than work shorter periods every day of the week.

The only hospital in which the intern's day deviates significantly from what I've outlined above is University Hospital. University is a hospital with a split personality. On the one hand, it seems like a laid-back, friendly community hospital nestled in a neighborhood of two-family houses; all the patients have private attendings (in sharp contrast to the two municipal hospitals, where the opposite is true), the nurses and the rest of the staff are like the boy and girl next door, and the pace is slow and relaxed. This makes University Hospital seem like a place you might actually like to visit during your summer vacation. However, the hospital is a major teaching affiliate of the Schweitzer Medical School and therefore is in reality a high-powered academic center. It's the place where many of the full-time clinical faculty of Schweitzer admit their "interesting cases" for special studies. As such, the hospital contains patients with rare and often deadly diseases who need vigorous, round-the-clock management. Trying to fit these two personalities into the same building is not the easiest job in the world. And who suffers because of this? The interns and residents, as usual.

There are very few teaching conferences and much more free time at University than at the other hospitals. During the day, the interns work as glorified secretaries. Each patient's attending really makes all the important decisions affecting the patient's care, but attendings are not permitted to write in the nurses' order book. The nurses are instructed to pick up and carry out only those orders written by an authentic intern. So any time an attending wants to change a medication or order a test, he or she must get hold of an intern and ask that an order be written. The interns rarely have the opportunity to argue with an attending's request. They simply have to write down exactly what's been dictated.

Although there are very few emergency admissions, interns on call frequently spend a good part of their night fighting with the lab technicians. University's community hospital personality carries over to its laboratory. At night there are very few technicians covering the hematology lab, the chemistry lab, the bacteriology lab, and the blood bank. Because of the shortage of personnel, the technicians are never exceedingly happy about running any tests in the middle of the night, and if an exotic test needs to be done, they can turn downright ugly! Since a fair number of the patients on the ward can be very sick, it sometimes becomes critically important to get tests done after midnight. And this often results in massive arguments.

The patients at University Hospital are exceptional, to say the least. One reason people who train in pediatrics are attracted to the field is because children are basically healthy; their recovery usually is rapid, and it's a rewarding experience for the doctor. But at University Hospital, you have a ward full of children with uncorrectable chronic diseases. The pediatric renal service is housed at University Hospital, and all the kidney transplants are performed there. At any one time the ward will have five or so kids whose kidneys don't work and who are either waiting for, in the midst of recovering from, or actively rejecting a renal transplant. Except for the patients who have recently gotten a new kidney, few of these children are acutely sick. That's a mixed blessing: The chronically sick patients don't require a great deal of concentrated hard work, but they usually don't get remarkably better. And that can be discouraging.

Interns find different ways of coping with the aggravating parts of working at University Hospital. Some get into fights with the patients and staff; some spend their time hanging out in the cafeteria; and some try to get out of there as early as possible. The interns spend only one month out of their year there, so the rotation doesn't usually cause any serious or long-lasting damage.

ANDY

September 1985

Friday, August 30, 1985

I'm out of the NICU; I made it, although I had some question about whether I would that last night when I had to supervise at the death of a full-term kid who had aspirated meconium [**meconium is the first bowel movement; fetuses who are stressed intrauterinely frequently pass meconium before birth; they then breath it into their lungs during their first inspiration and develop a severe meconium pneumonia as a result**] and who wound up on maximum doses of tolazoline, dopamine, and the highest respirator settings possible. He finally died at four in the morning. The rest of the month is all a delirious blur. I think I actually learned something, but I just don't know whether is was worth the price I had to pay.

And now I'm on the Adolescent floor at Mount Scopus. I've been told it's easy street, but I don't totally agree. Life is certainly better, though. The veins of these kids look like pipelines. No more four hours wasted trying to start an IV. So far I haven't been beaten or abused, and if I can get a good night's sleep tonight, I'll be rejuvenated for call tomorrow. You know, I've been so burned out lately, I just hope that maybe in the next few days I'll get excited and interested again.

I almost thought I was getting excited and interested today. We had rounds with Marilyn Connors, our attending. She was pretty laid back. I've heard that all the adolescent attendings are hyper and picayune, so we'll see.

There's this intern I'm working with, Margaret Hasson. She was hysterical today, the way you get sometimes when you're postcall and can barely stay awake. She was presenting a patient

83

she admitted last night and she got really out of line, making off-color jokes and stuff. When you get so tired you're falling asleep on your feet like that, you think things are hysterically funny when nobody else does. It was great. After rounds, she told me that after she spent July over on 8 West, she decided she totally hated her internship. She doesn't seem like she's in a bad mood now, though. She'd not demoralized or grumpy and she doesn't hate everything.

I'm having my first experience with teaching medical students this month. I was assigned a good student who's very conscientious, humble, and a hard worker. I try to get her to spend as little time as possible in the hospital. She should be home, reading. That's what all medical students should be doing. They should spend only enough time on the wards to get an idea of what goes on there. I didn't do that; I think I spent too much time on the wards. Maybe that's why I'm so burned out already.

Having a student is interesting. I'm finding I do know a few things. I didn't think I had picked up anything since I got here, that I was a complete dum-dum. But I'm finding that I can actually talk about subjects intelligently. I don't know if they're sitting there thinking, Gee, this guy's really stupid, he's saying things that are completely wrong. But the important thing is I actually learned something over the past two months. I don't remember it happening; it must have been by osmosis.

We've got these two residents, Nancy Rodriguez and Terry Tanner, working on Adolescent this month. Nancy and Terry seem real nice, but they're only second years; they were just interns a couple of months ago. They're only a few months ahead of me and they're supervising on a busy ward! It's scary. I couldn't do it.

Saturday, September 7, 1985

This is supposed to be an easy ward, but God, there're just so many goddamned frustrations! Like there was this patient admitted the other day, this cute little fourteen-year-old girl from Barbados with severe mitral stenosis [a tight closure of the mitral valve, the valve between the left atrium and the left ventricle of the heart; stenosis results in the atrium having to work harder to push an adequate amount of blood into the left ventricle and to the rest of the body] as well as pul-

monary hypertension [an irreversible increase in the pressure
in the blood vessels that carry blood from the heart to the
lungs; frequently the cause of death in children with congenital heart disease] and hemoptysis [coughing up of blood].
She's really sick, but all anyone cared about was fucking poli-
tics. Even though she could be dying, the administrators have
to decide whether she can stay in the hospital because she's not
a U.S. citizen and not eligible for any kind of insurance. I was
told that it would probably be okay if we said that she was here
visiting relatives and got sick, rather than that she came here for
medical treatment, which was the truth. I was told not to write
anything in the chart until administration had cleared it and that
I shouldn't exactly lie, but I should tell the truth in a certain
way, you know, make it sound like she's really more acute than
she is. I can't stand buffing the chart [buff: polish to improve
an appearance]; it really bothers me. But fortunately, I had
blown the cover the first day when I wrote in my admission note
that she had come to the United States specifically for medical
care. A lot of other people said the same thing in the chart, so
it wasn't all my fault. Anyway, Loomis, the head of Adolescent
Medicine, spoke to some big cheese and got the hospital to foot
the bill. It was really nice of him, actually, and it was nice of
the hospital, too. This's going to be a fucking thirty-thousand-
or forty-thousand-dollar bill. But all this time, at least a half
hour of attending rounds a day was being wasted on this bullshit.

Yesterday was just one of those bad days; I wasted the morning with the attending and the administrators trying to figure out
what we were going to do with this kid. Then later on, I was
told I was getting a patient with sickle-cell disease who was in
painful crisis. Nobody bothered to mention to me that the patient was on the ward until the kid had been there for two and a
half hours, lying in his bed down the hall and writhing in pain!
I was so pissed I ran over to the head nurse and yelled, "Why
didn't someone tell me this guy's been here so long? How come
I haven't heard about this?" And she said, "Well, it's not our
fault," and she looked at me as if it were my fault, that I should
have somehow instinctively known the kid was there. I was so
furious, it took me two hours to cool down because the main
thing was, here's this poor kid, he's in agony, and he didn't have
to be! What can I say? It was just one of those days.

I think I probably get flustered too easily. I shouldn't allow myself to get angry about these things. Okay, so the patient's lying there, writhing in pain. Complaining to the head nurse didn't do him any good, and it sure as hell didn't do me any good. I could have just very quietly, very calmly filled out an incident report that I wasn't informed of the patient's presence. I could have sent that down to administration and then, whoever's ass had to be cooked, let his or her ass be cooked! I shouldn't allow myself to get aggravated about stuff like that; there's more than enough other stuff to get aggravated about. That's easy to say, but I still get all fumy and angry whenever something like this happens because, really, deep down inside, I want to do a good job, and I don't want people to be suffering. It really pisses me off.

I also got into a fight with a lab technician last night. I admitted a teenager with leukemia at about 6:00 P.M. He came in because he had fever and the hematologists were sure he was septic [had a bacterial infection in his blood; especially dangerous in patients with malignancies because their white blood cells, an important line of defense against invading organisms, are usually markedly deficient]. He got sent up to the floor very fast; they had seen him in clinic but they hadn't even done any of the lab work. They were really worried about him, so they sent him up directly from clinic.

As soon as he got to the floor, I drew all the admission blood work out of his central line [a surgically created, indwelling intravenous site, usually located in the neck, that connects with a large or central vein; used in patients receiving frequent chemotherapy or in whom total parenteral nutrition is being administered] and sent it off to the lab stat [immediately]. Of course, I included a CBC [complete blood count] with diff [differential cell count: percentage of various types of white blood cells within the sample], and I wrote the diagnosis on the lab slip so they couldn't blow off doing the diff [the differential count requires some tedious microscope work; therefore it is done only in cases where there's an abnormal number of white cells or in cases of malignancy]. When I called the lab about an hour later to get the results, they told me nothing was ready yet. I called back a half hour after that and they gave me the CBC, but the tech said they hadn't done the diff. I said, "What do you mean, you haven't done the diff? I checked off 'diff' on the lab slip and wrote the patient's diagnosis.'' He said, ''We don't do diffs at night.'' And I said, ''What do you mean, you don't do diffs at night? I need a diff on this patient; he's got leukemia, for God's sake, and he might be septic. I have to have a diff! This kid could die.'' And the guy said, ''Lots of people die every day,'' and then he hung up. He fucking hung up on me!

I was ready to go down there and kill. But the senior I was on with said it wouldn't do anybody any good and that all I had to do was take another sample over to West Bronx's lab and they'd run it for me. I did that, and sure enough, the kid was neutropenic [**had a deficiency of the particular type of white blood cells most important in fighting off infections**] and septic. He's pretty sick. He may die. But the people in the lab don't care about stuff like that. They only know what the rules are.

The aggravations of being an intern are just endless. I would say nine out of ten interns say these same two words over and over again: ''Internship sucks.'' I've heard that particular phrase so many times in the past week or two.

I mean, think about it: To the nurses and most of the rest of the staff, we're nothing but another piece of shit. To the nurses, anything that goes wrong is the intern's fault. Somehow they're always innocent and the intern always is wrong. And nobody around here seems to give a shit! There are really only three good nurses on this ward. The rest are worthless, lazy, uncaring shitheads who spend most of their time sitting around on their fat asses in the back room, watching TV and eating junk food. They don't want to do anything. They certainly don't want to take care of patients. They're so fucking, incredibly lazy! Anytime you ask them to do anything, even take a patient's temperature, they either take it as a racial slur or as a personal insult. Oh, my God, it's a federal case to get a temp done! I'm used to being in a hospital where the nurses were superefficient; they'd fall all over each other to get an order filled. I'm not used to this attitude.

And there's another problem: There's a major cultural difference. Here I am, this white, upper-middle-class Jewish kid, and most of the nurses are black, working-class women. We're from completely different worlds. God knows what they're thinking when they look at me and the rest of us, but I definitely get the feeling that they think we're a kind of annoyance they have to put up with. There're so few of them who really want to make the effort to work together. Oh, well, what can you do?

We got a really fascinating patient last night. She's this poor little thirteen-year-old Hispanic girl, very cute and extremely suicidal. She was brought in by ambulance because she told someone she had taken a full bottle of asthma medication. She didn't have any symptoms and her theophylline level was zero, so she really hadn't taken anything. But she told the people in the emergency room that voices in her head were telling her to kill herself, so they admitted her. Poor kid, she comes from the original scrambled family. She's under the care of her grandparents, each of whom have attempted suicide multiple times. She's with the grandparents because her mother is a drug abuser who severely beat the girl when she was younger. She lives in a complete fantasy world; she told me about it in vivid detail. But other than listen to her talk, there wasn't anything I could do for her. What she really needs is a psychiatrist. It's sad, it's really sad.

Karen's been here almost a week now. She's doing an elective in Manhattan. I've spent maybe six or seven hours with her, total. Next weekend she's dying to go to Philadelphia and she wants me to come along for this party a friend of hers is throwing. But that would mean I'd have to do every other night on call and I'd have to trade with Margaret, who would have to work an extra weekend day. I don't want to ask her to do that; it's not fair to her and it's also not fair to me. It would mean having to sleep on somebody's floor or something, and I'd come back and have to do the every-other. I'd be completely fatigued and I wouldn't even get to see Karen for five whole days. And that's just to try to go to a little party in Philadelphia. In other jobs, you'd expect to have every weekend off, and it wouldn't be such a big deal to go somewhere and have some fun. As an intern, you can forget it.

This past week Karen has had a very difficult time adjusting to my life. She's been really upset at my absence, at the fact that the first night she was here I fell asleep four times over dinner. She had just had this interview at a program for a psych residency and it hadn't gone well. The place seemed extremely disorganized, the people were disinterested, and they didn't know a thing about her. She was upset and she wanted to talk about it and all I could do was fall asleep; I'm worthless to her!

So she was very frustrated. And since that night she's been getting angrier and angrier about the fact that two out of three nights I'm either away or asleep. Fortunately we have this weekend to be together. It's only Saturday afternoon now. I'm going to go to sleep for a while and then we'll have tonight and tomorrow together.

Friday, September 13, 1985

We are going down to Philadelphia tonight. I wound up having to go. I'm just waiting for Karen to come home. I don't know how I'm going to get through this, but I found myself in a position where I couldn't say no.

All the patients I'm taking care of now are psychopaths. Every adolescent in the Bronx is trying to commit suicide. They're either trying to do it by an overdose, by shooting themselves, or by starving themselves to death. The floor is chock full of anorexics and bulimics. There are two types: the "walkers" and the "liers." The "walkers" spend the entire day pacing up and down the halls. Whenever you need to find them, you just walk the corridors and there they are. They walk because they're trying to expend as many calories as possible, and this is about the only exercise they can get while they're in the hospital. They can't do their "jazzercise" four or five hours a day, so they just walk. The "liers" are worst off, though. They all look like concentration camp survivors; they're nothing but skin and bone. They're so debilitated, they can't do anything but lie in bed.

And there's nothing I can do to help them. I go and I try to talk to them, I try to reason with them about eating. They say they'll eat more but I know they're just doing it to get rid of me. They'll tell me anything they think I want to hear. Then they'll just go and do whatever they want.

I referred one of the psychopaths to my clinic today. A patient of mine, one of my suicide-attempt kids. He's nuts, but he's really a good kid. I think he just needs someone to look after him. I can't do a very good job of that as an intern, but I can at least be a little bit more of a support system. While I was making the appointment for him, I was thinking, Do I really want to do this? Do I really need this much of a problem coming to my clinic every week for the rest of the year? I hope I don't regret it.

My med student is turning out to be great. She told me I was great, too. She said I really cared about people. That's nice; I'm glad she said that. We pat each other on the back, and that's important because nobody else verbally applauds us. At first I didn't want her to do any of my scut, that's not what med students are for, but she was always willing to help and eventually I just got used to her being there when I needed her. I always tried to teach her things while we were scutting out, kind of on a one-to-one basis: I taught her how to do a gram stain [a test to identify bacteria in a sample of body fluid] and then when I needed one done, she'd run to the lab and do it for me. I taught her how to read an EKG [electrocardiogram], how to put in a Foley [a catheter passed through the urethra into the bladder, to monitor the output of urine], how to put in IVs. She liked that. She's going to be a great doctor.

Sunday, September 15, 1985, 1:00 A.M.

I just got back from Philadelphia. I went down there with Karen and some friend. We went to a big party at Brad's house, but I couldn't stay for the bash; I had to come back home so I could be on call tomorrow . . . later this morning . . . Sunday.

Last night—Friday, actually—I got home postcall and everybody came in after they'd gotten the car. They said they couldn't wake me up for ten or fifteen minutes; I wouldn't talk at all. I don't remember much, but I finally got out of bed and slept the whole way there. Soon's I got there, I went to sleep. I had a good time in Philadelphia; it was fun.

I talked to Ann while I was in Philly. She's a friend of mine from medical school. She's an intern doing pediatrics at St. Christopher's. Right now she says she just entered this phase of intense resentment and anger and depression and hatefulness. She hates her work, she hates her patients, and she especially hates anybody who's enjoying what they're doing. She says she doesn't think it's so bad because in three days she's going on vacation and she knows she can kind of get this way now. She says she didn't know what she'd do if she were in my shoes and had to wait another three months for vacation.

I'm starting to feel kind of apathetic, in a funny way. Does apathy follow depression? I don't have much more to talk about because I'm tired; tired and pissed. I'm also kind of sick of doing this diary, to be honest. I'm starting to feel kind of annoyed, I don't know why. I don't think I want to remember this fucking year.

Friday, September 20, 1985

I finally had a dream I remembered. I guess it's a good sign, but I think I'm better off when I forget them. The dream went like this: I was at work and the resident wanted me to check the potassium level on this patient who was taking a drug that depletes potassium. I kept making excuses, I don't know why, I kept putting off drawing the blood. Finally I was sitting in the library and a cardiac arrest was called. I went running in to find my patient dead and unresuscitatable. The rest of the house staff showed up and started yelling in unison that I had killed the patient. I woke up at that point in a cold sweat. I was terrified!

I can't exactly put my finger on what's wrong with me. I only have six patients now. Two of them are GORK who don't make any extra work, and one is just a suicide attempt. But it doesn't matter. I still seem to get killed almost every night I'm on call. And then I come home postcall and fall asleep and Karen glares at me. I spend three hours with her every third night. Last Monday night, a friend from home came to visit. We went out for dinner. I fell asleep three times during the meal. When is it going to start getting a little better?

AMY

September 1985

Monday, September 2, 1985, 11:00 P.M.

I just got Sarah to sleep and I finally have some time to myself. Today's Labor Day and I had the day off. We had a great time: We went to a zoo, we went swimming, and we just generally relaxed. It was something we all really needed! It was freezing last night; I had to put Sarah to sleep in a sweater. Summer's ending; I usually get depressed at this time of year, but this year is different. I'm actually happy summer's ending. It means I'll never have to be an intern in the summer again!

I started on 8 West on Wednesday and so far it's been a mixed experience. It's not nearly as calm as University Hospital. There are some interesting things going on but it's not so taxing that I can't get out early. So those things are good. But our resident this month is an idiot! He's completely useless. He can't teach, and when he tries, he gets it all wrong! On Thursday he told us that the peak age for SIDS [**sudden infant death syndrome: the unexplainable death of an infant**] was six months to one and a half years. That's completely wrong! I know a lot about the subject, I've made myself crazy about it since Sarah was born, and I know the peak age is two to six months. I told Barry [**the senior resident**] what it really was and he stammered and argued for a while and finally said, "Let's just drop it, okay?" I looked it up in Rudolph [**a textbook of pediatrics**] after rounds and showed him I was right. He still hasn't admitted he was wrong.

He's also not very good technically. He couldn't start any of the IVs I've had trouble with and he can't get blood on kids after

92

I've failed. So if he can't teach and he can't help, what good is he?

It's very upsetting having this guy in charge, but what can I do about it? So far what I've done is just ignore him. If I need help, I either ask Susannah, the other intern on our ward, or if she can't help, I go to the chief residents. The chiefs seem to understand our problem; they always come and help if we need it.

It's good to be working with Susannah. We were classmates at Schweitzer. She's got a ten-month-old daughter at home, so our motivation is pretty much the same: We both try to get out as early as possible. On days when I'm on call, I tell her to sign out to me as early as possible, and when she's on, I sign out to her as early as I can. Having this moron as our resident is mostly just a pain in the neck for Susannah and me. I feel bad for David, our subintern, and the medical students. They don't know how little they can trust Barry, and they might just believe some of the things he says. What this means is that Susannah and I are going to have to do some extra teaching this month to undo the damage caused by our resident.

I was on call Saturday, and it was quiet. I spent most of the day sitting in the residents' room watching TV. I got only one admission, in the afternoon, but we just about had to drag the patient up to the ward. It was a six-week-old who came to the ER with a history of a fever, a cough, and an eye discharge. The baby had been seen in some other ER the day before and was sent home, if you can believe that! Even I know that anyone under two months of age with a fever gets admitted to the hospital for IV antibiotics. But this bozo at the other hospital actually told the mother the baby was fine, he just had a little cold, and she should take him home. She brought him to Jonas Bronck the next day because he still had the fever. When the guys down in our ER heard it was a FIB [fever in baby] they pounced on him, did a complete workup, and got ready to admit him.

I wound up getting a few hours of sleep in the on-call room. The place is really disgusting; it's a tiny room at the end of 8 East with nothing in it except two sets of bunk beds and a telephone. Usually they don't provide pillows or blankets, so you have to steal linens from the clean-laundry cart, and you can do that only if the nurses like you or if they're not looking.

They know me, so there wasn't any trouble. So life's not bad. At least so far.

Sunday, September 8, 1985

This is the end of another terrific weekend. We spent yesterday and today with my father in New Jersey. Because of the way the schedule worked out, I had Sunday and Labor Day off last week and this whole weekend off. I feel like a banker, not an intern. And I've actually had a chance to spend quality time with Sarah without the sitter being around.

Marie and I are getting along fairly well. We're not exactly best friends, but I think we at least understand each other. I guess I've come to accept some of her mishegoss [Yiddish for craziness], and she's come to accept some of mine. I was concerned for a while that Sarah would come to think of Marie as her mother and me as someone else who happened to spend a lot of time around the house, but it's clear she knows who I am and who Marie is. Sarah's doing a lot of things now, rolling over front to back and back to front. She doesn't lie still for a second; we can't leave her alone on the bed anymore or she might roll off onto the floor. Then I'd have to take her to the ER for head trauma and they'd probably report me to the BCW.

I did bring Sarah to work with me last Wednesday. She had an appointment with Alan Cozza, and since his office is right off the ward, I figured we could get it in before work rounds. Alan told me Sarah's doing fine. She weighed over fourteen pounds. She's nearly doubled her birth weight in four months! And she got her second DPT [diphtheria, pertussis, and tetanus immunization] and OPV [oral polio vaccine]. I had to leave the room when Alan stuck her. It definitely hurt me more than it hurt her. Now I can understand how the parents feel when we stick their kids. Sarah cried for about twenty minutes after he finished. And that's after pretreatment with Tylenol!

Anyway, before rounds started, I sat in the residents' room with Sarah on my lap, and all the other interns and residents came over and oohed and aahed over her. A lot of them didn't even know I had a baby. It's so strange! Here are people I work with every day, I even sleep in the same room with them every third night, and they don't even know I have a baby! Of course, I don't know what's happening in their lives either. But this job tends to do that to you, it brings you into intimate contact with people who remain total strangers.

The work on the ward still is pretty easy. I've been getting out between three and four on the days I'm not on call; so has Susannah. The subintern's been staying until six or seven every night, but of course he's not really sure what he's doing yet, so naturally everything takes him longer. He also thinks he has to stay late to get something out of the rotation.

Everything would be perfect if it wasn't for that idiot Barry Bresnan! He really is dangerous. I hate work rounds in the morning. We do nothing but argue for an hour. He's got some very strange ideas about medicine, and most of the time they're wrong. One day last week, Susannah admitted a five-year-old with a hyphema [**bleeding into the anterior chamber of the eye; dangerous because it can lead to blindness**]. The boy had been hit in the eye with a baseball. Susannah did what the ophthalmology consultant told her to do: She put him in a private room, patched his eye, and kept him sedated so the eye would not get reinjured and bleed again. But on the rounds, Barry said there was no reason to sedate these kids; in fact, it was dangerous for some reason he never explained. He told us to stop medicating the boy and just let him run around and do what he wanted. Susannah told him he was crazy, that if the kid were to rebleed into his eye, it could cost him his vision, and that she was going to continue the medication because that was what ophthalmology wanted done. Barry yelled at her that ophthalmology wasn't running the ward, he was, and this is what he wanted to do. At that point Susannah figured it was useless to argue with him. She said "All right" and left it at that. She kept the patient sedated though.

Later in the day, when the chiefs made rounds with Barry, they told him the boy had to be kept sedated or else he might rebleed. So Barry came back to Susannah and said he'd changed his mind and she should start sedating the boy again. She told him she'd never changed the order in the first place, and that really pissed him off. But what could he do? He had been wrong and we had been right. He couldn't very well go to the chiefs and complain that the interns weren't following his orders, because his orders were wrong! He's so stubborn and so stupid. And he's dangerous. He could cause a lot of trouble for our patients. It's frightening!

Friday, September 13, 1985

I am really angry! That jerk is continuing to find ways to torment me. Every time Susannah or I make a decision, every time we try to do something to help one of our kids, he comes and tells us we're wrong and we have to change things, and we argue and get into a big fight. And it always turns out that we're right and he's wrong! It never fails! I don't know how he can be a resident and know so little! It's actually scary!

Today was the worst so far. We started off the morning fighting about a kid with asthma I had admitted last night. Nothing earthshaking or exotic, just a simple, straightforward eight-year-old asthmatic, something we see every day on the wards, and he found a way to screw up the kid's care!

This was a kid who gets admitted to the hospital four or five times a year. They gave him a minibolus of aminophylline in the ER. [Aminophylline, a drug that dilates the breathing tubes, is the mainstay of asthma therapy. In severe asthma attacks it must be given by vein either in boluses, when a large dose is given once every six hours, or by constant infusion or drip]. I started him on a one-per-kilo drip [a drip containing one milligram of aminophylline per kilogram of body weight per hour, the dose needed to maintain the blood aminophylline level] after checking the old chart and finding that that's what it took to maintain his level. I drew levels [blood samples to determine the amount of aminophylline in the blood] after the bolus and four hours after starting the drip, and they showed he was in the therapeutic range. By this morning he was much better, but still he was wheezing a little. On work rounds Barry asked me what we had done. I told him and he said, "No, you did it all wrong, that's not the way to figure out what dose of aminophylline to give an asthmatic." He then recalculated everything using this strange formula I'd never seen before and told me that we should have started him on a 1.5-per-kilo drip. I told him he was crazy, that if we put the kid on a 1.5 drip he'd get toxic [develop blood levels of aminophylline in the toxic range; signs of aminophylline toxicity include nausea and vomiting and convulsions] in a matter of hours and I certainly wasn't going to do that to my patient. He told me I was wrong, that he'd always used this formula and he'd never had any trouble with toxicity. That's when Susannah told him he probably just had been lucky in the past because she was positive that if we changed the dose to 1.5 per kilo, the kid would be vomiting by noon. She also happened to mention to Barry that she thought he was both full of shit and dangerous and that we'd all be better off without him. Although she and I had been thinking all of this since the very first day of the month, neither of us had said it to him before. He yelled back at us that we were the ones who were full of shit and that we could say whatever we wanted about him, but he was sure he had never seen two interns who cared less about their patients. I got really angry at that point and asked how he could say that. He said something to the effect that he had never heard of interns who left the hospital at three o'clock every afternoon.

Well, we were yelling loud enough at that point to get the chief residents out of the ICU, where they were rounding. Susannah said something about the fact that she and I were able to get out early because we had learned to be very organized and that maybe Barry's problem was that when he'd been an intern he hadn't learned anything and that was why he'd turned into such a bad resident.

That was when the chiefs separated us. Jon Golden pulled Susannah and me down the hall, and Eric Weinstein took Barry into the residents' room. Jon asked us what had happened, and I related the incident from start to finish. Jon said that Barry, as usual, was definitely wrong and that we were definitely right. He told us they were having a lot of problems with Barry, that he really did have some problem with his knowledge base and that, on top of it, he had no confidence in himself. "Of course he has no confidence in himself!" I told Jon. "He doesn't know anything! There's no reason for him to have any confidence!" Jon told us that may be true, but they were stuck with him, and we would have to try to make the best of the situation. He also told us we should try to be nice to him because it might help him with this confidence problem. That's not exactly what I wanted to hear and it wasn't what Susannah wanted to hear, either. She said there was something really wrong with all of this, that this guy was dangerous and he shouldn't be in a position where he had the chance to harm the patients. I said I thought he should be thrown out of the program. Jon kind of groaned and said that he really wasn't that bad and that we just should give him a chance. We just walked away at that point.

There was nothing else we could say. We weren't getting through.

I don't know what Eric told Barry, but he came out about a half hour later and didn't say a word to us. We finished work rounds without him and made all the medical decisions ourselves.

At about three o'clock I was signing out to Susannah in the nurses' station. I didn't have much going on; it's been kind of quiet. I only have six patients, and two of them are chronic AIDS patients. [**The back rooms on 8 West are reserved for children with AIDS and AIDS-related illnesses. On any given day there are four to six patients residing there. Most are not sick; they have come to live in the hospital because there's no other place for them.**] While I was signing out, Barry came up to me and said, "What are you doing?" I told him I was signing out and he said, "Look, you can't sign out at three o'clock." He said there had to be some work I still had to do. He said that I had a responsibility to teach the students and obviously they weren't getting taught anything if we were all going home at three o'clock.

I didn't answer him; I just continued signing out. After a while he said, "Didn't you hear me? Why don't you answer me?" I told him I didn't answer him because I didn't have anything to say to him. He looked really hurt and walked away. A couple of minutes later, Jon Golden came into the nurses' station and asked if he could talk to me in private. I had finished signing out and was getting ready to leave. He took me into the chief resident's office and said, "I know things aren't going well on the ward, but don't you think you could try to be nice to him?" And I said, "Why? He's not being nice to me!" I told him about what Barry had just said to me and he kind of sighed and just asked if, in the future, I would just play along with Barry, at least make him think I was being friendly. I said I'd try. And then I got up to leave and on my way out, I ran into Barry again. I said good-bye to him and this time he ignored me! Unbelievable!

There are two more weeks to go on this ward. If it hadn't been for this jerk, this would've been a very nice month. As it is, I can't wait until it's over!

Monday, September 23, 1985

Thank God the month is almost through. I haven't recorded anything in over a week. It's been too depressing. I hate going to work every morning and spending the whole day fighting.

It wasn't as bad in the beginning of the month because we weren't all that busy. But last week the place started to fill up and there are a lot of complicated patients around who need a doctor who knows how to make decisions. Susannah and I don't know enough, and since we've stopped talking to our resident, there's nobody to turn to except the chief residents, who aren't all that thrilled about being bothered with our trivial stuff every five minutes. But these cases are complicated and we can't manage them alone!

I now have nine patients. They include three asthmatics, one of whom was really sick and almost needed to be intubated [**had a breathing tube placed through the larynx and into the trachea to facilitate artificial ventilation**]; a four-year-old girl with nephrotic syndrome [**a condition in which the kidney fails to retain protein; the protein spills out in the urine and the patient becomes protein-deficient, which leads to severe swelling of the entire body**]; an eight-year-old girl who's GORKed out after being in a fire and inhaling a lot of smoke [**brain damage occurs in patients with smoke inhalation usually because of carbon monoxide poisoning**] and whose only sign of brain activity is her daily convulsions; two FIBs on antibiotics, one of whom probably has meningitis; and Winston and Salem, my AIDS twins (it's still hard to believe anyone would name a pair of twins "Winston" and "Salem," but there they are, on my ward). And even they're not doing so well. Susannah's got ten patients and the subintern's got six and we have to cope with an idiotic resident.

What happened today with Winston and Salem is a perfect example of what's going on. Salem developed some pimples on his chest this morning. I was pretty sure it was chicken pox and I had Susannah look at them and she confirmed it. And Winston's had a cold for the past day or two, now he's probably coming down with it also. Susannah and I got very worried. We both know that varicella [**the virus that causes chicken pox**] could kill them [**varicella, usually the cause of mild illness, can cause an overwhelming infection in persons who are im-**

munodeficient], but we didn't know what to do. Neither of us wanted to ask Barry; we knew he wasn't going to have anything helpful to say. So I went to Jon Golden right away and he said it probably won't be a problem because both of them are getting gamma globulin treatments [**a treatment modality that has had some success in children with AIDS**] and that the gamma globulin had antibodies to varicella so they probably wouldn't get an overwhelming case. Going over Barry's head worked out okay this time, but what's going to happen on those nights when there's nobody else around except him?

At least I have Sarah and Larry to come home to, and that makes me feel much better. Even after a day like today, ten minutes after I saw my baby, I was back to my old self. You know, when I started this internship I was concerned because I didn't know if I'd be able to be a good mother and a good intern. Now I don't understand how you can be a good intern without also being a good mother. I'll tell you, though, if I had to choose at this point whether I wanted to be a mother or a doctor, it wouldn't be a hard decision to make.

Sunday, September 29, 1985

I don't have much time. We're waiting for some friends to come for dinner. What can I say? I made it through the month, but it took a lot out of me. I'll never speak to Barry Bresnan again, that's for sure, but I survived it. It's now three months down, nine months to go. Eight if you count vacations. I'll survive it, I'm sure of it. I've managed to make things at work relatively easy for myself, but trying to be a mother and a doctor is taking a lot out of me. So far I think I'm doing a reasonable job at both; I just hope I can keep it up.

MARK

September 1985

Sunday, September 1, 1985

Ah, one day on call in the emergency room and suddenly I remembered exactly what it was that made me become a doctor in the first place. Yes, I'm sure the reason I became a doctor was so hundreds of mothers and fathers who don't speak a word of English could curse at me in their native tongues while expecting me to cure their little darlings completely within minutes. What a rewarding experience yesterday was!

Actually, it wasn't all that bad. It wasn't too busy. I spent most of the afternoon taking care of a six-week-old who came in with fever and a cough. Everyone, even a lowly intern, knows that a six-week-old with fever is an automatic admission. But apparently that's not something that's taught to the interns at BEPI [internese for Bronx Episcopal Medical Center, a voluntary hospital in the South Bronx] because this kid had been seen there a day before, had been started on amox [amoxicillin, an antibiotic], and sent home. Sent home, for God's sake! The mother brought him to Jonas Bronck only because his fever hadn't gone away and she happened to be visiting a friend in Jonas Bronck's neighborhood, so she decided to stop in and spend a few hours watching TV in our waiting room for a change. So not only did I have to do a whole sepsis workup [spinal tap, blood, and urine for cultures] on the kid, I also had to explain to the mother that the baby would have to be admitted. This must have sounded a little strange to her. After all, the kid was better than he had been the day before, and if he was so sick, why didn't the doctor at BEPI say that he needed to be admitted?

What can you say in a situation like that? "Oh, the doctor at

BEPI didn't admit him because he was a malpractice major at Our Lady of the Offshore University of Medicine and Hair Design"? It's hard to tell a woman that the last doctor to whom she trusted her kid was a moron who might have killed him! So I told her that some doctors are more conservative than others about these things and that keeping the child was mainly a safeguard. That's the first time I ever used the word "conservative" as a euphemism for "competent."

Anyway, the story doesn't end there. That was really just the beginning. I finally convinced her that the kid needed everything, including a workup and admission. I went ahead and drew the blood and did the spinal tap. I also did my first bladder tap, which is a pretty nasty procedure [**to do a bladder tap, a needle attached to a syringe is passed through the abdominal wall and plunged downward until urine appears in the syringe**]. So I finished all that and I told the mother to go back out to the waiting room and hang out until someone from the ward came down to pick her up. Up until that point, everything was fine.

I called the intern upstairs and it took her about a half hour finally to get down to the ER. It was Amy Horowitz. I sent her out to the waiting room to find the kid but she came back a few minutes later and said, "They're gone. Do I still get credit for the admission?" [**Admissions are distributed evenly to the two interns taking call on the inpatient wards at Jonas Bronck; they alternate, admitting every other one.**] I went out to look and I couldn't find them either. It looked like they had vanished into thin air. Bob Marion was the attending and he told me to try to call the woman at home using the number listed on the ER sheet. So I called and I got some woman who claimed not to be able to speak any English. I asked for the kid's mother by name and this woman on the phone said something about "no speeka de English." So I got one of the nurses to translate and she told me that the woman was saying that she had never heard of anybody by the name that was listed on the sheet. I figured I dialed the wrong number, so I hung up and tried again. I got the same woman on the line and we went through the same routine again. I was sure I was talking to the mother of the patient; I was positive she had decided that she didn't want the kid admitted, that she had never believed me in the first place, and that she had gone home and would deny that she had ever been to Jonas Bronck. It made me crazy! I told

Bob about this and he got angry, too. He called the number himself and told the woman in Spanish that the baby could be very sick and if she was lying about it and the kid did die, it wouldn't be his responsibility, it would be on the mother's head and not his. Amazing! I had never heard anybody using the concept of Jewish guilt translated into Spanish. It didn't work, so it may have lost something in the translation, because the woman told him he was crazy, that she had never heard of the people he was talking about, and if any of us tried to call her back again, she'd call the cops and have us all arrested.

Bob hung up, and his face was bright red. He yelled that I'd better call the police and have them go out to the address listed on the ER sheet and bring the baby back, dead or alive. That is, if the address listed was correct. So then I started trying to contact New York's finest. Jesus, what a day!

I called the precinct house in the neighborhood they lived in and spoke to the desk sergeant. He took all the information but didn't know what to do with it so he tried to connect me with his supervisor but somehow the phones got disconnected. So I called back and got somebody else, who reconnected me with the desk sergeant who again tried to connect me with the supervisor. While I was on hold, the senior resident came up to me and said, "The charts are starting to back up. When are you going to be done with this nonsense?" I started to answer but then someone picked up and I never finished my sentence. I had to give whoever was on the phone the information all over again, and he said, "Well, you understand we can't just go out there and arrest them. We can't drag them in against their will. If the woman doesn't want to come, we can't force her." I told him just to do his best; he said he'd try and asked for their address. When I gave it to him, he said, "That's in the projects, isn't it?" I didn't know, so he looked it up and said it was. Since it was the projects, it was out of the city cops' jurisdiction. He told me I'd have to call the Housing Police.

So I'm sitting in the emergency room, the patients are starting to pile up in the waiting room like the planes over Kennedy International Airport on a Sunday afternoon, and I'm getting a civics lesson in the structure of the New York City Police Department bureaucracy. I was pretty pissed off about all this. I called the number of the Housing Police and went through the same business again but finally a sergeant told me he'd send out a squad car to see what they could do.

I figured that phase of this mess was over and I went to pick up a new chart from the triage box but before I could even make my way to the microphone to call the next patient in from the waiting room, one of the nurses came running up to me and told me to follow her. She led me into the adult ER and there, in the holding area, lying on a stretcher, was the woman with the baby in her lap, both dead asleep. She had lost her way out to the waiting room, had come across this nice, cozy, empty stretcher, and had decided to use it to catch up on some sleep. I couldn't believe it! I went back to the ER, called Amy, and told her to come down and pick up her patient.

Then I remembered that a crack unit of the Housing Police was preparing to swoop down and make a raid on the woman's apartment. I figured it was my civic responsibility to try to prevent them from going on this wild-goose chase, but when I called, I found out I was too late; a squad car had already arrived at the projects and they couldn't be called back. About ten minutes later, two huge Housing Policemen marched into the ER leading this panicked little eight-year-old kid. "He said his mother wasn't home," one of the cops said. "He said she was still here with the baby." Bob and I explained the story to them very nicely. They weren't even upset. They didn't threaten to slug us in the mouth or anything. They even volunteered to take the boy back home. So the story had a happy ending. What a strange job this is!

I waste a lot of my time in the ER talking on the phone. If it's not the police, it's the labs. The lab techs don't give a shit about anything. There's this rule that before they give out any information to a house officer, they have to torture him verbally for a while. And if it's not the labs, it's a consultant from one of the subspecialty services who wants to avoid coming in to see a patient at all costs. And if it's not a consultant, it's the Bureau of Child Welfare. BCW's the worst! I never really knew what the term "terminal hold" meant until I made my first BCW referral. If putting people on hold were an Olympic sport, the BCW would be the gold medal winner. They can keep you waiting for twenty or thirty minutes without breaking a sweat. If all of us house officers could just see patients and not deal with the rest of the bullshit, there'd be no waiting to be seen in the emergency room.

Thursday, September 5, 1985

A week in the Outpatient Department has done me a lot of good. I'm more relaxed now, less on edge than I was on Infants'. Take Hanson, for instance. When I think about him I actually find myself laughing at some of the things that happened two and three weeks ago, how angry I got when he crumped. I guess with the passage of time, there'll come a point where I actually have fond memories of him. I can imagine: "Ahh, that Hanson, what a wonderful child, what I learned from him, how I wish I could take care of him again!" This is all kind of frightening. I think it's these kind of warped remembrances of internship by people in charge of training programs that keep us working every third night!

Sunday, September 8, 1985

I had this whole weekend off, and Carole and I sat down and actually tried to plan out my vacation. Carole can get only the second week of it off, so I'll have to figure out something to do the first week. We argued about it for a while; I wanted to go to some quaint New England village and just sack out, but Carole didn't like the idea of wasting a whole day in the car getting there and another whole day coming back. She wanted to go to some hotel in the Poconos. So we compromised: We're going to a hotel in the Poconos. Ahh, what the hell, it doesn't matter that much to me. Anywhere we go is fine. As long as there's a place to sleep and it's far away from here.

Working in the ER is fine. I'm seeing a lot of patients, nothing major or earth-shattering, just routine walk-in clinic pediatrics. I think I'm holding my own. I'm learning to do a lot of things I never knew how to do before. I'm even learning a little Spanish. I now can have three-year-olds refuse to open their mouths, stick out their tongues, and say "Ahhh" in two languages. Who says internship is not an educational experience?

Hanson keeps repeating on me like a bad hot dog you get from one of those umbrella carts. I got a call from Jennifer Urzo, the intern who picked him up when he came back to Infants' after being discharged from the ICU. She said he was doing fine, hadn't crumped in over a week, and wasn't he the most adorable thing I'd ever seen? I restrained myself. She said they're starting to think about discharging him and wanted to know if I had any idea how to get in touch with his mother. I told her I'd never set eyes on the woman, that she never once showed up during August, but if she was able to contact her, she should give me a call because there were a few things I'd like to say to her!

I have nothing much else to say. I can't wait till Thursday. Imagine, I'll be able to stay in bed past seven o'clock two days in a row!

BOB

September 1985

People who live outside of New York City carry a vivid image of what the Bronx is like. That image is based on a picture that appeared in newspapers around the country, a photograph of then-President Jimmy Carter standing amid the burned-out rubble of Charlotte Street. But the poverty and the dilapidation of the South Bronx is really only one view of the borough. At the opposite end of the spectrum, at the northernmost part of the Bronx, there's Riverdale, one of the wealthiest sections of New York City. And in between the North and the South there are numerous middle-class neighborhoods, each with its own special character and ethnic flavor. The people from all these communities share one thing in common: They receive their medical care at the hospitals in which our interns and residents work.

But the poor children of the South Bronx are by far the Pediatrics Department's biggest customers. They're the ones who crowd the waiting areas of our emergency rooms and fill past capacity the beds of our hospitals. Many of the problems from which these children suffer are directly related to the extreme poverty in which they live: They get anemia and growth failure because of inadequate diet, lead poisoning because they eat the paint chips that fall from the ancient walls and ceilings of their apartments, and asthma from inhaling the polluted air that hangs over the South Bronx like a deadly cloud. Other medical problems are indirectly related to the poverty: As young children they're physically and sexually abused and abandoned by their angry and frustrated parents and other adult caregivers; as adolescents, unable to find jobs or stimulation, seeing little to look forward to, they turn to drugs and sex, having babies when they themselves are still children and getting infected with venereal diseases and the human immunodeficiency virus in the bargain. And all these problems fall into the laps of our house officers, who have to work doubly hard to figure out how to relate to these abused children, sixteen-year-old mothers, and adolescent crackheads while very often functioning simultaneously as doctors, psychologists, and social workers.

The vast majority of the patients who come to the emergency rooms at Jonas Bronck and West Bronx hospitals are black or Hispanic. The vast majority of the house officers are white. Sometimes it's difficult for the patients to relate to these doctors who know very little about how poor people live or what makes them tick. When I was a resident, I saw a six-year-old boy who had come to the emergency room with a fever. I diagnosed an ear infection and prescribed an antibiotic in liquid form. I carefully instructed the boy's parents to give one teaspoonful of the medicine every six hours around the clock and to keep the container refrigerated. A week later, the child was back with the same symptoms. When I asked if they had given the medication as prescribed, the mother explained that she had tried, but since they didn't have electricity in their apartment, they couldn't keep the stuff refrigerated, nor was there enough light at night to measure it out. The therapy was bound to fail because I had no understanding of the social situation. It became necessary to treat the child with a capsule form of antibiotic to treat the infection effectively.

Dealing with these kinds of social situations is a huge problem for our house officers. As I've already mentioned, frequently social conditions are the direct cause of our patients' illnesses. The house officer can treat the asthma or the lead poisoning, but after the child is better, he or she will be sent back home and most likely will encounter the same environmental hazards that caused the illness in the first place. To provide really effective care, the home conditions would have to be altered, a monumental and frustrating task. Our overworked house officers wind up having to settle for treating the symptoms rather than the underlying disease, an unsatisfactory but necessary compromise.

Another big problem our interns and residents face is caused by their lack of understanding of their patients' cultural background. For example, people from certain areas of Puerto Rico have a very complex belief system based on hot and cold. Some illnesses are considered "hot," some are thought to be "cold." Similarly, remedies are believed to be effective for either hot or cold illnesses, but usually not for both. If a doctor prescribes what turns out to be a "cold" remedy for a "hot" illness, not only will the parent of the patient not use the medication, but also he or she will lose all confidence in that doctor.

Many of our patients speak no English and must rely on a doctor, nurse, or other patient to translate for them. In the emergency room, this slows down the doctors' progress through the pile of charts of patients waiting to be seen, lengthening the waiting time dramatically. The net effect of all these problems is that hostility builds between patient and caregiver.

Sometimes there's a great deal of hostility. Many of our patients use the emergency room as a kind of walk-in clinic, showing up at all hours of the day or night for problems the house officers consider trivial: belly aches that have been going on for three or four months, headaches for which no aspirin or Tylenol has been tried, mild gastroenteritis, complaints that the interns and residents know could be handled in a clinic setting, over the phone, or by the parents just using a little common sense. Since no one who shows up at the door of the ER can be turned away, the house staff winds up having to see these patients, getting backed up, and ultimately losing sleep because of what they consider this abuse of the system. And when one is chronically sleep-deprived, this can easily turn into resentment and anger, the ultimate effect of which is that the house officer will come to view the patient as an enemy.

Although hostility might exist between patient and doctor, it's nothing compared with the hostility that exists between a doctor and some of the other members of the staff. The best example of this is the relationship between the interns and the people who work in the laboratories. The intern knows, almost instinctively, that fighting with the lab technicians will only bring him or her misery. No matter what happens, arguing with a technician is a fight the intern can only lose. The lab technicians, after all, hold the key to the completion of the scut list; without the results of lab tests, the intern can never go home. But sometimes it's impossible to hold back.

As a house officer, I managed to hold back every time but one. When I was a senior resident, I was taking care of a sick preemie who was scheduled to go to the operating room the following day. It was my job to make sure that the child was pre-op'd, which included sending a specimen of blood to the blood bank for typing. The intern on call that night tried six times to get blood from this poor baby, who seemed to possess no visible veins in his entire body. I tried and failed four more times. Finally, on my fifth attempt, I succeeded; I managed to get about two cc's of blood.

I put the precious specimen in the proper tube, gave it to the medical student who had volunteered to carry it down to the lab, and went on with the rest of my work. About two hours later, a nurse happened to mention to me that the technician in the blood bank had called and said that because the tube and lab slip had been signed by a medical student instead of a doctor, it had not been acceptable. He had tossed the specimen in the trash and now was demanding a second sample.

Needless to say, I got angry. Trying to hold myself back, I ran down to the lab. I explained to the technician how difficult it had been to get that blood; I described in vivid detail how small and sick the baby was. He told me he was sorry, but rules were rules; unless a person with M.D. after his or her name has signed in exactly the right places, he had been instructed to dump the tube.

I got angrier. I started searching the trash cans in and around the blood bank. The guy caught me and said, "It won't do you any good. I poured it down the sink."

That's when I really lost it. Three years' worth of repressed anger at laboratory personnel was immediately released in a single, spectacular tirade. I cursed out this technician, I cursed out his mother, his father, the rest of his family and friends; I went on for at least ten minutes. He didn't say a word, he just continued doing what he had been doing when I had first appeared. When I finally ran out of steam, I went back up to the ward and tried to get another sample of blood from the baby. It took only three attempts this time, but I got it, carefully signed the tube and lab slip, and dropped it off myself.

This kind of explosion is not uncommon. Lab technicians have a great deal of work to do and have a lot of people on their backs trying to get results. It's impossible to make everyone happy, so frequently no one is made happy. Many house officers will tell you that dealing with lab technicians is the most aggravating of all their jobs.

Perhaps all of these little aggravations make working as an intern in the Bronx more difficult than working in some other area of the world. Battling the environment, the patients, and certain members of the hospital's ancillary staff while chronically overtired is no mean feat. Year after year our house staff does it, and they learn to do it well. But the question still remains: Is it all worth it?

ANDY

October 1985

Monday, September 30, 1985

I guess I'm starting to get sick of talking about internship. I don't talk about it to other people very much anymore; I used to think maybe I shouldn't talk about it, maybe people wouldn't be able to understand what I was saying, but now I just don't want to anymore. Nobody fucking understands.

I'm over at University Hospital now, into my fourth month. I'm going to lose my mind before I make it to my first vacation. I have three more months to go, so I'm now only slightly more than halfway there. I've finished a quarter of my internship year. If you include vacations, I've finished a third of it. Yeah, only eighty more nights on call, right?

My apartment has become disgusting. I have so many roaches, they're crawling all over the place. I turn on the faucet and the water goes in the sink and the roaches come cruising out. They all dive off the edge of the sink right onto you if you don't move fast enough, because they're trying to get away from the water. Too many roaches, no one to talk to about roaches; no one to talk to about roachy thoughts. I wish there were people on my team I felt buddy-buddy with, like last month. But there aren't any.

Thursday, October 3, 1985

I'm really tired. I don't have anything to say anymore. I've been feeling depressed and apathetic and ground down lately. Tomorrow I canceled plans to go out with a friend. You know what I want to do instead? I want to be by myself. Isn't that weird?

Tomorrow's a precall night, the only time I ever feel even a little rested, my only chance to have a little fun. And all I want to do is be by myself.

There were a couple of times today when I thought I should never have become a doctor. I just don't have what it takes. I don't know, it must not be true, people say I'm really good sometimes. But that's how I was feeling.

Putting in too many IVs . . . yeah . . . yeah . . .

Friday, October 4, 1985, 1:00 A.M.

Should I tell you about the baby who died the other night when I was on call? Should I tell you? Another one died, this one right in front of my eyes. A DNR baby [**DNR: "do not resuscitate": DNR orders are written only after careful consultation with all parties involved in the patient's care, including the child's parents**], very sick. She was born with multiple congenital anomalies and they couldn't figure out what caused them. She had terrible heart disease and it was only a matter of time.

She had been admitted the day before I was on call because she was severely hyponatremic [**had a marked deficiency of sodium, an essential electrolyte, in her blood**]. As soon as she hit the floor, all these consulting services came to see her: genetics, renal, neurology, and endocrinology, you name it, they came by. Harrison, the intern who had admitted her, signed her out to me, saying that nobody knew what the hell was going on with her but that it didn't really matter because she was DNR, and if she crumped, I wasn't supposed to do anything but stand by and watch. The only scut he told me to do was that if she died, I was supposed to call the neurologist so they could do a brain biopsy [**take a specimen of brain in hopes that studying it would suggest a diagnosis**].

It hadn't been a bad night; things were pretty quiet. Then at about eight o'clock, a nurse came and told me and the resident that the baby's breathing had stopped for a few seconds but then started again. The resident and I went in to look, and sure enough, she was having these long pauses in breathing. I did a quick physical exam and couldn't find anything specific that was different except the breathing pattern. We asked the nurse just to watch her, and we went back to the nurses' station.

About five minutes later, the nurse came running out again,

saying, "Now she's not breathing at all!" We went back into the room and found that the nurse was right; the baby wasn't breathing; she was also bradycardic [**had a slow heart rate**]. The resident grabbed an ambubag and started bagging her and the heart rate started coming up again. Then all of the sudden it hit me: We were resuscitating a DNR baby. By that point it was too late: The heart rate had come back to normal.

I felt bad; I mean, this might have been the baby's one chance to die, and by resuscitating her, we kind of screwed that up. No telling how much longer the baby was going to hang on now. I went back in to talk to the father, who had been sitting in the room this whole time, to tell him we weren't going to do any more resuscitation. The father agreed.

About an hour later, the nurse came to tell us the baby wasn't breathing. We went back into the room, but this time we just quietly walked over to the bedside and listened to her chest. She still had a heart rate, but there wasn't much respiratory effort left in her. She was white as a sheet; I've never seen a baby that white before.

We stood over her like that for a while, occasionally listening to her heart, and finally, after about fifteen minutes, it stopped. The baby was dead. I looked up to the resident, expecting him to say something, and he just stood there with a goofy look on his face. I was thinking, You're in charge, you've got to say something. But he didn't say a word. It was very uncomfortable for a while, and finally I had to say it. I had to tell the father that the baby had died. There I am again, having to tell a parent that his kid was dead. I still have no formal training in it, but once again, the job fell to me. Why am I always the one? At least this time, everyone was expecting it, so it didn't come as a shock. But it still made my skin crawl.

I took the father outside the room and let him sit by himself for a while. Then I had the nurses come back and together we cleaned the baby up, took out all the tubes and stuff that had been in her. We swaddled her in a blanket and cleaned up the room. I had learned to do this in the NICU; after babies had died in there, the attending always tried to put everything in order before letting the parents spend time with their child. It made a lot of sense to me. So when we were all ready, the father came back in, I handed him the baby and sat him down on a chair. He held the baby, and we all left the room so he'd have some privacy. Standing outside, I could hear him cry. I started crying a little myself.

After a few minutes, I went to call the neurology attending. She was a total bitch; she yelled at me for not calling when the baby had stopped breathing the first time. I told her I had been told to call her after the baby had died, not when the baby was dying. I thought I was doing them all a favor, and all I got for it was a bunch of abuse. She told me I might have ruined any chance of making a diagnosis because of the delay. Shit!

Well, that was my last night on call. I've been feeling a little better, though. I wasn't completely depressed at work today. I actually enjoyed myself a little bit. I realized there are two things that make me enjoy work: sleep and not being on call. Being on call is the worst because when you're on call, even if you get very tired and you have tons of work to do, you still have to do it, there's no one around to help you out. It's very stressful. Being postcall is next worst because you're really tired and you always have a fair amount of work still to do, but you feel some relief because you're finally off the hook. Of course, the best time is when you're not on call and you're not tired, like today. I really liked that, it was really nice. Internship could almost be good if there were more times like today.

Sunday, October 6, 1985

I just got home. I'm postcall, I got no sleep, it was a busy night. I admitted four patients, which isn't bad, but there was an AIDS patient who was exsanguinating [**hemorrhaging; losing all his blood**] on the floor, a renal transplant kid who was in the midst of an acute rejection crisis, and some other patients who were basically causing trouble. My admissions were hideously staggered throughout the day and night, and I didn't know what the fuck was happening.

I actually got a really interesting case last night: a little kid with argininosuccinicacidemia [**an extremely rare inborn error of metabolism caused by a deficiency of an essential enzyme that results in liver disease, neurologic dysfunction, frequent infections, and, often, death in early childhood**]. The kid is really sick, but he looks just like the Michelin Man. He's got layers of fat around his belly and arms and legs, and it looks like tires. It's hard to feel sympathy for him because I laugh every time I look at him.

Harvey Abelson, the director of pediatric home care, the service that manages all the chronically sick patients, is the Michelin Man's doctor. He's really nice and he's smart and he's a good teacher from what I can tell. Very intense, totally intense guy.

The transplant kid sounds like the beginning of a sad story. He got this new kidney in August. His mother donated it to him. There were some problems around the time of the transplant, but he pulled through. Now he comes in with rejection crisis. His blood pressure's about 180/140 [normal for this patient would have been about 100/60]. They're talking about having to take out the good kidney to bring down the blood pressure. The mother's beside herself.

Monday, October 7, 1985, 11:00 P.M.

I think I want to be Harvey Abelson when I grow up. He's hyper but he's a pretty impressive guy. He's right on top of everything all the time. You should see him working out what needs to be done with the Michelin Man. He knows everything! Yes, Harvey Abelson, that's who I want to be.

My brother got married today. He didn't want anybody else to be there, so he invited only a couple of people. My parents weren't invited, I wasn't invited, we were "uninvited." I wished I could have been there, but I respect their wishes. My parents, however, are major-league pissed off. My brother and his wife, they were going to do it in December but then at the last minute they decided to do it today. I heard about it, of course, from Karen. I don't know . . . there has to be a better way.

I had to stay late tonight to get my work done. My transplant patient seems to be better; his renal function's coming back and his mother's calmed down a little, too. But there was a lot of scut work to do so I had to stay until nearly eight. Now I'm going to bed. A solitary life, that's what I'm leading.

Let me check if there're any roaches in my bed. I've had roaches in my bed recently, roaches crawling in my bed. I woke up the other day and there was a dead roach underneath me. I must have rolled over and squished it.

I don't know how I'm going to make it until Christmas, when I have my vacation. I just don't know how I'm going to make it. It's just too long.

Some kid asked me what I was doing, who I was today. He asked me if I was a doctor and what kind of doctor I was. I told him I was a hospital doctor. Just a hospital doctor. Someday I'll look back on all this and cry. Has it always been this hard?

Tuesday, October 8, 1985

I've got to do something about this. I've been wallowing in this low- to moderate-grade depression for about the past month now, and that's all I'm doing is wallowing. I can't stand this feeling anymore. I've got to do something about changing my attitude. It's the only way, because if you can't go over and you can't bow out, you gotta go through it. And that's what I've got to do.

Thursday, October 10, 1985

I spent a long time teaching my medical student today, telling him about fluids and electrolytes. Very exciting! I feel like I don't know anything. I guess that's not exactly true, though. I do know how to teach about fluids and electrolytes. But that's about it.

And I got myself reorganized again. Started using my daily flow sheets again on all my patients, something I hadn't done for the past week because I was too depressed. I didn't give a shit, and I never really knew what was going on, and that made me more depressed and so I gave less of a shit. Getting organized should help. Getting organized will make things better.

I'm feeling kind of horny these days. Doesn't help having Karen two hundred and fifty miles away. Kind of get to eyeing the nurses, you know? But I don't think I'm going to follow up on any of that. Nope! Think I'll just stay true blue and all that stuff. It's just a couple more weeks; I think I can make it.

It turns out that Harrison Boyd, the other intern on our team this month, is completely insane. He's got a very funny, terrible sense of humor. Very bad jokes, the worst! And Laura Santon, who is always happy, actually looked depressed today for the first time. Maybe she was just spacing out, but she looked kind of upset. I was surprised.

Had pizza for the hundred and fifty thousandth time for dinner tonight. Seems that's all I ever eat around here, pizza. Missed the shuttle [the bus that travels between Mount Scopus, Jonas Bronck, and University Hospital], had to take a cab home, and got a free, unguided tour of the Bronx, because they always take some strange route. Very interesting, the Bronx at night. Very exciting. I could have done without it.

Sunday, October 13, 1985, Morning

I've had so many nights of sleep in a row, I practically don't know what to do with myself. Yessirree, I was on call Friday night and I got seven and a half hours of uninterrupted sleep, breaking all records heretofore known for all interns in this program. It sure is a record for me. And it was good timing because my parents are here this weekend, they came down on Saturday. So it was great.

I just came back from medical records at Mount Scopus. I had a lot of charts to complete and I had to go over today because they were threatening to withhold my paycheck if I didn't finish them. It's impossible to get over to the record room during the week when you're on the other campus. It's so weird: I went back to these charts, two of them for babies who died. One was on a baby that was born premature in the bed. When the baby had been born, I was the first one to get to the labor room, and I didn't know what to do. Here's this little chart and I'm supposed to fill out the discharge summary. There was the autopsy report; it said the baby weighed 460 grams and had atelectasis [collapsed alveoli, the air sacs in the lungs], visceral congestion [accumulation of blood in the circulation going to the internal organs], PDA [patent ductus arteriosus, a persistence of the opening of the structure that, in fetal life, shunts blood from the underdeveloped lungs to the rest of the body], and patent for amen ovale [a communication between the left and right atria of the heart that allows oxygenated and deoxygenated blood to mix]; no big deal. It was just a really preemie baby. Four hundred sixty grams, it might just have been SGA [small for gestational age]. At any rate, I still feel kind of sad about it. Maybe we could have done something, we could have resuscitated it. Months later and I'm still wondering. Well, anyway, it's sad. The chart was wafer thin. There wasn't much to it; a baby who was born and then died. All it had was a heartbeat; it never had an Apgar of more than one. **[Apgar: a scoring system used in the immediate newborn period designed to measure neonatal well-being. The baby is evaluated in five categories: heart rate, respiratory rate, color, muscle tone, and response to stimuli. Zero, one, or two points are awarded in each category, and the maximum score is ten. Babies are evaluated at one and five minutes after birth. Apgar scores above seven are considered normal. Less than five are definitely abnormal.]** It's very sad. The mother was a thirty-one-year-old woman, she has three living children, maybe she was happy this happened. Maybe eight months from now I'll get named in a lawsuit. Who knows?

You can't focus on the negative all the time, you know? That's what I'm trying to do now, that's my new approach. I still haven't found a way to focus on the positive. In fact, I'm still finding it hard to decide what is positive. I guess it's positive when things turn out well, and when you have a good relationship with a family. That's good. That's the most positive thing I can think of right now.

It's pretty nice having my parents here this weekend. My father rented this total junker of a car. It sounded like the wheels were about to fall off at any moment. It's tiny, you can park it anywhere. I took them down to Soho yesterday; that was fun, they had a good time. Then we went to the Upper East Side and had dinner at this really nice Italian restaurant; nothing fancy, just very nice.

Then I went to sleep and Karen called at some point, I don't know, I was half asleep, I don't remember anything she said. I've had so many conversations with Karen over the phone where I don't remember anything, or I remember hardly anything. It's disgusting, it's totally disgusting.

I found myself reassuring my parents last night that this neighborhood was really okay. Isn't that funny? Because just a few months ago I was telling them how much I hated it. I don't like it, really, but I don't feel threatened so much anymore. I don't think it's a really bad neighborhood; it's not beautiful, but . . .

I'm feeling better now, I'm not feeling depressed, I'm starting to feel like there's an end in sight. I know it's too early to be saying that, but if you look at it, there's twelve months in this year. A hundred divided by 12: That's $8\frac{1}{3}$ percent of the internship per month. At the end of this month, I'll have completed four months; that's $33\frac{1}{3}$ percent. If you add in vacation time, well, then you're at $41\frac{2}{3}$ percent. So at the end of this month, if you include vacation time, which is really free time, I'll have completed over 40 percent of my internship. Not bad! Not bad at all! Forty percent: That has a definite, hefty ring to it. Forty percent! That means I have survived the beginning. I really have, I've gotten through the hell of being an early intern. Whatever hell lies ahead, and I'm sure there's more, at least this has been survived.

Sunday, October 13, 1985, Late at Night

My parents have gone. I felt kind of lonely after they left. I sat down and did a little paperwork, paid a bill, wrote a letter to somebody, and I feel a little better now. It bummed me out because I have to go into work tomorrow and be on call. And I know I need a vacation, I know I need it, but I'll just have to wait. I know I'll make it.

> I'll just have to wait.
> It'll be so great.
> To be on vacation
> And to sleep late.

Friday, October 18, 1985

Postcall. Cleared my bed for roaches. In bed here, getting ready to make the big snooze after a rough night on call at University Hospital. Tomorrow I've got to decide what to do with my life. I've been talking with the director of the program I originally wanted to go to up in Boston. He says there's a place for me back there for next year if I want it. I have to decide if I should stay or if I should go. I don't know what the fuck to do, and I'm too tired to think about it now.

Yesterday I got my first kid with AIDS; actually it's ARC [AIDS-related complex], but still, it's the first kid I ever admitted with the big "A." I don't know, it's no big deal; it's just another horrible, fatal disease. Our team got a talk from the immunologist about the disease. Part of it was about health workers with AIDS, and every one of us started wondering if we had it. We were wondering whether we, the people who suck meconium [**the first bowel movement; when breathed in by a neonate, it can cause severe respiratory disease**] out of the mouths of newborns have gotten AIDS yet. Who knows? Sometimes I think maybe I should go and get myself tested or something. Then at other times I think, what difference does it make?

I had dinner tonight with Ellen. Bought a little Indian food and came back here and ate it. She conked out and went home. That's life when your only friends are interns.

Monday, October 21, 1985

I didn't get much sleep last night, less than an hour. It was a pretty hard night at University. Goddamn renal transplant patient came in! Nice kid for a whining three-year-old. Got his mom's kidney. Jesus Christ, I think the nephrology attendings sit around just thinking of more tests they can order. Anyway, they transplanted the kidney and the kid looked like a million bucks afterward. I hadn't slept all day, and I looked like about thirty cents! I spent two fucking hours in the recovery room; it seemed like I was in there forever. Before the kid came in, there were like a thousand people, a big commotion, everybody wanted to get involved. Then when they saw nothing too exciting was happening, they all split and all of the sudden it was me sitting there alone. All the nurses, all the nephrologists, all the surgeons, they were gone! There's just this kid and I'm in charge. It turned out to be no big deal; nothing happened. I had to make a couple of decisions, but hey, I think I know how to do that. But I didn't get much sleep.

And so what do I do? I get out of work, come home, and stay awake for like three hours! I could have gone to sleep at like seven or eight o'clock. I'm totally overtired. I slept through half of attending rounds today. I didn't even make any bones about it, I just leaned on my elbow and went to sleep. I must be crazy!

I don't know, I guess I just like to come home and pretend I have a life or something. So you know what I wound up doing tonight? I watched TV. I haven't sat and watched TV since well before my internship. Isn't that interesting? Very interesting. Interesting as a pond of mud.

Tomorrow's Tuesday, and Mike Miller is probably going to ask me what I'm planning to do next year. I don't know what the fuck I'm going to tell him. I don't know if I'm going to tell him the truth about this job offer in Boston or what. I'm still trying to make up my mind about it. It depends a lot on Karen, too. She has to decide whether she wants to do her internship in Boston or come down here to one of the real hot shit New York programs. I tried to call her tonight to talk to her about it, but she wasn't home.

My eyes are burning. Someone told me at work that they're really red. What do you expect? Christ, I lie down, trying to get an hour of sleep, and the nurses wake me up. Fucking transplant kid had a headache. I had a headache, too, for God's sake, and I didn't see why the hell they had to wake me up about the transplant kid. But no, they said he had a headache and they took his pressure and it had decided to hop up from 120 to 180.

So I called the renal fellow and told him the kid's pressure was up and he told me to give him a dose of captopril [an antihypertensive medication]. I gave it, the pressure immediately came down, and I went back to bed. About a half hour later, just as I was getting into some deep sleep, a nurse knocks on the door and tells me this other renal kid had a headache. It's an epidemic, for Christ's sake.

I went to see this second patient, and she said that not only did she have a headache but she also had fucking blurry vision. And her blood pressure was 200. So I gave her some captopril, too, and her pressure came down, but she was still complaining of the headache and the blurry vision. I thought about it for a while and I figured, screw it; if her pressure's down, there's nothing wrong. There wasn't anything else I could do.

I went in to talk to her and tried to calm her down. She said she'd try going to sleep. I went back to the on-call room but now I couldn't fall asleep. I was too worried about her.

So I got back up and went to her room and sure enough, she was sound asleep.

I kept getting woken up all night long for little things. It was a quiet night and I still couldn't get any sleep.

Another week to go at University Hospital. It'll be a great feeling to be a third of the way through the year, knowing I've completed four tedious months of internship.

Friday, October 25, 1985

I just woke up. I was on call the night before last and I'm on again tonight. I'm doing an every-other, which is okay, I guess, because I get the weekend off. Thank God.

Karen called last night, I think. I think she called and said she'd been offered a place in Boston at the program she wanted to go to. But I'm not sure. I was so tired! I've managed to hold them off here. Mike Miller asked me whether I'm planning to be a resident here next year. He offered me the job. I told him I wasn't sure yet, that I had to do some thinking. We've got to make a decision about this pretty soon.

Tomorrow is my last day at University Hospital. So what have I learned this month? I don't know. Maybe I've learned how to handle many patients all at once. I don't think I learned too much about kidneys, even though that's about all we see.

I better get up before I fall back to sleep.

Saturday, October 26, 1985

My last night at University turned out to be pretty shitty. Everybody on the ward was sick. They all had fever spikes and high blood pressure and headaches, and everything necessary to ruin my day.

And then in the evening, Henry got sick. I guess I haven't mentioned Henry yet. He's an eighteen-year-old with Down syndrome who's had end-stage renal failure for a long time. He's pretty high-functioning: He's no genius or anything, but he's a really sweet kid with a good personality, and everybody loves him.

Henry has a cadaveric transplant [**transplanted kidney obtained from a cadaver**] and hasn't been doing very well. He came in at the beginning of the month with rejection crisis.

We gave him steroids and he got better and went home. Then earlier this week he got admitted because he was rejecting the kidney again; he's been hypertensive and peeing tea-colored urine for days. We've been giving him these massive doses of antirejection medication but he seems to be getting sicker and sicker.

He got really sick last night. He'd been feverish in the afternoon, but we weren't told about it. The nurse who took his temperature called the renal fellow directly and didn't bother informing us. At about six o'clock last night, the fellow called to find out what the results of the sepsis workup were. "What sepsis workup?" I asked. That's how I found out that Henry had spiked a fever.

I went in to see him at that point. He was feverish to about 102 and was tachypneic [breathing rapidly]. He didn't look very comfortable. I ordered some Tylenol for him and told the nurses to sponge him down. As the night wore on, he became more and more tachypneic and his fever just wouldn't stay down.

At about ten o'clock, he was looking really uncomfortable. I ordered a chest X ray and drew a blood gas. I brought the blood gas down to the lab myself but I couldn't find the technician for about ten minutes. He was hiding in a back room somewhere. I finally found him and he ran the test grudgingly. The gas just showed a little hypoxia [the oxygen was a little low], so I went back upstairs, put Henry in 35 percent oxygen, and then went down to radiology to look at the chest X ray. It didn't look too bad, but when I got back to Henry's room, he was looking more uncomfortable. We turned up his oxygen to 50 percent and, after about another half hour, I did another blood gas. I ran it down to the lab, and again I couldn't fucking find the technician anywhere. I looked all over the damned place; the guy was nowhere to be seen. I spent at least fifteen minutes looking for him. And when I finally found him and told him that I had a really sick patient and needed the gas stat, he said, "I have something else to do stat. I'll get around to yours when I have a chance."

I was ready to strangle the guy! I had already wasted fifteen minutes looking for him and now he was telling me I was going to have to wait longer. And for all I knew, while I was down fucking around with this technician, Henry could have been arresting up on the ward. I was tempted to run the blood gas myself, but I knew that if I touched the machine the guy would have my head on a platter. And yelling at him was completely pointless because I knew that the more you yelled, the more hostile he'd become, and the longer he would take to run the sample. So I just sat on the stool feeling my blood pressure go through the roof.

Finally, the guy picked up the sample, strolled over to the machine, and did it. The gas was pretty lousy. I ran upstairs and showed the resident. Henry was going into respiratory failure in front of our eyes. He was just going down the tubes. And he was scared shitless.

We called the nephrologist and told him we were going to intubate Henry and bring him over to the ICU, and he told us to go ahead. We called the anesthesiology resident, and he did a great job of intubating him. We put him on a respirator and brought him down the hall [**University Hospital's ICU, located down the hall from the Pediatrics ward, admits patients of all ages**].

I spent the whole night in there with him. He was all squared away by about three in the morning, but we had to stay and monitor him constantly. At least he was stable on the respirator. He wasn't getting any sicker and he seemed more comfortable. And I didn't have to deal with that lab technician again because the unit has its own blood gas machine.

Then, this morning, we spent until about noon rounding. I felt like warmed-over shit. After rounds, I went back to the ICU to write a note in Henry's chart, detailing what had happened the night before, and as I was sitting there, one of the nurses called a code. There was this obese, middle-aged guy whose heart had completely stopped beating. He was in fucking asystole [**without a heartbeat**]! And there was no doctor around other than me.

I jumped up onto his chest and started doing compressions. After about ten minutes, the critical-care fellow showed up with a bunch of medical residents trailing behind. But all those guys did was stand around for a while and discuss what to do. They didn't even offer to help. Finally, they decided to shock him [**apply an electrical charge to the chest in hopes that this will start the heart beating again**], so I jumped off his chest. They got his heart beating again and they figured he was stable, so everybody disappeared. I sat back down and tried to finish my note, but fifteen minutes later the same nurse yelled out that the guy had arrested again. And again, nobody was around. So I jumped back on his chest and started CPR again. This time the critical-care fellow showed up with the code team really fast, but again, they all stood around talking while I was doing the resuscitation. Finally I said, "Does somebody else want to do this? I'm from Pediatrics, for God's sake!" I couldn't believe it.

Finally, one of them took over for me and I went to finish my note. They got the guy's heart beating again, but what would have happened if I hadn't been there? The guy would have fucking died because there wasn't a doctor around to do CPR. And I wasn't even supposed to be there. What kind of care are these patients getting?

AMY

October 1985

Saturday, October 5, 1985

I really needed things to calm down a little after last month ended, but it doesn't look like that's going to happen. I finally got away from Barry Bresnan, but I wound up on the Adolescents ward at Mount Scopus, and it's been terrible. I'm tired, and I'm fed up. I need a vacation. I have one coming up at the end of this month. I hope I'll be able to make it till then.

It's been really busy on Adolescents and it's very depressing. Half the beds are filled with fourteen- and fifteen-year-olds with leukemia, brain tumors, you name it. And the other half is all girls with anorexia nervosa who are completely crazy! It's impossible to talk to them, it's impossible to do anything for them. They just want to be left alone, do their aerobics, vomit in any secret hiding place they can find, and lose weight. They don't want anyone coming near them, especially not a doctor who might actually be able to do something to help them.

My most difficult patient is this eighteen-year-old girl with choriocarcinoma [**a malignant tumor derived from the products of a pregnancy**]. Two weeks ago, she was completely fine. She knew she was pregnant, and she was looking forward to having the baby. Then suddenly she started having some cramping and bleeding and she came to the ER where the gynecologist saw her. They figured she was having a miscarriage so they did a D and C. The stuff they took out looked strange. They sent it to pathology and found out it was cancer. She got admitted to me on Monday, the first day of the month. We did a quick workup that showed the cancer had spread all over the place, to her lungs, her brain, everywhere.

127

On Wednesday or maybe it was Thursday, she got sick; she had a headache and was vomiting. The oncologists figured it must have been due to mets in her brain [**metastases to the brain cause increased pressure within the skull, leading to symptoms such as headache, vomiting, irritability, etc.**]. We started chemo [**chemotherapy**] on Thursday afternoon, but that didn't help. In fact, she felt a hundred times worse; she spent all yesterday vomiting. It's pathetic.

I hate going into her room. On the one hand, I know her prognosis isn't bad, even with the mets; but on the other hand, I know what this girl's going to have to go through over the next few months: She's going to have a lot of chemo, her hair's going to fall out, she's going to be vomiting constantly, she'll have to spend a lot of time in the hospital. Also, if we can't eliminate the cancer with chemo, the next step is to do a hysterectomy. It's really sad. And so sudden; I mean, one day, she was looking forward to having a baby, the next day she finds out that not only is she having a miscarriage, but also she's got cancer that's spread all over her body, and if it can't be controlled with medication, she may have to have a hysterectomy and never be able to have any children. She's very depressed; you can't blame her. I haven't told her about Sarah. I don't know if it would be good for her to know I've got a baby. It might depress her more.

She's the worst, but they're all like that. I've got an eighteen-year-old who's got a brain tumor. He was fine until about six months ago, when he started waking up having to vomit every morning, with really bad headaches. He came to the emergency room; they did a CT scan, and it showed this huge mass. He's spent a lot of time in the hospital, getting the works, surgery, chemotherapy, radiation, but he's just gotten sicker and sicker. At this point he knows he's going to die and he doesn't want anything done anymore. He screams at any doctor who comes near him. He only trusts one person and that's one of the nurses.

The only good thing about working on this ward is that there're a lot of doctor types around, so nobody gets too many patients. We've got three interns and two subinterns on our team and the whole ward holds only thirty-five patients, so the most anyone can get is seven if things are equally distributed. But seven of these patients are worth fourteen University Hospital patients!

There is one other good thing about this ward: Susannah's working here this month, too. If she hadn't been around last month, I'm positive I would have gone crazy. As it was, I don't know how I survived it. So it's good to have her here. But I can see that neither of us is going to be able to keep the same hours we had last month. The days of getting out at three o'clock in the afternoon are definitely over.

Things at home are quiet. Sarah has a little cold, but I don't think it's too bad. I'm not worried about it. I've been feeling kind of sick myself, so I think we've probably got the same virus. I spent most of today sleeping. I'm on tomorrow, so I won't get to spend any time with her again. It's really impossible being a mother like this.

Thursday, October 10, 1985, 9:00 P.M.

What a week! This has definitely been the worst week of my internship. Every bad thing you could think of has happened to me. And it's not over yet. I've got all day tomorrow and I'm on Saturday.

First, Sarah got sick. She woke up last Saturday night at about 3:00 A.M., screaming her brains out. She had a fever of 103 and she just wouldn't stop crying. I was sure she had meningitis; that's what kept going through my head, "She's got meningitis, she needs a spinal tap, and she'll have to be hospitalized for two weeks and then she's going to end up retarded and I'm going to have to go to work tomorrow and every day from now on and try not to think about it." I somehow got her and myself dressed and we brought her over to the Jonas Bronck emergency room. She kept crying all the way over; she was inconsolable. Rhonda Bennett was the night float. She saw Sarah right away. I was sure she was going to examine her and turn to me and say she needed to draw blood and do an LP [lumbar puncture], but no, she found that all it was was a bad otitis [otitis media: infection of the middle ear, a common medical problem during the first few years of life]. She just gave us some Amoxicillin [an antibiotic used to treat otitis media] and Tylenol and said she'd be fine in a couple of days.

What a relief! We went back home but I didn't sleep a wink for the rest of that night. Sarah stayed up screaming until about five in the morning, when I guess the Tylenol started to work. She finally fell asleep, but I had to get up and go to the hospital and be on call like usual, as if nothing had happened. I was tired and nauseous and I couldn't concentrate on anything all day except Sarah. I called Larry about forty times. Sarah had a fever most of the day but it was gone by the night and Larry said she looked better.

I admitted this girl with conjunctivitis [**inflammation of the conjunctiva, the outer part of the eye; also called "pink eye"**] who turned out to have GC [**gonococcus, the bacteria that causes gonorrhea; gonococcal conjunctivitis can be very serious, potentially causing blindness, therefore the infection must be treated very vigorously**]. I washed my hands about a hundred times after I examined her but I was sure I got some of the stuff into my eyes. I was positive I was going to turn out to have GC conjunctivitis.

I got maybe an hour of sleep Sunday night and then I had to stay to start fresh on Monday. By that morning I was sick as a dog. I was vomiting and I was sure I had a fever. Larry was going to take the day off from work and stay home with Sarah, but he got called into his office on some emergency, so he had to leave her with Marie, who I'm not sure I trust with medication. I tried to get my work done so I could get home, but I was running at about 10 percent of my usual speed. Susannah told me just to go home, that she'd take care of my patients, but she wasn't feeling so well herself. Of course, nobody else volunteered to help, neither of the subinterns, who have a total of three patients between them; or the other intern, who I must say had to go to clinic that afternoon; or the resident. I plugged on and on and I didn't get home until about seven. By that point I felt like I was going to die. I didn't even care about Sarah anymore. I just got into bed and fell asleep.

When I woke up on Tuesday my eyes were glued shut. I had conjunctivitis. I was sure I had GC. I wanted to go to the hospital and scratch that girl's eyes out, but when I tried to get up I realized I wasn't going anywhere. I literally couldn't get out of bed. My arms felt like they weighed a ton each. I called Arlene, the chief who was on that day, and told her I had the flu and wasn't able to come in. She gave me a really hard time. "Are you sure you can't make it?" she asked me. "Are you really too sick to come to work?" I couldn't believe it!

Larry had to go to work again that day. Before he left, I had him go out and get me some medicine and I wound up staying home and fighting with Marie all day. We mostly fought over little things, but I'll tell you, it's a good thing I'm away at work all day because if I had to spend a lot of time with that woman, I'm sure it'd be the beginning of World War III. Of course, if I wasn't away at work all day, there'd be no reason for her to be coming into my house.

I couldn't face spending another day alone with her, so I went to work yesterday. I was also on call, and there's no way you can call in sick on a day you're on call. When I got to the ward, I found out nothing had been done on any of my patients the whole day before. They had left everything for me! It wasn't like everyone was busy or anything like that, they just didn't think to help me out. So I had a stack of labs to check, notes to write, consults to call, tests to schedule, tons of scut. I got yelled at by the oncologists for not doing something on one of their patients. How could I have done it? I was sick in bed all day!

And I found out that my patient with choriocarcinoma had developed a painful infection in her mouth. She got these sores last week and they were getting worse so I sent off a culture and it turned out to be monilia [a common type of fungus]. It was so painful, she hadn't been able to eat or drink for thirty-six hours! She couldn't chew or bite, and nobody had even thought to give her anything to make her feel better. When I went into her room, she was literally crying in pain. I talked to the oncologists, and they hadn't even been told about it. We decided to give her some morphine to see if that relieved the pain. I shot it into her IV and held her hand. Within three minutes, she was feeling better. What's going to happen to her when I leave at the end of the month?

Anyway, I didn't have a bad night, but I only got about three hours of sleep, and this morning I was feeling lousy again. I don't give a damn anymore about anything! When everybody showed up for work this morning, I just told them I was going home. I came home, went to sleep, and slept until a little while ago. Larry's home and Sarah's pretty much back to normal. I feel better myself today. It's not good being a sick intern. You never get a chance to recover. I can see that this flu is going to drag on until the end of the month because I'm just not going to get a chance to rest it out until then. I'm tired and sick, and I'm upset that I'm not able to be a mother to my baby. I really need this vacation. But even that's been a headache.

We're planning to go to Israel at the end of the month. I don't know if I've mentioned that Larry's whole family lives in Israel. His sister is getting married and we're going to the wedding. But Larry's mother gave me a list of things she wants me to bring for her; nothing expensive or anything, just things that are hard to get there. In order to get the stuff, I'd have to spend a whole day shopping. I don't have time for that. I can't just take a day off from work to go shopping! So I told Larry that unless he goes out and gets the things himself, we're just not going to be able to bring it with us. I'm sorry, but I don't think it was right of her to ask me to get it. It goes back to the fact that she doesn't understand what this internship business is all about. Nobody understands it. Nobody could possibly know what it's like to go through this unless you've gone through it yourself.

The other problem about going on vacation is my schedule. We've got tickets to leave from Kennedy International Airport on Monday, October 28, at 11:00 A.M. My vacation officially starts that morning, but of course I'm on call the night before. If I work that night, as I'm supposed to, there's no way I'll be able to make it out of the hospital before nine o'clock in the morning. And considering that I'll be signing out to interns who have never been on the ward before and don't know any of the patients, it'll probably be much later than that. There's no way I'm going to make it to the airport on time. So I'm trying to make a change. The only person I could possibly switch with is one of the subinterns. She says she'll think about it, but she's not committing herself yet. If she can't do it, I just might not show up that day.

Sunday, October 20, 1985

I got into a big fight with Marie on Wednesday. I was postcall and tired but I knew we needed some things, so I called before leaving the hospital and told her I was going to be stopping at the supermarket and was there anything special we needed? She said there wasn't, so I just got the things I knew we needed. Then when I got home, I found out we were out of Pampers. I went crazy! "Didn't you realize we were out of diapers?" I asked. She said she forgot, and I let her have it! The bottom line was that the baby had to spend the night without a diaper change because I was too tired to go out again.

Then Larry yelled at me for yelling at Marie, and I let him

have it, too. I told him I wasn't a superwoman, I couldn't do everything. I can't be expected to work and take care of the baby and do the shopping and the cooking. I told him he was going to have to pitch in more and do some of the things that needed to be done around the house. Then after I let him have it, I felt even worse because I hate fighting with him. He's one of those people who just doesn't fight back; he never seems to get mad. He's so calm, it drives me crazy! So we've been fighting a cold war since then.

And things are terrible at work. I hate my patients, except Lisa [**the young woman with choriocarcinoma**]; I hate the house staff I'm working with, except for Susannah, who's had the flu herself; but most of all, I hate the medical students. They're terrible. I've never seen anything like it. I've got this third-year student who's been assigned to me the past two weeks. He actually deserves to fail. He's an M.D.-Ph.D. [**a special track in which college graduates are accepted for a course of study that will ultimately grant them both an M.D. and a Ph.D. degree; Schweitzer accepts a handful of these students each year**], and he's got this attitude problem. He thinks he doesn't have to do anything, all he has to do is show up. I ask him to go and check labs and do other scut and he actually refuses. He says it's not in his job description.

And the subinterns are big pains also. I asked one to switch with me so I don't have to be on the last night of the month. At first she said she'd think about it. Then a few days later she said she'd do it. Then this week she told me she'd decided she couldn't switch for some reason. She didn't tell me why, but it doesn't matter. It was the one time this whole year I really needed somebody to help me out, and nobody would do it. So now I don't know what I'm going to do. Maybe I'll just walk out of the hospital early the next morning. I mean, I'm not going to miss my flight.

My patient with the brain tumor died last week. He had been in a coma for about a week. After talking it over with his parents, we all agreed to make him a DNR [**do not resuscitate**]. I don't think he was in much pain; his heart just stopped one night and they declared him dead. I never got a chance to talk to him. He was always so angry when he was conscious.

At least Lisa's doing much better. I'm glad about that. She's the only patient I care about right now. Her mouth sores are

better and she's able to eat again. She finished her first course
of chemo and she's not nauseous anymore. She's actually im-
proving; she's about the only patient all month who has gotten
better.

I told Lisa about Sarah on Friday. She asked me if I was
married and I told her about Larry and the baby. She said she
was happy for me and that she was really sorry that she wasn't
still pregnant because she really wanted a baby of her own. She
said she thought I must be a good mother because I'm a doctor
and I know what to do when children got sick. I don't know
about that, but it was a nice thing for her to say. She said she'd
like to meet Sarah sometime, so maybe tomorrow, when I'm on
call, I'll have Larry bring her over to the hospital.

Well, a week from tonight I'll be on call for the last time on
Adolescents. And a week from tomorrow, we'll be on our way
to Israel. I can't wait.

Saturday, October 26, 1985

I can talk for only a minute. I'm very busy tonight, but I wanted
to get this down on tape before I left on vacation. This is a
terrible story.

Tuesday I admitted this seventeen-year-old named Wayne
who'd had leukemia in the past but had been in remission for
years. He came to the hospital because of shortness of breath,
and as soon as he hit the floor, it was pretty clear that his leukemia had recurred. His shortness of breath was due to his
enormous spleen. His white count [**while blood cell count in
the peripheral circulation**] was over a hundred thousand [**normal is between five thousand and ten thousand**], and he was
anemic and thrombocytopenic[**thrombocytopenia: low platelet count; platelets are factors that aid in clotting of blood**].
The hematologists jumped on him right away. They gave him
all sorts of poisons to bring his white count down. He was sick,
but he was in pretty good spirits, considering what was happening.

Then yesterday morning, we were on work rounds and
Wayne's mother came to tell me he was acting funny. I didn't
think much of it, but I went to check him anyway. He was acting
really strangely. He was shifting around in bed making gurgling
sounds; he didn't respond to questions; it was like he was in a

coma, but his eyes were open and he was moving around. I got him to respond to pain, but he didn't respond to anything else. I called for help, and everybody came running. The resident noticed that his right pupil was fixed and dilated [a sign of an acute and serious change in neurologic function]. Then he arrested.

We all worked on him for about an hour. We were never able to get anything back. Everybody was in there: Alex George [the director of the intensive-care unit], the chief residents, everybody.

That was my first death. All I kept thinking about through the whole thing was Sarah. A patient's death always bothers you, but when you've got a baby, it means a lot more. I went home after work and just hugged her and hugged her. She'll never understand it. I don't think I'll ever forget it.

We're in the middle of packing. I've got to get everything done tonight because I'm on call tomorrow and there's no other time to do it. I explained the situation to the chief residents and they told me they were sorry but there was no way they could force anybody to switch with me against their will. They at least said that if everything was under control, I could sign out to the senior who was covering at 7:00 A.M. and leave. I'll still never have enough time to get home. So it looks like I'm going to be going on a twelve-hour plane trip after being on call. If it's a busy night, I may not even get a chance to change my clothes or take a shower. I'm really pissed off.

The fact that nobody'd switch with me when I really needed it has made me incredibly angry. It may be a little thing, but I'll tell you, I'm never going to help anybody around here. Except for Susannah, maybe.

MARK

October 1985

Friday, October 4, 1985

They're trying to kill me. I know they're trying to kill me. I'm just surprised I've survived this long. I've been at Jonas Bronck since Monday, and so far everyone's tried to kill me, the chief residents, the nurses, the elevator operators, the lab technicians, and especially the patients, but no one's managed to finish me off yet. They're all trying, so I know it's only a matter of time.

See what a vacation will do for you? It clears your head, makes you see things in a new light.

Actually, my vacation wasn't exactly what I'd call wonderful. No, wonderful is definitely not the word I'd use. How would I describe it? What word would I use? Lousy; lousy is definitely a word I'd use, lousy bordering on shitty.

It started off with my brother and me in my car driving south as fast as we could to escape from the Bronx. We didn't have any real end point in mind; I was just trying to reach a place where cockroaches don't exist. Actually, that's not true. We were heading for Cincinnati. We both have friends there, and we decided to go visit them. Yes, there's nothing more romantic than spending a week with your younger brother visiting friends in Cincinnati in late September. The whole experience almost made the Bronx seem nice.

Okay, so it wasn't romantic, but Carole and I sure made up for that in the second week of my vacation. We went to the romance capital of the East, Pocono Castle, a resort hotel catering to the honeymoon crowd. What a place! I knew we had made a big mistake when the first thing the bellboy showed us was the heart-shaped bathtub in our room. Carole said she liked it; I thought I showed great restraint by keeping myself from puking right there on the spot. But that wasn't the worst of it. We went down to the dining room for dinner that first night and discovered that everybody there, every last couple, was there on their honeymoon. It was Carole and me and four hundred new-lyweds! The place was disgusting; the food was horrible, the decorating job was ostentatious, the rooms were dirty, and it rained all week. All for two hundred bucks a day! Just the kind of relaxing environment I needed.

In the dining room, they put us at a table with another couple. These two were great: They had just been remarried for the second time. They were reformed drug addicts. We spent every meal chatting about AIDS!

And then we got back to the Bronx last Sunday night. I started on the ward at Jonas Bronck Monday morning and it's been hell, absolute hell! On Monday we started work rounds at eight o'clock and didn't finish until three in the afternoon. Seven solid hours of rounds! I'm sure all our names are going to be listed in the *Guinness Book of World Records* under the category of "World's Longest Work Rounds." Every time we'd try to leave one patient and move on to the next, some disaster would occur and we'd have to stop and sort things out and then try to start again. I picked up five patients: a pair of twins with AIDS who, if you can believe it, are actually named "Winston" and "Sa-lem" (as a result of taking care of them, I've decided to name my first two kids "Chesterfield" and "Lucky Strike"); a brain-dead kid who inhaled a little too much carbon monoxide when her apartment caught on fire; and the "specialties of the house," a couple of asthmatics. That wouldn't have been so bad, five new patients, but you've got to remember, this was my first day on the inpatient service at Jonas Bronck, and I never got a chance to get myself oriented. I didn't know where the labs were, I didn't know how to get results of anything, it took me a day and a half just to figure out where the damn bathroom was! I had to hold it in for thirty-six hours, which, if you've never done it, is not the most comfortable thing in the world. It got so bad, I started to feel like a water balloon. And to make matters worse, the intern who had been on the ward before me hadn't written off-service notes on any of the patients. How considerate! So even if I had had a chance to read the charts, which I hadn't, I still wouldn't have been able to figure out what was going on with my patients.

Then I was on call that first night. I picked up five additional patients and I didn't get any sleep. And the way the schedule worked out, I was on Monday and again on Wednesday and I was postcall on Tuesday and Thursday, so my brain's been in hyperspace for an entire week. I wasn't sure I could find my way back home today, let alone try to figure out what was going on with my patients.

I've been completely helpless. Mike Miller is my attending this month, and he and the senior resident have asked me a lot of questions on rounds and I haven't even been close on any of them. I feel like a real idiot, which I probably am. And since Miller's a friend of my family's, I've felt even worse about it. I mean, I'm sure I've gone a long way to convince him I got into medical school on the one scholarship given every year to the most deserving mentally retarded individual in the United States. I've also had this fantasy that he's been calling my mother at home every night and telling her what a moron I turned out to be.

But hey, it hasn't all been my fault. I've gotten some really sick patients over the past few days, and working in Jonas Bronck isn't exactly my idea of living in paradise! What a place! The elevators don't work; people have died waiting for them, and those weren't patients, those were interns! The people who work in the labs have a combined IQ of about 3. If you're nice to them, they'll screw you; if you're not nice to them, they'll screw you. I'm convinced they sit around up there trying to come up with the most difficult ways to give out results. If you call them on the phone they'll put you on hold for ten minutes and then hang up on you. If you call back and say you were cut off, they'll yell at you and say it's not their job to give results over the phone. I walked into the bacteriology lab Wednesday night at ten o'clock and a woman pushed me out of the door and said they were closed. They were closed! What does that mean? You're allowed to diagnose infectious diseases between the hours of nine and five only?

And the food stinks! That hellhole downstairs is the worst excuse for a coffee shop I've ever seen! I was wondering how they could get away charging only a dollar and a half for a turkey sandwich, so I tried one and I figured it out: They don't put any turkey on the bread; they don't sell turkey sandwiches, they sell mock-turkey sandwiches, for God's sake! And the place keeps the same hours as the bacteriology lab, which is pretty telling. So when you're up all night, when you really get hungry, you can't even get a mock-turkey sandwich.

And how can Miller and all those other guys who run this department and who say they're really concerned about our well-being not provide us with a shower? If I don't get to take a shower after a night on call, I'm worthless. I feel like shit! Just working in this hospital, you wind up covered with about an inch and a half of municipal hospital crud, and if you don't get a chance to wash that off, you just can't work effectively.

Well, now I've really depressed myself. I was in a pretty good mood when I started recording this, but listening to what I had to say, I have to admit, I must have been pretty crazy to have come back from vacation. I mean, a week at Pocono Castle was a picnic compared to an afternoon at Jonas Bronck.

Monday, October 7, 1985

I think I've finally recovered and gotten myself a little better oriented to Jonas Bronck. It was pretty rough there for a while. That's a real problem with this program: You work at so many places, by the time you feel comfortable at one hospital, they move you to another and you have to start from scratch again. It's the concept of perpetual confusion, an ancient form of torture developed, I believe, during the Ming dynasty.

Things have calmed down a little on the ward. I was on last Monday and Wednesday and then again on Saturday, but from here on it's every third for the rest of the month. (Oh, what joy, only every third night! How lucky can I get?) All last week was a blur. I admitted about ten patients, some of them really sick. It was interesting. They kind of came in groups: Monday was Leukemia Day. First I admitted this fourteen-year-old boy whose gums had started to bleed a lot when he brushed his teeth. He also had a slight fever, he was feeling kind of sick, and he had bone pain. He turned out to have ALL [**acute lymphocytic leukemia, the most common form of cancer in the pediatric age group**], and he's in the poor-prognosis group for everything—age, sex, race, you name it. He only stayed at Jonas Bronck overnight. On Tuesday we shipped him over to Mount Scopus, where he'll get started on a chemotherapy protocol.

Next, I admitted this eight-year-old who had had ALL diagnosed six years ago. He had been treated with chemotherapy for four years and had been considered cured. He woke up one day last week with a terrible headache. He was seen at every emergency room in the Bronx, and all the doctors told his mother the same thing: There was nothing wrong with him, and she should try giving him some Tylenol. He finally showed up to see his hematologist here at Jonas Bronck, and she noticed that he had a sixth-nerve palsy. [**The sixth cranial nerve, the abducens, runs the longest course in its path from its origin in the brain to its point of action in the eye. Because of its long path, the sixth nerve is sensitive to increased pressure within the skull. If pressure is increased, the sixth nerve will not work properly and is said to be "palsied."**] She arranged a stat CT scan that showed a golf-ball-sized mass in his frontal lobe, most probably a lymphoma but possibly some other terrible horrenderoma. [**I don't think the term "horrenderoma" requires defining.**]

So Monday was a really comforting night. I'm starting on a new service in a new hospital, and I picked up five patients who didn't have adequate off-service notes, so I didn't know what the hell was going on with any of them, and I admitted two kids with terrible prognoses. And I barely had time to recover from that night when I was on again on Wednesday, and that turned out to be Chromosome Abnormality Night. My first hit was this three-month-old who looked like she'd been dead for a few weeks already except for the fact that she'd just had fresh casts put on her legs to correct her clubfeet. Her mother brought her into the ER with a complaint that she was breathing too fast. The intern who saw her in the ER asked if she had any problems with her health, and the mother said, "No, there's nothing wrong with her." Turns out she's got trisomy 18 [**a congenital malformation syndrome caused by an extra chromosome No. 18 in every cell of the body**] and severe congenital heart disease, which had caused her to go into congestive heart failure and led to the breathing problem. [**Almost every child born with trisomy 18 has congenital heart disease. The heart disease is one of the factors that leads to early death in these patients. Eighty percent of trisomy 18 children will die before their first**

birthday.] The kid's got trisomy 18, and the mother says there's nothing wrong with her! When the intern got the old chart and found out the diagnosis, the mother still denied it. Sounds like she got some top-notch genetic counseling! Anyway, the kid was in congestive failure, so I started her on some Lasix **[a diuretic that rids the body of excess fluid; since fluid buildup is a major problem in congestive heart failure, treatment with Lasix often relieves symptoms such as rapid breathing]** and suddenly she started looking like a million bucks.

I don't really understand why this kid's got those casts on her legs. I mean, if she's got such a bad prognosis, what's the use of fixing her clubfeet? It doesn't make much sense. Of course, that doesn't mean anything; there aren't many things around here that seem to make much sense.

Anyway, later on Wednesday night (actually it was about five o'clock on Thursday morning) I admitted a fourteen-year-old with Down syndrome who was having an asthma attack. Now, asthma's pretty straightforward. At this point, I can manage asthma in my sleep. In fact, that's when I usually do the best job. But this kid was just a touch more complicated because, in addition to his Down syndrome and his asthma, he also had chronic renal failure. The problem with that is that aminophylline **[the mainstay medication used in the treatment of asthma]** is removed from the bloodstream by the kidneys. I could give the stuff to him and it'd probably help his asthma but he wouldn't ever be able to get rid of it. He'd probably wind up with toxic side effects; he'd stop wheezing and start seizing, and that wasn't going to be very helpful. We thought about it for a while and decided to turf him **[turf: internese for "transfer to another service"; also referred to as "a dump"]** immediately to University Hospital, where the renal dialysis unit is located. So I had to ride over to University Hospital in the ambulance with him and drop him off at the ward.

Well, I got over to University, brought the kid up, and introduced him to Andy Baron, who was the intern on call over there. He wasn't exactly happy to see me. What the hell happened to him? I mean, I haven't seen him in a couple of months. He used to be a kind of easygoing, friendly guy. He yelled at me when we got there. He accused me of dumping this kid on him, which of course I was. But, hey, that's not my fault. We weren't doing it to make Andy's life more miserable, we were doing it because it seemed to be the best thing for the patient.

It's kind of scary, running into people you haven't seen for a while. It's like going to see a horror movie and realizing that you and your friends are the main characters. You look at Andy and you see what kind of a monster he got turned into and you start to wonder if maybe the same thing hasn't happened to you, but you haven't noticed it because you live with yourself every day and it's hard to notice any changes. I don't know, it's pretty scary.

Anyway, Saturday was pretty quiet. I got only two admissions the whole day, so I had a chance to spend the day sitting in the residents' room watching TV and eating mock-turkey sandwiches. It was good; I needed a chance to relax a little and figure out who all my patients actually were. And today was pretty quiet, too. So right now I've got most of this straightened out.

I spent yesterday in the city with Carole. We went to a matinee. We saw *Cats*. I fell asleep four times and Carole had to wake me up because my snoring was disturbing all the people around us. I don't think I missed much; from what I saw during the short period when I was conscious, it looked pretty lame. I can't figure out how they get people to wear those silly costumes eight times a week. I guess if they can get me to do the ridiculous stuff I do, they can get anybody to do anything!

Thursday, October 10, 1985

As if my life weren't bad enough, Hanson's back. I couldn't believe it! I got called down to the ER to pick up an admission last night and all I knew was it was supposed to be a six-month-old with diarrhea and dehydration. I got down there and there he was. There was no doubt about it. No other six-month-old I've ever seen has that characteristic putrid look about him. His mother had brought him to the ER, and of course she didn't recognize me. During the entire month he had made my life miserable on Infants, she had never once come to see him. All I knew about her was that she was a drug addict. When I realized she was his mother, I almost said, "Oh, I'm sorry, I didn't recognize you without the needle in your arm," but I showed excellent restraint and tact and kept quiet. I'm getting really good at this patient-relations stuff. Anyway, poor little Hanson had been home maybe two weeks and had developed diarrhea again. I asked his mother why she didn't bring him back to Mount Scopus since, after all, all his records are there, and she said, "I don't like those doctors at Mount Scopus. They don't know nothing. They're all a pain in the ass." I guess she came to Jonas Bronck because she wanted a second opinion. Very smart!

Anyway, I figured I should try to get some history on his last days at Mount Scopus, so today I got in touch with Jennifer Urzo, the intern who discharged him from Infants. I said, "I just admitted Hanson," and I could hear her groan. It's amazing how one tiny baby can cause such a uniform reaction from everybody who's come in contact with him. Jennifer told me this weird story about how she spent the entire month of September working really hard to get him straightened out. Not only did she work on getting him relatively healthy, she also arranged for a bunch of outpatient follow-up appointments, home visits by the VNS [**Visiting Nurse Service**], social work involvement, the works. It sounded as if she genuinely liked the kid (there's no accounting for taste). When everything was arranged, Jennifer somehow got in touch with the mother and actually convinced her to come in and learn how to take care of the baby, which must have been a major miracle. The mother came a few times. Jennifer said she never felt really comfortable around her but that the nurses felt the mother knew what she was doing. So Jennifer told her she could take the baby home. She started going over all the appointments she had made and the mother said something about the fact that she was going to take the baby home and she'd keep most of the appointments but she sure as hell wasn't going to come back to see Jennifer because she didn't like her, she didn't think she was doing a good job with the baby. She said she didn't think she was a very good doctor. This obviously really hurt Jennifer. She even got tearful on the phone just talking to me about it.

Anyway, he seems to be doing okay now. I kept standing around his bed all night waiting for him to crump but he never did. He hasn't had any diarrhea since early this morning but we're still keeping him NPO. I started an IV last night. What thrilling memories that brought back! I'll tell you one thing: He may be a little bigger and two months older, but he still has shit for veins! I stuck him about a dozen times to get the line to stay in place. It felt so comfortable. Just me and him and a box of twenty-two-gauge plastic IV catheters.

While I had Jennifer on the phone, she told me what finally happened with Fenton, the kid on Infants whose grandmother was crazy and was getting him admitted to all the hospitals in the area for GE reflux that he didn't really have. BCW took the grandmother to court, and Jennifer had to testify, since she was the discharging intern. The judge decided the grandmother needed psychiatric evaluation and ordered that the kid be placed into foster care until that was completed. So there's another happy ending.

Anyway, there's not much else going on right now. I'm going to sleep so I can be bright-eyed and bushy-tailed for call tomorrow.

Wednesday, October 23, 1985

Nothing much has been going on. The ward's been pretty quiet, thank God, and I've been getting sleep most nights when I've been on. The most notable thing that's been happening is that Carole and I have been talking a lot about the future, which is starting to scare me to death. She wants to get married. I'm not so sure I do. I have to admit, she's been very good to me since I started this insanity. She's always been there when I've needed her, but marriage, that's a really big step.

I'll have to do a lot of thinking about this. Just as soon as I have enough time.

BOB

October 1985

In October of my internship, my wife developed severe abdominal pains. She went to a physician who did an upper GI series and diagnosed a gastric ulcer. The doctor started her on Cimetidine, a drug that decreases the amount of acid produced by the stomach, gave her advice regarding her diet, and told her to take it easy. With time, the symptoms disappeared.

I was pretty surprised when Beth told me about her ulcer. After all, I was the one with the stressful life-style; I was the one who wasn't getting enough sleep, who was taking care of critically ill patients and trying to cope with their families. All she was doing was working in her laboratory, the same as she had done for the previous three years.

Looking back on it now, it's clear that Beth's life at that time had become as stressful as mine. First, because I was in Boston and she was in New York, she had become a regular weekend passenger on the Eastern shuttle. Beth was terrified of flying, and these weekly excursions were rapidly taking their toll on her mental health. Second, upon finally reaching Boston after each of these hair-raising flights, she was finding that I, once a sensitive and loving human being, had been turned into a melancholy, self-centered wretch. She seriously questioned, at least to herself, whether this "new" me was a permanent change or whether it was just a temporary interruption in our relationship. And finally, she was worried about her work; it wasn't going as well as it should. She was expending so much energy worrying about me and our relationship that she just couldn't concentrate on what was happening in the lab. At the time, I didn't understand any of this. That's because I, like most interns, couldn't see past my own problems.

It's not surprising that Beth's ulcer first appeared in October. It's during October that internship begins to take its toll on everyone. To the intern, it's the start of the winter doldrums: The thrill of being a doctor is gone (that usually occurs back in July), the "newness" of the on-call routine has worn thin, and exhaustion has begun to set in; in addition, the intern realizes there's no end in sight.

October also is usually the time when interns lose all contact with friends and relatives. I clearly remember the routine that became established at about this time in my own life. I'd come home after shopping to pick up a pizza, take off all my clothes, climb into bed, and watch reruns of *The Odd Couple* and *The Brady Bunch* while wolfing down dinner. Then, by about eight-thirty or nine, I'd turn out the lights and quickly fall asleep. Unless forced, I would not leave my house; I didn't go out to movies or to dinner with friends or even to the supermarket to buy food. I didn't have the strength, and I didn't have the interest. I just wanted to be left alone.

Andy Baron is taking to internship just like I did. When I visited him on the ward at University Hospital early in the month, he said he couldn't talk to me. Figuring he meant he was too busy to take a break, I suggested we go out for dinner, and he said, "No, you don't understand. I can't talk to you, and I don't know if I'll ever be able to talk to you again. If I think about what's happening to me, I'll start to cry, and once I start crying, I don't think I'll be able to stop."

"So you don't think you ever want to talk to me again?" I asked.

"I'm not sure," he replied, and I could see tears starting to well up in his eyes. "For now, I just want to be left alone. I don't want to have to talk or think about anything."

I told Andy how much he reminded me of myself. I told him about my pizza and *Odd Couple* routine. He smiled at this and said it hadn't gotten that bad for him yet (he said his TV was broken).

To people like Andy, Mark, and Amy, who have long-term relationships, October can be a frightening time for loved ones. Because of the appearance of this first wave of depression, interns become introspective, largely ignoring everyone else; all an intern is concerned about is his or her ability to get enough sleep, enough to eat, and to find some kind of happiness without expending too much physical or emotional energy. And like Beth, this is a time when spouses begin to wonder what the future is going to hold.

That's certainly the case with Carole, Mark Greenberg's significant other. She and Mark have had a relationship that's gone on for years and weathered all sorts of storms. And now, four months into his internship, she finds that Mark has no time for her. He falls asleep whenever they go anywhere together; he talks about nothing but life on the wards while taking no interest in her work or her problems. Carole is looking for some answers: She wants to know if the change she's seen in Mark is permanent or temporary; she wants to know what effect all this will have on her life; and she wants to know if she and Mark will wind up getting married or not. Unfortunately, at the present time, Mark is in no condition to give her these answers.

Amy seems to be handling her life outside of work better than any of the other interns. From what she tells me, her relationship with Larry has not been adversely affected by her internship. I think there are two reasons for this. First, Larry is an exceptional guy; he's very patient and understanding, and he loves to spend time with his daughter, which is pretty important, since he's Sarah's primary caretaker most nights and weekend days. Second, Amy is reacting differently than everyone else; she understands that she can't come home, sit in front of the TV, and tune out life, because she has a second job that's even more important than being an intern: She has to come home and be a functioning and loving mother. So far, Amy and Larry seem to be holding things together.

But even their relationship has clearly been stressed. Amy told me about an argument she and Larry had concerning Amy's yelling at their baby-sitter. She said they almost never argue, but this one had occurred after a particularly bad night on call because Amy was overtired. So even for them, some small cracks have begun to appear in their ironclad marriage.

October also is a pretty hard month for the house officers who don't have ''significant others.'' During the middle of this month, I went to the Recovery Room, a bar across the street from Mount Scopus, with some of the senior residents. Ben King told me he was a little upset because he was planning to go to his ex-girlfriend's wedding this weekend. He and this woman broke up last year after a long-term relationship because she just couldn't take it anymore. She didn't like the idea of spending every night alone. "Even when I was there," Ben told me, "I was only about half there."

Usually, the only other single people unattached house officers come in contact with are other single house officers. There's almost no time for them to hang around places where nonmedical single people congregate, and during what little time is available, there is a great deal of pressure to "succeed." But most potential partners, like Ben's old girlfriend, don't want to put up with the bizarre hours interns and residents are forced to keep. So it becomes almost impossible to develop any kind of meaningful relationship that will last through training. For the men, this is just a major irritation; they figure things will straighten themselves out after their internship and residency ends. But for the women, it's a lot more terrifying: They say they can actually hear those proverbial biological clocks ticking away inside their ovaries, and as time passes, they tend to become more and more fixated on finding Mr. Right.

So the overall effect of all this is that a great many interns and residents feel depressed. This internal turmoil can have far-reaching effects, causing the person to decide to make major changes in his or her life. Some interns decide to leave medicine; some (very few) decide to leave life by committing suicide; others decide to leave their program. This last seems to be happening with Andy.

On the evening of October 14, our phone rang almost as soon as I got home from work. It was Andy; he said he needed to see me right away; it was important, and he couldn't talk about it over the phone. He asked if I could come down to the Bronx immediately.

I was worried. I knew Andy had been depressed, and I also knew that anything was possible. So without losing a minute, I got into my car and headed back to the Bronx.

Andy lives on the twentieth floor of the Mount Scopus apartment tower. He has a studio apartment with a terrific view. From the balcony, looking east, you can see parts of the Bronx, City Island, Long Island Sound, and, in the distance, the lights of Long Island and Westchester County. After showing me around,

Andy sat me down and said, "I guess you're wondering what's going on." After I told him that that was an understatement, he continued: "You have to promise not to tell what I'm going to say to anybody else, not even your wife. It's very secret and I could be extremely damaged if word leaked out."

After we negotiated a little and I finally promised, he told me: "I've been offered a job at another program."

I must admit it was kind of a letdown. I was expecting something juicier, something like he was having an affair with one of the other interns or possibly even with one of his ex-patients on Adolescents. He went on with the story; he told me that before this year had started he had talked with the director of Pediatrics at Boston Children's, the program he had originally ranked first on his match list last year, and had asked him about the possibility of coming back to Boston as a junior resident next year. The director had told him that no jobs were available at that time, but if one were to open up, Andy would be No. 1 on the list. Then yesterday the guy had called, had told him one of the interns was planning to leave and that Andy could have the position if he still wanted it.

Andy told me he was feeling very conflicted. There were a lot of things to think about. First, in spite of everything that's happened, he thinks our program is good and he's made some close friends; he feels bad about the prospect of leaving. Next, Karen is applying to some of the more impressive New York psychiatric residency programs and has a better than even chance of getting in.

"So stay," I said.

"It's not that easy," he replied. "My family's all in Boston. And I know I'll get a good education at the other program. And Karen and I are planning on settling in Boston. We want to have a family; staying in New York will just delay that."

I told him it sounded like a tough decision but that it wasn't a bad situation to be in; I mean, he's going to win either way. I told him I'd definitely be sorry if he decided to leave.

We talked for about an hour and a half. Of course, nothing was resolved. I'm not sure what's going to happen to Andy, but if I had to bet, I'd bet on his going back to Boston. There's simply more to draw him there at this point than there is to keep him here.

* * *

Every October, all the attendings who have contact with the house staff meet to discuss the internship group. This meeting serves two purposes: First, it identifies those people who are or may soon be having trouble so that some form of intervention can be planned; second, the meeting allows us to come up with some idea of who will be returning the following year and, more importantly, who will be leaving.

It's rare that all the interns come back as residents. Two members of each year's incoming group are accepted with the understanding from the very beginning that they'll be leaving for residencies in psychiatry, radiology, or other specialties in which a year of pediatric or internal medicine training is mandatory. A few more, people like Andy Baron, decide to change programs for personal reasons. So during this meeting, Mike Miller tried to get a head count of prospective junior residents.

The meeting this year was interesting. Mark Greenberg and Andy Baron were both viewed as very good. Andy, in fact, is considered by most people to be outstanding, an excellent candidate for one of the program's four chief resident positions. Since he had sworn me to secrecy, I didn't mention a word about his job offer in Boston.

The intern about whom there was the most discussion was Amy. She's apparently made more than a couple of enemies among the attendings. In addition to her problem in the emergency room back in July, she tends to do a lot of little things that get people upset, such as leaving the hospital early; complaining frequently and loudly; and criticizing other house officers, such as Barry Bresnan. I spoke up for her; I said I thought a lot of her complaints were justified and that she shouldn't be condemned for voicing them.

It was ultimately decided that Mike Miller would have a talk with Amy and explain the concerns that had been raised at the meeting. It wasn't thought that anything needed to be done, that her work was certainly good enough to justify being offered a position for the following year. I don't know how Amy is going to respond to this criticism, especially since I'm sure she won't think it's warranted. After all, I don't think it's warranted either; I think she should be commended for doing as good a job as she's done, considering all the pressure on her. And I'm going to tell her that.

ANDY

November 1985

Tuesday, November 5, 1985

I've pretty much decided that I'd like to go back to Boston for next year, but things still are up in the air. It looks like Karen might get accepted into Columbia's psych program, and that's going to be pretty hard to turn down.

This past week has been really, really hard, with this decision hanging over our heads, and we've both been incredibly stressed out. I'm in OPD [the Outpatient Department] now on the Jonas Bronck side, although I spend two days a week here at Mount Scopus for clinic. I've been on call it seems like an inordinate number of times already in the past week; I've already done two every-other-nights and I'm on call again tonight. I'm finding the Jonas Bronck ER a real drag to work in. The nurses are extremely hostile and critical and cold. They're very good nurses, very efficient, and they obviously know what they're doing. They're much better than the nurses in the West Bronx ER, but they all seem to have a chip on their shoulder. I've been told that there's some kind of war going on among them but, hey, you know, that's no excuse. That just makes it a drag for everybody else to work there.

The place is unbelievably busy. I end up getting out at four-thirty in the morning on nights when I'm on call. It's just fucked. You come home, you sleep for three hours, and you're supposed to be back at the hospital for the eight-o'clock teaching conference the next morning. Forget it! It's really unfortunate. I really was looking forward to the Jonas Bronck ER, and I do enjoy the work I do there. The pathology that walks through the door, the

151

patient population, the mix, it's unbelievable; it's fantastic. I'd love it except dealing with all these angry nurses is a real drag!

So far I've been thrown into that fucking asthma room a lot more than I think I should've been. Some of the other interns are going to have to help pitch in with that. [**In the Jonas Bronck ER, all patients with asthma attacks are placed in the asthma room. When things get busy, one house officer, usually an intern, winds up doing nothing but working in the room. That person may see nothing but asthmatics for four or five hours at a stretch.**] It gets really boring in there, seeing the same thing over and over again without a rest. I've already complained about it but I don't think anybody really cares. That's all; I've got to go back to clinic now.

Thursday, November 7, 1985

I'm in the P²C² [**Pediatric Primary Care Center, the pediatric clinic at Jonas Bronck**] conference room waiting for the conference to start. I have to talk quietly or they'll think I'm talking to myself. Nobody else is here yet.

Last night I was so tired, I slept eleven and a half hours straight. I could have slept another five easily. Can't work every-others, they just wear the shit out of you. And on both of those every-others, I worked in the ER till about 5:00 A.M. Then yesterday I had to work in the ER all day, from nine to five, Jesus Christ, this place is a goddamn zoo!

Karen's been here for the past few days. We're still trying to decide whether to go back to Boston or stay in New York. It's tough, there are a lot of things to consider, but so far it looks like we're both leaning toward going home. They've been really good about it here. Miller knows what's going on, and he's giving me the time I need to decide. He says he wants me to stay. It's nice of him to say it, but does he really mean it?

I've got to stop now; someone just came in.

Friday, November 8, 1985

I'm here in the thirteenth-floor conference room of West Bronx, where the pediatric OPD conference is supposed to be. I got here at eight, and I just found out it doesn't start until eight-thirty, so I'm about twenty minutes early now.

Today's an important day because after long and tedious deliberation, Karen and I have definitely decided to go back to Boston for the remainder of my residency. Karen's been getting internship offers from everybody. Every single place she's applied to is offering her a position. It's hard to turn opportunities like that down, but we've decided to go back. Karen feels she'll be happy at Boston University, the program where she'll wind up going, even though it's not in the same league as Cornell and Columbia.

The important thing that we've decided is that we want to be around family and friends. This year has been so hard for me because of the separation. I don't think internship can ever be easy, but I know I would have been better off had I stayed in Boston instead of coming to the Bronx. Plus, we both think Boston is a nicer and easier city to live in than New York, which is very exciting but also crazy and congested and stressful. So this morning I'm going to call up Scott Thomas, the director at Boston Children's, and tell him I'd like that spot if he's still got it. If he hasn't got it, I'm going to wring his little neck. Then I'll have to call Mike Miller and let him know that I've made my decision. Hopefully I'll get the contract and the whole thing will be signed, sealed, and delivered within the next week or so.

A couple of days ago, I thought for the first time that I'd ultimately like to subspecialize. It's not because I have some burning interest in any one field; I don't really. A lot of things interest me, but there's not any one field I'm that attached to or interested in. I want to subspecialize because I'm tired of being so inexpert at so many things. I don't think I could spend the rest of my life knowing a little about a lot of things, like many of the OPD attendings do. I need to feel like there's one area in which I have a great depth of knowledge. Someone just walked in; I'm going to have to stop now.

Sunday, November 10, 1985

Karen's still here. I'm finding myself getting all depressed again, and I'm not really sure why. I just can't put my finger on it. There's just nothing that's obviously wrong: I'm in OPD, and that's pretty easy, I'm not lonely. Something's just wrong.

I guess one of the reasons I'm depressed is that I made this massive decision about going back to Boston, and now there's a kind of letdown. It's official now: I called Dr. Thomas the other day and accepted the job. And Karen officially turned down Cornell and accepted the place at Boston University. On Monday, Thomas is going to call Mike Miller and discuss it with him, then he's going to call me back and let me know it's all sealed, and that's it! That's it; we're going back.

Last Friday was a horrendous day. I started working at my clinic at Mount Scopus at nine o'clock, and I began the day with a child-abuse case. A patient who requested me because they had seen me in the emergency room once, came in. I saw signs of abuse and reported them. That was a very unpleasant situation; they were very angry, and I can understand why. And then at noon, I went to the Jonas Bronck ER, and I was there until seven the next morning. I was so tired, I fell asleep taking a history! While I was talking to the mother, I just zonked out! Soon as I woke up, I picked it up with the next question I had in my mind, but I knew I had been asleep. The mother was sitting there staring at me with a strange look in her eyes that hadn't been there a second before (because it probably had been several seconds). Then I fell asleep listening to some asthmatic's chest several times. I kept wondering, Why is it taking me so long to get a respiratory rate? Because I kept falling asleep every time I put the 'scope on the kid's chest, that's why! So that was an abysmal night.

I guess all the shit I've been seeing at Jonas Bronck's depressing me a little, too. All the child abuse and the codes and all that, that stuff gets me down. And it's been really cloudy and nasty and rainy, and that doesn't help. And living in the Bronx is just a bore.

And there's something else: I've started to become obsessed that I've got AIDS. I've started waking up in the morning feeling anxious, thinking I'm going to die. That's one of the main criteria for major depression. I've been trying to go and get the test **[blood test for antibodies to the human immunodeficiency virus, the agent that causes AIDS]** but I haven't done it yet, initially because if I think rationally about it, there's no reason I should have it, and then because I realize I don't want to find out if I'm positive.

I'm getting a little bit of the feeling I used to have in medical school, that I'm trapped in a prison, and the rest of the world out there is beautiful and happening and I'm not in it. I saw *The New York Times* today; I read the headline saying that the Democrats had taken over the Senate, controlling fifty-five of the seats. I didn't even know there was an election. I didn't know until after it was over. So I feel very much isolated from the mainstream of humanity. And at times I feel like I'm not taking this seriously enough. I mean, each mother brings her kid in and the kid means all the world to her, but to me, it's just another set of wheezing lungs. I try to do my best with each one, I try to think of each one individually and I do, I know I do, but, I don't know, in some ways it all becomes a blurred mass of humanity flowing through the doors of the emergency room.

There are these two kids, I see them all the time, the mother calls me every week, she comes into clinic every week. She's a really good mom, maybe a little neurotic. She has a Down's baby; the other kid's normal. And she's really great. Seems like there are so few other patients and families I'm happy to see, though. That can't be right; you can't just like one family out of the hundreds who come through.

The streetlights are still on. It's the middle of the day but it's so dark that the lights are still on. I'm supposed to go shopping to get my brother and his wife a wedding present. I don't know what the fuck to get them.

Wednesday, November 13, 1985

It's cold outside, it's turning into winter. You can see your breath in the air. I'm still in the OPD. And I'm feeling better.

My depression has gone, for the most part. At least the acute exacerbation. I'm still left with the chronic, smoldering depression I've had since August. It turns out I was also getting sick. Got this goddamn viral syndrome from some kid and now I've got this residual cough.

Monday, November 25, 1985

I haven't talked into this for a while. Karen left yesterday, and when she's here, I usually talk less. I'd rather spend time with her than this machine.

Today's the end of the fifth month. I finished outpatient this afternoon. Tomorrow I start on 8 East at Jonas Bronck. And while part of me is relieved to get the hell out of that ER, which has just been a madhouse, I'm kind of dreading tomorrow because I'm on call and I have my clinic, so it's going to be a dreadful night. I'll be up all night, I'm already sure of that.

But I'm also looking forward to being back to the somewhat protected environment of a floor where I know what my work is. The work's cut out for you, and even if what most of the other interns have said about Jonas Bronck wards is true, that there are too few nurses up there and the nurses who are there don't want to work, in a lot of ways it's better than being out in the unprotected emergency room.

I've been paying more attention to some of the other interns lately. Some of them are a lot worse off than I am. Take Peter Carson, for instance. I've been working with him in the ER. My God, is he an angry man! He makes the rest of us seem like laughing hyenas. I'll give you an example. Saturday we were both on call. It was a horrendous day in the emergency room. The third year resident was Larry Brooks, and he said it was the worst day he'd ever seen in that ER. It wasn't because we had so many terrible things happening. We did have a few kids in the back [**the back: the trauma area of the Jonas Bronck emergency room**], but there weren't any real tragedies that took up a lot of time. It was because of the volume; it just never let up, and there were only three of us working until four in the afternoon when the evening float resident showed up four hours late (ooops). I literally had only ten minutes to eat during the entire nineteen hours I was there. It was exhausting. By 4:00 A.M. I was just going cross-eyed. I couldn't concentrate for shit.

Anyway, at 4:00 A.M. we were ready to get out of there, but the triage box wouldn't empty. Finally it got down to two charts. The night float was there, he was all alive and peppy, and we were getting ready to leave, but Larry came in and told us there were a couple more to see and I heard the night float say, "Just give them to the interns and go home yourself." Well, when Peter heard that, he went completely berserk. He started screaming, "That fucker! Let the interns do it? Let me at him! I'll rip his testicles off, one by one!" He was screaming so loud that everybody in the emergency room could hear him. A nurse came knocking on the door in a second saying, "You know, not everybody out here wants to hear about testicles being torn off!" But Peter was beyond help; he was so incensed, he just kept screaming. We were saying, "Peter, Peter, shut up or we're going to have to call security on you," and then he kind of calmed down, but only a little. He was wild. And then what ended up happening was that Larry told us to go home and he wound up seeing the last patient himself.

Peter and I split a cab back to our apartment building, and all the way there he was just cursing, saying how much he hates being an intern and how much he hates the ER. He was just absolutely infuriated. But he's back there every day, somehow or other. I guess I'm not the worst off, but I think I'm getting a reputation as being one of the depressed interns.

AMY

November 1985

Saturday, November 16, 1985

I'm not very happy about being back from vacation. We had a wonderful, relaxing time in Israel. I must have been in pretty bad shape before we went away. The frightening thing is I didn't even realize it until I had a chance to get away from it for a while.

Before we left, I was obsessed with being on call that last night of October. It became the most important thing in my life. As it turned out, it wasn't a problem. It was a very bad night; I admitted a new onset diabetic who was in DKA [**diabetic ketoacidosis, a buildup of acid in the blood caused by the inability of the body to use glucose as its energy source; insulin, the protein that allows the blood's glucose to enter the cells of the tissues, is either absent or abnormal in diabetics**], and I was up all night managing the boy's fluids and electrolytes, but Ben King, the senior who was on with me that night, threw me out of the hospital at seven in the morning. Just like that, he told me to leave and have a good time and not to worry about a thing, he'd take care of the patients and sign out to the new interns. So, after all that, I did manage to get home, take a shower, and change my clothes before we had to leave for the airport.

The flights were terrible both there and back. Sarah screamed the whole way. It didn't bother me that much on the way over; I was completely zonked and I slept most of the trip, so it was Larry's problem, not mine. But I couldn't believe it on the way back! I was sure the pilot was going to land and throw us off the plane. But outside of the flights, it was the best vacation of our lives. Larry's parents were great. They wanted to spend the whole time taking care of the baby; they left Larry and me alone, and they encouraged us to go out on our own and do whatever we wanted. I slept late every morning, and by the middle of the second week, I felt like I had finally caught up on my sleep. We traveled all over the country. I can't imagine a better vacation. The only problem was that the time just flew by. Before we knew it, it was time to pack up, get on the plane, and come back to work.

I've been working in the OPD at Mount Scopus. Things have been quiet. I've been getting out between twelve and one on the nights I've been on call. Things would be perfect if we weren't all so jet-lagged. When I'm not on call, I've been going to sleep at seven and waking up at three in the morning. And when I am on call, forget it; I have to use toothpicks to keep my eyelids open after nine. But I can see how much calmer I am now compared with before we left. I really needed that vacation, there's no doubt about it. It's just too bad I have to wait so long for my next one to come around.

Saturday, November 23, 1985, 2:00 P.M.

I had a very bad night last night. The ER was busy and depressing. I didn't get home until after three this morning, and I just woke up about a half hour ago. It's a beautiful day and we're going to take Sarah out for a walk in a few minutes, but I wanted to record this while it was still fresh in my mind.

At about nine o'clock, I picked up the chart of a three-year-old whose mother said she had had a bloody bowel movement earlier that evening. I didn't think much of it at first; bloody bowel movements aren't that unusual. It's usually due to an anal fissure [**a tear in the anal mucosa caused by straining; very common in children around toilet-training age**]. I called the patient in and I saw she was a cute, well-dressed, healthy-looking little girl. I took the history from the mother, who seemed appropriately concerned. Then I examined the girl. I noticed right away that her rectum was very red and it looked kind of . . . well, boggy is the best way to describe it. I did a rectal exam and I noticed that the tone of the sphincter seemed a little decreased. I was suspicious, so I called the attending and did the rest of the rectal exam with him in the room. The girl didn't even cry while I was doing it. There wasn't a peep out of her, which, to say the least, is not normal for a three-year-old.

I got a sinking feeling in my stomach when I was doing the rectal because I've taken care of little kids who've been sexually abused and I knew what was going to happen from here. I was going to have to question the mother, she would probably deny everything and accuse me of making it all up, we'd get into a big fight, and she'd eventually start to cry. Then I would have to call the BCW and report the case to them and they'd wind up doing a full investigation, which might end with them taking the child away from her mother. I knew that none of this was fun or interesting and it was going to take up most of the rest of the night.

Anyway, I started asking all the questions I had to ask. Did they live alone, or were there other people living with them? Did she watch the girl all the time, or did she leave her with other people? Was the girl's father around, and did he have anything to do with her? The mother knew something was up because she answered every question honestly and without too much expression. It turned out that the mother and the girl lived in a two-bedroom apartment with ten other people. Some of the people who lived there were relatives, like the girl's grandmother; some were friends of their family; and some were just friends of the friends. The woman's father had been a junkie and had died of AIDS the year before. The family had all been tested for HIV and the girl's grandmother had been the only other person who tested positive. But some of the other people living in the apartment were junkies, and they hadn't been tested. And there were two teenage boys who were cousins of the mother and who had been taken into the apartment when they themselves had been abused by their own parents a few months before. It was a very confusing, chaotic story, but I believed it because it wasn't all that unusual. I've heard lots of stories like this one since I started medical school.

The woman said she and her daughter slept in the same bed at night but during the day the mother went to school and she had to leave the girl with anybody who happened to be around. She admitted it was possible for anyone, especially her teenage cousins, to have sexually abused the girl while she was out of the house.

At this point the mother started crying and I had to leave the room for a minute. I was ready to cry myself.

I went over to talk to the attending and told him the story and he asked me one question: Why was the mother being so honest? I hadn't even thought about it before that, but he was right; having your child sexually abused by one of your relatives is not something anyone would be especially proud of. The only thing I could think of was maybe the mother wanted to get something out of this. I mean, here she is living with all these people in this chaotic apartment. Maybe she figured the BCW would do their investigation and decide that the girl should stay with the mother but that they should be placed in their own apartment. It was a pretty disgusting thought but completely possible.

I had to go back and tell the mother what was going to happen, and I had to do the rape kit. The attending told me I should draw some blood for HIV testing, just as a baseline. [**People who are exposed to the human immunodeficiency virus will test positive for antibodies to the virus a few weeks after the exposure. As such, Amy's patient should have been negative but may later convert to positivity if she had been exposed to the virus.**] I hadn't even thought about that, but it certainly was a possibility. Not only did this little girl get raped, but also the rapist might have given her AIDS! I didn't even want to think about it.

After I finished the rape kit, I started to make all the phone calls. I first called the social worker, and she said that I'd have to make it a joint response. [**Joint response: when a child's life is considered to be in danger, a report must be made simultaneously to the Bureau of Child Welfare and the New York City Police Department. The BCW's investigation does not get started immediately. Therefore, an immediate investigation by the police must be done to determine whether the child can return home.**] So I called the BCW and the police. The whole thing, from start to finish, took about four hours. By the time I was done it was after one o'clock in the morning and there were still a bunch of charts in the box. What finally happened was the mother and the girl were placed in a shelter for the night. I think they'll ultimately get placed in their own apartment.

I've been thinking about that little girl constantly since I finished with her. All through the rest of the night, all during the cab ride home, while I was trying to fall asleep and since I woke up, that little girl didn't leave my mind. It's really terrible. I'm sure I'll see her face in front of me for years and years to come.

MARK

November 1985

Friday, November 1, 1985

Yesterday was Halloween. I was on last night in the Jonas Bronck ER, and I learned an important lesson: If you want people to trust you, it's probably not a good idea to dress up like Bozo the Clown. I know that because I did dress up like Bozo the Clown yesterday and none of the parents of my patients wanted to have anything to do with me. I guess I can't really blame them; it's one thing to come to the ER and wait four hours to be seen by a competent, or at least a semicompetent, doctor. It's another thing to wait four hours and finally get called in to find out your kid's going to be treated by Bozo the Clown.

But, hey, it was Halloween, and we're supposed to be taking care of kids, aren't we? We all decided the day before to come in dressed in costumes. Peter Carson, who's about six feet three and weighs at least 250 pounds, came dressed as a ballerina, the chief residents were dressed as killer bees, Terry Tanner (a junior resident) was dressed as a witch, and I was Bozo the Clown. The kids seemed to like it even though their parents weren't ecstatic about it. And everything would have been fine if I hadn't had to tell a mother that her kid was dead.

It was about eight o'clock, right in the middle of the busiest time of the evening, of course. All bad things seem to happen when we're really busy. We got a call from the EMS [**Emergency Medical Service**] saying they were bringing in a traumatic arrest [**a patient who, as a result of some accident, was not breathing and whose heart was not beating**]. So Bozo the Clown; the six-foot, three-inch prima ballerina; the witch; and one of the killer bees stood around the trauma area waiting for the disaster to show up. It took maybe two minutes and they brought in this eight-year-old. He had run out into the street and had gotten flattened by a van. The van then stopped and the kid got pinned under the back wheels. They started CPR [**cardio-pulmonary resuscitation**] out on the street, but you could tell it wasn't doing him much good. He was pulseless and breathless, and when they hooked him up to a monitor, he was flatline [**he had no electrical activity in his heart**].

We knew it was probably going to be pretty hopeless, but we started doing everything anyway. The chief intubated him, Peter started pumping his chest, and Terry and I tried to get lines [**IVs**] into him. I somehow got one in his right arm, which was a miracle in itself, and we started pushing bicarb [**sodium bicarbonate, to reverse the buildup of acid in the blood**] and epi [**epinephrine, in an attempt to get the heart to start beating again**], but nothing happened. Then the surgeons came by and offered to crack the kid's chest for us [**perform an emergency thoracotomy, an operation in which the chest is opened so that the heart can be directly massaged**]. Hey, when five surgeons walk up to you with scalpels in their hands and say they'd like to crack a patient's chest, it's hard to say no. So the kid got his chest cracked and they found that he had a bronchopleural fistula. [**The impact of the van had caused the left main stem bronchus, the main windpipe to the left lung, to tear in half. Oxygen that was being forced into the boy's windpipe was ending up in the pleural space outside the lung, causing an ever-worsening tension pneumothorax.**] It was about then that we realized that this code was pretty much over.

I walked out of the trauma area, and the boy's mother was standing there less than ten feet away. She was literally being held up by one of the nurses. She said, "Doctor, how is he? Is he going to be okay?" I didn't see any way out; I was too upset to come up with a lie. So that's when I, wearing my Bozo wig; my Bozo makeup; my Bozo shoes; and my Bozo suit, which was now covered with blood, told the woman that her son had died.

She went crazy. She started crying and she fell down on the floor. I felt like a total idiot standing there dressed like that, and there was nothing I could do to change anything. One of the hospital administrators, the guy we call the administrator-in-charge-of-patients-dying because he always seems to show up when this kind of thing happens, came, and he, the nurse, and I lifted the mother up off the floor. The administrator led the woman out of the ER. I don't know where they went, but before seeing the next patient, I changed my clothes and took off the stupid makeup. I don't think I'll wear that costume again. The bloodstains kind of take all the fun out of it. And next year, if I'm on call on Halloween again, I don't think I'm going to dress up.

Tuesday, November 5, 1985, 10:00 P.M.

I'm feeling much better today. Sure, a weekend off, that's just what I needed. It gave Carole and me two whole days to fight about whether we should get married. It was a whole lot of fun. At least she didn't make me wear my Bozo costume while we argued.

I really don't know what to do about this. I don't want to get married during my internship. Can you imagine that? Falling asleep standing up right in the middle of the ceremony. And then the wedding night! Yes, the wedding night must be a memorable event for the intern's spouse. Eight continuous hours of snoring. Seriously, being married is hard enough when you lead a relatively normal life. I don't think it'd be possible for us to survive if we got married while I was doing this. But Carole thinks we should do it. She says if we got married, she'd be able to take better care of me for the rest of the year. I think I'll eventually wind up marrying Carole. We get along very well and we basically want the same things out of life. I just can't do it yet. I think I'll be able to think a little more clearly after this is over, but that's not for seven months yet. Well, what can I do? I'll just try to hold her off as long as possible.

And then, after that fabulous weekend, I got to be on call again last night in the Jonas Bronck emergency room. And what a night it was! We were five hours behind the whole time. We had two security guards stationed at the doors to protect us. Every five minutes, another angry customer would appear and want to know why his or her precious little child who had been sneezing for three days hadn't been seen yet. And what interesting patients I had to take care of! I got this four-day-old who, through some sort of screwup in our world-renowned Social Service Department, wound up getting discharged from the nursery with his psychotic mother who also happened to be a crackhead. Usually when a baby's born to a crackhead mother, Social Services picks up their hot line and gets a BCW hold slapped on the kid so that the baby can be kept in the hospital while the BCW figures out what to do with him. We usually have to keep them longer than three days anyway because the kids usually have withdrawal symptoms and need to be treated. But somehow Social Service missed the boat and sent him home early.

When the nursery's social worker realized the kid had been discharged, she called the cops and had them find the kid and bring him back. The cops did a great job: They went out and scooped up the baby, the mother, and, lucky for us, the father and brought them all in. Of course, they didn't mention to them what was going on. So not only did we have two psychotic crackheads roaming around the ER, we also had two psychotic crackheads who were paranoid and had no idea what was going on, which is a wonderful combination.

Well, it didn't take long for them to figure it all out. Once they woke up to the fact that we were planning to admit the kid and slap a BCW hold on him and that their chance of ever getting him back again was about the same as my chance of being elected president of the United States, they let their best qualities come to the surface. The father picked up the baby like he was a football and started to move toward the exit. The city cops, who were still hanging around, knew the mistake had been the hospital's and not the parents'. They also knew that the parents hadn't done anything wrong, at least not at that exact moment, and so they didn't try to stop them. The cops left, and that's when the hospital security guards stepped in. They caught the guy, brought him back, put them all in a room, and watched them for the rest of the night, but they weren't exactly happy to do it. They acted as if they had better things to do than baby-sit for a couple of ranting junkies.

I tried my hand at talking the parents down. I told them that putting the baby in the hospital was the best thing for him, that if he was hooked we could give him medication to make him better and slowly wean him off. It sounded great to me, but of course the parents, who were pretty crazed, didn't buy it. Then the social worker showed up and she talked to them for about a half hour. Obviously she made just as great an impact on them as I did, because when they came out, the mother was still holding on to the baby. We didn't know what to do next, so we had a priest come down and talk to them, we had some friend of the family's who had shown up talk to them, but nothing seemed to do any good. Finally, after about five hours of this nonsense, the mother said she had to get home right away because she needed something to steady her nerves. She handed the baby over to the social worker and she and the father kind of ran for the door. So we got the baby back. Her fix was more important than the baby in the long run.

We got out this morning at four-thirty. I didn't get home until after five, and I fell right to sleep. I didn't even get out of my clothes. I had two and a half hours of sleep. But it was quality sleep, so that makes a big difference. Yeah, right! And when I woke up, I was still wearing my smelly, dirty clothes. What a wonderful experience this internship is!

At least I got to go to my grandmother's for dinner tonight. My grandmother's good, she's doing fine. I'm sure she thinks I've lost my mind or something because I can't keep up even boring conversations with her and I keep falling asleep every five minutes. But she doesn't say anything. She just keeps the food coming.

I'm going to sleep now. Maybe when I wake up, I'll realize this has all been a dream.

Monday, November 11, 1985

I'm suddenly not feeling very well. I think I'm coming down with something. I've had this stomachache and a sore throat since this morning. I have the chills, too, so I probably have a fever. I can't understand why I'm getting sick. After all, all I do is hang around an emergency room, working twenty-hour shifts, seeing sick children who sneeze on me, cough on me, pee on me, shit on me, and vomit on me. What possible means would I have of getting sick?

My mother came to visit on Saturday. She walked into my apartment, took one look, and said something like, "Oh, dear, I hadn't heard anything about a nuclear attack in this part of the Bronx." (I get my sense of humor from my mother's side of the family.) I have to admit, I have kind of neglected the housework over the past few months. So my mother rolled up her sleeves, got to work, and spent the next six hours cleaning up my apartment. I had all sorts of great things planned; I was going to take her to lunch at the Jonas Bronck coffee shop. I figured she'd love those mock-turkey sandwiches. Oh, what the hell! We did go out for dinner at a nice Italian restaurant. It was nice to see her. And now I can be sick in a nice, clean apartment.

I took some Tylenol, but it hasn't done any good. I think I'm really sick.

Wednesday, November 13, 1985, 9:00 P.M.

I'm dying. I didn't expect it to be one of the patients who would finally get me, and I never thought they'd use germ warfare. But there it was, the most virulent GI [gastrointestinal] bug ever to exist, and now I'm sure it's only a matter of time.

I fell asleep Monday night at about seven. I wasn't feeling well Tuesday, but I made it to work and somehow I made it through the day. I took my temperature in the ER at about one in the afternoon. It was over a hundred. But hey, I'm an intern, and interns can do anything, including working a full fourteen-hour day when they're sick. I came home yesterday and fell asleep right away. I slept until 11 P.M., and when I woke up, I had the worst cramps in the history of the human race. I ran to the bathroom and stayed there for the next four hours. I got back into bed sometime after three and I fell asleep for a while. Then I woke up with worse cramps than before and tried to get up to run to the bathroom. My brain was strongly in favor of the idea but my body just wouldn't budge. I managed to crawl out of bed and make it to the bathroom just in time and I fell asleep in there until my alarm went off at seven-thirty. I still could barely move. At that point, something told me that I probably wasn't going to be able to make it to work.

I called Jon Golden [one of the chief residents] and told him what was going on. I told him I was on call and that I probably wouldn't be able to make it in. Calling in sick on the day you're on call is the biggest sin an intern can commit. But what could I do? I couldn't even walk! Jon told me not to worry, just to try to get well and make it back tomorrow.

I got into bed and fell asleep, but Elizabeth woke me up at about ten. She's on the Jonas Bronck wards this month. She'd heard I was sick and wanted to know if I was making it up just to cash in on some sympathy. I guess when she heard my voice, she realized I was serious. She asked if there was anything I needed; I asked for cyanide. She said she'd see what she could do. She asked if I thought I was dehydrated and I said I was easily about 10 percent dry. [**The main complication of gastroenteritis is dehydration. Five percent dehydration is enough to require hospitalization; 10 percent is serious, and 15 percent may lead to shock.**] She said I should come in and let her start an IV. I told her I hated pain, and knowing her technical skills, I would never allow her anywhere near me with a needle in her hand. She thanked me for the vote of confidence and said I must be feeling better to be making jokes. I said, "Who's making jokes?"

I am actually feeling better tonight, but I still fall down every time I try to get out of bed, and I don't think that's normal. I feel guilty about not going to work. I know the other people on call tonight are probably working their butts off and cursing me every chance they get. But what can I do?

This is such a screwed-up job. In what other profession would you actually feel guilty calling in sick when you really are sick? Lawyers get sick and take a week off, schoolteachers take days off like it's coming to them, which it is. It's only us interns and residents who feel guilty about it.

Sunday, November 17, 1985

I'm feeling 100 percent better. Well, maybe not 100 percent, maybe only 80 percent, but I'm feeling well enough today to go into the city with Carole to see a movie. I don't know what we're going to see yet, and it doesn't really matter. The only thing I care about is that the theater has seats comfortable enough for me to fall asleep in. Of course, after last night, a chair with spikes coming out of it would be comfortable enough for me to fall asleep in.

I won't say last night was bad but at about two o'clock there were still about ten charts in the box, and Peter Carson and I were seeing patients in the asthma room. Peter's kid was a really cute three-year-old girl. She was sitting there alone because her mother was out registering her and she was scared. But very shyly, she asked Peter if he was a doctor. "Yup," Peter said.

"And you don't ever go to sleep?" the girl asked.

"Nope," Peter answered.

"Never?" the kid asked, amazed.

"Never," Peter answered. And he meant it. Then we both ran out of the asthma room and cracked up. It seemed really true last night. I've got to get out of this ER!

Thursday, November 21, 1985

Did I say something the other day about having to get out of the ER? Well, the chief residents must have overheard me, because on Tuesday afternoon they called me into their office and told me that I wouldn't have to work in the ER Tuesday night. That would have been wonderful, except for the fact that they also told me that I had been selected, out of the entire intern group, to have the distinction of being the first person ever to take call in the new neonatal intensive-care unit that had opened that morning on 7 South. What a thrill that was! It sure is something I'll never forget as long as I live! And you know what? After one night on 7 South, I'm ready to spend the rest of the year in the ER.

What happened was, Val Saunders was supposed to be on that night, but she called in sick. Everybody said she wasn't really sick, she just didn't want to be on call the first night in the new unit, which was really very sweet of her if it was in fact true. Somebody had to work there, and since I was supposed to be on in the ER and there were four other people down there that night, the chiefs figured I was "it."

So there I was, sitting in the nurses' station on 7 South, waiting for some disaster to happen. I'd never even been in a NICU before, and here I was, taking care of twenty-eight tiny babies. Just looking at them scared me to death! And nobody knew how anything worked! They hadn't even figured out how to turn the heat on yet! They couldn't find the outlets to plug in the damn ventilators! And sometime during the move, somebody had misplaced the coffee pot, so we couldn't even make coffee! And I was supposed to cover all those babies! It's the kind of situation that'd make for an outstanding horror movie!

Somehow, the babies and I all made it through. I didn't get any sleep. I spent the whole night running from room to room trying to figure out what was going on, but nobody died, nobody even crumped, and when the morning came, I was still standing on my feet. I think I did pretty well. Maybe I'll go into neonatology.

By the way, after I finished yesterday morning, I went into the chiefs' office and they thanked me for filling in. I very graciously told them that if they ever pulled anything like that on me again, I'd reach down their throats, yank their spleens out through their mouths, and refeed it to them. I was very polite about it. I think they got the point.

BOB

November 1985

When I was a house officer, we occasionally saw children who were beaten or molested by their parents or other adults, but these cases seemed to be few and far between. I vividly remember one of the first abuse cases in which I was involved. In clinic one day during a month of OPD at Jonas Bronck, I found that I had been assigned a new patient, a little eleven-year-old girl named Brenda. As soon as I called her into the examining room, her mother began to tell me that Brenda never seemed to have any energy; she was always tired, was complaining of too many bellyaches, and seemed to be gaining a great deal of weight. When I started to examine the girl, it took less than a minute to diagnose the problem: Brenda was about six months pregnant.

Realizing that I now was going to have the gargantuan job of informing this mother that her daughter, a child herself, was going to have a baby, I told Brenda to get dressed and sent her out to the waiting room. I started the conversation awkwardly, asking if Brenda had begun to get her period yet and whether she had a boyfriend. Finally, after beating around the bush long enough, I blurted out the news to the woman.

She wasn't surprised. She told me she had seen her daughter's clothes get tight and had noticed that her breasts had become swollen. Then she told me an amazing piece of news: She knew who the father of the baby was. He was Brenda's fifteen-year-old brother, the person who was entrusted with caring for the girl after school when the mother was at work. The brother, apparently fed up with having been saddled with the responsibility of looking after his sister when he'd rather have been out with his friends, had taken his frustrations out on the girl.

172

I spent hours with that family. We talked about abortion, an option Brenda's mother rejected for religious reasons. We talked about the effect the pregnancy would have on Brenda and on her brother. We talked about what measures should be taken to prevent anything like this from happening again. Brenda's mother assured me that she would discipline the boy in her own way and begged me not to report the case to the Bureau of Child Welfare, the state-run agency charged with investigating possible cases of child abuse. After long discussions with the mother and the clinic attending, I decided to go along with her wishes. That might have been a mistake: I never saw Brenda or her mother again.

I think I made that mistake for the same reason I can remember Brenda so distinctly: Hers was one of the few cases of child abuse I was called on to manage during my residency. Now, several years later, an intern can't even make it through a single week in the OPD without getting involved with the BCW. Child abuse and neglect have definitely increased over the past few years. Rarely a day goes by now without a family of two or three or four kids who have been abandoned or beaten or sexually molested being escorted into the emergency room. I was working in the ER last week and the cops brought in a family of seven children ranging in age from ten months to eight years. The parents were both crack dealers; the mother had been arrested the previous Thursday, and the father had been taken into custody the day after that. These children had been left to fend for themselves for three full days. They were starving; dirty; and very, very scared. Medical care in their cases included food, baths, and hugs. The police had been called by a neighbor who had complained that the baby was crying too loudly. They were temporarily placed in a shelter.

Although child abuse is clearly on the rise in New York, there's another reason that so many more abuse patients are being identified. The house officers are far more sensitized to the signs and symptoms of child abuse than my fellow residents and I were in the early 1980s. Interns are asking questions I never would have even thought of asking, such as: Where does the child sleep? How many people sleep in the same room? Who watches the child during the day? And they're performing more pelvic and rectal exams in younger kids than we performed.

Through these means, they're finding evidence that we simply would have missed.

The net effect of all of this is that the Bureau of Child Welfare has become completely overwhelmed. The BCW always has had its problems. Calling their twenty-four-hour hot-line number to report a family has always been an exercise in frustration. They've been slow-moving in completing investigations. But this has all become worse since the current "epidemic" of child abuse hit. And new methods of guaranteeing the safety of at-risk children have had to be invented.

The "joint response" for reporting serious abuse involving children was only recently developed. When the examining doctor believes that a child has been abused and that his or her life may be in danger, both the BCW and the New York City Police must be informed immediately. A member of the sex crimes unit of the police force is then immediately dispatched to investigate the situation. The child, who may have been beaten by the mother's ex-boyfriend, may have been sexually molested by a relative who lives in the same apartment, or may have been removed from a home in which another child has been killed or seriously injured, cannot be released into the custody of the parents or other relatives until the results of the police investigation are known. Since most abused children appear in the emergency room during the evening or night, sleeping accommodations for the child must be arranged. This entails either admission to the hospital or, if possible, transfer to some shelter.

To the house officer, dealing with child abuse translates into pure aggravation. There's endless scut that must be done. In cases in which sexual abuse is suspected, a "rape kit" must be completed and followed to the letter so that the collected specimens can be used later in court as evidence; reams of medical and legal forms must be completed according to strict guidelines; telephone calls to agents who are themselves overworked and who aren't always the most caring or sympathetic individuals must be made; and careful explanations to hostile, suspicious, and often guilt-ridden parents must be given. All this must be carried out by doctors to whom child abuse is a particular anathema; these people, who become adjusted to death and disease, frequently become physically ill themselves while working with a child who has been abused.

The net effect of all this is that progress through the pile of

ER charts is dramatically slowed. A house officer can be tied up for an entire night reporting a single child abuse case. In an emergency room in which three or four residents are seeing all patients, the loss of one or sometimes two doctors can add endless hours to the waiting time. Parents sitting with sick children become angry and hostile as the clock ticks on. Often the whole situation ends with hospital guards being called to protect everyone from injury.

ANDY

December 1985

Wednesday, November 27, 1985

So I survived my first night on call at Jonas Bronck. It was busy, another night of sleep deprivation. Harvey Abelson announced in front of about six people that I was going back to Boston. Not in a real obvious way; no, he was very subtle. He said something like, "So I hear you're going to Boston next year!" He said it really loud, in kind of a nasty tone. So now I feel a little bit like a *persona non grata* around some people. What do people think when you leave a program? Do they think you're turning your nose up at it and, in a sense, at them? Can't they accept that you're leaving because there's something else, something more important than being in this program for you? Why can't they just accept that?

Friday, November 29, 1985

I'm on a flight to Boston, to spent the weekend at home. This is the first year I was away from my family on Thanksgiving. It was a real bummer. I was on call yesterday, and there was nothing to eat. Stupidly, I forgot to bring anything to the hospital from home. I should have known that there would have been nothing available to eat at Jonas Bronck, but I just didn't think about it. I mean, there was *nothing*. I starved during Thanksgiving. What an image! Well, it'll make going home even better. I don't know . . . I just hope I'm never on call for another Thanksgiving.

It's been an amazing few days. I started working on 8 East this week. It took only a few days for word to get around that

I'm leaving the program next year, and I've already noticed a big change in the way people are reacting to me. It's a funny thing; some people want everybody to know that I'm leaving. For example, Alan Cozza, the director of the pediatric service at Jonas Bronck, has referred to my leaving in front of a lot of people on a couple of occasions over the past week. He's not doing it with any kind of malice. I'm not really sure why he's doing it, whether there's a certain sense of pride he feels, like he's proud of this program and thinks that when I go to Boston I should reflect how good it is, or if he really wants to mark me as different from everybody else. It's a strange thing.

Thursday, December 12, 1985, 11:00 P.M.

I don't think I've put much of an entry into this thing for a long time. I think I've made it out of my month or two of depression, and I haven't felt the need to vent about things as badly. Even though I'll still wind up cursing about life, and I still hate being on call more than anything else I can ever remember hating, and I'm still chronically tired, I'm definitely not depressed anymore. I don't know why; maybe it's because I know vacation's coming up very soon. Maybe it's because I'm so goddamned used to working all the time now. Maybe it's because I like working on 8 East because of the social feel of the place; it's as if the whole staff is part of one big family. I just don't know.

I find myself looking back on the past six months and realizing that so far this is the month I've enjoyed the most out of all of them. Jonas Bronck and my month at University Hospital are definitely my two favorites. Isn't that strange? University Hospital was like a torture chamber half the time. But there were some really nice things about it, too. Cute nurses, that helped, but I think it was also because the patients were complicated and interesting. Or maybe it was just because it seemed like it was just us residents against everybody else. I think I like the idea of working in a tertiary-care hospital. Everything is right there, there aren't any interruptions from the emergency room or the clinics or anyplace else; it gives you a sense of self-containment. But I also like Jonas Bronck, which is just the opposite. It's hard to justify that, it's hard to figure how I can like two such different systems.

I have to present chief of service rounds again tomorrow.

[These rounds are held every Friday at noon at Jonas Bronck Hospital. An interesting case is selected, a summary is prepared and presented by the responsible intern, and the patient is discussed in depth by the faculty's expert in that particular field. It's a well-liked teaching conference, but it's a pain in the ass for the overworked intern who has to prepare the presentation.] I wish they'd ask somebody else. It takes a long time to get that stuff together. I did it once already this month and I had to do a grand rounds, too. [Grand rounds, held on Wednesday at noon, is occasionally constructed around an in-house patient. As in the case of chief of service rounds, the intern caring for the patient is responsible for preparing the case presentation.]

We've got a pretty good team this month. Our senior, Pat Cummings, has turned out to be okay. I actually like him; he's a good resident. He's kind of got a gruff, hard edge to him, but other than that he's a funny guy.

And I like my medical student. We spent a fair amount of time together today, doing scut. Makes all the difference in the world to do scut with another person. We had to stick some kid five times to get his IV in. I finally got it in, and it ran like a dream. I hope the damned kid doesn't kick it out tonight. It looked good enough to stay in a couple of days.

Last night wasn't too bad. I got four admissions and I managed to get a couple of hours of sleep. And I got everything done. For me that's good. I couldn't do that at the beginning of the year. If I got four admissions back in August, I'd be up all night, writing and writing and writing. Now I write less and go to sleep. By the end of the year, I should be able to do ten or twelve a night. Ten or twelve admissions a night—boy, is that a horrible thought.

I've got the FIB service [FIB: fever in baby]. I have six patients and they have a combined age of about nine months. And they all look and act alike; it's hard to tell one apart from all the others. It's not very interesting.

I ran into Mike Miller the other day. When he saw me, he kind of frowned. And I sort of frowned when I saw him frown. I said, "What's the face?" He said, "Well, I'm just sad you're going to be leaving and you're not going to be around here next year." I don't know if that's what he was really frowning about. At any rate, it was a nice thing to say.

This tape recorder's kind of annoying me; it's making weird noises. It's hypnotizing me . . . Well, you get the idea. Those sleeping noises go on for the remainder of this tape, which I'll be recording over now, because ten minutes of sleeping noises aren't very exciting. I fell asleep again, fell asleep while recording on this fucking tape recorder.

Sunday, December 22, 1985

I've actually wanted to talk into this machine for a few days but I ran out of tapes and haven't had a chance to get any until now. It wasn't that I was saving up anything much to say, just the sense of having something to say.

I've had this whole weekend off and in some ways it felt like my vacation actually started yesterday. I'll be on call tomorrow and then I leave on Tuesday morning. I'm tempted to wear a big button to work tomorrow that says, "THEY CAN'T HURT ME NOW!" I've told several people that no one's died on me yet this month, and everyone's said the same thing: "Don't be so smug. You still have one more night!" But I feel somewhat confident that I'll make it unscathed off this ward and that I'll always have fond memories of general pediatrics when it's provided in a place like Jonas Bronck, surrounded by lots of smart, nice people in a great environment without disasters.

Well, that's not exactly true; I did have one near disaster, a kid with asthma who I was supposed to admit to the ward but who wound up going to the ICU on an Isuprel drip [**Isuprel drip: a continuous IV infusion of isoproterenol, a drug used in cases of asthma when there is danger of respiratory failure**]. I was the one who started that Isuprel drip. I didn't know how to do that before. Hey! I now know how to do an Isuprel drip! Now I pretty much know everything.

We're going to New Orleans this vacation, I just found out yesterday. I got home postcall, turned on my answering machine, and there was a message from my brother saying he and his wife and Karen all decided it would be great fun to go to New Orleans and they asked if I wanted to do it and I said sure. I'd go anywhere. Just to get the hell out of the damn Bronx!

I know this sounds weird, but a lot of people I talk to say I'm the most enthusiastic person about the program. Isn't that ironic? Here I am, I've been depressed for months, and now I've even

decided to leave at the end of the year, and I'm the most enthusiastic of the interns! But it's true, I have been in a good mood
for the past month, and I've started to wonder why. I think it
had a lot to do with two things: first, being on 8 East, which
was really great; and second, knowing I've finally got this vacation coming up. I survived, I've made it through six long
months! I've reached the halfway point.

I feel like I've gotten a lot out of this first half of the year. I
think I've learned a lot. I don't know how I'll compare with
those second years at Children's when I start out there next year.
Will they be way ahead of me? Will they know a lot more,
having been in that highly academic environment for their internships? Will my vast ability to do scut really pay off at all?
Will it matter? I don't know.

Will my learned ability to manipulate the ancillary personnel
to get patient care done quickly and efficiently make any difference in a place where the ancillary services are actually good?
I mean, I've gotten good at working through this system, I've
finally learned how to get things done fast. I've just watched
how the third years do it and I've figured out you either stretch
the truth or you simply lie outright. You have to make everything
seem like an incredible emergency or people will ignore you.
You tell the elevator operator that you need an elevator right
away or else the patient's going to die. And they'll do it! That
elevator will be there in a second. It's too bad, but it's just the
way it is here, it's just a game you have to play if you want to
get things done or you want to take proper care of your patients.
You have to lie; they just don't give a shit any way else.

I'm learning to be efficient and how to be smart. Friday night
on call was pretty quiet, I didn't have a bad night, I only got two
admissions; one was a FIB, the other a UTI [urinary tract
infection]. I even got a couple of hours of sleep. So on Saturday
morning when I was postcall, instead of going right home, I sat
down and wrote four of my off-service notes on my chronic
patients. I put them in my clipboard, I'll bring them back tomorrow, date them, then I'll stick them in the chart, and I'll be
done with them. The fact of the matter is, I've got to get out of
there Tuesday morning and catch a plane, and I want to be able
to bolt at early as I can.

The UTI I admitted was kind of interesting. It was a one-
month-old who came up as a FIB. Of course, no one in the ER

had done a sed rate [**erythrocyte sedimentation rate—the rate at which red blood cells settle when left to stand in a capillary tube; an elevated sed rate is a sign of inflammation and therefore an indication of infection**] or a UA [**urinalysis**]; thanks a lot. It's always the second and the third years who send them in unworked up. So I basically did the whole admission by myself. Pat kind of danced in for a minute, copied down the history I took, poked and prodded the kid, then went back to sleep, and I finished the rest of the workup. I actually got one of the night-shift nurses to hold the kid while I drew the blood and did the suprapubic [**bladder tap**], and there they were on the unspun urine, sheets of polys [**polys: polymorphonuclear leukocytes, white blood cells that flock to the site of a bacterial infection**] and gram-negative rods [**the microscopic appearance of E. coli**]. So I decided what to do: I wrote the orders to start the antibiotics, went in, woke up Pat, and said, "Pat, this kid's got a UTI and I'm starting her on ampicillin and Cephotaxime [**two types of antibiotics**], a hundred per kilo of both. How's that sound?" He mumbled something like, "Huh? Fine," and went back to sleep. In the morning he said he was very impressed with the gram stain. I had done the right things. So how do you like that? I can now manage unbelievably simple problems all by myself!

You know, I might have been able to do all this a few months ago, but I sure wouldn't have felt right about it. Now I feel like I know what I'm doing. Watch, I'll come back and something horrible will have happened by Monday.

I played Santa Claus on the ward the other day. I put on the red suit and the hat and the big beard and the hair and stuffed a pillow under there and strapped it on with some kerlix [**rolls of gauze bandages**] and said, "Ho, ho, ho, ho, ho! Merry Christmas!" about three hundred times. I danced around on my toes. Everybody told me what a wonderful Santa Claus I was. And John Mason [**a four-year-old boy who is a long-term occupant of the AIDS section of 8 West**], who usually runs away from Santa Claus, thought it was a lot of fun this year and was totally thrilled. Filled with happiness. I was glad I could do that, make little John happy for a while.

AMY
December 1985

Sunday, December 1, 1985

This internship is really rotten. There's nothing about it that I like. The only thing that gives me any kind of enjoyment right now is Sarah, and I can't even really enjoy being with her because in the back of my mind I always know that I'm going to have to be back at the hospital soon. And when I'm in the hospital, I spend my time with all these nice children who have terrible things wrong with them, and I know I'm going to have to watch them get sicker and sicker for thirty-six hours at a stretch. I don't know, I have pictures of about a half dozen of these children burned into my mind. I haven't been able to forget the little girl I saw in the ER last week who was sexually abused; I've been thinking about her constantly. There's her, that leukemic who died on Adolescent, and a couple of others.

I've been thinking this weekend that if I knew then what I know now, I never would have done this internship. Everything's so hopeless; I'm so hopeless. It isn't even half over yet, I just got back from vacation, and I'm already so tired of all of it! I don't know what I'm going to do. I don't know what I can do.

Mike Miller called me into his office last week. He told me some of the people in the department were kind of upset with my attitude. Screw them! He said there were some people who thought I wasn't taking the job seriously enough. Terrific, just terrific! I asked Mike how many of these people had to take night call every third night with a baby at home. How many of them had to neglect their responsibilities as a parent in order to work in the hospital? I told him I was doing the best I could and if he or anybody else didn't like it, he should just fire me! He said it wasn't him, that he understood what was going on, but that this had come up at some meeting they had had and he had been the one who was supposed to have a talk with me about it.

He also asked if I wanted to come back as a junior resident next year. He said he needed to know within a few days. I told him I'd have to think about it. After what he'd said to me I was pretty damned angry and I seriously thought of going in and telling him to go fuck himself, that I wouldn't be coming back next year or ever again. But after I cooled off a little, I finally told him on Friday that I would be back. I don't know. I could have taken a year or two off; Larry was encouraging me to do whatever I thought was best, and for a while, taking some time off made a lot of sense. But then, after I'd been working in the emergency room for a while, I figured this wasn't too bad and I thought I could stick it out. I still have the feeling that if I were to decide to take some time off, I'd have a lot of trouble getting myself motivated enough to get back into it. But this whole weekend, I've been thinking, maybe I made a mistake. Maybe staying isn't such a good idea. The problem is, I don't know what I can do about it now.

I'm doing Children's at Mount Scopus this month. It was good to get out of the Jonas Bronck ER. The actual work there isn't so bad; it's just that there are so many bad things that happen to the kids who come in, like that sexually abused girl. Seeing kids like that every day gets to be too much pretty quickly.

Coming to Mount Scopus isn't great either. It seems like everybody has an attitude, all the nurses and the clerks. They all seem to resent having us around, like we're getting in the way of their work or something. This week, Harrison [**Harrison Boyd, the other intern on the Northwest 5 Children's team**] wrote a q4h order for Demerol [**an order for the painkiller Demerol to be given every four hours, around the clock**] for this five-year-old with sickle-cell disease who was in with a painful crisis. One of the nurses came up to him while we were on work rounds and said, "We don't give pain meds q4h on this floor." Just like that; she simply refused to do it. Harrison told her that the child was in a lot of pain and he thought she required medication around the clock. The nurse told him it didn't matter, the rules are that they can only give pain meds on a prn basis [**prn: as needed**]. So now this little girl has to feel pain and beg for her medication before someone will give it to her.

The nurses say they're afraid a q4h order will make the patient addicted. They say they're afraid they'll wind up turning the child into a drug addict. Turn a five-year-old into a drug addict? That's a lot of nonsense. But that's the way things are done at Mount Scopus, and there's nothing you can do to change it.

There aren't a lot of patients on the ward right now, and most of the ones who are there are just post-op cleft lips and palates **[Mount Scopus has a large craniofacial center]**. We do have a couple of fairly sick patients, and one of them is mine. She's a really sad case: She's a ten-year-old with neurofibromatosis. **[This is an inherited disorder in which, for reasons that are not yet clear, the affected individual may develop dark pigmented spots and a variety of tumors of the skin, optic nerve, the brain, and other internal organs. Most people with neurofibromatosis live a normal life; some, like John Merrick, the "elephant man," are severely deformed.]** She was perfectly well until last week, when she started having trouble urinating. Her mother brought her to the ER last Tuesday and they did a KUB **[X ray of the abdomen; called KUB for kidneys, ureters, and bladder]** and found she had a big mass in her pelvis. Then they did a chest X ray and found another tumor in her lung. She was admitted to Children's, and on Thursday she had a CT scan that showed she also had a brain tumor. They're taking her to the OR tomorrow to biopsy the pelvic and the lung tumors, but the oncologists don't think she's going to do very well. It's too bad, too; she seems like she could have been a nice, normal girl.

Wednesday, December 4, 1985

It's getting cold. It's really turning into winter, and I don't know if I'm ready for that to happen yet. I guess I'm kind of depressed, and the weather isn't helping things any.

Things on the ward are getting worse. This morning a little girl with sickle-cell disease died while we were on work rounds. She had been admitted a few hours before with what looked like pneumonia. Harrison had brought her up from the emergency room, started her on antibiotics, put her on oxygen, and went on with the rest of his work. At about eight-fifteen, while we were on work rounds, the girl's mother came up to us and said her daughter was breathing funny. We ran into the room and watched as she arrested. We called a code, and people started flying into the room from all over the place. We worked on her for over an hour, but we never got her pulse back. Her mother was hysterical. It was completely unexpected. After it was over, Harrison locked himself into the on-call room and wouldn't come out. It was terrible. And we still have no idea what happened or why it happened.

On Monday I admitted six new patients, which is busy for Children's. Most of them were pre-ops for Tuesday, but they still needed to be worked up and have bloods drawn and all the rest of the endless scut that goes with an admission. I tried to get my student to help, but she simply refused. I don't know what it is with these medical students; when I was doing my clerkships, I'd sooner jump out a window than tell my intern I wasn't going to do the things he or she asked.

Angela, that girl with neurofibromatosis, is not doing well at all. She went to the OR on Monday to have her tumors biopsied. They turned out to be different types of malignancies, which is very unusual. It's also terrible in terms of her prognosis. She spent Monday night in the ICU and then came down to the ward again on Tuesday. The oncologists are talking about what they're going to do with her; it looks like she's going to need both chemo and radiation, but they have to decide which order to do them in and when to start. Nobody's said anything to Angela yet. I think she knows, though. She's pretty smart and she seems very sad.

I went to talk to Mike Miller today about next year. I went up to his office, and when he saw me standing there, he said, "Amy, what's wrong?" I guess my face told him I was upset. I went into his office and we closed the door and I started telling him everything that had been happening, and about five minutes into it I started crying and I just couldn't stop. He held my hand and tried to calm me down, but I just couldn't stop crying. I cried for fifteen, twenty minutes. I knew he was starting to get bored with me so I tried hard to control myself and finally I stopped. I told him I wasn't sure whether I wanted to come back next year. He told me he understood and that whatever I wanted to do would be okay but that I had to sit down and give it some serious thought, taking everything into account before making up my mind. He said he'd hold off submitting my name for reappointment for another few days but I should try to get back to him by sometime next week. Then I left and went back to the ward.

That's the first time that ever happened to me. I'm not a crier. The last time I remember crying is when my mother died. This isn't nearly as bad as that was, so I'm kind of surprised. I don't know, maybe it's because I'm so tired, or because working in the Bronx is so depressing, or maybe it's because I miss Sarah so much and I know I'm missing so much of her infancy. All I know is, if the rest of internship is going to be like this, I'm never going to make it.

Sunday, December 15, 1985

I haven't recorded anything in a while. I've been going through a very difficult time. I think I'm finally out of my depression, though. I don't know why that happened. Nothing's changed; I'm not spending any more time with my family, the work on the ward is just about the same, but for some reason I'm feeling a little better.

Maybe one thing that made me feel a little better is that I finally made a decision about next year. I went to see Mike Miller again last week and told him I had decided to stay. He seemed relieved to hear it and then he said some nice things to me. He told me he had been very upset after our conversation the day I broke down in his office and that he was glad I had decided to stay because he thought I'd make a good resident. I don't know whether he meant it or not, especially after what he told me about that meeting the faculty had last month, but it still was a nice thing for him to say. It made me feel good to hear it.

Sarah stood up by herself for the first time yesterday. I was on call, of course, so I didn't get to see it, but Larry called me at work to tell me. He said he and Sarah had been sitting on the floor of the living room and at one point she just climbed up the edge of the couch and stood there. She isn't even nine months old yet! She's done everything early; she sat at five months, so I'm not surprised she stood by herself so young. She's like a miracle; it's absolutely amazing just to be around her and watch as she grows and develops. I've been so worried, but she seems to be a normal, well-adjusted little girl. Maybe she's better off with me at work; maybe Marie is doing a better job with her than I would have.

Things at work are about the same. Angela is getting worse; we started her on chemotherapy about a week ago, but it isn't doing any good. She had a seizure last week. We brought her out of it with IV Valium and Dilantin [an anticonvulsant medication], but the seizure wasn't a good sign. She had a repeat CT scan a few hours after the seizure and it showed the tumor was larger than it had been before the biopsy. Right after the seizure, her mother, who's been at her bedside ever since Angela got here, told me for the first time that she thought Angela was going to die. Angela's going to start radiation therapy next week. Maybe that'll help; everyone doubts it, though. I hope they're wrong.

Sunday, December 22, 1985

Tomorrow's my last night on Children's. After that I go into the nursery at Jonas Bronck. I'm not looking forward to that. Nursery's the one rotation I'm really frightened of. My month on Children's wasn't all that bad. It would have been great had I not gotten so depressed in the middle of it. Children's is a good place; most of the patients are pretty healthy and almost everyone gets well without much work from us. Angela isn't getting better, though, and we're all getting depressed about that. I guess we've all come to accept the fact that she's going to die sometime soon. I just hope she holds out till Wednesday. I'd really rather not have her die on my time.

MARK

December 1985

Tuesday, December 3, 1985

Well, I finally figured out how they decide what ward a kid'll
go to when he gets admitted to Mount Scopus. If he still sleeps
in a crib, they put him on Infants'; if he's out of the crib but
hasn't committed any violent crime yet, they put him on Children's; and once he's committed his first violent crime, he automatically goes to Adolescent. Yes, what a wonderful
experience it is to take care of ten- and eleven-year-olds wanted
by the police in three states for armed robbery.

Okay, so maybe I'm exaggerating, but only a little. What a
weird place this Adolescent ward is! As I see it, we've got three
groups of patients. The first are those kids with truly medical
problems; these are mainly kids with different types of cancers;
they really make things pretty sad. The second are the girls with
eating disorders like anorexia nervosa and bulimia; what a thrill
it is to take care of eighteen-year-old girls who weigh seventy
pounds and think they're too fat, and who spend the entire day
exercising and trying to find places to hide their vomit. And the
third group are the drug addicts who come in for detox and for
antibiotics for their skin abscesses. Yes, this is all a very rewarding experience.

And, of course, everybody's got VD. I've had to do pelvic
exams on everything that's come through the front door! At least
on every female; I haven't had to do one on a male yet, but hey,
the month's still young, and anything can happen. It doesn't even
matter what they come in with, they always wind up having PID
**[pelvic inflammatory disease, the common name for infec-
tion of one or more pelvic organs, usually caused by gono-**

188

coccus, the bacteria that causes gonorrhea; PID is diagnosed by pelvic exam and confirmed by culture results].

Take this afternoon, for instance. I was on call last night so I wasn't supposed to get any admissions today, but there were a lot of electives scheduled and the other intern was at clinic, so they asked me to take a kid who came in at about three. Her only problem was an ASD [atrial septal defect, a "hole" in the structure that separates the right and the left atria], and she was coming in for a cardiac cath. [This is a test in which a catheter is passed through a blood vessel in the thigh and fed up to the heart. In pediatrics, cardiac caths usually are done on children with ASDs and other congenital malformations of the heart to define better the anatomy in preparation for surgical repair.] A pretty straightforward case, right? Sure, until I started taking the damn social history. I made the mistake of asking her if she was sexually active, and she said she was. (At least she didn't say, "No, I just sort of lie there." Someone once told me they actually had a patient who said that.) Then I asked if she used any form of contraception and she said she didn't. So I asked if she wanted to be pregnant and she said no, and I started to go into my "If you don't want to be pregnant, you have to use contraception" speech, but she interrupted me and said that she knew about that, and in fact, every time she does get pregnant, she just has an abortion. "In fact," she said, "I had one just last month and, now that you mention it, ever since, I've had this smelly, white discharge. Do you think it might be serious?"

That's when I realized that even this, even this simple, straightforward cardiac cath admission, was going to require a pelvic exam and that even though I was postcall and exhausted, I was going to have to stay late and do it myself. But what could I do? You can't put something like that off; if she's got PID, we'd have to cancel the cath and start her on antibiotics. And a pelvic exam isn't something you can sign out to the person on call: "Oh, yeah, the cardiac cath I admitted needs to have her pre-op bloods checked [all patients having any kind of invasive procedure must have a complete blood count, a specimen of blood sent to the blood bank in case transfusion becomes necessary, and a urinalysis to make sure a urinary tract infection is not present], and I think she might have PID. So would you do a pelvic exam?" I don't think that'd go over real well, although I'm sure some of my cointerns have tried to pull stuff like that.

Anyway, I did the pelvic and it turned out she didn't have PID, just some nonspecific vagitch [**internese for vaginitis, an acute inflammation of the vagina**], and that wasn't going to keep her from having her cath. But it did keep me from getting home until after seven. I missed going to my grandmother's for Tuesday night dinner. And now I'm so tired, all I can think about doing is going to bed.

You know, all these pelvic exams reminded me of something. When you're in college and medical school, you read all these books like *House of God* where the interns are spending half their lives in bed with the nurses, the social workers, and all the other females who populate the hospital. By the time I started this damn internship I knew those kind of things didn't really happen, but I did expect to continue to have at least some semblance of a sex life. But this week, spending so much time in the gynecology room doing pelvics diagnosing PID, I actually realized I have less interest in sex now than I ever remember having! It's scary. All I care about is getting to sleep. This might be the reason Carole hasn't been spending too much time with me over the past few weeks. I hope this is reversible.

Well, I'm going to sleep now. I've got to get my eight hours every other day or so.

Tuesday, December 10, 1985

I am furious! I can't believe they're doing this to me! I tried to be nice to them, to do them a favor when they needed it, and they wind up screwing me, *screwing me* in return! I just might kill the chief residents, all four of them. I know I've said that before, but this time I'm serious! I think I'll spend the next few hours figuring out exactly how I'm going to do it. Yeah, that might calm me down a little. I just can't believe they're really doing this to me!

It all started this afternoon. I was sitting around the nurses' station on Adolescent, saying how I couldn't wait for the month to be over because next month I'm scheduled to be on Children's and I love Children's. And Arlene, one of the chief residents, said, "Oh, haven't you heard? We had to pull you from Children's next month and put you on 6A." She said that, after all,

I had already done July on Children's and that there were some interns who were never scheduled to work there and it wouldn't be fair if I wound up doing two months and other people wound up doing none. I very calmly reminded her that I had only done a month on Children's because the chief residents needed some-one to fill in when one of the subinterns didn't show up and they had promised that if I did them the favor, they wouldn't pull me from my regularly scheduled month. Arlene said she hadn't heard anything about that; all she knew was, I would have to spend the month on 6A. I should have pulled her head off right there while I had the chance.

Not only are they going to do this to me, not only are they going to take me away from the best rotation in the system, but also they're going to deprive me of working with Amy Sorenson; Amy Sorenson, who, in addition to being one of the smartest and friendliest of all the residents, also happens to be one of the best-looking. I've waited all year to work with her; I've even dreamed about it. It's one of the only things that's been keeping me going. And now they're making me switch to 6A, where my resident'll be Attila the Hun. And not only are they taking me from the best ward with the best resident and putting me on the worst ward with the worst resident, but also *they weren't even going to tell me about it until I showed up at the start of January rotation*! So what this means is I'm going to wind up doing a total of five weeks on 6A and three weeks of Children's. I'm getting screwed, and I'll tell you one thing: Even if I don't wind up killing the chiefs, you can bet I'll never be caught dead doing a favor for them again!

Friday, December 13, 1985

I'm waiting for Carole to come by. We're going out for dinner with Bob Marion and his wife, so I've got to make this quick. It looks like I won my battle, and I didn't even have to use force. When I showed up for work on Wednesday ready to go up to the chief residents' office to reenact some of the more gruesome parts of *The Texas Chain Saw Massacre*, Arlene came up to me in the hall and said, "Oh, we made a mistake. You don't really have to work on 6A next month after all." Apparently the chiefs talked it over and decided they really couldn't screw me like that. That's kind of nice, but it threw me off guard. I mean, it's

completely against their nature to be nice to interns. I have to
assume they're setting me up for something. So now my problem is, I'm sure they're going to try to ambush me, but I'm not
sure when. It would have been easier if they had forced me to
do the month on 6A and I had just killed them; it would've taken
all the guess work out of the next few weeks.

Well, the bell just rang. I guess that's Carole.

It's still Friday night, or maybe it started being Saturday
morning already. Yeah, it's twelve-thirty. I just got home. Carole
and I had a big fight. What else is new? I'm such a wonderful
conversationalist, so nice to be around. All I ever do is complain
about work, and all she ever does is complain about me. Tonight
she started in on me about my apartment. We went to this sea-
food place on City Island and she asked Bob and his wife if they
knew of a place where I could move that didn't have roaches. I
don't want to move! I like my roaches; they give me someone
to talk to. So I said, "I don't want to move!" and that started it
off. She said she understood I was working hard but that she
was a person, too, and if I wanted her to be part of my life, I
was going to have to make some time for her in my busy schedule. I said that life is hard enough right now for me without
anybody making demands on my time. Bob's wife looked kind
of uncomfortable through this, but Bob was eating it up. He
wants to make this year into a book, so he was salivating with
all this intimate social stuff. We fought for a while but then we
made up around dessert. So now we're friends again.

Carole's given up on getting married, at least for right now.
I don't know what's going to become of this, but I do know one
thing: If this relationship can make it through this year, it can
make it through anything.

Wednesday, December 18, 1985

Last night something really funny happened. It almost made it
worthwhile being on call. Wow, what a weird thing to say. Nothing could ever make being on call worthwhile. Anyway, here's
what happened: I admitted this fifteen-year-old girl who had
been found unconscious in the street. Someone called EMS
[Emergency Medical Service] and they rushed her to West
Bronx. It was quickly figured out that she had overdosed on a

combination of crack and heroin. They worked on her for a while in the ER and got her stabilized, then decided to admit her to Adolescent. So I went down to the ER to pick her up. That's when she woke up. Lucky me.

She wasn't what I'd call the friendliest patient I'd ever seen. What she was was abusive. She cursed out anyone who came within ten feet of her, me, the nurses, my medical student, everybody. I couldn't examine her, I couldn't even get close enough to get her vital signs. So I called the senior and she came, and after she got cursed and threatened for a while, she said, "No way! I'm not touching her!" So here it was, nearly two in the morning, and we've got this lovely young woman in our treatment room who isn't exactly happy to be there, and we're supposed to do something to make her better. So the resident said, "If we can't examine her, we have to call the person who has ultimate authority. Who's that?"

I said it was the attending. She said, "Well, call him and tell him to come in and see if he can talk to her." And then she left. Very helpful.

Well, I called the operator and got Hal Loomis's home number. I felt a little funny calling him that late for something like this, but when I told him the story, he said, "No problem; I'll be there in a half hour." He actually seemed happy I had called him at home and woken him up! These attendings are really weird.

About an hour later, Hal walked out of the elevator and onto the ward. I led him into the treatment room and pointed to the stretcher. She seemed to be asleep, but when we got close to her, she opened her eyes and started yelling at us. "You stay where you are, you fucking son of a bitch. Don't come any closer or I'll kick you in the balls, you asshole." And, without missing a beat, Hal yelled back at her, "You watch what you say, you little bitch! We don't want to have anything to do with you either, but you're here and you're sick and it's our job. So you better let us do what we have to do or we're going to tie you down and do it anyway. Now, which way do you want it?"

Well, it was great logic, and I think it would have worked if she'd been in her right mind, but, of course, she wasn't. So when Hal and I got close to her again, she started punching and kicking and biting us. But with him there holding her down, I at least could get some sort of a physical exam done. After about a half hour of that, I said I was finished, and we tied her down to a bed in one of the rooms with leather restraints. Then Hal headed back to Westchester, I got a couple of hours of sleep, and this morning she was a real pussycat, believe me. She's just fine today.

So I didn't mind being on call last night. If I could watch an attending make a fool of himself every night I'm on call, I think I wouldn't even mind being an intern.

One more week to go on this damn ward. One more week and the year's half over. I can't wait!

BOB

December 1985

This month marks the halfway point in the interns' trip through this horrible year. The first half of internship officially ends on December 28, and I'm sure that on that night, as they lie in their beds trying to fall asleep, or sit in nurses' stations around the Bronx trying to finish yet another admission note, many of our interns will take a minute or two to reflect on what's happened to them since July 1 and try to work up enough enthusiasm to propel them through next June.

The pediatric department's annual holiday party was held on Wednesday night, December 18. Most of the interns managed to turn out. That's surprising when you consider that a third of them were supposed to be on call and another third were postcall and many of these guys probably hadn't slept in a couple of days. So the fact that so many were there was nice.

Just watching them, it was clear that something had changed since the last time this group had met at a prearranged site for a party. At the first orientation party, the interns had seemed isolated, nervous, and scared to death. Now, six months later, they were a strong, unified group. Tight bonds had formed among them from the mutual sharing of the good times and bad that have occurred over the past six months. On the dance floor, at the bar, sitting at the tables, there was a lot of backslapping, a lot of laughing, and a lot of inside jokes. These guys have built a strong support network for themselves; they're there to help each other out. That's exactly the way it should be at this point in the year.

Thinking back on it, these people have definitely changed. They've gone from being frightened, untrained, technically awkward but very concerned medical students to competent, overworked, and chronically overtired interns. It no longer takes them all night to start an IV or all morning to draw the routine bloods on their patients. They've become masters of scut; they've learned how to manage their time so that they no longer have to stay until eight or nine o'clock on the nights when they're not on call, as they did when the year first began. They've learned the shortcuts that are necessary to survive.

They're also beginning to feel comfortable being around critically ill patients. They no longer feel the impulse to run away as fast as they can when they hear that a three-year-old who's in the midst of a convulsion or a six-month-old with signs and symptoms of meningitis has appeared in the emergency room. They've started to be able to formulate a plan of management by themselves, not relying as much on the residents or attendings to tell them what to do and when to do it. And they're beginning to develop good instincts; they're now able to figure out which patient is truly critically ill and in need of immediate attention, and which patient is not so sick and can wait. But these skills are still in an embryonic state. It'll take a few more months before any of the interns feel confident enough to reject advice given by an attending physician. But one day that will happen. They'll suddenly realize they can do it all themselves.

That's how it was for me. I remember the night everything seemed to come together. It was the middle of March and I was working on the general pediatrics ward: the worst night of my internship. Starting in the afternoon, I had admitted patient after patient, each sicker than the last. By the next morning I had trouble remembering them all; there had been at least eight of them, with three sick enough to quality for admission to our hospital's ICU.

It was at about five-thirty in the morning when it suddenly hit me. The sun was coming up and I was finishing with my third ICU admission, a fourteen-year-old girl who was comatose and near death due to acute inflammation of her brain. She had been sick with chicken pox the week before and had now developed postvaricella encephalitis, a very rare, devastating, and often lethal complication. I had admitted her and done the entire workup by myself, including putting in an IV, drawing the bloodwork that I thought needed to be done, and performing a spinal tap. I had decided on a plan of management and had confirmed that plan with all the appropriate consulting services. And as I sat to do my admission history and physical, with the girl's vital signs finally stable, after this long and terrible night, I realized all of the sudden that I could actually do this stuff. I could be left without someone looking over my shoulder and the job would get done. And once I came to this conclusion, I knew for the first time all year that I would survive my internship.

But it wasn't until March that I reached this conclusion. It's only December now and, although Mark, Andy, and Amy have come a long way, they still have a long way to go.

Mark came to the Christmas party with Carole. They seemed to have fun, but Carole has to have a tough time at events like this: She has to feel like something of an outsider, not being involved in medicine and knowing few of the people. And Mark has to feel a little uneasy, trying to share the experience with his intern pals while at the same time making sure that Carole is enjoying herself. They spent most of the night off to the side by themselves.

Andy didn't show up at the party until after nine. He had gotten out of the hospital late after a busy night on call, and he had stopped at home to take a shower and change his clothes before coming over. He was wearing a bolo string tie, had his hair slicked back, and was wearing a pair of horn-rimmed glasses that he hadn't worn since sixth grade. The effect of all of this was that he looked as if he were on his way to a costume party.

Andy immediately joined in with a group of eight other interns who stayed together through the rest of the evening. This group is composed of the interns who had either started the year alone, without "significant others," or, like Andy, with significant others who lived outside the New York area. These people have supported each other through the first half of the year, and they have formed very tight, close friendships.

The interns in this group have little to worry about. They may not each be feeling great right now, or be extremely happy about the prospects for the rest of the year, but they know they've got each other and they know that no matter what happens, the others will be there to help them through any bad times.

At the Christmas party, the house officers traditionally put on a skit. This year, the senior residents presented a little play about what life must have been like in the Jonas Bronck ER back in the "Days of the Giants," the phrase facetiously used to de-

scribe the times when the current attendings were doing their
training. The myth about the "Days of the Giants" goes something like this: "Back when we were interns, we worked much
harder than they do today. We were on call every other night,
and we loved it. And when a tough case was admitted, we fought
to be able to take care of that patient. We wanted to impress our
chief with how good we were."

In the skit, senior residents were Alan Cozza, Mike Miller,
Alan Morris, and Peter Anderson. They ran around a pretend
emergency room trying to prove how *macho* each was. They
got into arguments and ultimately fistfights about who would
admit the critically ill patient (played by another senior resident)
who was brought in by ambulance.

But the residents also went on to depict what actually occurred once those Giants got those really tough cases: They
didn't know what the hell to do with them. Because the reality
of the situation is that back in the "Days of the Giants," there
wasn't a tenth of the technological advances that are commonplace today. In fact, pretty much all the Giants could really do
was fight over the patients; there was very little that could be
done to cure many of the problems presented. The skit ended
with a very bitter and melancholy song about the life of the
residents.

The other attendings and I all left the party early; that's also
become traditional. The latter part of the Christmas party belongs to the house staff, a time for them to let loose without
having to worry about being judged by their bosses standing off
in the corners. The morning after, there were a lot of exhausted
but happy interns running around the Bronx. They've got six
months to go. In many ways, these last six months are much
tougher than the first six.

ANDY

January 1986

Sunday, January 19, 1986, 1:00 A.M.

I started my vacation, as planned, in Portland [Maine] with
Karen and her family. We were there for Christmas. I ate like it
was going out of style, I vegged out and slept a lot, and I got to
know Karen's family a little better. Three days never went so
fast.

After leaving Portland, we went back to Boston but we only
stayed overnight. We had originally planned to go to New Orleans, but we went to California instead. We decided not to go
to New Orleans because we saw in the newspaper that it was
forty-five degrees and rainy down there and we heard that one
of the big college football teams was going to be in town for a
bowl game and there were going to be millions of crazed football fans running all over the place. So we spent a week out in
Santa Barbara instead. We stayed at Karen's sister Kathy's house.
Kathy was still out in Portland with Karen's parents. My brother
and his wife, Debbie, and Karen and I shared this little bunga-
low with a porch in the backyard where you could sit and look
out and see the Pacific Ocean in the distance. It was very quiet,
very beautiful, and warm. We did a lot of walking that week;
we walked on the beach and in the hills and around town. It was
really a good kind of meditative thing to be doing. I had a chance
to look back and think about what had happened to me over the
past six months, what this internship had done to me. We
watched a million movies on Kathy's VCR, just one after the
next. I slept a lot, and that was very good, too, just having the
chance to catch up on some of the sleep I've missed. And I
balanced my checkbook, which I hadn't done in six months. I

brought all the stuff out with me because I knew I wouldn't do it otherwise. And I felt like my life was a little more back in order again.

At the end of the week, we were all very sad to go home. Karen and I were still enjoying each other's company a lot. We went back to Boston, where it was frigid and bitter cold. I had a few more days there. I saw a couple of old friends, and then Karen and I packed up all our stuff and got ready to come back to New York. Karen has come out to stay for two whole months. She's doing a subinternship in psychiatry in Westchester.

I came back from vacation relaxed and happy, and I was hoping my mellowness would carry me along for a couple of weeks, at least into February, when I'm scheduled to be in the ICU. The depressing thing is that the pace of being back in the ER, the aggravations of being an intern, the frustrations that come with taking care of patients all mounted very rapidly, and it took only a couple of days before I felt like I'd never left. And it's kind of a drag. I mean, here I am, only back for a week and a half, and already I'm feeling aggravated.

Most of the patients I've been seeing have been really abnormal children, really abnormal! During OPD, I spend two out of five weekdays in clinic, and that's what's killing me! All the kids I follow now seem to be abnormal; I've picked up tons of patients who've been discarded by other doctors. I've got kids with MR-CP [mental retardation, cerebral palsy], kids with seizures, kids with weird syndromes, psychotic adolescents I picked up while on the ward; you name it, I've got one of them in my clinic. I seem to have no straightforward, healthy children at all.

And in the ER, well, we do see relatively normal kids there, but it's such a bad situation. The parents are exhausted, they're frustrated, they've had to wait no less than forty-five minutes before they're seen; most of the time they have to wait a couple of hours. Half of your interactions with parents in the ER are not very good. I try so hard to make things go off well, but it's so hard. By the time they get to see you, the parents are so aggravated that you get aggravated. It's just a vicious cycle.

There were a couple of bad things in the ER today. I had one kid who came in and got worse right in front of my eyes. We wound up nearly coding him. And then we had a kid with 20 percent second-degree burns to the perineum [the diaper region] that didn't look very nice. How do you think those got there? It was another abuse case, of course.

Then a thirteen-year-old stab victim came in. The stories are always the same with stab victims: They say they were just going to the store to get their grandmother some ice cream or something like that when somebody out of the clear blue came up to them and stuck a knife into their chest; they're always innocent. This kid wasn't really that bad. And he was about the worst we had today. I didn't have to do any pelvics. So that made it a pretty good day.

I used to get upset about doing pelvics, but I really don't care about them that much anymore. They really aren't so bad as long as you've got a kid who isn't going to be hysterical. That's about one out of every five kids. I'm not wild about doing the other hysterical four, but one of those will be only semihysterical, and only one of the other three will be completely off the wall. But you really can't blame them; most of them are twelve years old and they've never had a pelvic before, and then they find out they're pregnant. Uhh, God forbid! Anyway, it happens all the time. And sexual abuse, you know—what can I say?

We had this attending on today who was driving me up a wall! She was so indecisive, I wish I'd never asked her anything! I think she made more trouble for me than anything else. But I kind of liked her, she was really very nice, and she actually gave me a little off-the-cuff talk on pharyngitis that was very good. But every other time I asked her for help, she just wound up making everything very confusing.

I'm getting to the point where I don't want to bother with the attending, I just want to ask other residents for advice. The attendings usually wind up mucking you up, unless they're really good, and that isn't too often. I'm realizing that it's best just to listen to their advice as a suggestion and then do whatever you want to do. Shit, it's my name that goes on the bottom of the ER sheet, not theirs! [**Although the attending is supposed to be supervising the care of all patients in the ER, the house officer is the one who signs the chart at the completion of the patient's care.**] I'm the one who's really responsible!

I really can't complain about anything tonight. First, I got home at a great hour. I mean, I left that emergency room at twelve-thirty. That's almost unbelievable! And I have the next two days off because Monday is Martin Luther King's birthday [observation] and all the clinics are closed. Hallelujah! What will I do with myself with all this spare time? Sleep, probably.

Sunday, January 19, 1986, 11:30 A.M.

I was just lying in bed here thinking about how no one tells you, really, how to be an intern. They tell you what to do, when to do it, how much to do it with, and how you're not doing it fast enough, but no one tells you really how to be an intern. For instance, where do you draw the line between your own decisions and those of your superiors? Over the past few months I've come to feel comfortable with making decisions; I can deal with a lot of issues on my own now. But when the attending tells you to do something and you don't think it's exactly the right thing to do, what are you supposed to do? After all, it's your name that's on the paper, not the attending's. A lot of times it seems like the attendings don't really fully understand the case, and they make snap decisions with only a half or a three-quarter understanding, and you're the one who's supposed to carry out their orders. So what it all comes down to is, you have to decide for yourself. You're not a medical student anymore, you're really a doctor, even though you barely know how to function as one. That's what no one can tell you. It's something I can barely tell you myself.

The other night I examined a little three-year-old girl who came in with a vaginal discharge. The history wasn't suspicious at all, and there were only a couple of very, very subtle things on the physical exam aside from the vaginal discharge, but the first thing you're supposed to think of in a case like that is sexual abuse. And that's exactly what went through my mind.

But I found myself getting talked out of reporting the case to the BCW because it wasn't all that clear-cut. The attending argued that the discharge could have been caused by something other than sexual abuse. I had to agree. And I felt really pressured by the attending and the social worker, people who have had years and years more experience than I, just to let it pass, to sign it out as nonspecific vaginitis rather than sexual abuse. We talked about it for a long time, and they told me to think about what reporting it would do to the family; the child would be removed and placed in a foster home. The parents would be labeled as criminals, whether anything really happened or not.

It might be years before these people's lives would return to normal. And with all that pressure, I decided to go along with them.

Now I'm regretting it. I've been thinking about this kid ever since. The attending told me to be sure to follow the girl carefully. But let's say this was a case of abuse: What if they don't come back for their follow-up appointment? What can I do then? And, of course, I called the bacteriology lab at Jonas Bronck today and was told that they have no record of receiving the GC [GC: gonococcus, the bacteria that causes gonorrhea] cultures. Great! I'll keep looking for them; I'm sure they'll turn up sooner or later. I hope to God the messenger didn't throw them down the elevator shaft or something like that. But if they don't show up and we never find the cultures, what can I do? And what'll happen if this girl comes back dead next week because whoever molested her decides to whack her over the head with a hammer? It'll be my fault, because I listened to the attending and the social worker rather than doing what I thought was the right thing.

This feeling I have, that I have to start making up my own mind and not relying on other people, it's really something that can't be taught beforehand. I'm just realizing it myself, and I've been doing this for six months now.

I got on the elevator in the DTC building [the clinic building at Mount Scopus] the other day and the elevator stopped at one of the adult floors. This middle-aged man came on with these two middle-aged women, and he said something like, "All they see when they look at you is dollar signs." Then he said, "Look at their mistakes. They fill the graveyard. They don't give a damn. All they care about is money. I don't trust doctors one damn bit anymore." This guy was standing three inches from me! And I was really biting my tongue. I felt like saying, "Look, there are some bad apples out there who suck, who are only in it for money, and who don't give a shit about people. But most of us really do care about our patients."

I don't know, I find myself feeling defensive about organized medicine and at the same time being more disillusioned about it than ever. I do look at the mistakes that are made and the horrible outcomes that result, and yes, our mistakes do end up in the graveyard, but they dot them, they don't fill them.

Well, I've gotten a little off the subject. Anyway, I don't think there's any way that people can be taught about what it's like to be in the uncomfortable position of having to start to use their own mind but having very little to base decisions on. There's just no way anybody could have prepared us for this transition from the little puppy dogs who do everything the attending tells us to independent doctors who wind up being very uncomfortable with some of the decisions we have to make. I'm constantly feeling as if I've got a green belt in karate, that I know enough to kick someone but I might break my own foot doing it.

AMY

January 1986

Friday, December 27, 1985

It snowed yesterday for the first time this winter. Sarah's amazed. We took her out in her stroller a little while ago and she kept looking down at the ground and looking up at Larry and me as if to say, "Where did all the grass go?" It's funny to watch.

I've been in the nursery at Jonas Bronck for a few days now. So far it's been a mixed experience. I'm assigned to the well-baby nursery, which is nice. I spend most of my time examining newborns and talking to their mothers. That's what I really liked about pediatrics in the first place, and it's nice to have the chance to do it without all the other nonsense that usually takes up our days. So that part of it is good. What I don't like, though, is that my night call is in the neonatal ICU. It's frightening in there! And it's harder for me than for the other interns because, since I'm only in the NICU at night, I don't know the sick ones very well. All I know about them is what the interns sign out to me, and it's impossible to get a really complete sign-out on a patient who has a hundred different problems. So that's frightening to me, but what can I do? It could be worse; I could have to spend all my time in the ICU.

Another bad part about working in the well-baby nursery is that we're always on call to the delivery room. If there's a premature baby being born or a baby who's in distress, the resident and I get called to come to the delivery. It's not really that bad, though, because during the day there's usually a fellow [**neonatal fellow, a physician who has completed a pediatric residency and is getting specialty training in neonatology**] or an

205

attending around, and one of them usually comes in with us. If they weren't there, it would be terrifying!

I have to admit, I've been lucky with my schedule over the past couple of months. I've worked with very good residents and I haven't been on the hard wards or had a lot of bad patients. I guess I should say that I finished on Children's last week and Angela [**the young girl with neurofibromatosis**] was still alive. I heard she got worse the day after I left, though. She had another very long seizure and they had trouble stopping it, so they transferred her up to the ICU. They had to anesthetize her to get the seizure to stop [**general anesthesia is used as a last-ditch effort to stop intractable seizures only after every other treatment modality has failed**]. The intern who picked up my patients told me they don't expect her to survive much longer, only another few days at most. It's really sad; one month ago, she was a completely normal child. Now she's almost dead. That's not supposed to happen to children.

I was on call Wednesday, Christmas Day. It wasn't so bad, since we don't celebrate Christmas, but it was like working an extra weekend day. The hospital was completely dead, even deader than most Sundays. But babies don't know anything about holidays; they crump whenever they feel like it. I did get a couple of hours of sleep that night and I guess I should be thankful for that, but I can see that night call during this month is going to be terrible.

I had only one admission to the unit on Wednesday, a thirty-weeker [**thirty-weeker: a baby born ten weeks prematurely**] who did pretty well. We were in the DR when he was born. The obstetric residents thought he was only going to be about twenty-six or twenty-seven weeks; my knees were shaking while I stood in the delivery room waiting for him to come out. The resident and I were very relieved when we saw such a big baby come out. He weighed about thirteen hundred grams, which is gigantic for the NICU. And he didn't get too sick: He had a little bit of respiratory distress but nothing terrible. All he needed was a little extra oxygen, so we put him in a headbox [**a cylindrical Lucite box that covers the head of an infant and through which oxygen can be provided**] with 40 percent oxygen. [**Normal room air contains 21 percent oxygen; therefore 40 percent oxygen provides about twice the normal concentration of oxygen.**] He never retained CO_2 [**babies with respiratory**

distress syndrome, a major complication of prematurity
caused by underdevelopment of the lungs, develop a buildup
of carbon dioxide, or CO_2, in the blood], so we didn't have to
intubate him. He should do fine. His mother is seventeen years
old and already has a one-and-a-half-year-old at home. She lives
with her mother, who essentially takes care of her and the baby
as if they were siblings. It's a funny social system here in the
Bronx. Most of our mothers are under twenty, and most live
with their mothers, who wind up taking care of the children.

Well, the apartment is quiet. Sarah's asleep, Larry's watching
TV in the living room. I'm going to go to sleep. I've got to be
up early tomorrow morning so I can be on call.

Saturday, January 18, 1986, 10:00 P.M.

I haven't recorded anything in a while. I've been very tired and
very busy. I'm really enjoying working in the well-baby nursery;
it's the first thing this whole year I could actually see myself
doing for the rest of my life. The problem is, there's no way to
do it without doing a fellowship in neonatology first, and that is
something I definitely do not want to do. So once again, I'm
kind of stuck.

I've gotten along very well with a lot of the mothers. They
seem to trust me. They trust me even more when I tell them I've
got a baby of my own who's almost nine months old. I guess
they feel they can identify with me. Frankly, I'm not sure how
you can be a pediatrician and give advice to mothers without
having your own child. Anyway, it's been a very rewarding experience.

I've pretty much gotten my work down to a routine. When I
arrive in the morning, I look at the list of babies who were born
the night before. All of these kids need to have physsies [physs-
ical exams; all babies get examined within twelve hours of
delivery and then again right before discharge]. I find the babies and do the exams. When I'm done with those, I find the
list of babies who are supposed to be discharged that day. I find
those babies, and one at a time take them out to their mother's
bedside and examine them right in front of their mothers. I
found that that gives the mothers the chance to ask about anything they don't understand or anything they're concerned about.

It's amazing how many strange things these women come out

with. I had this one woman, a nineteen-year-old who had had
her first baby, who asked me about the strawberry hemangioma
on her baby's back. [Strawberry hemangioma is a birthmark
composed of a mass of blood vessels; they are very common
and usually are of no medical significance; most disappear
by the time the child is six years old.] I told the mother it was
just a birthmark and that it wasn't anything to worry about. She
asked me three times if I was sure that that was all it was, and
each time I told her I was positive. Finally, I asked her why she
was so worried about it. She wouldn't say anything at first, but
finally I got her to tell me the story. She said she had heard that
some people with AIDS had a skin disease that might be the
first thing that's noticed. I told her that was true, that the skin
disease was called Kaposi's sarcoma. I also told her that babies
almost never got Kaposi's and then I asked why she was so
concerned. At first she said it was because the baby's father had
been using drugs for years and she was worried that he might
have AIDS, that he might have passed it along to her, and that
she might have passed it along to the baby. I worked on her for
a while, and I finally got her to admit that she had used drugs a
few times about a year ago and that she and the baby's father
had sometimes shared needles. Ever since, all through this pregnancy, she had been scared to death that she had AIDS.

I spent over an hour with her. I asked about all the signs and
symptoms that might indicate AIDS. She didn't have any of
them, and I told her that was a very good sign. But she said she
had been having trouble sleeping at night for a few months because she was so worried and that it was starting to affect her
schoolwork. She goes to Bronx Community College. She told
me she wanted to be a lawyer but she honestly didn't think she
was ever going to make it because she was going to die of AIDS.
And then, when the baby was born with the strawberry hemangioma, she had become convinced that not only was she going
to die of AIDS, so was her baby. She started crying and I held
her hand and comforted her.

I waited until her crying stopped and then I told her that if
she wanted, I could take some blood to see if she had antibodies
to HIV [human immunodeficiency virus, the virus that causes
AIDS]. She told me she'd thought a lot about getting tested but
she was afraid to. She said she didn't know what she'd do if she
turned out to be positive. I told her that was a problem, but I

pointed out that she was already suffering and it might all be for nothing; there was a good chance, after all, that she'd turn out to be negative. So I guess I talked her into letting me do the test. I had her sign the consent form [**HIV testing can be performed only after the subject has signed a form stating that they understand the purpose of testing and that they want it done**], and then I drew her blood. I wore gloves when I was taking it. I felt funny putting on the gloves; it was as if I were saying, "I've been telling you I don't think you have it, but I'm not taking any chances." She didn't say anything about the gloves. I don't know; maybe we make too much out of feeling guilty. So far, whenever I've worn gloves, none of the patients or their parents has said a word.

Anyway, I think I did some good for that woman. Here she had been coming to obstetricians for months, always with this dread fear, and nobody had found out anything about it. And just because I spent a little extra time with her, I was able to discover that her life was being completely disrupted by something that might be totally avoidable. I haven't gotten the results of the blood test yet. But I'm going to see her and the baby in clinic sometime next week, and hopefully by then I'll have the answer. I felt really good about that one.

I've had a couple of cases that didn't turn out that well, though. And one of those made me feel as bad as that last case made me feel good. During rounds our attending, Joan Cameron, always tells us we should try to push breast feeding whenever we get the chance. I have mixed feelings about breast feeding. I mean, I know it's the best thing for the baby; it's supposed to be helpful in preventing infections and things like that, and it's also supposed to help the bonding process between mother and infant. But it's not the easiest thing to do. A woman really has to be committed to breast feeding, and she has to have a lot of support from the people around her. If she's kind of wishy-washy about it, it's just not going to work out.

Anyway, last week I was talking to this woman who asked me about breast feeding. I gave her the party line: I said yes, it's the most important thing you could do for your baby. Then she asked if I had breast-fed my baby (I had already mentioned to her about Sarah). And I had to say that I did it for a few weeks only and then stopped because I had to start my internship. And she said something like, "You doctors are all alike! You tell us to do things you wouldn't be caught dead doing yourself!'' And she said some other things that weren't very nice. Basically she called me a hypocrite and she immediately asked for a bottle of formula.

I knew she was right, and she hit a nerve. I mean, I would have liked to have breast-fed Sarah for longer if I'd had the chance. It makes me pretty angry. Here we are, being told by our attendings that we should advocate breast feeding, but there's no way I would have been able to do it with my own baby. How can you breast-feed if you're on call every third night and there's no place in the hospital to keep your baby while you're working? That woman was right, it *was* hypocritical for me to suggest she do something I couldn't do, and it's very hypocritical for our faculty to try to get patients to do something that's best for their babies and not give the house staff the same opportunity. So that situation didn't work out so well. And I'm still angry about the whole thing.

My night call is just about what I expected. I've only gotten sleep a couple of times on nights I've been on call. I'm finding something out: I really need only about two hours of sleep to function well the next day. But those two hours have to be between four and six in the morning. If I'm up between four and six, I'm just about worthless the next day. If I sleep those two hours, even if I haven't seen the bed the rest of the night, I'm fine.

And doing night call in the NICU hasn't made me feel any more comfortable about working with these tiny babies. If anything, I've become more terrified. The unit is brand new; it just opened a couple of months ago, so everything is state of the art. And these babies are so sick! We've had three deaths so far this month—two preemies and one full-term kid. I was on call the night the full-term kid was born. That's something I won't forget for a long time!

We were called to the DR because of thick mec [mec is **meconium, the medical term for the baby's first bowel movement. The passage of meconium by the fetus near the end of pregnancy is a sign of fetal distress. In addition, meconium can be breathed into the lungs with the baby's first breath and can then cause severe respiratory problems and a condition called "persistence of the fetal circulation," which can lead to death]** and late decels [late decelerations: a pattern on fetal heart tracing indicating fetal distress]. The obstetricians decided to do a stat C section and they pulled out the baby, who was covered with mec. I tried to suction her mouth while she was still on the table, but I guess I didn't get all of it out because she was in respiratory distress almost immediately. **[Actually, the baby had probably already aspirated meconium prior to delivery; in this case, suctioning of the oropharynx probably didn't provide any help in preventing what subsequently happened.]** Eric Keyes was the senior on call with me, and he was on the baby as soon as she hit the warming table **[the table in the DR on which the baby is placed following delivery]**. He intubated her and started suctioning out her airway through the ET tube. He was getting tons of thick mec out. In the meantime, I was listening to her heart. She was really bradycardic **[had a low heart rate]**, so Eric told me to start a line and get ready to push meds. I hadn't ever started a UV **[umbilical vein]** line myself, so he talked me through it as he was suctioning out the trachea. When I finally managed to get something in, we changed places so Eric could push the first round of meds. The airway was pretty clear by that point, so I started bagging the baby **[pushing oxygen through the endotracheal tube, using an ambubag to generate pressure]**. The heart rate came up a little, to about 80 **[the normal heart rate for a newborn is 120 to 140 beats per minute]**, and Eric decided that we'd better get the baby out of the DR and into the ICU right away, so we put the baby in the transport incubator and ran with her down the hall to the unit.

We worked on her all night. We called the neonatal fellow at home, and he came in to help. She had severe respiratory distress and PFC **[persistence of the fetal circulation]**. We were having trouble ventilating her and getting her blood circulating. We put her on a ventilator and had it turned up to very high settings. **[To ventilate a child with mec aspiration, it's often necessary to use a great deal of pressure with which to push oxygen into the lungs. Meconium causes the lungs to become very stiff, and the pressure is necessary to get them to expand.]**

At about four in the morning, she crumped. Eric decided she had a pneumothorax **[a collapsed lung, caused, most likely, by the high ventilator pressure that was being used to force air into the baby's lungs]**, so he put a chest tube in and she immediately looked better. But she was still hypoxic [lacking oxygen] all night, and at about five in the morning Eric and the neonatal fellow decided to start her on tolazoline, which is supposed to help PFC. It didn't do her much good. She crumped again at about eight, just when the day crew started showing up. It was another pneumothorax. I didn't stay any longer than that. I had to get out to the well-baby nursery and start doing my physsies. The baby died a little later that morning.

It was terrible. She had been completely normal. If she hadn't gotten all fouled up with meconium, she probably would have been a normal child.

That baby's mother was put on the gyn ward, so I didn't get a chance to talk to her. They did that so it would be easier for her; it would have been very hard if they'd put her on the regular postpartum ward and she had to be surrounded by all the new mothers with their healthy babies. I don't know what I would have said to her if I had gone to talk with her. Nothing seems right.

I heard that Angela died a little over a week ago. She spent her last couple of weeks in the ICU at Mount Scopus, comatose. I never thought there'd be so many deaths in a pediatric internship!

Anyway, I've got to go to sleep. I'm getting tired and I'm on call again tomorrow, so I've got to get a good night's sleep. I've got another week to go in the nursery, then I have two weeks in the OPD and then vacation. I hope I make it until then.

Sunday, January 26, 1986

There are so many crack users around. There are six babies who've stayed in the nursery the entire month. The mother of each of these babies is a crackhead and the babies have been taken out of their custody by the BCW. They're all waiting for foster placements, but it's hard to find homes for these kids because there's a good chance they're infected with HIV. All of them spent their first few weeks of life withdrawing from drugs. It's sad. For a lot of these children, their lives are already over before they even had a chance to start.

The ICU has been pretty quiet over the past week. There was an outbreak of naf-resistant staph [a type of bacteria that is insensitive to nafcillin, the antibiotic that is most effective in treating staph], so they had to close two whole rooms [**closing the rooms and cleaning them is the only effective way to prevent sick newborns from getting infected with the bacteria**]. That cut the census by about half, so taking call in there wasn't so bad. I even got a few hours' sleep the last two nights I've been on. So all in all, it's been a pretty good month.

We're going out to New Jersey to visit my father this afternoon. Sarah was nine months old yesterday, so my father's going to have a little party for her. We haven't seen him in over a month; he's starting to feel like we're trying to avoid him. He still doesn't understand what it's like to be an intern. He thinks I've got a lot of free time and that we're just doing other things rather than coming out to see him.

Well, I'm going to stop now. Tomorrow I'll be back in the Jonas Bronck ICU. Seven months down, five more to go.

Oh, one more thing: That woman who thought her baby's strawberry hemangioma was a sign of AIDS showed up at clinic this week. I called the lab to get the results of her HIV testing, and guess what? She tested negative! When I told her, she hugged me and kissed me. That's the first time this whole year when I really thought I had done somebody some good. And it happened only because I took the time to sit and listen to what she had to say. It had nothing to do with medicine.

MARK

January 1986

Thursday, December 26, 1985

I was on call Tuesday for the first time this month, and it wasn't too bad. It should have been great: It was Christmas Eve, the ward was quiet, and I had only one admission. I should have gotten six hours of sleep at least, right? Wrong! It was one of those cases where if anything can go wrong, it will go wrong. It was a two-and-a-half-year-old sickler with pneumonia. She was called up from the ER at about eleven-thirty, so I figured great, I'll go down, bring her up to the floor, do the workup, start her on some antibiotics, and be in bed by one. Of course, that's not even close to what happened. First, I got down there and found that no one had been able to get an IV into her. Everyone had tried and everyone had failed. So they figured what the hell, let old Mark take the kid up to the ward and have a crack at it. How nice of them! But it turned out okay, because you know what? I got it in on the first stick. That's right, the very first stick! I'll tell you, I'm becoming the King of Scut. It just shows you that if you take a plain, ordinary, moronic intern and make him do the same things over and over again until he loses his mind, you can teach him to do almost anything. I think that now that I've mastered IVs, I might take up neurosurgery in my spare time.

I'm getting off the track here because I'm a little tired. Anyway, so I brought her up to the floor and got the IV in and did the whole workup, and by two o'clock everything was done except a urinalysis. I spent most of the rest of the night chasing after her with a urine cup, trying to get some of her precious body fluid. Yes, my mother sure would have been proud of me!

They hadn't been able to get any urine from her in the ER. I didn't want to start her on antibiotics until we had a sample of urine because she had had a UTI [urinary tract infection] in the past, and if she had one again, we needed to know about it. I wasn't having trouble getting the urine because she wasn't peeing; it was that she wasn't real happy about peeing into any kind of container. Right after we got her up to the floor, she was standing on the scale in the treatment room and she let loose a stream, so I ran over with a cup just in time for her to pee all over my hands. No urine ended up in the cup, of course. Then we decided to straight-cath her [place a sterile catheter through her urethra and into her bladder in hopes of obtaining clean urine], but just as soon as I got close to her with the catheter, she started to pee straight up into the air. I managed to catch some of that in a cup, and I ran off to the lab to analyze it. It turned out that her urine was clean as a whistle. By that point it was about five in the morning. I got a total of two hours of sleep.

I found out later she was a patient I had taken care of in August on Infants. Now she's graduated to Children's. These kids keep following me all over the place. Next thing you know, Hanson'll show up again. Hanson! Now, there's someone I haven't thought about in a while! You know, no one's heard anything about him since I discharged him from Jonas Bronck in October. But I know he'll turn up again, you can be sure of it. It'll be the busiest night of the year; there'll be hundreds of admissions to take care of, and he'll come toddling in and take one look at me and crump right there and then!

I've been totally and completely terrified of Alan Morris [the attending in charge]. Monday, on the first attending rounds of the month, he asked me to tell him about my patients. I went to present my first kid and I started off by saying, "This is a six-month-year-old-month old . . ." I just couldn't get the words to come out right. I got so tongue-tied I finally said, "Forget it! I can't present anybody to you! You make me too damn nervous!" That was good because it loosened everybody up. Alan seems to make a lot of people uptight. I'm not sure what it is about him that does it. Maybe it's the whip he brings to rounds with him. Or the buzzards who are always circling over his head. I don't know why, but he definitely makes me uptight. He's a great teacher, though; so far, rounds have been excellent. I had to present my sickler to him this morning and I managed to get the words out, but I was still nervous. Then we wound up talking about sickle-cell disease and he happened to hit on the one area I actually knew something about. He grilled me for about a half hour and I think I did a pretty good job. In fact, he must know I need some positive reinforcement, because for the first time since I've been here, I actually heard him give someone—in this case, me—a compliment. He said something like, "I don't care what everybody else is saying about you, I think you're doing a reasonably good job." Talk about a vote of confidence! I guess it's better than having him say he thought I was a complete idiot!

The floor was a real disaster today; poor Ron was getting creamed! There were four admissions, and each one had a bizarre story. One of them was an eight-year-old with subaortic stenosis [an obstruction to the flow of blood below the aortic valve; this obstruction prevents blood from getting from the left ventricle of the heart out to the rest of the body] who was only mildly symptomatic but who was admitted for surgery anyway. Ron and Amy, our resident, did a complete workup, history, physical, labs, the works. When they had drawn his type and hold [a specimen of blood to be sent to the blood bank so that blood for transfusion could be prepared], the mother said, "What are you doing that for?" Martha told her it was for the blood bank and the mother said, "Well, you don't have to send it. Don't you know we're Jehovah's Witnesses? There's no way you're going to give my child any blood, and that's final!"

They went crazy. Ron was ready to reach into the cardiologist's mouth and tear out his vocal cords. And then this whole big thing started with the cardiothoracic surgeon, two or three anesthesiology attendings, the cardiologist, and us. The Anesthesia Department refused to do the surgery without the option of using blood if it was needed. They had to call the hospital lawyers and wait for a ruling. The whole thing took hours, and the end result was that the kid wound up going home. Amy and Ron were pissed off, the cardiologist was pissed off, the CT surgeon was pissed off, and the anesthesiology people weren't exactly happy.

I sat through all this in kind of a daze because I was so tired. I've got to try to get more rest. Well . . . maybe next year.

Tuesday, December 31, 1985, 11:30 P.M.

I know it seems pretty strange, but here it is, eleven-thirty on New Year's Eve, and I'm lying in bed, talking into this stupid machine. I'm too tired to go out, so I'm here all alone. Carole went to a party by herself. I was supposed to go with her, but I called her a couple of hours ago and told her I was just too tired to make it. I'm pretty pathetic!

I had a long night last night. It took forever to finish my work today, and just as I was about to leave, a nurse came running out of a room yelling, "Hurry up, she's not breathing right!" So I calmly got my stethoscope and walked into Cassandra's room, and there she was, sure enough, breathing at a rate of eighty to ninety. Now even I know that eight-year-old girls aren't supposed to breathe at a rate of eighty to ninety. I wasn't sure what was happening. She's got osteogenic sarcoma [a malig-nant tumor of the bone] and she isn't expected to live very much longer, but I at least expected her to make it into 1986. When I came in and found her breathing that fast, I figured maybe she was having a pulmonary embolus [a clot in one of the lung's major arteries; dangerous because they prevent blood from reaching oxygen, thus causing widespread hyp-oxia throughout the body]. But she had equal breath sounds. We did a whole workup and didn't find anything. She's not my patient, but we've all gotten to know her. I just called and found out that she's still alive and she seems to be reasonably com-fortable, which is reassuring.

I don't know about these terminal patients; it's really draining taking care of them. You don't even want to go near the room because you know there isn't anything you can do to help, and whenever you do go in the room, it's to do something terrible, like draw blood. It's very frustrating. The only thing we can do is try to make the last few months as comfortable as possible for her. If we can do that effectively, then we've really done our job. Dealing with these kinds of issues is really the hard part of this year.

There, now I've really cheered myself up! I'll tell you, I'm not sorry to be seeing 1985 end. In 1986 I'll be an intern for only half the year. That's not so bad. I'm going to sleep. Good night. And Happy New Year, tape recorder! Now, that's really pathetic!

Tuesday, January 7, 1986, 9:00 P.M.

This has been an interesting couple of days here. On Friday morning I had to get some blood from a patient before attending rounds started. I was late, and I was worried that Alan was going to yell at me. He still scares me to death. I was postcall and really crazed and I guess I hadn't eaten in maybe sixteen hours. So I went into the patient's room and started drawing the blood, and pretty soon I started realizing that I was feeling kind of light-headed. Really light-headed! So light-headed, in fact, that I grabbed on to the patient's mother, who was helping me hold the kid down. She, of course, thought I was coming on to her, but I reassured her that I wasn't trying to do anything nasty, I was merely trying to prevent myself from collapsing in a heap on the floor. I told her I'd be fine just as soon as I finished drawing the blood. I'm sure that reaffirmed her faith in me as her child's physician!

Anyway, I drew the blood, got it into the tube (which I consider quite a save, considering how hard a stick this kid was), and then I started to kind of sort of lie there on the floor feeling very dizzy. Everyone came running; I thought they were going to call a code and start full-scale resuscitation on me. But they didn't; I guess they realized that I hadn't arrested, I had just fallen over, so they got me into a wheelchair, and the nurses checked my blood pressure, which was normal, and then they put me in the house staff room, where I collapsed on the couch. I felt dizzy every time I tried to lift my head. This was, needless to say, somewhat anxiety-provoking.

I stayed in there for a few minutes and then I tried to get up so I could get to attending rounds. I got myself in a sitting position and started to cave in again when Alan Morris showed up. I said to him, "You know, I'm really not feeling too well." And he looked at me with a very serious face and asked what was wrong. I said, "Well, I've been dizzy for the past fifteen minutes." Then he said (in a formal-sounding voice), "I suggest you continue to rest; if this persists for a few more minutes, I recommend that you be brought down to the emergency room for evaluation." All in his usual righteous tone of voice.

Well, he went out and came back a minute later with the wheelchair and said (in the same formal-sounding voice), "You know what? On second thought, it's been long enough. If you had been out in the street somewhere or in any place other than a hospital, you would have already been brought here by ambulance. I think we'll take you down to the ER,'' which he did. By the time I got down there, I was completely white and really uncomfortable. They slapped me down on one of the stretchers, they stuck an IV in me (at least I didn't have to do that one myself), they drew blood; I got examined by one of the ER attendings, I got examined by one of the residents in neurology, and God help any of us if we really have a neurological problem and we have to be taken care of by a member of the neurology house staff, because this guy turned out to be pretty hopeless.

Well, hours and hours passed; many people came and went (actually, it was nice to get all that sympathy). My student, who generally is a moron, stayed with me the whole day and was very sympathetic. And finally, at the end of the day one of the adult neurology attendings came by. I told him what had happened, he did a quick exam, found everything to be normal, and told me I'd hyperventilated and that I should stop consuming anything with caffeine in it.

Hyperventilation—how about that? He probably was right, too. I was pretty crazed when I was drawing that blood, I was worried about what would happen if I made it to attending rounds late. But can you imagine an intern having to eliminate caffeine from his diet? Caffeine is the only thing that's been keeping me alive. If I stop drinking coffee, I'll just lapse into a coma and never wake up.

Anyway, so I left the ER at about six and Carole, who was coming to see me for the night, picked me up and carted me home. Ever since, I've been getting total abuse from my "friends." That was my emergency room event for the year. It was actually really interesting being on the other side of the bed. As a patient, you realize how sensitive you are to what everyone is saying and how they're saying it. Really, it was a very interesting experience to have had. And I hope I don't have it too many more times.

I was on call Sunday. It was a pretty good day, only two admissions. Then yesterday, I got home after being on call and I found out my phone wasn't working. It turns out it was some problem with the phone company's cable, but I didn't know that; I thought it was something wrong with my phone. I called them and made an appointment for someone to come to my apartment today at four-thirty. So I was in a rush all day, I knew I had to get out of the hospital early. And, of course, when you're in a rush, everything goes wrong: I went out to my car this morning and found that the damn thing wouldn't turn over. The battery was dead. I'm sitting out there fuming, it's freezing cold, and the damn battery's dead! I called the AAA and wound up getting to work forty-five minutes late. All because I was in a hurry.

And then attending rounds went on forever! We would have gotten done early because there had been only one admission last night, but then my moronic medical student asked Alan for a lecture on static and cidal levels of antibiotics [**cidal: the concentration of antibiotic needed to kill bacteria; static: the concentration needed to prevent the bacteria from reproducing**], something I'd heard eight times already. And, of course, I couldn't get up and leave. No, I had to sit there or face the Wrath of Alan. It took a whole two hours before we were done.

Then I called the telephone company to tell them I was going to be late, and could they come later, and they told me "Oh, didn't you hear? The problem was on our side, not yours. Your phone works perfectly now!" So I built up all that serious aggravation for nothing!

So, to review the past week, I've had one episode of hyperventilation, which earned me a trip to the ER; one episode of phone failure, which nearly earned me a nervous breakdown; and one episode of battery failure, which I've taken care of by getting a new battery. And who's to say what lies ahead over the next couple of days; or months; or years, for that matter, in this exciting borough I hope to get out of sometime soon, or at least before I go completely crazy! I'm telling you, one day I'm just going to get this enormous ulcer and bleed right out on the floor! It's only a matter of time!

Wednesday, January 22, 1986

Fine. Now I've developed an allergy to something. My nose has been running and my eyes have been itching like hell all night long. I may not survive this month. If I were an insurance company, I certainly wouldn't allow me to take out a policy!

I guess you can say yesterday was just another typical day. I admitted this kid who was dehydrated. They thought he had mononucleosis in the ER, but when his CBC **[complete blood count]** came back, it showed pancytopenia **[lack of all types of blood cells]** and lymphoblasts **[immature white blood cells]**. A diagnosis of leukemia was entertained (what an ironic expression). And unfortunately, this morning the diagnosis was confirmed. Of course, the family's really nice.

Sunday, January 26, 1986

So tomorrow I start my month in the NICU. I'm ready to jump out the window. It won't be too bad, though. I have clinic tomorrow afternoon, so hopefully I won't be around long enough to get *really* nauseated. **[Obviously, an afternoon in clinic exempts the intern from the hospital for the time he or she is scheduled to see outpatients in the clinic.]**

I guess I'm going to miss Children's. It really is a good place to work. Alan Morris was an excellent attending. Even though he still scares me to death, I really learned a lot from him this month. When I went up to him on Saturday to thank him for the month, he told me I should have more confidence in myself because he thought I was a good intern. I think I've figured out what it is about him that makes me nervous: He reminds me of my father, whom I was always terrified of. I was always afraid he was going to yell at me for not eating my vegetables or something.

The main reason I liked Children's this month, though, was because of the resident. The resident was wonderful. She's just totally wonderful in all ways. She's smart and she's an excellent teacher. She's calm and she doesn't get upset no matter what happens or how many mistakes I make. And she's great-looking, too, which certainly helps. It's just too bad I won't get the chance to work with her again this year. And I swear to God, if she weren't married . . .

BOB

January 1986

We're getting into the seriously depressing part of the year now. New Year's Day marks the beginning of Intern Suicide season, the time when we really have to start worrying about the house staff's mental health. There are a number of reasons why January and February are so bad. First, exhaustion is cumulative, and the interns have now built up a six-month supply. They're chronically overtired and can't get themselves too enthusiastic about anything. This exhaustion affects all aspects of their lives: They don't have energy to socialize, so they completely lose contact with family and friends; they eat too much junk food and get little or no exercise, so they wind up gaining a ton of weight. This causes them to feel down about themselves and to lose confidence.

Second, although everybody around them is celebrating the end of one calendar year and the beginning of the next, the end of the internship year hasn't even yet appeared on the horizon. There's just about nothing for these guys to look forward to right now other than another half year of the same shit over and over again. So they develop a feeling of desperation, and that feeling is compounded by the fact that they know there's nothing they can do to make the time move any faster.

Finally, the environment seems to be conspiring against them. The weather this time of year is horrible. It's constantly freezing cold, and the city is frequently getting pelted with snowstorms. It gets dark so early that the house officers can go for weeks without ever actually seeing sunshine; they get to the hospital so early that it's still dark and they come home again at night, after the sun has set. So the house officers live in a constant

222

world of cold and darkness, and there's nothing more depressing than that.

Although January is bad, it's nothing compared with February. In January, there's still some semblance of a "spark" left within the bodies of the interns, the last vestige of the excitement that accompanied the holiday season. The department's Christmas party did the whole staff a lot of good; there were a couple of weeks during which everyone seemed a little happier and a little calmer. But it was really short-lived. And usually by February 1, any spark of excitement has been snuffed out.

A fair number of pretty strange things happened during January. The strangest involved Andy Ames, one of the interns who's in Andy Baron's circle of friends. The story started like this: At the beginning of January, Andy Ames and one of the female senior residents were working together on the Jonas Bronck wards one night and admitted a six-week-old girl with fever. Because a significant percentage of these infants will be shown to have a serious bacterial infection in their blood or spinal fluid, it is policy that all babies under two months of age who come to the emergency rooms with fever routinely get admitted to the hospital. Blood, urine, and spinal fluid cultures are taken, and the infants are started on intravenous antibiotics.

Anyway, Andy Ames and the senior resident were trying to get a sterile specimen of urine from this little girl by doing a straight catheterization, a procedure in which a plastic tube is inserted into the urethra and passed up into the bladder. The cath went pretty well, and they managed to get an adequate sample of urine for culture and urinalysis. But the mother, who was standing in the treatment room the whole time, went nuts when she realized what Andy was doing. She accused him of sexually molesting her daughter and of "ruining" her for life. The mother yelled and screamed for most of that night, becoming more and more agitated as time passed. Early the next morning, she went to Alan Cozza and the hospital administrators to complain. When the situation was assessed, it was carefully explained to the woman that what Andy had done was completely aboveboard and standard treatment and did not in any way constitute sexual molestation. The mother continued to yell that Andy had "ruined" her daughter and that no man would ever want her after what he had done. The administrators continued throughout that day and the next to try to calm her and explain the anatomy of the procedure to her. When it finally became clear to the woman that she wasn't going to get any satisfaction from the hospital employees, she decided to take matters into her own hands: She began to threaten Andy Ames with bodily harm.

From then on, things became exceedingly weird. While the baby was in the hospital, the mother told Andy every time she saw him that she was going to sneak up behind him when he wasn't expecting it and stick a butcher's knife into his back. She also told this to everyone else who was hanging around the ward, the house staff, the medical students, the nurses, even some of the other parents. Since the baby was better and no sign of bacterial infection had been found, Alan Cozza decided to discharge the child a day earlier than usual. He hoped that with the baby and her mother out of the hospital, some of the pressure would be removed from Andy, who, needless to say, was feeling quite persecuted by all this. But discharging the baby didn't help; the woman managed to find other ways to drive Andy crazy.

After discharge, the baby's mother began to call the ward asking for Dr. Ames. When Andy got on, she'd repeat the threats. She somehow got the number of the residents' room and left cryptic messages for him with Lisa, the house staff secretary. She even managed to get Andy's home telephone number and left messages on his answering machine.

At about this time, Alan Cozza, concerned about what was happening to his intern, began investigating this woman's background. Not surprisingly, he found that she had a long psychiatric history and had been diagnosed as having paranoid schizophrenia. Then, about a week after the baby was discharged, a call came for Andy in the residents' room. The person identified himself as the woman's psychiatrist. He explained that the woman had told him exactly what had happened and had laid out in explicit detail exactly what she was going to do to get back at "that intern who ruined my daughter." He told Andy that he was concerned about his well-being because she was angrier and more agitated than he'd ever before seen her.

This was all Andy needed. If he hadn't been worried about all this before, the psychiatrist's call certainly pushed him over the edge. And apparently there was very little at that point that anybody could have done. The woman wouldn't voluntarily consent to hospitalization in a psychiatric facility because she didn't think of herself as sick. Her psychiatrist, although truly concerned about Andy, was unwilling to proceed with forcing her into institutionalization against her will. He said he simply hadn't accumulated enough evidence yet to justify such a move. And so, during January, after work every day, one of the other members of the house staff had to walk Andy out to his car in the parking lot. The interns took turns staying over at his apartment. He had his phone number changed and made sure the new one wasn't listed. And all of this certainly took its toll on him. He began looking terrible: He was already exhausted from the usual intern routine, and he barely had enough strength to get through a typical day. But now he was no longer able to sleep even on the nights when he wasn't on call because he was so worried.

The story finally came to a head in early February. The baby's mother showed up in the residents' room at Jonas Bronck one day, demanding to see Andy and wanting to know why he wasn't on the ward where he belonged. Lisa, the secretary, told her that at the end of January he had rotated onto another service and was no longer at the hospital. The woman demanded to know where he was, and when Lisa, who was well aware of the situation, refused to tell her, the woman pulled a big knife out of her pocketbook. One of the residents who had been sitting in the outer office ran to get the security guard who was stationed on the pediatric floor. The guard ran into the room, surprising the woman. In the confusion, he was able to overpower her and force her to release the knife. No one was hurt, thank God, and the woman was taken to the psych emergency room in handcuffs. She was ultimately admitted to Bronx State Psychiatric Hospital. Andy, who was working on the Infants' ward at Mount Scopus, was relieved to hear this news, to say the least. He went home that night and had his first good night's sleep in weeks. And within a week or two, the whole incident was forgotten.

This melodrama is certainly not an everyday occurrence. But when something like this does happen, you can be sure it'll occur in January or February.

ANDY

February 1986

Sunday, February 23, 1986

All in all, the two weeks I spent in the Jonas Bronck OPD were pretty good, even though it was so frustrating. My prior ER experience at Jonas Bronck had been horrendous, and I had expected the same. But it was much quieter this time; the asthma room wasn't constantly packed, it wasn't constantly filled with screaming, wheezing children who were vomiting all over the floor, making the place smelly and sticky and making the whole emergency room so noisy because of the sound of the oxygen coming out of the wall tanks. Instead, it was much quieter, and on call nights we'd get out of there at twelve or one o'clock, instead of at four or five in the morning. And the chiefs, thankfully, were really nice to me for some reason. They gave me no Friday nights [the night without a night float] and the only even slightly hard thing I had was neurology clinic, which is bad only because there always are so many patients.

Even dealing with the ER staff was easier in January. I really felt like I was getting along well with the nurses for a change. When I had worked in the ER last there was this one nurse named Eve whom I didn't like at all. One day during my first month there I just said to her, "I've had it with you! I'm not going to ask you for any help anymore. All you ever do is give me a hard time! As far as I'm concerned, you're not even here! I'm not talking to you anymore!" And she said, "Fine." So we left on horrendous terms. She was in a really bad mood because she was going to be quitting at the end of November and at that point she hated being in the Jonas Bronck ER. And then one day I was seeing a patient in my clinic at Mount Scopus and I walked out of the examining room and there she was, there was Eve, whom everybody else loved and I hated. We were standing there, staring at each other eye to eye, and she kind of looked afraid. It was a strange thing; I had never seen Eve like that, she'd always been so nasty and aggressive. She had an almost scared look in her face. And I kind of just laughed and walked past her and said, "Oh, *you're* here!" And she said, "Yeah, I'm working here now, I'm one of the nurses here." And we both laughed, and she said, "Don't worry, I'm not going to be such a bitch because I don't know what I'm doing yet."

Things still weren't exactly great. But then, the next time I saw her, we talked for a little while and then we went out to lunch and now we've become friends. She's really a good nurse, she's fast and efficient, and she's funny. Now I even like her.

I should mention one patient I had in neurology clinic. He was a seventeen-year-old autistic, severely mentally retarded, violent guy who had been sent over from Bronx Developmental Center [a residential facility for moderately and severely developmentally disabled children and adults] for evaluation because he was becoming increasingly depressed and had been losing weight. He was on all kinds of phenothiazines [a class of tranquilizers], but nothing was helping. I brought him into the examining room with the health care worker who had come with him. While I was looking through his old chart, he suddenly started to become extremely agitated. He got up and began stomping his feet on the ground and then he started slamming his head into the green tile wall over and over again. I looked over and realized there was blood on the wall, and there was blood coming out of his mouth. He had actually knocked a couple of teeth loose!

Then he started going completely wild; he attacked the health care worker and turned around and slugged me in the ribs a couple of times. Then he went and smashed his face against the wall again. The health care worker, a large, matronly black woman, grabbed him and tried to hold him still. All this time, he was screaming and making unintelligible grunting noises. Pretty soon he began flailing around, and the health care worker, who was getting kind of panicked, looked over and said, "He doesn't like to be in tight spaces. We need to get him out of here!"

I thought I had been very calm up until that moment. I opened the door, walked out, and everybody was looking toward the door because there had been a lot of ruckus in my room. I said, "I have a problem here." We got the kid out of the room and into the hallway, where apparently he didn't feel so enclosed, and we called security and I sat down with the neurology attending to whom this guy had been referred and said, "Why did you put me in that room with him? You knew exactly what was going to happen." And she made some comment like, "Well, you have to learn to take care of these kinds of patients," and I thought, No, I don't. As a resident, I don't have to take care of severely disturbed, autistic, retarded, violent patients who've been referred to a specific doctor for evaluation. In fact, the neurologist didn't want anything to do with him either. She finally said, "You know, we just can't evaluate him." So we sent him back with a letter saying sorry, there's nothing we can do. It was too bad, but we had nothing to offer.

I've thought about that patient a few times since this happened. I'm wondering how I would have reacted to the whole thing if this had happened back in July instead of in January. I think in July I would have tried a little harder, maybe looked farther through the chart or pushed the attending a little more. I don't know, the kid was crazy, he was dangerous, but when I was in OPD last July, I did some things for patients I don't think I'd do now: I stayed late to finish the workups on patients, things like that. I don't know if that's bad; it's just that it's a real change in me.

Anyway, those last weeks in January were very nice and I began regretting my decision to leave the Bronx. And on my last day in the ER, I said to the nurses on the afternoon shift, "This is the last time I'll ever be in Jonas Bronck." (My schedule at that time had been set so that I spend the rest of the year at Mount Scopus.) And they said, "What are you talking about? You'll be back next year." I said, "No, I won't." And they all said how much they'll miss me and stuff. It was very nice. Very nice and very sad.

I just finished my month in the ICU at Mount Scopus. It was a terrific month. We had a great team: Alex George was the attending, Diane Rogers was the senior resident, Terry Tanner was the junior resident, and we had a couple of good cross-coverers at night. The ICU was tremendously exhausting but somehow I didn't feel as overwhelmed as I had in the NICU, where I never got any sleep. There were a few nights this past month when I didn't get to bed either, but I got at least some sleep most nights I was on call. And I slept for seven whole hours my last night.

I seemed to have the same luck in the ICU that I've had all through the rest of the year. I seemed to get the sickest patients with the most dismal prognoses, and Terry got a lot more of the acutely ill, rapidly recovering patients with relatively good prognoses. It became kind of a standing joke that if I were there to admit a patient, the patient would either wind up dead or with some kind of severe permanent deficit. I guess I've got a lot of bad luck.

There were three patients who were the saddest patients I'll remember for a long, long time. The worst was Ronnie Morgan, this wonderful, beautiful, redheaded boy. When I met Ronnie Morgan for the first time, he was intubated, with a shaved head, a swollen face, and a dozen lines running in and out of his comatose body. Ronnie Morgan was a little two-and-a-half-year-old who had been doing really well until three months before I met him, when he became ill with some minor symptoms and was found on a routine blood test to have an outrageously high white blood cell count. He was admitted, a bone marrow biopsy was done, and a diagnosis of ALL [**acute lymphocytic leukemia**] was made. Soon thereafter, he had a bout of ARDS [**adult respiratory distress syndrome, a condition in which the lungs fill with fluid and respiration becomes extremely difficult**] and a systemic fungal infection. He was admitted to the ICU at death's door, recovered, went through some chemotherapy, and finally was thought to be going into remission. Although his disease and his chemotherapy turned him into a cranky and irritable little kid, his mother always remembered him as being a beautiful, wonderful, happy boy. And then a few days before I first saw him, he was leaving his hematologist's office after a routine visit and fell and hit his head. That's not so unusual; he was a toddler, and toddlers fall a dozen times a day; that's why they're called toddlers. But when he fell, he happened to have a very low platelet count because of the chemotherapy, and he got an occipital hematoma [**a large, blood-filled bruise in the back of his head**]. So he was admitted to the hospital for a transfusion of FFP [**fresh frozen plasma, a blood product containing the** elements of the blood essential for blood to clot] and platelets because it was feared he could bleed out into the hematoma.

Over the course of the next thirty-six hours, he became progressively more lethargic, his mental status deteriorated, and with that concern he was brought down for an EEG [**electroencephalogram, a test to examine brain waves**]. While he was in EEG, he began to seize. He was then rushed to a CT scan, where a massive intracranial bleed was found [**intracranial bleed: a hemorrhage in the skull**]. At that point, he was immediately brought to the operating room for emergency neurosurgery. There, a huge intraparenchymal [**within the body of the brain**] and subarachnoid [**below the inside layer of the meninges, the tissue that surrounds and protects the brain**] hemorrhage was evacuated, along with a good part of Ronnie's brain, something that happens when you do that kind of surgery. He was then brought up to the ICU on a ventilator and became my patient.

I knew Ronnie was a goner from the moment I saw him. He had a horrible problem, a subarachnoid and intraparenchymal bleed, and that diagnosis on its own was horrendous. And then you add to it his age and his fragility with his leukemia and the low platelets and all the rest and he really had no chance at all. And everyone in the ICU identified so much with him and his parents, who were young, white, middle-class, articulate people.

He was with us for about ten days. After maybe the fourth or fifth day, he had a sudden, uncontrollable rise in the pressure inside his skull. We had been able to keep the intracranial pressure down prior to that time with various maneuvers and drugs, but that day it just became uncontrollable. And with that it was felt that he was essentially brain dead, and yet his body wouldn't die. It was all so horrendous, continuing to take care of this boy who had no prognosis at all. His father understood the situation; he knew how bad things were, and he was trying to mourn his son's death before it actually occurred. But his mother was too defensive and wouldn't accept it, and in a sense was preventing the father from doing his mourning. I never really got to know these people very well; when I first picked up Ronnie as a patient, I saw all the people who were gathered around the parents and I felt that my availability as a support person would not be needed. I didn't see the need of intruding myself into these people's lives when they had already made acquaintance with Alex George, a hematologist, and some other members of the staff. And while it was true that there was nothing extra I could have offered them, I think I missed out on something and I wish I'd had the opportunity to learn how to help these people grieve.

The day his ICP [intracranial pressure] skyrocketed, we were standing by his bedside, and Alex said that Ronnie had died, that the bleed inside his head and the pressure had completely destroyed his brain. In the bed right next to him, separated only by a flimsy curtain, was a fourteen-year-old girl who had been diagnosed with a horrible brain tumor and who was going to die of that tumor within the next year or so. She had just undergone some surgery and she was a little off the wall and her mother, who had been sitting here, suddenly said, "I can't take this, this is too much for me!" and left the room. It was just a little too close to home for her.

Finally Ronnie did die. He died a couple of hours before I came in one morning. I had been postcall the day before and he'd been doing very badly; I left knowing it was only a matter of time. I didn't go to his funeral, but I wish I had. I think I've been mourning his death ever since he died; not often or always, but whenever I think about him, I get very sad. But it's strange: I never did know him as a person; I only knew him through the eyes of the people who loved him. Still, I know I'll remember him and be sad for him through maybe the rest of my professional career.

I had another patient, Kara Smith, a little four-month-old who broke my heart. Her first three months of life were normal, and then she came down with pneumococcal meningitis [meningitis caused by the bacteria *Streptococcus pneumoniae;* this type of meningitis causes particularly devastating effects]. When I picked her up at the beginning of the month, she was just this little seizing baby who was in renal failure, on peritoneal dialysis [a procedure performed on patients in renal failure; dialysis rids the body of the waste products of metabolism that normally are removed by the kidneys], getting multiple antibiotics, and who had a very abnormal neurologic exam. To make a long story short, Kara was the patient who should have died but didn't. Her mother agreed to a DNR [Do not resuscitate] order. I actually first brought up the idea of DNR with Ms. Smith. I told her it was something she should consider, and she decided that it would be best if Kara just died. It sounds cold-blooded saying it like that, but it really would have been the best thing that could have happened. We decided we'd just do supportive care and nothing heroic, but even that division became increasingly unclear.

One afternoon she had an acute respiratory attack; it was probably just mechanical, just her [endotracheal] tube slipping down her right mainstem [bronchus, the breathing tube going to the right lung], and she began deteriorating. She became cyanotic [blue], and her heart rate dropped. We readjusted her tube and she recovered a little but she still looked shitty. I felt really uncomfortable doing nothing, and yet, to bag her back [force oxygen into her lungs using an ambubag] was kind of a resuscitation. It was very unclear. And there was a senior, Eric Keyes, sitting there, and he said, "Forget it, just leave it, don't do anything." It was so easy for him to say that, it was nothing for him, he was just looking at her and thinking, This kid's just a GORK, forget her. But I felt bad doing nothing. She was my patient. I'd made a pact, in a sense, to support her. So when she continued to deteriorate, I in fact did bag her a little. And then, after a while, she was fine again. I'm still haunted by that issue. It's one of those very gray areas of medicine.

I talked to Karen so many times about this baby. One night after a really long discussion, she said, "Listen, you have no medical basis for what you're doing with this kid. Why don't you just put down the side rails on the bed and let the baby fall to the ground and die? Is that any different from letting her electrolytes get out of whack because you're not doing blood tests on her? Why not just put down the rails?" In fact, putting down the rails wouldn't make any difference; the baby never moved anyway. But she was right; there was no medical basis for so many of the decisions that were made. Everything seemed so arbitrary and based on emotions rather than facts. I think we were very much guided by the fact that the mother just didn't want that baby anymore, she didn't want a baby who was so severely damaged. We consulted the mother at many points along the road, we involved this poor woman who had no support system and who had other kids at home to worry about, and these decisions were difficult for her to make. One day I asked her to come in because we needed to talk about something; she showed up late at night, hours after the time I had asked her to come. She came with this young guy, about seventeen, who looked scared and a little intoxicated, and it turned out to be the baby's father. I had never seen him before; he had been nowhere near the hospital for at least two and a half weeks. We sat in the family room for a long time and talked; we talked about DNR and the new thing we were going to withdraw and she said, "Go ahead." It was as if she were saying, "Please don't let this baby live!"

It didn't really hit me how dismal Kara's prognosis was until I saw her CT scan. Her brain looked like a minefield; there was more space and fluid than there was brain tissue. This little baby had so little substrate to build her life on. But by then it was too late, all the miracles had been done on her; she just wouldn't die. I eventually got her off the ventilator and off the dialysis. I got her electrolytes corrected, I got her to feed, we stopped the antibiotics, and she became just a baby in a basinette. And one day we needed a bed in the unit and she was the most stable patient, so she was shuffled off to the Infants' ward.

The third patient was Emilio Diaz, a really adorable three-year-old with AIDS who had done so well for so much of his life. Emilio spent his first year in the hospital because there was no place for him to go. He was finally adopted by one of the nurses who had taken care of him when he was a baby. This woman really loved him. She married Emilio's father, an IV drug user who had AIDS so that she could legally adopt him and take care of him. She had done a lot to try to give Emilio as full a life as possible. He'd gone to Puerto Rico to visit relatives, he'd gone for trips all over the place, he'd done a lot more than your average Bronx three-year-old. And then he became sick and was admitted to the ICU and rapidly deteriorated. He had terrible pneumonia; he became ventilator-dependent and reached ventilator settings that nobody had ever seen before in the ICU. And he just kept getting worse until finally I had to have that horrible discussion with the parents about DNR on him, too. In Emilio's case, though, it was his parents who first asked about DNR. I suppose it's not surprising, since his mother is a nurse and very medically sophisticated. But one day she came to me and said, "He's suffered enough; we want to make him DNR."

Emilio died one evening just after I left for home. He was there the longest of all three of these patients; he was my patient for a good three and a half weeks. It was so sad taking care of him. There finally came a point, around the time that he officially was made DNR, when I felt very, very depressed. Every time I had to go over to his bedside, every time I had to write a note in his chart or I had to look at his bedside clipboard or call for his lab results, I became severely depressed. It was really sad. Really sad.

Well, anyway, I learned a lot of medicine from those three patients and from the other patients I took care of in the ICU. I learned how to put in A lines [**arterial lines; like IVs, except going into arteries instead of veins**], I got good at intubating, and I learned about Dopamine and Dobutamine drips [**a class of drugs known as pressors, which raise blood pressure; they're used in critically ill patients who cannot maintain their own blood pressure**]. And I did a lot of thinking about ethics and the fact that, basically, we can keep just about anybody alive for an indefinite period of time but that keeping people alive may not be such a good thing. That's a hell of a lot to pick up in one month! And I think one of the reasons I was able to do all that was because of the people I worked with.

Diane was a great resident. She's very, very bright; extremely capable; and very talented. She has a very wry sense of humor. We were on call together five of my nine nights, and we had a lot of fun. I thought she was kind of attractive, too, but of course that was something I couldn't really tell her. Her body is very similar to Karen's, and I found that very erotic. I told her that the morning after the last night of the month we were on call together. I was kind of delirious and I don't know how it came up but I said something like, "You know, you're very erotic," and she said, "What's wrong with you? You must be completely out of it!" And I said, "Yeah, I guess I am," but in fact I had been thinking about it for a while. But I couldn't say it until then because we'd been on call and slept in that little on-call room so many nights together. Not that it would have mattered, for God's sake. Anyway, it would have been an inappropriate thing to have done.

Alex is a great attending, and he really was very supportive. He'd come up, give me these big bear hugs during the day, and ask me how I was doing. He said he was worried about my psyche all the time because I was taking care of all these very sick patients. He was a good teacher, too. And he has a really big heart, he really cared about so many of the patients. He was somehow able to be a very devoted and involved ICU director, there all the time, always available and really involved, and yet he could keep some distance and let the residents try to run the place.

On the last day of the month, Alex took us all to lunch, which no attending has done for me before. He was a role model for me. I felt maybe I could actually do this kind of thing for a living. Even though it was depressing and even though taking care of critically ill children is so far removed from what I originally thought I'd wind up doing, I felt having someone who really cared made a big difference. When you think about it, all you really need in the ICU is a good technician who knows how to run all the machines and monitors. You don't *need* an Alex George to run a unit. But I think his heart makes a big difference; Alex is what makes that place seem human and not just a mechanical torture chamber. I'm sure his being there has helped a lot of families. I know it really helped the house staff; his fatherliness, his caring attitude, it really made a difference.

And finally, there were the nurses. I really got to like those nurses. They're superb; they're fun to work with, they've got a great sense of humor. I learned to depend on them totally and to trust them. They do a lot of things that need to be done without you ever knowing about them. They ask you to write the orders for them after they've finished. They know so much, they're each like a doctor. Many times we'll be sitting there, scratching our heads, trying to figure things out, and they're flipping the dials, running the lines, drawing up meds, making decisions they are confident with. And they just say, "This is what you want, isn't it?" as they push it in the line. So they are real lifesavers, and I'm going to miss them.

AMY

February 1986

Sunday, February 2, 1986

All year, anytime anybody's asked me to do something, I've done it without an argument. It seems it works only one way, though, because whenever I've asked someone to do me a favor, nobody's willing to help out. It's disgusting.

This is what happened: I started my two weeks in OPD last Monday. I had only two weeks to go before my vacation, so I figured it would be a cinch. But when I got home from work last Monday afternoon, Marie told me she thought Sarah was coming down with something. She hadn't eaten well during the day, which isn't like her, she'd been kind of sleepy, and she had a runny nose. Sure enough, I put her to bed at about nine and she woke up at a little after eleven, screaming at the top of her lungs. Larry and I ran into her room and found that she was burning up. I took her temperature: It was a 103.4°. It took about twenty minutes to get her to stop crying, and when she finally calmed down, I checked her over. I couldn't find anything specifically wrong, her ears looked fine and everything, but she still had rhinitis [**runny nose**] and she was coughing a lot, and I noticed the whites of her eyes were red. I figured it was just the virus that was going around. I gave her some Tylenol and rocked her back to sleep, and she finally dropped off at about midnight.

She woke up again at 2:00 A.M. She was screaming, and her temperature was back up. I gave her more Tylenol and tried to calm her down, but this time she just wouldn't stop crying. I was sure she had meningitis and I told Larry to get dressed because we had to take her to the emergency room, but just as

236

he finished getting his clothes on, she quieted down and fell
back to sleep. I guess the Tylenol had kicked in. Anyway, she
slept the rest of the night, but I didn't; I stayed awake in her
room, watching her constantly. I was sure something terrible
was going to happen.

On Tuesday morning, she woke up in a much better mood
and her fever was gone. I figured whatever was wrong had
reached its peak and now she was getting better. When Marie
came, I told her about what had happened and made sure she
knew how much Tylenol to give if the fever came back. I had
clinic that morning and was going to be in the ER that afternoon
and night, so I left Marie a schedule of where I'd be if she
needed to contact me, and I left for work.

I should have called in sick, but I went to clinic anyway.
Marie called at about ten-thirty to tell me that Sarah's fever was
back and that she had this rash all over her. I told her I'd be
home in a few minutes and I rushed through the rest of my clinic
patients. I was done by about eleven and I ran home to find
Sarah's fever back up to 103. She was miserable; she was coughing and sneezing and covered with snot, and she had a whopping
conjunctivitis [**inflammation of the membranes that line the
eye; also called pinkeye**]. And she had a raised red rash on her
face and chest. I wasn't sure what it was, so I called Alan Cozza.
He told me to bring her right over.

Well, to make a long story a little shorter, Alan took one
look at her and said, ''My God, she's got the measles!'' I
had never seen anyone with measles before; kids just don't
get it, because we immunize them. Alan brought some of the
other interns who were on the floor in to see Sarah just so
they'd know what measles looked like. I have no idea where
she got it; she's a baby, she doesn't go outside, she doesn't
hang around with other kids except sometimes when Marie
takes her down to the lobby, but that's rare. But anyway, she
had it. Alan told me to take her home and give her Tylenol
and fluids and just make her as comfortable as possible and
that it would pass in a few days.

By that point it was nearly one o'clock. I was supposed to be
in the ER starting at one, and since I was on call that night, I'd
be staying in the ER until maybe three or four in the morning.
So I decided to stop in and talk to the chief residents; I figured,
hearing that Sarah was so sick, they'd naturally say, ''Well, why

don't you just stay home with your daughter tonight?'' Yeah, right!

What they said was that two people who were supposed to be on call that night had already called in sick and they had to pull one person from the emergency room to cover and although they sympathized with me, they just couldn't let me off. If I didn't show up, there'd only be two house officers to staff the entire emergency room, and they just couldn't allow that to happen. They told me I should try to switch with someone who was scheduled to be on the next day, if I could find someone who would be willing to switch, but there was just no way they could give me the night off.

How nice of them! After all the abuse I've taken through these seven months! After everything I've done for them! Whenever they've asked me to do anything, I've always done it without a whimper! I filled in for other people, I covered wards I'd never been on before because somebody was out, and I never complained. I've repeatedly put my job ahead of my family, and this is the thanks I get! The one time my daughter is sick, the one night I need to take off, of course no one would do a thing for me. I asked everybody if they'd switch, if they'd cover for me this one night, and they all had some excuse. I should have just gone home. I should have taken Marie and Sarah home and stayed there and when they called me to find out where I was and why I wasn't in the emergency room, I would have said . . . I don't know exactly what I could have said. But, of course, I didn't do that. What I did was, I brought Sarah and Marie home and went back to the hospital.

The rest of that day was ridiculous. We were short-staffed in the emergency room; the place was like a zoo. Everybody in the Bronx was sick with the flu and had fever and vomiting and coughing. There was a six- to seven-hour wait to be seen through most of the afternoon and night. I rushed around that emergency room until four in the morning, and during all that time I didn't see a single patient who was as sick as Sarah. I really resented being there, and I must have told that to the nurses and the rest of the staff at least a thousand times.

Marie kept calling me all through the afternoon. She didn't exactly feel comfortable taking care of a baby with a fever that ranged between 103 and 104, and I can't say I blame her. I'm sure she was afraid Sarah was going to have a seizure or something. That idea crossed my mind a few times. So she called every half hour or so, saying, "Her fever's still up. What should I do?" or "Her eyes are getting very glassy. Are you sure you can't come home now?" Even she had a hard time understanding why I couldn't just come home to take care of my baby. And there wasn't anything I could say to her to make her understand because I wasn't sure I understood it myself.

I finally got out of the emergency room at about four. Larry was wide awake; he hadn't gotten any sleep, having been up with Sarah all night. Her fever was still up, and she was very irritable. She'd sleep for maybe a half hour and then wake up howling. It's so strange seeing her like this; she usually has such a good personality. And she was absolutely covered with the measles.

I was all set to call in sick on Wednesday, but Larry had already made arrangements to take the day off, and he told me I should go in. I went, and in the morning Alan called to ask me how Sarah was doing. I gave him a piece of my mind! I told him about how the chiefs had made me work the night before, and he seemed amazed by it. He said he'd go have a talk with them, but a lot of good that's done me! I'm really so angry. I'll tell you, this episode has really taught me a lesson. Let them ask me to do anything, let anybody ask me to cover or to switch; my answer is going to be *"NO!"* I don't care what it is or who it is, I'm not doing anything for anybody ever again! I've had it with these people! I've got to look out for my own interests, because no one else is!

Sarah's better now. The rash is starting to fade. Her temperature came down to normal on Friday, and she's not irritable anymore. By tomorrow she should be back to her old self. But I'm not going to forget this. You can bet they're going to regret making me work Tuesday night!

Saturday, February 8, 1986

I've just finished packing. My vacation starts after I finish my call in the ER tomorrow night, and we have a ten-twenty flight to Fort Lauderdale on Monday morning. I really need this vacation. I'm physically and emotionally exhausted. We're spending two weeks in a condominium near Fort Lauderdale; two weeks of lying in the sun and sleeping late. I can't wait!

Things have pretty much returned to normal. Sarah is back to her old self. The measles have disappeared, and the only things left from the whole episode are my anger and resentment.

MARK

February 1986

Monday, January 27, 1986

Today was my first day in the nursery. What fun I had! I love staying until ten-thirty, running around like a chicken with my head cut off, having no idea in the world what the hell I'm doing. It was a million laughs! I can't wait to go back there tomorrow!

Well, let's see: How can I describe what the day was like? I came in at about eight o'clock, and Ed Norris, the director of the neonatal ICU at Jonas Bronck, tried to give us an orientation lecture. He certainly made things very clear; it was like listening to a lecture in Swahili! I couldn't understand a good 50 percent of the things he was talking about. He kept referring to the inhabitants of the unit as "your patients." You know, "your patients this" and "your patients that." And then we walked around and he showed us these so-called patients. My God, those things weren't patients! They'd have to quadruple their weight to be classified as patients. Right now, they're mostly tiny portions of buzzard food with lots of ridiculous wires and tubes coming out of them. This is going to be a long month!

They gave me eight of these things to take care of. For most of them, the kid's chart weighs more than the kid does, which is a very bad prognostic sign. And, of course, I didn't have a clue about what the hell was going on with any of them, so I spent the whole day sitting in the nurses' station trying to read these ridiculous charts, which were filled with words I had never seen or heard before and numbers I couldn't even attempt to figure out. I was trying like hell to make sense of all of this before one of these things wound up dying. At least I didn't have to go to clinic this afternoon; it was canceled. Thank God, because there's no way I would have made it anyhow.

I really can't believe this! It's ten-thirty, I'm just getting home from work, and this is my good night! It's just amazing! I have eight patients, they're all stable, and none of them is really that complicated, but even uncomplicated preemies have this long, annoying history, most of which I don't give a damn about. I mean, truly, I just don't care! There was a point there, about five o'clock tonight, where I swear I was this close to just taking all the charts, throwing them out the window, and saying, "Forget it! I'm sorry I ever applied to medical school! I never really wanted to be a doctor anyway!" I just couldn't take it anymore: just all these little runts who shouldn't be alive in the first place! Damn! Really annoying! But hey, I stuck it out, because I have such great self-control, and here I am, celebrating by eating my favorite food, Sno-Caps. This is the first thing I've placed in my mouth since breakfast. That was over fifteen hours ago! Working in this damned ICU is like being on a self-imposed fast! I feel like Gandhi, for God's sake!

I better try to eat neatly. This looks like it's going to be one of those months where I'm not going to get to wash the dishes or do the laundry! Maybe I'd better just start using paper plates right now. It's too bad they haven't invented paper clothes. That'd be perfect: disposable clothes for the house officer. Maybe if they could be made edible, that would solve both problems at once. I'm not making any sense anymore. I've got to get some sleep!

This place really sucks. What am I going to do?

Wednesday, January 29, 1986

Well, I'm home again. It seems like only yesterday I was last here, but actually it was the day before yesterday. I'm exhausted. I was on last night and I didn't get any sleep. No one ever gets any sleep in the nursery, so saying you didn't get any sleep on a night you were on call is redundant. I spent the whole night running around from bed to bed, doing stuff I didn't understand on babies I didn't think were human, for reasons that are totally beyond me. What a rewarding experience.

Here are a few more of my thoughts about the neonatal intensive-torture chamber. What a fun place it is. Starting to work in the NITC [neonatal intensive-torture chamber], or the NICU, as the neonatologists like to refer to it, is like being thrown into prison in a foreign country where you have no idea what the fuck's going on. I really don't know anything! I've never even taken care of well babies before. I can barely tell the difference between the respirators and the babies. Before Monday, I'd never seen a kid with jaundice. [Neonatal jaundice is caused by immaturity of the liver, the organ that removes bilirubin from the bloodstream; it's a common problem in infants and is treated with phototherapy, placing the infant under banks of fluorescent lights.] I don't know when to turn on the lights, when to turn off the lights. I don't even know what a normal bilirubin is for a baby!

And I don't know what you're supposed to feed these things. I don't know how much they're supposed to eat, how much they're supposed to pee, nothing! If it weren't for the nurses, who, thank God, seem to know what the hell's going on, I'd probably have managed to kill off every last kid by now!

And even if I did know all that simple, obvious stuff, there's all this other information I don't even have a clue about. There isn't one word that they use in there that even sounds like anything I've ever heard outside the unit. It's like they make up terms just to make our lives more miserable, if it's possible to be more miserable than I already am! Every one of those kids has biochemical rickets. What the hell is biochemical rickets? I have no idea! And besides that, who cares?

As you can tell, all these little annoyances aside, I'm really having a lot of fun. I'm really enjoying taking care of these bags of protoplasm. My favorite patient is this kid Moreno. He's a three-month-old with congenital hydrocephalus. [Hydrocephalus is a condition in which an excessive amount of cerebrospinal fluid, the substance that normally bathes and protects the brain and spinal cord, accumulates in the skull. Usually it is due to obstruction of flow of the fluid from the brain, where it is produced, to the spinal cord, where it is absorbed. When hydrocephalus occurs at birth, it is usually caused by an abnormality in the formation of the brain.] This kid is all head! He weighs twenty-five hundred grams, and about twenty-three hundred of those are housed above his neck. And of those twenty-three hundred grams, 99 percent of that is fluid. His cerebral cortex looks like a ribbon around a water balloon. And that's after he had a shunt put in that seems to be working. [A shunt is a piece of plastic tubing, one end of which is placed in the brain, the other end of which is placed in either the abdominal cavity, the chest, or the heart, that drains the cerebrospinal fluid out of the brain in patients with hydrocephalus.] His head circumference today was forty-nine centimeters. [Normal head circumference for a newborn is thirty-five centimeters. At three months, the head circumference should be about forty centimeters.] This kid's got a great prognosis!

So anyway, Moreno's mother called me today. I wasn't in a very good mood, having been up all night and not having understood anything anybody has said to me in nearly three days, so I wasn't really in much of a mood to put up with her. She calls every few days to ask what the kid's head circumference is. She's fixated on his head circumference. I told her it was forty-nine centimeters this morning and she got all panicky, saying it was only forty-eight centimeters on Sunday and now it was a centimeter larger, and wasn't I worried about it, and what was I going to do about it? I calmly explained to her that no, I wasn't worried about it because it had been forty-nine centimeters when I got there on Monday and it was still forty-nine centimeters now and he wasn't irritable or vomiting and he didn't have any of the other signs of increased intracranial pressure, and since the neurosurgeons and the neurologists had been by to see him and neither of them had been upset by his head circumference, I wasn't going to do anything about it. I think I also told her that I was happy that his head circumference was forty-nine centimeters, I was pleased as Punch, and if she wanted to find someone who wasn't happy, I suggested she call the neurosurgeons or Ed Norris to see what they think. I think I said that, but I'm not sure because, like I say, I was kind of tired and I haven't been making much sense over the past few days. But I'm pretty sure of one thing: I don't think Mrs. Moreno is going to be calling me much during the rest of the month!

Well, there is one saving grace about working in this torture chamber. Some of the night nurses are extremely cute. One in particular: dark, brown hair, really beautiful. Damn! She almost makes it worth staying up all night. But not quite. Nothing could really make it worth staying up all night.

I must say, my progress notes have deteriorated significantly.

I never really wrote very good notes in the first place; in fact, my progress notes have been voted among the worst ever seen at Mount Scopus Hospital. Recently, no one's been able to read any of them. But at least they used to be short. Now, because of all the problems these kids have, instead of my usual three or four lines of unreadable scribble, I now write whole pages of unreadable scribble.

What a stupid thing to do to us, throw us in the middle of this unit when we don't know what the hell we're doing. And Norris screams at us that they're our patients! Bullshit! He should be thrown in jail if he really thinks they're our patients! None of us knows what the hell we're doing with them. All right, show us around, give us a week or two to figure out what's going on, then you can think of them as if they were our patients. At this point we can have virtually nothing to do with their care, because we know virtually nothing about how to care for them.

Hey, but the jury's not in yet. I'll give it a little more time to see what it's like before I make up my mind. I'm on call Friday night with a senior resident who sort of drives me crazy. She's reasonably intelligent and she seems to know what's going on, but she really lacks self-confidence. It wouldn't be so annoying if she didn't keep turning to me for reassurance. Me, can you believe that? I mean, I have absolutely no idea what the hell is going on! The other night she did something that I think was probably wrong. She wanted to intubate this kid for having one bad blood gas. And she asked me if I thought it was the right thing to do. I said, "No, it doesn't sound right. I think you should just turn up the oxygen and repeat the gas before you do anything." That was just common sense; this kid was perfectly pink at the time. I hope I'm not that unsure of myself next year, when I'm in a position of authority. Hah! Boy, we're all going to be in trouble when that happens!

Thursday, January 30, 1986

It's nine o'clock and I just got home. Things are looking up: I cut an hour and a half off the time I finished on Monday night. Why, if this keeps up, I'll have so much free time this month, I may actually get to cook my own dinner one night! I think washing the dishes'll still be out of the question, though. That'd be just too much to shoot for.

Here's some news on the Moreno front: Today's head circumference was forty-nine and a half centimeters, up one-half centimeter from yesterday's closing. And you know what? I don't give a shit! I just don't care!

I don't like the neonatal ICU. I'm not positive, but I just don't think I'm going to grow up to be a neonatologist!

I've got this nervous feeling in my stomach all the time. I stopped at a drugstore on the way home and bought this great big bottle of Maalox. Either I'm coming down with gastroenteritis or I'm beginning to burn a big hole in my gastric muscosa [getting an ulcer].

Monday, February 10, 1986

I'm postcall. There's nothing like being postcall when you're in the NICU. It's at least a hundred times worse than being postcall anywhere else in the world, including Infants', which until this month had won the prize hands down as the Most Horrible Postcall Experience in the Bronx. I should be asleep now, but I haven't recorded anything in over a week. I've wanted to; I just haven't had enough strength to push down the ''record'' button on this silly machine. I don't want to let this fabulous experience escape immortalization on cassette tape, so, at great expense (at least ten minutes of precious sleep), here goes.

Working in this nightmare has now settled into a nice, regular, predictable routine of devastation and misery. Take yesterday, for instance. It was Sunday and I was on call. I walked through the doors of 7 South with a smile on my face at seven-thirty and was completely and overwhelmingly depressed by eight o'clock. Iris Davis, who'd been on call Saturday, signed out to me. She was in a great mood. When she gets real tired, she starts to cry, so it took her about an hour and a half and at least three boxes of tissues to get through sign-out. All I got out of it was a scut list about a mile long and a terrible headache.

Most of what Iris signed out to me was checking bloods that had been drawn earlier in the morning. So I started calling the labs to get the results, a very rewarding experience. Each lab had a different and very novel explanation for why the results weren't available. The chem lab claimed they had never received any samples, even though Iris assured me that she hand-delivered them. The hematology lab said that all the specimens, every one of them, was QNS [**quantity not sufficient**]. That's a polite way of saying, "We poured the blood down the sink, so you're going to have to draw them all over again." And the blood gas lab said the machine was broken and they wouldn't be able to run any samples for at least another hour. What this all meant was that I was going to have to spend the next two hours redrawing all these bloods and then spend another half hour delivering the samples to all the different labs.

Okay, so I did all that, and then I got to spend the next six hours writing progress notes. I love writing progress notes! You have to write a note on every patient every day or else the administrator on duty swoops down at about midnight and puts an evil spell on you. And these notes aren't just "Patient still alive. Plan: Make sure he stays alive until tomorrow morning." These notes go on and on, listing problem after problem. Each one can take an hour.

It wouldn't even be so bad if all I had to do was the scut and the notes, but that's all broken up by the endless rounding. First the attending showed up at about eleven so that he could view the patients close up for about an hour. He also has to fill his daily quota of yelling at the house officers. Then in the evening, there were rounds with the senior resident, who managed to come up with a whole new list of scut for me to take care of during the night. So I got to draw some more blood, have more fights with the lab technicians who have perfected the art of denying having received blood samples you handed them not an hour before, and write more long notes in the charts documenting what the results of those fights with the lab technicians have been.

And even all that would have been okay if it hadn't have been for the fact that the DR [**delivery room**] kept calling us to come down to deliveries. That's the real ulcerogenic part of this job. The rest is just irritating, but the DR is downright frightening. At any moment, without so much as a minute's warning, you could be called down there and find yourself face to face with a brand-new four-hundred-gram wonder whose only goal in life is to make your next two or three weeks completely unbearable. Also, there are all these little emergencies that come up in the unit, like kids deteriorating or spiking fevers, stuff like that. It's all such fun!

Last night, I actually got myself in a position to go to sleep at about three o'clock. I was in the on-call room, in my winter coat, getting ready to lie down on the cot. The on-call room is an interesting place. They recently rebuilt the entire ICU and they made us this very nice place to sleep. The only problem is, they forgot to put any heat in there. The average temperature is about forty to forty-five degrees. Sleeping in there is like camping out in Alaska.

Anyway, I was on the cot, getting ready to lay down. I was lowering my head toward the pillow and just as my hair made contact with the pillowcase, my beeper went off, calling me to the DR stat. I went running down there to find it was an uncomplicated problem, a little meconium-stained amniotic fluid. The baby was out by the time we got there and he was fine, just fine. There was nothing we needed to do. So I went back to the unit, got back into the on-call room, put my coat back on, and actually got about an hour of sleep. At five o'clock, I got another stat page. We went running down to the DR, and what did we find? An obstetric resident with her arm, up to the elbow, thrust inside a woman's vagina. What a romantic sight!

It turned out, this woman had wandered in off the street with a prolapsed cord. [**The umbilical cord had come through the cervix and was lying in the vagina. The danger of this is that if the cervix should close up again, blood would stop flowing through the umbilical cord and the fetus would suffer from lack of oxygen, causing either death or severe brain damage.**] The resident was trying to push it back up into the uterus while two other people were preparing to do an emergency C section. The whole thing took about an hour, and when the baby came out, he was just fine! By that point it was eight o'clock in the morning and time for the day crew to show up. I finished with the work on that patient, started drawing the morning bloods, and then started rounds with the rest of the team.

We went on work rounds and then we had attending rounds. I tried to write my notes during all this because I had clinic this afternoon and I didn't want to have to come back to the unit again after clinic was over. So I got to clinic at Mount Scopus at about two and I got home a little while ago, at about six. A typical thirty-four-hour day; at least I got one whole hour of sleep!

I've had some really terrific experiences in the unit over the past week. Really terrific! I've got these two kids who are essentially brain stem preparations. One weighed 525 grams at birth and from the very beginning had virtually no chance of surviving. So what do we do? We use everything we have to keep him alive. And all that comes out of it is a great deal of work for me and the other interns. The other kid was good-sized at birth, a thirty-three- or thirty-four-weeker, but the mother had an abruption [**abruptio placentae: a condition in which the placenta tears itself off the wall of the uterus, leading to a great deal of bleeding and a severe deficiency of blood in the fetus**] and the kid was severely asphyxiated, with Apgars of 0, 0, 3, and 3. [**Apgar scores are given at one and five minutes after birth. If the scores are low at one and at five minutes, additional scoring is done at ten and at twenty minutes. In the case of Mark's infant, the score was 0 at one minute, 0 at five minutes, 3 at ten minutes, and 3 at twenty minutes.**] Not what you'd call very good. Where I come from, we have a name for children like this: stillborn. So this kid is basically brain dead but we're keeping the body alive to have something to keep us busy. As if I already didn't have enough to keep me busy!

This rotation continues to have only one redeeming feature, that being the nurses. These nurses are fantastic. They're young, real attractive, and real good at their job. Last week one of the night nurses handed me a prescription form. It looked like this:

CITY OF NEW YORK
HEALTH AND HOSPITAL CORPORATION
———————— HOSPITAL

Name Mark Greenberg, M.D.   Age 26
Address————————————Date 2/4/86
Rx

        1 date with me

Physician's Signature ————————   555-0826

I've been carrying it around ever since. I had lunch with her last week. She seems nice. I don't want to jeopardize my relationship with Carole; Lord knows it's already suffered enough! So I don't think I'll actually take this any farther. But it sure was nice to get that note. It made me feel . . . it made me feel almost as if I were a human.

Tuesday, February 25, 1986

I haven't recorded anything in a couple of weeks. I look upon these tape recordings as kind of a funny running monologue, but I haven't felt very funny over the past two weeks. Working in this unit has been terrible, just terrible, much worse than I ever imagined. We've had a lot of deaths and, even worse, we've had a lot of survivors, babies who should never have been allowed to live. I don't want to think back on what's happened, I just want to look ahead. In just a couple of days I'll be done with the NICU, and then I've got a month in OPD at Mount Scopus, two weeks of vacation, and two more weeks of OPD after that.

Every month so far there have been a lot of bad memories, but there have also been some good ones, funny stories I'll carry with me probably forever. This month there have only been bad memories and worse memories. Moreno and his steadily increasing head circumference; the wasted, dying preemies hanging on much longer than they should be allowed to because of all the machines we have to use on them; the bigger kids with PFC [**persistence of the fetal circulation**]; the brain-dead baby with the abruption; these were terrible, terrible things. I've been finding that I just can't defend myself against them. It's been just brutal.

I don't want to make this sound too sappy, but I knew I was in trouble when I cried in the hospital last week. Iris, the other intern, has been crying just about every day, but last Thursday I had been up the whole night before with this PFC'er who had done really poorly, and when he finally died, I just couldn't take it anymore. I went into the bathroom, locked the door, and just cried my eyes out. I'm really starting to fall apart. That was the first time I'd cried all year. I know most of the other interns have cried, but I kind of prided myself on the fact that I could control myself. Not this month.

Maybe sometime in the future I'll be able to come back to this and fill in some of the blank spaces I've left, but I can't do that right now. I need a nice vacation. I think I'll take my vacation in the West Bronx emergency room over the next four weeks.

I'm going to sleep. Maybe when I wake up, things'll start being funny again.

BOB

February 1986

Mark Greenberg and Andy Baron worked in ICUs during February, and both had experiences caring for patients who were being kept alive thanks to technological advances that had been developed over the past few years. It's always been true that technology has run way ahead of ethics in medicine. With every advance that's been made, be it the development of antibiotics, the iron lung, present-day respirators, chemotherapy and radiotherapy for cancers, or the ability to transplant organs, physicians have been able to take discoveries made in the laboratory and apply them to humans. The immediate result of these advances has been that patients who the week before would surely have died have been given the opportunity to survive, at least for some period of time. But we've often learned that survival may not always be the best outcome for the patient or for society. The question of whether these fruits of medical technology should be utilized has to be addressed. In many cases, answering this question can be more difficult than developing the technology in the first place.

In no place is this truer than the neonatal intensive-care unit. Although there has always been interest in the very premature baby, until the 1960s these infants were considered little more than curiosities. Rather than being cared for in specially designed intensive-care units where all their life functions were meticulously monitored, these babies used to be warehoused in circuses and freak shows, and exhibited to the public for a price. If they lived for very long, it created more interest. If they died, usually because of respiratory failure, it meant only that they needed to be replaced.

Unlike most other medical specialties, which gradually evolved into existence, neonatology had a sharply demarcated beginning, largely the result of a specific event. In August 1963, Patrick Bouvier Kennedy, the premature son of President John and Jacqueline Kennedy, died of respiratory distress syndrome at Boston Children's Hospital. For a few days, an intense media spotlight was shone on the special problem of babies who were born too soon. Although, sadly, this event ended with the death of the infant, it resulted in millions of dollars of national grant funding being devoted to research into the special problems of the premature. And therefore the death of Patrick Bouvier Kennedy led to neonatology as we know it today.

The major advances in the field occurred early. By the mid-1970s, using respirators, intravenous medications and fluids, specially developed dietary formulas, and very aggressive care, it became technically possible to keep alive infants who were born as much as fourteen weeks prematurely and who weighed as little as twenty-eight ounces. Some of these infants did well; they've gone on to lead relatively normal lives. Most of the other survivers, though, have been left with significant physical and developmental problems: Some developed cerebral palsy and required orthopedic intervention and braces to help them walk but were otherwise spared; others were found to have suffered extensive brain damage and, in addition to cerebral palsy, were left with mental retardation and seizures; still others were so extensively damaged by the consequences of their prematurity that they wound up leading a vegetative existence, many residing in institutional settings. And so the question was raised, "Although technically possible, is any of this justified?" Neonatologists and medical ethicists have been struggling to answer this question ever since.

Neonates with problems can be divided into three groups. A first group includes those who have an excellent prognosis right from the beginning. This group includes the "garden variety" preemie who weighs two pounds or more and who is born without any problem other than prematurity. Most everyone in the field of neonatology would agree that everything possible should be done to support these infants.

A second group is made up of those infants who are born with such severe defects that survival is not possible no matter what is done for them. Included in this group are babies with anencephaly, a condition in which the skull and brain fail to develop; all of these infants are either stillborn or die within the first days of life. Also included in this group are babies born before twenty-four weeks of pregnancy. Most but not all neonatologists feel that these infants should be made as comfortable as possible and be allowed to die without intervention.

The third group of infants with problems is the most difficult ethically. It is made up of those children who fit between these two extremes: babies born weighing less than two pounds but above the twenty-fourth-week-of-pregnancy cutoff; and infants with major birth defects that are not necessarily lethal. The medical community is divided about what to do with these babies. Many neonatologists would do everything possible to offer these infants the opportunity to survive, knowing that possibly for every surviver who turns out to be normal, there'll be an infant or two who will wind up significantly damaged. Others would provide limited care, reasoning that the "strong" will survive and the "weak" will die off (the problem with this reasoning is that some in the former group who would have led a normal existence had aggressive care been provided will wind up damaged as a result of this method). Finally, some would argue that nothing should be done for this middle group and that nature should be allowed to take its course; physicians who think this way are clearly in the minority.

In neonatology, there's a tendency to lose sight of the end point. Sometimes a neonatologist who understands that he or she has the tools to keep any newborn alive for as long as he or she wants, may decide to flex his or her technological muscles and play God, keeping alive children who should be allowed to die. Neonatologists might argue that these exercises are good in the long run: By learning about keeping these children alive even for a brief period today, it might someday be possible for some to survive. And there might be some truth to this; after all, the argument that nothing should be done could have been made twenty years ago concerning babies who weighed twice what the babies who survive today weigh. But the question is, What price is being paid for this?

During his month in the NICU, Mark was kept awake night after night caring for babies some of whom he considered brain dead, one of whom weighed only a little over seventeen ounces.

Discouraged because of all the inevitable deaths, he asked, "What possible good am I doing here?" It didn't seem as if many of the babies were benefiting from the intensive care. The parents, who were seeing everything done for their infants, were being given false hope; they reasoned, "If they're doing so much, they must believe that my baby has a chance to survive." This winds up making coping much more difficult for the parents when the baby ultimately does die.

Taking care of patients who have no chance of surviving is extremely frustrating and anxiety-provoking. You're asked to do things that don't make sense to you; you're called upon to counsel parents without having the picture clear in your own mind. But this state of mind is not limited to working in the NICU. These problems also occur in other intensive-care units.

Physicians working in ICUs that care for older patients must deal with many of the same issues as the neonatologist, but the situations are often radically different. Patients in the pediatric or adult intensive-care units are not neonates; they come into the unit with a life history. They have relatives and friends who know them and love them, not just for what they might be in the future but also for what they've been in the past. They have personalities and desires, and often specific requests about what should and should not be done. The intensivist must often decide whether to honor these requests, or the requests made by the patient's loved ones, or to do whatever he or she thinks is in the patient's best interests. And that can be very difficult.

During his month in the pediatric intensive-care unit, Andy became involved with three patients for whom "do not resuscitate" orders were ultimately written. Actual orders stating that a specific patient should not be resuscitated in the event of a cardiac or respiratory arrest are new at Mount Scopus Hospital. Prior to the time that the present interns began their year, plans for patients who had no chance of survival were formulated through conversations among the physicians, the family, and, if possible, the patient. If it was agreed by all parties that resuscitation should not be attempted, the word would be passed to all members of the care team. The concept of a patient being a "no code" developed; then the concept of a limited or "slow code" (the situation in which cardiac arrest leads to limited efforts at resuscitation) evolved. Verbal "no codes" were troublesome; to many members of the care team, it seemed like a sham. Notes and orders were being written in the patient's chart that did not truly reflect the thoughts of the care providers or the wishes of the patient and his or her family. But DNR orders could not be written; they raised legal and ethical questions that had not yet been answered.

The use of written, formalized DNR orders arose through the efforts of a committee composed of the hospital's lawyers, ethicists, and physicians. Now the true plan for a specific patient can be spelled out in the chart without fear of legal or ethical retribution. The actual order must be written by the patient's attending physician and must be reordered every week. Once a DNR order has been written, it leads to conflicts of another sort: Now that we've stated that the patient is expected to die, what should and what should not be done for that patient?

Here's an example that'll help explain this conflict: A patient who is DNR develops a fever. Normally, hospitalized patients who develop fever are managed very aggressively; a "sepsis workup" consisting of blood and urine and sometimes spinal fluid cultures is done, and antibiotics are immediately begun. Failing to treat a patient with fever may lead to overwhelming infection and ultimately to death. But what should be done if the patient is DNR? Should antibiotics be started on such a patient, or should infection and its consequences be "encouraged"? If antibiotics are going to be withheld, should cultures be obtained? These questions must be considered in every case. Often, under the reasoning that to treat an infection would be to prolong life artificially, antibiotics will not be given and cultures will not be obtained.

But using this reasoning, one could argue that feeding the patient would also lead to artificial prolongation of life. Therefore, should DNR patients receive the nutrition they require for life to continue, or should they be allowed to starve to death? Most physicians would agree that the withholding of nutrition should not occur. Implicit in DNR is that the patient should not be allowed to suffer. Starvation is a painful and drawn-out way to die. Therefore, most intensivists would make sure all patients were receiving an appropriate number of calories to sustain life.

These are only some of the issues Andy and Mark agonized over during their month in the ICU. And they are not alone. The conflicts that arise for young physicians at the edge between life and death are universal. And they lead to a great deal of mental and emotional stress and anxiety.

ANDY
March 1986

Tuesday, March 11, 1986

For the past two weeks I've been in the OPD at Mount Scopus and West Bronx. It really hasn't been too bad. I've come to realize that I've had to start acting more like a resident; I have to depend more on my own impressions and make my own decisions. The past few weeks have been the first time I haven't felt that the residents and the attendings were giving me good answers or helping me solve problems very well. So it's been a kind of stressful learning experience, but I think I've been doing okay at it so far. I guess this is how you learn to become a resident.

The other night in the Mount Scopus ER was memorable. It was my last official night in the Mount Scopus ER. I was supposed to have another whole month of OPD on the west campus, but I switched to be at Jonas Bronck. Working in the Jonas Bronck ER is a better learning experience. So it was my last on call; I can't say I'm not happy to get it over with.

It was also one of the worst nights I can remember. There was a tremendous volume of patients; they kept just coming in. It was nuts! At one point we were fifteen charts behind, which is a lot for that place, but we couldn't make any headway because we had about a half dozen acutely ill children. And the place has only four rooms; we were spilling over into the adult ER. Let's see: We had two head traumas in various states of coma; we had a diabetic with sickle-cell disease who was in the middle of a painful crisis *and* in DKA [diabetic ketoacidosis, **the buildup of acid in the blood of diabetics caused by high sugar in the blood and inability of the cells of the body to**

258

use the sugar for its normal processes]; we had a little baby sickler with fever; we had a couple of vaginal bleeders and a drug overdose. All of these were occurring pretty much simultaneously. And it was just me and a senior resident who was not the greatest doctor you ever saw. We couldn't get help from anybody. The attending was over in the West Bronx emergency room. Every time we'd call with a problem, he'd say, "Well, it doesn't sound *too* bad. Call the senior in the house [the resident in charge of the inpatient service at night] if you're worried." He wasn't even concerned! What a shithead!

I never ran as hard as I did that night. Finally at one point the nurse, who was fabulous, said to us, "Please call for some help!" So we did. And then slowly but surely we got some of the docs who were on call on the floors down there, and we cleared the place out. But it was still crazy the rest of the night. Right before we were going to leave, this fourteen-year-old girl who's an asthmatic and has been intubated twelve times came in tight as a drum. [She was not getting air into the lungs. Asthma is caused by narrowing of the air tubes. When these air tubes are slightly narrowed, wheezing will be heard in the chest; when they become very narrow, as they were in this patient, no breath sounds are heard and the patient is considered "tight."] We had to intubate her in the ER. I didn't get out of there until 3:00 A.M., which is late for Mount Scopus.

Karen left a couple of weeks ago after nearly two months of that subinternship she was doing. It was sad taking her to the airport. Fucking LaGuardia Airport; I really hate that place! I've felt very blue since she left. I've been missing her a lot and it's been a real drag being apart like this. She's doing obstetrics/ gynecology now; she has to be on call every third night, and our schedules are completely out of whack. We've been able to talk only a couple of times in two weeks. It's weird. But we'll be together soon. It won't be too long before this insanity is over.

Last Tuesday was my birthday. I was postcall and I felt terrible, and I didn't want to celebrate at all. I went to visit my friend Gary and his roommates out in Brooklyn. I had a good time. The next day I went out with my friend Ellen. We went into Manhattan and had a wonderful time. Anyway, the weekend was pretty good.

I've been kind of reflecting on what's happened over the past few months. I've been thinking about what's changed. One thing is, I really don't feel much like a medical student anymore. Occasionally I get into situations where I remember what being a student felt like, when I have no idea what I'm supposed to do. That's what being a medical student is all about, always with an undefined role. When that happens now, I remember how frustrating it was. I am more comfortable with making decisions now, but I don't think I'm ready to dictate those decisions to other people the way residents do. That's still frightening to me.

I'm starting to realize what I need to do to become a better doctor. I've got to become faster and more selective, be able to narrow things down quickly and home in on the diagnosis, because those are the things I'll need to be good at when I'm a resident.

So anyway, I guess I'm starting to become a master of internship, which is supposed to happen around now. I've become damn good at being a scut puppy, a data gatherer. I have a couple of tough months ahead: Infants' (pain and torture but with some good people); and a month in the Jonas Bronck OPD, which will be great but tough; and then my last month here, 6A. What a good-bye kiss!

Thursday, March 13, 1986, 1:30 A.M.

I got back from the West Bronx ER a little while ago. It was a typical West Bronx night. As soon as I walked in, Andy Ames signed out a child-abuse case to me. It took the usual form of no one understanding where the second-degree burn on the child's right leg came from. The social worker who called in the case had naturally gone home, and Andy was also gone, so that left me in charge. When the father came in angry and hostile, he couldn't find anyone but me to threaten. Everything was getting out of hand, and then the police showed up to start their investigation and that led to more havoc. Christ! Anyway, the BCW finally decided that since there was no obvious perpetrator—that is, no one had come forward and said, "Yes, I did it, I was the one who burned the baby," they let the kid go back home with the parents. I said, "Fine! Let him go home. What the hell do I care?" That's typical of the BCW! And what usually winds up happening is the kid'll show up next week or next month or next year dead. But what can you do? You can't fight the parents *and* the BCW. That's a little too much to take on.

The rest of the night was the usual. We had a bronchiolitic [**a child with inflammation of the bronchioles, the small airways leading from the larger bronchi to the lungs; children with bronchiolitis are usually under one year of age, and have respiratory symptoms that are very similar to those of asthmatics**] who probably has pneumonia [**since bronchiolitis is caused by a viral infection, it's not unusual that pneumonia, or inflammation of the lung itself, is often an accompaniment**] who bought himself a bed on 6A. I also saw this girl, a skinny seventeen-year-old who had hematuria [**blood in her urine**] and stabbing pain in her right lower quadrant. When I told her I had to do a pelvic exam, she refused. She said she'd allow it only if someone from Gynecology did it. I paged Gynecology three times and they didn't answer. The next thing I knew, the patient's uncle was calling from a phone booth on Jerome Avenue. He said the girl had got fed up with the whole thing and just walked out of the ER and he followed her down to Jerome. So he was calling very apologetically to say that she wouldn't come back. Right under our noses, she just walked. She was actively bleeding from somewhere; whether it was her vagina or her uterus, God only knows. But she up and left. Unbelievable! So I got on the phone with her and said, "Look, you know you're leaving against medical advice. I advise you to come back to the emergency room right away." She said, "No way! No fucking way!" So I said, "Promise me one thing: If you start to bleed profusely, you'll go see another doctor." She said, "Well, maybe." That was it. She just walked!

At about ten o'clock, the ER filled with exhaust fumes from the ambulances parked outside the emergency entrance. Exhaust fumes! That was great for the asthmatics. They thought they had come in to get treatment for their asthma; they wound up leaving in worse shape than they'd been in when they first got there! And the place was scorching hot for several hours; it must have been in the mid-eighties in there. God knows why! I felt very rundown and I had no appetite. I ate nearly nothing the whole night. I didn't want dinner. That whole child-abuse case was getting me down; it killed my appetite. But we finished at one, which isn't bad, and I came back home and listened to the messages on my machine. I ate some food and I'm listening to this music now and suddenly I'm on vacation. Tomorrow I'll be home! Strangely, I'm not that excited about it. I am excited about seeing Karen and my parents and everything, but I'm not excited about the idea of going home itself. It's funny, I think it's really starting to bother me that I'm going to be leaving the Bronx for good in a couple of months. I'm starting to feel that I've made some good friends here and I know I'll have to leave them and I'm already getting sad about it, three and a half months ahead of time. Isn't that terrible?

AMY

March 1986

Wednesday, February 26, 1986

It's the last night of my last vacation of internship. Tomorrow I start on 6A [at West Bronx]. I haven't worked there before, but I've heard it's a real killer. And of course I'm on tomorrow night. So I've gotten myself really depressed.

These past two weeks have been very special to me, very relaxing and calming and restful. This was the first time I've been able to be a full-time mother, twenty-four hours a day, seven days a week, without interference. Since I started my internship, Larry and I have never been alone with Sarah for such a long stretch of time. There's always been someone else around. This was my first opportunity to get to know my daughter. I did everything for her: I changed her diapers and fed her her meals, I got to talk to her and to watch her go through her normal activities without any interruptions. And I actually managed to watch her take her first step! It happened about a week ago, while we were in Florida. She's been cruising for a while now [cruising: **walking while holding on to a surface, usually a bed or a table**], but one morning last week she just let go and took three steps without holding on. It was great.

So I really got the chance to know what being a mother is about during this vacation. And I liked it. I liked it a lot. It sure is better than working in all these damned hospitals where nobody cares about anything except themselves. I really don't want to go back. I just don't want to go back to work tomorrow.

So what else can I say about the vacation? We stayed at a condominium in Fort Lauderdale. We went to the Miami Zoo, we went to the beach, we went out on day trips, we did a lot of things. I caught up on some sleep, and I had a lot of time to think about what's happened over the past few months and especially about what happened at the beginning of February. The more I think about it, the angrier I get. I really was taken advantage of! There was no need for the chiefs to do what they did to me. They definitely could have let me go home and found somebody else to cover the ER that night. It wouldn't have meant that much to them, but it sure meant a lot to me! I thought that going away, taking some time off, would make me ease up on this. But it didn't. I can't forgive them. And I can't forget it.

Well, I'm going to put Sarah to sleep now and then I'm going to try to relax a little. I'm really very tense about tomorrow.

Saturday, March 1, 1986

So far, 6A hasn't been as bad as I thought it would be. The census is low and it's a good thing because the chief residents are trying to screw me again. It may actually work out in my favor this time. I'm sure they won't be too happy about that!

What's happening is, there are usually four interns working on 6A. It's a big ward, there's the capacity to house fifty patients, so when it's busy, you really need to have four interns. But this month, we're one person short. That's because the fourth intern is supposed to be a psych rotator [**psychiatry residents have to work for four months on either internal medicine wards or, if they're interested in child psychiatry, on general pediatric wards during their internship year**], and he's not going to be showing up. The reason he's not going to be showing up is that the people who run the psych program felt he was too "psychiatrically unstable" to do a rotation on a ward as stressful as 6A. So rather than having four people covering, we have only three people. It's too stressful for the psych rotator when there would have been four, but nobody's concerned about how stressful it's going to be for us now that there are only three. That's typical, typical! But I just might luck out because of the solution the chiefs have come up with.

What they're doing is this: Usually the interns are divided, two working with a senior resident, the other two working with a junior resident. Because we were short, the chiefs decided that the other two interns would work with the junior resident and I would work alone with the senior resident. The senior this month is Ben King, who is one of the best people in the program. He was the person who let me leave the morning after my last night on Adolescents' so I could catch the flight to Israel. So I'm very happy to be working with him. The junior resident is Dina Cohen, who's one of the worst people we have.

Because there's only one intern on our team and two on the other, we started off the month with only one third of all the patients. And not only that, but on that first morning, Ben was smart enough to realize that most of the patients who were assigned to us didn't belong in the hospital in the first place. I started Thursday morning with seven patients. When we made rounds, Ben decided that three of them could be sent home right away, so I was down to four. I got only one admission Thursday night, and one of the other patients went home yesterday, so tomorrow I'll start with only four patients. That's not bad for 6A; that's not bad for anywhere. And none of them is what you'd call sick. Two are preemie growers. [Six-A serves as an "overflow valve" for the neonatal intensive-care unit; when the unit gets crowded, preemies who have outgrown the problems of prematurity and only need to gain weight, are transferred out to the ward. These babies frequently continue to have more problems than normal, healthy babies of the same age, however. Caring for a preemie who graduated from the unit is not just a baby-sitting service.] One is a kid with AIDS who's here just because he's got no place to go. And one is a six-month-old with meningitis who's doing pretty well; he's just in the hospital to finish his two-week course of antibiotics. So, so far I don't have much to do. I'm not complaining about it. I know it won't stay like this for long.

Thursday, March 6, 1986

I was on last night with Dina Cohen. Jesus, what an airhead that woman is! She's completely incapable of making a single decision. She's totally incompetent. Yesterday afternoon, Margaret was signing out and she told me she had this adolescent girl who had come in the night before with abdominal pain and a positive urine pregnancy test. An emergency sonogram had been done that showed something around the right ovary. Ben was sitting next to me, and when he heard Margaret say all this, he got very upset because he knew the girl had to have an ectopic pregnancy [a pregnancy in which the gestational sac implants some-place other than in the wall of the uterus; it is dangerous because it can cause a massive hemorrhage]. Ben asked if Gynecology had come to see her, and Margaret said, "No, they haven't even been called yet." Ben just about blew his top! He ran over to Dina and asked her about it and she said, "Well, the ultrasound attending said it wasn't a conclusive study. He thought it could either be an abscess or a cyst or an ectopic—" Ben interrupted her and yelled, "It is an ectopic! You have to call Gynecology right now!" And Dina said, "Well, I'd rather be sure first. I think we should do a beta HCG [a blood test for pregnancy; more accurate than the usual urine pregnancy test], but you can't get one done until tomorrow morning. Can you imagine? You can't get a beta HCG done in this hospital after twelve o'clock—" Ben stopped her right there and said, "Dina, think a minute! You've got an adolescent with abdominal pain, a positive urine pregnancy test, and a finding consistent with an ectopic on ultrasound. You don't need a beta HCG. What you need is a gynecologist. They have to take her to the OR right now or she may bleed out before tomorrow morning!" Then Dina said, "Well, I thought we should do more tests—" And Ben said again, "You have to call Gynecology right now. Don't you understand?"

He finally convinced her to make the call. They came and saw her at about five o'clock and took her to the OR almost immediately. Of course, she had an ectopic. If Dina had waited and hemmed and hawed a while longer, that girl might have bled out right there on the ward!

Needless to say, I didn't feel very comfortable being alone with Dina for the rest of the night. The girl with the ectopic did okay. She stayed in the recovery room for a few hours and then came down to the floor at about midnight. And luckily, it was a quiet night; I only got one admission, and that was an asthmatic who didn't require any kind of expertise in his management. So I didn't ask Dina for any help all night long. I didn't even see her after midnight; she went off to sleep in her on-call room.

Sunday, March 9, 1986

It was seventy degrees today—really spring. We spent the day out on the grass in front of the apartment building. Sarah loved it. She got a chance to toddle around and see some of the other children. It was a really nice day.

Things on the ward are okay. I'm still getting along well with Ben. He's just great, the best resident I've ever worked with. He's got good judgment, he knows what's important and what isn't, and he's got a good sense of humor.

But the other team is having a lot of trouble. Because Ben knows when to send patients home and Dina doesn't, they now have almost all of the patients on the ward. And to make matters worse, the interns are finding it very stressful to work with Dina. Laura's doing okay; she's a very good intern and she doesn't have to rely on anybody for much help. But Margaret isn't as secure about herself and she's having a very hard time with Dina. On morning rounds on Friday, Margaret completely fell apart. She started crying, saying she couldn't go on. She refused to work up a patient. She wound up spending a few hours in the chief residents' office. She just needs more help than Dina can give her. I think there's also a lot of other things going on in her life now. But that's true of all of us, isn't it?

The chiefs decided that they had to get Margaret out of the hospital for a few days. How nice of them! She's stressed, so they give her the weekend off. My daughter gets the measles and is sicker than most of the patients who come to the emergency room but I still have to work! That's typical! Oh, what's the use? What's the use of talking about it and thinking about it over and over again?

Anyway, Margaret got to go home Friday afternoon and didn't have to come in for her call on Saturday. She's got a great medical student, Susan, who's running the service for her. Susan took Margaret's call on Saturday and did a good job. She did as well as a lot of the interns. I wish I had a student like that. I haven't had a good student all year. All my students have ever done is complain. They don't want to do scut, they don't want to run to the labs, all they want to do is stand around and be spoon-fed information twenty-four hours a day. Susan isn't like that; she's willing to work. A student like Susan can make internship a whole lot easier.

Actually, having a good student doesn't matter for me right now. I've still been having great luck on call. I've gotten only one or two admissions per night. I left yesterday with only three patients, and one of those is probably going to go home tomorrow. That'll leave me with only my AIDS patient, who's really just a social hold, and one of the preemie growers I picked up when I started. Neither of them requires any real work. I should be able to leave tomorrow right after work rounds. I'm planning to go home at ten o'clock in the morning! It's amazing!

Saturday, March 15, 1986

I just finished putting Sarah to sleep. This is my weekend off. It's been a strange week. Work's fine, there's no problem there. But Larry got called away on business on Monday. He's in Switzerland and he'll probably be gone all next week. It's been hard for me. I've had no relief in taking care of Sarah at night. Usually, when I'm postcall, Larry handles her 3:00 A.M. wake-up; usually I don't even hear her cry. But on Wednesday it was all me, and I was tired. I don't know how I got through it.

We got Marie to stay over on the nights I don't come home. She wasn't very happy about doing it and it's costing us an arm and a leg, but what else could I do? Someone has to be with Sarah; I can't take her to the hospital with me. I'll be happy when Larry gets back. His being away like this makes me realize how much I depend on him!

I haven't been feeling very well, either. I've been very tired. And I've lost my appetite. I think I've just made it to the point in the year where I'm simply exhausted all the time. I know a lot of the other interns have gotten to this point already; I'm surprised it's taken me this long to get here. And being tired sure isn't making it easier to take care of Sarah by myself!

My luck has been holding: I got two admissions last night; and when I was on this past Tuesday, I didn't get any. But that doesn't mean I've been getting a lot of sleep. The other team's been getting killed on their on-call nights. They've got a lot of patients, and some of them are really sick. So I still wind up staying up, doing scut on their patients all night long. More IVs fall out on 6A than anyplace else I've ever worked. I don't know what it is about that ward! Some of the other interns say the nurses actually pull the IVs out, but I don't believe it; to pull out an IV would mean the nurses were actually touching the patients. So far I haven't seen one come that close.

Friday, March 21, 1986

I know this is going to sound crazy. It doesn't make much sense, but it's true. I'm pregnant! I found out today. I think it's great, but I know everybody else is going to think I'm crazy.

I've been feeling lousy for a couple of weeks now. I've been run-down and a little nauseous all the time, but I just figured it was internship finally getting to me. And my period didn't come last week, but that's not so strange; it happens to me a lot. I saw Susannah in clinic last week and I was telling her how bad I was feeling and she said, "It sounds like you're pregnant. Is that possible?" I hadn't really even thought about it until then. I told her it was certainly possible, and she told me to send off a urine sample. I found out this afternoon that it was positive. Unbelievable!

Larry came home from Switzerland yesterday. I told him a little while ago. He thinks it's wonderful. We're both very excited. We'd talked about waiting until I was a junior resident before we tried again. I'm about six weeks now, which means I'm due sometime around next November. Sarah will be only about eighteen months then. That's closer than we had planned. And it means that for the last year and a half of my residency, I'll have two babies to worry about instead of one. But what the hell? One thing I've learned over the past few weeks is that we have to do what's best for us, and I think having this baby is the best thing for me, for Larry, and for Sarah.

I'm not going to tell anybody about this just yet. A lot of things can happen. I had a miscarriage in my first pregnancy, and that can certainly happen again. And anyway, the chiefs probably are not going to be exactly thrilled when they hear about this. But I don't care. That's their problem. I really don't care what they or anybody else thinks.

I just hope I can make it through next month in the neonatal intensive-care unit! If I continue to feel the way I do now, it isn't going to be easy.

MARK

March 1986

Sunday, March 16, 1986

It's taken me a while to get back to normal, but here I am, having as much fun as I had during the first six months of this nightmare. Yes, even though I came that close to doing a triple gainer off the top of Jonas Bronck Hospital just two short weeks ago, life's now become a barrel of laughs again.

This last month has really been pretty disturbing. I mean, I always had this idea that I was immune to getting depressed or something. I really didn't think anything could get me down. I guess I just happened to stumble on the secret recipe for major depression: You take one garden-variety intern, deprive him of sleep for a couple of months, make him eat take-out pizza every meal during that time, and force him to take care of the sickest babies on the face of the earth. Mix well and let him marinate in his own juices for three weeks. Then you collect the pieces in a body bag and send them off the morgue. I guess I managed to interrupt the process right before I made it to the final step.

I really can't take credit for saving myself. Carole really did it. She took care of me, and I'm really thankful to her. Our relationship had been going down the tubes over the past few months. And it's all been my fault; I mean, I've kind of had other things on my mind, like sleeping and eating, and I haven't been paying much attention to her. So things hadn't been great between us. I was starting to have some doubts that our relationship would make it through the year; of course, I was also having some doubts that *I* would make it through the year, so my concerns about the relationship were not exactly at the top of my list of things to worry about.

Anyway, over the past few weeks Carole has just about moved into my apartment. She's somehow figured out how to get rid of all the cockroaches. I have to admit, things are nicer without all the wildlife even though they had kind of become my pets. She's been here every night when I came home from work and she's been really understanding, listening to me complain about everything imaginable, from how much I hate my patients to the fact that the West Bronx coffee shop was closed down by the Health Department because of "unsanitary conditions." (The amazing thing is, that was the best coffee shop in the system. I guess mouse droppings and rat hairs really do make everything taste better.) I know I wouldn't have gotten back to normal, if you can possibly call what I am now normal, if it hadn't been for her being here when I needed her. Well, enough of this; it's starting to sound like a sermon or something.

So for the past couple of weeks I've been working in OPD on the west campus. It certainly has been a welcome relief compared with the neonatal eternal-care unit. I like the emergency room because it gives you the chance over a very short period of time to torture a large number of children who, if you're lucky, you'll never have to see again. That's a unique opportunity. It almost makes being an intern seem like fun. Not quite, but almost.

I was on call on Friday and it turned out to be Fascinoma Night in the West Bronx ER. Every patient who came in between the hours of 5:00 P.M. and 8:00 P.M. had some bizarre diagnosis or some record-breaking laboratory result. The very first kid I saw was this one-month-old whose mother said he had vomited every feeding since he was discharged from the nursery. Every feeding! Now, I immediately recognized that there was some sort of problem here. I mean, I may not be Sir William Osler [a **famous physician of the nineteenth century who was known for his legendary clinical acumen**], but I do know it's not normal to vomit every single feeding of your entire life. At first, I was a little skeptical about the story. It's a little hard to believe something like that, so I asked the mother why she had waited so long to bring the kid in. She said she hadn't waited long at all, that this was the fourth time she had been in an ER, and that no one seemed to want to do anything to find out what was wrong with the kid. Okay, so then I figured the woman had to be a fruitcake or something. I mean, any doctor seeing a baby who had vomited every single feeding of his entire life would get very concerned and do something definitive, wouldn't he?

I guess not, because when I saw the baby, it became pretty clear the mother had to be right. I couldn't believe it. He looked like a baby concentration-camp survivor. He looked worse than Hanson did on Infants', which is pretty damn bad! This kid was a pound and a half below his birth weight, for God's sake! I did an exam and I didn't find anything. Then I sat and fed him for a few minutes. He seemed to do fine right away, but about ten minutes into the feeding he started to cry, and the next thing I knew there was baby vomit all over my sneakers. Great! So I ran over and got the attending and showed him my shoes and told him I thought the kid had pyloric stenosis. [**This is a condition caused by enlargement of the muscles at the junction between the stomach and the first part of the intestine. Because of the muscle enlargement, flow of partially digested food is obstructed, and once the stomach fills, the feeding is vomited. Pyloric stenosis is surgically repaired.**] He refused to help me clean off my sneakers, but he did come see the kid and we felt the abdomen, and sure enough, the kid had an olive [**a mass in the abdomen overlying the site of the stomach**].

But the pyloric stenosis isn't what made the kid so interesting. What made this kid a fascinoma was the fact that because he was so sick, I sent off a blood gas to see how alkalotic he was. [**Because the infant with pyloric stenosis is vomiting stomach contents that contain hydrochloric acid, these children frequently manifest alkalosis, or lack of a proper amount of acid in their blood.**] It turned out he had a pH of 7.76, the highest recorded pH in the history of the pediatric chemistry lab at West Bronx. I think as a result of having my name on the lab slip as the doctor of record, I'm supposed to get a commemorative plaque or something. As a result of having the record-breaking pH, the kid is getting a no-expenses paid trip to the ward at West Bronx for fluid and electrolyte therapy before the surgeons take him to the OR tomorrow to fix his stomach.

And that kid was just the beginning. A little later we got a call from one of the orthopedic attendings who told us that a patient of his was coming in. He told us, matter-of-factly, that the kid had been bitten by a horse. A horse! Where the hell is a kid from the Bronx going to find a horse to bite him in the middle of March? I mean, we're talking about the South Bronx here;

this isn't the Kentucky Derby! So the story seemed a little peculiar to begin with. And then the kid showed up, and it got even stranger.

I didn't actually see the kid right away. I heard her first. The sound she made was very much like the sea lion tank at the Bronx Zoo around feeding time. And that was just her breathing! I walked over to see what was going on and the mother said, ''Don't intubate her, she's got a problem with her trachea, she always sounds like this.'' It was at that point that I started to get a little suspicious. It turned out, this was the orthopod's patient. She was this five-year-old with some horrible disease called metachromatic leukodystrophy, a really rare metabolic disorder. She was followed by one of the neurologists. So I'm sure this is the only case in the history of recorded medicine of a kid with metachromatic leukodystrophy having been bitten by a horse. At least having been bitten by a horse in the South Bronx during the month of March.

I have to admit, the story kind of piqued my interest, so I asked the mother how the kid got bitten. She told me the girl was involved in this therapeutic horseback riding program and she had been out for a ride that afternoon. At the end of the ride, the girl usually feeds the horse a carrot. She did it this time but she forgot to pull her hand away after the carrot was gone, and the horse, not understanding the difference between carrot and hand, continued to nibble. So she got bitten. Right; that made all the sense in the world. I'm glad she cleared that up for me!

Luckily, the kid wasn't too bad off. The horse had broken the skin on the back of her right hand a little, but it didn't look like any bones were broken. The orthopod came in and we did some X rays, which were negative. He put a dressing on the hand and asked me what antibiotic I'd recommend to cover the bacteria from a horse bite. Since I've had so much experience with treating horse bites in the past, I decided maybe I should look it up. You know, in all the pediatric and infectious disease textbooks I could find, not one of them even listed horse bites in the index! Unbelievable! It's such a common complaint, I thought there'd be long chapters on it wherever I looked. Anyway, we decided just to treat her with broad-spectrum coverage and see her back in a couple of days.

I go to talk to this kid's mother while we were waiting for the

X rays to be developed and she told me the kid had been completely normal for the first year and a half of life and then started to deteriorate. She's been going downhill ever since. It's really a horrible story. There's nothing anybody can do to help her. It's only a matter of time now. It's really sad.

Anyway, so that was Fascinoma Night in the ER. And we didn't even get out late, which is probably the biggest fascinoma. I like nights like that. Maybe "like" is too strong a word. I can tolerate nights like that. They don't make me want to jump off the roof after I'm done with them.

I had this weekend off but I'm on again tomorrow. I've got to get some beauty rest now. At this point, I'm at least six months behind.

Friday, March 21, 1986

Things have been pretty quiet, but I was on call last night and something did happen that I really want to get down on tape. At about eight last night this one-year-old came in with a fever. I called him in and started getting the history. He looked really familiar, but his name didn't ring a bell. He was brought in by this woman who was his foster mother who said he'd spent the first five months of his life in the hospital. She said that she wasn't sure what exactly had been wrong with him but that he had been really sick for the longest time and that all the doctors were sure that he was going to die. It was then that I realized that I was standing over Baby Hanson.

Hanson! I only have to say the word and I get nauseated and want to run to the bathroom to throw up. But he looked great. That puny, disgusting, horrible bag of piss-poor protoplasm had grown into what looked like a fairly normal kid. He got taken away from his biological mother and placed with this foster mother in December, a couple of months after I had last seen him, when he was admitted to the ward at Jonas Bronck. The foster mother didn't know anything about the biological mother, so I don't know why he had finally been taken away from her. The foster mother had given him her last name, and that's why he was now Rodney Johnson.

It was amazing! He was sitting up, he could stand holding on, he wasn't even that delayed. He could even say a few words, although he couldn't say "crump," which really should have been his first word. And he still didn't have a vein in him. I looked all over, just out of curiosity. Amazing! If you would have told me back in August that Baby Hanson could have grown up into this kid, I would have called a psych consultant for you. But there he was!

He only had an otitis **[ear infection]**, and I sent him out of there with some amoxicillin. But I learned something from seeing him. I learned that no matter how horribly disgusting and wretched a baby is, there's always a chance he could grow up into a seminormal child. I never would have believed it.

I finish in the OPD next week and then I go on vacation. Carole and I have decided to go to Cancún. We were thinking about going back to that hotel in the Poconos we went to during my last vacation, but Carole decided against it. She thought I had been tortured enough for one lifetime over the past few months. I still think that maybe we should go. I mean, if I go someplace nice and actually have a good time, how am I going to be able to come back to the Bronx to finish the last couple of months of this wonderful experience? But who knows? Maybe Cancún will be hit by an earthquake or some other natural disaster, just to keep me in shape!

BOB

March 1986

In 1981, three reports of an apparently new disease appeared in a single issue of the *New England Journal of Medicine*. The articles described a series of patients who had become sick over the previous few years with some serious and unique symptoms. The patients shared a great deal in common: Each had been in excellent health before the appearance of the illness; each had developed pneumonia caused by *Pneumocystis carinii*, a parasite that only rarely caused problems in otherwise healthy individuals; many had also developed unusual malignancies, such as lymphomas and Kaposi's sarcoma; and, in retrospect, all were gay men. These articles, which at the time appeared to be the result of chance coincidence, would have incredible implications. They signaled the beginning of the age of AIDS.

The story of acquired immunodeficiency syndrome in children began at our hospitals. In 1979, two unrelated children were referred to the pediatric immunology clinic at University Hospital with serious, recurrent bacterial infections, including pneumonia. These children presented a puzzling picture of immune deficiency not previously seen in the pediatric age group. By the time those first articles on AIDS appeared in the *New England Journal of Medicine*, five children had been identified with symptoms that were identical to those reported in the gay men. In addition to their recurrent infections and immunological abnormalities, these five kids shared one common factor: All had been born to women who were drug addicts. And these women were also becoming sick, developing symptoms very similar to those of their offspring.

The widespread acceptance of the fact that AIDS could occur

in children did not occur until 1983. But whether accepted as fact or not, by 1983 it had become clear to everyone working in the Bronx that something terrible was happening.

Although pediatric AIDS started with a handful of cases, by the mid-1980s a full-fledged explosion had begun. The Centers for Disease Control in Atlanta estimate that by 1990 a total of three thousand children in the United States will become sick with AIDS. Scientists who have watched the epidemic develop believe this figure is an underestimate.

What this means to those of us working in the Bronx is that there are many infants and children who are or soon will become sick with AIDS and who will ultimately die because of it. At this moment, there are currently ten to twenty children with AIDS and the AIDS-related complex hospitalized in Jonas Bronck, Mount Scopus, University, and West Bronx hospitals. These children are in the hospital for one of two reasons. Some are critically ill; these patients have serious infections, cancer, and chronic lung disease. They fill beds in the ICUs for extended periods, draining resources and causing the staff who care for them severe emotional distress.

Other children with AIDS who are hospitalized are not sick, at least not initially. These kids live in our hospitals because they have no place to go. Their parents are drug addicts, many of whom have become sick themselves, and some have died. Grandparents and other family members have abandoned them; they've become pariahs because of their disease. Although some manage to escape from the hospital for some short period of time, most members of this group wind up living out their short lives knowing no home other than a steel crib in a three-bedded room at the back of 8 East or 8 West at Jonas Bronck Hospital, knowing no family other than the nurses, house officers, and medical students who provide their care.

But these hospitalized patients are only the tip of the iceberg. There are over a hundred sick children in our system currently being followed by the immunologists. Another hundred have already died. And these numbers are growing daily. Unless a cure is miraculously found, all these children will presumably die.

There's no question that AIDS has altered every aspect of modern medicine. It has radically changed residency training in virtually every specialty, including pediatrics. When I was an intern, there were few deaths on the pediatric wards. In fact, one of the reasons I chose to specialize in pediatrics was because children tended to recover from illnesses. But thanks to AIDS, all that's changed.

Amy, Mark, and Andy, as well as every other intern and resident in our program, have each been involved with at least one sick and dying AIDS patient. Over the past couple of years, about one child with AIDS has died every month. Occasionally the death seems almost like a blessing; these children are alone, with no loved ones; they are comatose, lingering on day after day in a vegetative state, with no hope of survival. But most of the time the death of a child, any child, is a tragic, deeply disturbing, and anxiety-provoking event for the house officers, nurses, and other staff members who care for the child and who stand by helplessly watching, unable to do anything to alter the course, as the child grows sicker and weaker until he or she ultimately dies.

But the inevitability of the death of the patient is only one factor that's changing the way house officers approach their charges with AIDS. The second and perhaps dominant force is tied to our current knowledge of the way in which the human immunodeficiency virus, the agent that causes AIDS, is transmitted. House officers know very well that if they stick themselves with a needle that has been in the vein of an HIV-infected individual, they can become infected. And becoming infected is equivalent to a death sentence.

When I was an intern, we drew blood, started IVs, even did mouth-to-mouth resuscitation without giving it a second thought. We knew of few risks and little harm that could come to us from stabbing ourselves with a needle or breathing in secretions from a patient who had had a respiratory arrest. Now it's mandatory that all house officers wear gloves whenever sticking a needle through the skin of any patient, regardless of whether the patient is thought to have AIDS or not. This increased use of gloves has caused a worldwide shortage of rubber. New types of gloves advertised as being resistant to HIV are being marketed. In the emergency rooms, nurses have been issued goggles to be worn over their eyes when around a patient who is bleeding profusely. Some residents don surgical gowns and masks just to enter a patient's room. And forget mouth-to-mouth resuscitation! What was once knee-jerk reflex is now something that house officers, with good reason, try to avoid at all costs.

Even though these precautions are being taken and everyone is being very careful, there is still a great deal of fear about AIDS within the ranks of our house staff. I went out for a couple of beers with Andy Baron one night early this month. He looked terrible: He has lost at least ten pounds since the start of internship, and he was barely able to keep his eyes open. It was pretty clear he was depressed. During our third beer, he let me in on why: He's convinced that he's infected with HIV. "I've stuck myself with so many needles, there's no way I don't have it," he explained.

I told him he shouldn't worry so much, that every intern and resident has stuck himself or herself multiple times over the past five years and so far nobody's tested positive for HIV. Andy replied that the key phrase there was "so far." He's sure that it may not be today and it may not be next month, but within ten years he and most of the rest of the interns in his group are going to wind up coming down with AIDS.

"How do people get AIDS?" he asked. "Drug addicts get it from contaminated needles that have been used by people who are infected with the virus, right? If we stick ourselves with needles that have been stuck into the veins of children who are infected, why shouldn't we get it? We're no different from drug addicts. We don't have any magical protection."

There's really no way to argue with his reasoning. I think it's pretty safe to say that at this point in the year, most of the interns would agree with Andy. This fear of AIDS has definitely changed the way the members of the staff approach patients. And it's not something that will go away or change in the near future. AIDS is here, apparently to stay.

ANDY

April 1986

Saturday, March 29, 1986, 11:30 P.M.

I'm not going to talk for long because I've got to go to sleep; I'm on call again tomorrow. I'm on Infants' [NW5—**Infants' ward**]; I started a couple of days ago and of course I was on the first night. I got totally fucking killed. I was assigned six kids to start and then I got six admissions and a transfer that first night. It was like thirteen admissions, because I never had a chance to get to know anybody. In any case, it was terrible; I was up all night with a cross-covering resident who was really pretty mediocre; he didn't help organize things at all. Then the next morning was a nightmare; I couldn't present to save my life, it was like being a third-year student all over again. I was tired and they stole my scrubs and . . . it sucked. I felt disorganized, panicky, and I got chewed out by Alan Nathan for delaying giving an antibiotic to a patient. And there was so much scut I couldn't get anything done; I didn't have any progress notes written, nothing! I barely got my admission notes done. I finally got to sit down and write my progress notes at seven o'clock. I had two days' worth of notes to write! I was postcall and I had to try to make some sense out of what had happened over the past thirty-six hours! I didn't get out until after ten-thirty, and that was my postcall night! Ten-thirty at night! I was there for thirty-six hours without a wink of sleep, working my butt off the whole time. I'm still tired, and tomorrow I'm on call again. I think that was probably . . . that may have been the worst call I've had all year. What a fucking nightmare.

Anyway, I'm sure my senior resident, Eric Keyes, whom I like a lot, thinks I'm a complete idiot by now. He probably won't trust me for the rest of the month. First impressions are pretty important.

Tomorrow I'm on call with another idiotic cross-coverer. I won't mention names, but tomorrow I'm on with one of the worst, least-liked second-year residents in the program. What a pain in the butt! You know, they don't give a shit when they're cross-covering, because they're out of there the next morning. They don't have to face up to things; I do! I have to clean up the mess through the entire next day! And then my next call after that is on Wednesday, the day I have clinic. Then I'm on next Saturday. You know what that's like? It's like having four lousy calls in a row. It sucks! I hate it. I really hate this so much. If tomorrow's anything like yesterday and the day before, I don't know how I'm going to get through this month. It's absolutely torture.

Right after vacation to come back to this! I can't tell you! My vacation was pretty good. I'll talk about that some other time.

Monday, March 31, 1986, 8:30 P.M.

I'm postcall again. Not so angry this time and not so unbelievably tired. I had a really easy night, actually; I got only one hit. It was easy, but still I was running scut until midnight. The guy I was on with turned out to be a completely obnoxious blowhard who at least is pretty smart. He's a total zero as a human, though. Two calls and two total-zero cross-coverers. But now that I got these two over with I'm scheduled to be on with really, really good people during my next two calls. It's just too bad it's worked out in this order.

The nurses are great on Infants'; I really like them. But the place is a zoo; the private patients drive me up a fucking wall. They make me wonder what I'm doing going back to a privately run system. This lady today told me she didn't want me to draw her baby's blood. Jesus Christ! These parents are so uptight and nervous, they always want to come in and see the procedures being done. They can't accept the fact that they shouldn't be in the room. What do they think we're going to do, break their kid's arms? I have to think of nice ways to say, "No, you should wait out here, we'll be back when we're done, it's best for the child, and it's best for you, too. So don't come in!" Usually I don't get nervous when I'm doing procedures, but this lady today was making me crazy! And I couldn't get the blood. It was the first time that's happened to me in months!

I got these new medical students today. Brand-spanking-new students, never been on a ward before, I have this big, hulking guy named Ronald; he seems very nice. God knows; maybe he'll turn out to be a tyrant surgeon a few years down the road. He looks like one. He looks like he's going to be an orthopod. Anyway, I did my best to teach him stuff today, to get him over the jitters of being on the floor with real patients for the first time.

I've been hanging around the hospital too much. I stay too late. I was there until seven tonight. It's ridiculous! Finally Keyes said, "Get the hell out of here, you're just making work for yourself." He was right! What you're supposed to do is write your notes and get the hell out of there and let the person on call hassle with your patients. I think I'll do that tomorrow. I say I'll try, but I never can; I'm never able to get out before five.

I'm already in bed. It's eight-thirty and I'm already in bed, can you believe that? I'm going to sleep, I don't care. I'm always sleep-deprived; sleep's like going out of style for me. This job is so damn stupid! It's just stupid!

I spoke to Karen tonight for the first time in about a week, because of my stupid on-call schedule.

There I go; I fell asleep again. God! So, I spoke to Karen tonight. She's doing all right. We didn't talk for a long time. I miss her. I can't stay awake any longer.

Monday, April 7, 1986

For some reason, I've had all these revelations over the past week. At least they seemed like revelations at the time. Coming back to them now, they really seem like just a bunch of mundane thoughts. I seem to have them on the scut run between the chemistry elevator and the hematology elevator. I have no idea why, but over and over I get these things popping into my mind while I'm in the back corridor by the back entrance to the kitchen.

One of the things I realized was that, at this point in the year, I feel like I'm getting stupider, not smarter. I know it's not true, but I think maybe it has to do with the fact that the barn door has swung open to the world of knowledge. I guess I'm just realizing what you really need to know to be a decent resident.

It's unbelievable; I just feel so stupid. And it doesn't matter whether I read or not; I don't remember anything an hour after I'm finished with it. But I've got to keep persevering. It's funny; I thought I was smart a couple of months ago. I'm not!

I also had this thought about nurses and how night nurses seem to be universally weak in all places except maybe the ICU, where they're still good. I don't know why this is. At night, there seems to be a certain stereotype: the middle-aged, fat, black nurse who's kind of disgusted and noncommunicative. And while she may not be all those things, the stereotype of being noncommunicative and disgusted seems to hold true. I don't know why, but from hospital to hospital, it seems to be the case. And it's kind of distressing because at night there's nobody else there, and sometimes you need to talk to somebody about a patient, and these nurses, they just don't want to talk about anything! Everything seems to be an effort when you ask them to do something.

Monday, April 14, 1986, 2:00 A.M.

It's 2:00 A.M. and I've woken up for some reason from my precall sleep. I really should be asleep. I have insomnia. I keep thinking terrible black thoughts because last night I wrote up the protocol for the M and M Conference [**Morbidity and Mortality Conference, a teaching conference run much like chief of service rounds in which a patient who has died is presented; the clinicians discuss the disease process, and the pathologists bring the autopsy report and describe what really happened**] on Emilio, my patient with AIDS who died when I was in the ICU in February. Yesterday I got Emilio's chart from the record room and I wrote up a summary of what happened to him over the weeks I took care of him. It really hurt to do it, to go through that chart again and to see that he was deathly ill the minute he arrived and never improved and that he finally, finally, by the grace of God, died. I remembered how he suffered and how his mother would come and sit by the bedside for hours. About a week before he died, she told me how at times when the Pavulon [**a paralyzing medication**] was wearing off, before he got his next dose, she would see tears forming in the corners of his eyes. She knew he was suffering terribly. But of course he couldn't cry out because he had a tube between his vocal cords and because he was more paralyzed than not. And we constantly would do horrible things to him in our effort to save him from certain death. So I wake tonight with these terrible black thoughts that I'm going to get AIDS, die the same death that poor Emilio died, having my lungs pumped with ventilator air every second, and my limbs poked with needles by young physicians in training, and my neck or groin poked by the fellow trying to put in a line, or my lungs needled and cut, while I hear the doctors saying crass and horrible things about my death and illness, making fun of my debilitated state, while I'm lying naked on a table and shitting on a blue chuck [**a pad made out of the same material as disposable diapers and that are placed under incontinent patients**], the way poor Emilio did, with no dignity. Just pain. How he must have hurt.

And I think about the Infants' ward I have to go to tomorrow on call and all the sick children I have to take care of there, two of whom are trying to die on me all the time. I don't feel up to taking care of these fragile little things. I'm tired of being abused by the system, of having my sleep taken away every third night, of the stress I'm put under and the illness I'm exposed to, and the pain I have to see and cannot heal. I'm tired of dealing with parents whose pain I can never completely understand because there's never enough time. The only time I have to try to understand what's happening to them is the time I take away from my own sleep. It's a constant battle. The doctors who do the best with their own lives, who get the most sleep and get out the earliest, are the ones who don't talk to the families, who don't play with the children, who don't thoughtfully consider things. But I'm not that way; I'm not efficient. I spend time with the families, I talk with them, and so I get sleep-deprived.

Tuesday, April 15, 1986, 9:00 P.M.

There's something I haven't talked about yet, something that's really hard about training that most people outside of medicine don't have to deal with, and that's the sense of loss of social skills that happens after you've been working all night. You then have to interact with people in a complex fashion. You have to go on rounds and talk to other members of the staff. I very often find that I have no idea how I'm coming off to anybody else. If people laugh, I can't tell if it's because I said something funny or if I've done something really dumb and embarrassing and that's the only reaction they can have. Am I offending anybody? Do I curse too much? Should I just fart and get it over with? A lot of times I just can't tell, I can't judge what people are saying to me: Are they being serious, are they making a joke?

It's not so bad with other residents. They understand, they can say, "Hey, he's been up all night, he's just postcall." But what about the parents of my patients? What the fuck do they think is going on? I might be acting really weird. Do they understand it's because I haven't slept in two days? They must think I'm just batty or something. And that's not good, because here they are, trusting me with their most precious thing in life, and I'm acting really flaky. It's an ill-defined concern of mine, but it really bothers me.

Today my student had to give a presentation of a patient. It didn't go too well; it was very rough, to say the least. I like Ron, he's a good guy. He reminds me of how I was as a student. Real nervous, disorganized, can't think on his feet, that's just how I was when I started out as a third-year. Shit, I still get like that sometimes. Anyway, after rounds, Mike Miller, who's our attending, came up to me and said, "Andy, I think you guys have to work on your student's presentation. It really isn't very good." And I told him I would, it was on the top of my list of priorities. So a little while later I sat down with Ron and we went over how to write up an H and P [history and physical exam] and how to present it on rounds. I can imagine what he was feeling: defensive, embarrassed, humiliated. It's one of those awful rites of passage. I don't know, I didn't get much sleep last night, I was really tired, and I wonder what he was thinking. I don't know if I was coming off as a hard-ass, if I was being condescending. I didn't mean to be; I kept saying to him over and over that you're not expected to know this, nobody ever teaches you this. I spent about twenty minutes talking to him about this, telling him the same stuff over and over again. He probably thought, You asshole, stop repeating yourself! I hope he learned something from it, and I'll tell you, the next time I'm on call, next Friday, he'll just have to take the admission and just go over it with me first. When I'm done with him, he'll sound like a master.

It's a beautiful, sunny spring day today. I came home and I really wanted to sit out on the porch with some friend and drink some beers, but I didn't feel like calling anybody; I guess I really wanted just to be by myself. I'm too fucking tired to talk anymore.

Saturday, April 19, 1986, 11:30 P.M.

Last night one of my patients coded and died. It really hurts to go through the story again, but I suppose I'll try.

It was a little five-month-old with bad heart disease, doesn't matter what type, who had been admitted several times before for congestive heart failure. This time she was coming in to get a cardiac cath done so they could plan her surgery. When I first saw her, she was in some failure: She was puffing away and a little cyanotic [blue], but her mother said she always looked that way. And so I got her plugged in and talked to her attending and he also told me not to worry because this really was her baseline, so it wasn't necessary to start oxygen. The cath was scheduled for the next morning. In the evening, she spiked a temp; there was no obvious source, and it was only a low-grade fever. I figured maybe it was the start of a URI [upper respiratory infection; cold]. The resident who was covering looked at the kid and said she had an otitis [otitis media, an ear infection]. She didn't have an otitis, no more than I did. But the resident insisted, so we gave her some amoxicillin and some Tylenol and she defervesced [her fever went down]. But she had spiked and it was the day before her cath.

She went for her cath bright and early yesterday morning and she came back at about ten. We were on attending rounds. I saw her for a moment, at about noon. She had fallen asleep in her mother's arms, and her mom asked me not to disturb her. I told her I'd come back and see her later, after she'd slept for a while. When I came back, she looked a little uncomfortable, but not bad. I got called away to do something else before I had a chance to finish my exam.

At two o'clock we were called to see her because the nurse had noticed she was looking worse. We went in: There she was, pale, tachypneic [breathing rapidly], with cold extremities. She looked clamped down and shocky. We had a devil of a time getting a line in. Before we did, we got a blood gas: It showed she was quite acidotic, with a pH of 7.21. But after we got the line in, we gave her a small amount of fluid and she seemed to become more comfortable. Her repeat blood gas was improved; she was less acidotic.

A little later we decided we should give her a little Lasix [a diuretic] so she wouldn't go into congestive failure or pulmonary edema. When I went to give it she looked comfortable, breathing at sixty instead of eighty. I spent the afternoon darting in and out of the room; basically she looked okay. We put her in 60 percent oxygen by headbox to help her out. Her attending also kept coming in and going out all afternoon. He was concerned that she had suffered some sort of ischemic event [damage to the heart muscle due to lack of oxygen], but he didn't know when. He told me I might have caused it by drawing blood and introducing an air embolus, something I'd never heard of before. That sounded like a really ridiculous idea. He said it might have been that or it might have been the cath, but he sort of kept stressing that I had done something.

Anyway, at about five o'clock he was there, and he chastised Eric. He told him how foolish and unobservant he had been. He told him that the child was in respiratory distress, grunting and flaring, and that he'd noticed it an hour and a half before, but that he didn't seem concerned. During the afternoon, the baby had spiked to 40.5°C [almost 105°F]. We were very worried, so we got a chest X ray, drew some blood, and started the baby on antibiotics. Her attending told us the fever was just a "dehydration fever." I saw him put his hand on Eric's shoulder and say condescendingly, "I've been in this business for a long time. I can tell you that's all it is." He didn't want us to start the antibiotics. But we did nonetheless.

At about six-thirty I was writing my sign-out, trying to get home; Eric was with Kelly Jacobs, the other intern, almost at the end of evening rounds. Eric remarked to Kelly that the baby had a "preterminal look." She had a heart rate of ninety, which is slow. Suddenly her heart stopped, right in front of their eyes, a witnessed cardiac arrest!

When I first heard the scream "Call a code!" I jumped up; I knew it was my baby. I ran into the room; they were starting to position her to start CPR. I turned around and helped the nurses haul the crash cart in. Eric intubated the baby and I took over managing the endotracheal tube while he ran the code. I started ventilating the baby while Kelly started sternal compressions. He was counting "One one-thousand, two one-thousand," up to five, and I forced a breath in every time he got to five. Meanwhile, the nurses had ripped open the crash cart and people began to fill the room from everywhere. And we began to code the baby.

We did everything we could. We pushed four rounds of meds. Jon, the chief resident, came and stuck a line in the baby's external jugular vein. We poured in fluid and kept pushing meds. But every time we stopped the CPR and looked up at the monitor, there was nothing. Flat-line. Finally we put her on an Isuprel drip. Even that didn't work. Then Eric tried intracardiac epi. And when that didn't work, after twenty-five minutes, they called the code and declared her dead.

At one point, well into the code, I remember looking up and seeing the mother, horror-stricken, with her hands to her mouth, bent at her hip like she had been punched in the stomach, screaming with horror. And then Jon had pulled the curtain so she couldn't see in. When we stopped the code, Eric pushed me out of the room and told me to tell the parents. He said, "You go first, go tell them." Just for a moment I stood in the baby's room terrified that I'd have to go through this experience again; I've already had to tell three sets of parents that their child had died. But this would have been the worst of them, because this was my patient, I had admitted her, and because this was a baby who wasn't supposed to die.

But I was spared giving the news this time. By the time we left the room, the mother already knew. Word got out very fast; one of the nurses had told the baby's grandmother, and the grandmother had told the mother.

We went out of the room as the nurses came in to clean up the mess. As we passed through the hall, there were shocked, terror-stricken looks on all the other parents' faces. Then we saw the mother. She was panicky and crazed. She wanted to run in and see the baby. We had to hold her back; we kept telling her that she shouldn't go yet, that she should wait until everything had been cleaned up. She was screaming that she had to see the baby and we couldn't keep her from her baby! But we told her again that she shouldn't see her baby now, with all the needles and the mess.

Someone found a wheelchair and we got her into it; with a lot of effort, we pushed her into the house staff lounge. We got the father in and we got everyone else to leave, and we told the parents exactly what had happened. That's when they began to cry. We told them we had done everything, everything possible, and that nothing had worked; there was never a response. They just couldn't understand.

Then finally one of the medical students came in and said it was okay for them to come and see the baby. The mother darted out of the room and we followed behind her. We stood in the hallway and we called for the attending and we called for the priest and we called for the social worker. There were a lot of crying, hysterical relatives filling the hallway, filling the ward, and panic-stricken parents of the other children stood uncomfortably at the edge of the doorways, not knowing what to say or how to act. It seemed to go on forever.

The father didn't stay in the room long; he couldn't bring himself to look at the baby. The mother stayed. When she finally came out, we took her, and the father, back to the house-staff lounge and we sat and talked for a long time.

After a while I left the room. I had to try to finish my work so I could go home. It was hard to concentrate on my other patients, but somehow I did it. At some point, Jon came in and asked me if I would go back and sit with the parents while he and Eric went to attend to some other business. I went in. It was just the parents and me. They sat there, upset but now calm. They asked me, "What will happen to our baby now? Where will you put her?" I told them the baby would stay in the hospital until they had decided what they wanted to do. They asked me if I thought an autopsy should be done, and I said yes, I thought one should, so that we could find out exactly what had happened. But they shook their heads no.

A little later, Jon and Eric came back with the autopsy permission form. They urged the parents to consent to an autopsy; the parents said they would think it over.

Before I left for the day, I pulled Jon aside and began to cry. I couldn't stop; I cried for the baby and for all the other children I'd seen die. I told him that I'd had other patients who had died and that I was beginning to feel like a death cloud. We went and talked and he reassured me it wasn't my fault.

Then the family met with the priest and the social worker. Phone numbers were exchanged; I didn't give them mine, but I thought that someone else had given them my number. Now I

worry that I've lost touch with the parents forever. I wish I could
be available to them.

When the family left, Jon, Eric and I were standing in the
house-staff lounge. Eric cursed about how terrible this all was
and then, in a very serious and angry tone, he said, "This job
sucks!" We sat there silently, morose and upset. But then Eric
began to imitate and make fun of some of the attendings in the
most merciless way. And pretty soon, we were all laughing, and
it felt so good to laugh because it had seemed like forever since
I'd last done it. But as I was sitting there laughing, this terrible
sadness came over me; I started feeling guilty for laughing at
such a serious time. Then I began to sense a horrible, black
feeling coming over me.

I left after that. The baby's attending had never shown up. I
was exhausted, so exhausted. It was a very bad night, a night
during which I thought about quitting. And so I got up, and
walked home.

I tried to call someone, just to talk about what had happened.
All I kept getting was answering machines. So I tried to get
drunk, but I could barely finish two beers because I was so tired.
It's been over twenty-four hours since it happened, but all day
today I've been feeling depressed and upset. And I feel guilty
as hell about it, even though I've been told over and over again
that it wasn't my fault.

Mike Miller had me over to his house. He told me over and
over that the baby's death was not my fault. We talked for hours.
I really think Mike cares. He told me that the whole thing had
happened under the eyes of the attending and that I was not to
feel responsible for the baby's death. And yet I do feel responsible. I feel terribly guilty and terribly sad. And I need to find
some place for this inside of me so that it won't eat me up, so
that I can live with it. This was definitely the worst death of all
deaths this year.

AMY

April 1986

Monday, March 31, 1986

I'm in the neonatal ICU at Jonas Bronck now. Most of my patients shouldn't even be alive. They're so small and sick, I can't understand how any of these things are going to grow up to be anything like a normal child. Most of them don't even seem human. It's such a contrast for me. I spend the days running around doing all this worthless work on these premature babies and then I go home and see Sarah. Sarah's a real person now, she's walking around and talking. It's great to watch her and to be part of the process, but then I go back to work the next morning and I realize that no matter what we do or how hard we work, it'll never be possible for most of my patients to do any of the things my baby can do. I feel very sorry for them but I also feel sorry for myself, because I'm being forced to take care of them and I don't want to have to take care of them. I stand back sometimes and realize that we're not really doing anybody any good. But that's not for me to say. I'm supposed to do what the attending tells me.

And things are even worse this month because I'm feeling so bad. I'm nauseous all the time now and I'm always completely exhausted. I get to a point around three o'clock every afternoon where I have to lie down for a few minutes. Trying to get a half hour or so off in the middle of the afternoon in the NICU is not the easiest thing to do when all your patients are in critical condition and dying and there's still a ton of scut that has to get done. So far this pregnancy is a lot worse than my pregnancy with Sarah. I'm feeling a lot sicker. It's probably because I started out this one so chronically exhausted.

I still haven't told anyone in the program except Bob Marion that I'm pregnant, so I have to cover up how I'm feeling and make excuses about why I need to go off and be by myself for a while. I don't think anyone's caught on yet, but I'm sure it's only a matter of time.

I've got a total of eight patients. Four of them started out weighing less than eight hundred grams [**one pound, twelve ounces**]. Two of these are relatively new preemies and are extremely sick. Both are on ventilators; one has NEC [**necrotizing enterocolitis, a serious infection of the intestine**] and sepsis and all sorts of other problems. I spend most of my time trying to keep these two from dying. My other two preemies have been around longer; one's about a month and a half old and the other's nearly four months old. I remember the four-month-old from the last time I worked in the unit; he was very sick back then. Now he and my one-and-a-half-month-old are stable but they're both really damaged. They both have grade IV IVH [**intraventricular hemorrhage, a hemorrhage into the ventrical of the brain; IVH is graded from I to IV, with IV being the most severe**], and one has bad hydrocephalus. The four-month-old has been abandoned by his mother. The mother hasn't been around in over a month. I don't know if I can say I blame her. I'm not really sure what I would do if I were in a situation like that. God forbid! But the nurses are really attached to this kid. That seems to be something that happens a lot when babies spend so many months in the unit.

I've got another patient, a six-month-old, who was born with congenital hydrocephalus. He's been in the nursery his whole life! His head is enormous; it looks like a basketball. He's had five shunts placed, but none of them seems to have done any good. All he can do is suck, breathe, and keep his heart beating, so he won't die for a long time, but he also isn't going to be leaving this unit. It's really sad. His mother visits him every day. She's kind of a pain; she always asks about his head circumference and tries to find out what his last CT scan showed. I feel sorry for her. She's really devoted to him. I don't think she has much of a life outside of here.

Then I've got this whole assortment of crack babies who live in the ICU. We had some in the well-baby nursery when I was working out there but they were mostly just social problems. These babies in the unit are all very sick. They all started out addicted and SGA [**small for gestational age**]; a couple of them have had convulsions. And all of them have either been abandoned or have been taken away from their mothers by the BCW. They're all very pathetic. They start out sick, and even when they get well, they have no place to go.

So that's my service so far. I don't understand how I'm going to have enough motivation to get up every morning and go to work. I'd rather just stay home and lie in bed all day than go to that horrible ICU.

Saturday, April 5, 1986

One of my patients died last night. Dying was definitely the best thing that could have happened to this baby; he had almost no chance of survival. But dealing with the mother was very hard.

It was a baby who had been born two days ago with severe malformations. At first we weren't sure what the baby had, but we knew it was something really bad. She was very abnormal-looking; she had a loud heart murmur; and she didn't respond to anything, including pain. Bob Marion came to see her and said the baby had trisomy 13. [**This is a disorder caused by an extra copy of the thirteenth chromosome. Children with trisomy 13 have so many malformations, both internally and externally, that almost all die within the first few months of life.**] He told us we shouldn't do anything heroic to try to prolong life, so we didn't, we just let the baby be and kept her comfortable. It took her over twenty-four hours to die; she waited until everybody else had gone home, so it was only me and a senior resident who was cross-covering.

The baby's heart just stopped beating. One of the nurses called me over and told me she was dead. I listened and didn't hear any heart sounds. At least she chose a reasonable time to die; it was about eight-thirty. At least the nurses didn't have to wake me up at four in the morning to declare her.

The mother was out on the postpartum ward and I went out to her room to tell her. She was really upset. Bob Marion and Ed Norris, our attending, had talked to her a few times since the baby had been born, so she knew what was wrong and that it was only a matter of time, but still she got very upset when I told her. It was really sad. She's thirty-nine years old and this was her first pregnancy. I sat with her for about a half hour, trying to calm her down. She told me she really wanted this baby, that she had had a lot of trouble getting pregnant and had gotten to the point where she didn't think she'd ever be able to conceive. And then, just when she had just about given up hope, she became pregnant with this baby, who turned out to have trisomy 13. I had absolutely no idea what to say to her. What can you say at a time like that? I don't even want to think about it, especially not now. So that wasn't the easiest thing in the world to deal with.

The rest of the night wasn't bad, though. I even got a few hours of sleep. Most of the preemies behaved themselves and didn't do anything stupid while I was on. Still, all night, I kept thinking about that mother. And so even though it should have been an easy night, it wasn't.

Friday, April 11, 1986

Yesterday was the official opening of the neonatal intensive-care unit on 7 South. The unit's actually been open for months now, but that's beside the point. They had this big celebration, and Mayor Koch, a group of other officials from the city, and all these reporters were here. Ed, our attending, who's the director of the nursery, took the mayor on a tour and showed him some of the six-hundred-grammers. The mayor was, to say the least, a little put off by the appearance of some of our patients. He didn't volunteer to kiss any of them, the way most politicians kiss babies.

I was on last night, and I had a terrible night. At about 1:00 A.M., we got a call from the DR that they had this woman who had just walked in off the street who was ready to deliver and had had no prenatal care. They weren't even sure when her LMP [last menstrual period] was, but they thought the baby might be about twenty-six weeks. Luckily, I was on with Enid Bolger, who's the senior in the unit this month. Enid also happens to be very good. We went running down to the delivery room just as the baby was coming out. It was tiny! I was positive it was too small to survive. Enid thought so, too, so we just gave it some oxygen and didn't do much else. It was only about eleven and a half inches long, so it was probably about twenty-three weeks [about three weeks too early for the baby to live independently outside the uterus]. But the baby came out with a heart rate, so we had to take it back to the ICU and wait for it to die.

That was pretty bad, but it could have been worse. Enid was very good about it; she didn't go crazy, like some of the other residents do. Some people would have done everything: intubated it, put it on a respirator, started IVs. But it wouldn't have accomplished anything. That baby never had a chance. It weighed only 520 grams [about one pound, two ounces]. So it was good to have someone like Enid in charge; I agreed with her completely in how this baby was managed. When the heart finally stopped beating, Enid and I went down and talked to the mother. She didn't seem too upset. I don't think she had really thought of it as a baby yet. I'm not even sure if she had realized she was pregnant before that day. She has three children at home. I don't know, I'm fairly sure it was for the best.

But I didn't get much sleep, and I've now had two deaths in one week. That's a lot, even if you're expecting the baby to die. I hope my luck changes.

I got into a fight with a mother last night. It was the mother of my patient Moreno, the six-month-old with hydrocephalus. I was in the middle of doing my evening scut and one of the nurses told me that Mrs. Moreno wanted to talk to me. I told the nurse I was busy just then and I'd try to stop by later. It was a very busy night and I completely forgot to go back to find the mother, and about an hour and a half later the woman came up to me and said, "Didn't the nurse tell you I wanted to talk to you?" I very nicely explained to her that I had a lot of work to do and I couldn't talk just then. She then got nasty, accused me of neglecting her child because I didn't think he was as important as the other babies, and said she was going to go right down to the patient advocate's office to make a formal complaint against me. I felt so lousy and I was so fed up with everything that I just told her, "Go ahead! Go and complain! What can they do, fire me? Let them fire me! I'd be glad if they fired me!" And I went on like that for a while. The woman didn't say another word, she just walked off the unit. I guess she went and complained. I haven't heard anything about it, but I'm sure I will. The nurses told me not to worry, though, because since the baby's been in the unit, she's complained about four other doctors. Still, I don't think I should have been so nasty to her. But what can I do?

Thursday, April 17, 1986

I don't think I want to work in that unit anymore. Too many bad things have happened in that nursery. I don't like taking care of those things. I just want to stay home with Sarah.

I had another death last night. That makes three on my time in three weeks. This last one was the worst of all of them because it was my four-month-old preemie, the one the nurses were really attached to. He had been doing poorly all along, and last night at about two o'clock, one of the nurses went in to check him and found him dead. Just like that. He was cold already. There wasn't anything we could do for him at that point. The nurses were really upset about it; some of them cried. I've never seen a nurse cry before for a patient who had died. At least I didn't have to go through the stress of talking to the mother, but spending the rest of the night with the nurses who were in a rotten mood might have been even worse.

Mrs. Moreno did complain about me to the patient advocate. I got called down there on Monday, and one of the administrators asked me to explain what happened. I told him the whole story and he told me that this woman was very angry about what had happened and what was happening to her baby, and she was blaming the entire staff for everything. He said it was a bad situation but they were trying to keep her calm and that for the rest of my time in the ICU I should try to be nice to her and put up with all her craziness. He didn't fire me. I was hoping I was going to get fired or at least suspended for a week or two. No such luck.

There's only one more week to go, so it looks like I'm going to make it through the month. I go to the OPD next, and that should be easier. And I think I'm starting to feel a little better. I didn't feel like I had to vomit once all yesterday and today. So maybe this part of the pregnancy is coming to an end. I know that'll make things easier.

MARK

April 1986

Tuesday, April 15, 1986

Well, I'm back from another wonderful vacation. I don't know what it is about me and vacations, but no matter how hard we try or how much in advance we plan, things always seem to turn out as if we were characters in one of those low-budget disaster movies.

This time Carole and I went to this beautiful hotel right on the beach in Cancún. It was a gorgeous place: great rooms, delicious food, and an amazing view. Everything would have been perfect, absolutely perfect, if two weeks ago hadn't turned out to be Mexican monsoon season. I didn't even know they had monsoons in Mexico, but I could have sworn that's what it was. We got off the plane at the airport in the pouring rain, and the rain continued the entire time we were there! An entire week of looking out the window at rain falling on a beautiful beach. Very exciting! And of course this place didn't have any indoor activities. Why should they have indoor activities? It never rains in Cancún, the weather's always perfect, isn't it? Sure it is, it's always perfect, except, of course, when I go there on vacation!

Everyone I've met since I got back to the Bronx has mentioned what a nice tan I got. Nice tan? There's no way I could have gotten a tan! There wasn't enough sun to get tan, the sun never came out, not for the entire eight days we were there! The only way my skin could have turned color is if maybe I started to rust. That must be what it is, I went away on vacation and got a nice rust!

Well, at least I got some rest. And I did get to spend a lot of time alone with Carole. That was very nice; we had a good time together. And I even got to read a book while we were away. An actual novel, not a pediatric textbook. It's the first nonmedical book I've read all year. It was getting to the point where I was starting to think I wasn't allowed to read any sentence unless it had at least one six-syllable word that had a Latin root in it. Reading this novel was tough at first. I'm so conditioned by reading medical stuff that I kept falling asleep after reading one paragraph. But I finally managed to get through it. I guess there's still hope for me.

Well, so much for my fond memories of our trip. It's now the middle of April, and the big news is there's only a little more than two months of this misery left. Yes, winter's over, the snow's all melted, the leaves are starting to appear on the trees, the addicts are starting to hang out on the street corners again, and the cockroaches are mating. I guess the cockroaches are always mating, but I swear, I got back to my apartment after flying back from Cancún and there were at least four times the usual number of roaches hanging around. We had managed to cut down the number remarkably for a while but now they're back in full force. It was an awe-inspiring sight, opening the front door, happy to be home after narrowly escaping being killed in the floods, and looking inside to see that my apartment had turned into Cockroach Heaven! I've been fighting the war ever since, but it looks as if they've definitely established a foothold. It's time to start thinking about moving out of the Bronx! I think Carole may ultimately win this battle. She's wanted me to get out of here for months.

I'm spending the last two weeks of the month in the OPD at Jonas Bronck. I've been on call two nights so far and it really hasn't been bad. We've left the ER at the stroke of midnight both nights, which is kind of amazing. We seem to be between seasons right now. Respiratory infection season has ended, and diarrhea and dehydration season hasn't started yet. At least that's what all the attendings keep saying to explain why it's so quiet. They talk about it like these diseases are sports. You know, in a couple of weeks I expect the chairman of the department to come down to the ER and throw out the ceremonial first diarrhea and dehydration patient to open the season officially. Well, whatever's causing it to be quiet, I'm not complaining. I just hope it keeps up.

I'm assigned to neurology clinic on Friday mornings. What

a lot of fun that is! The clinic is held on the fifth floor of Jonas Bronck, and you get there at about nine o'clock and the waiting area is already filled with what looks like hundreds and hundreds of kids seizing and shaking and yelling at the top of their lungs. Every kid has a chart that contains at least five thousand pages, and you have to read the entire chart to figure out what the hell is going on. And because there are so many patients scheduled, you have to move really fast or else you wind up staying all afternoon. This is the first time I've been assigned to neuro clinic this year, and I'm glad I have only a couple of sessions there before the month ends. If I had to imagine what hell might be like, I don't think I could come up with anything worse than being permanently assigned to neuro clinic. Get the feeling that I'm not going to be a neurologist when I grow up?

Over the past few weeks, I've started thinking about what I'm going to do when I'm finished with this internship and residency. The more I think about it, the worse the headache I wind up getting. I can see the advantage of specializing in something, but I also can see the advantage of not specializing in anything. I could go right into practice after I'm done, or I could do a fellowship. So far the only thing I've definitely decided is to put off making a decision about this for as long as I can. It's really very early. I don't even have to start panicking until about next year at this time. I've got all the time in the world.

I'm also getting a little worried about July. In July I'm going to be magically transformed into a junior resident. I like the idea of not being an intern anymore, but I'm not so sure I like the idea of being a resident. I mean, residents are people the interns turn to when they have questions and concerns. Residents are figures of authority. For some reason, I can't seem to imagine myself as an authority figure. I can't imagine giving interns advice. I wouldn't trust advice I gave to myself. Of course, that sounds kind of ridiculous.

BOB

April 1986

During the course of training, each doctor develops his or her own individual style of dealing with the family of a patient who has died. The evolution of this style occurs mostly through trial and error; with enough experience and having made enough mistakes, you gradually develop a method that makes both you and the family comfortable. There's no way this can be taught in a classroom or through reading books or articles.

Some doctors find that they feel most comfortable sitting down and having an open and frank discussion with the family, explaining to them in an honest and supportive way the events that led up to the death of the patient. This method is used most often by physicians who have had a lot of experience and who have a great deal of confidence in their skills. Young house officers have difficulty being very frank when discussing the death of a child with parents. Often there are many questions in the minds of the intern and resident about what actually led to the patient's death; they worry that they might have missed something important that could have saved the child's life, or that some task for which they were responsible was overlooked and contributed in some way to the patient's death. So interns usually don't feel comfortable having long discussions with the parents of a child who has died.

Some doctors overstep the traditional role of the physician and cry along with the parents of a child who has just died. This isn't necessarily a bad thing; the parents often appreciate the fact that their grief is shared by others who knew and cared a great deal for their child.

This style certainly described me as a house officer. While

on the oncology ward in May of my internship, I cared for a twelve-year-old boy with leukemia. Tom's disease had been diagnosed the previous September, and coincidentally I had cared for him during that admission as well. Now we were both back on the ward, and on the first morning of the month, Tom was once again assigned to me.

It was a shock to see him after all that time. Back in September, he had been a strapping, healthy-looking young adolescent; by May he had been reduced to a wasted, comatose vegetable, unable to speak or eat or react to any outside stimulus. His mother, with whom I had become friendly during his first admission, stayed with the boy constantly during the time he spent in the hospital, guarding over him for what proved to be the remainder of his life.

I was on call the night Tom finally died. His vital signs had become very irregular during the evening; his nurse had called to tell me this news, and I had left what I was doing to come. We stood silently over him, his mother at the foot of the bed, the nurse to the left, and me on Tom's right, and we waited for his breathing to stop. That finally happened about an hour and a half after I had first entered the room. I was the one to declare him dead.

I had spent all that time in Tom's room not because I was his doctor; there was nothing I had learned in medical school or during my internship that could in any way have altered the course of events. I knew that, and Tom's mother knew that. I had stayed in his room because I was a friend; I had known him and his mother for nine of the most difficult months of their lives, and I was with them at the end out of respect for that friendship. I think my being there meant something to Tom's mother; I know it meant an awful lot to me.

But some doctors find that they can't deal with death at all. They equate death with failure, and they have trouble dealing with and accepting their own failures. Once the patient dies, these physicians simply wash their hands of the whole affair. They leave the counseling of the family, the "mopping up after," to others.

In the case of Andy Baron's little patient, it seems as if the child's attending fell into the latter of these three groups. Unfortunately, the job of talking to the parents fell to Andy and the other house officers who happened to be around. At this stage in his training, Andy is looking to people such as that attending to guide him through this process. I'm almost positive Andy did a good job with these parents; I know him well enough at this stage to understand how sensitive and sympathetic he can be. But still, the attending's absence at this critical time must have been very difficult for the house staff as well as for the parents, who were looking for answers that couldn't possibly have been given by anyone other than the attending.

I know it must have been difficult for the parents, because I've been on their side of the fence. Last year, my wife delivered a stillborn baby. Beth had started having what she thought were labor pains one evening about two weeks before her due date. We had gone to the hospital with all our stuff, figuring our baby was about to be born. When we got to the labor floor at University Hospital, a nurse listened to Beth's abdomen with a fetoscope, a special stethoscope designed to amplify the fetal heartbeat. She couldn't hear a thing. Without a word to either of us, she left the room, and about five minutes later, a resident appeared at the door, pushing an ultrasound machine in front of her. She introduced herself and told us that she was going to do a sonogram. And without saying anything else, she went about her work.

I've watched over five hundred fetal sonograms. I have a pretty good idea of what's occurring on the ultrasound machine's screen. And while watching the scan that the resident did, I could make out our daughter's head and her chest, her abdomen and her limbs, but I could not see her heart beating. After a few minutes of searching, the resident picked up the ultrasound machine's transducer, turned off the power, and said she'd be back in a few minutes.

"I didn't see the fetal heartbeat," I said.

"I didn't either," she said quietly, startled at my statement. "I'm going to call your attending."

Beth and I sat in the room crying; no one came to explain what was going on or what would happen next. Finally, after about a half hour, Beth's doctor appeared at the door. He told us that it seemed as if the baby had died. He talked with us, answered our questions, and told us what the most appropriate management plan was. Since the labor pains that had begun this whole episode a few hours before had completely ceased, Beth agreed to wait until natural labor resumed, an occurrence her doctor assured her would take place within the next week or so. And so, devastated, we prepared to go home.

After leaving the labor room, we approached the nurses' station. The nurses and the resident who had done the ultrasound were having an animated conversation, laughing and apparently enjoying themselves, but as we approached, they became silent. I was used to this; I had been part of this kind of behavior, especially during my time in the neonatal ICU. But now I was experiencing it in a different way; Beth and I were the opposition now, and this behavior made our grief just a little bit worse.

I've learned something from this experience, and accordingly I've altered the method I use when talking with the families of children who have died. This isn't an experience I would recommend, but it did help me understand a little more about what goes through the mind of a parent whose child has died.

ANDY

May 1986

Wednesday, May 7, 1986, 7:00 P.M.

I finally finished Infants'. It was a horrible, depressing month. About a week after the baby with heart disease died, I had another patient who got very sick and had to go up to ICU. I intubated him myself. He deteriorated so fast, he almost died on the ward before we could get him up to the unit.

Now I'm in the OPD, and all the details are starting to blur. I suppose if I spoke into this thing religiously every day, I could tell you endless story after story about all the kids and their various problems. But what does it matter? It's all just a horrible blur, one after the next, made up of all these poor, sick kids.

Thursday, May 8, 1986, 10:00 P.M.

It's become really hard to continue keeping this diary. Over the past few months I've lost touch with my inner self; I'm not sure completely why that's happening, but I think it's because I'm defending myself against all the bad feelings I've had about being an intern. It relates to a lot of different issues having to do with the general feeling of being abused and mistreated, and the fatigue and the sleep deprivation, and the death and the morbidity of my patients. So certainly that's one reason I haven't been talking. I'm out of touch with myself, and it's hard to know what exactly to talk about. The other thing is, the thrill and excitement and novelty are gone, and they've been replaced by a more realistic perception of what I think medicine is. And for some reason, there's something in me that doesn't want to relate all

304

those stories about all the various patients. Talking about it makes me feel like I'm back at work, and I hate even to think about being at work.

Saturday, May 10, 1986, 4:10 A.M.

I just spent the last six hours in the Jonas Bronck ER working on a fucking child-abuse case. I really hate them; I hate them more than anything else in this job. I think I've seen enough child abuse for an entire lifetime. I don't want to see any more, thank you. They never go well, they're always difficult.

This one, I just pulled the chart from the box, I didn't even read the triage note, and I called the kid in. She had a bandage on her forehead. Oh, great, I thought. A laceration. I asked what happened and the mother gave me this story that the girl was lying on the floor and playing and she bumped her head and cut herself on the hinge of her glasses or something weird like that and cut her forehead. I asked her to go over that again and the mother gave me basically the same story. So I took the glasses off the kid's face and I tried to find a way to make the hinge hit up against the forehead. I couldn't do it. The frames were plastic and they were totally intact. I thought, No way! No way the kid could have done this!

So I decided I'd better do a complete examination. I got her undressed, and lo and behold, she had big contusions across her back and across her upper right thigh. I just thought, Oh, fuck! You get a feeling down in the pit of your stomach when you finally figure out what you're dealing with, and I got it at that moment.

Then I examined her vagina, and it looked kind of red and smelled bad, and I thought, Oh fuck! again. To make a long story short, I reported the kid to the BCW and the cops as a suspected physical and sexual abuse case. And I had to fill out only about a thousand forms among the chart, documenting the living shit out of it, the BCW 2221 form, and the rape evidence kit [documents and materials that will be needed when the case goes to court].

The whole thing was horrible. The parents were crazed; at one point they tried to take the kid out. They started to dress her and said they were going to take her to Washington Hospital [a municipal hospital in the South Bronx]. Give me a break! I called security at that point. Once I called security, that was it, they knew the jig was up. They knew they had been caught. Oh, man! It was horrible. I hate it. After I called security, I was shaking and nervous for a while because it's such a bad thing to have to deal with. I don't want to help take kids away from their parents! Kids don't want to be taken away from their parents; they love them even if they are horrible! So even though the parents have done something terribly wrong, I'm the one who feels like he's committing the crime.

Anyway, it takes so long to do everything, God knows what the kid's disposition will be. I don't know what to say. I hate it, I hate child abuse so much, I wish it never existed.

Wednesday, May 21, 1986, 9:30 P.M.

It's been a typical wild month in the Jonas Bronck ER. I'm getting out of this month exactly what I wanted: I'm learning how to manage trauma, and I'm learning how to see multiple patients in a short period of time. I'm a lot better at it than I was; I'm still not able to be as accurate as I'd like to be, but I can see some improvement every day. I can be fast when things aren't too complicated; I still haven't gotten good at seeing a complicated patient and a couple of uncomplicated patients at the same time. But I have another week in the ER and maybe I can get a handle on that.

I can't remember anymore what I've talked about and what I haven't talked about. I don't know, there are so many stories, so many stories of frightened mothers and frightened children, sick children, and I don't know why, I just don't want to talk about any of it anymore. I've had some bad nights, I've had some good nights. I'm sorry . . . I'm sorry this is deteriorating. But the year's almost over, it's just another five weeks or so and I'll be moving back to Boston. I really need to start making arrangements. I haven't done that yet. I'll have to take a day off from work to get that squared away.

Everybody seems to be calling in sick all the time now. Except me. There's one intern in particular who's always calling in sick, or coming late to clinic. I'm thinking that maybe I'll fucking call in sick one morning and get everything arranged for the move. But I think maybe this is another fantasy of mine. I haven't missed a day of work yet this year and I probably won't start changing and calling in sick with so little time left. It pisses me off a lot when other people call in sick. It's totally irresponsible and everybody always winds up having to work a little harder to make up for the person who calls in sick, and that's not fair.

My clinic's going fine, and I have a couple of specialty clinics including renal, which I think I like a lot. I think I could actually do renal. I'm not sure yet, I'll have to try it again when I'm in Boston, but there are a lot of good things about it: It's interesting, it isn't a lot of hard work, and the people seem nice. I don't know, it's something I might be able to be content with for the rest of my life.

People have been saying a lot of nice things about me over the past few weeks. They tell me how much they're going to miss me and that I've added a lot to the program. A couple of the attendings have said that I'd make a good chief resident. That's all very nice and very flattering; part of me likes that fantasy of staying here and being asked to be chief, even though I know it's just a fantasy, and part of me now is very slowly, very slowly recognizing that I'm actually going to be leaving soon. I haven't started thinking of myself as being a resident in Boston next year; I don't have an emotional attachment to that program yet. I can see myself as a junior resident here much better than I can see myself as a junior resident there. I really wonder if I'll be ready for the demands of that place.

Next week I start my last month on 6A. My last month! My God! You know, this is going to sound tacky and very clichéd, but the year really has gone by fast. Two hundred ripped-off nights!

The chief residents' beeper party was today, and I missed it. I'd been looking forward to it for months. I even went out this morning and bought a blueberry pie to bring. Then I got stuck in the ER with a fifteen-year-old who got hit by a car and was dragged twenty yards. He was a mess; he had a basilar skull fracture, a hemotympanum [**blood behind his tympanic membrane, a sign of skull fracture**], blood in his urine, a laceration over the eye. I was fuckin' stuck with him and I missed the party but I learned a little about handling multiple trauma. I wanted to go so badly, I really was pissed off. One of the highlights of the year, and I missed it. Too bad. There'll be new chiefs the day after tomorrow. New chiefs: No more calling Jon, no more calling Claire, no more calling Arlene, no more calling Eric. I wanted to thank them, I wanted to thank them all, and now I don't know if I'll get the chance. I'll miss them, and I'll remember them. They were really great.

The tape's running out. So I'll stop now. One more month to go. One more month.

AMY

May 1986

Sunday, May 11, 1986

Sarah's been taking a lot more of our time and attention lately. She wants to be read to constantly. She's always toddling over to Larry or me, holding a book in her hand. She has two favorites: *Goodnight Moon* and *Green Eggs and Ham*. She can listen to them over and over again for hours. But they do start to get a little boring after the fifteenth or sixteenth reading.

It's getting harder for me to keep up with Sarah because of how tired I've been feeling. My nausea's just about all gone but I'm always so tired, all I want to do when I have a free minute is go to sleep. And Sarah isn't very happy about that. She doesn't like to see Mommy in bed. Lord knows, she sees so little of me, at least I ought to be able to play with her when I do manage to get home from work.

Things have been very stressful and aggravating for me lately. First, it was the month in the NICU. God, that was terrible. I never want to spend another night in there! As far as I'm concerned, neonatology is a complete waste!

And when I finally finished getting aggravated in the NICU, it was time to start fighting with the chief residents and the rest of the administration about maternity leave. I know this might sound like a very old story, but it looks like they're trying to screw me again. Last week, they sent out these things called "Schedule Request Forms" for next year. We're supposed to fill them in and make requests for when we'd like our vacation time. Since I'm already in my third month of pregnancy and some people have already started asking me whether I'm pregnant, I figured it was time to bring the issue up with the chiefs.

So last Tuesday I went up to their office and had a little talk with them.

Jon and Arlene were sitting at their desks and I walked in and said, ''Hi. Guess what? I'm three months pregnant. I'm due next November and I need to arrange maternity leave.'' Just like that. You should have seen the looks on their faces. I thought Arlene was going to fall out of her chair. Of course, whether I'm pregnant or not doesn't really make any difference to them; they're not going to be here after June 1, so it isn't their problem, it's the new chiefs' problem. But they certainly were stunned just the same. It took them about five minutes to recover enough to congratulate me. In some ways it was worth suffering through these weeks of nausea and exhaustion just to see the looks on their faces!

Anyway, what's been done in the past is that a three-month period of maternity leave has been created by taking the one month of vacation and the one month of elective without night call we're entitled to [**senior residents have a one-month period called free elective; during this month, because they have no night call, they can travel to other cities to do electives**] and adding another month of elective with night call. I told the chiefs that that's what I wanted to arrange, but they immediately started giving me a hard time. They said that as far as they knew, all I could get was my one month of vacation. They were unwilling to give me the other two months; they told me three months off would cause enormous problems in the schedule, and they just couldn't afford to do that. I've found out since then that three other women are pregnant and expecting at about the same time I am, and if they give us all two or three months off, it just might destroy the schedule.

Well, I don't care if my having a baby does destroy their precious schedule. I'm finished worrying about everybody else. What it comes down to is they're trying to discriminate against me and I'm not going just to sit back and stand for it this time! I'm tired of being pushed around and doing things just because the chief residents or the attendings or someone else tells me that that's the way it's got to be! So I made a call to the CIR [**Committee of Interns and Residents, the house officers' union**] office in Manhattan. I got the vice president on the phone and asked him exactly what the policy was for maternity leave. He told me that I'm entitled to six weeks of leave above and beyond any vacation or elective time I might have coming. That means that what I'm really entitled to is six weeks of maternity leave, four weeks of vacation, four weeks of elective without night call, and another four weeks of elective with night call. That's a total of four and a half months, and you can be sure I'm going to take all of it! If they hadn't tried to screw me over in the first place, I would have settled for three or maybe even two months. Now I'm going to take four and a half months, and if they don't want to give it to me, I'm just going to file a grievance with the union!

I went back to tell the chiefs about this on Thursday and they said they'd have to talk with the higher-ups before they could give me an official response. I got a call on Friday from Mike Miller's secretary, setting up a meeting for tomorrow. It looks like I finally got some action! After all this time, I finally figured out how to get things done around here. It's too bad everything has to be done through threats, though.

Wednesday, May 14, 1986

On Monday I met with Mike Miller about my maternity leave. He was very nice about the whole thing. First, he hugged me and told me how happy he was to hear the news. He seemed really sincere about it. Then he told me how upset he had been when he found out what the chiefs had tried to do to me. He said that in our program, we've always been very liberal about maternity leave. He went into a whole lecture about how we as pediatricians were supposed to be advocates not only for children but for their parents as well and how it would be hypocritical for us not to allow the residents proper time to be with their newborns. He was being nice to me, so I didn't start up with him about breast feeding and how it was hypocritical that none of us could ever breast-feed our children because we weren't provided with the proper facilities to ensure its success. Anyway, he told me he would guarantee that I got at least two months of leave after the baby was born and that I'd have easy rotations both the month before I was due and the month I came back after the baby was born.

Mike's always been nice to me, and I think he really meant what he said. I don't think he was saying those things just to try to prevent me from filing a grievance with the union. So I'm going to take his word for it. I'm going to trust him and I'm not going to speak to anyone from the union, at least not until next year's schedule comes out at the beginning of June. But you can be sure, if two months of leave are not written into that schedule for November and December, I am going to be on the phone to the CIR so fast it'll make your head spin!

I was a little distracted when I went in to talk to Mike because I've been really worried about my father. I called him on Sunday night and right near the end of this very nice conversation, he happened to mention to me that he had passed some bright red blood with a stool earlier in the day. Just like that, very matter-of-factly he said it. I immediately got upset and I asked him what he was going to do about it. He said, "Nothing."

I almost went crazy! He always does this to me. I yelled at him that he had to go to see a doctor the next day, and if he wasn't going to make an appointment, I would call his doctor and make the appointment and then come out to New Jersey and drive him to the doctor's office to make sure he got there. I think he got the message because he said he'd try to make the appointment but told me that his doctor was a very busy man and he might not be able to get to see him for weeks.

Anyway, right after I came out of Mike's office, I called my father at work. He said he had been able to make an appointment for this morning. He called a little while ago to tell me that the doctor had seen him, had done a full examination including a sigmoidoscopy [an examination of the sigmoid portion of the large intestine], and that the bleeding had been due to hemorrhoids. Everything else was fine. So I felt a lot better. My father told me I had made him worry for nothing. I told him that we didn't know it was nothing until we checked it out. It might have been something, and if he had ignored it, it might have cost him his life.

The doctor did tell my father that he did have to have the hemorrhoids removed as soon as possible because there was a possibility that there could be massive bleeding. He said he could arrange for the surgery to be done next Monday, and amazingly my father agreed; he's not admitting it, but he must either be in a lot of pain or really be scared about this. Whatever it is that's causing it, I'm glad he's acting so reasonably about it. But now I have to try to get next Monday off so I can go out to New Jersey to be with him. It shouldn't be too much trouble.

Then again, you wouldn't expect it to be too much trouble to get a day off to stay with your baby who has the measles and a fever of 103, would you?

I've been feeling better over the past few days. My nauseousness is completely gone, and I'm not so tired anymore. I think I've made it through the worst part of this pregnancy. When I was pregnant with Sarah, once I made it through the initial yucky part, I felt wonderful until about three weeks before I delivered; then I felt like a blimp and couldn't move at all. So it should be smooth sailing for me over the next few months. There's only one more month of this internship left. I haven't enjoyed most of this year; maybe I'll be able to salvage this last part of it.

Tuesday, May 20, 1986

They did it to me again! I can't believe it! Yesterday was the day my father had his surgery. I had been trying since last Wednesday to get the day off. I thought it would be easy. I should have known better.

There were lots of problems from the beginning this time. First of all, I have clinic Monday afternoon, so I went to the director of the clinic and asked if I could switch my patients to another day just this once. I'd never asked her for a single favor in the past and I'd done lots of things for her like covering for other doctors who were sick. She hemmed and hawed for a couple of minutes and then when I explained that I needed to go to be with my father who was having an operation, she said she'd see what she could do. She called me on Thursday to say that she'd tried everything but there was no way she could cancel or reschedule the patients.

Fine. I understood what that meant. What that meant was that I wasn't going to be able to approach this whole thing as a grown-up. I was going to have to call in sick and lie about it. And because of that, I didn't even go to talk to the chiefs about switching my night call. I'd just call in sick and leave them hanging in the wind.

Well, yesterday came, and that's exactly what I did. I called everyone I had to, the chiefs, the clinic, and the emergency room, and I told them I had gastroenteritis and I couldn't make it in. Then I got dressed and got ready to leave for New Jersey.

But just as I was about to leave the apartment, the phone rang. It was Mike Miller. He asked me if anything was wrong. I thought for a minute: Should I tell him the truth, or should I continue the story I made up? I decided to tell him the truth. It was obviously the wrong decision, because after I got finished telling him about my father, he said that they were strapped today, that a lot of people had called in sick, and if I didn't come to be on call at least that night, there would be only one person in the emergency room from five until midnight. So he made me a deal: He told me he'd let me take that day and the next day off if I came in to be on call that night. He said they were depending on me. He was so nice and so straight about it, I didn't see that I had much of a choice. So I went out to New Jersey and sat outside while my father had the surgery and stayed in the recovery room. I had to leave to come back to the Bronx just as he was going back to his room. It was so stupid; I didn't get to spend any time with him at all.

At least I knew he had done well during the operation. But all during the night, while I was seeing patients in the emergency room, I kept thinking how stupid this was. I mean, my father's not a young man; an operation like that can cause complications. And he had nobody else in the world to stay with him except me. So what was I doing while he was waking up from the anesthesia? I was seeing kids with runny noses and ear infections. I didn't need to be there; Evan Broadman, who was the senior resident, could have seen everyone by himself.

Well, I spent all day today at my father's bedside. He's in a lot of pain. The surgery's very uncomfortable. He didn't say anything about my not being there last night, but I knew he would have liked me to have been there. And I would have liked to have been there, too.

Monday, May 26, 1986

I was trying to think last night if I'd learned anything this year. I was taking care of a six-year-old girl who had been hit by a car. She had about a five-minute loss of consciousness but seemed to be fine by the time she reached us. I handled the entire case myself. I started an IV and sent off a CBC [complete blood count] and a set of lytes [examination of blood electrolytes]. I got skull films [X rays looking for a skull fracture], which were negative; I did a UA [urinalysis] and found some blood in her urine, so I arranged for an IVP, which also was negative [any patient who has had significant trauma and is found to have blood in the urine must have an intravenous pyelogram, an X-ray evaluation of the kidneys, to make sure that no damage has been done to the kidneys]. I cleaned out her forehead laceration and sutured it myself. Then I called the intern up on the floor and admitted the patient for observation. I think that was pretty amazing! Considering I couldn't start an IV or put in a suture when I started last July, I think you'd have to say I've come a long way. It's funny, though; you never see it that way while you're doing it. While you're working, you're only aware of the things you don't know, not the things you do know.

MARK

May 1986

Thursday, May 1, 1986

My mother told me I should always try to find something nice to say about a situation. I started my rotation at University Hospital last Monday, and ever since, I've been trying to figure out something nice to say about the place. I finally came up with something: The food is good. No, that's not even exactly true. It's not actually good, it's just plentiful. Plentiful and easily available and free; they give us meal tickets so we can eat three meals a day. And that's it. Outside of the food, I haven't found anything I've liked at University Hospital.

I've been on call one night and so far I've had one patient die. It was a patient I'd met before: the kid I saw in the West Bronx ER a few weeks ago who got bitten by the horse. Her name was Melissa Harrison, and she had this horrible disease, metachromatic leukodystrophy. She'd been going downhill for a while. She came in on Monday in status epilepticus [**the state in which constant seizures are occurring**]. Dr. Ruskin, her neurologist, came in and spent about an hour and a half talking to the parents. At the end of the meeting Ruskin came out and told me they'd decided that this was going to be it. We weren't going to do anything heroic, just fill the kid with enough morphine to keep her comfortable and then wait for the end to come. The end happened to come when I was on call Tuesday night.

This wasn't exactly the most comfortable situation I'd ever been in. I mean, I didn't know this kid from a hole in the wall. And here I was, being called on to stand by her bed and let her die without doing anything to prevent it from happening. Ruskin might have felt comfortable being in that situation, but she wasn't standing there at the kid's bedside. I was, and I felt pretty bad about the whole thing.

This kid's mother was a saint, though. I guess she saw I was pretty uncomfortable, and she spent a lot of time trying to calm me down. She told me about what Melissa had been like before she started going down the tubes. Isn't that wonderful? The mother of this dying girl had to spend the last minutes of her daughter's life calming down the intern who had gone completely out of his mind. Well, listen, it isn't completely my fault that I'm berserk; I'll be the first to admit that I might not have started out this internship with a full complement of marbles, but most of the berserkness I've been demonstrating recently is the result of the deep frying my brain's been receiving over the past few months.

Anyway, Melissa's mother was really great. She's a real Mother Teresa type. I can only imagine what kind of hell her life's been over the past few years.

So that was a great way to start out the month. I'm on again tomorrow, and since I seem to have become the Intern of Death, I wonder which one of my panel of patients will be tomorrow's selection in the Meet Your Maker sweepstakes. Will it be Nelly, the three-year-old with AIDS who has PCP [pneumocystis car-inii pneumonia, a common cause of death in patients with AIDS]? Will it be Jesus, the one-year-old with yet another bizarre metabolic disease, the name of which I can barely pronounce? Will it be one of the parade of renal transplant patients who are constantly marching onto the ward to get treated with medication that might stop them from rejecting their transplanted kidney? Or will it be a completely different patient, one I haven't even met yet, one who's waiting in the wings to make my life completely miserable over the next forty-eight hours? Only time will tell. And I don't think I want to know.

I'm going to sleep now. Maybe I'll sleep through tomorrow and the entire next two months, and when I wake up, I won't be an intern anymore. I can always hope!

Sunday, May 4, 1986

Great news! I was on Friday night and no one died. Nobody; no patients, no nurses, not even me! At least if somebody did die, I wasn't told about it.

Actually, Friday night was nice, if any night spent in any hospital can be called ''nice.'' I didn't get a single admission. I even got five hours of sleep in University Hospital's very lovely intern on-call room. The on-call room is in reality a closet with furniture; it's about six feet by six feet and it's got a door, a telephone, and a cot. When they were building this hospital, they obviously decided to spare no expense when it came to the comfort of the interns. I shouldn't complain, though. I heard that as of four years ago, the interns didn't even have this closet to sleep in. They had to sleep in empty patient beds. That's always very dangerous, especially here at University Hospital, where there's an actual blood-drawing technician. There's always the chance the tech will find you lying in bed some morning, mistake you for a patient, and suck out all your blood.

I discovered another good thing about University Hospital. There's this porch attached to the cafeteria that you can actually go out on and get some sun. Actual sun in the Bronx! Anyway, I found this porch at lunchtime on Friday and I spent an hour out there on Friday afternoon. It was really beautiful. The weather's been great all weekend, too. The temperature's been in the seventies. Yesterday Carole and I went to this inn about an hour north of here. It was great, really relaxing, and we weren't caught in a rainstorm, a monsoon, a tornado, or any other natural disaster. Amazing! Maybe my luck is actually changing. Nah, it probably was just a fluke.

I don't really have too much to say tonight. I just wanted to show that it's still possible for me to be in a good mood. See— there's hope for me yet.

Tuesday, May 6, 1986, 9:00 P.M.

I was on last night. What a good time I had! What a wonderful learning experience it was! I had such a good night last Friday, I thought I was actually going to like the rest of my month. I thought it was going to be really quiet and restful. Then I was on last night and now I feel as if somebody dumped a fifty-pound bag of excrement on my head.

And I feel better now than I did a couple of hours ago! At six o'clock I was a genuine basket case! I was ready to manually extract the spleens of each of the chief residents without the use of anesthesia. But then I went over to my grandmother's. She fed me a nice dinner and calmed me down. Thank God for Grandma! Thanks to her, the chief residents will live another day.

When I talk about it, I don't think it'll sound like last night was all that bad. I mean, I had six admissions, which is kind of bad, but all of them were electives and none of them was sick, so it should have been pretty easy, right? It would have been easy had they all come in at a reasonable hour. It would have been easy had at least a few of them come in at a reasonable hour. Did any of them come in at a reasonable hour? Of course not! Why would anyone expect a kid who's scheduled to have surgery the next day, who needs to be seen by residents from at least three services [**pediatrics, surgery, and anesthesiology**], and who needs to have blood work and all kinds of other tests done, to come into the hospital before nine o'clock at night? What a silly idea that is!

Well, anyway, they started to arrive at about seven-thirty and they continued to show up until nearly midnight. I couldn't believe it: A six-year-old who was scheduled to have a T and A [**removal of tonsils and adenoids**] this morning didn't show up until midnight. A normal six-year-old shouldn't even be awake at midnight, to say nothing of a six-year-old who's scheduled to have an operation a few hours later! I was pissed, the anesthesiology resident who came to see the kid was pissed, the surgery resident was pissed, everyone was pissed except the kid and his mother, who couldn't understand what we were all so upset about. To them a six-year-old coming in for an elective procedure at midnight was completely natural.

So it took me until after two-thirty to finish all my scut work on six lousy electives! And of course just when I was finished and I should have been able to get to sleep, Nelly, my AIDS kid with pneumocystis carinii pneumonia, decided to try to die on us. Boy, how happy I was to see that! It's me and Diane Rogers [**the cross-covering senior resident**] in a hospital that doesn't have a pediatric ICU, trying to keep alive a kid who's trying her best to get to heaven. It was amazing: She was perfectly fine one minute, and the next minute she was dropping her pulse to sixty and her blood pressure to sixty-five over forty-five. It really looked like the end was near. We stood around scratching our heads for a couple of minutes, trying to figure out what the hell was going on and what we should be doing about it. Her blood gas was still okay, so we knew it wasn't a ventilatory problem. Diane finally figured maybe we should try some Dopamine [a **drug that increases blood pressure, among other things**] to see what that did. I didn't understand the reasoning (of course, there isn't much reasoning I do understand), but the Dopamine seemed to do the trick. Nelly was good as new after that.

So there we were, with a kid with AIDS and PCP, who was going into shock, getting a Dopamine drip while on the regular ward. I had to stay with her for the rest of the night. I didn't get any sleep, and then I had to start rounds so I could have my usual morning fight with the blood-drawing tech who was refusing to draw blood on everyone. This has become a regular part of my day, I've kind of become addicted to it. Fighting with the blood-drawing tech is like drinking coffee.

So much fighting goes on at this hospital, it's unbelievable. Working at University Hospital is definitely like being drafted into the army during wartime. It's us against them, with the "them" being everybody who's not a house officer: the attendings, the nurses, the lab techs, and especially the patients and their mothers. Work rounds in the morning are more like a prebattle strategy session. We plan out the tactics we're going to use that day. But there are a lot of situations you can't plan for; things like sneak attacks. They tend to keep you on your toes.

Friday, May 9, 1986

I really don't know what to make of this place. This hospital definitely has some schizoid tendencies; sometimes it seems like the nicest place in the world. There are some afternoons when it's so peaceful and quiet, you can relax, sit out on the sun porch, even take a nap. And then there are some days where the patients all get sick at once, there are millions of admissions, and all you do is fight with everybody you can find. Take yesterday afternoon. At about three o'clock, the whole team got stat-paged to the adult ICU. We had one patient in there, an eight-year-old who had been hit by a car a couple of days before and had been unconscious ever since, so we all were sure she had arrested. We went running into the ICU and found she was fine, but the neurosurgery attending and one of his residents were standing by her bedside. As soon as we pulled up, the attending started yelling about how poorly we were managing the patient and how embarrassed he was that a patient who had been referred to him was getting such lousy care. She wasn't getting lousy care, she was getting great care. We all knew that. It's just that this guy has this quota: He has to yell at at least one house officer a day.

It was really hard to keep a straight face while this guy was yelling at us because he was sucking on a lollypop the whole time. It's hard to take this neurosurgeon seriously in the first place, but when he's got a lollypop in his mouth, it's damn near impossible!

And that wasn't even the end of it. Today, when we were on work rounds, we ran into the neurosurgery team. In spite of how poorly we had managed the kid, she had awakened out of her coma last night and seemed just fine today. Now her prognosis is excellent, and the neurosurgery chief resident told us we had done a great job with the patient. The attending immediately yelled at him, saying, "How can you tell them they did a great job less than twenty-four hours after I yelled at them for doing a lousy job?" The chief resident apologized and told him that since he hadn't been on rounds yesterday afternoon, he didn't know the attending had yelled at us. Then the attending got real pissed and said, "Next time I yell at somebody, I want the whole team there. I don't want to have to yell at people twice for the same thing!"

So last night I had a really quiet night. No admissions, just some coverage, and almost everyone remained stable. This was mainly due to the fact that Nelly, the AIDS kid, got transferred over to the ICU at Jonas Bronck. When Al Warburg, the daytime senior resident, found out that we had a patient on the ward on a Dopamine drip, he picked up the hot line to the chief residents' office and told them they had to transfer Nelly. So after I had been up all night with the kid, she got whisked away to Jonas Bronck. Don't get me wrong, I'm not complaining.

I guess the sickest kid on the ward right now is José, a one-year-old with this weird metabolic disease called argininosuc-cinicademia. The name of this thing is longer than the kid is! Anyway, having José on the ward is like taking care of an unremitting Hanson. He's constantly crumping and then stabilizing and then crumping again. He's lived in the hospital for the past couple of months, and all the nurses have come to love him. That's always a bad prognostic sign.

This disease has something to do with the urea cycle, and the kid is being treated with all these weird chemicals that make him smell really strange. I spent a few minutes standing at his doorway yesterday, sniffing his bouquet, trying to figure out what in hell it was he smelled like. It took a while, but it finally came to me: He smells just like the bottom of a birdcage. The kid smells like parakeet droppings! It's the strangest thing, but that's exactly what it is. Since I figured that out, I've become fixated on thinking of him as a parakeet. I'm waiting for him to start singing. And I'm sure it won't be long before he sprouts wings and just sort of flies away.

When you start sniffing the patients, I think it's safe to say you've been an intern too long. I think it's time to get out of here!

Sunday, May 18, 1986

Well, I haven't recorded anything for over a week, and nothing much has happened. Working at University really isn't so bad if you like taking care of kids with diseases whose names you can't pronounce. It's not like the other hospitals; they actually hire people here to do some of the scut work we're normally expected to do. So workwise there just isn't that much to do. But you more than make up for it in aggravation.

This is definitely the weirdest place I've ever worked in! At all the other hospitals, you really know what the score is. The rules are simple: They try to pile as much shit on your head as they can until you collapse, at which point a chief resident comes along, pats you on the shoulder, and gives you the weekend off to recover. Here the work isn't that hard, but you always have the feeling that you're missing something. You don't have control over anything. There are always attendings around who are trying to do things without telling you, and the parents always know more about what's happening with their kids than we do. It's very frustrating.

Nobody wants their kids touched by an intern. The parents all want the private attending to come in and draw the blood or start the IV. That's pretty funny because most of these private attendings haven't started an IV on a kid in years. People always naturally expect the more senior people to be able to do everything better than the interns. I'll tell you, at this point in the year there are very few people who are better than the interns at starting IVs, doing spinal taps, drawing blood, doing any kind of scut. But the parents still want to know why the private attending isn't coming in to do the stuff. So even though there's lots of time to sit out in the sun, I think I'd rather be in the wasteland of Jonas Bronck.

Well, there's only a little over a week to go and I'll be out of here. And then there's only one more month of internship left. That's pretty unbelievable, but I'm finding the idea of me being a resident even more unbelievable. In a little over a month there is going to be a group of poor, innocent interns who are actually going to look up to me with respect. They're even going to think they can trust me! My God, what a frightening thought!

Wednesday, May 28, 1986, 8:30 P.M.

Well, it looks like I made it. I just came home, which means I'm done with University Hospital. The rest of my internship consists of one measly month in the NICU at West Bronx. It'll be a cinch compared with last night.

I had the feeling last night that what was going on wasn't real. I figured this had to be a setup for *Candid Camera*. But nobody told me to smile, and no short, fat, bald guy came out and shook my hand. So I think it must have been real.

I was supposed to be on with Diane Rogers, but she called in sick and there was nobody to cover for her. So the chiefs asked if I would mind working on the ward by myself. Me mind covering a ward filled with twenty-five sick kids by myself? No, no way I'd mind it. I told them I looked forward to challenges just like this, that I welcomed just this type of adversity. In fact, I even told them I'd be happy to work every night next month by myself because that's the kind of guy I am. I don't think they realized I was being cynical, because somehow at around ten o'clock last evening I found myself rounding on the ward by myself. I even yelled at myself a couple of times for not following up on some scut I was supposed to do.

Anyway, everything was going fine, mostly because there hadn't been any admissions in a couple of days and the place was really quiet, but then at about four o'clock this morning I got a call from one of the neurology attendings, who told me he was sending in a kid with a brain tumor who had been in status epilepticus for about four hours. Status for four hours! I told him fine, I welcomed these kinds of patients, that I looked forward to challenges just like this, and that I'd be waiting for him. Then I calmly hung up the phone, ran for the staircase, and started moving in a downward direction. I was getting out of there; I might be crazy, but I'm no fool.

When I hit the third-floor landing, something weird happened. I got this sudden rush of guilt and I realized I'd have to go back. So I slowly climbed back up, told the nurse what was happening, and got ready.

The kid got there at about four-thirty. He was seizing, all right, there wasn't any doubt about it. I had no trouble figuring out he was seizing; what I had trouble figuring out was what I was going to do about it. So I called the neuro attending at home, and the first thing he did was yell at me for waking him up. I was expecting that; the first thing everybody does when you call them from University Hospital is yell at you. But then I asked him what I should do, and he said, "You've got a kid who's seizing. What the hell do you think you should do?"

My neurons turned on and I waited a couple of seconds for an answer to come out of my mouth. When it finally did, it was, "Give him an anticonvulsant?" The neurologist said, "Brilliant," so I knew I was on the right track. I said, "Should I start a line, give him some Valium, and then load him with Dilantin?" He told me that that sounded like a wonderful idea, so that's what I did. I got the line in, I pushed the Valium, and the kid suddenly stopped seizing. It was great. By six-thirty I had him stabilized, lying in bed, sleeping, which was a lot more than I can say about myself.

This was pretty amazing. I have a lot of trouble believing I was capable of working by myself for a whole night and even admitting a seriously ill patient and not making any major screw-ups. I guess now that I've got pediatrics perfected, it's time to try another field. Maybe I'll become a heavyweight boxer.

BOB

May 1986

At the beginning of the month, Amy Horowitz told the chief residents that she was pregnant and needed to arrange maternity leave. Her announcement was met with the release of an explosion of venom aimed at her by the chief residents, who weren't about to give any special treatment to Amy just because she happened to be pregnant. This reaction of the chiefs produced the release of an equal explosion of venom from Amy, who, fed up with what she viewed as the chronically poor treatment she'd received all year long, decided to call the Committee of Interns and Residents to find out exactly what she was entitled to. The situation, which was escalating, was finally defused by Mike Miller, who managed to put Amy's ire to rest, at least for the time being.

The issue of maternity leave for house officers is a relatively new one. In the 1950s, residency training programs didn't have to worry about developing specific policies regarding leaves of absence for new mothers for two reasons: First, at that time, there were very few women in medicine; and second, many programs strictly prohibited house officers of either sex from being married. Over the past thirty-five years, however, this situation has changed dramatically: Today over 50 percent of the 105 house officers who make up our program are women, and the majority of these women are married. In recent years we've averaged about five new babies born to female house officers annually. As a result, a definite plan regarding maternity leave has been developed, with the intern or resident receiving about three months away from the hospital around the time of delivery.

The development of this plan has been met with mixed reactions from the house officers, both male and female. After all, if one person is given three months off, someone else is going to have to fill in for her. An attempt is always made to spread the coverage evenly, but often a few people wind up doing what they consider more than their fair share. This leads to resentment directed toward the person on maternity leave, resentment that may stay with her through the rest of her training.

But the problems that female doctors face are certainly not limited to these issues surrounding maternity leave. Discrimination against all women in medicine is rampant. Although the foundation of this discrimination is rooted in the past, when medicine was exclusively a male profession and when house officers were referred to as "the boys in white" and specialists such as ear, nose, and throat surgeons were called "ENT men," the image lives on in the public's mind. It lives on mainly because the medical establishment, which at this time is composed of those "boys in white" of the 1940s and 1950s who have grown up and taken charge, perpetuates the myth. And so the acceptance of women as medical equals of men is a difficult goal to attain.

It's easy to see examples of discrimination. In our emergency rooms, any male who has contact with a patient is immediately referred to as "Doctor" by the patient's parents, regardless of whether he is a doctor, a nurse, a medical student, or a clerk. Any female, no matter how senior or expert, is automatically assumed to be a nurse. At the beginning of the year, the female interns take great effort to correct the parents; they explain that they've gone to medical school, have graduated, and are just as much doctors as any man; but as time passes and it becomes clear that these explanations are doing little to change the public's conception and actually are creating hostility between doctor and patient, the women try to ignore what they consider this slight, managing just to cringe a little and swallow hard a few times when it happens.

And patients often believe that women can't do as good a job as men when it comes to the technical aspects of medicine. I've seen it a hundred times: parents refusing to let the senior resident, who happens to be a woman, draw blood, do a spinal tap, or start an IV on their child, demanding that the male doctor in the next examining room, who happens to be an intern, try the procedure first.

But the patients clearly are not the only ones who discriminate against female doctors; it's also firmly entrenched in academic bureaucracy. Thus far, few women have achieved positions of authority at medical schools in the United States. As an example, only a handful of the chairmanships of pediatric departments, the specialty with the largest percentage of practitioners who are female, are held by women. Part of this is due to the fact that until recently there weren't many senior physicians who were female, but part is definitely because qualified women are frequently not offered a job when an equally qualified male candidate is available.

Also, it becomes difficult for female doctors to deal with nurses, the majority of whom also are women. A good intern has to be aggressive, but aggressiveness is not a trait that is viewed as acceptable in women. When a male doctor orders a nurse to perform a task for his patient, it is viewed positively; he is just carrying out his responsibility. When a woman is the one who requests that a nurse do something, she is regarded as "uppity" and a troublemaker. It's a bind that is difficult for the female house officer to resolve satisfactorily.

These issues present an enormous identity problem for the female intern. On the one hand, she's not getting equal treatment from her patients or from the nurses; on the other hand, she has few or sometimes no role models to guide her in her training. Very often this second problem is more serious than the first.

Take Amy's problem as an example. Amy has done an amazingly good job. She has worked for an entire year as an intern, fulfilling all or most of her responsibilities. But at the same time, she's also had to be a mother to Sarah, trying her hardest to fulfill the responsibilities of what clearly is a second important full-time job. She's done all of this without anyone pointing the way for her; there are few faculty members around who could share their experiences as an intern and a mother with her. And although she's had some help, mainly from her husband and her baby-sitter, she's found little support within the system. The chief residents never wanted to know how sick her daughter was or what family obligations she had; they weren't even happy or excited when Amy told them that she was pregnant; they only wanted to know that she'd be at the assigned place at the assigned time and that her job would get done.

And there are very few options open to female residents with children. The attitude is basically this: If you want to have a baby and you want to spend time with your baby, you should take a year or two off; if you want to work, you should put off childbearing until after residency training is completed. A happy medium—that is, working as a house officer halftime and spending the rest of the time as a mother—is at present available at very few hospitals.

Changes are occurring, but they're occurring slowly. Eventually the young women who are house officers today will move into positions of authority, and the concept of medicine as a private club for men will gradually fade away and ultimately die out. At that time, a more realistic attitude toward women in medicine will evolve. And innovations such as shared residencies with two or more people fulfilling the responsibilities of one house officer, day-care facilities within hospitals, suitable facilities to encourage breast feeding, and fair maternity leave policies, which today are considered radical and expensive luxuries, will become commonplace. But as of now, Amy and her sisters in medicine must bear a heavy load.

ANDY
June 1986

Tuesday, June 24, 1986, 5:15 P.M.

My internship ends in three days. I'm moving back to Boston on the twenty-eighth. I can't believe this is finally going to be over so soon.

This has been a tremendously long year, in some ways feeling more like three separate years than just one. The first year stretched from when we started back in June to when I finished on Adolescents at the end of September; that first period took me from the time when I was enthusiastic and up about medicine to the point where I reached my first real depression. The second year included University Hospital and my first three months at Jonas Bronck; this was the best time for me. I was "up" for a lot of it, I managed to get myself organized, I pulled some things together for the first time, and I really began to see that the experience was eventually going to turn me into a doctor; the time I spent on the east campus was the most optimistic period for me.

The last period, which has been the most difficult, took up about the past four or five months, from the time I first walked into the PICU until now. I've gone through hell these past five months; I became emotionally wrecked, much worse than I ever thought I could. It's affected every aspect of my life, including my relationship with Karen, which I've always thought was unshakable. There was a time earlier this month when things had gotten so bad that we were seriously considering splitting up. This last period of internship has turned me into a very selfish and self-centered person. Thank God I've gotten some insight into what's been happening. I think Karen and I have patched things up pretty well now, but it was very disturbing there for a while.

The hardest period of this year happened during the last half of May. I hit the big burnout. I really didn't give a shit about anything; all I wanted was to be left alone by everybody. This lasted through the first couple of weeks of this month. At one point about two weeks ago, our attending sat me down and said, "You know, Andy, when you go to that new institution, it's going to be very important for you to make a good impression during the first couple of weeks. Everyone is going to judge you for your entire stay there on how well you do at the very beginning. So snap out of this!" He realized I was just going through the motions, and it was nice of him to talk to me about it. I've pretty much recovered from that burnout now. I don't know how, maybe it was because of what the attending said to me or maybe I just kind of woke up and realized what was happening on my own, but now I can behave myself most of the time without cursing and being moody and driving everyone crazy.

Over the past week or so I've started listening to some of the tapes I made back at the beginning of the year, and I noticed something: It seems like I remember the bad things much more vividly than I remember the good. I've forgotten a lot of the good things, the successes, the patients who have walked out of the hospital and have said, "Thank you" and have shaken my hand. Those people have been crowded out of my memory by all the ones who died or who did poorly, the ones who wound up breaking my heart.

Internship is supposed to be an important educational experience, but I'm still not sure what I've learned. One thing I've accomplished this year is I've managed to develop my own personal style as a doctor. I've turned out to be more compulsive than I thought I would be. I've gotten very efficient; I'm more able to decide what's important and what's not than I was a year ago, when I don't think I really knew how to prioritize at all. And probably a year from now, I'll look back and realize how little I know about what's important right now. I also think I somehow managed to retain my sense of humanity and my sanity among the inhumane environment of the hospital and the insanity of everything we do and the craziness of the Bronx. Thinking about it like this, I guess I really did pick up a lot this year.

But I definitely don't feel ready to be a second-year resident yet. I don't feel ready for that next step, that sudden acquisition of great responsibility where I'm the one who has to make the decisions and oversee the interns. I've gotten pretty good at doing what I've been called on to do as an intern. I have my own opinion now about how things should be done, but I don't argue much if I disagree with the residents or the attendings. They've got their jobs to do and I've got mine.

The other day we got new medical students. Brand-new, green, third-years, who've never been on a ward before. Our resident took great pains to explain carefully everything that was happening to these guys, like what a FIB is and what tests were done in a CBC. I was bored to tears.

We were all on our best behavior during rounds, but as rounds were ending, the other interns all tried to impress the students with how jaded and how cynical they had become. I stood there for a while as this discussion began and I just thought, Listen to all this bullshit! After a few minutes I couldn't take it anymore; I didn't want to be a part of this scene. So I just walked off. This kind of thing, trying to impress these poor third-year students, gets old really fast.

But I had fun with my stud [**student**] the rest of the day. I caught him in the library reading at about noon and I said, "Give me a break! What are you going to do, put on a nice clean shirt and tie every morning and spend the entire day sitting in the library reading textbooks? You're not going to get anything out of sitting in the library." So I forced him to get up and follow me around. I showed him some of the ropes. This afternoon I asked him to write a progress note on one of the patients he picked up and he wrote one of the worst notes I've seen in my entire life. It's so funny. He had absolutely no idea what was expected of him or what was supposed to be written in the chart. It kills me because he seems to be so bright and eager to work, but he just doesn't understand how to do anything yet. So tomorrow I'm going to have to really start to teach him things from scratch. But it's so hard to try to get my mind back to where a beginning third-year student is. I just can't put myself in his place.

Friday, June 27, 1986, 8:00 P.M.

My friend Ellen always used to talk about the need to process what was happening to all of us. She told me recently that it wasn't until the last few months of internship that she's been able at least to start to fit some of the pieces together and begin to understand what had happened inside her. I guess I've been able to do that only a tiny bit so far. I'm still standing too close to things to have any real insight. There's a lot of my internship I haven't talked about on these tapes. There have been things that were just too painful to go into; they would have been too damaging to bring up at the time, and now I've forgotten a lot of the details. But they've had their effect on me.

I'd like to think that overall this has been a good year, but I can't. It has been good in the professional sense. I was transformed from a medical student into a doctor. I've learned a great deal about patient management and how to think on my feet while half asleep. I think internship did all that extremely well. Thank you, Schweitzer Peds Department. All of you helped me make that transition.

Internship was also good in providing the battlelike atmosphere that brought me close to a bunch of strangers, my fellow interns, and very close to a few people to whom I'll forever have a bond, no matter how infrequently we communicate, no matter how physically far apart we drift. In all other respects, though, my internship was a draining, dehumanizing, destructive experience. It's almost like we started out in July smelling of cologne and perfume, and dressed in freshly laundered formal evening clothes, well-mannered and even-tempered with warmth in our hearts and great expectations, but by the end of the year we had become tattered, unshaven, smelly, cynical, snarling survivors of a long and somewhat meaningless struggle with ourselves and the rest of the world.

AMY

June 1986

Thursday, June 5, 1986

So far, this has been the best day of my internship. Today's the day of the Pediatric Department picnic; the attendings all cover the wards so we can all go out to some park somewhere and have a good time. That's not exactly what I decided to do. When our attending showed up and told us we could leave, I came right home, picked up Sarah, and took her to the Bronx Zoo. Just the two of us; it was the first time all year I got to be alone with her during a workday. I'm so glad I decided to spend the day with her instead of going to the picnic. I'm really missing the best parts of her childhood.

The Infants' ward is pretty much what I expected. In some ways it's like being in the NICU except there aren't any really tiny preemies around. There are a lot of babies who graduated from the NICU. The ones with any real chance of a normal life go home; the disasters come to Infants'.

Of three babies on the ward who are DNR's, I'm taking care of two of them. One is Kara Smith, an eight-month-old who got meningitis about four months ago. She spent most of February in the ICU upstairs; she had everything wrong with her, there were problems with every single organ system, and all the doctors who had anything to do with her were sure she was going to die. But she didn't die, and eventually they transferred her down to Infants', to the DNR room, where she's been living ever since.

It's really sad; she's completely vegetative; she can't do anything. She has no head control, she can't smile, she can't suck. The nurses feed her through a G-tube [**gastrostomy tube: a** tube inserted through the abdominal wall and into the stomach; G-tubes facilitate feeding of children who are neurologically impaired enough not to be able to suck or swallow]. Five times a day they squirt blenderized baby food into her, and an hour or so later they change her diaper. She also has a trach so she can be suctioned [babies with no gag reflex will not swallow the normal secretions that build up in the back of their throats; as a result, if these are not removed mechanically, the children will choke]. And pretty much, that's the extent of her care. Since she's a total DNR, we don't draw bloods on her for anything, we don't culture her if she gets a fever, and we're not supposed to start her on any antibiotics. Eventually she'll probably develop pneumonia and die. But it's already been four months and she hasn't gotten pneumonia yet.

One of the nurses who's really attached to her told me that Kara's mother used to come every day when she was first moved down here. Eventually she only came every other day, then a couple of times a week. Now she comes maybe once a week. I haven't met her yet; usually she shows up late at night, so I suspect some night when I'm on call I'll run into her.

My other DNR baby is Lenny Oquendo. He's six months old. He's never been out of the hospital, and it looks like he never will be. He was one of the NICU disasters; he weighed a little less than six hundred grams [one pound, five ounces] at birth and spent three months on a ventilator. He has a grade IV IVH [the worst type of intraventricular hemorrhage, a hemorrhage into the brain], severe hydrocephalus, and about a dozen other problems. He also has a G-tube and a trach. Lenny's mother hasn't come to see him in months. She seems to have completely lost interest in him.

There's a third DNR baby in the same room, but he's Ellen O'Hara's patient, and I don't know much about him. But that room is so depressing! The nurses and the rest of the staff buy these kids clothes and toys and things to try to liven up the atmosphere. But it doesn't help, it only makes everything that much sadder; the clothes and toys only make you realize how different these kids are from normal children. Just going in there and seeing those three hopeless and helpless babies lying in their cribs, it makes you want to cry! But at least they aren't much trouble. The only thing we have to do for them is rewrite their orders once a week and remember to sign them out to the intern on call.

The rest of the ward is filled with assorted disasters. There are three babies with spina bifida who have shunt infections [infection of the ventriculoperitoneal shunt, the device that drains fluid from the brain into the abdominal cavity] and are getting IV antibiotics, there are two babies with infantile spasms [a severe form of seizures] who are being treated with ACTH [the medication used in this type of seizure disorder], there's a nine-month-old with AIDS who was in the ICU last week with PCP but who's getting better. There are even a few normal children who have bronchiolitis [an inflammation of the small airways, causing respiratory distress; caused by a viral infection].

Working on this ward really takes a lot out of you. It's emotionally very taxing. So having today to spend with Sarah was especially good. It raised both our spirits.

I'm on call tomorrow night. I'm going to stop now and actually cook dinner.

Sunday, June 8, 1986

I've been in a good mood this weekend. The schedule for the next year finally came out on Friday. They actually came through with what they promised: I'm scheduled to have my CERC rotation [a month spent learning developmental pediatrics at the Children's Evaluation and Rehabilitation Center on the east campus; CERC is a calm, nonstressful experience] in October, my vacation in November, a month of elective without night call in December, and my neuro selective [a rotation learning child neurology; like CERC, neuro is pretty laid-back] in January. They gave me what I wanted. Finally, after everything that's happened this year, I wound up getting something without getting screwed!

It's hard for me to believe that I have only three more weeks of internship left. At this point in time, I'm fairly sure I'm going to be able to make it the rest of the way. I hadn't been able to say that before this week. I'd been dreading working on Infants' for months; I'd heard only bad things about it. But actually, although I can't say I'm really enjoying the patients I'm following, I am having a good experience here. We have a very good attending, Alan Morris. He's an excellent teacher and I've been learning a lot from him on attending rounds. And we have a strong team: Ellen O'Hara and Ron Furman are the other interns, and they're a lot of fun to work with. And our senior resident is my very favorite person in this whole program, Ben King. Ben's a little burned out at this point; this is his last month of residency, and I don't think he really wants to be in the hospital. Yesterday, on work rounds, he got into a wheelchair and made Ron push him around the ward. He's funny and he makes working easy because he's got excellent judgment. So, probably for the first time all year, I'm actually part of a team I like being on.

I was on call with Ben yesterday. It was a very quiet day. I had only two admissions, an eight-month-old sickler with dactylitis [**inflammation of the hands and feet, usually the first painful manifestation that occurs in children with sickle-cell disease**] who didn't require any work, and a nine-month-old with bronchiolitis who was admitted from the West Bronx emergency room but who Ben immediately sent home. It was really funny: I went down to the ER to get the baby at about three in the afternoon and he really didn't look that sick. But I didn't question it, I just brought him up to the ward. Then Ben came by to see him and he said, "Why did they admit this kid?" I told him I didn't know. He listened to the baby's chest and said, "This kid doesn't have bronchiolitis. He's healthier than I am! Send him home before something bad happens to him!" Just like that. His mother got him dressed and they left. I don't know any other resident who would have done that. But if you ask me, it was the right thing to do.

So all in all, I haven't been too overly stressed on Infants. Calls haven't been bad, and I've been getting out at a reasonable hour: not three or four in the afternoon, but usually no later than five. It's staying light out until seven o'clock now, so when I get home I can take Sarah out onto the lawn in front of the apartment building and just sit out there with her. It's nice. It's too bad the rest of the year hasn't been like this.

Sunday, June 15, 1986

Kara Smith died Friday night. She had developed a fever on Thursday; Ron was on, he examined her, and he thought she had pneumonia. He didn't do anything about it, just wrote a note documenting it in the chart. Then on Friday during the day her breathing became very labored. She must have been hypoxic. I felt very uncomfortable. I kept coming into the room to check on her. I knew she was DNR, but just sitting around doing nothing really bothered me. I wanted at least to get a blood gas and maybe start some oxygen, but the rules are no treatment.

Then finally on Friday night, one of the nurses called me around midnight to come to see her. She was blue and gasping for air. Her heart rate was down to about forty, so I figured the end was near. I called the resident on call to tell her what was happening, and she came down and checked Kara; she agreed with me that she was dying. We didn't do anything; we just sat by and watched.

She finally stopped breathing at about twelve-thirty. We covered her with her blanket and just walked out of the room.

I called the mother. I had met her last Saturday night. I had been on call and she came in at about eight o'clock. She didn't say much to me, only that she was pleased to meet me. It wasn't much, but at least I knew who she was and she knew who I was.

I got her on the phone and told her that Kara had died. She didn't cry at first. She seemed very composed. She asked if I thought Kara had felt any pain; I told her I didn't think so, that she had seemed comfortable the whole time. She asked if I knew what the cause of death was, and I told her about the fever and the breathing problems and the fact that she had probably developed pneumonia. Then the mother said, "I guess she's up with the angels now," and that's when she started to cry. I couldn't think of anything to say; I just sat at the nurses' station with the receiver up to my ear.

When she finally stopped crying, she apologized to me. She told me she'd been prepared for Kara's death for months and that she didn't think she would cry when the time finally came, but that she just couldn't help it. She said, "They told me she was going to die and I came to accept it, but I never really believed it." She started crying again at that point, but only for a minute or so. After we hung up, the rest of the evening was quiet; I didn't get any admissions, and the ward was calm. I went to the on-call room but I couldn't get to sleep. I kept thinking about Kara's mother.

Tuesday, June 24, 1986

Tomorrow's my last night on call as an intern. I've made it! It's hard to believe, but I actually survived. Believe me, it's not something I'd want to do again.

Looking back at the year, there have been a lot of things I've disliked; I didn't like the way I was treated by the chief residents, I didn't like the fact that I had to be on call every third night, I didn't like being tired and exhausted all the time, and I didn't like having to take care of sick, sick children. But definitely, the thing I disliked the most was being away from Sarah. I know I've said it before, but it's still true: I've missed some of the most important moments of my daughter's childhood.

I've asked myself a lot lately whether I'd have done this internship if I knew then what I know now. I'm not sure what the answer to that question is; over the past few weeks I've tended more toward, "Yes, I would do it." But there are some days, when things are very stressful, when the answer is, "No way!" I guess it's silly to ask the question, though. I mean, it doesn't really matter. I've done my internship, I'm finished with it, and I never have to do it again. That's all that's really important.

MARK

June 1986

Sunday, June 1, 1986, Noon

I just got back from my first night on call in the neonatal intensive-care unit at West Bronx, and I'm really starting to get the feeling that I'm not going to become a neonatologist when I grow up.

I got to the unit a little before eight yesterday morning. I got sign-out from Elizabeth, who was on the night before. I wouldn't say she was exactly sad to be leaving. Then she left and I started running around, and I continued through the night. I ran to the labs, I ran to the DR, I ran to the babies who were trying to die. The only time I sat down during the entire twenty-four-hour stretch was when I had to write those endless, pointless progress notes that go on for pages. It's a total waste, me writing notes. It's definitely gotten to the point where I can't even read my own handwriting anymore. Anyway, the whole day was horrible. Yesterday made my month in the nursery at Jonas Bronck seem almost pleasant!

Monday, June 2, 1986, 8:30 P.M.

I just got home. It's eight-thirty and this is supposed to be my good night, and I just walked through the door. Oh, this is a nightmare. But do I care? No, I don't care at all. Why don't I care? Because I just stopped at the supermarket on the way home and found blueberries. When blueberries appear, the end of the year is nearly here. They can do whatever the hell they want to do to me, but I don't give a damn anymore. Because I've made it. I've made it to the blueberry season.

So what's life like in the NICU? It's wonderful, great, like a vacation in Cancún during the rainy season. The unit is really very small. You can walk from one side of it to the other in about ten or fifteen steps. But packed into those ten or fifteen steps are some of the sickest patients you could possibly imagine. It's one disaster after another. There's a roomful of preemies who don't do anything all day but seize and try to die; there's a roomful of cardiacs [babies with congenital heart disease who are being evaluated for or are recovering from cardiac surgery] who only rarely seize but who always are trying to die; there's a room of miscellaneous disasters; and a fourth room, filled with social holds.

And the unit continues to stay full, mainly because of the top-notch obstetric service. OB is run by a team of killer midwives who are really heavily into what they call "the psychosocial aspects of childbirth." What that means is, they encourage the mothers to hold their babies right after birth to make sure they bond, no matter what's happening to the kid. On Saturday, Eric Keyes [a senior resident who was cross-covering the unit] and I were called to the DR stat for fetal distress. We got there and found this tiny midwife pushing on the belly of an enormous pregnant woman. The midwife told us she was applying external abdominal pressure. This pregnant woman must have weighed at least three hundred pounds, and the midwife weighed ninety at most. As she pushed down, it looked as if the midwife was going to be swallowed up by the pregnant woman. Anyway, we looked at the fetal tracing and saw there were late decels [late decelerations: a heart pattern indicative of fetal distress], so Eric suggested maybe they should think about doing a C-section. The midwife gave him a look I was sure would instantly turn Eric to solid rock but apparently it didn't, because seconds later, when the membranes ruptured and meconium started splattering all over the room, Eric immediately said, "Holy shit, let's get ready to intubate!" A little while after that, this tiny baby came flying out. The midwife caught it, wrapped it in a towel, and immediately handed it over to the mother.

I thought Eric was going to blow out his cerebral artery right then. He looked at the midwife for a second, then he looked at the baby, who was blue and not breathing, and he yelled, "What the hell is going on here?" The midwife turned to him and said, "Bonding. Shut up and go away!" Eric immediately grabbed the baby away from the mother, brought it over to the warming table, and we started working on it. The kid wasn't breathing. Eric intubated and sucked out a huge glob of meconium and then we started to bag the kid [**blow oxygen through an endotracheal tube directly into the baby's lungs**]. The baby picked up at that point and cried for the first time since birth. His heart rate came up, he started breathing on his own, and he turned pink, which looked much nicer on him than his original blue. It looked like a save.

But that wasn't the end. Just as we were finishing, the midwife came over and started yelling at Eric, telling him his grabbing the baby away like that severely disturbed the mother-child relationship. Eric said something like, "Oh yeah, sure, anoxic brain damage would have markedly improved the mother-child relationship, right? Bonding to a blue baby is much better than bonding to a pink baby. How stupid of me to interfere." They then got into a real big shouting match, right there in the DR [**delivery room**]. Eric told me later the midwives are always like that. He said you can expect to get into at least one argument with them a night. He said he thought there must be a required course in blue-baby bonding in midwife school.

Thursday, June 5, 1986

Today was the Pediatric Department picnic. The people in charge actually gave us the whole day off just to go and have a good time. It's so out of character, it's almost frightening!

This morning at about eight-thirty, our attending, Laura Kenyon, showed up and told us just to sign out to her and get the hell out of the hospital. Elizabeth and I were out of there instantaneously! If an attending's offering, we aren't about to give her a chance to reconsider. So we drove up to this camp in Chappaqua where the party was going to be. When we got there, we couldn't believe it. It was acres and acres of green grass and trees. It was great!

The picnic was actually a lot of fun. Just about all of us were able to go. We played softball, ate hamburgers and hot dogs, and drank much too much beer; in other words, we did all the things normal people might do if they were on a company picnic. We did a good job of pretending we were normal, at least for a few hours. It gave us hope that someday we might be able

to shed this schizophrenic outer coat we've grown and return to
the Land of Normalcy.

Anyway, on the way to the camp, we passed Peter Anderson's
house, the place where we had orientation almost one year ago.
Boy, that's amazing! It's hard to believe that orientation happened a year ago. It seems more like something out of a different
century. There were the Middle Ages, the Renaissance, and
orientation at Peter Anderson's house, not necessarily in that
order. Well, what difference does it make? In another couple of
weeks a whole new group of interns will be deposited on Peter
Anderson's doorstep, sweating bullets. I bet they're all sweating
bullets right now. I remember last year at this time, I was scared
to death. By the way, if you haven't guessed by now, sweating
bullets was the completely correct reaction. I wouldn't trade
places with those guys for all the money in the world!

I left the picnic at about three-thirty because I had to get
Elizabeth back to the hospital. She's on call tonight. Elizabeth
wasn't exactly in the best mood today. It's kind of hard to enjoy
yourself when you know that in a couple of hours you're going
to be face to face with your worst nightmare.

I'm going to watch some TV now. Yes, it's been the kind of
day normal people have, and I'm going to end it the way normal
people end their day. I'm going to watch *The Tonight Show*!

Twenty-three days to go. But who's counting?

Sunday, June 8, 1986

Carole and I are getting along really well. It's kind of frightening. Either I'm over my internship depression, or she's slipped
into a serious state of depravity. Anyway, it looks like our relationship has weathered the year. I'm glad it did, I guess. I like
Carole a lot.

I just got off the phone with Elizabeth. She's on call tonight.
She said her foot is feeling better, but it's still not great. I don't
know if I mentioned what happened to Elizabeth last week. She
was on on Friday night and there was a code about 3:00 A.M.
She told me she was in another part of the unit, trying to teach
one of the cardiac kids how to breathe like a human, when the
alarm went off in the preemie room. She went running in there
but tripped on an electrical wire on the way and flew about ten
feet into the air. This is a new Olympic event, the Preemie

Resuscitation Slalom Course. She must have made a perfect landing, because she said the judges gave her scores of 9.5 and above, but she came down on her ankle, which got all twisted up. A couple of hours later, after she had made sure the preemie who had coded would live to face another sunrise, she was drawing the morning blood and noticed her ankle was hurting. I got there about that point and we rolled down her sock and both noted that her ankle had become the size and color of a ripe eggplant. At about that moment she said she was feeling a little queasy. I noted that her face had turned a sickly shade of green. That was right before she passed out.

"Yes, I'll tell you, they just don't make these interns like they used to! At the first sign of adversity, they all find it necessary to fall over. They're just not as durable as they used to be in the Days of the Giants!"

Anyway, we got her a wheelchair and I took her down to X ray. There weren't any fractures. Laura Kenyon got hold of an orthopedic surgeon who examined her, said it was just a flesh wound, and wrapped her ankle in an enormous Jones dressing **[a bulky dressing made of three layers of Ace bandages]**. She was up and caring for the clients in less than two hours. What a trooper!

I'm finding it very difficult to concentrate on my patients. They've all become a blur to me at this point. I get one preemie mixed up with another; all the cardiacs seem the same; I just can't keep them straight anymore. I think I've got spring fever. I'm going to stop now.

Saturday, June 14, 1986

It hasn't been such a bad week. There are these bugs **[bacteria]** flying around the NICU that seem to be resistant to every antibiotic known to man. I don't know how they got into the unit, but I'm glad they did, because it means we're contaminated and closed to all admissions.

If I had known closing the unit would have been that easy, I would have brought the bugs in myself. I must have some type of bacteria resistant to every antibiotic known to man living in my apartment. I seem to have everything else living here. I can see a great future in the bacteria-resistant-to-every-antibiotic-known-to-man mail-order business. Interns all over the world would beat down my doors trying to get enough bacteria to close down their particular ICU. What a great concept!

Anyway, the infection hasn't done my old patients any harm. Of course, these kids are so sick, it's kind of hard to tell whether something does them harm or not. But it has caused us to have a nice, leisurely week.

Saturday, June 28, 1986

Well, it's over. It's all over. I am no longer an intern. As of nine o'clock this morning, I officially became a junior resident. No more internship! Ever! No more daily progress notes! No more blood-drawing! No more IVs! No more fighting with lab technicians! No more fighting with elevator operators! No more mock-turkey sandwiches! No more patients who are as sick as Hanson! No more Hanson!!

I think you can see here that I'm exaggerating a little. I think you can also see that I'm completely out of control! And I don't care! Because I'll never have to be an intern anymore, never again. Hooray!

This morning at about eight o'clock, I was drawing the morning blood and whistling. Yes, I've been whistling on blood-drawing rounds over the past few weeks because it's such fun! Anyway, I'm walking around the unit whistling and jabbing great big needles into my wonderful patients because I love them all so much and this guy who looked lost and scared to death came in and asked, "Is this the nursery?" Guess who he was? He was . . . an intern. He was the intern who was on call in the NICU today! And I didn't know who the fuck he was! Because he's brand-new!

I told him he was in the right place and I showed him where to get a set of scrubs and then I showed him the patients. While I was doing this, I stayed between him and the door at all times because I was sure that at some point or other he was going to bolt, leave the hospital, and never come back, and I'd have to stay and be on call again. But he didn't leave. He was really nervous, but he seemed very enthusiastic. It was like I was talking to a member of a completely different species on the evolutionary tree. He took notes on this clean pad on this brand-new clipboard. He didn't ask any questions, and I'm convinced he didn't understand a single word I said to him.

Anyway, I finished rounding with him at about ten and then we all gathered in the West Bronx library and the party started. A bunch of us were sitting in there, drinking champagne and getting soused. At ten in the morning. We stayed until about eleven, when the bar across the street opened, and then we all went over there for brunch. It might seem strange that ten or twelve interns would be sitting around a bar drinking at eleven o'clock in the morning, but hell, we weren't alone. The place was packed! It wasn't only pediatrics that changed over today; medicine and surgery changed also, and everyone was getting loaded. Anyway, we stayed there until about two. I just came home to take a nap and get ready for the real partying, which will start tonight.

I thought when it was all over, I'd have all these great, profound thoughts about internship. I've been trying to think of something profound to say all day, but I can't come up with a single thing. Internship sucks, that's all there is to it. It just flat-out sucks. But hey, it's not my problem anymore. I'm no longer part of that lower class of humanity! I'm pretty sure that if you come to me in five years and ask me if I thought my internship was a good or a bad experience, I'll probably tell you it was bad but that there were a lot of good things about it. That's what happens to people when they stop being so depraved. Right now, I can assure you there is absolutely nothing good about internship. Nothing.

Well, that's not exactly true. I've worked with a whole bunch of nice people whom I never would have come to know had I not been here. And I had a lot of good times. And I had two wonderful vacations I'll remember for the rest of my life.

See, it's been over for only five hours, and already my mind is warping. Do you think there's any hope for me?

EPILOGUE

Bob

Wednesday, February 25, 1987

About seven months ago, on a sunny Wednesday morning near the end of last June, as Amy, Andy, and Mark were beginning to celebrate the end of their year of internship, I got into my car and drove up to Peter Anderson's house in Westchester County. At about eleven o'clock that morning I found myself sitting on the grass outside Dr. Anderson's front door and asking three scared-to-death interns-to-be what most worried them. My question was met by an intense silence that lasted for what seemed like minutes. Finally, one of the new interns, a guy named Anthony D'Aquila, meekly said, ''The thing I'm most worried about is the night call. I just don't think I'm going to be able to survive a whole year of being on call every third night. I can't understand how you can be up all night every third night and still be able to function the next day.''

Slowly, the other two interns joined in, agreeing with Anthony. Then one of the others, a woman named Andrea Zisman, said that she was worried about what internship would do to her social life. She told us that she'd had a steady relationship with a guy for the past three years; he was a lawyer, and she was concerned that the life-style of an intern would completely destroy this long-term relationship.

We spent about an hour talking together in that group. As the time passed and as the list of anxieties I was recording on the piece of paper in front of me grew longer, I could feel at least some of the nervousness, some of the tension, gradually die away. By the time Mike Miller finally came to call us all to

346

lunch, I had the sense that these three had made some progress; they were ready to begin the year.

I saved the anxiety list from that morning's group and brought it home with me. I compared it with the list that Andy, Mark, and Amy had generated exactly one year before. The lists were almost identical. Not in the same order, not in the same words, but the concerns, the issues, the worries all are universal. Although Andy, Mark, and Amy have moved on, we attendings are dealing with the same problems, counseling away the same anxieties, coping with the same fears in a new group of interns.

Nineteen months have passed now since the day in June 1985 when I asked Mark, Andy, and Amy if they would like to participate in this project by keeping a diary of their internship year. Today those three interns are more than halfway through their junior residency and more than 50 percent finished with their mandatory three-year period of training. And even those three interns with whom I sat at orientation in June 1986 have only four months left until they say farewell to internship. Like the interns who came before them and like the interns who will follow them, they're at present trapped in the depths of the February depression. But I've told them to take heart. The light for them is beginning to appear at the end of the tunnel.

A lot has happened to the public's conception of internship over the past year. Various cases of suspected medical malpractice caused in at least some small part by the fact that unsupervised, overtired, and overwhelmed interns had allegedly made errors in judgment at critical junctures in the management of patients have received a great deal of publicity. The effect of this media attention has been that the lay public's eyes finally have been forced open to the fact that young doctors are often required to work over a hundred hours a week in a system that's antiquated, unnatural, and unhealthy for both the patients and the physicians themselves.

The state of New York has looked into the issue of internship training. The New York State legislature has proposed placing limits on the number of hours a house officer is allowed to work. There are two mechanisms for doing this that are currently being studied. The first of these limits the total number of hours a house officer can work in a single week to eighty; the second limits the number of hours that a physician can work in a single day to twenty-four.

Limiting the number of hours that can be worked in a single day to twenty-four would mean that interns would never again have to work thirty-six-hour shifts; overnight call would be illegal. However, because the wards and emergency rooms have to be staffed twenty-four hours a day, additional house officers would have to be hired. Although the state of New York has announced that funds for these new physicians would be forthcoming, there is a real question whether adequate numbers of medical school graduates could be found to fill these new slots. If sufficient personnel could not be recruited, the new regulations would ensure that interns would wind up working six or possibly even seven days a week. In discussing this possibility with our house officers, almost all state that they would much rather work thirty-six hours at a stretch knowing that they'll have a day off rather than work shorter hours without a day away from the hospital.

But limiting the number of hours an intern can work to eighty a week seems like a viable option. This would essentially outlaw the every-third-night call schedule, replacing it with a more human every-fourth-night scheme.

These reforms are long overdue. But the changes will take time to establish and to institute. So for the time being, at least, internship and residency proceed as they always have.

Early on the morning of June 29, 1986, I drove to the Bronx and stood out in a drizzle as two enormous guys loaded all of Andy Baron's possessions into an Avis rental truck. Andy, Karen, and I stood out there during the hour it took to get everything loaded, getting soaked by the rain. We didn't say much to each other. I knew there were a lot of things going on inside Andy's head, but apparently he didn't want to let either Karen or me in on them. So we just stood there, getting wetter, and silently watched Andy's furniture disappear into the truck.

The two guys were finished by about ten. Andy paid them, and then he and Karen got ready to climb into the truck. Before he got behind the wheel, I put out my hand. Still in silence, Andy came toward me and gave me a bear hug. After a few seconds he released his grip, turned, and climbed into the cab of the truck. A minute later I watched as the truck disappeared down Gun Hill Road, heading east toward the entrance to I-95 and his junior residency at Children's Hospital in Boston.

I've kept up with Andy since that day, speaking with him and Karen by phone a couple of times a month. In some ways, this year has been like a second internship for Andy: He's had to prove himself all over again, he's had to make a whole new group of friends and learn the ins and outs of an entirely new system. Everything about his new program is different from Schweitzer: The patients are mostly private and are referred to the hospital because of the special expertise of members of the faculty. The diseases they have are, for the most part, less common. ("We've got zebras here," Andy told me. "No horses, just zebras.") And the ancillary services are worlds better than ours. It took some period of adjustment, but now Andy is feeling comfortable. Before he left, he had some concern that he would be ill-equipped to work at Children's, that his knowledge and skills after a year of training here in the Bronx would leave him wanting when compared with those of the house officers in Boston. He's told me that that fear has turned out to be unfounded. He feels that he knows as much as if not more than the other junior residents in the program.

Recently, most of Andy's thoughts have been taken up with the future. Specifically, he can't figure out what the hell he's going to do after he finishes his senior year. He's jumped from wanting more than anything to get some subspecialty training so he can know a great deal about one particular area of medicine that very few other people know about, to wanting to be a good primary-care pediatrician, serving the needs of a large number of children and their families. In our most recent conversations, Andy's been leaning back toward specializing. His current favorite area is nephrology. Maybe someday he'll come back to Schweitzer to take care of all the kids at the University Hospital with chronic renal failure.

While in deep sleep during the early-morning hours of Wednesday, November 12, 1986, after nearly two weeks of maternity leave, Amy Horowitz spontaneously ruptured her amniotic membranes and immediately went into labor. Larry, awakened by the rush of warm amniotic fluid that engulfed the bed, immediately jumped up and started to get dressed. They briskly walked the two blocks from their apartment to University Hospital, stopping a few times along the way when the contractions came. Amy was admitted to the labor and delivery suite in active labor. She delivered her second child, a perfectly

formed, beautiful boy, just before eight o'clock in the morning.
Amy and her son, who was named Eric, stayed in the hospital
for three days and were then discharged to home, to spend the
next six weeks together until Amy had to return to work.

I spoke with Amy last week. She told me that she can't believe how quiet and well-behaved Eric is. Apparently he never
fusses, he rarely cries, and he demands almost no attention. A
typical second child! Amy also told me that Sarah loves her baby
brother and wants to help with his care whenever possible. "Her
biggest goal in life right now is to carry the baby around," Amy
said. "But since she weighs about twenty-five pounds and Eric
already weighs about twelve pounds, it doesn't look like that's
ever going to be possible."

Since her return from maternity leave, Amy has worked very
hard and seems to have a serious, no-nonsense attitude about
her responsibilities. And her reputation has changed with this
apparent change in attitude. I was talking with Eric Keyes and
Enid Bolger, two of the chief residents, about Amy last week.
Amy was in the emergency room and had just called up to tell
them about an adolescent with DKA [diabetic ketoacidosis]
whom she apparently had managed superbly. Enid said, "I never
worry when Amy's down in the emergency room. She's got a
good sense about things. She knows what to do, and when she's
in the ER, I know I don't have to worry." Amy's becoming a
mother for the second time has apparently caused her to do a
great deal of growing.

And what of Mark Greenberg? Of all the people in the internship group, he's probably the one least changed by his transition to junior residency. He's still making everybody laugh.
But he has become a leader, which is what a good resident needs
to be.

There is another thing that has changed in Mark's life. In July,
a few of the house officers were invited to Mike Miller's summer
house on Candlewood Lake in Connecticut. Because of Mark's
childhood friendship with Mike, he and Carole were invited to
come. In the afternoon, Carole and Mark got into Mike's row-
boat and rowed out into the middle of the lake. When they
stopped, Mark reached into his pocket and pulled out a jewelry
box. From the box, he produced a ring. And then he asked
Carole to marry him. Old cynical Mark, proposing marriage in

probably the most romantic way possible. Carole accepted the ring. They plan to be married this coming summer.

What is there left to say? My own internship was the hardest, most devastating year of my life. It's been eight and a half years since I finished that year, and some of the pain, the anger, the exhaustion, and the anguish is still with me. I don't think my experience, or the experiences of Andy, Amy, and Mark, are unique. Everybody who lives through an internship is forever changed by the experience. The intern learns about medicine and the human body; he or she truly becomes a physician. But in the process, through the wearing down of the intern's spirit, that person also loses something he or she has carried, some innocence, some humanness, some fundamental respect. The question is, Is it all worth it?

GLOSSARY

abruptio placentae Separation of the placenta from its attachment on the wall of the uterus. Dangerous because it deprives the fetus of oxygen.

acidosis Buildup of acid in the blood.

acute abdomen Term used to describe condition in which an abdominal catastrophe is occurring. Causes of acute abdomen include ruptured appendix, and inflammation of the pancreas and gallbladder.

agonal rhythm A pattern of electric activity generated by the heart just prior to death.

A-line Abbreviation for arterial line, a tube placed in an artery used for sampling blood.

ALL Abbreviation for acute lymphocytic leukemia, a common form of childhood cancer.

AMA Abbreviation for "against medical advice," the situation in which a patient signs out of the hospital before his doctor considers it safe to do so.

ambubag A device used to force air into the lungs; consists of a mask that covers the mouth and nose and a rubber bag that, when squeezed, generates a gust of air under pressure. Used in respiratory arrests.

aminophylline Drug used for treating asthma.

aneurysm of the ascending aorta A ballooning out of the aorta, the main artery bringing blood to the baby.

antecubital vein A vein at the elbow that usually is most accessible for blood drawing.

APGAR scores A scoring system, designed for use in the newborn, that monitors fetal and neonatal well-being. Maximum score is 10.

ARC Abbreviation for AIDS-related complex.

ARDS Abbreviation for adult respiratory distress syndrome, a condition in which respiratory failure occurs.

argininosuccinicaduria A rare inborn error of metabolism that leads to mental retardation and often to premature death.

aspiration The act of breathing in; aspiration pneumonia results from the breathing in of foreign substances, such as meconium in the newborn.

atelectasis Collapse of the lung.

ATG Abbreviation for antithymocyte globulin, a drug used in patients who are rejecting transplanted organs.

bagging The act of forcing air into the lungs of a patient having difficulty breathing.

BCW Bureau of Child Welfare, the New York State agency charged with investigating and acting upon cases of suspected child abuse.

Benadryl An antihistamine used in treatment of allergic reactions.

beta HCG A blood test to diagnose pregnancy; more accurate than a urine pregnancy test.

bicarbonate A drug used in patients with acidosis (*see above*).

bladder tap Procedure in which a needle is passed through the lower abdominal wall and into the bladder so that an uncontaminated sample of urine can be obtained.

blood gas A test done on a sample of arterial blood that tells the amount of oxygen and carbon dioxide within the body.

bradycardia Abnormal slowing of the heart rate.

bronchiolitis Inflammation of the bronchioles, the small air passages leading to the lungs. This is a condition that resembles asthma and occurs in children under a year of age.

bronchopleural fistula A leak in the main air tube that causes air to leak into the pleural cavity, causing a tension pneumothorax.

BUN Abbreviation for blood urea nitrogen, a substance that builds up in renal failure and in dehydration.

CAC Abbreviation for "clear all corridors"; a general request, announced over the loudspeaker, for help at a cardiac arrest.

cadaveric transplant A transplant performed using an organ obtained from a person who has died.

cardiac cath A procedure in which a catheter is placed in an artery or vein and threaded up to the heart, at which point a dye is inserted. Used to define the nature of heart disease.

CBC Complete blood count. A blood test to examine the content of hemoglobin, red blood cells, and white blood cells within a sample of blood.

central line A tube placed in one of the major blood vessels, usually in the neck or the groin.

cervical adenitis Swelling of the lymph nodes of the neck.

chemo Short for chemotherapy.

chief of service rounds A weekly conference in which an interesting case is presented and discussed by an expert in the field.

choriocarcinoma A cancer that develops from a molar pregnancy.

CIR Committee on Interns and Residents, the house staff union.

CP Cerebral palsy, an abnormality usually caused by lack of oxygen around the time of delivery.

CPR Cardiopulmonary resuscitation; technique used at cardiac arrests to keep the patient alive.

cracking the chest The surgical opening of the chest wall to gain access to the heart and lungs.

creatinine A substance in the blood that's elevated in cases of kidney failure.

crump To deteriorate rapidly.

CSF Cerebrospinal fluid, the liquid that bathes and protects the brain.

CT scan An X-ray procedure; most CT scans examine the head, looking for specific defects of the brain.

cutdown A surgical procedure in which a vein is isolated and a tube is placed into it for access. Used when no superficial veins can be found.

CVA tenderness Tenderness at the costrovertebral angle, the area of the back under which the kidneys are situated. CVA tenderness is present with many types of renal disease.

cyanosis Blue discoloration of the skin usually due to lack of oxygen in the blood.

dactylitis Swelling of the hands and feet; usually the first presentation of sickle-cell disease in an infant.

DKA Diabetic ketoacidosis; a severe metabolic abnormality that occurs in diabetics who have a marked buildup of sugar in their blood. If not cared for correctly, it may lead to death or brain damage.

DNR Do not resuscitate.

double footling breech Condition in which baby is heading out of the birth canal feet first; dangerous because there's a chance the fetal head can get caught, leading to the baby being unable to be born.

DPT Two meanings: (1) immunization given to young children that protects against diphtheria, pertussis (whooping cough), and tetanus; (2) a mixture of Demerol, Phenergan, and Thorazine used to sedate children who are having some painful procedure.

dual response Procedure used in cases of child abuse in which the child is considered to be in danger. The police and the BCW (*see above*) are informed, and an immediate investigation is carried out.

dysplastic kidneys Condition in which the kidneys did not form normally and therefore cannot function well. Often leads to chronic renal failure.

E. coli A type of bacterium.

ectopic pregnancy A pregnancy occurring in a location other than the womb.

EEG Electroencephalogram; a test in which the electric activity of the brain is examined.

EMS Emergency Medical Service; the agency that staffs the ambulances.

endotracheal tube A tube passed through the larynx and into the main breathing tube that allows the individual to be placed on a respirator.

epinephrine A drug used in patients whose hearts have stopped beating.

ER Emergency room.

extramural delivery Delivery of a baby that occurs outside of a hospital.

fascinoma An interesting case.

febrile seizure A convulsion caused by a marked elevation in fever.

FFP Fresh frozen plasma; a part of the blood that sometimes is used as a transfusion.

FIB Fever in baby; all babies under two months of age with fevers should be admitted to the hospital and treated with antibiotics.

Foley catheter A tube that has an inflatable balloon at the end; Foleys usually are passed into the bladder to help monitor urine production.

fundoplication A surgical procedure used to correct gastro-esophageal reflux (GER—*see below*).

gastrostomy A surgical procedure in which a hole is made in the abdominal wall and the stomach so that feeding through a tube can be accomplished without the patient's having to suck and swallow.

GC Gonococcus, the bacterium that causes gonorrhea.

GER Gastroesophageal reflux, the regurgitation of stomach contents back into the esophagus.

gonococcus The bacterium that causes gonorrhea; also known as GC (*see above*).

gram-negative rods The appearance, under the microscope, of certain bacteria when stained with dye using a special technique. *E. coli* (*see above*) is the most common form of gram-negative rod.

G-tube A tube placed through the opening of a gastrostomy and through which blenderized food is squirted.

guaiac A test looking for blood, usually in a sample of stool.

Haldol A drug used in patients with psychosis.

H and P History and physical; the admission note that must be completed on all patients staying in the hospital overnight.

headbox A Plexiglas box that fits over the head of an infant and through which oxygen in high concentrations can be administered.

hemifacial cellulitis Infection of the skin on one side of the face.

hemoptysis The coughing up of blood.

HIV Human immunodeficiency virus; the agent that causes AIDS.

hydrocephalus Dilatation of the ventricles of the brain, which can lead to increased intracranial pressure.

hyperbaric chamber The center on City Island in New York

City where the barometric pressure can be increased. Patients who have inhaled smoke and have a high level of carbon monoxide in their blood are sent there for treatment.

hypoxia A deficiency of oxygen in the blood. May lead to brain damage.

infantile spasms A particularly severe and damaging type of seizure disorder.

interosseous infusion Procedure in which fluids or drugs are injected into the bone; used in dire emergencies when an IV cannot be started.

intracardiac infusion Procedure in which drugs are injected directly into the heart; used as a last-ditch effort to save a patient's life when IV access cannot be established.

intracranial bleed A hemorrhage into the brain; usually causes brain damage or death.

intubation Procedure in which an endotracheal tube (*see above*) is inserted through the vocal cords and into the main breathing tube.

Isuprel drip Constant infusion of isoproterenol, a drug used in severe asthma.

IVDA Abbreviation for intravenous drug abuser.

kerlix Rolls of bandages, often used to restrain little children.

KUB Abbreviation for kidneys, ureter, bladder; a type of X ray in which the abdomen is examined.

Lasix A diuretic drug used in hypertension and heart disease.

lidocaine A local anesthetic.

LMD Abbreviation for local M.D. The patient's private doctor.

LMP Last menstrual period. Important because it's used to determine how premature a baby is.

LP Lumbar puncture; a procedure in which a needle is inserted through the back and into the spinal canal so that a sample of CSF (*see above*) can be obtained for study. Also known as spinal tap.

main-stem bronchus One of the two main tubes connecting the trachea and the lungs.

M and M conference Morbidity and mortality conference, a teaching exercise at which a patient who has died is discussed.

meconium The baby's first bowel movement; when meconium is passed while the baby is still in the womb, it often is a sign of fetal distress and can lead to respiratory problems if it is aspirated.

mediastinum The central part of the chest that houses the heart.

membranes The structures that contain the fetus, the placenta, and the amniotic fluid. Rupturing of the membranes, followed by a gush of amniotic fluid, often causes the onset of labor.

meningomyelocoele A defect in the spine, present at birth, that often is associated with hydrocephalus, neurologic deficits of the legs, and urologic abnormalities. Also called spina bifida.

methotrexate A chemotherapeutic agent used in the treatment of some cancers.

"mets to the brain" Metastatic cancer affecting the brain.

mitral stenosis Tightness of the valve that separates the heart's left atrium and left ventricle.

monilia A type of fungus that frequently causes diaper rash in infants; also affects patients with immune deficiencies such as AIDS.

NEC Abbreviation for necrotizing enterocolitis, a severe disorder affecting the intestines of some premature babies.

nephrotic syndrome A condition affecting the kidneys that results in the inability to retain protein.

neuroblastoma A relatively common form of cancer that affects children.

neurofibromatosis A genetically inherited disorder that can cause abnormalities of the skin, the central nervous system, and other organs. Also known as the Elephant Man Disease.

NICU Abbreviation for neonatal intensive-care unit.

night float A resident who is scheduled to work the overnight shift in the emergency room.

NPO Abbreviation meaning "nothing by mouth." Ordered for patients with intestinal abnormalities and patients who are pre-op.

occipital hematoma Hemorrhage into the back part of the skull or the underlying brain.

OPD Outpatient Department, composed of the ER and clinics.

orthopods Internese for orthopedic surgeons.

osteogenic sarcoma A type of cancer affecting bones.

otitis media Infection of the middle ear. Very common cause of fever in infants and young children.

oxacillin A type of antibiotic.

painful crisis A complication/result of sickle-cell disease; sickling of red blood cells leads to lack of oxygen reaching the tissues and results in development of severe pain.

pancytopenia Deficiency of all types of blood cells, both red and white.

patent foramen ovale An opening between the two atria of the heart. If untreated, it might eventually lead to pulmonary hypertension (*see below*).

Pavulon A drug that paralyzes the recipient; used in patients on respirators who are agitated and said to be "fighting the machine."

PDA Abbreviation for patent ductus arteriosus, a congenital defect of the cardiovascular system that is common in premature infants.

perineum The genital region.

periorbital cellulitis An infection of the skin surrounding the eye. Dangerous because it can lead to infection of the eye (orbital cellulitis), which can lead to infection of the brain.

peritoneal dialysis A procedure performed to "cleanse" the blood in patients with kidney failure, in which fluid is placed into the abdominal cavity and later drained out.

PFC Abbreviation for persistence of fetal circulation, a complex physiological abnormality encountered in newborns who have aspirated meconium.

pH Measure of acid in the blood. Determined routinely as part of a blood gas (*see above*).

phototherapy A treatment for jaundice of the newborn in which the infant is placed under ultraviolet light; through a mechanism that's not clear, this therapy lowers the level of bilirubin in the blood.

physsies Internese for physical examinations of the newborn performed in the well-baby nursery.

PID Abbreviation for pelvic inflammatory disease, an infection of gynecological structures. Often caused by gonococcus (*see above*).

pneumococcal meningitis An infection of the spinal fluid caused by a very virulent and damaging form of bacterium.

pneumothorax Collapse of a lung; must be treated by placement of a chest tube that drains out the accumulated air.

PRN Abbreviation used in medication orders meaning "as needed."

prolapsed cord Condition in which the umbilical cord passes out through the cervix before the baby. Dangerous because if the cervix narrows, blood flow to the fetus can be blocked, leading to hypoxia (*see above*) and brain damage.

pseudomonas A virulent bacterium.

P²C² Abbreviation for Pediatric Primary Care Center, the clinic at Jonas Bronck Hospital.

pulmonary hypertension Increased blood pressure in the pulmonary arteries, usually as a result of heart disease. Is a nonreversible condition that eventually will lead to death.

pyloric stenosis Narrowing of the lower part of the stomach, leading to inability to pass stomach contents into the intestine. Occurs most commonly in first-born male infants during the first two months of life.

q4h When written in a medication order, means "every four hours."

QNS Abbreviation for quantity not sufficient.

rales A particular sound heard when listening to the lungs through a stethoscope and that implies the presence of pneumonia.

renal biopsy A technique in which a needle is passed through the back or side and into the kidney. Allows sampling of kidney tissue and therefore diagnosis of specific diseases affecting the kidney.

'roids Internese for steroids, an anti-inflammatory class of drugs.

scut A collective term for the routine work that an intern must do.

sed rate Short for erythrocyte sedimentation rate, a test used to determine if an inflammatory disease is occurring.

sepsis Bacterial infection in the blood.

SGA Abbreviation for small for gestational age. Used for babies who have not grown to adequate weight while in the womb.

sickle-cell anemia An inherited disorder in which an abnormality of hemoglobin, the protein that carries oxygen, causes deformation of the red blood cells and serious consequences. (*See* painful crisis, *above.*)

sigmoidoscopy Examination of a portion of the colon using a device called an endoscope.

spina bifida Synonym for meningomyelocoele (*see above*).

status epilepticus Condition in which patient is having constant, uncontrolled convulsions.

straight cath Passage of a tube through the urethra into the bladder to obtain a sterile sample of urine.

strawberry hemangioma A purplish birthmark; these often disappear by the time the child is six years old.

subarachnoid hematoma A collection of blood between the arachnoid membrane and the brain.

subinternship A two-month rotation in the fourth year of medical school in which the student acts as an intern.

suprapubic tap Synonym for bladder tap (*see above*).

tachypnea Rapid breathing.

thrombocytopenia Deficiency of platelets, structures that aid in the clotting of blood. One of the features of pancytopenia (*see above*).

tight as a drum Phrase used to describe a patient with asthma who, because of the disease, is having difficulty breathing.

tolazoline A drug used in persistence of fetal circulation (PFC— *see above*).

tox screen Short for toxicology screen. A test done on a sample of blood, vomitus, or urine obtained from a patient in whom ingestion of a toxic substance is suspected.

TPN Abbreviation for total parenteral nutrition, in which all the nutritional requirements are supplied via an intravenous route.

transillumination Technique used to "light up" a particular structure. Used to diagnose pneumothorax (*see above*).

traumatic arrest Cessation of cardiac activity caused by a traumatic event, such as an automobile accident.

triage box The place in the emergency room where the charts of the patients waiting to be seen are piled. Patients are triaged according to how sick they are.

trisomy 18 A condition caused by an extra No. 18 chromosome; patients with this disorder are born with multiple anomalies and usually die before their first birthday.

turf Internese for sending a patient to another service.

UA Two meanings: (1) abbreviation for urinalysis, a test performed on urine to see if a UTI (*see below*) is present; (2) abbreviation for umbilical artery, a blood vessel in the umbilical cord that carries blood from fetus back to mother.

URI Abbreviation for upper respiratory infection. Also known as the common cold.

UTI Abbreviation for urinary tract infection.

UV Abbreviation for umbilical vein, blood vessel in the umbilical cord that carries blood from placenta to fetus.

vagitch Internese for nonspecific vaginitis, an inflammation of the vagina.

varicella The virus that causes chicken pox.

V-fib An abnormal cardiac rhythm, the next stage after V-tach (*see below*).

VP shunt A plastic tube inserted into patients with hydrocephalus and that drains excess spinal fluid from the ventricle of the brain to the peritoneal cavity of the abdomen.

V-tach An abnormal cardiac rhythm that, if untreated, can lead to death.